## Critical acclaim for Jeff Gulvin

'So detailed, so accurate in its depiction of terrorist and counter-terrorist activities, that had it been written as a piece of non-fiction, the Government would almost certainly have tried to ban it'
*Time Out*

'*Storm Crow* is that rare bird – a meticulously researched thriller with a gripping and ominously plausible plot'   Dr Bruce Hoffman, Director of the RAND Corporation's Washington Office

'This rattles along at a fine pace, yet has time for the detail which not only adds authenticity but demonstrates the author's thorough research and sound knowledge of his subject'   *Shots*

'. . . the labyrinths of betrayal and personal responsibility are as important as the mechanics of the thriller plot. Gulvin's main aim is to keep the pages turning (and here he scores a palpable hit), but he is fastidious in his characterisation, and his villain in particular is something of a unique creation'
*Good Book Guide*

# JEFF GULVIN

# NOM DE GUERRE

ORION

An Orion paperback
First published in Great Britain by Victor Gollancz in 1998
This paperback edition published in 1999 by Orion Books Ltd,
Orion House, 5 Upper St Martin's Lane, London, WC2H 9EA

A CIP catalogue record for this book
is available from the British Library.

ISBN: 0 75282 736 7

Printed and bound in Great Britain by
Clays Ltd, St Ives plc

*This novel is dedicated to*
*the 'brick agents' of the*
*New Orleans FBI field office*

The author would like to thank:

Special Agent Ken Piernick, Domestic Terrorism, FBI.

The New Orleans Field Office, FBI.

Rex Tomb and Ed Cogswell, Fugitive Publicity, FBI.

Also:
Tony Thompson
Bruce Hoffman
&
Freer Richardson

# GLOSSARY

| | | | |
|---|---|---|---|
| ANO | Abu Nidal Organization | DST | Direction de Surveillance Territoire |
| ARV | armed response vehicles | ERT | evidence response team |
| ASAC | assistant special agent in charge | ETA | estimated time of arrival |
| ATF | Alcohol, Tobacco and Firearms (Bureau of) | FEMA | Federal Emergency Management Agency |
| BKA | Bundeskriminalamt | FEST | Foreign Emergency Search Team |
| Box 500 | MI5 | | |
| Box 850 | MI6 | | |
| CAD | computer-aided dispatch | GBI | Georgia Bureau of Investigation |
| CASKU | Child Abduction and Serial Killer Unit | GS15 | government service grade 15 |
| CJIS | Criminal Justice Information Services | HRT | Hostage Rescue Team |
| CP | command post | NCIC | National Crime Information Center |
| DEA | Drug Enforcement Administration | NCIS | National Criminal Intelligence Service |
| DIA | Defense Intelligence Agency | NOPD | New Orleans Police Department |
| DOD | Department of Defense | NYPD | New York Police Department |

| OP | observation point | SO19 | Tactical Firearms Unit |
| SAC | special agent in charge | SOG | special operations group |
| SEG | special escort group | SSU | special secure unit |
| SFO | specialist firearms officer | SWAT | special weapons and tactics |
| SIOC | Strategic Intelligence Operations Center | TOC | tactical operations center |
| | | UCA | undercover agent |
| SO11 | Directorate of Intelligence | UFAP | unlawful flight to avoid prosecution (warrant) |
| SO12 | Special Branch; also SB | | |
| SO13 | Antiterrorist Branch | VICAP | Violent Criminal Apprehension Program |

**I**

Ismael Boese hung upside-down like a bat. Matthews and Thompson bench-pressed, across the floor of the gym; one lying flat, one standing ready to lift the bar back into position. Boese watched them out of upside-down eyes, the heat of blood in his face. Terlucci stared at him through the wired glass of the window.

In the showers afterwards, Boese let hot water roll off his skin, standing with his head slightly bowed, resting his forehead against the limescaled chrome of the pipe. Behind him, Matthews and Thompson discussed how much they could lift. Armed robbers, both of them. Violent men. They were all violent men in here. Boese rubbed cheap shampoo into his scalp. Thompson was speaking to him, though the words were unintelligible through the fall of the water. He raised his voice. 'I said, you're like a fucking bat in there.'

Boese turned the shower tap off and stared at him. He did not reply, merely lifted his towel from the hook. For a moment Thompson held his gaze, with his lip lifting against his teeth. Boese stared calmly back, black eyes, like marks of death in his face.

Dressed again in his own clothes, one of the benefits of the special secure unit, he crossed the tiled floor where Morgan was playing pool with McClellan, the IRA man. He and Boese should have had much in common, but they didn't. Now and again McClellan tried to talk to him, but Boese spoke only fleetingly with anyone. McClellan's cronies, Butcher and Gibbs, came out of the workshop under the eye of wardens in the control room. Gibbs had a visitor coming in the morning, and already he had passed his spare set of clothes for inspection. Morgan was a murderer, who had escaped from both Dartmoor and Parkhurst in his time, a Welshman whose blood family now lived in Scotland. Boese caught his eye as he bent to play his shot.

Griffiths, one of the wardens, was standing by his cell on the north side of the building, minus his red book. He was running an evaluation on him for the authorities, and he wrote his comments and observations down in the red book. Boese walked right up to him. 'State of mind calm,' he said. 'Accommodating if uncommunicative. Non-disruptive. Mixes reasonably well, without being buddy-buddy.' He paused, watching the rush of colour in Griffiths's cheeks. 'Does not instigate conversation. Seeks no company in particular. Plays chess. Works out in the gym, and has the strange habit of sleeping on the floor.' He took half a pace closer and looked deep into Griffiths's eyes. 'Appears to show no remorse for the two hundred and eighty people he killed in Rome.' He showed his teeth in a smile and stepped into his cell.

He lay on his bunk; once the doors were open in the morning, they remained that way all day. Only ten of them in here: three Irish terrorists and himself, Morgan, the Blues Brothers, as he had nicknamed Thompson and Matthews, Terlucci and a couple of others. Morgan was the brightest, he also kept to himself like Boese. Terlucci was the one they would use. Boese stared at the wall as he considered how to deal with it. Nothing. No pictures, just the same pale blue paint over brick as the rest of the building. Reading Prison special secure unit, built in the shape of a plus sign; with the sterile area and visitors' room tacked on to the southern hall, by the entrance. Terlucci was a Mafia hit man. He had been arrested in London after carrying out a contract, placed on a rival by his Sicilian father. A knifeman by reputation, he liked to

2

get close to his victims. That would be how it was, a knife. Not kill him, just enough to make sure he knew who they were.

Griffiths was still at the door. 'No remorse?'

'What?'

'You said, no remorse.'

'I did.'

Griffiths seemed to need to say something. 'Why did you do it?'

Boese laughed then and shook his head. His face closed up again.

'There must have been some reason other than the money?' Griffiths scratched the hair that grew out of his ear. He was middle-aged, one of the wardens that did it for the love of the job, one of the few who really believed he might make a difference. He wore the Ichthys fish of the 'born again' in the lapel of his black jacket. In summer he transferred it to his shirt, as if to emphasize his allegiance. 'Why go to all the trouble of doing what you did in London, only to get yourself caught?'

'Mr Griffiths,' Boese swung his legs over the edge of the bed, bare feet cold on the tiled floor, 'I'm not in the mood for talking.'

Griffiths nodded, again his finger drifting to his ear, as was his habit. 'OK,' he said, and smiled. 'When you are, I'm always ready to listen.'

Boese lay back on the bed, forearm over his eyes. Six months and silence. No visitors. No letters. No calls. He had made none, not written to anyone and had asked for no visitors. That was important. They would come, make their request from the outside. A priest, a social worker, prison visitor maybe. But so far, no one and nothing. He stood up and pulled on some shoes. The mirror over his tiny wash basin showed a dark, lineless face and close-cut hair. He had not aged. From the concourse in the middle

3

of the block, he could hear the clack of pool balls as somebody fired one hard into a pocket. Mindless game, strange that Morgan should be so adept at both pool and chess. Morgan beat everyone at chess, even the Irish freedom fighter, McClellan, who thought he was James Joyce. Morgan had been inside for fifteen years now, having served half his sentence. Age in his face, his hair, lines under his eyes, and a sallow yellow to the skin that stank of a life with no air. The exercise yard was twenty metres square, encased in steel mesh, sides and roof. You could only see the sun through little squares of wire.

Boese recalled the words that police officer had told him, leaning across the table at Paddington Green: Swann, Jack Swann, whom they had used up and spat out for the birds. 'Thirty years,' he had said. 'You'll only be able to walk forty-two paces in any one direction for the next thirty years.' He had been right, Boese had counted.

That had been after the news broke in Rome; just when they thought they had beaten him, a taxi belonging to the unknowing, all-trusting Giancarlo Pasquali had belched pirillium E7/D10 into the crowds outside St Peter's Square. Before that, a chemical bomb in London to send the City into a panic and force the entire population to run for their lives. And then nothing. A hoax, a huge sigh of relief and then his arrest and suddenly hell breaking loose in Rome. Two hundred and eighty dead. None injured. The derivative kills or leaves you alone. There are no injured. He had made the activities of Aum Shinrikyo look foolish. And the sweat on Swann's face as he told Tal-Salem to 'go to work' on the telephone. Confusion, the sudden fear that comes with ignorance, standing out in his eyes.

He heard a movement outside his cell, and then a sudden quietness; the pool game was over. Somebody's foot scraped over the tiles. Boese lay where he was, arm still shading his eyes. Two voices back in the hall, half-whispered words. He felt a tick rise under his left eye and the saliva drained from his mouth. Every muscle was tense now, but still he lay where he was. Somebody filled the door, he detected the subtle change in atmosphere; the smell of the Italian's hair gel. Strange, he thought it would have been in the kitchen. Why he did not know. Perhaps it was the association with knives. Louder voices now, Thompson and Matthews in the hallway, laughing. The fresh clack of pool balls. Still he lay there, arm across his face, and felt the shadow as Terlucci stepped towards him. Boese sat bolt upright. The Italian paused, three paces from the bunk, a filed-down knife cupped in his right palm. Boese ignored the knife, and looked him straight in the eyes.

'Your name is Gianluca Terlucci,' he stated quietly. 'Your father is the head of the Palermo Terlucci family. He has business in New York and Miami, but never leaves Sicily. You used to go on his behalf, but you don't any more.' He did not get up, did not move, just continued to stare in Terlucci's eyes. No fear, voice low and calm, the words like chips of ice from his tongue. Twenty-four-year-old Terlucci, and sudden incomprehension in those eyes. 'You have killed three men,' Boese went on. 'All with a knife.' He indicated the home-made weapon still half-concealed by fingers. His voice dropped another octave. 'You do it quietly, from behind. Your signature.'

The Italian moved the tip of his tongue to moisten his lips. Three paces still; as if there were some unseen barrier between them. 'You got married at nineteen to Sabrina, your childhood sweetheart,' Boese told him. 'But before you came here, you had four different mistresses. Would you like me to tell you who they are?' He slowly got to his feet. 'You have two daughters, twin girls: Eva and Marianna. They're nearly five years old. You married your wife because you got her pregnant and the Catholic faith

5

of your father would not allow an abortion. Your daughters are pretty little girls, black ringlets in their hair. They go to Mass on Sundays, the Church of St Peter, Father Vittorio Bintempi. Every morning they're taught kindergarten by the Sisters of Mercy at St Teresa, Palermo.' He paused then and again looked at the knife. 'Shall I tell you what their bedroom looks like?'

The Italian stared at him. Outside the pool balls rattled over the table. Boese held Terlucci's eye, saw the line of sweat break from the oiled hairline and roll down the side of his face. He moved closer to him, close enough to smell the morning's tobacco on his breath. 'Next time, come from behind me,' he said.

# 2

Swann wiped his mouth with a palm and listened to the echo of voices resounding through the high-ceilinged gymnasium. Webb was chatting away to one of the other climbers while Swann stared at the wall. Why was this so difficult? There was a time when he would swarm up without so much as a second thought. He felt Webb's hand on his shoulder, and kicked the sole of one friction boot with his other foot.

'Can't get my head round it,' he said.

'It's a route, Jack. It's on a climbing wall.' Webb lifted the belayed end of the rope. 'You can't go anywhere.'

Swann was acutely aware of the sweat on his face and he almost walked away. Webb held his eye, smaller than he was, with round, bright blue eyes that had a way of cutting away the bullshit.

'Go on. Get to it.' Webb pushed out a cheek with his tongue. 'I haven't given up an evening of drinking and whoring to hold a rope for someone who isn't climbing.'

Swann smiled then and again slapped the soles of his boots. Dipping his fingers into his chalk bag, he rubbed away the gathered moisture and looked at the long-legged female student who swung up the knots of stone like a monkey. Swann glanced left and right; most of those climbing were a lot younger than he was and he wondered why he was still doing this. He thought he had got over it all last year, but now he knew he hadn't.

He climbed, aware of just how good the girl was on his right, crabbing her way up with a four-fingered mantelshelf, while using her feet as a pressure point. Swann laboured; he could hear the uneven rasp of the breath in his chest as Webb kept the rope tight below him. It was hooked through a bolt ring at the top of the wall. If he peeled off, he would fall no distance at all. Yet the sweat stood out in thick globules against the wrinkled skin of his forehead, and the chalk did nothing for his grip. He slipped, kicked away and dangled above the floor like a broken spider. Slowly he shook his head and Webb lowered him down.

Webb sang in the shower as he always did. Swann was silent. He soaped himself down, rinsed off and got dressed. They crossed the road to the Irish pub on the corner, Swann feeling in his pocket for change for the cigarette machine. October and a biting wind chased itself through the lamplit street. Buses chugged back and forth and the rattle of diesel engines fogged like a muggy weight in his mind. Webb bought the Guinnesses and brought them over. Swann bought a packet of Marlboro and tore off the cellophane.

'You're supposed to be quitting. You even promised your kids.' Webb set the dark beer before him and settled into the seat opposite.

'Don't, Webby. I'm really not in the mood.'

Webb sat back and watched him, drumming square fingers on the tabletop. A siren sounded right outside the door. Swann was thinking suddenly about Pia, or rather Brigitte. He must stop thinking of her as Pia.

'I still call her Pia in my mind,' he said.

'It was her name.' Webb shrugged. 'You've got to forget about it, Jack. It's not doing you any favours. Believe me.'

Swann frowned at him. 'Has somebody said something?'

'Not in so many words.' Webb drank half the Guinness in his glass.

Swann sat back then and stubbed out the cigarette, only half smoked. Immediately he wanted another one. He pushed a hand through his short-cut hair and thought about it. He had been in the Antiterrorist Branch for almost five years now. It was a five-year posting and he should be moving on. He didn't want to move on though, what other kind of policing was there after this? He needed to be careful. He did not need George Webb to tell him that things were not right. Clements, his DI on the investigation squad, Bill Colson, the operational commander, they had all given him a bit of leeway after Storm Crow. The terrorists had suckered him in, using a woman who became his lover for eighteen months, so they could be ahead of the game when the time came for them to act. That act had been a bogus chemical bomb right in the middle of the City, then a real attack in Rome. Ismael Boese, Storm Crow, the protégé of Carlos, was on remand in Reading.

But there is only so much slack a man can have. It was a job, a profession. He had to be professional. Right now, if the shit really hit the fan, how much of a liability would he be? He closed his eyes at that thought; feeling the tension taut all at once on his brow. He looked across at Webb's quiet face and saw sympathy for a friend, but equally the cold professionalism that goes with the job. Two years ago, Webb had saved his life on the Springfield Road. They were undercover in West Belfast; telephone engineers, with false passports, credit cards, driving licences; watching two men who were the mainstay of an IRA active service unit in Hayes. They were compromised, to this day RUC Special Branch could not tell them how, but the back-up team was ten minutes away. They left the pub as soon as Swann realized they were blown, and tried to make it back to their car. Two men approached them, singled him out, one of them with a hand on his arm when Webb buried the muzzle of his Glock into his belly. 'On yer way, sunshine,' he had offered in his best northern brogue. Swann was clicking the transmitter in his cuff for back-up.

Swann jumped as Webb snapped his fingers under his nose. 'Come on.' Webb stared at him. 'Where were you?'

'Springfield Road.'

Webb pursed his lips. 'You know Caroline doesn't even know about that.' He leaned forward. 'I've only just told her I go over there.' He waggled his empty glass. 'By the way, it's your round.'

When Swann got back to the table, Webb was looking thoughtfully at him. He leaned forward and tapped the chipped wood of the tabletop with his forefinger. 'You remember Springfield Road then, Jack.'

'What d'you mean?'

'Not many people could've held it together in that situation.' Webb lifted his eyebrows. 'Wrong word, wrong move and gone.' Again he clicked his fingers. 'Just like that. No time for the ninjas to dig us out.' He stroked the condensation from the side of his glass. 'You remember *that* when you wake in the middle of the night.'

Swann lit another cigarette and drew the smoke in deeply. 'You're right,' he said. 'I've been losing it, haven't I.'

Webb looked at him and nodded. 'You had a bad time. Pia, or rather Brigitte Hammani stiffed you.' He lifted his shoulders. 'Shit happens, Flash. You're not the first and you won't be the last. Put it behind you. Move on.'

It was the way they had got to him that really stuck in his craw. They wanted a weak link and had found one. A few years previously he had killed his climbing partner, cut the rope and dropped him to his death on Nanga Parbat in the Himalayas. He still heard the screams at night. He had told Pia, one night in Scotland; poured it all out, and afterwards he felt as though he had got some degree of sanity back in his life. But she betrayed him. She was not

10

who she claimed to be, so his confession, if that's what it was, was null and void. The guilt was back ten fold.

'Listen.' Webb laid a hand on his forearm. 'You have to deal with this, Jack. Go and see someone if you have to, doctor, counsellor, whatever. If you don't – the way things are going – you're going to have problems.'

Swann was at his desk early the following morning, getting up at six and catching the tube in from Waterloo. The late turn was over and it was that transition period at the early part of the day. A date was due to be set for Ismael Boese's trial and he still had bits and pieces of evidence to sort out. He sifted through it now and saw again Boese's cold eyes across that table in the interview room at Paddington Green. They had arrested him the previous afternoon on the M1 motorway; a rolling takeout from SO19, expertly executed with three attack cars, and the surveillance team blocking the traffic five miles back. Boese had been as impassive then as he was the following morning, when Swann had interviewed him. Swann was back in that room now, with those haunting black eyes across from his, recalling how this man had sent him a photograph of himself with a bullet hole in his head. It was Boese's right to have a solicitor present and he had asked Swann to call a firm called Reeves & Company in Islington. Swann had handed him the phone and watched those eyes as Boese said three quiet words: *Go to work.* He would never forget that moment, the quiet malice in the voice, the deadness of the eyes. Within one hour, people were dying in Rome.

Boese had been put back in the cells and local uniforms were sent to the offices of Reeves & Co. When they got there, they were straight on the radio to the central command complex at the Yard; and Swann, Webb and Campbell McCulloch raced north to Islington. Already, there was blue tape cordoning off the doorway that led up from the high street. The solicitor's practice, what looked like a one-man affair, was situated in the office above a television and radio repair shop. Swann showed his warrant card to the uniform standing guard.

'The doctor's upstairs now, Sarge,' the uniform said to him. 'We were told to leave forensics to you blokes.'

Webb was already dressed in his white forensic suit and pulling on rubber gloves. He followed Swann up a flight of steep uncarpeted stairs, the soles of their shoes scuffing on the linoleum. Two more uniformed officers were standing in the outer office. Swann moved past them and gazed through the open door to Reeves's office. The pathologist was kneeling beside the body, curled on its side in an almost foetal position, bald-headed with one long strand of hair falling away at the ear. Swann could see he had been shot through the middle of the forehead.

'SO13?' the pathologist said as he squatted back on his haunches.

Swann nodded, his gaze being pulled to the heavily made-up woman, who sat upright behind the desk, with a trickle of dried blood running down the right-hand side of her nose. Two drops on her chin, two more on her blouse. The back of her head was scattered across the high-backed chair. He was aware of the hollow sound of his own heart. Webb was over by the desk, where papers had been shifted to one side, as if somebody had sat there. He peered at the ashtray where two cigar butts and a roll-up lay in a smattering of grey ash. He took a pair of tweezers from the small plastic box he carried, and lifted the butt of the hand-rolled cigarette from the ashtray. 'Spliff,' he said.

They looked at one another for a moment. 'Tal-Salem,' Swann said.

There was no doubt. Tal-Salem sucked his joints hard and he always smoked before he killed someone. They had recovered DNA from traces of saliva left on the end of the butt. It matched that found by the DST in France, at the scene of the 1995 assassination of the Italian banker called Alessandro Peroni, in Paris. It also matched a sample being held on file by the BKA in Germany. The perpetrators in France were known to be Pier-Luigi Ramas and Tal-Salem, a two-man hit team employed by Storm Crow to kill Peroni. Ramas had been shot dead by SO19 at Heathrow Airport, the previous May. Tal-Salem was still at large.

Swann flicked through the other information he was putting together. He picked up a photograph of a meal receipt in Paris. It had been taken by an undercover FBI agent in Idaho, who was watching the compound of Jakob Salvesen, the Christian Fundamentalist, who'd employed Boese to attack London and Rome. Poking out from under the receipt was the slip of paper with the scraps of handwriting on it. Bits of words. Swann was sure they were Winthrop directions to a dead drop. He sifted through other stuff, some of the forensic bits they had gleaned from the car they had stopped on the motorway: a Ford Mondeo, one that Boese had bought a year previously and left in underground storage. Again Swann hesitated, aware of a presence in the squad room doorway. He had asked himself the same question a dozen or more times – why had Boese gone back for that car? He must surely have known they would track it. It did not matter now, Boese was in the special secure unit at Reading Prison; a building all on its own, housing only ten prisoners, with a razor wire fence, then its own outer wall, a second wire fence and the main perimeter wall. Even Storm Crow could not fly that particular nest.

He looked up to see DSU Colson watching him. 'You're an early bird, Jack.'

'Things to catch up on, sir.'

Colson put his hands in his trouser pockets and strolled

across to the window. They were the only two in the room; Swann could feel some kind of question, statement perhaps, weighing on his boss. He was aware of a tingling sensation, sudden butterflies in his stomach.

Colson spoke without looking round, gazing at the still-darkened city skyline – the Palace of Westminster and Big Ben, clock face illuminated. 'Everything all right with you, Jack?' He said it casually, but Swann could sense the slight edge in his voice. He got up and walked over. Front it out, he told himself. Best way. He paused beside Colson, who looked round, a big man with an open, intelligent face. He raised the knuckle of one forefinger to his lips, leaning his elbow against the window. Swann was conscious of both their reflections in the glass.

'I've had a bit of a bad time, sir.' He looked Colson squarely in the eye now. 'Things to deal with.'

Colson nodded. 'Your kids still living with you?'

Swann shook his head. 'They're back with their mother now.'

'You must miss them. What was it – almost a year?'

'Thirteen months in the end.'

'Where are they now?'

'Muswell Hill.'

'Not too far.'

'I see a lot of them.'

Colson was quiet for a moment, then he said. 'How long have you been up here now, Jack?'

That was it, what Swann had been waiting for, feared almost. What was it he had heard one time, some psychologist or other. *You move towards your dominant thought.* 'Five years almost.'

Colson kept his eyes on him, face open; no furtive glances, no avoidance of the eye. 'You've been good, Jack. Very good.'

Swann felt something break in his chest.

14

'And you're right. You did have a bad time.'

'Look, sir. I know I haven't been at my best, but I'm dealing with it.'

Colson held his gaze. McCulloch came in clutching two bundles of files, with a polystyrene coffee cup balanced precariously on one of them. Colson moved away from the window. 'If you want an extension on your five years, I'll back you,' he said.

Swann could hardly believe his ears. Two minutes ago he was sure Colson was going to ask him to transfer out of the Branch. 'Thank you, sir. I do.'

'Good.' Colson patted him on the shoulder and made his way to the door. 'By the way,' he said, 'Chrissie Harris has been doing some spade work on a team she thinks might be looking to cause us problems. I'll put you on it when the time comes.'

'Great.' Swann moved back to his desk.

'You OK, Macca?' Colson asked McCulloch.

'Not bad, Guv. Piled high with paperwork.'

'What is it?'

'Operation Airwaves. The Iraqi group in Bayswater.'

Colson nodded. He turned to both of them. 'By the way, we've got a visitor coming this morning, the assistant commissioner's bringing him down.'

'Who's that, then?' Swann asked.

'Dr Benjamin Dubin.'

Ben Dubin was an academic, formerly of the Jonathan Institute in Israel, an organization that studied terrorism, set up after Benjamin Netanyahu's brother was killed leading the raid on Entebbe. Swann had only heard of him through Louis Byrne, the FBI agent who had led the Foreign Emergency Search Team that came over after an American was killed in the Storm Crow incident. Apart from Byrne himself, Dubin was the leading light on Storm

15

Crow. Swann remembered that it was Dubin who had put forward the theory that Storm Crow was the protégé of the Jackal.

Swann had heard a lot about Dubin from Byrne: allegedly, he was the best theoretical terrorism expert on the planet. Byrne had rumoured that he once worked for the US government, but would not elaborate. Now he was director of the centre for study of terrorism at the University of St Andrews in Scotland, and had headed the RAND Corporation in the late 1970s. Swann had no idea what to expect, none of them did, even how old he was. Colson brought him down to the squad room; a small wiry man, with the darkened complexion of a Middle Eastern birth. Byrne had told them he was fluent in both Hebrew and Arabic. Swann put him in his early fifties, though he was tight-limbed and lean. He wore a checked cotton shirt, brown tie and a brown corduroy sports jacket, and circular tortoiseshell glasses pressed the bridge of his nose. Swann looked for the leather patches on his sleeves, but could not find them.

Colson introduced the team to him and explained that they could only tell him so much about the Storm Crow investigation, as Boese was still on remand.

'I understand. Don't worry.' Dubin spoke with a heavy New York accent. 'Gotta keep it pure. Nothing that'll prejudice a prosecution. Get it with the FBI all the time.' He smiled a wide smile, showing a set of crooked, off-white teeth. His hair was intact and his beard still dark, just a few salt and pepper flecks here and there.

'You're Swann?' he said, shaking hands. Swann nodded. 'Louis Byrne told me all about you. I guess you two worked pretty closely on this one, huh?'

'Pretty closely, yeah.' Swann folded his arms. 'I wasn't aware you'd left the Jonathan Institute.'

'End of the last academic year.' Dubin dragged fingertips

16

over the desktop. 'Mutual decision, I think, though I guess the fact of it is I fell out with them.'

'The Israelis?'

'Kinda.' Dubin indicated the desk. 'Mind if I . . .'

Swann swept an arc with his hand. 'Be my guest.'

He squatted on the edge, one foot on the floor. 'Between you me and the wall,' he explained, 'I'm not too keen on Netanyahu's policies. Don't get me wrong here, I'm Jewish.'

'But not an Israeli,' Christine Harris from the Special Branch cell observed.

Dubin smiled at her. 'Right. New York City born and raised. Did my Ph.D. at Columbia.'

There was an ease about him that warmed Swann to him. Webb too was relaxing. They had had academics on the fifteenth and sixteenth floors before, most of them about as streetwise as a statue of Louis XIV. Often, they pontificated on the politics behind the violence. John Garrod generally gave them short shrift, which was why they were left to assistant commissioners to handle. As far as the Branch was concerned, terrorists were criminals. Police officers arrested criminals. That was the end of the story.

'You're in Scotland now?' Harris asked him.

'Right. I went back to RAND for a few weeks, but I'm settled north of the border now.'

'I remember reading something you wrote,' she went on. 'After the Tripoli bombings.'

Dubin nodded. 'That was just before I left RAND. Guess I fell out with the Reagan administration.' He laughed. 'Seem to fall out with everybody these days. Age creeping in, I guess. Must be getting cantankerous.' He looked again at Harris. 'I had a public row with Reagan over the Tripoli air strikes.'

'Why?' McCulloch spoke for the first time.

'Because fundamentally they didn't work. I knew they

17

wouldn't at the time. I tried to tell the government, but they didn't listen. Told me to butt out in the end.'

Swann motioned for McCulloch to get some coffee. 'Anyways,' Dubin went on. 'I was right, of course.' He smiled again. 'I generally am. Reagan claimed that the Tripoli attacks would halt the state sponsoring of terrorism by Libya. Far from it. Between 1987 and 1988 Libya funded at least twenty-three separate acts. That was more than they'd done period, before Reagan hit them. Qaddafi also hiked up his supply of arms to the IRA, because you guys let the F15s take off from British soil.' He made an open-handed gesture. 'Well, matter of fact, I got pissed off with the States and went to Israel for a while. I worked at the Jonathan Institute, took my data base with me. But then I started to question what they were doing, how accurate their information was, and in the end I took up the post at St Andrews.'

Swann moved off the desk. 'You said data base?'

Dubin looked at him over the rim of his glasses. 'That's right. I got a data base listing every terrorist incident in the world, going back to the Irgun in 1945.'

Swann and Webb showed him round the rest of the floor. The squad room, senior officers' rooms and the SO12 cell where Harris linked with upstairs. Finally, they went to the Buckingham Palace end of the building, exhibits, where things that went bang were dealt with.

'And bomb data?' Dubin asked, when they had shown him the weapons and various other devices they had on the wall of the anteroom, next to the evidence cages that each officer kept. Webb showed him the mortars from the two Heathrow Airport attacks by the IRA.

'We log everything,' Webb explained. 'Link up via the Trevi Committee; BKA, DST, FBI, whoever we can share information with.'

'The relationships are good, then?'

18

'Now they are.'

'The French?'

'Yes, even the French.'

Back in the exhibits office, the three of them sat down and Colson came through to join them. Dubin leaned forward with his hands clasped together, black hairs disappearing up his sleeve from his wrist. He looked keenly at Swann. 'You arrested Storm Crow,' he said.

Swann looked evenly back at him. 'Ismael Boese, yes.'

'Rome,' Dubin said. 'Not to mention what he did here. The political shock waves are still reverberating throughout the world.'

'I'm not surprised,' Swann said. 'That incident proved the very fear that was generated by Saddam Hussein back in February.'

Dubin nodded slowly. 'Only much much worse.'

Swann sat forward then. 'You were the one who first put forward the idea that Storm Crow was a protégé of Carlos, is that right?'

'I guess. Louis Byrne agreed with me.'

'You know him well?' Webb asked.

Dubin chuckled. 'Pretty well. As good as one gets to know anyone from FBI HQ. Byrne's a good agent. What they call a "Blue Flamer" in the FBI field offices. A suit from D.C. on the fast-track career programme.'

'But it was you who thought Boese was linked to Carlos,' Colson stated.

Dubin sat back and placed his hands behind his head. 'Yes. I've always thought so. Carlos is in prison in Paris now.'

'We know. We interviewed him last year.'

Dubin nodded. 'So did I.'

Swann stared at him then. 'The DST let you in?'

'I asked to see Carlos. He agreed. The authorities vetted

me and I passed. If Carlos wants to see me – I can see him.'

'The only person who ever interviewed Carlos was Assem El Jundi, the Syrian poet,' Swann said.

Dubin nodded. 'I think he must've got up Carlos's nose, because he ended up getting shot for his trouble.' His face lost its smile. 'Anyway, after the French convicted him of the Rue Toullier murders I was allowed to interview him. I've just finished a full biography.'

'And Storm Crow,' Webb said. 'Did Carlos confirm your theory?'

'He neither confirmed nor denied it.'

'But he knew Ismael Boese,' Swann said.

'Oh, yes. He definitely knew him. Boese was there in 1982. I've had two independent witnesses over and above Carlos, who have separately confirmed the young man from America, whose parents were SLA, and whose mentors were Provisional IRA. Entirely separate accounts. When Carlos declared war on the French government over Magdalena Kopp being imprisoned, Ismael Boese was there. I think his first real blooding was the Paris–Toulouse express.' Dubin paused. 'If my theory is correct, Boese learned a great deal from Carlos, not just about the terrorist act. Carlos wrote a letter to Gaston Defferre, the French Interior Minister, on the 25th February 1982. He proved he was the sender by enclosing a set of his fingerprints.'

'Identity,' Swann said. 'And vanity.'

'Right. Carlos revelled in the glory. Most of what's been attributed to him is pure fiction. He could not have possibly done all that's been claimed about him. One argument is that he was a CIA/KGB disinformation exercise who started to believe his own publicity.'

'And Boese learned from that,' Swann said.

'Yes. To keep his identity secret.' Dubin looked from one to the other of them. 'Funny thing is, if Carlos was not responsible for much of what was claimed about him, Storm Crow *was* responsible for everything that was claimed about him. Not only that – he did keep his identity secret for almost ten years.'

'Until last year,' Colson put in.

Dubin lifted his shoulders. 'Everybody gets careless. What was it, a set of prints from a beer glass or something?'

'ATF in California,' Webb told him. 'Louis Byrne located them.'

'You're certain that Boese is Storm Crow,' Swann said.

'Aren't you?'

'I wasn't.' Swann glanced at his colleagues. 'Until last May.'

Dubin nodded. 'Boese's Storm Crow all right. All the evidence points to it.' He smiled and scratched the palm of one hand with the fingernails of the other. 'I suppose there's only two people in the world who can say with *absolute* certainty, though, and one of them is Carlos.'

'And the other, Boese himself,' Webb said.

'Yes.' Dubin pursed his lips. 'That's why I want to interview him.'

# 3

Gibbs had a visitor. Boese always took a quiet interest whenever anyone had a visitor. Since he had been here, there had been quite a number: Gibbs three, McClellan one, Butcher three. Brynn Morgan, the Welsh murderer, had been visited regularly by his sister in the past, but apparently she had not come for a year now. The day before Gibbs's visitor came, he sent his spare clothes through to be searched and laid ready for him in the sterile area. The wardens were vigilant. Since the IRA break-out from a similar special secure unit at Whitemoor Prison, they had doubled their searches. The routine was much the same, however, the ten prisoners in the unit had their days pretty much to themselves. They worked if they wanted to, at a metal and woodwork shop. Although the product of their endeavours was strictly scrutinized, Terlucci had still managed to fashion himself an excellent replica of the Italian stiletto knife. Boese watched him as they ate breakfast at the tables in the dining area. The cover was still on the pool table and Terlucci sat with his back to it. He was on his own this morning. Normally he hung around the Blues Brothers, but they were deep in some conversation of their own. Boese watched him and Terlucci avoided his eye.

Information is power. Boese had been taught that even before he could walk. His parents had taught him many things that other people did not get taught. Subsequently, he never looked at any situation as another person might; his mind concentrated on the minutiae of detail. It was how he had avoided capture for as long as he had. He listened, observed, and picked up snippets of conversation. Terlucci was troubled now, confused at how a man in the SSU, with no outside contact whatsoever, could know so much about him. But like most Latinos, Terlucci was a talker. Boese had never spoken directly to him, but it was not difficult to pick things up. A word here, a word there. In the six months that he had been here, he had gleaned enough information to frighten the life out of most of them. He had no need of violence; reputation was all. He did not have a clue what his daughters' bedroom looked like, but right now Terlucci believed he only had to whisper to harm them.

Gibbs was looking forward to his visitor. He talked openly at the next table to Butcher and McClellan. Somebody from over the water, no doubt hopelessly vetted by the authorities. In the past it had been family members who visited, but today it was allegedly Gibbs's priest. Boese would watch with interest.

He lay on his bunk and meditated; mind working back over itself, the little details of the year gone by. Tal-Salem was in Spain, waiting as he was. Ramas had been sacrificed. The woman. He smiled when he thought of her, all those nights with Swann, and priceless snippets of information. He thought about the panic in the country, the people fleeing London, the Prime Minister, and then all the backslapping and relief when they realized they were only dealing with water. And then, all at once – Rome. He sat up and moved to the corridor. Morgan was sitting at the freshly cleared breakfast table, with the chesspiece box open before him. Terlucci was watching kids' programmes on TV. Boese could see the flickering screen through the open lounge doorway.

Morgan set up the pieces while Boese leaned against the metal doorframe to his cell and watched him, head slightly to one side, eyes hooded. Nobody volunteered to play with

23

him. Very carefully, Morgan set the pieces in their places, the whites facing away from him, then he sat for a moment with his knuckles gripped under his chin. A thickset man, square-faced and flat-fingered, red hair cut high on the neck and freckles creeping over the creases in his face. He had been convicted of beating a nightclub bouncer to death in Cardiff.

Boese walked casually over to the table and leaned with his hands fisted before him. Morgan did not look up. Boese studied the board, aware of Griffiths's gaze from the control room. Any moment now he would be reaching for the red book. Morgan looked up eventually. 'I never played you,' he said quietly.

Boese did not reply, merely eased himself into the empty seat across the formica-topped table and stared at the pieces. He moved a pawn. Morgan looked over red fists, blond hairs growing on them. 'White moves first.'

Boese just stared at him.

They played slowly, Boese watching the workings of Morgan's mind. He was not particularly intelligent, but he had a methodical mind. He studied every move for three minutes or more before moving his pieces, always in the same position, unshaven point of his chin resting against his knuckles. Boese could hear him breathe. The Blues Brothers played pool right next to them and the dull smack of wooden balls seemed to irritate Morgan. He shifted in his seat and glanced now and again at the players from under one cocked eyebrow. Boese ignored them, concentrated on boxing Morgan in. It was not difficult. The man took so long over studying each move, his own response was predictable. Boese beat him easily, but he made it look difficult. He could have won inside a few minutes, but he chose to jockey and then gradually wear him down. It was the first time anyone had beaten Morgan. Everybody was aware of it and a silence descended as Boese uttered the word, 'Checkmate.' For a long time Morgan sat across from him, still with his fingers interlocked, still studying the end of the play. At last he breathed out, long and audibly, then sat back. He stared into Boese's eyes. Boese stared back, then Morgan scraped his chair away from the table. He hovered a moment, fist clenching and unclenching, then very meticulously he began collecting the pieces.

Gibbs's visitor arrived at two-thirty. Visitors had their own entrance, twin sets of airlocked doors with a dead space between them. Two wardens showed them into the suite, where they waited while the inmates remained in the sterile area. Gibbs went in, the only one with a visitor. Boese watched him from the television room. His spare clothes were waiting for him. He was strip searched and his existing clothes removed, then he dressed in those he had passed for inspection the previous day. When he was ready, he was led through to the visitors' suite. Restless all at once, Boese went to the gym. Terlucci was lifting weights with the Blues Brothers.

Boese worked out, pumping weights, running and boxing, anything to get the blood flowing. His mind was working overtime and he needed the flow of adrenalin. At four-thirty, Gibbs came back to the unit. He looked pleased with himself and Boese noticed the wardens were edgy. He wondered who Gibbs's priest had been.

He waited all evening, cooking supper, a chore they took turns at. Nobody complained about his food. Boese served Butcher, he served McClellan and then Gibbs. Momentarily, he caught Gibbs's eye. Nothing. In his cell later, he sat crosslegged on the floor and stared at the space between his knees. He heard a movement in the hallway, a light step outside.

'Go away, Mr Griffiths.'

Griffiths cleared his throat. 'Somebody has telephoned about you.'

Boese stilled; his hands, loose in his lap, tensed imperceptibly. Slowly, he looked up. Griffiths's eyes were watered blue, yellow at the edge due to his age and the artificial lighting they perpetually lived under. He plucked at his ear. 'Somebody wants to talk to you.'

Boese half lifted one eyebrow. 'I don't know anybody.'

'His name is Benjamin Dubin. Dr Benjamin Dubin.' Griffiths studied the slip of paper in his hands. 'St Andrews University in Scotland. He's a professor of international terrorism.'

Boese looked beyond him, past the black of his uniform to the blue-painted wall and the tiny chips in the brick. 'Why does he want to see me?'

'He's written to the governor and asked for permission to conduct an interview with you, for academic research, if you are willing. We have no objection. The man is internationally renowned and has been cleared by the Home Office.' Griffiths came closer, a lop-sided smile on his face. 'Do you want to see him?'

Boese said nothing, his gaze still on the brick wall. Tal-Salem in Spain, and the others – waiting. 'I'll see him,' he said. 'But he is not allowed to tape anything or photograph my face.'

Swann fastened the knot of his tie and jerked the cuffs of his suit jacket down over his shirt. He could smell his own aftershave. The suit was new, a black, three-button two-piece. He had bought it off the shelf and it fitted well. The flat was empty, had been since the children went home. He missed them terribly. The phone rang on the small table under the window.

'Swann.'

'Hey, Jack. What's happening?'

Swann smiled and sat down on the settee. Cheyenne Logan. He recognized her voice immediately, the southern

26

drawl from her childhood in Alabama, still evident. She had been part of the Foreign Emergency Search Team that the FBI sent over last year. They had spoken half a dozen times since then. He imagined her as he sat there; black skin, long legs and very pretty. She favoured red suits and red nail polish, and her hair, the last time he had seen her, had been shoulder length, the colour of soot and brushed away from her face.

'Hello, Chey. How are you?'

'Just fine, Jack. Had a note on my desk about Jakob Salvesen and I thought about you. How you doing?'

'Oh, I'm surviving. Going to a works do later tonight.'

'Your kids OK?'

'Back with their mother.'

'Probably best for them, honey.'

'Yes, probably.' Swann transferred the phone to his other hand and scrabbled in his pocket for cigarettes. 'How's Lucky Louis?'

'Got promoted, Jack. Unit chief now. Heads up the International Terrorism Ops Unit.'

'Give him my congratulations. What's happening with Salvesen?'

'Arraignment's only just coming up. Takes a while over here.'

'Tell me about it. Boese's still on remand.'

'We're interviewing Salvesen again, Jack. Particularly about the UK connection. Does anyone from SO13 want to speak to him?'

Swann made a face. 'Not right now, I don't think. We've got Boese and enough evidence to get him thirty years. We don't need any more.'

Suddenly he missed her. He didn't really know her and yet he missed her – soft and warm and feminine. He sat forward, scraping a match for his cigarette. 'Have you got any plans to come over here, Cheyenne?'

27

'Not real soon, Jack. Why?'

'I'd like to buy you dinner.'

'So get on a plane. It's only a couple hundred bucks.'

Swann laughed. 'I'd love to. But the chances right now are slim to nothing at all.'

'You and me both then, huh.'

'I suppose we could have a transatlantic telephone relationship,' he said.

'You trying to tell me something, honey?'

'Only if you want me to.'

'When I do, you'll know.'

'I'll look forward to it.'

Neither of them spoke for a few moments; Swann could hear the echo down the line. 'If I do get the chance to come over, I'll phone you, OK, Chey?'

'You better.'

They chatted some more and Swann began to feel that familiar warmth spreading through him – the softness of a woman's voice, her interest in his life. He recalled her touch. The night they arrested Boese, they were celebrating in Los Remos. Cheyenne wore her clothes well, colours to set off the black sheen of her skin. He remembered how she smelled.

'Gotta go, Jack,' she said in the end. 'Bureau's paying for this and I got a meeting to go to.'

'Good to hear from you, Chey. Listen,' Swann sat up straighter, 'tell Louis we've finally met Ben Dubin. You know, his contact from the Jonathan Institute. Tell him Dubin is going to interview Boese.'

Boese was strip searched. He passed his clothes through the day before Dubin was due to arrive and the following morning they strip searched him. When it was done, he dressed in the fresh clothes, face set cold, and sat in the sterile area waiting for Dr Benjamin Dubin, the inter-

28

national academic he had heard on radio stations throughout the world.

Dubin was alone, but their conversation would be monitored, as it always was, by a warden. Chesil: tall, young, thin face with pockmarks still evident from his youth.

Boese was led into the interview room at the far end of the main visitors' suite and found Dubin waiting for him. For a long time they stared, neither one of them speaking, the table between them, but neither one of them sitting. Chesil stood at the door like a guard from Buckingham Palace. Dubin finally extended a hand. 'Ben Dubin,' he said. 'St Andrews University.' Carefully, Boese took the hand, held it for a moment, then released it. Dubin gestured to the vacant chair. 'Please.'

They sat and regarded one another across the short expanse of tabletop, Dubin leaning forward, his elbows on the wood, beaten leather briefcase resting against the leg of the chair. Boese studied him minutely. He dressed like an academic – the briefcase, the badly ironed slacks, and the cuffs on his shirt were ever so slightly frayed. Yet his eyes. His eyes were not the eyes of a professor. Boese felt his pulse rate quicken a fraction. 'Why did you want to see me?' he asked.

Dubin clasped his hands in front of him. 'I'm the director of the centre for the study of terrorism and political violence at St Andrews University. I'm writing a book, almost finished. A biography of Carlos.'

Boese thinned his eyes. 'Where were you before the university?'

'The Jonathan Institute.'

'In Israel.'

'Correct.'

'Where else have you been?'

'The RAND Corporation. US government think tank in California.'

Again they studied one another. Boese thought he could detect a slight nervousness in Dubin, but he was not sure. He had a way of slowly rubbing his hands together.

'What did you do in Israel?'

'Same as I always do. Studied terrorism.'

'The Israelis are terrorists.'

'That's an opinion.'

'You don't share it?'

'They've committed terrorist acts. Begin was a leader of the Irgun. The Stern gang. They blew up the King David Hotel, hanged two captured British army sergeants.' He gestured openly with his hands. 'It's certainly an opinion.'

Boese still sat perfectly still, hands in his lap, slightly back from the table. He was aware of Chesil's gaze. Chesil was unintelligent; this conversation should go over his head. Choose words carefully.

'How long were you in Israel?'

'I went in 1986, just after Reagan bombed Tripoli.'

Boese screwed up one eye a fraction. 'And left?'

'Just after you killed those people in Rome.'

Silence. Boese sat a little closer, his gaze fixed on Dubin, who returned the stare impassively. 'You are Storm Crow, aren't you,' Dubin said. It was a flat, almost monotone statement. Boese looked at him carefully, scanning every millimetre of his eyes. He said nothing. Dubin smiled. 'I didn't expect you to confirm it, but I believe you *are* Storm Crow.' He picked up his pen, where it lay across his pad of paper on the table. 'Do you mind,' he said, 'if I take a few notes?'

'I don't give interviews.'

Dubin looked slightly concerned. 'They told me no tapes, no tapes or pictures.'

Again Boese was silent. Dubin scratched his nose and looked keenly at him. The fluorescent light reflected off his glasses. Boese saw his own face in them. 'What do you wish to know?'

'As much as you're prepared to tell me. I'm particularly interested in the time you spent with Carlos.'

The Jackal. Fat Venezuelan fool. Boese lightly tapped his fingers on the tabletop. 'Ilyich Ramirez Sanchez.' He shook his head. 'He worked for Wadi Haddad in the Yemen. Saddam Hussein over OPEC. The PFLP. I never met him.'

Dubin frowned heavily. 'You were his protégé, Mr Boese. Paris 1982. You were present when he wrote his letter to the Minister for the Interior, Gaston Defferre, declaring his intentions over France. I have separate accounts from two of the "Friends of Carlos" that state as much.'

Slowly Boese shook his head.

'Magdalena Kopp,' Dubin went on. 'Bruno Breguet.'

'I don't know them.'

'Kopp was arrested with Breguet and imprisoned in France. Carlos declared war unless they released her. In 1982, you bombed the Paris–Toulouse express.'

'I wasn't there.'

Dubin sat back again. 'OK,' he said. 'Maybe we can come back to that.' He looked round the room. 'Your motivation for the attacks last year, was that purely money?'

Boese merely looked at him.

'OK.' Dubin lifted both eyebrows. 'Where did you first meet Carlos?'

'I told you. I do not know him.'

'So my information is incorrect.'

'What do you think?'

Dubin held his gaze. 'I don't think it is.' They sat in silence for a few minutes after that, then Dubin changed tack. 'You killed Bruno Kuhlmann, didn't you. You may

31

have known him as Richard Gravitz. Healey Hall Farm in Northumberland. Was that a deliberate sacrifice – to see if the derivative you had worked, or was it just an accident?'

Again Boese said nothing. He was waiting, waiting. Chesil was listening.

'What was your connection with Jakob Salvesen's militia?'

Boese still did not reply.

'I understand.' Dubin held up his hands. 'You're going to trial, you don't wish to prejudice yourself. Forgive me.'

Boese stared at him now.

'Let me ask you a different question. Much has been written about Carlos. But we know he was not actually responsible for anything like what has been attributed to him. He was more a product of the Cold War than anything else. He was in the pocket of Iraq and Syria particularly, perhaps Libya. Countries, regimes were his paymasters. Did you learn anything from that?'

Boese eased back on the legs of his chair. The Jackal had been in it for the money like the rest of them. He had no cause. He played one country off against the other. Boese watched Dubin's eyes. Leaning forward, he clasped his hands together, their faces close now. At the door Chesil stirred, but Boese ignored him. 'What did you do in Israel?'

Dubin looked slightly taken aback, but he smiled. 'I tell you what,' he said. 'Let's trade information. I'll tell you what I do, if you confirm some of these questions of mine.'

Boese considered. 'The Jackal will have told you nothing,' he said. 'You asked him the same questions?'

Dubin nodded.

'And he said nothing.'

'I asked him about you, about Storm Crow. Who gave you the name? The first recorded incident is—'

'Israel,' Boese finished for him. 'In 1989.'

'The US Ambassador's motorcade.'

'Brigitte Hammani and Said Rabi. In Israel,' Boese said again.

Dubin scratched at his pad with the pen, laid it down and sat back. 'I was there. It was during my time with the Jonathan Institute. As far as I was aware, the name did not come from the press like "the Jackal", it was your preferred *nom de guerre*. Where did you get it, Tolkien's *Lord of the Rings*?'

Boese looked puzzled.

'The Riders of Rohan,' Dubin explained. 'The wizard, Gandalf Stormcrow. He only ever showed up when he had ill-tidings to bear.'

Boese did not reply.

Dubin sighed and sat back again. 'This all began with your parents, didn't it. They were active with the SLA. After your parents were imprisoned, how did it feel being handed to a couple you hardly knew? That must've had a profound effect on your life. Has anyone ever considered that all you ever knew in your life was terrorism? SLA, IRA and then Carlos the Jackal.'

Boese stood up and turned to Chesil. 'That's it,' he said. 'I've finished.'

Dubin stared at him. 'I'm sorry . . . I err . . .'

Boese stared back at him, past the glasses into his eyes. There was something about those eyes. Dubin stood up. 'Look, perhaps we can meet again . . .'

Boese followed Chesil out of the room.

# 4

'Remember,' Vaczka said, blue eyes moving from one upturned face to the next. 'The Stanislavsky method.' He held up a stiff index finger. 'It's why we're here. De Niro, Pacino, Dustin Hoffman, James Dean; even Marilyn Monroe tried to learn the method. You *are* the character. You don't so much act as become them. Daniel Day-Lewis, nowadays, is probably the best European exponent. Think of him in *The Boxer*, trained by Barry McGuigan, he could acquit himself in most rings in the country. Total dedication. Becoming that person.' He paused, pressing the bottom of his tight black T-shirt deeper into his sweatpants. 'Ask the question – who are you?'

Amaya Kukiel caught his eye and smiled. He ignored her, deliberately, just leaving his gaze there long enough to catch the swift change in her expression. He liked how she looked today, with her dyed blonde hair piled on her head so braids fell and danced about her ears.

'Pieter,' he said, clapping his hands. 'Show me.' He sat back on the tall stool then, one foot on the rung, the other on the floor, toes scrunched into black jazz shoes. He folded hairy forearms across his chest. Pieter Jeconec stood up and moved to the centre of the floor, while the others all eased themselves to the side. For a moment, Jeconec looked at the floor and then shifted his chin to his chest, half lifting one arm, the fingers spread out. He started speaking, weary-voiced, Miller's *Death of a Salesman* – the scene where Willy tells Linda how much he loves her – looking at the studio wall as if it were her face.

Vaczka nodded to Kukiel, who stood up, smoothed

hands over her flanks and moved to a mock mirror where she put on an imaginary hat. She laughed softly to herself. Jeconec continued, talking about his loneliness, his fears for the future, his desperation at not selling, having nothing to leave for his boys.

The scene ended and Vaczka stood up. 'Good. Good, Pieter. Excellent.' He smiled at Kukiel. 'Thank you,' he said, and gestured once more at Jeconec. 'Willy Loman. He was Willy Loman.' He paused then, hands on his hips, blue eyes scanning every pair that looked so expectantly back at him. 'OK, that's it till next time.'

He stood poring over his notes and heard Amaya behind him. He could smell her, the faint hint of perspiration. He half turned, reached out a hand and clasped her fingers, drawing her to him. She touched him lightly on the buttocks and nuzzled into his neck.

'Everybody gone?'

'Yes.'

He straightened. 'Good. Lock the door.'

She stared at him. 'Jorge, we can't . . .'

'Lock the door, Kukiel.' He always called her by her last name; he liked to – it added to the feeling of power he knew he had over her. He moved towards her, aware of the hint of moisture gathered at the seamhead of her leotard, red and skin-tight over black dancing pants. He liked them free and supple for movement at this stage in their endeavours. Costumes could come later.

They were in a classroom on the top floor of the POSK, the Polish university complex on King Street in West London. The floor was deserted, the theatre auditorium was being renovated and this studio was the only room in use. Vaczka moved past her to the door, locked it with a twist of the key and pulled the blind down over the reinforced glass. Amaya giggled. Vaczka leaned against the stool once more, a quiet smile on his lips. She looked at the clock on the wall. 'I'm due in the cafeteria.'

'Not for fifteen minutes.' Again he smiled. 'That's enough time to fuck me.'

He moved towards her, reaching out with a finger to tug at the top of the leotard. Her breasts were swollen against the Lycra, nipples suddenly erect under his gaze. He stirred in the loose-fitting sweatpants he wore. She reached up, wrapping both arms about his neck, mouth puckered towards his. He kissed her softly at first, then pressing down he could feel her teeth edged against his. Her lips were full and very red; they always were after class. She could not act, but she was keen and that was all that mattered to him.

He eased fingers inside her leotard and it came away, down the line of her shoulders, exposing the fullness of her breasts and high-pointed nipples, that lifted with a covering of gooseflesh. Vaczka bent to them, tugging each one in turn with his teeth, while she moaned in her throat and rubbed herself against him. He pressed her, walking her back against the wall, and hoisted his T-shirt over his head.

'What if someone comes . . .' He crushed the rest of the words from her mouth with his. He took her against the wall; sweats round his ankles, her tights off, and dark pubic hair under his fingers. And then inside her, pushing up and in until she gasped so loudly he had to put his free hand over her mouth.

Afterwards, he dressed again and watched her, still half-naked, slumped on the floor, looking at him dull-eyed, with her legs splayed and the mound of pubic hair pushing up at him. He always hated her afterwards and could never understand why. 'Get dressed.' He looked at the clock. 'You'll be late.' Then he laughed as he pulled on his T-shirt, and added, 'And I'm hungry.'

'Bastard,' she said.

Vaczka looked down at her. 'If you don't want it hard, you shouldn't pout at me in class.'

She was on her feet now, fiddling with her knickers and pushing the fallen hair from her eyes. 'I don't pout at you,' she said.

She was late, and Carmen, the manageress, a big woman in her forties with blonde hair and too much lipstick, tutted at her as she fastened her apron. Amaya's face was flushed, sweat still glistened on her brow, and Carmen could smell the sex on her. Vaczka was already seated at one of the green and white tables, drinking thick black coffee and flicking through the newspapers. Carmen looked at him with lust in her eyes; he must be nearing her age and his body was still firm. Jeconec came and sat next to him.

'Good?'

Vaczka did not acknowledge the comment, leafed through a few more pages until Amaya came over with a plate of *bigos* for him. He spooned meat and cabbage into his mouth, dripping gravy on to his chin. He glanced at Jeconec. 'You know, you were not bad in there just now.'

Jeconec lifted an eyebrow. 'How the fuck would you know?'

Vaczka laughed through his gravy. 'Exactly. But I'm Polish. I talk a good game and I have the right certificates. What more do they want?' He glanced over at the counter to where Amaya was dishing dark, jammed doughnuts on to a plate for the one-legged man who always came in on Tuesdays. 'Besides, the students love me.'

He spooned more stew into his mouth and spoke while he chewed. 'Any word?'

'None.'

'What about Blunski?'

'Nothing.'

Vaczka frowned. 'Funny,' he said. 'It's been a while now.'

Jeconec looked at Amaya's breasts through her shirt.

'Go and have a look in the window,' Vaczka told him.

'Now?'

'Yes. Now. We need to look every day.'

For a second, Jeconec squinted at him as if he were about to protest, but he did not. Instead he got up and walked outside, down the steps on to King Street. He glanced at the kids milling about the entrance to Latymer High School and walked the short distance to the corner of Ravenscourt Road. A few people wandered down from the tube station and a few more were gathered outside the newsagent's window, scanning the hundreds of little postcards which all but filled the glass. Everything you could think of was advertised there, from lawnmowers to piano lessons; and all of it was in Polish. Two men, whom Jeconec recognized but did not know, eagerly scanned the cards. Jeconec looked for a wholly different reason, picking out each card in turn and carefully reading the contents. It took him twenty minutes, then he sighed and walked back to the POSK.

Vaczka was flirting with Carmen while she loitered over clearing his table. His mobile phone rang and she moved off, allowing Jeconec to resume his seat. Vaczka spoke softly in Polish, then switched the phone off and laid it on the table. He sucked at the strings of meat between his teeth.

'Well?'

Jeconec shook his head. 'Who was that on the phone?'

'Herbisch.'

'Anything?'

'Not a word.'

Behind the counter Amaya watched them carefully, but she could not tell what they were saying. She had seen Jeconec go outside and watched him from the window as he made his way to King Street. She knew what he would be doing. He had done the same thing every day for two weeks now. Vaczka was agitated (or as agitated as she had seen him) over something, but she did not know what it was. He must have felt her gaze for he looked up and stared into her eyes. There was something about those eyes that disturbed her, a cruelty deep within them that she had experienced from time to time. He studied the newspaper once more and then he yawned and sat back.

'How much time shall we give it?' Jeconec asked him.

Vaczka looked witheringly at him. 'What sort of a question is that? We wait. Tell the others. We just sit and wait.'

Jeconec scraped his chair back and got up. 'See you later, then.'

'Tonight, yes.' Vaczka was looking towards the counter again. 'I think I'll fuck Carmen,' he said. 'See if it pisses off Kukiel.'

'Carmen's fat,' Jeconec said.

Vaczka looked up at him with a glint in his eye. 'You know what they say about fat women.'

Amaya finished work at four and, collecting her bag, she wandered outside. It was raining now and almost dark. She hated this time of year – damp, cold and dark, the streets of London smelling of garbage and too many people in too many cars; even the wind had the resinous tang of the river. She walked towards the tube station, passing the boarded-up offices, which had still not been let. She only lived a couple of streets away, but she wanted to look in the newsagent's window. Vaczka was long gone, back to his flat or his friends or whatever other jobs he did. His work at the college was only part-time, and she knew now he did not have the appropriate qualifications. There was no problem with looking in the window of the newsagent's; everybody did, every Pole in the neighbourhood; seeking

39

work, buying, selling, whatever. Mini-crowds would gather all day long, with bits of paper and stubs of pencil, jotting down what it was they thought they needed to know.

Amaya looked hard, but she did not know what it was she was looking for exactly. She had seen Jeconec looking day after day, not just him but Blunski too, and on one occasion, the blond-haired silent one called Stahl. As she was scanning the window, she was suddenly aware of somebody watching her and for a moment she thought it was Vaczka. She turned with a start, but none of those near her was taking more than a cursory interest. She shook the feeling away, then glanced further afield at the buildings across the road. Then she turned towards Ravenscourt Park tube station and saw Julian leaning in the doorway, watching her. He was not alone. The woman, Christine, was walking down the road towards her. Amaya felt her heart sink. It was a month since she had seen either of them and she was just beginning to hope. That hope faded now, and, glancing at her watch, she turned back along King Street and made her way towards the park. A train thundered above the arches as she got there, heading back into central London. There was nobody sitting on the benches, no children playing in the sandpit or the playground. It was too cold and too dark to do anything other than cross the park purposefully on your way somewhere. Amaya thought about pausing under the arches, but a glance over her shoulder told her to keep walking. Christine was following her.

Four months ago they had approached her. She was working as a barmaid then, in the Stonemason's Arms, just off Hammersmith Broadway. First it was just him; Julian, he had said his name was. He used to come in and chat to her, ask lots of questions. She was free and easy with her conversation; over here doing an academic course. She had been born in Gdansk and her father was one of those who

40

fought with Lech Walesa for freedom. She was not study-ing at the POSK, no, but at the University of London, eighteen months into a three-year degree course. When she was qualified, she hoped to go back to Poland and teach.

He had been very nice to her, tipping her occasionally and buying her drinks. She thought that he had just been chatting her up, as so many punters did. She ignored most of them and always refused when they asked her out on a date. Julian never asked her out, however, and he never talked about himself. It was always her, what she was doing, who she was seeing, how her family were, how her studies were progressing. Then one night he came in with a woman. They sat at a table and talked together and Amaya got the strangest feeling that their conversation was about her in some way. Julian did not say much to her that night, polite enough when he ordered drinks, but said very little. Three nights in a row the two of them came in and then one night they approached her.

She was leaving work and a car was squatting on double yellow lines a little further along the road, close to the UPi building. She thought nothing of it, but as she made her way down towards the Broadway, the car suddenly drove up alongside her. Julian was driving.

'Let me give you a lift,' he said. 'I'm going your way.'

'Have you been waiting for me?'

'No.' His face was open and smiling.

It was late and she was tired. 'OK, then.'

Reaching behind, he opened the back door and she got in. The woman he had been in the pub with was sitting there.

'Hello, Amaya,' she said. 'My name's Christine.'

They drove her back to Ravenscourt Park and her converted bedsit off Ravenscourt Road. They were careful about being seen, but insisted she invite them inside. The room was small, a tiny kitchenette off it and a shared bathroom upstairs. Julian sat on the bed.

'What is this about?' Amaya could feel the nerves in her lower belly fluttering like the wings of butterflies. Christine was pretty, but cold-faced. Julian was still all smiles. He sighed before he spoke.

'Your visa runs out at the end of the year, Amaya.'

'I know. I must get it renewed.'

He nodded slowly. 'So you can finish your course?'

'Yes. It's very important to me.'

'Teaching.' Christine spoke to her.

'The course first, but then teaching.'

'Make a lot of money in Poland, do they, teachers, I mean?' she asked her.

'Quite good, yes.' Amaya had her hands in her lap, knees drawn up, rubbing the sweat with her fingers. She looked at Julian. 'What is this about? I haven't done anything wrong.'

He smiled at her in an almost fatherly manner and reached out to pat her knee. 'Of course you haven't. Don't worry.'

She looked at them then, each face in turn, tugging at her lip with her teeth. 'Who exactly are you?' she said.

'We work for the government, Amaya,' Christine told her. 'Nothing for you to worry about.'

She stood up then and picked up a set of family photographs that were standing on the mantelpiece, and pointed to a man in his late forties with a shock of grey curling hair. 'Father?' she said.

Amaya nodded. 'Please, what is this about? I'm very tired and I have to work tomorrow.'

'Pleased with you, is he – your father?' Christine replaced the photograph on the mantelpiece. 'Glad you have this opportunity to study in England?'

'Yes, he is. Very. It's a chance he never had.'

42

'I'm sure.' Christine sat down again and laid a hand on her arm. 'You know a man called Jorge Vaczka, Amaya?'

Amaya squinted at her. 'I know who he is. I see him sometimes at the POSK.'

'Your other job.'

'In the cafeteria, yes.'

'Do you like him?'

'He's OK to talk to.'

'Fun?'

'I suppose.' Amaya was aware of her need to go to the toilet. She crossed her legs, intertwining fingers in her lap.

Christine sat back on the bed and rested a fist on her knee. Her clothes were dark, expensive. Amaya could smell the scent of her perfume.

'Jorge Vaczka teaches drama,' Julian said. 'Small classes, the Stanislavsky method.' He paused for a moment, as if considering whether to broach a subject or not. He glanced at Christine.

'Amaya,' she said. 'We need you to help us.' She smiled then for the first time. 'You're a pretty girl. Has Jorge ever asked you out?'

'For a date? Yes. I said, no.'

Julian laid a hand on her arm. 'We've watched you, Amaya, for a long time now. We've watched Jorge. He'd like to take you out. He'd like to take you out very much.' He paused momentarily. 'We'd like you to give him some encouragement. We'd like you to go out with him.'

Amaya was looking from one to the other now, incomprehension on her face.

'I don't understand,' she said. 'Why should I go out with him? Why are *you* interested in him?'

They told her then; Vaczka was involved in something illegal, or so they believed. They needed her help to get information. They were, she realized now, some kind of agents for the security services. They told her that if she

43

wasn't able to help them, then she might have some trouble with her visa renewal. And it would be such a shame to have to go home to Poland without her qualifications.

Christine walked alongside her now, past the withered flowerbeds, the earth rock hard behind the wire-meshed borders. 'What news, Amaya?' she said without looking up. There was no one on the path save an old man a hundred yards ahead of them. Another tube train thundered over the bridge at their backs. Glancing behind, Amaya saw Julian under the arches, the other side of the fence.

'No news.'

'Nothing?' Christine made a clicking sound with her tongue. 'You're not doing very well, are you, my dear.'

Amaya felt the shallows of her belly knot together; the old helplessness welling up inside her. 'He's doing something. Jeconec is always talking to him. He takes calls on his mobile phone.'

'Who from?' Christine squinted sideways at her. 'Stahl? Herbisch?'

'I don't know. Herbisch, I think.'

'What about the newsagent's?'

'Jeconec looked today. I looked today. You saw me. But there was nothing there.'

'Has he mentioned anything to you about Ireland?'

Amaya stopped then and looked directly at her. 'No. Nothing.'

Christine sighed. 'Something is happening, Amaya. We know that from other sources. We need you to find out what. Sleep with him. Men talk in bed, especially when they're satisfied.'

'I *am* sleeping with him.' Amaya wrung out her hands. 'What more can I do?'

'That's up to you.' Christine's face was cold now, black-gloved hand clasping her bag, the collar up on her navy cashmere coat. 'Think about your visa, Amaya. Think about your father and mother in Poland. Think about all their expectations. I'll be in touch.' She turned and walked on.

Jack Swann sipped coffee from a plastic cup and placed it on the conference room table on the sixteenth floor of New Scotland Yard. Colson had summoned him and Webb to a briefing given by Christine Harris. The situation she had been watching had moved on enough to bring the Branch in. Harris was speaking. Next to her sat Julian Moore from MI5. On the table between them, a slide projector hummed quietly.

'It's been a joint Box/SO12 operation thus far,' Harris was saying. 'Julian?'

He cleared his throat. There were only a handful of them there: Swann and Webb, DI Clements and Colson. 'Our colleagues from Box 850 gave us the original information. Jorge Vaczka was resident in the UK.' He made a face. 'We didn't know him before then. I suppose he had always been small time.' He stood up and switched off the lights. Harris picked up the handset to move the slides and slotted the first frame into place. A man's face appeared on the expanse of white wall at the head of the table.

'He looks younger than forty,' Webb said.

Harris nodded. 'Ladies' man, George. Keeps himself in shape. Right now, he teaches the Stanislavsky method to drama students at the Polish Centre on King Street, Ravenscourt Park.'

Swann scraped his fingers across the wood of the table. 'Nice work, if you can get it,' he muttered. He studied Vaczka's face – cold, blue eyes and dark, short-cut hair, bright with the sheen of gel.

The next slide was a younger man, again with short-cut hair, and puffy cheeks, full-lipped, and unshaven as

Vaczka. 'Adam Herbisch,' Harris went on. 'He runs the support group, premises, vehicles, employment. He has huge contacts within the Polish community here in London.'

She paused and flicked to the next slide and Moore spoke again now. 'Innocent looking, isn't he,' he said. Swann stared at the boyish, blond-haired man with blue eyes and a mischievous grin on his face. 'Robert Stahl,' Moore went on. 'According to our colleagues at Vauxhall Cross, he's responsible for at least three killings in Eastern Europe. Over here he's responsible for operations.'

Harris moved the slides on to other faces. 'Blunski,' she said. 'Looks after their intelligence. Jeconec. Vaczka's personal eyes and ears.'

When she was finished, Moore put the lights back on. 'Professional,' Swann said.

'And well funded.' Moore folded his arms and looked at Colson. 'We believe they're backed by Sabri al-Banna, alias Abu Nidal. The Abu Nidal Organization's been around for years. Nidal himself lived in Poland between 1981 and 1984, and he's got a multinational arms company based there. His group, as we know, has been used by Syria, Iraq, Libya. There've been others, though. His Palestinian links are all but gone now and he's pretty much for hire. Mossad first alerted 850 to this Polish element years ago; they infiltrated the ANO way back.'

Swann toyed with his coffee cup. 'Is Vaczka's team directly linked to Nidal?'

'Funded by, I suppose, is a fairer term. Or at least they have been. They run weapons for him predominantly, but they have all the attributes, structure etc., of a terrorist group in their own right. Intel', support activity and ops.'

'Just like us,' Webb commented.

'The game's the same, isn't it.'

'What's Vaczka doing over here?' Colson asked him.

Moore sighed heavily. 'That bit we don't know. Like we said just now, he teaches at the POSK, but he has no qualifications. He's got all the right bits of paper, but he's never been near a drama school.' He glanced at Christine Harris. 'It's a cover. The ANO pay him indirectly. He lives on Lime Grove, a ground-floor flat with stripped floors, basement study and a landscaped garden.' Again he looked at Harris.

'We've suborned an informant,' she said. 'Somebody close to him. Female.'

'Pillow talk,' Webb said.

Harris smiled at him. 'That's the idea. You know how men like to talk in bed, George.'

Swann flinched. Harris caught his eye and coloured. Quickly she turned to Moore.

'Box 850's original information was related to Ulster,' he said. 'The word was he might have links with some of the underground Loyalist factions.'

'Weapons from Abu Nidal?' Swann curled his lip.

'Wouldn't be the first time, would it.' Colson pushed back his chair. 'So, what've you got from your snout?'

Harris sucked breath. 'That's the difficult bit. We haven't got much. All she can tell us right now is that something is going down. Vaczka contacts the rest of the cell through advert cards in a newsagent's window. It's simple and effective and safe. Every day hundreds of Poles gather on King Street and look at them. It must be how things are done in Poland. I don't know.'

'The activity is high right now,' Moore put in. 'We know that much. Something is moving and we need to keep tabs on it. We're briefing you chaps now, so if we need to move quickly, you'll be ready.' He looked again at Harris. 'That's about it, yeah?'

She nodded. 'Jack, I'll liaise directly with you down-stairs, if there's anything else we need to talk about.'

47

'Fine.' Swann got up, tossed his coffee cup in the bin and followed Webb out of the room.

Boese watched Terlucci disinterestedly across the woodwork shop. He was fashioning the prow of a boat. Five minutes till they were exercised like hounds in the yard. Boese bent to his own work, a small wooden image of Geronimo the Apache. Boese bunched his eyes, aware of the knot of thought at his temple. He considered again the little man from Scotland, with the New York City accent and questions about the Jackal. Six months of silence and then the visitor with eyes that did not belong. Boese had seen eyes like that before, and the beginnings of an anger burned inside him. Yet he could not be sure. He could never be sure. He stopped then, scuffing at a burr of wood on the muzzle of the Springfield rifle that Geronimo held across his chest. He carved the wood from memory: an old photo of the renegade standing by a train with Naiche. The slash of his mouth and the cunning cruelty in his eyes; he was the very last one to be captured, back in 1880. He could sense Terlucci's confusion and, as he looked up, the Italian knifeman looked away. Boese allowed his own gaze to linger for a moment or two, just to remind him. He did not know what Terlucci had said to the Blues Brothers, but no one was bothering him now.

Morgan was in the exercise yard, collar up on his jacket, pacing with his hands in his pockets like a polar bear trapped in a zoo. Again, Boese remembered Swann's words: *Forty-two paces in one direction and then you have to turn.* He looked up at the sky through the grim slits of wire and tried to remember what the pale sun looked like without lines of grey running across it like scars. Irritation; his calm was broken and he knew it. He sought Morgan's face as they moved past one another in opposite directions. The warden watched from the doorway, leaning with his back to it, his coat buttoned and his breath coming as steam. Morgan held his eye, the same coldness reflected in the darkness of his own.

Inside, they sat across the chess table from one another. Boese had played him once since he won, and was able to lose without it looking obvious. Morgan was pleased, the desire to win was evident in the clipped tension in his jawline. Afterwards, he had almost managed a smile. Now they sat across from one another again and Boese studied the board. He knew that the wardens were watching them from the control room and he spoke without looking at Morgan's face.

'Take your tobacco out and drop your cigarette papers on the floor.'

Morgan did not answer him, his arms folded against the tabletop, scrutinizing the move Boese had just made with his second knight. He said nothing. Boese said nothing, and then Morgan reached behind him to his jacket pocket and took out his tobacco. The packet of Rizla papers fluttered to the floor under the table. As he bent to retrieve it, Boese let go two papers himself. Morgan retrieved them and scraped them under the tin as he placed it on the table. He quietly rolled a cigarette and returned his attention to the game. Boese beat him, then went back to his cell.

Brynn Morgan recalled Griffiths's response when he had asked him to send the money for a train fare to his sister. Initially, his expression had been one of suspicion, because she had not visited in a year. But then Morgan explained his motives, his desire not to lose touch with the only family he had. What would happen to him when he eventually got out, if he did? Now he laid the two flimsy papers with one glued edge on the bed. Picking up the paperback novel he was reading, he slid both papers against the page and leaned on his elbow to read.

# 5

A week after Boese and Morgan played chess for the third time, Morgan's sister came to visit. Morgan did not mention it. Boese only found out when Morgan was strip searched before being allowed in to the visitors' suite. Others had visitors – McClellan and Gianluca Terlucci. Boese worked out in the gym while Morgan saw his sister. Calm again, he hung upside-down as he liked to, allowing the heat of blood to pucker the skin of his face and soak into his brain.

Morgan spoke quietly to his sister across the table in the visitors' suite. Nothing unusual in that, he always spoke quietly, said little. It was a habit he had perfected during early stretches inside. An old lag had advised him, avoid the quiet ones who look as though they would not hurt a fly. His sister was fifteen years younger than him; Cathy, the only member of the family who had not disowned him. She had a son of eleven; her husband having run off as soon as he knew she was pregnant. They spoke about life outside, what was going on, how she was doing, how her son, Ieuan, was getting on at school. Halfway through the conversation Morgan took out his tobacco, rolled himself a cigarette and laid the green package of Rizla papers on the table. The warden was gazing disinterestedly at the wall, twirling a set of keys round the end of his finger. Morgan looked in his sister's eyes and tapped the green packet with a bitten-down fingernail. She sat forward and covered the papers with her hand, then fished in her pocket for her packet of Golden Virginia. She laid a fresh packet of papers on the table and Morgan rolled a cigarette for her, before slipping the packet inside his tin.

October had been cold, November was much better. The Cambrils beachfront was empty, though the sun shone low above the greenish blue restlessness of the Mediterranean. A few English expatriates wandered along the footpaths that flanked the flat pale sand, and mini, white-foamed breakers crawled at the edges of rocks. Tal-Salem sat at an aluminium table in an aluminium chair outside his favourite bar, where the Turkish waiter made him Café Arabi. Cigarette smoke drifted in the light breeze, and he flapped open the pages of the *International Herald Tribune*, as he had done once a month since the summer. Today was the fifth, bonfire night in England. He perused the pages, sipping thick, dark coffee and sucking at the end of his cigarette. He found the advertisements and read each one very carefully. He did not know exactly what he was looking for, but he would know if he found it. His gaze settled on a strange collection of words.

TO SELL BOOKCASES TO ENGINES TO
XYLOPHONES.
AND SHORTLY TO BE IN YORK AND
BIRMINGHAM AND BRIGHTON.
IN KENDAL NEXT YEAR. FOR BEDS OR QUEEN
ANNE OVAL MIRRORS, XYLOPHONES OR
VIOLINS, CALL BRITISH AND ANGLIAN.

Tal-Salem stared at the page, aware of the pulse heightened against his temple. He finished his cigarette and, folding the newspaper on the table, summoned the waiter for more coffee and a sheet of paper and pencil. The coffee came and he lit another cigarette before settling down with the pencil. Very carefully, he went through the advertisement again and started picking out letters; the first in every other word. TBEXSBYBBKYBQOXVBA.

He paused and sat back and smoked some more, watching a girl in shorts walk down to the sea with a pair of white tennis shoes in one hand. A seagull hovered in the wind and cried above her head, as if it were expecting her to throw some bread or fish. The same breeze caught her ink-black hair as she stared at the boats, dotted like chips of paint against the grey of the horizon. Tal-Salem looked back at the letters, then wrote out two English alphabets beneath them, beginning the second one under the D of the first one. It was a code they had agreed on, very simple, but nonetheless effective. It had been used centuries before, when Caesar wrote covertly to Cicero. When he was finished, a little chill ran through him and he sat back. The cigarette had burned low in the ashtray. He stared at what he had deciphered. WE HAVE BEEN BETRAYED.

Amaya Kukiel sat on the rug that Vaczka had placed in front of his smokeless fire. He stood before the rectangular mirror that dominated the wall above the mantelpiece, combing wet hair. Through the bay window Amaya could see the dark strip of hedge and the windows of the houses opposite.

'Where we going?' she asked.

'Just for a drink.'

'Where?'

'The Bush Ranger. They've got a band tonight.'

'Just us?'

'No. A couple of friends will be there.'

'Do I know them?'

He stopped combing his hair and looked down at her, one hand on his hips. 'Robert, Adam, Pieter maybe. Some girls, I guess. I don't know. I just said I'd meet some people. Go home if you want to. You don't have to come.'

She stood up and slipped her arms about his waist. 'Course I want to come.'

'Then why ask so many questions?' He pushed her arms off and took a clean T-shirt from where it lay on the tallboy. Briefly, he inspected the dusty leaves of the rubber plant and then went into the kitchen for water. Amaya stared at herself in the mirror and saw the nervousness in her eyes. This was her state of mind these days; it had been ever since that night when those two security officers wandered into her life. She had no idea such things were possible in a liberal democracy like this. Poland before Solidarity, yes. East Berlin and Moscow before the Wall came down. But this was England. Her visa, and with it her future, hung perpetually in the balance.

Vaczka came back and bent down to lace his shoes. 'Get your coat, if you're coming,' he said.

Silent Stahl, with the laughing eyes and boyish grin, was already sitting at a table. Next to him were Jeconec and Blunski. Three girls, only one of whom Amaya recognized, were also there. She looked about for others and saw Herbisch at the bar. This was different, she thought; never had she seen all of them together like this. Occasionally, she would see Jorge with one of them, maybe Herbisch and Blunski together, but never all three of them, and rarely with Stahl at all. Herbisch crossed the dusty wooden floor and placed a tray of drinks on the table. On the far side of the pub, a girl was plucking at the five strings of her banjo, plinking the note, then tightening the string. Seated at the bar with his back to them, a bearded, dark-skinned man smoked Turkish cigarettes.

Vaczka was in a good mood. The band played their first set and the dark-skinned man swivelled on his stool to watch. The girl's voice was good – sweet, deep and mellow in her throat. She sang with a low passion and seemed to look above the faces of the audience as she did so. The set ended and she put her banjo down, spoke briefly with the guy on the guitar and bought a drink at the bar. The dark-skinned man lit another cigarette, finished his vodka and bought another. Now and then he would glance out of the window, then his gaze would fall momentarily on to the gathering at the table behind him. Vaczka; Stahl was with him. Herbisch and Blunski too. And women, a particularly pretty girl, blonde hair and big eyes. She sat close to Vaczka with her palm between his thighs. Her drink looked untouched on the table before her.

Just as the band was about to start up again, a slim-built man in his twenties stumbled along the bar, with his Japanese girlfriend attempting to steady him. His hair was long, well past his shoulders and heavy over his face. He kept sweeping it back with his hand. He carried a glass of pale beer which slopped on to the floor as he lurched. The music began and he clicked his multi-ringed fingers to the beat, and jogged against Stahl as he turned to watch. Stahl pushed him away and beer slopped over the long hair's leather trousers.

'Fucking . . .' He shook his head, hair falling over his eyes. Tal-Salem watched Stahl gather his fingers into a fist. The long-haired guy stared at him and then down at his trousers. 'Fucking tosser,' he muttered and made a loose gesture with his right hand, curling the ends of his fingers and thumb together.

Stahl was half out of his seat, when the weight of Vaczka's hand on his arm stopped him. Vaczka leaned over the table and spoke to the long hair, holding out a five-pound note as he did so. 'Buy yourself another,' he said, voice lifting over the music. 'Drink it at the other end of the bar.'

The long hair snipped the note out of his hand, made the gesture of shooting a pistol at Stahl and staggered away. Vaczka sat back, and then his eyes met those of the bearded

54

man at the bar, who held his gaze for a moment, before turning once more to his drink.

'You should've let me take him outside,' Stahl muttered.

'That would be really clever.'

Amaya squeezed his hand, as if to remind him she was there, but he ignored her. He looked at the bearded man's back, then shook his head and picked up his glass. He drank, wiped his mouth and lit a cigarette. Stahl was brooding, half watching the band, half looking for the long-haired guy. Blunski shifted in his seat and looked up at Vaczka.

'So, what do you know?' Vaczka asked him quietly.

'Nothing.'

'You sure?' Again, Vaczka was looking at the man at the bar.

'Certain.' Blunski sucked froth from his beer. 'We're clean, safe. Nobody is looking at us.'

Vaczka looked up at the bar. There was a space where the bearded man had been.

Tal-Salem sat in the car he had rented and smoked Lebanese gold in a long, loose joint. He liked to roll them loose to allow the tobacco some breath and let the smoke thicken before entering his lungs. The streetlights were dull, and his breathing easy as the hashish gently probed his veins. He could feel the fragment of sweat at his hairline and the slight weight in his eyes, as he watched the walkers approach. One of them, the man, had metal-tipped soles and Tal-Salem could hear him clip-clopping through the slight gap in the window. He slouched lower in his seat and saw them walk up to the front door of the ground-floor flat. The street was quiet, though the traffic still moved on the Goldhawk Road. The blonde girl was still with him. He would have to find out her name.

*

Swann could not sleep. He got up and went to the roof of his building. He had a small roof garden, fenced, though he did little to keep the plants in any kind of order. When he had had the children living with him, the nanny used to tend to them, but since they had gone so had she, and the plants were left to themselves. He put on a dressing gown and stood in the freezing November air with the weight of winter cloud stretching over the city, and smoked a cigarette in the darkness. He could hear the vague movement of traffic on Waterloo Bridge, but his street was quiet at this time of night. The flat felt soulless and empty.

He recalled the day Rachael, his former wife, came and took the children away, reminding him that he could go back to the life he had had before with Pia. Little did she know then that Pia Grava was really Brigitte Hammani and Brigitte Hammani was owned by the Storm Crow. He thought about her a lot; those eighteen months had felt real and he could not just drop them from memory. At night, nights like these in particular, he could sometimes smell her in his bed; a hint of how it used to be, the soft nakedness of a woman; warmth when he woke from his dreams. Ironically, in a way, he had not dreamt for ages. Perhaps he *had* exorcized some of the demons when he poured his heart out to her that night, last winter, in Scotland. She had listened intently, had touched him, stroked his face, told him everything was all right; but it did not feel that way. Right now, he felt as though he had opened himself up for no reason. Nothing was sorted out, everything remained as before, fractured; like the broken pieces of some interminable jigsaw puzzle that he had been trying to finish for years.

Back downstairs, he looked at the telephone, the need to speak to somebody was all at once acute. Sweat gathered on his brow and he felt vaguely feverish. He let go a stiff breath and told himself to get a grip. He wondered then at how lonely he felt. He had rarely felt this lonely before, except perhaps when he woke that awful morning, high on the Diamir face of Nanga Parbat, having killed his climbing partner. This feeling was reminiscent of that, part of that, inextricably linked to that. Swann picked up the photo of his two girls, both of them smiling in that exaggerated way children do when faced with the lens of a camera. Rachael was living with her boyfriend now and he was back to every other weekend. He hated the thought of some other man bringing up his children. He glanced at the telephone once more and thought of Cheyenne Logan. She had called him out of the blue. He looked at his watch – too late. He only had her number at FBI headquarters, not her home phone. Switching off the light, he went back downstairs to his bed, and lay there till morning, staring at the patterns woven by streetlights on his ceiling.

Tal-Salem, skin dyed black, perused the Polish bookshop, listening to the clatter of dishes in the café next door. The assistant asked if she could help him and he smiled, but said no, he was only looking. His nose was a latex prosthesis and his hair was nappy and kinked like an Afro-Caribbean and the assistant gave him barely a second glance. He was pleased. Boese had taught him well and the sensation of power this generated set the adrenalin pumping. He asked the assistant if the poetry, Polish one side and English the other, was any good and she told him it depended on his taste. He nodded, smiled and thanked her, then went through to the green and white cafeteria. Vaczka was there with the one called Jeconec, seated at a table eating potato and flour balls filled with meat. The fat waitress served them, all lipstick and dyed blonde hair.

No sign of the girlfriend, and then she appeared, hair moist, from the shower no doubt. Her skin was flushed with the red sheen of hot water and sweat. She sat down with Vaczka and ordered a cup of coffee. Tal-Salem watched her, gaze flitting from Vaczka's face to the waitress and the street outside. He sipped from his own cup and considered. Earlier he had wandered the building, free to look around according to the receptionist. He had witnessed Vaczka's class through the glass door of the studio and nodded to the workmen in the theatre auditorium. Vaczka and Jeconec carried on their conversation as if the girl was not there. Tal-Salem got up and wandered back to the street. The newsagent's on the corner of King Street intrigued him; all those people gathered outside the window, looking at adverts placed on cards against the glass. He crossed the road and paused outside the high school. From here he could see the cafeteria; Vaczka and Jeconec still seated at their table. No sign of the girlfriend. And then he saw her, walking down towards King Street.

She paused outside the newsagent's, giving a cursory glance at the cards before moving on to the tube station. Tal-Salem followed her, hands in the pockets of his raincoat. On the platform heading east into London, she seemed in a daze and if she noticed the black man who had been in the café, she did not show it. Tal-Salem got in the same carriage, but further up, a seat against the window, and flapped out a copy of *The Times*. The girl seemed lost in thoughts of her own, a troubled expression crowding the beauty of her face.

She got out of the train at Victoria and went up to the main line station. Tal-Salem followed at a discreet distance, wary of his exposure now to any third eye looking out for the girl. He followed her outside and into the winter sunshine, a frost on the pavements this morning and a biting chill to the air. Tal-Salem had travelled down Victoria Street before, but that had been in the back of a taxi to collect an economist named Jean-Marie Mace. Not long after, Mace's children were orphans.

The girl walked hurriedly now, purpose in her stride, her hair blowing out at the sides of her face, pink and yellow striped bag dangling from one shoulder. Fifty yards behind, Tal-Salem passed the Army & Navy Store and then McDonald's, and then she crossed the road and went into Pret A Manger. He slowed now; there was plenty of time and he could learn all he wanted from this side of the street. He drew parallel with Pret A Manger and saw the girl sitting at one of the circular metal tables with another woman. She was neatly dressed in a two-piece jacket and skirt, dark hair, and had an earnest look on her face as she sipped cappuccino. Tal-Salem had seen the signs before. He knew now what had happened.

Amaya sat with Christine Harris and nibbled a sandwich. Harris stirred her coffee and scanned the street outside. 'They were talking last night,' Amaya was saying. 'The four of them, together at the house. Stahl, Herbisch, Blunski and Jorge.'

'What did they say?'

'Something about time, waiting. They seemed very frustrated.' Amaya flicked hair from her eyes. 'I'd already gone to bed and I had to listen through the wall. Then I got up and went to the door, but I couldn't stay too long in case they came out. They were drinking beer, getting up and down to go to the toilet.'

'What exactly did they say?' Harris asked her, eyes on the other lunchers.

'I only heard a few snippets. But they've been waiting for something, some word. I'm sure it's due to be posted in the newsagent's. Jeconec looks every day.'

'Did they say anything about guns, Amaya?'

Amaya lifted her shoulders, lips turned down a fraction at the corners. 'If they did, I didn't hear it.'

Harris sat back and studied her. 'I need more than that.'

Amaya glared at her suddenly. 'This isn't easy, you know. What am I supposed to do? Hey, Jorge, tell me what's going on, will you? The secret service wants to know.'

'Keep your voice down.' Harris's eyes were suddenly cold.

Amaya looked away, bit her lip. 'How much longer does this go on?'

'Until we get what we need.'

'You're blackmailing me.'

'No we're not, Amaya. We're helping you, helping you get the qualifications you need, so you can go home and help your family, your country's economy. This is a gesture of magnanimity.'

'Oh sure, right.' Amaya slipped off the stool. 'You know what. Maybe I'll finish my degree in Moscow. They'll let me alone there.'

Tal-Salem sat through a lecture on Polish architecture in the POSK auditorium and looked at his watch. Ten minutes to twelve, ten minutes and the method acting class would be over. He smiled at the elderly Pole sitting next to him, a beaten-looking man with coarse white hair and watery eyes that leaked now and again at the corners. He dabbed at the spillage with lean, blackened fingers and he smelled of life on the street. Tal-Salem wore his Muslim costume, complete with full beard, and keffiyeh tied Yasser Arafat-style. He could hear the drone of the lecturer's voice as he indicated various wonders of pre-war Polish construction with his laser pointer, but he wasn't listening. He sat with his hands in his lap and his eyes half-closed, until his watch read a minute to twelve. Then he rose, nodded to the dishevelled figure beside him and slipped out of the room.

Vaczka was teaching in one of the basement studios and Tal-Salem hovered about the stairwell, looking at the original oils that lined the walls, until the hubbub of conversation crescendoed as the would-be actors and actresses crowded up the stairs. As soon as the door opened, he moved up one more flight, and from there witnessed who passed and who did not. He was only looking for one face, the girl he had seen in Victoria. She came up second to last, talking with another girl whom Tal-Salem did not recognize. He could still hear voices as he walked down the final flight to the black-walled basement studio. The door was open and he saw Vaczka and the one called Jeconec deep in conversation. Vaczka looked up and frowned. 'Can I help you?'

Tal-Salem walked inside and closed the door. For a moment he did not say anything. Jeconec hovered a little awkwardly.

'What can I do for you?' Vaczka said. 'If you want to enrol, I'm afraid you'll have to wait till next term.'

Tal-Salem looked from him to Jeconec. Jeconec looked away. 'I would like to speak with you in private,' he said.

Vaczka paled, then he motioned to Jeconec, who moved past Tal-Salem and closed the door.

When he was gone they stood in silence, Tal-Salem, the Arab, looking closely at Vaczka's face.

'Do I know you?' Vaczka asked.

'No.'

'Of you?'

'No.'

'Then . . .'

Tal-Salem pulled the blackout down the window in the door and stepped forward. Vaczka stepped back, eyes suddenly tight in his face. Tal-Salem looked coldly at him.

'You've been careless,' he said.

'What?'

'Every day Jeconec looks in the window on King Street. You might as well have broadcast on the television.' His voice was chill and he was looking for a reaction, trying to decipher just what exactly was what.

Vaczka's face blanched. 'We've been waiting.'

'Yes, but there is waiting and there is waiting. Have you been contacted at all?'

'No. Nothing since before May.'

'Not a word?'

'Absolutely nothing.' Vaczka lifted a hand. 'Believe me, I'd know.'

Tal-Salem considered for a moment, his tongue tasting the inside of his teeth. 'You have a leak in your organization,' he said.

Vaczka's eyes widened. 'How do you know?'

'Because, unlike you, I remain vigilant.' He could see the sweat break out on Vaczka's brow.

'Is that why there's been no contact?' Vaczka said. 'Were you aware of something, then?' He was trying to sound apologetic.

'The leak is close to you,' Tal-Salem told him. 'Yesterday I followed Amaya Kukiel, your girlfriend. I followed her from here to Victoria, where she met somebody from the security services. Your hosts seem to know about you.'

'Amaya?' Vaczka felt the blood thud in his temple. 'Who did she meet?'

'It doesn't matter who. It will be MI5 or Special Branch. British security services.'

Vaczka could feel the sweat gather under his arms. He was cold and hot at the same time. He knew when he had accepted this job what the price of failing was. When he had passed the information of the approach back, he had been told by Abu Nidal himself: *If you mess up, don't look to me when they come for you.* Tal-Salem could smell his fear. It disgusted him; he was filled with the desire to kill the Polish fool just for being so stupid. But there was a bigger picture here and things he had to resolve. Vaczka too was thinking hard and quickly. 'What do we do now? How can we proceed if they're watching?'

Tal-Salem snapped a glance at him and then looked at the floor. 'You cannot. You'll have to subcontract,' he said. 'The financial loss will be yours.'

'Of course.' Vaczka was breathing again.

'Think about what you must do. I will contact you again.' He turned then and walked out of the room. On the stairs he almost bumped into Amaya coming down them. He bowed and apologized and felt her eyes on his back as he climbed the rest of the stairs.

Vaczka took Amaya back to his flat. She was not working in the cafeteria today, having taken a few days off so she could concentrate on her studies, and she was talkative and lively. He wanted to strangle her; strip her naked first, fuck her really hard and, just as she was about to climax, put his hands about that white throat and shake the life out of her. His mood showed, but not that much. She sensed the quietness in him and asked what the matter was. He told her: nothing, everything was fine, he was just conscious of the leap of faith the class needed to take if they were to progress now, and he was not sure if they could make it. She accepted his comment and traced lines on his chest with long fingers, letting her hand slip down to his groin. He stirred when he did not want to. He knew he could not take her to bed, because if he did, he would definitely kill her. So he feigned tiredness, suggesting that she go home and take the time to study.

After she had gone, he watched the road from behind the curtains, but saw no one. Then he showered and changed and went out. Surreptitiously, he scanned the parked cars for people who shouldn't be there, but again saw no one and knew he had to quash this sudden paranoia. Stopping at the phone box on Goldhawk Road, he fished in his pocket for change, then considered the box, its

63

proximity to his flat and moved on to the next one. He watched cars, looked at the faces of the people paying in the petrol station, the shop windows, those people sitting on the common, and shook away the thoughts. Fool, he told himself. Get a grip. At the next box, he phoned Stahl on the cloned mobile he used. This, at least, was secure.

They had an appointed meeting place for non-social gatherings, the cinema complex in Leicester Square. It did not matter what was playing. Vaczka arrived first and paid his money, then sat in the seats farthest from the entrance of Screen 2. Ten minutes after him, Stahl came in, looked round the half-empty auditorium and sat next to him. He sucked Coca-Cola through a straw. Vacska told him what had happened. 'We need to subcontract,' he said. 'Any idea who?'

Stahl sucked noisily, eyes on the screen – a woman's features filled it in close-up, huge green eyes and the softest hairs on her cheeks. The image cut to a street where two men sat at traffic lights on motorcycles. He passed the carton of Coke to Vaczka. 'Yes,' he said. 'I have.'

# 6

The black man flipped the butt of his cigarette out of the truck window and rolled it up again, the sudden blast of chill November air cutting across his shoulders. He slowed out of Anderson and took 81, which he knew would rejoin Highway 29 if he took the right fork for Hartwell. She would be waiting on the bridge that crossed the Savannah River. The old Chevy rattled and shook as he ground the pedals, and thick, oily smoke spluttered from the muffler as he changed down. The towing gear clattered behind him, the swing hook coming loose yet again from its housing. He looked behind – no traffic, no state trooper or sheriff's deputy, he'd leave it till he got to the river.

He did not see her car, parked at the back of the old iron bridge, until he pulled off the new bridge and swung down towards the riverbank. The water was deep here, perhaps twenty feet, which would suit his purpose later. The slope down from the twist in the road was gentle. Slender silver-trunked trees, bereft of their leaves, lined the road on either side and the world was quiet save the choked cough of the diesel. She was driving a blue Toyota with dark-tinted windows, and stood at the end of the iron bridge, with a camera in her hand like any other Yankee tourist. Blue-black hair cut short to the neck, she wore tight-fitting jeans and a heavy checked overshirt. The black man gunned the dying truck once more and then pulled off on to the unmade road that used to be the highway. He sat a moment in the cab and waited. She stood at the end of the bridge with her camera, looking out over the still water, the bank sloping sharply with willow trees all but down to the paint-black surface.

The black man watched a pick-up truck highball across the bridge, then slam gears before taking the hill at another run. After that there was silence and he climbed down from the cab, lit a cigarette and looked at the woman. She was walking towards him now and he ambled down the slope to her car. He did not know her name, he did not want to know her name. She did not know his. She did not speak, but lifted the tailgate on the Toyota and dragged aside the carpet covering the spare tyre. The black man looked on as she pulled out the neoprene tool bag and slipped the elastic over the top. A Sig-Sauer pistol slid out as she upended it, together with a length of thick electrical cable. The woman gestured with one hand and he nodded. She put the gun and cable back in the tool kit and refixed the housing. The black man looked beyond her once more to the stillness of the water and the twin sections of iron framework bridge, that was all that remained of the original. 'Three days,' he said, and walked back to his Chevy.

He came into Royston from the east, truck burbling and belching oiled smoke every time he put his foot on the gas, and bumped over the railway lines. Immediately on his right were autoshops, motorcycles standing outside one of them, and a little further on – King's Auto Line. Duncan Tires faced him as he chugged up the hill on 29 and came to the lights. On red, he put on the brakes and knocked the gearshift into neutral, watching the handful of white faces on the street. They stared at him briefly, a couple of them looking at the truck, and then the lights changed and he crossed Church Street. Glancing to his left, he saw the pharmacy and a sign saying 'Tri-County Industrial and Hardware'. The road bottomed out down a small hill and he passed the Pruitt funeral home and a red brick church with white-silled arches for windows. He drove slowly past the Tri-County Medical Center and glanced at the set of self-storage units on the other side of the road. Ty Cobb, the old baseball player's name was everywhere. Beyond the sprawling Chevy and Oldsmobile dealer's on the left-hand side, was city hall and then the Royston motel on the right. The black man pulled off the road and parked the truck.

An elderly white woman greeted him in reception, vertical creases of age above and below her lips pinching her mouth into a mean grin. She looked at him out of cat's-eye glasses pushed high on her nose.

'Can I help you?'

'I think I'm gonna need a room, mam. My truck's about to bite it.' He rubbed his arm and the black skin of his hand.

'How many nights?'

'A couple, I guess. Depends if I can get my truck fixed.'

'I'll need picture ID.'

He showed her his fake driver's licence. 'Where can I get my truck fixed?' he said, leaning dirty elbows on the reception desk and looking right up in her eyes. She stepped back.

'Well, there's lotsa places, I guess. Y'all head on back thataway to the railroad tracks and you'll see King's Auto Line.'

'Thank you, mam.' He stood up, wiped grimy palms on dirty jeans and took the room key from her.

The room was neat and functional. He looked in the toilet and in the shower, making sure there was paper and soap, then he went back to his truck. He saw a couple of black faces, but not many. The western end of town was richer, nice white men's houses, with porches and verandahs and steps leading down to the yard. It had clearly been built long after the far end by the railroad tracks. He had a look, making sure he knew the route out towards 85, and then swung the truck round and headed back to the autoshops. His truck kicked smoke and fumes as he killed the engine in front of King's. A mechanic in worn overalls looked up from under the hood of a Chrysler, as the black man jumped down from the cab. He looked again at the engine he was working on, then at the Alabama plates on the tow truck.

'Hey, what's up?' the black man said. The mechanic did not answer at once, but picked up a rag and wiped the grease from his hands. The black man glanced to his right as a police department Ford bumped across the railroad tracks and headed out of town.

'You got yourself a problem there, buddy?' The mechanic spoke slowly, a pinch of snuff lumpy under his bottom lip.

'All but broke up, my man. I'm pissing oil ever' which way. Got to get back to Birmingham, and I ain't gonna make it like this.' The black man took a cigarette from the crumpled pack of Lucky Strikes in the top pocket of his jacket and popped a match on his thumbnail.

The mechanic looked behind him, sighed and walked outside. He glanced underneath and then straightened. 'Look, buddy. I can't look at her now. Leave her where she's at and I'll see what I can do in a while.'

'Whatever you say, bro. I ain't going no place.'

The black man left him then and wandered across the railroad tracks to the benches set in the shade of two oak trees, and flipped away the butt of his cigarette. The mechanic would look and tell him he was burning oil not losing it, and the head was letting a little water into the oil. More than that, right now he had a problem with the exhaust system which was adding to the loss of power. He would be able to fix it up, but it would take a couple of days, as they were busy with work from the Chevy dealer up the road. The black man knew. He had checked long before he arrived.

The sun came out as he walked up Highway 29 to the intersection with Church Street running off to his left. He turned up his collar against the nip of the wind and wandered along Church Street. Two middle-aged women watched him suspiciously from the doorway of the pharmacy and he smiled at them and touched his fingers to his temple. They looked away hurriedly. Across the road was a Western store and half a block down on this side, the place he was looking for. He felt a quickening of his pulse as he saw the sign sticking out at right angles to the window: 'Casey's, dealers in fine jewelry'. He looked out of the side of his eye as he passed; the woman was there, bending over the half-empty display cases in the window. She was slim, maybe fifty, maybe more. She wouldn't weigh very much. Directly adjacent to the store was a gap, like a grass-floored alley running fifty yards back between the jeweller's and the fashion store, with the parking lot out front. Beyond the alley, the undergrowth got tangled and a water tower dominated the skyline.

The black man kept walking, a bank on his right, and in the distance, the spire of a church clipped at the sky in grey tiles over white. He paused for a moment as a lot opened on his left, two blocks down from the jeweller's store, and he saw an aging policeman leaning against his Ford, talking to a young buck deputy with a cocktail stick in his teeth. He hid his smile and thought of similar events in the past, and the need to smoke tickled the back of his throat.

He lay in his motel room and watched Fox news disinterestedly, waiting for the call from the autoshop. As he wandered back past the medical center and city hall, he had noticed a sign declaring a city residents' meeting for the night after this one. Nobody spoke to him. He saw few black faces; the black/white thing here was not as bad as Louisiana or Mississippi, but it was bad enough. He tried to imagine being black and growing up here, with Confederate flags still flying from some of the houses.

The call from Donny, the mechanic at King's, came just after lunch. 'Gonna take at least a couple of days, but I'll get to it. Y'all can take it like it is, if you wanna, but you won't make Alabama.'

That evening, he looked for a bar but could not find one, in the end having to settle for beer from the Winn-Dixie and drinking in his motel room. He bought food to go, watched television and slept. The following morning he walked back up the street, through rain that slanted in grey stripes at an angle of thirty degrees, spraying his jacket and soaking the front of his jeans. He wondered how his hair would look in the wet. Again, only the woman was in the jeweller's. He opened the door and a little bell tinkled. She looked up with a smile on her thin, white face, and then the smile faltered, then faded to nothing.

'How y'all doing?' she asked.

'Just fine, mam.' He smiled at her, showing his teeth.

'Can I help you with anything?'

'Necklace. I'm stuck here for a couple of days. My truck's broke.' He pointed in the direction of the railroad tracks. 'I wanna get something for my girl, 'cause she's pissed at me for not getting home.'

She looked at him with an expression on her face that said she had an idea of just what kind of girlfriend he would have, and then looked at the glass display cabinets before her.

'Gold or silver.'

'Gold.' He was enjoying himself now. 'Thick gold chain is good. Yeah, thick gold chain.'

She showed him an assortment and he ummed and ahhed for a while, telling her he wasn't sure and he would

70

probably have to think about it for a while. The telephone rang from behind her and she excused herself and opened the door at the back of the store to answer it. He moved away from the counter, watched the street for a moment, counting cars going by. Then he looked back again. She was leaning against the doorjamb with one hand hooked in the crook of the other arm, as she talked. He smiled at her and glanced briefly beyond. He could see a small sort of sitting room, probably where she took her lunch, and beyond it a back door which must open on to the little strip of land that separated her from the building behind, bordering the grassed alley. He motioned to her that he was going to think about the chain for a while and stepped back on to the street. The aging chief of police was watching him from the lot two blocks down. He was seated in his cruiser, waiting to pull on to Church Street. The black man gave him a brief glance, then crossed the road to the Western store, which seemed to be permanently closed. He could feel the cop's eyes on his back as the Ford gunned its way to the lights.

The mechanic called him the following afternoon, his third day in town, and told him he could collect the truck. The black man checked out of the motel and shouldered his overnight bag, before walking one final time along the main street. A couple of rednecks were stowing fence-post wire and a shovel in the back of their Dodge as he crossed Church Street, and gave him the eye. He ignored them, waited for the lights to change and wandered down across the railroad tracks to the autoshop, where his red tow truck awaited him. He paid for the work with a credit card and tossed his gear into the back.

'Should get y'all home,' the mechanic told him, 'but you wanna get that head sorted out real quick.'

'Appreciate it, bro.' The black man shook hands with him and climbed up into the cab. He fired up the truck and ground into first, the rumble from the muffler stiller than before. Hauling the wheel round, he drove back out of town the way he had come and swung a path through the gentle hills, with their grey-green grass and scattering of naked trees.

The woman was waiting in the blue Toyota, just off the highway by the old bridge. The black man drove down the hill, checking his rearview mirror and the road ahead. The highway was deserted. As he got close, the woman waved her arm and he rolled the truck off the road and down the slope to the old bridge. He did not cut or slow the engine, just kept her going, steering with one hand and opening the door with the other. At the last minute he jumped, and the truck rolled into the river with a hiss from the hot metal. He stood a moment, watching it lurch and boil, the black water cuffed into slapping, white-lipped surf, as the river took hold and dragged the Chevy down. It was gone in twenty seconds.

Still no cars passed on the highway. The woman with the blue-black hair and cold eyes slid into the back of the Toyota. The black man jumped into the warmth of the driver's seat and glanced once behind, as she fed herself beyond the back seat and into the trunk. The roll top was across and she couldn't be seen from outside. On the floor by the passenger seat doorwell was a set of New Jersey licence plates.

The black man drove back towards Royston, the clock on the dash reading nearly ten after five. She closed the store at exactly five-thirty, before driving to the far side of town where she lived. Her husband worked at the Chevy and Oldsmobile dealer's, selling used cars. He had watched her stop by as she drove home from work the previous evening. He could not help but think that this was a strange place to end up, given everything she had been through. He parked the Toyota on Church Street, a block up from the jeweller's. Traffic moved across the 29 intersection, but there was no sign of the police chief. He did not lock the driver's door, but walked quickly up to the jewellery store and stepped inside. He could feel the length of electrical cord against his breast. The Sig was stuck in the waistband of his jeans, a switchblade in his back pocket.

'Y'all come back for that chain?' she greeted him. 'Somebody else looked it over just this afternoon.'

He did not answer her, but reached behind him and turned the key in the lock. He could see the pocket of air convulse in her thin throat, and a strip of unease light up in her eyes.

'Matter of fact, I'm about to close up now,' she stuttered.

From his pocket he took a pre-rolled joint, sniffed the glued-down paper and put it in his mouth. He popped a match on the glass top of the counter and lifted the gun from his belt.

'You're already closed,' he said.

Vaczka placed the advert in the personal section of *Back Street Heroes*, and bought the issue, when it came out, from the newsagent's on King Street. There were various lonely hearts in there. One made him smile: 'Long-haired male with 650 Bonny Chop, 30, fat, dirty, bad teeth, and a face like a bulldog chewing a wasp, seeks slim willowy blonde, 18–25, for visits to the opera, French cinema and escorting to cocktail parties.' He read on, scanning the page till he saw it. 'Looking for heroes to wave the flag. Get in touch boys. It's been too long.' He had given Stahl's cloned mobile number.

Back in the flat, he found Amaya hovering in the hallway and regretted giving her a key.

'I thought you had college today,' he said, jaw set in a line.

'I have. I'm going now.'

'What're you hanging around here for?'

'I'm not hanging around. I was waiting to ask you something.'

'So ask.'

She came into the living room and dropped her bag on the floor. 'What's the matter with you, Jorge? You've been really on edge these last few days.'

'Business,' he said. 'Nothing for you to worry about.'

She touched his face, cupping a cheek with long fingers. 'You can talk to me, you know. We're a partnership after all.' She paused then. 'Although sometimes it doesn't feel like it.'

Again he fought the desire to put his hands round her throat, and he bit his lip. 'Sorry,' he muttered, turning away. 'Things on my mind, that's all.'

'What sort of things?' He felt her hand move on the knots of his spine. He tensed, then relaxed, mind working.

'Just things, bits of business here and there.'

'Business with Stahl?'

He turned to her now. 'Yeah, stuff with Stahl. We're trying to set up a couple of deals.'

She nodded, suddenly not looking him in the eye. 'Anything I can help with?'

'No. I may have to go up north, though. But I don't know when.'

'What sort of business?'

'Oh, nothing important.' He took her by both shoulders and squeezed. 'Just things I do over and above teaching you lot. What I get down there hardly pays the phone bill.'

She went to college and he watched her walk the length of the street until she disappeared round the corner, the beginnings of an idea in his head.

Fifty Triumph motorcycles rode two abreast across the Tyne Bridge in Newcastle. They had gathered from all corners of England in the early hours of the previous morning, the hardcore from Hounslow in West London. They were following the hearse that carried the remains of their 'brother' to his final resting place. He had been killed in an accident with a lorry in South Shields. They rode with no helmets, their mark of respect, and a police car followed the last of the bikes in escort. High on the old bridge, a video team from the BBC took close-up shots of their faces. Below them, leaning against the ironwork next to his unmarked police car, John Newham smoked an Embassy Regal.

David 'Dog Soldier' Collier rode his Thunderbird at the head of the twin lines, his feet resting on the customized forward footpegs, the wind ruffling his short-cropped hair. They all wore colours – a rarity – the death's head between two crossed M16 rifles; and leather chaps over jeans. People stared from their cars as they passed on the other side of the road. North of the city, they stopped at the little church on the council estate close to the A1, where their brother's family had worshipped for years. Gringo guarded the bikes while the rest trooped into the church.

Back at the old bridge, Newham stood with his hands in his pockets, collar turned up against the wind, and waited for the camera crew to come down. He shook hands with the cameraman. 'I'll get it copied and let you have it, John. Soon as I can, mate. All right?'

'Sound,' Newham said. NCIS had contacted his Special Branch office yesterday morning, telling him that intelligence sources had informed them about the funeral ride. No helmets, a new biker gang, and a chance to get their faces on video. Ten minutes later, Newham had set it up.

After the service was over, Collier shook hands with the brother's parents and they all headed to the bridge over the A1, where they stood as one and looked out at the four lanes of motorway. A full two minutes of silence and then

Collier raised a fist to the road, before turning back to his bike. The key was in the ignition, and he was about to turn it over when a soldier from the Manchester platoon came alongside him and unrolled a copy of the latest issue of *Back Street Heroes*. 'Somebody wants to talk,' he said.

Jim Poynton took the stack of ballpoint pens from his shirt pocket and placed them, as he did every night after work, in the top drawer of his desk. Then he made sure that no paperwork was left out and the 'in' and 'out' stack of plastic trays was square, before he wiped the line of sweat from his brow with a handkerchief. He glanced at his watch, strapped across his thick, tanned wrist, and got up. Outside, he inspected the door to his Grand Am, which looked as though it was marked, but no, it was just a trick of the light. A blue Toyota, with dark-tinted windows, cruised west out of town. He looked again at his watch, already late for the meeting at city hall. They wanted to talk about litter patrols and he knew somebody was going to raise a question about highway work details from the correctional center. That would be Mad Martha again: she still reckoned, despite the two guards with a twelve-gauge and .357 apiece, that she was going to get raped by the inmates every time she drove over to Hartwell. Martha was seventy-seven years old. Maybe she was just hoping.

The meeting dragged on longer than he wanted it to and he hoped Mary had got the steaks on. He sat there at the back, doing his duty by the town, and all the time he was thinking about T-bones with onions and mushrooms and hot barbecue sauce, sizzling in a skillet on the stove. But when he finally got home, Mary's Buick was not in the driveway. He pulled in anyway, thinking that maybe she was doing her paperwork, as she sometimes did in the back room at the store. That had been a godsend, getting to manage that place when old John Casey got too old to run it any more.

Mary was not in the house and no cooking smells greeted him and, worse than that, the T-bones still sat on waxed paper in the icebox. Poynton pulled a Coors Light from the six-pack and ripped off the ring pull, sucking on the froth that bubbled up from the hole. He called out, more than once, yelling at the top of his voice. Then, slipping the open beer can between his thighs, he drove up to the store. Her car was parked out front, but the door was locked. He paused and knocked, tried his own key, but couldn't get it in the lock. Then he began to worry. She was still good-looking for her age and so much slimmer than him, and she hardly ever let him get on top of her these days. What if she was in the back right now, getting her rocks off with one of the local boys. He bit his lip, swallowed the rest of his beer and crushed the empty can in his palm. Tossing it on to the back seat of his car, he went round to the back of the shop. The dumpster was pushed against the wall and he had to shift it to get to the back door. It was heavy and he had to wiggle the wheels in the grass.

The back door was unlocked and slowly he turned the handle, a lump the size of a golf ball in his throat, waiting for those telltale sighs or little moans that would let him know for sure. He heard nothing though, and the back room was empty. Stepping through into the store itself, he was aware of the traffic passing outside, as the rest of the townsfolk went home from the meeting. She was not there, nothing was out of place. He scratched his head. Maybe she was next door with Jeanie-May in the fashion store or having a cup of coffee with the ladies from the pharmacy. There must be a simple explanation. The only thing that really bothered him, now he knew she wasn't being spread from behind, was the ache of hunger in his stomach. He'd go on home, cook up the T-bones and wait for her to come in. Even now, there would more than likely be a message on the answer machine. As he turned to go, he paused and sniffed the air – a pungent aroma, tangy, resinous, almost like cigarette smoke, but not like it. Maybe she'd had a pipe smoker in, old Mack perhaps; if he wasn't chewing Copenhagen, he was smoking.

Back at the house, however, there was no message. The last caller had been Ray Cavanagh's number from work, but no message. Poynton took another beer from the icebox and sucked on it while he moved the T-bones around in the skillet. There would be no sauce. He could peel and chop onions, mushrooms for sure, but he couldn't make Mary's barbecue sauce.

When she wasn't home by nine o'clock, he started to worry. He wanted to call somebody up, but felt foolish. He tried to watch TV, thinking she would show up at any minute, but she didn't. In the end, he scoured the phone-book for her friends and almost apologetically began calling them up. One by one they told him they hadn't seen her. Her car was still outside the jewellery store. Yes, he knew that. He put the phone down to the last caller and a tick started in his heavy, reddened cheek. He drank another beer and then got back in his car and drove up through town. It was dark now and quiet on the street, little to do save watch *Jeopardy* on TV. Her car was still there and he stood in front of the store with his hands in his pockets, as if just by peering through the darkened window he would see her and everything would be all right. But he couldn't see her and it wasn't all right. Turning, he crossed the road and went into the police department.

The chief wasn't there, only Regan, the young officer who liked to chew on gum and toothpicks. Poynton had had little to do with him and suddenly felt foolish telling him about his wife not coming home. Regan listened to him, sitting back in the chair with his arms folded, and licked his upper lip when Poynton had finished speaking.

'You sure she ain't just off with the gals someplace, Mr Poynton. I mean it ain't late or nothing.'

'I've called up all her friends,' Poynton said. 'Guess I came on over here 'cause I can't think what else to do.'

Regan pushed out his lips, then he stood up and lifted the heavy black flashlight from the desk. 'Why don't y'all show me the store, Mr Poynton, then I can figure out whether or not to call up the chief.'

They crossed to the store and Poynton led the way round the back, bumping against the green dumpster as he opened the door for Regan. Regan held the flashlight upended over his shoulder and shone it around the back of the store like a detective, then he moved inside. Poynton put on the lights and opened his hands wide. 'Nothing here,' he said.

Regan went into the store front and immediately stopped and sniffed. 'Somebody's been smoking weed in here.' He turned and studied Poynton out of the side of his eye. 'Your wife like a little bowl now and again, Mr Poynton, sir?'

Poynton stared at him. 'Don't be a fool, boy. She don't even smoke tobacco.'

Again, Regan sniffed the heavy atmosphere that hung like an unseen mist in the room. 'Think I'll call me up the chief.'

The two of them wandered back across the now-deserted Church Street and Regan telephoned his boss. 'Yeah.' Poynton cringed as he spoke. 'Somebody's been smoking weed in the store front, Chief. I can tell you that sure as Ty Cobb hit a hardball.'

Old Mack, the chief of police, met them at the jewellery store and stood with his hands on his hips, heavy-jowled, glasses slipping down his nose and a police issue baseball hat sitting high on his head. He chewed a plug of tobacco, yellowed jaws working like a cow at the cud. 'You sure she ain't but run off, Jimmy?' he asked with a twinkle in his eye.

'Now don't say that, Mack. This is bad enough as it is.'

'Mack.' Regan's voice called from outside the back of the store. The chief turned and saw Regan crouching in the grass, shining his flashlight on the ground. They walked outside. Regan nodded to the whitened butt of a hand-rolled cigarette. He picked it up and sniffed it. 'Weed,' he said, then looked up at Poynton. 'Your smoker was out here.'

Poynton scratched his head. It did not make sense. None of it did. Who did his wife know who smoked dope. He could not think, unless of course she didn't know him. For a moment he stared at Regan who in turn looked at the chief. The chief was looking at the dumpster. 'That one yours, Jim?' he asked.

'Yes.'

The chief nodded and spat tobacco juice into the alley. He lifted the lid of the dumpster. Mary Poynton's crumpled body was squashed down in the garbage.

'Oh, sweet Jesus Christ.' Poynton physically reeled backwards. The chief looked down at her – eyes open, her head pushed to an awkward angle where her body was pressed up against the side of the dumpster. Her shirt was ripped open, left breast mutilated, and blood was congealed in brown stains on her belly and skirt top. Regan stood and stared, then Poynton recovered himself enough to look again. For a moment he could not make out what had happened. Then he realized her left nipple had been cut off. Twisting away, he vomited into the grass.

The chief laid a hand on Regan's shoulder, the young officer's own face was paling to green. 'Boy, go call the sheriff in Carnesville.'

# 7

Officer Regan wound blue and white tape across the parking lot and alley, which led down the side of the jewellery store. Poynton sat in the doorwell of his car and listened to the wail of sirens coming up Highway 29 from the other side of town. Within minutes, three brown sheriffs' cars pulled up, and Poynton noticed for the first time the people who had gathered on Church Street. Absently, he tried to think of the last murder that had taken place here. He had been born and raised in this town, before leaving for the army and the surf of California, then eventually coming back again. He could not remember a murder. Old Mack crouched down in front of him, with a crack of his aging knees.

'Hang in there, Jimmy,' he said.

Poynton looked at him briefly, face awash with grey, little lines of red prickling the edges of his eyes. The sheriff came over, a big burly man, with a low-slung Magnum on his right hip. His belly bulged over the band of his trousers and he could not do up the zip on his jacket. 'Where's she at, Mack?'

The chief pointed to the back of the shop and the sheriff looked down at Poynton for a moment. 'This guy her husband?'

'Jim Poynton.'

The sheriff nodded and crouched down. 'Sir, I'm Van Clayburgh. Franklin County Sheriff. A couple of my dicks'll be along in a minute. You figure you might be up to talking to them?'

Poynton gazed beyond him to the swirling strobe lights

81

on the ambulance which had pulled over across the street, and said nothing. Two men in green overalls were crossing to where Regan stood by the tape. Clayburgh squinted at Mack, patted Poynton lightly on the shoulder and eased his bulk under the tape.

'Not pretty, Van,' Mack said, as the two men moved down the grassy alley to the dumpster, where the paramedics were waiting.

'Don't touch anything yet, fellas,' the sheriff said. 'Let my crime scene boys take their pictures. If this goes to Athens, I don't want GBI dicks giving me horseshit about evidence contamination.'

The crime scene team arrived and began their work, taking photographs, dusting the inside of the back room of the store, but leaving the body of Mary Poynton in the dumpster until the ME got there. The medics had already confirmed their 'obvious death determination' and were standing around waiting for the ME like everyone else. Eventually, he arrived and ordered them to lift the body on to the gurney so he could begin his work. Mack and Clayburgh stood to one side, Mack's tired jaws working at his tobacco. Every now and then he would spray a thin green jet of juice into the grass.

'Been chief of police for twenty-nine years, Van,' he said. 'Ain't never had a murder in this town, not in all that time.'

'You any idea who might've done it?'

Mack shook his shoulders. 'Nope. Boy Regan, there, reckons somebody was smoking dope, though.'

'Dope?' Clayburgh scratched the red veins in the side of his nose.

Mack nodded. 'Found the butt end of a reefer in the grass, right there.' He pointed to the dumpster.

'Sheriff.' The medical examiner was on his feet, stripping off the tight-fitting surgical gloves.

Clayburgh and Mack walked over to him. 'Make sure your man Regan talks to my dicks about that weed,' Clayburgh said. He looked down at the body once more, lying flat now on the gurney. 'What we got, doc?'

'Strangled, I think. Ligature marks on her neck.' The ME pulled a face. 'I'll be able to tell you more later, of course, but there's one thing that bothers me already.'

'What's that?' Clayburgh glanced behind him as he said it. One of his young detectives, wearing a dark, two-piece suit with his tie undone, walked up behind them, a notepad in his hand.

The ME nodded to Mary Poynton's mutilated left breast. 'I've heard about that before,' he said. 'I think you're gonna need the GBI on this one.'

The sheriff eased his breath out in a sigh. 'Yep. Kinda figured on that myself.'

Harrison leaned against the bar in the Jazz Café and sipped draught Budweiser from a 'to go' cup. He moved the lump of chew from his lip to the hollow of his cheek and scratched the rat tattoo on his upper arm, as he watched Maria swing her hips in that long slow loop that she liked to do when she was singing way down low. The rest of the band clicked on and Harrison closed his eyes. Her voice rose again and the strains of 'Rainy Night in Georgia' lifted above the hubbub out on Bourbon Street. The Sweet Sensation Band were playing, as they generally did, on a Sunday night. Maria finished up and came round with the bucket. Harrison dropped in a five-dollar bill and shifted his worn denim jacket to his other shoulder. 'You gotta sweet voice, honey.'

She smiled at him and touched him lightly on the chest with red-painted fingernails, then moved on. He watched her from behind as she moved along the line of drinkers, ninety per cent of them tourists. Then he slipped his jacket back on and went out into the night.

Three cops were walking along Bourbon Street. Black guys all of them, from the Vieux Carre Precinct in the old bank building. One of them gave him a second glance as he wandered west and flicked his ponytail out of the back of his jacket, where it was stuck at the collar. He was watching Rene Martinez, part black, part Hispanic, from the projects up by Interstate 10 and the graveyards where the corpses were buried above ground. It was the first thing he had noticed when he came down here, or rather the first thing Lisa noticed. *Hey, Harrison. Look.* She had pointed to the cemeteries filled with white and grey stone, above-ground tombs. *I guess the ground's too swampy to bury people in.*

Cochrane had confirmed it when Harrison was officially reassigned. He was Louisiana born and raised, served in the military, then spent twelve years as sheriff of St Charles Parish before joining the FBI. *Dig a hole, JB, and it starts filling with water.*

Harrison thought about Lisa now, as he watched Martinez bullshitting with a waitress from the bar on the corner. He leaned against a wall of the restaurant where the Recycled Cajun band was playing behind him. Accordion music in his ears, with the metallic slide of the skiffle board. He plucked a Marlboro from his shirt pocket and lit it, letting smoke trail from his nostrils, and watched Martinez trying to hit on the girl with no luck. She said one final word to him, then wandered away. Harrison looked back down the street as a mule-drawn sightseeing wagon trundled up behind him. Martinez was on the move again, walking down past the two NOPD Crown Victorias parked on the junction of Bourbon and St Peter. Harrison looked up, above the three-storey buildings of the quarter, beyond the wrought-iron balconies where revellers looked down on the street. The sky was smoky with cloud and he could smell the rain in the air.

Martinez took off down St Peter towards Royal. Harrison waited a half-minute or so and followed him. He was touring the bars, looking for someone. Harrison had an idea who that someone was, but he needed confirmation. Martinez was easy to track and this November night the French Quarter was humming as it was every night, save Mardi Gras, when you could not move on the street for floats and women showing off their titties, and pickpockets helping themselves to your hard-earned dollars. Harrison wore jeans, a faded jacket and the battered two-tone boots that he had bought years before in Idaho. Strapped inside the right one was his gun; nowhere else to put it when he was walking the quarter at night.

He watched Martinez in a bar on Royal, and sat there drinking Dixie beer with Franco and his girlfriend. Franco waited tables at the Café Sbiza and Harrison ate there at least once a week. The company was good cover, because Martinez had clearly increased his search and was looking over the tables with more care than he had done before. Harrison had his back to him, but could still see what he was doing in the mirror behind the bar. He knew the rounds and could afford to take a little time here with Franco. After this, Martinez would do the first two bars on Decatur, and if they weren't any good, he would end up in Jean Lafitte's. That was the information and Penny's sources were good.

Franco and his girlfriend left him then, telling him to meet them in Pat O'Brien's later. Harrison said he might, but there was a poker game upstairs on Rampart and he might check that out for a while. The clock on the wall ticking towards one-fifteen told him it was time to go and follow Martinez. He worked out how long he had been in the bar and figured that he might as well try Lafitte's right away. If he wasn't there, he could walk on down to Decatur. Martinez was there and he was with the man Harrison recognized, but whose name he did not know. Dark-skinned Caucasian, could've been Italian or even Spanish. He had those nasal native tones of an Orleanian, which reminded Harrison of the street agents he knew out of New York City. When he'd first met Franco, he swore he was from New York; but no, he was New Orleans born and raised. A couple of guys in the office spoke the same way. Then there was Cochrane and one or two others who were from out in the parishes, with that southern drawl that Harrison liked to mimic so much. He sat at the bar and talked to Katie, who had just broken up with her boyfriend. Katie was young and pretty; Harrison more than old enough to be her father. He plucked a menthol-flavoured Merit from his shirt pocket and popped a match on his belt buckle.

'You wanna Bud, Harrison?' Katie asked him.

'Thank you, Miss Lady Mam.' Harrison cringed inside as he said it. He had thought that phrase was for Lisa Guffy only, but somehow it hadn't turned out that way. He had known it wouldn't work out as soon as they left Michigan. That had been vacation time, fishing the big lake as he had done with his grandfather years ago. They had a cabin on the shore and cooked the fish they caught on the barbecue, drank beer and talked deep into the night. But then there was D.C. and Tom Kovalski's debrief with the domestic terrorism team, the commendation from the Director and all the fuss that went with it. The analytical research team proudly told him that the militia were running a poor-quality picture of him on their web sites, warning their number against infiltration.

The result had been a good one and he had all the evidence he needed, what with Salvesen having videoed his 'common law court' trial, not to mention the T-17

86

transmitters that Harrison had wired in himself. The suits at headquarters were particularly pleased because this had dealt a massive PR blow to the militia movement in general.

Katie brought him his beer in a 'to go' cup and Harrison squeezed the sides as he drank it. Martinez and his contact were still deep in conversation. Harrison saw Katie looking at them and he leaned forward. 'Honey, who is that guy with Rene. Face is familiar, you know what I mean?' She rested both elbows on the counter and freshened his ashtray for him.

'Name's Manx, Harrison. Alls I know, honey. I only ever seen him with Rene.'

'What's he do?'

'Baby, I don't know that. Why, you looking for a job or something? We need a bus boy right here, if you want it.'

Harrison laughed then, crushed out the Merit and rolled a Marlboro between his fingers.

He woke to Louisiana rainstorms, the shutters open in his room on Burgundy and Toulouse, and the rain hissing off the asphalt in grey waves. He got up, yawned and leaned his head out of the window, looking left and right. Only the street cleaner was out, done up like some dirty beacon in his yellow ankle-length slicker. Harrison turned his face to the haze of misted cloud which filled up the sky. It would rain all day, and probably all night as well. He looked at the clock by his cot, a little before seven. Switching on the coffee pot, he stuck a cigarette against his lip. He missed Lisa most in the mornings; like now, for instance. He had woken up next to her warm flesh for two years or more and it was hard getting used to being alone again. Still, he had been that way for most of his forty-nine years and he would probably die that way. But he missed her in the morning, especially when he woke up with an aching weight in his loins.

He dressed in last night's clothes, except a fresh T-shirt. It was wet but not cold and he would drive over to Poydras in his truck. His FBI car was permanently on the lowest level of the car park. The bosses had parking spaces on the fifth level. The assistant special agent in charge was Kirk Fitzpatrick, who'd been working in the computer support center in Pocatello when Harrison had been up in Idaho. That was part of the reason he had come to New Orleans in the first place. They were looking for a good guy to work with the special operations group, either semi-under-cover or at least surveillance. Harrison had all the qualities needed, and he had refused pointedly to cut his hair, so Tom Kovalski had spoken to Fitzpatrick. Harrison brought Lisa down for a week in the quarter and she loved it, but wouldn't live there. She was old enough to know she would hate the heat and miss the mountains, so she went back to Idaho. Harrison was faced with the same choice he had always been faced with – the woman or the job. Even with only five years till retirement, he chose the job. As he looked now on to the rain-washed street, with thunder crackling over the crescent of the river, he wondered why. The contents of the room and the black '66 Chevy were all he had in the world.

He parked in the underground lot below the Mobil building on Poydras and Loyola, next to the humming, red surveillance van used by the NOPD. It had ladders racked on the roof and was plugged into the wall by a yellow cable in order to keep the electronic equipment fully boosted. Harrison took the freight elevator as he always did. With his cover in the quarter, he thought it best. The FBI office was on the twenty-second floor and Charlie Mayer, the special agent in charge, was still trying to get something going on the construction of their own building. There was only a year to go before they had to move out. Being here was totally impractical. Suspects had to be shipped upstairs, via this freight elevator, for interviews in the three rooms on the twenty-first floor, and their holding facilities were non-existent. Not only that, the Department of Justice was pretty unhappy about a major field office being situated in the middle of a commercial building, especially with so many groups apparently gunning for them. Harrison waited for the elevator and smoked a final cigarette before the sanitized environment of upstairs. One of the guys from 7 Squad was doing the same thing, standing over by the two black Suburbans, tactical operations centers used by the SWAT teams.

On the squad floor he bumped into Penny, his partner, by the open door to the interview room.

'Hey, babe,' Harrison said. 'What's happening?'

Penny sneezed and indicated the rain. 'Got me a chill out running is what's happening.' He pointed at the all but blacked-out window. Sometimes, when it rained like it was today, you could look down from the floor up here and not see the ground.

'Told you all that exercise was bad for you.' Harrison took a tin of chew from his pocket. 'His name's Manx,' he said.

Penny paused, handkerchief to his nose, and looked over his hands at him. 'You know?'

'I know.' Harrison told him what had happened last night, and they went through to the long, open-plan squad room and sat down at Penny's desk.

Penny was at least fifteen years Harrison's junior, a marine lieutenant before joining the FBI. He could speak French and had worked in Haiti when the troops were 'invited' in. He always joked about the French being helpful down in bayou country, because he could order a beer in Cajun. He worked 10 Squad: drugs; the marine base supply routes, his cover. He was trying to close in on the main operators *actually* supplying the base, by appearing to set up in opposition. Harrison was being assigned to the SOG, but until that happened he was Penny's partner.

Fitzpatrick, the assistant special agent in charge, walked the length of the squad room and paused to speak with Deacon, one of the bean counters who worked with the white-collar crime unit. The Bureau was recruiting accountants and lawyers in droves. The only problem was that when the shit hit the fan, they thought they should be at home with their families. Harrison wondered at it all, as did other old-time 'kiss my ass' agents like John Earl Cochrane, whom he had known for years. Cochrane still drove his four-year-old Caprice because he didn't want to squeeze into a Ford. Goddamn Bureau is hiring dweebs, he would say. Come outta Quantico these days, you got your creds, your gun and a fucking lap-top computer.

Fitzpatrick wore his gun openly, strapped on his hip. The only agent in the office who did so. Some had shoulder holsters, most had ankle rigs, but Fitzpatrick liked to wear his openly, another throwback to the old days, perhaps. He walked past Penny's desk and flicked Harrison's ponytail. 'Hey, hick. Get a goddamn haircut.'

'Kiss my ass.'

Fitzpatrick laughed out loud. 'Cochrane's looking for you, JB,' he called over his shoulder.

Harrison squinted at Penny. 'What does Cochrane want?'

'I don't know. But he's pissed.'

Harrison sat back. 'Pissed at me? What the fuck did I do?'

'Not you, Harrison. He's filling in as media rep again and he thought he'd done with that.'

'Where's Tomason?'

'Seconded to Hoover High. He's doing a whole bunch of work on CODIS.'

Harrison looked blankly at him. 'What the fuck is CODIS?'

'Jeeze, baby. You been undercover too long. Combined DNA Index System. He's re-evaluating the data base. Anyways, that's why Cochrane's combining his 7 Squad stuff with media rep.'

Harrison went upstairs, leaving his partner to consider how they should go about either pissing off Manx or getting a meeting with him. Harrison quite liked the idea of direct competition, that would be interesting in the quarter.

The twenty-second floor housed the senior agents' offices as well as the media representative. Cochrane, a white-haired man from an old St Charles Parish family, was on the telephone, behind a mountain of paperwork that more than covered his desk. He wore a white shirt and red tie and his stomach was just beginning to bulge at his waistband. He nodded for Harrison to sit down and eased himself forward on his elbows, ploughing a path through the papers. Harrison lifted one boot to his knee and knocked his Zippo lighter against the heel. Cochrane put down the phone and ran fingers over his face.

'What's up, John Earl?'

Cochrane shook his head. 'Ever spoken to an assignment editor, Johnny?'

'Can't say I've had the pleasure.'

'I forgot how they can be sometimes. You know, we're pretty damn fair with information up here, but some of the young ones.' He tapped the desk with a red-knuckled finger. 'The women are the worst. Talk about pushy, or what.'

'You gonna be doing this for a while?'

'Not if I can help it.'

'So who's VICAP co-ordinator now then?'

'I am.' Cochrane tapped his chest. 'As if I haven't got

91

enough to do. That's what I wanted to talk to you about.'
He sat forward then. 'We got a joint task force going, John.
Two years back, a gal was found up by the levee off 310,
strangled and mutilated. Breast cut up, post-mortem. St
Charles Parish sheriff's office deal. Joe Kinsella is the
chief of deputies up there, used to be one of us. New York,
Miami, and a while up there at the puzzle palace. Anyways,
Joe does his stuff and puts the information on the national
computer. The Drug Fire Scheme boys get on it and they
come up with a similar murder. Same thing has happened
in Desoto Parish, between Mansfield and Shreeveport.
Since then, there's been three more killings, all the victims
women, all of them strangled, all of them mutilated in a
similar way, post-mortem. They sent the information to the
Violent Criminal Apprehension Program.'

'And they contacted you to set up the task force.'

'Right. The guy is going interstate. They're gonna need
us for a UFAP warrant, anyways.'

'Not if he's from round here, they won't. Didn't you tell
me that Louisiana fugitives are easy to locate. What was it:
*They always come back to momma*.'

The wind drove sheets of rain against the window.
Harrison glanced sideways and then looked back at Cochrane. He was restless, having been in the office too long,
and he wanted a cigarette. 'What d'you want from me,
John Earl?'

'There's been another murder.'

'Another one here?'

Cochrane shook his head and checked the note on his
desk. 'No. Not here. In Georgia. Quantico took a call from
an Agent Chaney of the Georgia Bureau of Investigation
in Athens. Apparently, a woman called Mary Poynton was
murdered in Royston, Georgia, last weekend. She was
strangled and her left titty was cut up, before she was
chucked in a dumpster.' He paused. 'That's a factor too;

four of the five victims that the CASKU has profiled to our guy were found in dumpsters. Press have nicknamed him "The Garbageman". All the murders have been within a day's drive of Shreeveport.'

'You can't say that about Georgia.'

'No. But somebody needs to go up there and take a look, anyways,' Cochrane said. 'I should go as VICAP coordinator and the fact that it's my case.' He held out his hands. 'But I can't, Johnny. I'm up to my neck with all this extra stuff and Maddie's not good.'

Harrison's eyes clouded. 'She getting worse, John?'

Cochrane blew the air from his cheeks. 'Put it this way, buddy, she's not getting any better. I really don't want to fly up to Georgia. We're talking a night away, at least. The kids are all in college and there's nobody but neighbours. I don't like to leave her.'

Cochrane's wife had leukaemia. Harrison stood up. 'No problem, John Earl. I'll go. You got a contact for me at the CASKU? I guess they're gonna send a profiler down.'

'Special Agent Mallory.' Cochrane took a business card from his wallet and passed it across the desk.

The Child Abduction and Serial Killer Unit had twenty-nine agents working out of its office at the Quantico complex. Mallory was one of them. Harrison took a flight from the airport in New Orleans to Atlanta and then got a ride with a probationary agent from the Atlanta field office, who had been assigned to cover the killing. They were due to meet Mallory at the crime scene. The agent from Atlanta was young and white and keen. Harrison squatted in the passenger seat with the window rolled down, smoking a cigarette, despite the red 'No Smoking' sign that dangled from the rearview mirror. The agent's name was Collins and he was pissed about the cigarette; that and the way Harrison looked. 'Goddamn, man,' he had said as Harrison lit the Marlboro. 'I couldn't make the sign much bigger.'

Harrison squinted sideways at him. 'What's your point, bubba?'

'Don't call me bubba.'

Harrison blew smoke from the side of his mouth. 'How long you been graduated?'

'Three months.'

'So, you're still a probationer.'

'Yeah, but that doesn't . . .'

Harrison held up a palm. 'I got you on age. I got you on experience. So quit whining.' Reaching over, he ripped off the 'No Smoking' sign and tossed it into the back.

They drove in silence after that and Harrison hoped Special Agent Mallory would be better company. Mallory was a woman and they were in Hicksville, Georgia. He shook his head and smiled when he met her and Agent Chaney at the GBI office in Athens, about twenty miles south of the crime scene. Chaney was a big, square-jawed man who chewed cigars to the butt, and had clearly been round the block a few times. He had been the one who informed the Violent Criminal Apprehension Program co-ordinator at Quantico about the crime scene similarities.

Now, Harrison seemed to find it a little hard listening to Mallory, all of twenty-nine, with her fine bones and clean hands and lap-top computer. She was pretty though, which was a diversion. She had tried to keep her expression clear when Harrison introduced himself, his hair falling over his shoulders, thinning now and grey, face battered about the mouth and eyes, and smelling of cigarettes. He explained that the New Orleans case agent was not able to make it, but he was there to assist. She looked more than a little doubtful, which seemed to amuse Chaney.

They looked over the evidence that the technicians from the Franklin County sheriff's office had collected before the GBI evidence response team got there. Harrison studied the plastic bag containing the butt end of the joint and a

94

sheet of white paper, part of a notepad, which had the indented letters *TJ CC* marked on it.

'What does this mean?' he asked.

Chaney shook his shoulders. 'Don't know. We thought she might have written it, but she didn't.'

Mallory looked thoughtful. 'The killer wrote it and tore the page off, leaving this here?'

Chaney nodded. 'We think so.'

'A person, a place, or what?' Harrison asked.

'We don't know. Could mean anything.'

Mallory sat down and studied the medical examiner's report, chewing at her lower lip. Harrison stood by the open window with Chaney, smoking. 'You guys got called in pretty quickly then, huh?' Harrison said.

'Day one, which is good. Some of those county dicks have a habit of treading on evidence.'

'Find much else?'

Chaney ran a calloused hand over his hair. 'The note, the bitty reefer you got there. A couple of bootprints we lifted from the grass. Took some effort to haul her into the dumpster. The print is pretty good, but won't give us anything distinguishing.'

Mallory looked over at them, pushing her fine auburn hair behind one ear. 'I'm going to want to talk to the ME,' she said. 'Can you set that up for me?'

Chaney reached for the phone on his desk. Harrison flipped his cigarette out of the window and moved over to her. He could smell her perfume, and standing over her he could see the soft white skin of her chest, flat above her breasts at the collar bone. He squatted down on his haunches. 'What you got, Mallory?'

She showed him the autopsy report. 'Ligature marks,' she said. 'At the throat, indicating a rope or cable, some kind of garrotte.'

Harrison bit his lip. 'That doesn't match. Our boy uses his forearm or something, right?'

She seemed amazed he had read the file. 'Big boy,' Harrison went on. 'Not too old, between twenty and thirty, you reckon.'

'Nearer twenty.'

He stood up then, knees creaking a fraction. Collins leaned with his palms behind him on the windowsill. 'Less planning,' Mallory went on. 'The dump sites are dumpsters right by the scene.'

Harrison nodded. 'The closer, the younger, huh.'

'Exactly. The more planning used generally suggests an older man. I think our "garbageman" is nearer twenty than thirty.' She looked again at the report. 'This victim is at least fifteen years older than the others have been. They were all between thirty and thirty-eight. Mary Poynton was fifty-three.'

'Rape?' Harrison asked her.

'No.'

'But the breast mutilation's the same.'

'Yes.' She laid the report down.

'The doc'll meet you at the sheriff's office in Carnesville, mam,' Chancy told them.

Collins drove, Harrison and Chaney in the back, with Mallory up front, still reading the report. It was about an hour's drive from Athens to Carnesville. They rode in silence for a while, Harrison looking out the window at the broken-down shacks they passed. 'Real *Deliverance* country,' he muttered. He looked at Chaney again. 'You come up with any possible perps yet?'

Chaney scratched the back of his hand with bitten-down fingernails. 'One black guy. Truck driver from Alabama. He was here three days, had his truck fixed at King's Auto Line, over by the railroad tracks in Royston. We ran checks on him, truck payment, motel room, usual kinda thing.

96

Credit card was a forged duplicate. He visited the shop, so the husband told us; wanted to look at a necklace. His wife remembered because he was the only customer she had all that day.' He swallowed tobacco juice. 'Royston ain't exactly a heaving metropolis.'

'Anybody talk to him?'

'Nope. He left the morning she got killed, drove back to Alabama. We haven't been able to trace him or the truck.' He sucked juice and swallowed again.

The Franklin County Detention Center was situated behind the small shopping complex on James Little Street, in Carnesville. The GBI agent explained to them that the murder of Mary Poynton had taken place right where three counties meet: Franklin, Hart and Madison. If it had been a couple of blocks in either direction, it would have fallen into Hart or Madison's jurisdiction. 'Don't suppose they have too many murders way out here in the boonies,' Harrison muttered. 'County dicks musta been pissed when you got involved.'

The medical examiner was sitting with the chief of deputies and the investigating detective who had worked the case before they involved Chaney and the GBI. Sheriff Clayburgh came through from his office when he heard them arrive. He looked at Mallory with a hint of scorn in his eye, then at the clean-cut young buck from Atlanta, and finally rolled a cursory glance over Harrison. 'You all FBI?' he asked.

Harrison nodded, and took a pinch of chew from his pocket and stuck it under his lip. Clayburgh looked at Mallory. 'You the profiler?'

'Yes. Child Abduction and Serial Killer Unit. CASKU, in Quantico.'

'Right.' Clayburgh scratched the hairs that jutted from above his collar. 'Y'all think we got us one here then, a serial killer, I mean?'

97

Mallory smiled at him. 'Sheriff, I don't know anything yet. I want to check a few details with the ME.'

'Y'all go ahead.' Clayburgh sat down and folded his arms, watching Mallory's skin redden at the base of her neck.

Harrison had to hand it to her, she controlled it well. She would be a psychology graduate, probably Master's level. The team that they had up in Quantico were all about as good as it gets. He could imagine the jokes flying when she got back; toothless, redneck sheriffs and hill-billy cops all spitting tobacco juice. She spoke carefully and clinically to the ME, going over every inch of his report. Then she spoke with the crime scene team that had attended the scene from Carnesville, then Chaney again in detail. Both she and Harrison wanted to view the crime scene, but the sun was fading now and they had to find a motel. Collins stayed with them and they ate dinner in the small diner by the BP station. Chaney had gone back to Athens.

'It ain't the same guy, is it,' Harrison said to Mallory as she picked at her salad, the fork held loosely between forefinger and thumb.

'I don't think so. But I need to see the crime scene.'

'The method of strangulation is different for starters,' Harrison continued. 'The file I got from John Cochrane indicates that the bruising marks are different. He's used his forearm or something.' He made a gesture like a wrestler. 'Some kinda headlock, anyways. He's never used a rope or a cord.'

'This is a cord,' she said, 'probably plastic-coated. There are no rope burns, the bruising is smooth.'

'But what about cutting off the nipple, that's exactly the same?' Collins drank mineral water.

Harrison looked across the table at him as he chewed. 'You got a point, bubba.'

'Quit calling me bubba.'

Harrison winked at Mallory, then looked back at Collins. 'Come on, man. Lighten up.' He leaned forward then. 'The breast mutilation is the same, yes, but the rest is different. The age of the victim, the distance from the original crime scene, which was Desoto Parish, Louisiana. Every other killing's been within a day's drive of that parish.'

'Maybe he changed his job,' Collins went on.

'Maybe he did.' Mallory looked squarely at him. 'But he got the method of strangulation wrong. All we've ever released about this guy is the fact that the victims were strangled. We couldn't keep that quiet, anyways. There're telltale signs that the press, who managed to get pictures, would know about. Burst blood vessels in the eyes are a giveaway.'

'You released the post-mortem mutilation stuff, though,' Harrison interrupted her.

She nodded. 'We did. In consultation with the victims' families. We hoped it might trigger something in somebody's mind.'

'And did it?' Collins asked.

'About five hundred phone calls.'

'All of 'em dud, right?' Harrison sucked cigarette smoke.

'Right.' Mallory sipped water. 'We did not, however, let out the fact that all of the victims had been killed in exactly the same manner. Just that they were strangled. We concentrated our efforts, after Fugitive Publicity got involved, on the big men that were reported to us. Louisiana men.'

'All go home to momma,' Harrison muttered.

'What?' Collins glanced at him.

'It don't matter. The dope,' he went on. 'That's a first too.'

'It is. Nothing we've got so far has indicated somebody using drugs. The opposite, matter of fact, in many ways.'

'What about as a facilitator?' Collins asked. 'Like Bundy

and booze. From what I read he couldn't kill unless he was fucked up.'

Mallory glanced at him. 'It's possible. We've just not seen any evidence of it till now.'

'The black guy in the truck's more than just coincidence,' Harrison said. 'Three days in town. Alabama plates. And no sign of either him or the truck since.'

'Casing the joint properly,' Collins put in.

'Three-day surveillance.' Harrison made a face. 'You must want her pretty bad to go to all that trouble.' He gestured at Mallory with his fork. 'Who was she, anyway?'

'I've not done any digging, Harrison. The GBI'll be doing the full background stuff. I guess she was insured. Maybe the husband paid somebody.' She smiled then. 'That bit's not our problem. We're here to establish an indisputable link with what we've seen in Louisiana. I want to look at the crime scene, but I'm almost positive there is no link. Somebody killed Mary Poynton for reasons of their own and made it look like our guy.'

# 8

Boese walked in circles, edging the wire-meshed double fence of the exercise yard; hands in his jacket pockets, his collar turned up against the breeze that came in flat from the west. Morgan walked the other way and they passed each other every circuit, bars on all sides, bars above their heads. Boese could hear the rumble of lorries from the other side of the wall. Yesterday, Morgan's sister had visited him. Since then he had waited, watched, wondered. Terlucci appeared to be growing bold again. The Blues Brothers, perhaps, goading him about not having the guts to do what he always bragged to them he would do. If he came at him again, Boese knew that the ice in his words would not be enough. He wanted to avoid trouble, though, particularly now. He watched Terlucci as they exercised, hands in his pockets like everyone else. He ambled behind Morgan, the Blues Brothers behind him. Boese watched his hands, and considered what kind of weapon he had in those pockets. Terlucci was always armed. Morgan passed him and for a second their eyes met. Boese felt the sudden surge in his veins.

The half-hour of exercise was over and they trooped back inside, the grey, wintry sky left behind. Boese went back to his cell, then came out and found Morgan setting up chesspieces. Terlucci was watching him from the pool table. Boese caught the eye of one of the wardens in the control room, and the man seemed to be intent upon Terlucci. Maybe they could sense the air of uncertainty that weighted the atmosphere. Boese had to watch Terlucci, but he was distracted by Morgan and Morgan's sister.

Terlucci had lost considerable face. Maybe the story had leaked to the outside and he faced ridicule and dishonour within his own brotherhood. Boese knew he would have to do something about him, before the Italian lost it completely. For the moment, though, he played chess. Morgan played with the level of seriousness he always applied, but slipped a cigarette paper to Boese as he took his queen. The game finished quickly after that, Boese allowing him to win. Morgan looked in his eyes, as if it was becoming more obvious. Boese left him to clear away the pieces.

In his cell, he lay on his back and read a book, one of those they brought round from the library, carefully vetted so as not to incite any emotions that would be inappropriate in a place such as this. Boese ignored the printed words on the page, studying instead the coded message from Tal-Salem.

DO YOU ORDER ANY BASIC FORM BUYING AT
ONE OF ANY HOME-BASED MULTI-XEROXING
MACHINES?
ANY FINE QUEST MACHINE GENERATES WITH
ZEST AND ZEAL.

Lying on his bed, he selected the pertinent letters in his mind, and as he did so, the hairs lifted on the back of his neck. DOBBOABXAQGZZ. Swinging his legs over the edge of the bed, he sat upright and looked again. Now he took the pencil from his pillowcase and marked out the words, suddenly oblivious to the risks. GREER DEAD TJ CC.

Jorge Vaczka walked into the pub with Stahl. They bought bottles of Becks and sat at the bar to drink them. Outside, cars moved up and down the A3. Two motorcycles had been set on their side stands in the car park. Both of them new Triumphs. Vaczka looked in the mirror beyond the bar for faces seated behind them. Two men sat on their own in the corner, both in leathers, no patches, colours, or markings. Both of them had short-cut hair. Vaczka sucked on his bottle and then ordered two more, and they walked over to where the two men were sitting, both on the same side of the table. They had just finished a meal and the waitress cleared the dishes away as Vaczka and Stahl sat down. Nobody said anything for a moment or two. One of the bikers took a tin of tobacco from his pocket, rolled a cigarette and licked the glued edge of the paper before twisting up both ends. Stahl flicked a match for him.

Vaczka looked at the other man – grey-eyed, short-cut hair, leather jacket and jeans, nothing to suggest anything about him. His eyes were cold and one of his hands lay fisted on the table. 'We're looking for a hero to carry the flag,' Vaczka said softly. The man did not register that he had heard, his gaze falling beyond them to the bar, eyes moving steadily over drinkers and diners alike, before he looked in Vaczka's face. 'You found him,' he replied.

Back in New Orleans, Harrison gave the details of what he had learned in Georgia to John Cochrane. 'Gal from the CASKU's happy it's not your "garbageman", John Earl. We left it with the GBI.'

Cochrane took the file notes from him. 'Nothing I need for the 302?'

'Not as far as I can figure. It's background stuff. I guess you could refer to it when you finally pop this guy, but none of it's testimonial.'

Cochrane looked gratefully at him. 'Thanks for going up there, JB. Saved me a whole buncha trouble.'

'No problem.' Harrison left him then and went back downstairs. He looked for Penny and was told that he was getting something from his car. That gave Harrison an excuse for a cigarette and he took it.

Penny was bending over the trunk of the car. Harrison came out the backstairs and plucked a cigarette from his shirt pocket. He popped a match on his fingernail and Penny jumped at the sound. He came up with 'Excalibur' in his hands. 'Jesus, Harrison. Don't do that.'

Harrison grinned at him and flapped out the match. The day was warm, the sun full in the sky and it reflected across the flat concrete floor like a mirror from the building across the street.

'What you doing?' Harrison asked him, nodding to the sniper's rifle cradled in Penny's hands. They were both SWAT-trained, and formed a sniper observer team, Harrison watching Penny's back. The black, hand-made 308 was Matt Penny's baby.

'Just sorting through my gear.' Penny held up the gun. 'The sponge is coming off.' He indicated the cheekwell space on the stock, where he had fixed a piece of sponge so he could lock in position quickly and without looking, then fire accurately at will.

'Use that thing in Montana?' Harrison asked him. Penny had been at the eighty-one day stand-off with the Freemen, as part of the regional response team.

'Took her, never fired a shot.' Penny replaced 'Excalibur' in her case. All the FBI sniper rifles were hand-made, specifically designed to fit their owners, by ex-US marine armourers who now worked for the FBI at Quantico. It was a 308-calibre with a 10 power scope. The barrel was free-floating, set in glass, and the recoil was your shoulder. Penny prided himself on being able to separate someone's brain stem at two hundred yards. He closed the lid and snapped the catches shut.

'What's happening?' Harrison asked, sucking on his cigarette.

Penny took a pinch of snuff from his tin and placed it under his lip. 'Martinez got busted last night.'

'No kidding. Dealing?'

'Possession.' Penny leaned on the edge of the trunk. 'Two grams of heroin, Harrison. Was driving like he was drunk and a road unit pulled him over on Sugar Bowl Drive. He's downtown right now.'

'Shit.' Harrison took a Merit from his shirt.

'It ain't shit, ponyboy. It's brilliant.'

Harrison squinted at him.

'Possession of heroin'll get him five to ten on a federal rap,' Penny said. 'If he helps us nail Manx, then maybe that five could be a two or even just probation.'

'So, what you thinking?'

Penny shook his head at him. 'Under Louisiana state law, possession of heroin gets you life in Angola.'

Harrrison's battered face cracked open in a smile. 'No shit,' he said.

They walked back to the stairs and Penny's gaze wandered to the tattoo half exposed at the sleeve of Harrison's T-shirt. Both of them had been in the military, fifteen years apart; though Penny as an officer, and he hadn't seen any action. 'What was it like down there, Harrison? In Cu-Chi, I mean?'

Harrison shrugged his shoulders. 'Dark. Snakes and spiders and stakes stuck in the ground.'

'Just you and your gun, huh?'

'You, your gun and him.'

Penny shook his head. 'Goddamn. What you got running through those veins, man, ice water?'

'I'm older now, homeboy.'

Penny kicked Harrison's boot where the gun was strapped. 'Sure you are,' he said.

They went back upstairs, Harrison suddenly aware of how he was thought of down here. When he had first arrived back in the summer, there had been all sorts of cracks about his appearance. He never wore a suit, never wore a tie, just jeans and T-shirts and his battered Idaho boots. The rat tattoo provoked conversation when it was visible and everyone knew that Agent Johnny 'Buck' Dollar, better known as Harrison, was the UCA who killed three men in a mine in Idaho. The jokes about his hair and his clothes were just that: underneath it all, most of the other street guys were in awe of him. The beaners and the dweebs did not even try to understand him.

'You gonna talk to the DA's office about Martinez?' Harrison said.

Penny nodded and picked up the phone.

Harrison went out to take a leak and when he came back from the men's room, Kirk Fitzpatrick was talking to Penny. 'There y'are, hick,' he said as Harrison came over. 'I've been looking for you.'

'What's up?'

'I got Tom Kovalski upstairs. He wants to talk to you.'

Harrison lifted one eyebrow. 'What's he doing this far south?'

'Visiting me. I'm responsible for counter-terrorism down here.'

Harrison followed him upstairs and found Kovalski sitting at the conference table in the ASAC's office. 'John, how are you?' Kovalski stood up and offered his hand. He was roughly the same age as Harrison, with a lined, leathery face and thick brown hair. Harrison had known him a long time, right back to his rookie days after joining the FBI from the border patrol in New Mexico. He had done more than one undercover job for the Domestic Terrorism Section, the last one being in Idaho. Kovalski was deputy section chief now, and, unlike some of the other suits in D.C., he had been a damn good field agent.

'See you didn't cut your hair, then.' Kovalski adjusted the knot of his tie and gestured to the chair alongside him. 'What you working, SOG?'

106

'Will be. Right now I'm helping out on the drugs squad.'

'In the quarter?'

'Got myself a room north of Bourbon Street.' Harrison smiled wickedly. 'I like the challenge at night.'

Kovalski looked at him for a moment. Harrison was still lean and mean-looking in his faded denims and ponytail. His grey hair was thinner now and his eyes were wrinkled hollows of light, but they could still pierce you at ten paces. Kovalski thought about his grandchildren and gently shook his head. 'You don't change, Johnny.'

'Yeah, I do. I'm old and creaky. Especially when it's raining.'

'Tell me about it.' Kovalski paused then. 'The arraignment date for Salvesen will be set next week.'

'Good. I'm looking forward to seeing that sonofabitch go all the way to the bottom.'

'And talking of which . . .'

Harrison looked at him carefully. 'You got some information for me, Tom?'

Kovalski sat forward. 'I spoke to Louis Byrne.'

'About me?'

'He was in London with the Foreign Emergency Search Team, wasn't he.' Kovalski fiddled with his fountain pen. 'Matter of fact, he came to me. He'd heard the whisper that you were mad as hell about who might have compromised you, and he spoke to me.' He laid down the pen again. 'I gotta tell you, John, and I'm happy to be doing it, it's nobody in the Bureau.'

'You know for sure?' Harrison cocked his head to one side.

'Byrne does.'

'How come?'

'Right about the time you got burned, he was in Paris checking on Jack Swann's girlfriend.'

'Swann's a British antiterrorist guy?'

107

'Yeah. It was his girlfriend who was feeding information to Storm Crow. She knew he was in Paris, Johnny. He called her up and told her he was going.'

'The meal receipt I found in Jake Salvesen's office.'

'Precisely.' Kovalski sat back and spread his fingers. 'The timing fits, John. As soon as she knew he was going to Paris she would've known why.' He broke off for a second. 'And one phone call later . . .'

Harrison got up and walked to the window. He thought back to the spring, when he had been on surveillance, watching the militia leader's compound, and all of a sudden Salvesen's men came gunning for him. He remembered sitting in their mock courtroom when they laid their charges of treason – for being a federal agent – against him. Then he remembered the flight through the tunnels that Salvesen had built in the hillside, and Dugger's Canyon and the Magdalena mine where three men had died at his hands. Jack Swann, a blabby-mouthed English copper responsible for almost getting him killed. He turned back to Kovalski.

'Makes sense, doesn't it,' Kovalski said.

'Yeah, I guess it does.'

'Doesn't make you feel any better though, huh?'

Harrison snorted. 'I'm alive, aren't I.'

He was quiet as Penny drove back from their meeting with Rene Martinez. Penny had good contacts on the NOPD drugs squad, and they knew he was trying to break the ring supplying cocaine on the marine base. Manx was the key to the bigger fish and Martinez was the way to get to Manx. If he got busted for possessing two grams of heroin, everything could fall apart. They did a deal with the assistant DA. If Martinez came up with the goods on Manx, he would get a federal charge and all the mitigating circumstances. If he didn't, Penny and Harrison would leave him to the New Orleans dicks and he'd spend the rest of his life getting butt-fucked in Angola. Penny pulled up outside Louise's bar off Canal, where they liked a beer after work. Cochrane and Fitzpatrick were there, together with some guys from the reactive squad, who were celebrating an armed robbery bust they had made the previous day.

Harrison sat at the table, with them and not with them, sucking cigarette smoke and blowing rings at the ceiling. Penny was laughing with the rest of them and making wisecracks about the waitress who kept them supplied with drinks. He sat back though, taking the last of his chew from the tin, and caught Harrison's expression.

'Hey, ponyboy, what's up?'

'Oh, nothing, kiddo. Just thinking is all.'

'Not good for you, man, not a guy of your age.'

Cochrane, too, had noticed Harrison's mood. He knew the story; the two of them were old friends. Harrison had stayed with John and Maddie for the first two weeks down here, before he got his room in the quarter. 'Kovalski give you some news, JB?'

Harrison looked at him. 'Yeah. Guy that got me in trouble up in Idaho was a UK cop. Somebody called Jack Swann. Louis Byrne worked with him on the FEST they sent over.'

'That chemical thing in London?' Penny asked.

Harrison looked at him and nodded. 'Storm Crow, yeah.'

Penny blew out his cheeks. 'And this guy Swann burned you?'

'Not on purpose, but it amounts to the same thing.'

Cochrane pushed a hand through his thick white hair. 'At least you know for sure now.'

Harrison nodded. 'I ought to be relieved that's all it is. I was thinking we had some internal problem to deal with.'

'That would've gone down real well, after the shit we got thrown at us the last couple of years.'

'Tell me about it. Still gets you in the guts though, anyways. Maybe one of these days I'll take a vacation in London, find this fucker Swann and have a couple of words.' They all laughed and Harrison stood up. 'Guys, I'm gonna split,' he said. 'There's a gal in the Jazz Café I wanna try and poke tonight.'

January 1999. One year until the new millennium. Swann thought about it as he drove into the Yard. Up on the fifteenth floor, he found Webb talking to DI Clements in the squad room. Clements was subject to tenure, and about to leave the department and go back to uniform. He was not exactly enamoured with the idea. They looked up as Swann dumped his case on the desk and went to pour some coffee.

'You all right, Jack?' Webb asked him. 'Caroline wanted to know if you fancied dinner tonight. Couple of pints on the way home, first? What d'you reckon?'

'Yeah. I suppose.'

'Jesus.' Webb shook his head. 'Mr Enthusiasm.'

'Sorry, Webby. Didn't mean it to sound like that.'

'Well cheer up, anyway,' Webb said, punching him lightly on the arm. 'We've got a date for Boese's trial.'

Swann looked up sharply. 'When?'

'February 5th.'

'Hallelujah. Time that bastard went down.' He thought for a moment. 'There's nothing the defence can pick holes in, is there, Webby? The last thing we need is Storm Crow flying away.'

Webb laughed at him. 'Jack, you know what, just because you're paranoid, it doesn't mean they're not after you. Relax,' he said. 'We've got every scrap of forensic evidence we need.'

'You sure?'

'Positive. Leave it to your uncle George.'

Swann sat down and rested the sole of his shoe against the desktop. 'You know, I don't think I'll be happy till that bastard knows he's doing thirty years.' He shook his head. 'Maybe it's because of Pia, maybe it's what he did in Rome, but no one has got under my skin like that guy.'

They went up to the sixteenth floor, where Christine Harris had called them in for a meeting. No Julian Moore this time, just Harris and another DS from SO12.

'Just an update, chaps,' she told them. 'The Vaczka gang.'

'You've had spotters on them?' Swann asked her.

'Not a full team, Jack. Not yet. The intel' is still too scant.'

'The snout not up to it?'

'I think she's up to it. She's about as close to him as we could hope to get somebody, but Vaczka's a pro. Remember his links with Abu Nidal. That's a serious connection. He lets very little slip.'

'So have we got anything fresh or not?' he asked her.

She stared at him for a moment, the snap of irritation in her voice. 'Yes, strangely enough, we have. That's why I called a briefing.'

Swann flushed red and held up a hand, palm outwards. 'Sorry, Chrissie. Ignore me. Probably time of the month.'

She blew air softly from her cheeks and shook her head at the others. 'See what happens when cousins marry?' she said.

The tension was only partially defused and Swann was aware of DSU Colson's gaze on him. Harris went on to tell them that Vaczka had met up with an Arab, or at least somebody dressed as such.

'That could tie up with the ANO thing,' Swann said.

'Possibly. But this guy wore headgear like Yasser Arafat.' Harris paused then. 'Somehow that doesn't make a lot of sense, does it. If you're a contact man for Abu Nidal, you don't swan around West London looking like an oil sheik, do you.' Nobody answered her. 'Vaczka's also spending more and more time openly with his three lieutenants. That's Stahl, Herbisch and Blunski. He is definitely planning something, only we don't know what it is.'

'What about the original information we got from Box 850?' Swann asked her.

'They know no more, or if they do, they're not telling us.'

'A possible connection with the disaffected Loyalists?'

Harris nodded. 'Vaczka has said something about a deal up north, he may have to go away for a while.'

'He told her that?' Colson said. 'I don't suppose he said when.'

'What about spotters now, Chrissie?' Webb asked her.

She shook her head. 'My guv'nor won't go for it, George. All the time we've got a snout in so close, you can't really blame him.'

'So we just sit tight as usual,' Swann stated. 'See if any of the spinning plates fall to earth.'

'That's it for the time being. The reason I'm telling you now is because when whatever they're doing happens, it'll be sudden and we'll need to roll very quickly.'

'Have you thought about briefing an SFO team, Chrissie?' Colson asked her.

'What could I tell them right now, sir?'

Tal-Salem sat and read the paper at his favourite café, wearing only a loose-fitting shirt and chinos. His feet were bare and his sleeves rolled back, the Rolex hanging from his left wrist where the strap was loose. The waiter poured him the Arabian coffee and he cast an eye over the beach, the sun warming the sand at his feet. Above his head, a gull cried and for a moment he looked along the line of the horizon, bunching his eyes against the brightness of the day. Then his gaze settled on the advert.

QUESTIONS ABOUT ORDERS?
NOT FOR THE XANADU AUTOMATIC INDEX.
EVERYTHING CAN BE BOUGHT BY YOU DIRECT.
CONSIDER XANADU FOR YOUR SANITY AND
BUDGET.

Carefully, he picked out the letters and his pulse rate quickened. QOFXICBYCFSB. TRIAL FEB FIVE.

He laid the paper aside and sipped his coffee. Then he took a pre-rolled hashish joint from his shirt pocket, cupped his hands to the match and drew smoke into his lungs. He breathed very deeply, aware almost of the movement of his diaphragm. His eyes glazed just a fraction and he could smell blood in his nostrils.

Vaczka lay back in bed, hands pressing into Amaya's hair as she sucked his penis. His eyes were closed and the skin gathered in wrinkles at the corners. She lifted her head, drawing damp trails on his belly with lips and tongue, and her hair tickled his skin as she worked up to his face. He took her by the hips and guided her body down until he brushed against pubic hair and then moisture and warmth, and a gasp escaped his lips. She flicked her hair from her eyes, sitting up, shoulders back, with the points of her breasts rising and falling as she worked his hips. He could feel the pressure of her pelvic bone as she moved herself forward again, falling on to her hands either side of him, so her breasts hung in his face. He lifted his head, straining the muscles of his neck and brushed hard nipple with his tongue. He came with a cry in his throat and the muscles of his face twisting almost in pain. She worked herself a little more and then fell forward on top of him.

Vaczka's eyes were closed; he was breathing hard. He

could feel the sweat gathered between their bodies. Then she eased herself off him, and curled into his chest with her knees against his hip. He kissed her hair, stroking her back, fingers feeling a path over the knots of her spine. Then he opened his eyes and stared at the ceiling.

'I'm going to be away for a few days,' he said.

'When?'

'Soon. I'm not sure exactly when. I'll have to cancel the class.'

She pushed herself up on one elbow. 'People are going to be disappointed.'

'Well, it's only the one class. I'm sure they'll get over it.' He moved the pillows against the headboard and scraped a cigarette from the packet beside the bed. Amaya sat up next to him, one leg crossed under the other. He lit the cigarette, flapped out the match and blew a steady stream of smoke at the ceiling.

'Is it work?'

'What?'

She swept the hair from in front of her eyes. 'Are you going away to work?'

'Yeah. A little sideline of mine in Liverpool. Theatre workshop.'

'Can I come?'

'You've got a degree course to do, Amaya. You'll never get it if you keep taking time off to follow me round the country.'

'You'll let me know when you're going, though.'

'Of course I will, dummy. I've got to cancel the class.' Vaczka put out the cigarette and cupped her left breast with a palm. 'What time do you have to be gone?' he said.

Tal-Salem flew into London on a Chilean diplomatic passport. He was well dressed for London in February – double-breasted wool suit and a cashmere overcoat that

114

reached to his ankles. He took a cab from Heathrow into London and checked into the Hyde Park Tower in Bayswater. He had posted a parcel to himself and collected it at reception. Upstairs, he laid his case on the bed and unwrapped the parcel. Inside were two Beretta automatics. He took the twin leather shoulder holsters from his suitcase and adjusted the straps when the weight of the weapons was in them. Then he took both guns to pieces, cleaned them with oil and put them together again. He had five spare clips and he popped each bullet out and then replaced them one by one until the spring mechanism would go no further. After that he lay back, smoked hash and watched the news on television.

Vaczka spoke to Stahl on the cloned mobile telephone, and set everything up. The following day, Friday, he cancelled the next week's lesson. He and Jeconec ate lunch in the cafeteria and he watched Amaya leave early and head down towards the station. He glanced at Jeconec and quietly shook his head. From across the road, one of Blunski's team, Rafal Kestin, followed her.

Amaya met Christine Harris by the statue of Robert Burns in the Embankment Gardens. It was lunchtime and people were eating sandwiches in the sunshine that had lifted the icy temperatures of the last couple of days. 'He's going to Liverpool next week,' she told her. 'He's cancelled Friday's drama class.' She paused then, as Harris considered the information. She had been running and her sweatpants were rapidly cooling against her thighs. 'If you arrest him for something, he's going to know this has come from me,' Amaya said, her mouth pinched and tight about the words.

Harris laid a hand on her arm. 'No, he won't,' she said. 'Besides, we'll look after you.'

Amaya looked at her with the edge of her lip raised over

her teeth. 'I'm not doing this any more,' she said. 'This is the last time you'll see me. You can do what the fuck you like with my visa. I've had enough. I might just go back to Poland, anyway.' She turned then and walked away. Kestin stood on the Embankment and watched them.

The week before Vaczka cancelled his drama class, Adam Herbisch stole nine motorcycles from different parts of the country. Through the network, he arranged for a target to be chosen, lifted, and then stored ready for the number plates to be changed. When he had the full complement, he passed the word to Stahl, who subsequently told Vaczka. Herbisch then stole a skip lorry and a Range Rover with tinted windows, and stored them in a lock-up in Highbury. He phoned Vaczka when everything was ready, and told him the preparations, routes in and out, everything. Vaczka switched off his mobile, confident that the authorities could not listen to conversations on cloned mobile phones, then left the flat for the POSK. Jeconec was waiting for him, eating meat-filled flour balls which only Carmen seemed able to cook properly for him.

'You should sleep with her,' Vaczka told him when he sat down. 'Better still, marry her. Look at the way she cooks.'

Jeconec laughed and glanced out of the window. Two men were working on the road; they had been there for three days now. He nodded towards them and Vaczka spoke without looking up. 'I know. I spotted them too. Interesting that the council should dig up the road just now.'

At the counter, a young couple in baggy coats and university scarves held hands as they ordered some coffee. They sat down at the table next to Vaczka and looking lovingly into one another's eyes.

'Amaya not working today?' Jeconec asked.

116

Vaczka shook his head, watching the men working outside. 'College.'

'She a good fuck?'

Vaczka looked witheringly at him.

'Sorry,' Jeconec said.

Vaczka sat back and spoke in soft tones, suddenly aware of the young lovers at the next table. 'Everything is now ready,' he said. 'All I need from you is the truck.'

Jeconec smiled widely and placed the last meatball in his mouth, looking across Vaczka at Carmen. 'No problem,' he said.

Tal-Salem picked up the stolen Range Rover from the lock-up and drove it north out of London. He was meticulous in his covert antisurveillance, arranging for the keys to be left for him at the hotel in Bayswater, then watching reception for two full days before actually picking them up. After that, he checked his maps very carefully, working out exactly what the layout of streets was around the immediate vicinity of the lock-up. Only when he was sure of that on paper did he undertake his first physical reconnaissance. Again he disguised himself as the black man, an appearance he was now beginning to appreciate. The application of stage make-up, something he had only perfected since he had worked with Boese, came much more easily to him. He made the pass in a taxi and checked to see what was close to the garages. They were set on their own in a side street, fully enclosed in a warehouse, which was overlooked by the back windows of a row of residential properties. Tal-Salem gave them a cursory once-over, but knew he would have to return to look more closely. This he did the same evening, and keeping to the shadows of the warehouse, he scanned the windows of the houses with an infrared scope, looking for the telltale silver disc of a video camera. He found none. No cars were parked close by. He even inspected the doors on the warehouses on the other side of the road. Only when he was absolutely certain of his security did he move the Range Rover.

Returning to his Chilean diplomat's disguise, he parked the Range Rover in Bayswater and watched the permit area for two days, having paid his fee to the hotel. Again satisfied, he made the trip out to the M3 and the service area at Hook. Two motorcycles, both of them British Triumphs, were parked by the steps leading up from the car park. The two riders were easily picked out, seated by the window in The Granary, watching both the entrance and the road. Tal-Salem sat at the table behind them, not acknowledging their presence, and observed them for half an hour. When he was satisfied, he reached over the back of his seat and looked into the hard grey eyes of David 'Dog Soldier' Collier.

Boese watched Terlucci, watched his face, the way he moved his hands, where he moved his hands; the depth of his conversations with the two bank robbers, Matthews and Thompson. He watched Terlucci and counted days. Morgan's sister visited him once more in late January and Boese played chess with Morgan the afternoon before. This time Boese beat him and Morgan left the table with a smile on his face. On 3 February, Boese found himself assigned to the kitchen with Gianluca Terlucci. Thompson was supposed to be cooking with him, but he was suddenly sick, and Terlucci took his place. When Boese saw the alteration on the roster, he took precautions. In the metal-work shop he had crafted a slim blade of his own, which he kept wrapped in toilet paper in the hollow tube of a barbell in the gym. Before the preparation began for the evening meal, he worked out as he did every afternoon.

The last piece of equipment he used was the metal-shafted barbell.

Terlucci was in the kitchen before him, and glanced sideways as Boese put on his long, white apron. The guard hovered about the doorway for a few minutes, then left them. The kitchen was next door to the showers and Boese could hear Matthews and Thompson washing themselves down after their workout. Butcher and Gibbs were playing pool, the others were either in their cells or watching TV. Boese could see the tension in Terlucci, etched into his shoulders like additional packed muscle. The vein was high in his neck, and his eyes were everywhere as he took the peeler to his potatoes. The dull-edged cutting knife, which you had to press so hard to get through anything, lay on the stainless steel work surface next to him. Boese was behind him, his own home-made blade, sharper than a razor, pressed against the skin of his arm, held in place by his sleeve.

One glance at the door was all he needed, then two paces and Boese was at Terlucci's back, with the knife sliding into his grip. He slammed Terlucci against the work surface, and pressed the blade into the soft, fleshy skin beneath his chin. 'Think about it,' he hissed. 'Between your jaw, through your tongue, the roof of your mouth and up into what little brain you possess.' He paused, feeling the sudden trembling in Terlucci's flesh. 'You cannot compete with me. Do not even try.' With that, he drew a line of blood under Terlucci's chin and stepped back. 'Get a plaster,' he said. 'You cut yourself.'

# 9

Swann and Webb formed part of the surveillance team that watched Jorge Vaczka. Amaya Kukiel, the informant, had phoned Christine Harris with the news that they were leaving for Liverpool on the morning of Friday 5 Feb. The fixed observation point was set up in the flat across the road from Vaczka's, on the Monday before. Posing as television delivery men, they arranged their equipment in the first-floor bedroom. The owner of the flat was retired, ex-Navy, and he was only too happy to help them. Special Branch and MI5 had primed their human sources in both Ulster and the Republic, but none of their informants had anything particular to report, which puzzled them even more. On the Thursday morning, Rafal Kestin, one of the lesser-known players in Vaczka's team, arrived outside the flat in a hired Luton Box van. The two men in the observation point called the information back to the Yard, where Swann picked it up from the baseman. Sitting at his desk, he began to make inquiries. Liverpool meant the ferry crossing to Dublin, so he called the booking office to find out if the Luton van was booked to make the crossing, but they had no record of any vehicle bearing that registration mark.

He imparted that information to Harris and the full surveillance team that had gathered for the afternoon briefing. Harris talked them through it, giving the information as it had been received. Two members of SO19's specialist firearms officer black team were also present, the skipper Mick Rob and his second, Tommy Lane.

'We'll want you from 1800 hours onwards,' Harris

explained. 'We don't know what time they're leaving, but there's three of them, all main players, at target one's house now. We've just had that confirmed from the observation team. The original Box 850 intel' was weapons, possibly from Abu Nidal to some Loyalist faction in Ulster. But it's been sketchy all the way through. What we do know is they've hired a Luton van and they've loaded boxes into it this morning from a lock-up rented by Pieter Jeconec. We don't know what's in the boxes, but it took two men to lift each one and there's two dozen of them stacked in the van right now.'

The surveillance team was over thirty strong and a great convoy of vehicles would move tomorrow if the van started rolling. Both Swann and Webb were due to give evidence at Ismael Boese's trial, but the opening statements would take a few days, and they were not required till midway through the following week. SFO black team would accompany the surveillance, three men to a car. They would be in plain clothes, but armed with Glock handguns and MP5 carbines.

Harris was more than a little apologetic. 'I'm sorry this is a bit messy,' she said. 'But Vaczka's a pro'. He's set up his organization to stop infiltration, and apart from his section heads, none of the bit players know who their team mates are.' She lifted her palms. 'To be fair to the source, every bit of information we've had has proved to be good so far. Dates, times, everything. Vaczka's been here a few years now, so has his team. We weren't even aware of them until 850 gave us the tip-off. They could've been supplying the Irish splinter groups on both sides of the fence, for all we know.'

'How far do you want to follow them?' Webb asked. 'I mean, before doing something about it.'

'Depends. We'll let them get as far as Liverpool, if indeed that's where they're going, and then see what

121

happens from there. We'll have to adapt as we go, Webby. Usual story.'

'What if they do get on a ferry?' Swann cut in.

'Follow them, put bodies on the boat and prime the other side. Drop people in the Republic if we have to.' She lifted her eyebrows and glanced towards Colson. 'Not that we do that, of course. The Republic's a foreign country.'

Vaczka, Stahl and Herbisch played cards at the kitchen table, a case of Becks at their feet. At eight o'clock they sent out for pizza, and Vaczka scanned the street and buildings opposite as he paid the delivery man on the doorstep. He could not see any signs of surveillance, but he had a feeling they were there all the same. Years of experience had taught him that when you can't see them, that's when they're probably watching. He looked for signs of cameras, but it was dark and the windows across the way were half-hidden in the dull orange of streetlights.

Tal-Salem watched the caretaker take one last look around the vacant lot, which once had been the bus depot on Hanwell Broadway. He was widowed, in his sixties, spending each day in his little kiosk, watching the empty spaces around him. He walked back towards the kiosk now, jangling the set of keys he carried round the index finger of his right hand. Tal-Salem eased the stolen Range Rover in through the west gate on Jessamine Road. The caretaker looked at him for a moment, then, lifting a hand, he shouted across the freshly concreted paving. Tal-Salem ignored him and drove the Range Rover up behind the huge advertising hoarding to the left of the gate that led on to the Broadway itself. Traffic was still heavy on the other side of the vertical wooden planking.

'What d'you think you're doing? You can't—' The man stopped, words caught in his throat, like breath too tight to exhale. Tal-Salem stared at him and levelled the 7.62 PSS silenced pistol at his chest. He smiled, thinly, briefly. Then he shot him. Barely a sound – sudden surprise in the old man's watery eyes as he was knocked against the cold brick of the wall, blood popping in a thin ribbon of red from the little hole in his chest.

Tal-Salem dragged him in front of the Range Rover and laid him on the ground, then he climbed back into the driver's seat and picked up his mobile phone. Ten minutes later, a yellow skip lorry pulled into the car park and came to a stop beside the Range Rover. Tal-Salem smoked a slim hashish joint, leaning against the door, aware of the smell of the old man's blood still in the air. His breath was visible, thickening the smoke he exhaled from the joint. Two men climbed down from the cab of the truck. Both had short-cropped hair, no earrings, no tattoos. Both wore grey flying overalls and tight-fitting lace-up boots.

Flipping away the stub of his joint, Tal-Salem placed one foot on the wheel of the lorry and swung himself up to the heavy skip, housed between the pole and chain at the back. Heavy-duty tarpaulin was stretched across the top. He lifted it and shone the torch he had taken from the glove compartment in the Range Rover. Squatting in readiness in the base of the skip was a PKS machine gun, twin belts of 250 7.62 × 54mm rounds. Next to it, a large industrial angle grinder. He replaced the tarpaulin cover and turned to find the two men laying long canvas work-bags out on the floor of the yard. One of them noticed the dead caretaker, gave him a brief glance and continued. Tal-Salem knelt, as the first man unzipped the canvas bag and began to place its contents on the ground for inspection. Ten RGN Russian antipersonnel grenades, each weighing 290 grams, 97 grams of which was the RDX explosive filling. They were spherical and smooth, made with internally pre-fragmented casings, producing 2000 fragments, and were lethal within a radius of eight to ten metres. A small safety pin was attached to the fuse casing, with a fly-off lever, and a detonating delay of three to four seconds. Tal-Salem picked one up, held it, smooth and cold against his palm, then set it back on the ground. The man produced five more and set them to one side, exactly the same as before except these did not fragment: they were phosphorus and burned. Next, he handed Tal-Salem a Vikhr 9mm submachine gun. These he had used before, in the old days before Ramas was sacrificed. They had been developed by the Institute of Precise Mechanical Engineering in Kimovsk, Russia; originally manufactured as a Spetsnaz weapon. The gun was designed to fire normal 9mm ammu-nition, but equally the 57N 181SM 9 $\times$ 39mm special round. Tal-Salem checked the magazine and nodded appre-ciatively. They were loaded now, a twenty-round clip; the shell capable of penetrating thirty layers of Kevlar, 1.2mm of titanium plate or 6mm of steel plate at a range of 200 metres. Between 700 and 900 rounds per minute was more than enough for the purpose he had in mind.

'Good,' he murmured. 'Very good indeed.' He got up, slid the Vikhr across to the passenger seat of the Range Rover and adjusted the pistol in his belt. The two men got back into the cab of the lorry. Tal-Salem climbed into the back of the Range Rover, where he settled down to sleep.

Swann was on his way to join the surveillance team when his pager vibrated against his belt. He upturned the display and squinted at it, one hand on the wheel of his car. *Call Reserve now.* He picked up the mobile phone and dialled.

'Swann here, Macca.' McCulloch was baseman that evening. 'What's up?'

'Colson wants you here tomorrow, Jack. Boese goes to trial and he's decided he wants you in London.'

'What about the Polish plot?'

'Got enough already. Webby's on it, and Tania.' Swann heard him exhale breath. 'Old man's orders, Jack.'

'Shit, I don't mind. Who wants to sit in a car all night waiting for some toe rag to drive off in a van. I'll be at the Yard at six-thirty.'

He hung up, turned his car round and headed back to his flat.


Three a.m., and somebody spoke into George Webb's earpiece as he snoozed, head against the misted glass of the car window. He was awake in seconds. 'Go ahead.'

'Target on the move.' It was the spotters in the observation point across the road from Jorge Vaczka's house.

Webb looked over his shoulder at Christine Harris who occupied the back of the car. 'You snore,' she said. 'How does your wife put up with it?'

'I don't know, Chrissie. I'm usually asleep at the time.'

'It's because you're fat,' she went on. 'Your airway gets blocked. You need to lose some weight, George.'

'Lecture over?' He started the engine. 'Then let's go, shall we?' He could not see the Luton Box van, parked as they were in a parallel street. There were thirty vehicles in all, dotted here and there, covering the available routes away from the target premises.

'All units, from fixed OP,' the voice said again in his ear. 'Confirming three occupants in subject vehicle – Cabbage Patch, Cindy and Barbie.' That meant Vaczka, Stahl and Herbisch; three of the four main players.

Webb glanced in the rearview mirror at Harris's face, pensive now; he could almost see the cogs turning. She spoke into the encrypted Cougar's microphone attached to her collar. 'Four/two from Kilo, respond?'

'Four/two. I have eyeball. Target heading north on Wood Lane.'

Harris looked at Webb. 'A40,' she said.

Webb nodded. 'The chopper'll give us their position. I reckon the M40 and M6 probably. No reason to take a circuitous route.'

The surveillance convoy rolled, the motorcyclist ahead with eyeball, above them a circling helicopter. The motorcycle would leave at the A40M and another vehicle would slot into place. The rest of them would keep back for now, but they would stay together; all the way to Liverpool if they had to. Next to Webb, Mick Rob, the SO19 team leader, sat with his MP5 between his knees.

Six-thirty a.m., and Boese ate a cold breakfast on his own. Though not very hungry, he ate for the benefit of the guards. Two of them watched him: Chesil and the concerned Griffiths. None of them spoke. Boese did not look at them, but ate slowly, chewing milk-soaked cornflakes with a deliberate, almost mechanical action. Chesil was watching him. Boese looked into his eyes for a moment, a cold black glance, and continued eating. He sipped his coffee and Chesil studied his watch. 'That'll do. Time to get changed.'

Boese rose and they marched him across the hall to the sterile area. He undressed while they watched him, carefully laying out each item of clothing, which they searched thoroughly. Griffiths was meticulous. He had been at the SSU in Whitemoor when the three IRA men had broken out. He had had to suffer the indignity of the Antiterrorist Branch taking up residence for six weeks. He could still remember the questions, the embarrassment at the fact that guns had been smuggled in, bolt-cutters even. Chesil strip searched Boese, who stood with palms flat against the wall, while Chesil stretched surgical rubber gloves over his fingers with a slapping sound. Boese stared at the peeling blue paint on the wall.

*

Across the yard from the newly built special secure unit was the main prison block and the interview and briefing rooms for the special escort group. The SSU had only been built the year before. The new Labour government had been concerned about the level of Irish prisoners either on remand or serving their sentences in the units at White-moor, Belmarsh and Parkhurst prisons, and the Home Secretary had instructed that a new one be constructed to the west of London. Reading, given its proximity to the M4, was chosen. In the yard, the three-and-a-half-ton prison truck was standing ready, along with two 827 Rovers, a Range Rover and four motorcycles. The vehicles carried respirators for the crew, together with smoke can-ister distraction devices. The officers from the SEG had travelled up from Lambeth an hour before, and were gathered for the briefing, now given by Chief Inspector Cranham.

'Ismael Boese,' he said, flashing up a slide of Boese's face. 'Responsible for the abortive chemical attack in the City last year, and the deaths of two hundred and eighty people in Rome. When he's served his time here, they'll extradite him to Italy, so he won't be doing anything for the rest of his life.' He paused and smiled. 'Initially, I thought this would be a fully armed operation with an SFO team along for the ride.'

'But it's not.' Phil Nicholson was the operator in the lead car. His job was to read the maps, plot the route and the alternatives, and keep the convoy moving at all times.

'No, Phil,' Cranham said. 'Boese has been on remand for eight months. In that time, he has had only one visitor, has received no mail and no phone calls. He hasn't sent any mail or made any phone calls.' He lifted his shoulders. 'According to his assessors, he's been the model prisoner.' He broke off for a moment and cleared his throat. 'As I

127

said, given what the wardens have told us, I perceive there to be a general but not a specific threat.'

'We're more likely to be attacked by the public after what that bastard did,' one of the other officers observed.

'I've taken tactical advice,' Cranham went on, 'and decided that we will do this without SO19, although we will have an additional MP5 man in each car. That takes the pressure off you, Phil, and the other guys in the passenger-seats. Merely a precaution, but a necessary one.'

The word came through that Boese was ready and being held in the sterile area, awaiting them. Cranham looked at his watch. 'He's due in court at ten o'clock,' he said. 'It's seven-fifteen now. Whatever happens, we're in rush hour, so let's roll.'

They moved out to their vehicles, three men in each car, one on a special swivel seat in the back of the Range Rover, Heckler & Koch carbine across his knees. If anything went wrong, he could drop the tailgate and fire. Two more in the cab of the prison truck, and a further two in the separate, pod-like cubicles which made up the back of the truck. Boese would be isolated in a third, sitting on a plastic bench, surrounded by walls, with an escape hatch centrally locked above his head. The driver of the lead car fired up the Rover's engine and Nicholson checked the planned route. M4 into London, A4 and then on to the Old Bailey from there. He had the contingencies agreed should they need them.

He looked in the wing mirror as the two prison wardens brought Boese out. He was dark-skinned and dark-haired and much smaller than Nicholson would have thought. The press had tagged him the most dangerous man in the world, but he looked pretty insignificant from where Nicholson sat. He watched as Boese was marched to the waiting truck and the two officers who would secure him in the back. Once they were set, the word would come through and

128

then it was down to him. He could feel the adrenalin pumping, as he always could on jobs like this. Today, the bridges over the motorway would be lined with pressmen. They would have choppers up, but there would be a flight exclusion zone around India 99, their own helicopter surveillance unit, which Cranham had ordered in. The press were gathered outside the prison walls already. Nicholson wished there was some way they could keep these trial dates secret. They were only released a day or so before, but that was more than enough time for the world's media to gather. He checked through to the City firearms unit on the radio. They were already assembled and waiting outside the Old Bailey, and on the ring of steel approaches. Boese had tried to bomb them out of Snow Hill and they were looking forward to this.

Jack Swann was trawling through evidence at his desk on the fifteenth floor of Scotland Yard. He looked up at the clock and calendar on the wall, thought for some reason about the little 'shrine' that the Bomb Data Centre had on Carlos and wondered whether he or Boese was the worst. Bomb data had one of his guns, a bunch of notes, and some other stuff that they had exhibited after Carlos was sentenced to life imprisonment in Paris. It occurred to Swann that if the DST had caught him back in 1975, when he killed their agents in the Rue Toullier, he would have been guillotined years ago. He touched his throat briefly and went back to his notes. His heart was high in his chest this morning. He was not due in court for days yet, but he was anxious. Something about this one, something about Boese. This man had singled out his life for interruption.

He went to get coffee from the vending machine and then wandered upstairs to where Campbell McCulloch was baseman again. A couple of guys from SB were milling around and Swann noticed two operatives from Box, one of whom worked closely with Julian Moore. 'What's happening with the Poles?' Swann asked McCulloch.

'Heard nothing. The plot rolled at three o'clock this morning. They'll be almost in Liverpool by now.'

Swann went to the window where the day was breaking over London. He looked at his watch: seven-fifteen. Boese's trial began at ten, but he would have to be there for discussions with his QC at least an hour before. The special escort group would be on the move from Reading Prison about now.

Webb yawned, smoothing the palms of his hands across the steering wheel. They were well north now, the van labouring along in the nearside lane, with a spotter ten cars back. 'Wish we'd been able to get sound in that cab,' he said to nobody in particular. 'Film's boring without the soundtrack.' He glanced at the SFO team leader next to him and winked.

They were north of Stoke-on-Trent and the van had not deviated from its course. Once they had crossed from the M40 to the M6 at Birmingham, they had trundled along at a steady fifty miles an hour – one hired van and thirty surveillance vehicles, including three motorcyclists braving the February chill in pursuit. The day was cold, with a sharpness to the air that kept the heater on in the car, but the sky was clear and the sun weak but full behind what little clouds there were. At junction eighteen of the motor-way, the van suddenly turned off. Webb glanced behind at Harris as the word came in from the lead car. They followed it down through Middlewich and Kelsall, before it turned suddenly north for Ellesmere Port. Webb shook his head at himself in the mirror.

The SEG convoy left Reading Prison in a shower of flashes from long-range press photographers. India 99, rotor blades

130

whirring above them, kept the TV crews at a safe distance, and the motorcycle outriders moved up to block the first traffic junction. Nicholson had his MP5 between his knees, his Glock 17 handgun strapped against his hip, and was studying the map book closely. They wound their way down to the M4 intersection, motorcycles moving ahead. All the vehicles had sirens yowling and the blue strobe lights whirling on their rooftops. The lead car blocked the oncoming traffic on the roundabout that led them on to the M4 itself. The driver, with the window rolled down, had his arm extended to keep the traffic back. Nicholson was checking the convoy behind him – front car, then the truck, and behind that the Range Rover, out in the lane to stop anyone coming alongside. The bikes kept traffic well behind them. *Police Convoy* and *Do Not Overtake* signs flashed in the back of their vehicles. Nothing between the lead and front cars. The block was in and the engine idling. 'Come to me. Come to me.' Nicholson spoke to the drivers behind in his back-to-back headset.

The lead bike was ahead of them at the top of the slip road. 'Move up. Come to me.' His voice crackled in Nicholson's ear.

Nicholson squinted at the map, then back to the convoy again. 'Move up. Move up.'

The driver nodded to the cars backed up round the roundabout, keeping his arm out, palm upraised, then slipped ahead of the front car, and they rolled up on to the motorway in convoy. The first bike became the last, as the traffic was blocked to let them on. All lanes were occupied, the vehicles shifting out at speed to overtake slower traffic in the nearside lane, bikes and cars bunching unwilling drivers all but on to the hard shoulder.

Rafal Kestin drove five hundred pounds worth of battered Volvo on to the M4 at junction two, where the elevated section began, and checked his mirrors. Already the rush-hour traffic was gathering. Before him lay the business buildings that dominated this area of London, company head offices, many-storeyed buildings climbing in white and beige and brown, crowding the gunmetal grey of the carriageway. He took a cigarette from the packet on the passenger seat and popped it in his mouth, then pressed the lighter in on the dashboard. Amazingly, it worked. He lit the cigarette and drifted across the road. He was midway between junctions one and two now, and suddenly he hauled the wheel to the right and ploughed into the Audi next to him. The driver of the Audi fought with the wheel, but the car got away from him and hit the concrete barrier on the raised section of motorway. The two cars fishtailed together and came to a jagged halt, coupled into one another at the bumper. Kestin braced himself, but still shot forward against his seat belt as a car slammed into the back of him. His cigarette was still alight, still in his mouth even, and he sucked on it before tapping away the ash, then climbed out of the car. The Audi driver was staring at his front end, the colour in his cheeks beginning to burn crimson.

'Oh, God. Look, I'm really sorry.' Kestin stood with his hands on his hips, shaking his head at the Audi. Behind him, the third driver was climbing out of his car. Kestin watched him, then glanced back along the twin lanes of carriageway as the traffic began to back up. He reached into his car for his mobile. 'I'll call the AA,' he said to the stricken driver.

Tal-Salem took the call, seated as he was, knees hunched behind the wheel of the Range Rover, which was still parked behind the hoarding that faced on to Hanwell Broadway, between the clock tower and the lights at Church Road. He acknowledged it, pressed the red button on the phone, then dialled the watcher on Southall Lane Bridge. Beside him on the passenger seat, the collapsed stock of the Vikhr poked out from under his coat. The driver of the skip lorry was watching him through the window.

'SEG from MP,' Nicholson heard the traffic operator's voice in his earpiece, talking to him from the central command complex at Scotland Yard. 'Accident on raised section of the M4, between junctions two and one.'

'Acknowledged, MP. Alternative route. A40 through Hangar Lane.' He looked at the map in front of him. They could continue a good way along the motorway, taking advantage of the three lanes, before threading a path up to the A40. He had considered the A4, but that would already be getting choked up with people leaving the M4 at every available exit. He glanced at his driver and then passed on the change in plan to the rest of the convoy.

Four men, in black leather, smoked cigarettes through the mouth-pieces of their silk ski masks, crash helmets set on the wall in the car park of the Viaduct pub, just on the Hanwell side of the River Brent. One of them had his leathers half undone and the butt of his 9mm Gyurza poked out. One of the others noticed it and nodded to him, indicating that he should push it out of sight. As he did so, a mobile phone rang and he answered it, spoke for a few minutes, then switched it off. 'It's on,' he said quietly. 'Stage one is complete.'

A man with short-cut hair drove the three-and-a-half-ton flatbed truck along the A40, whistling to himself as he drew closer and closer to the underpass at Hangar Lane roundabout and the North Circular Road. He watched the traffic, heavy now, and thought how pissed off everyone was going to be. In his pocket he fingered the small pair of wire-cutters. He slowed the truck as he approached the downward slope into the underpass, then slowed it some more and flicked on his hazard warning lights, before bringing it to a stop right in the heart of the tunnel. He sat in the outside lane, having made no attempt to cross to the inside carriageway, and people were honking their horns behind him. He jumped out of the cab, waving to the irate drivers behind, then dropped to one knee. He half slid under the engine by the offside wheel and snipped the reservoir pipe, which kept the airbrakes off, close to one end. The brakes seized on with a hiss of escaping air. He smiled and shook his head. The police had a Land-Rover, which could pump up deflated airbrakes so a truck could be towed. They would have a problem with this one. Moving back to the solidifying traffic behind him, he lifted his hands in a hopeless gesture and unclipped the mobile phone from his belt.

Webb smoothed the ends of his fingers over his moustache, as they followed the Luton van up through Ellesmere Port. The van passed a transport café on the right-hand side of the road, drove a bit further, then swung all the way round the roundabout before turning back into the car park of the café. Webb's was the eyeball car and he drove on, ignoring the van-full of Poles, and crossed the roundabout before heading a few hundred yards up the road. He gave the location of the van to following cars and then pulled off a mile further on. They had a Transit van as part of the pursuit. The driver would pull into the café and go and get some breakfast. Webb yawned and leaned over the back of the seat. 'I wish we had that sound, Chrissie,' he said.

The traffic operator at the Yard passed the information regarding Hangar Lane to Nicholson. 'Fucking wouldn't you know it,' he said to his driver. He scratched his head then and glanced at the convoy behind him. They were travelling at seventy miles an hour, with the Range Rover in the middle lane, a car's length back from the prison truck, ensuring that nobody could try to pass. Nicholson looked at the map again. 'Keep close,' he said, as the front car fell away a fraction. 'Hangar Lane is closed. We're going to take the Uxbridge Road. Come off at the Heston Services.' He spoke ahead to the Yard, asking them to make sure that the M4 control point had the barrier lifted so they could get through.

The press were gathered on the bridges above the motorway, filming the convoy as it passed. One man stood with a camera on North Hyde Lane where it crossed above the motorway, and watched the grouping pass beneath him. He had his mobile phone to his ear, the line already open to Tal-Salem in the Range Rover on Hanwell Broadway. 'They're leaving at Heston,' he said. He moved then to the northern end of the bridge and watched to see what would happen.

The convoy wound its way round the back of the services, lights flashing, and passed the M4 motorway control building and the red chequered barrier beyond the lorry park. The ground opened flat before them and the lead car raced up to the junction with North Hyde Lane. 'Taking the offside,' Nicholson told the others, as his driver blocked both lanes of traffic and allowed the convoy to filter out. 'Come to me. Come to me.' Nicholson was watching the road, residential here but quite wide. He wanted the shortest route he could get to Uxbridge Road. 'Right on Fern,' he said to the driver.

From the bridge across the motorway, the man watched them turn right into Fern Lane. That road was traffic-calmed and he knew it would take them a while to get to the far end. He spoke to Tal-Salem once again.

Tal-Salem drummed his fingers on the steering wheel of the Range Rover. They had taken the only sensible route they could. M4 gone. A4 gone. A40 gone. There was only the Uxbridge Road left. He stopped drumming and tightened his fingers a fraction round the wheel, and stared at the closed gate ahead of him – vertical wooden slats between the advertising hoardings. He looked to his left at the men in the skip lorry. One of them climbed out of the passenger seat and hoisted himself into the back, folding the tarpaulin over his head.

A workman standing at the bus stop by the Hanwell Car Centre answered the call on his mobile phone. He wore grey overalls, one piece, and a bulky donkey jacket over the top. In his pocket he had a black ski mask, and he had been careful to ensure that no shop had street-surveillance CCTV before he took up his position. Hanging on its sling under his jacket was the 380-millimetre-long Vikhr submachine gun, the rounds of which would pass through body armour like a hot knife through butter. Across the road, his colleague nodded briefly, his back to the plywood door with 105A scrawled in red paint on it. Behind that door, two other 'workmen' checked the rounds in their clips, the three spares they each carried and the fragmentation grenades on their belts. The door led to an alley between the buildings. At the far end was the flat, but before that an archway covered two more doors on the right, leading to the garages at the back of the shops. The service road ran parallel behind the shops and came out on to Church Street. Four of the stolen bikes were parked there, helmets straddling the seats. At the far end of the alley, just before the Church of Christi St Mellis, another bike squatted, two men on it, rider and pillion. The pillion carefully worked the action on his Gyurza pistol, and then replaced it inside his leathers.

The convoy bumped along Fern Lane, came through the narrowed section at the end and pulled out on to Norwood Road. Much wider here and they accelerated again. Then the outriders blocked the oncoming traffic and they crossed into Tentelow Lane. A man walked his dog on Norwood Green. As they passed, he lifted his mobile phone.

Nicholson blocked the roundabout at Three Bridges and they filtered on to Windmill Lane, round the second roundabout then slowed for the right turn under Iron Bridge, which led them on to the Uxbridge Road. They had not stopped anywhere en route, not at a junction, or roundabout, passing straight through every set of red lights with the lead car blocking the oncoming traffic. The traffic controller at the Yard told them that Uxbridge Road was busy, but traffic was moving. All local units had been informed they were coming and traffic cars were in position to assist them should the need arise. Nicholson glanced in his rearview mirror as they blocked Uxbridge Road. 'Come to me. Keep close,' he said into his radio. They moved off again, the bikes opening the traffic ahead of them.

In the prison truck, Ismael Boese sat on the plastic bench in the single locked cell and stared at the escape hatch, locked above his head.

Webb listened to the radio. The Poles were out of the café, in the car park, smoking cigarettes and talking. Vaczka was looking at his watch and glancing up and down the road. The sun had gone in and the clouds were ice-grey, threatening snow rather than rain. Webb shifted in his seat. Next to him, the SFO team leader rubbed the barrel of his carbine with a cloth. The Transit driver had left the café and a motorcyclist had taken his place, the rider now sitting in the café drinking coffee, watching what was going on outside. The Poles were still talking, Stahl kicking at a battered Coca-Cola can mashed into the tarmac. A Renault van pulled off the road and parked next to theirs. The observer whispered into his radio. 'Stand by. Stand by. Blue van. Renault. This could be it, boys.'

Webb stared out of the windscreen. No booking to Dublin. Box had had no word of anyone over here from the other side, who they didn't already know about. No activity, no movement from London or Manchester or Birmingham. The SFO commander spoke to his men; half the team had been deployed on standby, in cars fifty yards down from the car park. The other half were already moving up. Webb looked back at Christine Harris. 'What d'you want to do?' he asked her.

The SEG convoy pulled on to Uxbridge Road and, as they did so, a man on a motorcycle watched them from Mc-Donald's car park on the other side of the bridge. He spoke into a mobile phone. In the car park behind the Viaduct pub, the pillions climbed behind the riders as two 900cc motorcycles were started and the engines revved gently. They moved to the lip of the turn behind the pub.

Tal-Salem nodded to the driver of the skip lorry, who backed his truck down towards the west gate on Jessamine Road. Tal-Salem climbed out of the Range Rover and opened the north gates, swinging them back between the hoardings. A couple of people looked at him briefly from the pavement. He caught the eye of the man with the bulky workman's jacket, at the bus stop by the car centre. Then he got back in the Range Rover and started the engine. The helicopter had already made a pass and was swinging away to the south of them. At the far end of the road, by the church, the other motorcyclist started his engine. Then rider and pillion pulled ski masks over their faces and strapped on their helmets.

The traffic was bunched where the Uxbridge Road narrowed from two lanes to one each way. The convoy was already in the outside lane, passing the old St Bernard's Mental Hospital, which was now some upmarket apartment building, and then the Ealing Hospital. After that was the narrowed road, then the bridge over the Brent and the hill up to the lights and Hanwell clock tower. 'Take the offside.' Nicholson moved the Glock where it was digging into his hip. The traffic was heavy here. The driver switched the siren from the yowl to the long drawn-out wail to shift the traffic.

Up ahead, the helicopter had circled and was making a pass, fifteen hundred feet up, swinging back over the Broadway. The driver and passenger of the skip lorry were outside, checking the tarpaulin as it passed above their heads. Nicholson called the convoy on, taking the offside path after the outriders, pushing oncoming traffic to the side as they made their way across the river bridge and past the Viaduct pub. The lights at the clock tower intersection were red and an outrider blocked the lanes. The lead car pushed ahead. 'Come to me,' Nicholson said into his radio. 'Come to me. Keep up.'

Two motorcycles with pillions pulled out of the pub car park and ambled along the road, skirting the bunched traffic on the nearside lane. They followed the police Range Rover, at a distance of fifty yards. Ahead of them were the two rear outriders, still blocking the red lights.

The lead car crossed the clock tower intersection; 150 yards now to the second set of lights. The gates to the vacant lot on the right-hand side were open, a maw between the hoardings. Halfway down the open concrete lot, the driver and passenger tensed in the skip lorry, engine running, gears engaged, the clutch beginning to burn. Tal-Salem held his phone to his ear, but he could see the workman at the nearside bus stop. The lead car passed, moving up on the wrong side of the road, the outriders already controlling the next intersection. Behind the lead car, the front car. The skip lorry began to lumber across the open concrete lot. Tal-Salem watched the man at the bus stop, now holding a crumpled ski mask in his left hand. The front car was at the gates, crossing in front of them.

'Now.' Tal-Salem spoke into his mobile phone.

The skip lorry suddenly accelerated and raced through the open gate. No oncoming traffic, the road already cleared by the outriders and lead car. It bumped down the pavement and careered across the road, smashing into the side of the prison truck. The truck driver lost the wheel and the truck lurched across the road, leaping on to the pavement. People started screaming at the bus stop. The two workmen pulled on ski masks and ripped open their jackets, revealing the Vikhrs. Seven hundred rounds a minute: they sprayed the street in a burst of suppression fire. They were joined by the other two gunmen from the door to 105A. One firing, one loading, a continuous burst of gunfire.

At the intersection ahead, the outriders froze for a second. As they did so, a motorbike pulled out from behind the church and the pillion shot one of them in the chest. The other saw his colleague fall and screamed off up the road.

Tal-Salem gunned the Range Rover and backed it round and out of the gate. Already the driver of the skip lorry was out and on top of his cab, attacking the roof of the prison truck with the angle grinder. In the back, tarpaulin off, the other man hoisted the belt-fed PKS and sprayed rounds at the helicopter.

In the lead car, Nicholson heard the bang and lurched round in his seat. 'Jesus Christ,' he said. Then on the radio, 'SEG. Hanwell Broadway. Repeat. Hanwell Broadway. We're under attack. Urgent assistance required. Repeat. Urgent assistance required.'

Already his driver was backing the car at speed, the window rolled down so he could direct the traffic in the built-up area. In the front car, the officers were already dead. No time to get out, no time to raise their guns. Four men, two from either side of the road, no more than ten yards away, sprayed their car with bullets that went through the doors and windows, passing through body armour like water, kicking their bodies in the seats so they jerked and leapt like marionettes. Windows shattered, the sound of glass breaking, ringing out with the gunfire. People fell screaming, some of them running for cover, some of them hit by bullets that pinged off concrete and walls and the roofs of the car and prison truck.

At the church end of the Broadway, Nicholson and his driver reversed hard. A motorcyclist raced alongside them. His pillion lobbed something into the driver's lap. Nicholson screamed, a high-pitched wail above the wail of the siren, long and icy, like a vixen screeching in the night. The grenade blew – phosphorus – and three men and their car were burning. Nicholson, on fire, voice torn away by the pressure wave bursting his lungs, lurched from the car, as it crashed into another parked by the side of the road. He could not hear. Before the flames took his eyes he could see the carnage, but it was silent, no sound – the blast had deafened him. His clothes were on fire, hair on fire, gun melting against his hip. The others couldn't get out; the driver burned into his seat by the magnesium heat of the incendiary, his legs shattered by the explosion. Nicholson flapped at his face with arms ablaze and couldn't cry out. He thought of his wife, his children, his parents, then he pitched forward on to the pavement.

The police Range Rover raced forward as soon as the occupants saw the skip lorry cross the road. The MP5 man kicked open his tailgate with the heel of his boot, ready to spring out as soon as the car stopped. As he did so, two motorcycles suddenly accelerated at him, shots rang out, and the two outriders, still at the first set of lights, pitched off their machines. The MP5 man tried to level his weapon, but the car swerved and his eyes balled as the bikes got to him at speed. And then the pillion, arcing back his arm, lobbed the fragmentation grenade into the back of the car. Desperately, the officer searched for it, saw it, reached, and it rolled. Two seconds, three, four, the bike was screaming down the road, already doing seventy miles an hour past the burning lead car. The grenade blew out the windows on the Range Rover, the doors billowing with the pressure and blast impact. The roof buckled upwards; the car was lifted off its wheels and dumped on to the ground. The MP5 man looked at his lower body where his legs should have been and all he could see was the hole in the floor, where the blast had impacted.

The policeman in the passenger-seat stumbled on to the road, hands to his ears, fighting the blood that rushed into his mouth from ruptured lungs. The driver sat where he was, head rolling to one side. The four men on foot stopped firing. Sirens cried in the distance. The policeman from the Range Rover stumbled into a shop doorway and reached for his radio. It came away useless in his hand. He sat down, no sound. People, he could not hear, crying; faces broken up with shock and fear. He looked at his tattered uniform, pulses of blood pushing from cuts in the cloth all over his body. He looked up into eyes that hunted him from behind a black ski mask. The man wore grey overalls, like a flying suit. The policeman fumbled for his Glock, somehow managed to draw it. Then a spray of shells ripped through twenty-four layers of Kevlar and tore his body to shreds.

Tal-Salem had the Range Rover backed up to the prison truck, and was watching the precision of the suppression fire. He looked at the second hand of his watch, while the man on the roof cut away with the angle grinder. He was through, reached down and flipped the lever. The roof popped on all three cubicles and he offered his hand to Ismael Boese, the Storm Crow. Boese was up, on the roof of the truck, pausing for one moment to take in the scene of devastation: two burning police cars, one so shattered by gunfire that there were more holes than bodywork. He leapt on to the back of the skip lorry, then into the Range Rover. The man with the angle grinder looked down at the two unarmed SEG men in the second and third cubicles of the prison truck. He took out his pistol and shot them both in the head. Then he leapt to the ground and into the back of the Range Rover. The other man was already there; the PKS, complete with uplifted tripod and ammunition belts, on his lap.

Tal-Salem looked at his watch. Ninety seconds from start to finish. Police cars were arriving. One of the men in the back of the Range Rover lobbed an incendiary device into the back of the skip. 'For later,' he said and sat back. Tal-Salem drove quickly, tearing across the open concrete lot. Boese sat alongside him, silent, eyes cold, no smile. Down Jessamine Road and left on to the one-way system at Boston Road. Fifty yards and they went right, across the zebra crossing, past Murphy's Bar and then left down the narrow, terraced confines of St Dunstan's Road.

On the Broadway, the motorcyclists were gone. The four gunmen raced through the passageway of 105A and cut into the road at the back. They shouldered their weapons and pulled on crash helmets before tearing off north,

143

separate escape routes. The last one took Church Street just as the police outrider returned to the scene after making his report on the radio. The gunman looked back once – too long perhaps. Instinctively, the officer braked hard, one foot on the floor, and wheeled his BMW round as hard as he could, heel kicking up concrete dust as he did so.

Above them the helicopter was moving again, trying to follow the final four bikes. But they burst in four different directions. The gunman being pursued rode hard. Glancing behind in a life-saver move, he spotted the policeman hard on his heels. He gunned the engine, dipping the clutch and lifting the stolen Yamaha into a wheelie, front end almost above his head. He dipped through traffic, shoulder dropping, knee out and back again. Behind him, the officer watched almost in awe at the man's skill – popping through gaps that weren't there, without the benefit of lights or siren.

Tal-Salem braked hard at the end of St Dunstan's Road and swung right on to St Margaret's, before accelerating to the end of it and hauling the wheel left with a screeching of brakes, and a whine and hiss from tyres biting deep into tarmac. He slowed then and cruised down Green Lane into the little bit of Hanwell village, past the Fox pub where the road ended by the canal at Oak Cottages. A white Escort van was parked there, and next to it, two Trials motorcycles. They all got out of the Range Rover. The man with the PKS loaded it into the back of the Escort, which was filled with rubbish from somebody's house. He handed out three crash helmets from the front seats, then got back in and drove off. Tal-Salem passed one to Boese. Already, the other man was on a bike, engine going and revving. 'Teniel Jefferson,' Tal-Salem said. 'He fixes cars in Carson City, Nevada.'

Boese nodded, hands on the straps of his helmet. '*El Kebir*?' he said.

Tal-Salem shook his head.

Boese was on the back of the bike, Tal-Salem got on the other one and they rode down to the canal, turning sharp right before taking off at speed, past the lock gates and along the wide towpath, with a screeching of engines and a blast of blackened exhaust fumes. They tore along the towpath and were past the Three Bridges before the first police car stopped at the carnage on the Broadway. A woman walking her dog was almost knocked into the water, as they screamed past at eighty miles an hour. The day before, the lead rider had ridden this route twice on his mountain bike. He knew that the Glade Lane Bridge would mean up the steps and around the house. They were there in under ninety seconds. He bumped the bike to the right, dropping his knee and almost flipping Boese off. Tal-Salem followed, up to the bridge, round the house, then back on to the towpath again. Forty-five seconds later they were at the recreation ground where the towpath petered out, beyond the Old Oak Tree pub. The fruit and vegetable van was already waiting for them, engine idling, back doors ajar. Leaving the engines still running, they ran the bikes into the canal with a hiss of steam. Then Tal-Salem and the other man threw their helmets into the water: only Boese kept his.

In the back of the van now, moving slowly along the common, Boese pulled on a set of leathers and took the batch of documents from Tal-Salem. At the top of the road another biker was waiting, this time squatting on a CBR 900 Fireblade in black and yellow, with fumes rising from the massive exhaust. Boese jumped down, climbed aboard and two minutes later they were weaving a path through traffic, past the Western International Market that had been opened along with Nine Elms when Covent Garden closed down, and then hard left and the junction with the M4. The driver took the roundabout at speed, with Boese perched high on the back, head forward, the tarmac coming up rapidly as the bike was laid as low as it would go. Up again, flipping to the other side and accelerating with the front wheel off the ground. Up the slip road and roaring on to the motorway. One junction later, they were racing east on the M25. Two junctions further on and in less than four minutes, they were banked over, like an aircraft, on the approach to the M3.

The policeman on the BMW chased the biker hard through traffic. Voices crackled over his headset. Mass shooting, explosions on Hanwell Broadway, but he kept his eyes ahead, lights and sirens going, and watched his prey as he weaved his incredible path. He raced all the way north on Greenford Avenue, then hit the Ruislip Road west without even looking, his knee scraping at the kerb as he decked the bike sideways. The policeman was after him, but losing ground. The biker rode on, straight down the middle of Ruislip Road, with traffic fading either side of him. He stormed across the lights at the junction with Greenford Road and only just missed a van coming the other way. The policeman stormed after him. They flew along Ruislip Road, other cars and bikes joining in the pursuit, and they were gradually bearing down on him. The policeman could hear his chief inspector talking in his ear, the suspect on Ruislip Road was the only one they had. He leaned on the tank and wound the throttle open.

The roundabout with Margaret Road came up so fast the biker barely had time to see it. He leaned left and right, not slowing, and as he faded left off the roundabout, an old man in a Mazda pulled out from a side road. The biker saw him too late, eyes suddenly wide against his visor. He hit the red Mazda full on and went cartwheeling across the road, with the bike spinning after him. He did not remember landing.

The police rider pulled up, foot down, skidding his bike

to a stop. He leapt off. The biker was a crumpled mass of grey boiler suit, his arms askew, one almost ripped off with the impact. His head was at a difficult angle, hunched up against a car door. He wasn't moving.

Swann was still up on the sixteenth floor, talking to some colleagues from SO12, when the CAD started chattering in front of Campbell McCulloch. Swann could hear it whizzing through the printer, and he stopped talking, looked at the SO12 officer and then over his shoulder. 'Sounds busy, Macca,' he said.

McCulloch did not reply, his eyes fixed on the dispatch print-out in front of him.

'Macca?' Swann was on his feet. 'What've you got?'

McCulloch looked up at him then, the colour lost from his face. When he spoke, the words chipped drily from his lips. 'SEG's just been hit.'

Swann felt a cold sweat move through his hairline. 'Which SEG?'

'The one from Reading Prison.'

# 10

Swann drove, McCulloch alongside him in the passenger-seat, out of the underground car park and along Victoria Street, blue strobe light flashing against the windscreen where it was mounted on the dashboard. Neither of them spoke, each lost in his own thoughts, Swann silently cursing as cars got in his way and he whipped along the wrong side of the road. He had never driven faster. The initial reports were that the SEG had been massacred, that was the word from the operators in the central command complex. It rang now like a death knell in Swann's head, the weight in his gut, like a stone which would not dislodge. He saw again the faces of the crowds who had evacuated the capital in the wake of Boese's bomb.

They arrived at the scene on Hanwell Broadway twenty minutes after the attack. The uniformed officers guarding the cordons told him that an incendiary device had gone off five minutes after the first assistance got there, sending yet another shock wave through them. Mercifully, no one else had been hurt, but they did not know whether there were any other bombs. Phil Cregan, the explosives officer from Cannon Row, was already there, along with a colleague. Swann stood with Cregan, just inside the inner cordon, and surveyed the scenes of urban desolation that greeted them. The three marked police cars were wrecked, the lead vehicle burnt to a cinder, with smoke still rising from the ruptured metalwork. The second Rover was so full of bullet holes that it looked like some macabre pincushion.

As he walked slowly along the Broadway, McCulloch

next to him, Swann saw two paramedics lifting the lifeless bodies of the three SEG men who had occupied the Rover on to the pavement, where they were immediately covered with blankets. Swann paused by one blanket-covered corpse and could smell the thick, ugly scent of burning flesh. He glanced to see where the bulk of the newsmen were gathered farther down the road, then squatted on his haunches and drew the blanket back. It had been a police officer. Now the scorched shell of something vaguely human clutched at the pavement, limbs drawn up, face gone, hair gone, most of the flesh burned off, revealing reddened tissue, black and crisp at the edges. Swann looked for a long time: a colleague, a fellow officer. McCulloch drew breath sharply. Swann laid the blanket back over the bits of matted hair that stuck to patchy black skin on the back of the man's head, then he got to his feet. He looked at the shop windows, blown out or shot out. Ten ambulances in all and still more arriving. He had no idea how many civilians had been killed or wounded. He looked at McCulloch and McCulloch at him. Superintendent Colson arrived with Garrod, the security group commander, walking in long coats, hands in their pockets, faces grim and grey and chipped stiff by the sight that greeted them.

Swann crossed to the smashed remains of the prison truck, the armoured glass in the windscreen shattered. The street was littered with shell casings. God only knew how many rounds had been fired. He could hear someone moaning and saw another team of medics working on a man slumped in the doorway of one of the shops, the windows of which were merely tatters of glass, like rags, hanging from their housings. Swann crossed to where they were trying to save his life – jacket open, blood pulsing from twenty different wounds. His face was the colour of salt and his eyes opened and closed, body spasming now and again with the shock. Blood had spilled from his ears and his mouth, congealing in heavy brown lumps at his jawline and over his lips. The blast from a pressure wave. If he survived, he would be deaf. The man's eyes flickered then, widened a fraction, seeming to focus on Swann, whose own features were stretched into a taut, hard line. They looked at one another and Swann saw sudden fear in the wounded man's eyes. Then his head dipped and he died. For a moment the paramedics worked on, then one sat back, placed his hand on his partner's arm and shook his head.

Swann moved back to the road, where the Range Rover was buckled, doors blown out of shape, roof rising like the peak of a mountain. The paramedics had lifted what was left of the rear MP5 man on to a stretcher, part of one of his legs still hanging out of the back window. Swann looked up where the *whump whump* of a helicopter diverted his eyes. He could see a TV crew filming from the open fuselage doorway. Colson came up behind him.

'Jack?'

Swann turned.

'They've got one alive.'

'One of the attack team?'

Colson nodded. 'Motorcyclist. Some of them got away on bikes, according to India 99. This one was chased by one of the SEG outriders and hit a car on some roundabout out to the west. They've got him on life-support at Ealing Hospital.' He paused. 'I want you to get down there. This is an exhibits job now. Once the fatalities are cleared, we'll need to zone the area.'

'You going to let the press in?'

'Not for a long time yet.' Colson's voice stuck in his throat. The skin of his face was pallid like bad parchment. So was Garrod's, who was talking on his mobile phone by the advertising hoardings that boarded the vacant lot.

'How many dead?' Swann asked.

'The entire SEG, bar the one outrider who chased the suspect.' Colson pointed to the doorway where Swann had seen his fellow officer die. 'They did their job thoroughly, no police witnesses. That guy in the doorway was the last one. All the others are gone.'

Swann popped air from his cheeks. He looked at the prison truck with the roof seals sticking up at right angles. 'The two guys in there?'

'Shot in the head.'

'And Boese gone.' Swann voiced his own thoughts, their combined thoughts. The words slipped out and a coldness went through him again. Boese out, gone, on the loose all over again. Storm Crow. He saw once more the photo that Boese had sent to him, his face with a mock bullet hole punched in his skull.

Swann looked up as Garrod switched off his mobile phone and walked over, face pinched, lips a line of colourless tissue. He looked directly at Swann. 'That was the Yard,' he said. 'We've just received a crow's feather. It was addressed to you, Jack.'

The Fireblade raced down the M3. Boese, knees buckled up, perched like a bird on the raised part of the saddle, his face forward, looking over the shoulder of the driver as they screamed along the outside lane. He saw no traffic cops. They were doing over 120 miles an hour. The exits flashed by, Hook and Fleet and then Basingstoke, and before very long they were winding through the big bends past Winchester. Less than an hour since he climbed out of that truck. The driver lay on the tank again, as they exited on to the M27 and headed east for Portsmouth. Boese glanced behind him, the G-force nearly wrenching him from his grip; but he was lithe and fit and had spent eight prison months sleeping on the floor of his cell, preparing himself for exertions he knew would follow.

Halfway to Portsmouth, they left the motorway and crossed it again from the slip road. The driver glanced left and right, then pulled into an industrial estate. Boese climbed from the back of the bike and stripped off his helmet. He could see Morgan's sister waiting, with her son, in an estate car, parked by the Litho Supply building. The biker didn't look at him, didn't say anything, just twisted the throttle and cruised back out to the motorway. Boese walked over to the car and got in the passenger side. The young boy handed him a bag from the boot and Boese stripped off his leathers and passed them back. He did not say anything, but merely placed the documents in the glove compartment as she drove back to the motorway.

Twenty minutes later, they were queuing for the ferry to take them across the channel to Le Havre. He was driving now; Morgan's sister, his wife, according to the tickets, in the passenger-seat and their young son in the back. The helmet and leathers had been discarded before they reached the terminal, wrapped in a black plastic bag, then deposited in one of the large wheeled dustbins for the council to remove. Boese wore chinos, an Aran sweater and sports jacket. He wore no make-up, no facial disguise, save a pair of heavy spectacles. His papers were in order and his manner as relaxed as it had ever been. Their turn came and their tickets were inspected by the officer at the gate, then they were waved into another queue ready to join the ship. One hour later they were boarded, car chained down, and Boese was standing at the stern rail with his arm round Morgan's sister, watching the grey waves toss the foam in the ferry's wake.

Webb followed the blue Renault van into Liverpool. The Poles were long gone, having headed, presumably, back to London, with their load of weighty boxes transferred to the other van. They stayed with the cargo, moving the entire

surveillance team to the van and its two unknown occupants. Initially, they headed towards the docks and Harris
was on the phone to contacts in the Irish Republic, but
then the van changed course and instead drove right into
the city centre and pulled up outside a charity shop. A
motorcyclist passed the parked vehicle, confirming its
position. One car dropped off three people to keep the
eyeball on foot, and they confirmed two boxes being
unloaded. The crew of the van came out again and climbed
back into the van, then drove off once again. Two streets
away, they stopped outside the Deep-sea Fishermen's
Mission and unloaded two more boxes. Back at the charity
shop, one of the female spotters wandered in and began to
peruse the racks of clothing. Behind her, two little old
ladies were busying themselves at the lid of the box. The
observer watched them unpack a bundle of second-hand
clothes.

Harris looked at Webb's eyes looking back at her in the
rearview mirror. 'Old clothes,' she said. 'What the hell's
going on? It's bad enough being cooped up with a bunch
of dinosaurs like you lot, without someone taking the piss.'

They followed the van for another hour until the last of
the boxes had been delivered. They had been to half a
dozen Polish missions or charity establishments of one
kind or another. Webb's pager vibrated. The message was
to call the Reserve. Harris dialled while he drove. Mick
Rob, the SO19 firearms team leader, sat slumped in his
seat with his arms folded across his chest, an expression of
abject boredom dominating his face. Harris spoke to the
SO13 baseman. Webb half watched her face, half watched
the road ahead. She spoke quietly, asked what was going
on, then her voice stilled and the colour died on her cheeks.
'OK,' she said. 'We're on our way back now.'

'What?' Webb said, as she hung up.

For a moment she did not speak, looking out the window, eyes knotted amid the smooth skin of her face. She flicked at an irritating strand of hair that tickled her jawline. 'The SEG's been massacred,' she said. 'Storm Crow escaped.'

Swann sat in the waiting room outside the operating suite at Ealing Hospital, half a cup of machine-vended coffee between his palms. Boese's face stalked the recesses of his mind. He could smell the oil in the black feather he had not yet even seen. McCulloch shifted his position next to him. They were watching the lunchtime news on the television set above their heads. The waiting room was empty, save the two of them. Swann got up and turned the sound up. He could see Garrod in the background, talking to Colson, as the reporter spoke into the microphone.

'I'm here at the scene of the worst shooting incident in the history of the Metropolitan Police Force,' he said. 'Today, Hanwell Green, this quiet corner of West London, witnessed scenes of violence more akin to the streets of Los Angeles. Sixteen members of the special escort group were murdered this morning, by a gang of gunmen whose intention was to stop Ismael Boese, the international terrorist known as Storm Crow, from going to trial at the Old Bailey. Boese, as you will remember, was allegedly responsible for the chemical-bomb alert that saw the capital evacuated last spring. And for the subsequent attack in Rome, where two hundred and eighty people lost their lives, after being contaminated by the deadly nerve agent, pirillium E7/D10.' He broke off and the camera panned the street scene behind him. 'Three civilians were also killed and seventeen others wounded, six of those are critical. Eye-witnesses talk about the skip lorry, you see in the foreground, coming at speed from the old bus depot and crashing into the prison truck that was holding Boese. Gunmen then opened fire with machine guns, from these

154

two bus stops here. One woman, who looked from her flat window above this shop,' he pointed, 'talked about seeing something from a Hollywood filmset, with glass flying and guns firing for a full minute or more. So far, the forensic experts have yet to tell us anything, but two of the three escort vehicles appear to have been attacked by grenades.'

Swann looked at McCulloch. The commander was then interviewed, his face closed. He talked about terrorists, he talked about a concerted plan carried out with what appeared to be military precision, and then he talked about Storm Crow on the loose again. An all-ports warning had been issued within one hour of the attack. Only one of the assailants had been apprehended and he was currently undergoing emergency surgery in hospital. Swann stood up and switched the set off. McCulloch reached into his bag and brought out the transparent nylon evidence bag, which housed the automatic pistol they had recovered from the biker. 'I haven't seen this before,' he said.

'Neither have I. Why not get it down to Lambeth now, Macca. Get something going, at least. It doesn't take two of us to wait for the fucker to wake up.'

McCulloch nodded and got to his feet. He blew out his cheeks stiffly. 'They should've had a firearms team,' he said.

Swann shrugged his shoulders. 'Maybe.' He looked into McCulloch's eyes. 'But would it have made any difference?'

He sat on his own for another hour after McCulloch had gone, and then finally the surgeon came out, stripping blood-streaked rubber gloves from his hands as he did so. The mask hung loosely from his neck and he pushed his thick-lensed glasses higher up on his nose. Swann looked at him and understood. 'I'm afraid he didn't make it,' the surgeon said.

*

Louis Byrne was up at six-thirty, as he was every morning. The sun was just beginning to break between the cracks in the slatted pine shutters that covered the inside of their bedroom windows. He lay in the silence, listening to Angie sleeping next to him. Their bedroom spanned three windows of the first floor and he loved the space it afforded. Getting up quietly, he ran a finger over the muslin drapes that were tied back to the four iron posts of the bedframe, and stretched. Angie stirred. He looked at her, deciding to bring her coffee before waking her. She was moody in the mornings at the best of times, and she was due in court by nine.

The *Washington Post* was half sticking through the letterbox and he had to open the front door to get it. February and cold, no snow here yet, but there was a storm warning for later in the week. Tennessee and West Virginia were already without power where the snowfall had been harshest, and parts of the Virginia coastline were flooding. Some beach houses had had the stilts ripped from under them. Byrne scratched the raised stubble on his chin and glanced the length of the block, where Prince Street ran into the Potomac River. It was rising, no doubt about that. Shaking his head grimly, he recalled last year when it had swept half the length of their street. Fortunately, the town house was the last but one on Prince and Lee, so the river had a block and a half to rise before getting to them. The Oyster Bar on Union Street got it last year, though, and they'd be worrying now.

It was cold. He closed the door and went into the kitchen to make coffee. Angie was stirring when he took the cups upstairs. He touched her nose with the tip of his tongue and she flicked at the moisture with a finger. 'Wake up, honey,' he said. 'Time to get up.'

His wife opened one eye, rubbed at her forehead with

156

long-nailed fingers and sank deeper into the pillow. 'Aw, shit,' she said. 'Is it today already?'

Byrne laughed then and wafted the smell of coffee under her nose.

He left her and showered in the en suite bathroom. It had a black marble floor with a garden-sized bathtub, and a black marble shower unit with solid brass fittings. Angie had chosen it, to suit her moods she had told him; morning moods, no doubt. He stood at the end of their bed as she took a shower, and watched the early morning news from CNN while he fixed his tie. Images of London filled the screen, and, turning the volume higher, he sat down slowly in the Henry VIII chair that stood on the edge of the rug. He sat very still, tie only half fastened, while he stared at the images that Swann and McCulloch had witnessed an hour earlier.

Angie came out of the shower, a towel about her hair, another wrapped round her from above the breasts. 'Louis . . .' She stopped and looked at the screen, her husband hunched forward in his chair, the skin of his neck bunched above his collar. 'What's up?' she asked him.

Byrne did not reply, eyes intent on the screen. The last words of the newscaster: 'Storm Crow is on the loose again.'

Angie stepped in front of him. 'Escaped?' she said. Byrne was not listening, a frown deepening the lines above his eyes. 'Louis?' She shook his shoulder. 'Louis.'

'Sorry.' He stood up sharply. 'Jesus Christ. I thought we'd got rid of that sonofabitch.'

'What happened?' She looked back at the screen.

'The worst massacre in the history of British law enforcement is what happened.' He stepped past her, finishing his tie and lifting his jacket from the back of the chair. 'You're in court today, right?'

157

'Yeah. Leaman's trial's starting. But I doubt we'll get much beyond the opening statements.'

'I might be late.'

'We're out tonight, remember. The French Ambassador's reception.'

'I haven't forgotten.' Byrne looked past her to his reflection in the mirror. Only two people from the FBI had been invited to the White House, along with a whole bunch of foreign and US dignitaries: Louis Freeh, the Director; and himself, the man who put Storm Crow behind bars.

He flipped the electronic doors on the underground garage and drove up on to the cobbles. Right on Lee, he headed out of old town Alexandria and into Washington D.C. itself. Forty minutes later, he parked in the space allotted to him as unit chief of the International Terrorism Section, and went up to the fifth floor and his office. Leather desk, leather furniture, replacing the old stuff that Randall Werner had left behind when he moved to his last posting as SAC in San Diego. Byrne had taken over from him. He picked up the phone and dialled Scotland Yard, plucking Jack Swann's card from his pocket. Somebody answered, but it wasn't Swann. 'This is Louis Byrne from the FBI,' he said. 'Can you get Jack Swann to call me as soon as he comes in.' He put the phone down, clasped his hands together and looked at the photograph he kept on the wall – himself at Fort Bliss in Texas, with a bullet hole in his head. Next to it, the black feather from a crow.

Swann was in the briefing on the sixteenth floor. He had been there for four hours now. Webb and the surveillance team were back, and Webb was sitting next to him, his hands across his stomach, eyes dull for once. No one was speaking. Bill Colson, the operational commander, had just switched off the video they had taken of the scene. Fittingly

158

almost, there was no sound with it and the silence accentuated the devastation.

'They should've had SFO back-up,' Tania Briggs, from the exhibits office, observed quietly. 'The SEG were only ever traffic guys with guns.'

Swann looked sideways at her. 'They took tactical advice, Tania. The chief inspector was a passenger in the front car. He got killed as well.'

'What was the tactical advice?'

'Only a general threat. If they'd identified anything specific, they'd have had a full SFO team on it, maybe ARVs as well.'

'They face a general threat every time they move someone from PIRA,' Webb added quietly.

Colson waved at them to be quiet. 'There is absolutely no point in raking over what no one can do anything about. The chief inspector made his decision based upon the information available.' He leaned his knuckles on the desk then. 'The bottom line is that Boese is out.'

'Probably long gone by now,' Webb said. 'How long before they got the all-ports warning out?'

'Over an hour. We didn't get the CAD until ten minutes after the last shot was fired.' He looked at Swann. 'Just so you all know, we received another feather, his way of ensuring we understand exactly what went on. The feather was addressed to Jack.' All eyes swung in Swann's direction and he looked at the wall beyond Colson's head. 'This was planned to the minutest of details,' Colson went on. 'Whoever was behind it, knew exactly what they were doing.'

Webb sighed heavily and looked across the room to where Christine Harris was sitting with Julian Moore from Box. 'And half the fucking Branch were chasing a bunch of alleged Polish gun-runnners on a charity mission to Liverpool.'

Harris coloured. 'I wasn't to know that, George.'

Webb shook his head. 'I'm not criticizing, just pointing out the coincidence.'

Everyone was silent after that. Then Colson looked at Harris. 'It *is* a coincidence, isn't it?'

She sat forward, casting a brief glance at Moore, who cleared his throat. 'I put Chrissie on to Jorge Vaczka,' he said. 'Some of you already know that we had a whisper from MI6 that this guy was in the UK. We weren't aware he was here or of his existence until they pointed him out to us. Subsequent checks indicate he's been resident here for some three years.'

'How did they know about him?' Swann asked.

'Jack, they don't tell me that.' Moore spread his palms wide, elbows resting on his knees. 'They'd had word, I suppose. Like us, they have their sources. Vaczka's gang were organized. The more we've looked at them, the more we've come to appreciate that. Jorge Vaczka himself has been around. He's done some time, albeit briefly, in the United States.' He sat back again. 'We had a source close to him whose information was good. This morning was the first time that information was bad.'

'Again, a hell of a coincidence,' Swann said. He looked at McCulloch. 'Macca, any word from the gun room at Lambeth?'

McCulloch shook his head. Swann rested an ankle on his knee. 'How the hell did Boese organize this?' he said. 'He's not been in contact with anyone since he's been on remand.'

Harris squinted at him. 'No visitors at all?'

Swann was quiet for a moment. 'He did have one,' he said. 'Dr Benjamin Dubin.'

Back at his desk, he saw the note to ring Byrne and he showed it to Webb. 'Lucky Louis must've seen the news,' he said. 'He'll be well pissed off. Cheyenne told me he'd got a promotion on the back of this.' He picked up the phone and dialled. Byrne's phone was diverted to the Strategic Intelligence Operations Center, who located him in Quantico.

'Jack,' Byrne said, when they finally put him through. 'How's it going?'

'It's been better, Louis. No doubt you've heard the news.'

'This morning. I put a call in to you as soon as I hit my desk. What exactly happened, Jack?'

Swann sat back and lifted one foot to press the edge of his desk. He watched Webb across the squad room as he spoke. Webb was looking at the wing feather they had received, wrapped now in an evidence bag. The phone rang alongside him and he picked it up, glanced at Swann, then, facing the window, he picked up a pen and scrawled something on a sheet of paper. Swann sat forward, doodling on the pad in front of him.

'You saw the TV news, Louis. Boese got out.'

'But how?'

'We don't know yet.'

He heard Byrne sigh. 'Look, I'm sorry to hassle you so soon. It's just that this has implications for all of us. Did Boese see anyone in prison, visitors or anything?'

'Only one person,' Swann told him. 'Benjamin Dubin. Your mate from the Jonathan Institute.'

Byrne was quiet then. 'What did Dubin want with him?'

'He's written a book on Carlos, hasn't he. He thinks Boese is Carlos's protégé. I guess he wanted to find out from the horse's mouth.'

'You're going to talk to him?'

'What do you think, Louis?'

Swann arranged to keep Byrne posted on anything that he needed to know, then he hung up. Webb was deep in conversation with Colson. Swann went across to them. 'Louis Byrne,' he said as Colson looked round. 'Just as anxious as we are.'

Colson smiled crookedly. 'Built his reputation on him, didn't he.' He turned back to Webb once more, who was holding a sheet of paper. 'What've you got, Webby?'

Webb handed him the paper. 'Word just came in from the gun room at Lambeth. Russian. A 9-millimetre Gyurza, which means snake or viper.' He looked across the room to the fax machine which had started whirring. 'They're beaming across some details.'

Swann crossed to the fax machine, collected the specification sheet and read it. 'Special forces pistol,' he said. 'Fires armour-piercing rounds, 9 by 21 millimetre, RG-054. They can penetrate body armour.' He passed the sheet to Colson.

McCulloch came over from the far desk by the window, where he had taken another call. 'That was the gun room again,' he said. 'They've identified the shell casings.'

'And?' Colson said.

'Probably from a machine gun called a Whirlwind, Russian name – Vikhr. It's evil. Like a Kalashnikov, but more effective. The poor bastards in the front car didn't stand a chance. Those rounds can clear thirty layers of Kevlar at two hundred metres. They were only feet away.'

Amaya Kukiel served *bigos* to an old man who lived in a bedsit on his own. He came in three times a week and always ordered the same thing. She wondered if these were the only hot meals he had. She piled on a little extra, which he appreciated, smiling widely and showing her the gaping holes in his teeth. His chin was pointed and the stubble that clung there was the gathered fluff of the elderly. Carrying his tray in both hands, he shuffled to the table farthest from the door and settled himself down with a spoon. Amaya watched Vaczka watching her and fought to keep the colour from her cheeks. She wanted to urinate, something she had been doing a lot of since yesterday evening. Christine Harris had contacted her and told her about Liverpool and now she was nervous as hell. Had he been different since he got back? She did not know the answer. She did not know if she thought he had been different the last couple of weeks or so before he went north. Their love-making was as regular, more regular in fact; he seemed to want it every time he saw her. Was there something in that? She did not know. She had never experienced anything like this before and she was scared.

He surrounded himself with so many people, faces she knew and lots of others she did not, but the British intelligence services would not be interested in him for the purpose of idle curiosity. She wondered who he was and what they knew about him. He had never done anything for charity in all the time she had known him, let alone hiring a van and delivering clothes on behalf of the Polish mission. And now she had this deep sense of fear, right in the bowels, right there, where you could feel it as pain – a hollowed-out sensation that had been with her when she finally fell asleep, with her when she woke up, and with her now as she met his eyes across the floor of the cafeteria. He smiled at her and she could not tell what his eyes were telling her, if anything. She could feel the paranoia setting in and that frightened her all over again. The door to the street opened and Stahl came in. He glanced at her, staring for a second or so it felt, then he slid into the chair opposite Vaczka. Amaya went out to wash some dishes and calm herself down.

Vaczka looked at Stahl. 'Have you got it?'

'Yes.'

'Does it look legitimate?'

'It's in three parts. Bikes purchased, shipped to Poland

on the instruction of the company.' From his pocket he produced the copy invoice and slid it across the table to Vaczka. The final payment was to be electronically transferred, like the previous five. Six in total, nicely spread out and for amounts that varied considerably. 'Our US account to theirs.'

Vaczka stuffed the invoice into his jeans' pocket. 'I'd rather have paid cash.'

Stahl hunched his shoulders into his neck. 'Nobody wants cash any more.'

Vaczka stirred the dark coffee in front of him and nodded. 'Things have changed, my friend. Things have certainly changed.' Kukiel was back behind the counter again. He smiled sweetly at her.

'Have you decided what to do about her?' Stahl spoke from the side of his mouth.

'Not yet, but I will. She's a good fuck. I'll leave it at that for a while. Just think how obliging she's going to be.' He leered at Stahl, then sat back. 'This is the last meeting. Same for the others. Pass the word. Disappear, until I tell you otherwise.'

Stahl looked briefly at him, nodding once. Then, scraping back his chair, he stared very coldly at Kukiel and went outside again.

The following morning, Webb went out to Reading to begin the process of interviewing the remaining inmates of the special secure unit. The pathologist's report on the biker was not in yet. They had his fingerprints and were checking to see if he had served any time.

Swann flew to Edinburgh, then hired a car and drove over the Forth Bridge towards Perth, before turning off for St Andrews. With Boese gone, their case had gone too and they would have to start all over again. That meant retrawling through everything they had amassed over the past couple of years, relooking at every Storm Crow incident worldwide, and every known contact. Tal-Salem figured in this somewhere, Swann was certain of that. He thought again of the dead French banker and the solicitor and his secretary. Tal-Salem liked killing. You could tell, because of the hashish he smoked while he was doing it. Some killers might need to get high on hash in order to carry out their crimes, like others got shit-faced on booze. The orginal Hashinin, that Byrne had told him about, got high to generate the courage to assassinate, but Swann had the feeling that Tal-Salem just liked combining two pleasures.

Before he had left early this morning, Webb had walked past his desk. 'He always knew he could get out, Webby,' Swann said to him. 'And he always knew he *would*.' Swann picked up the polythene-encased feather and rubbed its stem through the plastic. 'That's why he sent this to me again.'

'What, sort of giving you the finger?'

'Yes. Like he did in that interview room.' Swann put down the feather. 'Remember when we nicked him? Remember how cool he was over it all, how calm he was at Paddington?' He twisted his lip. 'He's been ahead of the game, right from the off.' A thought struck him then and he stood up. 'If he hadn't been arrested, he would never have been able to look me in the eye and make the phone call, which sparked off the thing in Rome. He would have missed all that drama. Webby, this was planned long before we caught him.'

Webb leaned against his desk. 'What about the plans, what about getting the word out from inside?'

'It's been done before.'

'No mail. No visitors. No phone calls.'

'Apart from Dubin.'

'Yeah, but you don't really suspect Dubin, do you?'

'Why not?' Swann flapped his arms at his side. 'He's

165

the only person who's spoken to Boese since he got banged up.'

'Yes. And he has monthly meetings with the assistant commissioner.' Webb shook his head at him.

Swann drove into the old university town, past the Old Course Hotel on his left and the modern university buildings, off the roundabout, to his right. Dubin had said up South Street, on to North Street and pull over by the clock tower. Swann saw the tower and the pedestrian entrance under the arch, and swung the hire car into a parking space at chevron angles to the camber of the road. Dubin had mentioned parking vouchers to him. Swann pulled the Met fuel-record book from his bag and stuffed it against the windscreen. He locked the door and looked across the road. Students were milling about everywhere. He could smell the sea beyond the height of the old grey stone quad, where Dubin's office apparently was. He crossed the road, walked under the arch and came out on to a square of grass: the quad with four sides of three-storey buildings dominating it. He asked at the gatehouse and was told to cross to the far door. Dubin's secretary would meet him.

He waited in the stone-floored, high-ceilinged hallway, with the wide stone staircase rising before him. A woman in her late thirties appeared on the stairs. She had dark hair and was wearing a tweed skirt and nice, sensible shoes. 'Sergeant Swann?' she called. Swann followed her up the stairs.

Dubin's office was on the third floor, the last of the three doors between two sets of double fire doors. An essay box was fixed to the wall. The secretary knocked on the door and Dubin's voice called for them to go in.

'Sergeant.' Dubin stood up as Swann went in. 'Nice to see you again.'

'Doctor.' Swann glanced about the room. The US Stars and Stripes flag was draped behind the desk on the window

166

blinds, a globe dominated the desk already dominated by papers, a computer screen to one side and books. The walls were lined with racks of shelving and every available space filled with one box file or another. 'Some of what I brought from RAND,' Dubin explained.

'There's more?'

'God, yeah. Two rooms full of the stuff.'

'Terrorist events.'

'Yes.'

Swann looked across the desk at him. Then Dubin moved round to the easy chairs and the coffee table between them. He wore a tweed tie and corduroy trousers, his glasses perched on the end of his nose. 'Your assistant commissioner has been speaking to the families of the officers who got killed,' he said quietly. 'I've just phoned him myself to offer my condolences.'

Swann stared coolly at him. 'That's nice of you. Thank you.'

'Sixteen police officers and three civilians dead.' Dubin sat down heavily in the easy chair.

'Five,' Swann corrected him. 'Two more died this morning.'

'That's too bad. I'm really sorry.' Dubin looked at the floor, then up at Swann, eyes dark and intelligent. His gaze was almost penetrating, as if he would be the interviewer and not the other way round.

'Dr Dubin, you're the only person from outside the prison to speak to Boese since he was placed on remand,' Swann began.

'Is that right?' Dubin rubbed his nose. 'No other visitors?'

'Not only that, but no mail and no phone calls, either given or received.'

'Then how did he plan the escape?' Dubin cocked one eyebrow.

'That's what we'd like to know.' Swann shifted himself in the seat, then asked: 'What did you talk to him about, exactly?'

Dubin thought for a moment, looking beyond him to the window and flag behind the desk. 'The meeting didn't last long,' he said slowly. 'And it was nothing like as successful as I'd hoped. I spoke a little about my interview with Ilyich Ramirez Sanchez.' He broke off, looked at Swann and made a face. 'Basically, he wouldn't give me the interview.'

'How long were you there?' Swann said.

'Not very long. I couldn't tell you the exact amount of time, though I guess you could check with the prison.' His face was open. 'They'd know, wouldn't they.'

Swann thought for a moment, then said: 'Did you have any trouble getting Boese to see you?'

Dubin shook his head. 'I wrote the prison. They wrote back. Then I called and they told me he had agreed. I guess they checked me out, then I received a letter telling me a date and time.'

'So you didn't have to try and persuade him at all?'

'No. He seemed to be quite keen. He stipulated no tapes and no pictures, but apart from that he would see me.'

'But when you did meet him, he refused to be actually interviewed.'

'Well, it wasn't quite like that. We talked a bit, I guess, but it didn't go where I wanted it to. He denied what I knew to be true.'

'That he had been with Carlos?'

'Yes.'

'That's not surprising really, is it?' Swann cocked an eyebrow. 'I mean he was still on remand.'

'I suppose so, yeah. He seemed to want to see me, but what was the point if he wasn't going to talk to me.'

Swann made a face. 'Seems odd, doesn't it. I mean, I

168

guess he knew who you were. If he knows the major players worldwide, then he'll know about the bloke who chronicles them.'

'I don't chronicle them, Sergeant, so much as their activities.'

'It's much the same thing.'

'Is it?' Dubin looked at him carefully. 'I'm not sure that it is.'

Swann pressed on. 'But it's likely he knew who you were.' He gestured with one hand. 'You must have told him who you were in the letter.'

'Of course. I gave the prison my full background.'

Swann dabbed at his upper lip with his tongue. 'So he agreed to see you, talks some, then effectively declines a formal interview. I find that very strange, don't you?'

Dubin crossed one leg over the other. 'I do, yes. It was strange.'

'And then a few months later, he gets out.' Swann made a face, twisting his mouth down at the corners. He stood up then and stretched his legs, not speaking, walking to the window. 'Can I see the rest of the data base?' he asked.

'Sure. Why not.' Dubin collected his keys from his desk and led the way down the corridor to the far end of the building.

'How could he get out, Dr Dubin?' Swann asked him.

'You mean, who would he use?' Dubin looked over his shoulder. 'Christ, now you're asking.' He scratched his head as he walked. 'He's Storm Crow, isn't he,' he said. 'Who couldn't he use? Boese's had links with all the major groups you could think of.'

'What about Abu Nidal?'

Dubin pulled a face. 'It's possible, I suppose. Why, d'you have some reason to think that the ANO might be involved?'

'We're not sure of anything yet.'

169

Dubin showed Swann into an anteroom which housed hundreds of box files and two desks with computer screens standing on them. Two students were working at the respective keyboards. Dubin introduced him and Swann walked up the three steps which opened into a long, thin room, with a full-size window overlooking the back of the university and the estuary beyond. He leaned against the glass.

'Best view in the building,' Dubin told him.

Swann looked back at him, observing the calm expression in his big, dark eyes, then beyond him to the boxes and boxes of information: every terrorist event, every terrorist gang perhaps, going back fifty years.

## 11

Swann sat at the bar of Finnegan's Wake and watched the news on television. Webb and Harris were with him, together with Phil Cregan, the explosives officer. The carnage at Hanwell Broadway had been cleared, Webb and Cregan supervising the shipment of the wrecked vehicles to the Defence Research Agency at Fort Halstead in Kent. Webb had fully zoned the area for evidence and the forensics team had packed all that they could recover into nylon evidence bags, before wrapping the vehicles in sterile tarpaulin. The attack was still the main headline, with the name of Storm Crow dominating every newspaper and every half-hourly bulletin. Already, alleged sightings of him from France to Germany and Switzerland, and as far away as Chile, had been reported on national television. Swann took them all with a pinch of salt; over two hundred calls had come into the Yard that morning alone.

He lit a cigarette and one for Cregan and they all watched the news. Five-thirty, and the bar was filling up with workers from the various offices in and around Victoria. Normally they drank further away from the Yard, but with the ceasefire still holding, fears for personal security had calmed considerably. Benjamin Dubin was being interviewed, the reporter standing with him in the quad at St Andrews University, where only days before Swann had also talked to him. The camera was close up on Dubin's face: dark skin, bearded. His hair was still black and he looked fifteen years younger than his actual fifty-five.

'Dr Benjamin Dubin,' the reporter was introducing him, 'recognized by security services the world over as the leading civilian authority on terrorism. Ten years with the RAND Corporation, then another five with the Jonathan Institute in Israel, before coming here to St Andrews.'

Dubin stood behind him, hands in the pockets of his chinos.

'Dr Dubin, what can you tell us about Storm Crow? How could such an escape have happened? The worst attack the Metropolitan Police have ever suffered. Not even the IRA, who were at war with the UK mainland for thirty years, have ever engineered such a massacre.'

Dubin scratched his beard along the jawline. 'Storm Crow is nothing like the IRA. It's important to establish that fact immediately. Matter of fact, he's nothing like anybody the Western world has really come across before. Before his arrest in May of last year, Storm Crow had never been identified. That had always been his greatest asset. In the seventies and early eighties, Carlos, Ilyich Ramirez Sanchez, was reputed to be the ultimate enemy of Western governments after what he did with the OPEC ministers in 1975, the Rue Toullier and, of course, the hijacked aircraft that the Israelis liberated at Entebbe. But the security forces always knew who Carlos was. No secret was made of his identity. Although a considerable number of myths were created.'

He stopped talking, the wind coming off the sea to ruffle his hair. Students walked behind him, and Swann suddenly thought of the narrow upstairs room, where his two assistants logged every terrorist event in the world on computer.

'You have a theory that Storm Crow was a student, the word "protégé" has been used, of Carlos the Jackal,' the reporter said.

'I do. I know for a fact that Ismael Boese was part of the group known as the "Friends of Carlos", who were responsible for attacking the Paris–Toulouse express train in March 1982. The group were a mixture of nationalities,

German predominantly. But there was one young man, half-caste, whose national origins were unknown. It was always believed that he was a favourite, and I have had first-hand information from two members of the group that this man *was* something of a protégé. He did not stay with them for very long, however, but again, intelligence sources have confirmed that he and Carlos have remained in contact over the years.'

'And this man was Ismael Boese?'

'Yes.'

'You're positive?'

'Oh, yes. There can be no doubt.' Again, he glanced at the camera. 'Where the crow flies, bad news follows. That's Ismael Boese.'

'But how could he have planned such an escape?'

'Storm Crow has access to all the major players world-wide. There may've been a state sponsorship behind this. We'll only know for sure when he resurfaces, which, I'm afraid, he will.'

The pictures returned to the studio and Swann crushed out his cigarette. 'That what he told you, Jack?' Cregan asked him.

Swann snorted. 'I wasn't asking his opinion. I wanted to know what he and Boese talked about.'

Harris bought a fresh round of drinks and then her pager sounded. She frowned and glanced at the display, then, making her excuses, she left.

Amaya Kukiel finished her packing and sat on top of her suitcase. She glanced at the meagre bedsit and listened to the trains on the District line rumble over the bridge outside the window. She thought of her classes, the degree she would not now finish and what she would tell her father when she got back to Gdansk. The doorbell rang and for a moment she ignored it, then she slid off the bed and went

173

down to answer it. She could see two figures outlined through the frosted glass and her heart sank. Her fears were confirmed when she opened it. Moore and Harris pushed their way into the hall. She looked at each one in turn, sighed, and led the way upstairs. Harris lifted one eyebrow when she saw the suitcase. 'Leaving us, Amaya?'

'I told you. I'm finished.' Amaya's eyes smarted. 'If I leave, you can't threaten me about my visa.'

'Nobody ever threatened you.' Moore's voice was soft, but his eyes were cold.

'No?' She sneered at him. 'That's not how I saw it.' She stood now with one hand across her belly, gripping her other elbow. Then she picked up a packet of cigarettes and, hands shaking, she lit one. Moore walked to the window and looked out across Ravenscourt Park.

'We need you to stay, Amaya.' Harris lifted the suitcase off the bed and sat down.

'Too bad.' Amaya picked up her plane ticket from the mantelpiece and flapped it under his nose. 'I'm flying home tomorrow. You can keep your fucking visa and your fucking degree course. They're not worth the risk.'

'There is no risk.'

Amaya snapped air, audibly, from compressed lips. 'You want to swap places? Jorge Vaczka tells me something which I tell you. He then delivers charity clothes all over the north of England. He's never done a charitable thing in his life.' She broke off for a second. 'You don't see the way he looks at me.'

'We'll protect you.' Moore had turned from the window.

'No, you won't. Because I won't be here to protect.' She took a step towards him. 'You can't stop me leaving. I've been to the Polish Embassy, told them exactly what you made me do. I'm flying out tomorrow and if you try and stop me, I'll tell everything to the newspapers, how British MI5, or whatever it is you are, blackmailed *me*,' she tapped herself in the sternum, 'a poor, impressionable student from Poland over a perfectly legitimate visa.'

Harris glanced at Moore. 'OK, Amaya. If that's what you want to do. No one's going to stop you.'

Outside, Moore took a deep breath and sighed. 'Some you lose,' he said.

George Webb parked the Ford in the main car park inside Reading Prison. A special escort group truck was parked by the side of the compound, with a motorcycle outrider alongside it. Again, images of the wrecked vehicles burned themselves into his mind. He got out, looked across the roof at Tania Briggs, and closed the door. The afternoon following the attack, a team from the office had swarmed all over the special secure unit, which he could see now – a grey concrete building in the shape of a plus sign, behind its own wall and razor-wire fence. The other category A inmates had been locked in the cells while the SO13 officers took Boese's apart. Webb had found a note under the thin mattress, which the wardens said he never used, wishing them all the best in their search. Boese had known beyond any doubt that he would never reach the Old Bailey on the morning of 5 February.

They made their way across to the SSU entrance where Griffiths, the warden with the embarrassed face, was waiting for them. Slate rain rattled the concrete from an ash-coloured sky. Webb could smell the wet tarmac. Briggs carried their gear, not much of it now. Today, they were checking the records and hoping to talk to some of the other prisoners. Boese, according to the wardens, had not been particularly popular and perhaps they might make some headway. Webb knew the three PIRA men would not speak to them.

Inside, the governor was waiting for them. Webb had met him before. He had been assistant governor at Wormwood Scrubs, where Webb had interviewed some prisoners in the past. They shook hands and, for the second time in two days, Webb and Briggs were ushered through the airlocked doors into the dead space between them. On their left, the officers in the control room looked through smoked glass, caught their eyes and looked away. Webb chuckled softly to himself and winked at Briggs. 'Nothing like someone else's discomfort,' he said.

They were greeted by Maureen Bryant, the supervisor, a tall well-built woman, one of four in the team of ten wardens. She took them into her office, which looked directly across the dining area and pool table. The inmates were all locked in their cells. They would remain there all day while Webb and Tania carried out their investigations. One by one they would be exercised, like dogs, for half an hour. Webb laid his case on the desk and looked across at Bryant. 'We want to check the assessment logs,' he said. 'All of them. Then I want to talk to the officers who had the most contact with Boese.'

'That'll be most of us, then,' she said, holding his gaze evenly.

'Griffiths seemed to have a lot to say yesterday,' Briggs put in.

'Michael always tries hard with the prisoners, Constable.'

'We'll need to talk to him.' Webb smiled across the table at her. 'What about the inmates themselves?'

'They won't talk to you.'

'Well, there's a surprise.'

Bryant smiled. 'Well, that's not quite true, actually. One of them might. Gianluca Terlucci.'

Webb's eyes lit up. 'Our very own Mafia hitman. How many knives has he got in here?'

'Only the ones in the kitchen and they're counted daily, Sergeant.'

176

Webb leaned across the table and smiled at her. 'Why him, anyway?'

'Because we think he had a run-in with Boese on the night before the trial. Terlucci got cut, superficially.' She touched the fleshy skin under her chin. 'Said he cut himself shaving.'

'And did he?' Briggs asked.

Bryant lifted her eyebrows. 'At five in the afternoon, peeling potatoes in the kitchen?' She leaned both elbows on her desk. 'Terlucci has family in Italy, two young children and a wife. He's trying to get the Home Secretary to let him serve his sentence back home.'

'He stabbed a man to death in Hyde Park,' Briggs said.

'That's right. A rival, warring factions of the same family.'

Webb stood up. 'Let's talk to him, then,' he said. 'Then I want the little red books to look at.'

Terlucci was brought to the office they were using and Webb sized him up across the table – a slim, thin-faced man with slicked-back hair, jet black; so black in fact, it looked as though it had been dyed. His eyes were tight, scrapings of coal set deep in a prominently boned skull. He tapped long fingernails on the desk, a signet ring in gold on the third finger of his left hand. Webb studied the reddened line under his chin.

'Cut yourself,' he said.

'Shaving.'

'Of course. Careless. Boese did that to you, didn't he?' Webb leaned his weight on the edge of the table as he said it, pressing both arms flat and looking into Terlucci's eyes. 'You were having a pop at him or something.'

'Pop? What is pop?'

'Pop.' Webb leaned and brushed the Italian's jaw with his knuckles. 'Either that or sharper,' he said.

'You think so?'

'Yes, I do.' Webb sat back again. 'What was going on in here, Luca, what was happening?'

Terlucci seemed to consider then, perhaps thinking that if he did get out and back to Italy he had nothing really to lose. He pressed his lips down at the corners and made a gesture, lifting both palms to the ceiling. 'He is a bad man, this Storm Crow. He kill a lot of people in Roma. My country.' He poked himself in the chest.

'You had words with him about this?'

'Not so much. He speak to me. He like to laugh at me, at the misfortune of my country. He talk about Roma. The Pope. It was St Peter's Square where it happen.'

Webb nodded. 'What did you do about it?'

'I speak with him, of course. I say not to be so foolish as he is being. This is a small place. There are English here and Italian.'

'And Irish,' Briggs put in.

'Yes, but the Irish they don't care. England is bombed by the Storm Crow. Italy is bombed also.'

'What're you telling us, Luca?'

'Nothing. I just speak with him. "Take a little more respect, Mr Storm Crow."' He wagged his finger from side to side.

'And?'

'Well, he don't care, does he. He is the Storm Crow. He threatens me, my wife, my children. He know where we live. He know where we say Mass, where the children go to classes. He know everything about me.'

Webb was silent. 'You have visitors in here, Luca?'

'Of course. I have big family.' Again, the Italian touched himself on the chest. 'They love me.'

'Do you talk about the visits?'

'Pardon me?'

'When they're gone, do you talk about the visits?' Webb shook his head at him. 'Come on, Luca, all you Italians love to talk. Boese probably listened to you. You got photographs of your children?'

'Of course. Lots in my cell.'

'At church, school, home?' Webb pushed himself back from the table. 'It's not difficult to frighten someone if you really want to. You should know that, Luca.' He paused for a moment then. 'Who did Boese get on with?'

'Get on with?' Terlucci looked puzzled.

'Like. Who did he like?'

'Nobody.'

'Pool?' Webb glanced through the glass partition to the cloth-covered table. 'Did he play pool?'

'Sometimes.'

'Partners? Did he play partners with anyone?'

'No.' Terlucci sat forward then. 'He play chess, a lot of chess.'

'With you?'

He snorted. 'He don't play nothing with me. Morgan. He play chess with Morgan all of the time.'

They talked again to Griffiths, while Webb flicked through the log assessments that the wardens ran on each prisoner – watching his actions, behaviour, assessing how he was coping with prison life, whether or not he showed any early signs of disruption.

'In many ways he was the model prisoner,' Griffiths told them, 'if a little strange. He used to sleep on the floor of his cell, he never once used the bed.' Webb squinted at him. 'He used to put the blankets on the floor and sleep there. Very strange. Never seen it before.'

Webb was looking at the Ichthys fish on his lapel. 'Did you talk to him?'

'I try to talk to all of them. The Irish are the easiest in many ways.'

'Well, they've got religion, haven't they,' Webb said.

179

'Something in common.' Griffiths coloured, but said nothing. 'What did you talk to Boese about?'

'The usual concerns. Part of my job is rehabilitation, Sergeant, especially in here.' They looked at one another across the table.

'What did Boese talk to you about?' Webb asked him.

'Not a lot. If you want to know, most of his comments were based in sarcasm. He seemed to delight in sarcasm.'

'Maybe he worried you,' Briggs put in. 'Did he worry you?'

'Not especially.'

'Was he worse than anyone else in here?'

'He was intelligent, Constable,' Griffiths said. 'The intelligent ones I can handle well enough. They're predictable and not so given to spontaneous bouts of violence.'

Webb was looking at Boese's log book. 'Tell me about Morgan,' he said. 'Boese seemed to play a lot of chess with him. Were they friends?'

'Boese had no friends, Sergeant. He kept himself to himself.'

'But your assessment says he mixed.'

'He did. Pool, and the chess, obviously. He wasn't isolated particularly, he just didn't generate conversation with anyone. He liked the gym. He used to hang upside-down on the parallel bars. Let the blood run to his head for ages.' Griffiths opened his eyes wide. 'Weird man. Very weird man.'

'But he played chess with Morgan. He didn't play anyone else?'

'Initially, he did. But I don't think anyone else was good enough for him, Sergeant.'

'Was Morgan good at chess?'

'He beat everyone apart from Boese.'

Webb nodded and scribbled a note on his pad. 'I'd like to see Morgan's assessment log,' he said.

180

Griffiths brought it, then left them alone. Together, Webb and Briggs studied the two books, looking at dates and checking to see what did or did not correspond. Morgan was serving life for murder. He had never denied it, but equally had shown no remorse. He had always been considered a threat to other prisoners, because of his capacity for violence. Eleven of his fifteen years prison time had been spent in one of the four other SSUs in the country. He had been transferred out of Barlinny, in Glasgow, after clashing with other inmates. Webb looked at his visitor record and felt excitement well in his breast.

'Look at this,' he said. 'Morgan's only living relative is his sister. She lives in Hawick in Scotland. Family is Welsh, but moved to Scotland when they were both kids. Their father was based on the Clyde. Navy.' He paused and rubbed his chin. 'She visited him for the first time in almost a year, last October.' He tapped the page with a pudgy finger. 'Morgan had to pay for the train ticket.' He hunched himself over the page then. 'Bloody hell, Tania. Listen. *Morgan* requested the visit, said he wanted to make contact again because he could be due to come up for licensed release in another year. Record here says he was concerned that if he had no outside help, he would slip back into the old ways.' He looked sideways at her. 'This is the man who showed no remorse whatever for the previous fifteen years. He gets about a fiver a week in here, buys tobacco and papers and that's it.'

'What was the date of the visit?' Briggs asked him.

'The 4th.'

Briggs ran her finger over the page. 'On the afternoon of the 3rd, Boese played chess with him.'

Webb looked again at Morgan's assessment log. He discovered that after travelling down from the Scottish Borders with the payment being met by her brother, Morgan's sister came once a month until February. They

181

checked Boese's activities and found that he and Morgan had a game of chess on each afternoon preceding the day of the visit.

Swann leaned against the wall in the mortuary while the pathologist worked on the body of the biker. Disinfectant was thick in his nostrils, along with the other smells that were indistinct from one another – death or cleanliness or the imagined smell of death, he could never decide which. The corpse had been badly smashed in the motorcycle accident; hitting the old man's car at something like eighty miles an hour. The police outrider had only just been able to stop himself. The chest cavity had caved in and ribs had penetrated one lung, causing it to collapse, and the victim had bled profusely from the mouth and nose. His internal organs were savaged by the impact and both legs had been wrecked, along with his right arm, which was left hanging by sinew and bloody thread in the torn sleeve of his flying suit. Swann had examined his clothing in detail: grey, one-piece flight suit, the flame-retardant type used by the military, black Hi-Tec boots, like some of the ninjas preferred in SO19, and a pair of leather, knuckle-protected, military-issue gloves.

He looked across at the face where the pathologist was cutting into the skull, and grimaced at the sound of the electric saw. He stepped closer and studied the man's features. The face was intact, saved by the quality of the black Shoei helmet he had been wearing. Already they had analysed the suit, helmet and silk balaclava, and found traces of firearms residue. The man had once been good-looking, with chiselled, even features, black, short-cut hair and a distinctively styled beard – again, very black, and shaped round the lips and chin and rising in two points along the jawbone. Swann was vaguely reminded of Robert De Niro in *The Deer Hunter*. He looked for other distinguishing marks, and narrowed his eyes at a small tattoo on the man's right ankle: *ORHNEG*. 'What's that?' he asked, pointing.

The doctor looked at him over the lip of his paper mask and his eyes creased at the corners. 'Blood group,' he said. 'O. Rhesus-negative. He's got another one tattooed on his elbow.' Swann bent to his knees and saw the same marking on the man's right elbow.

'Soldiers sometimes do it,' the pathologist explained. 'Two places is always good, in case one gets blown off in battle. Saves a heck of a lot of trouble with blood transfusions.'

He met Webb back on the fifteenth floor and they both went up to the briefing that Colson was giving. Webb spoke first and told them what he and Briggs had discovered at Reading Prison, concerning Boese's possible link with Brynn Morgan's sister. 'She lives in Hawick,' he explained. 'That's a long train ride to Reading, costing seventy-five pounds return, plus the bus from Hawick to Galashiels to catch it. Morgan paid for her first visit, so either she was stuck for cash or he really wanted to see her. According to her visitor-suitability record, she's on income support, living in rented accommodation with a ten-year-old son. There's a part-time job in the Spar shop, but nothing else. I don't suppose she's what anyone would call flush.'

'Seventy-five quid?' McCulloch put in.

'Right.' Webb counted off on his fingers. 'Morgan pays for the October visit, but then she shows up in November, December, January and the 4th February.'

'The day before Boese's trial,' Swann said. 'Do we know if she went home?'

'Not yet. No.'

Colson looked at Webb, resting his chin on a fist, arm

crooked about his waist. 'OK, George. I'd like you and Campbell to take a trip up to the Borders and have a look at her, see what you can come up with. If it looks worth while, we'll consider putting a team on her.' He paused and turned to Swann. 'Jack?'

Swann looked at his notes. 'Our dead biker,' he said, 'he could ride most definitely. The solo who chased him verified that. If it hadn't been for that Mazda, he would have got away.' He paused. 'He could also handle weapons. We don't know where he was in that attack, but he *was* part of the team.' He broke off and looked across at Webb. 'How many do we reckon?'

'A lot. Witnesses say there was firing from both bus stops, either side of the road. The amount of shell casings found and the angle of trajectory indicate more than two, maybe two each side. There's twenty rounds in the Vikhr clip, and the word on the street was continuous fire. Suppression. That would mean one man loading while the other fires, and vice versa. Four then, on foot. Then there's the skip lorry, two in that. Getaway car for Boese. One more, maybe. Then the other two SEG vehicles: the Range Rover was hit with an RGN grenade and the lead Rover with phosphorus. It takes at least two more people to do that.' He paused for a second and studied the Annacappa chart on the wall, the events they had so far, the evidence recovered, timings, bodies, witness sightings. 'We know that four different motorbikes were parked in the alleyway behind the shops. That alleyway can be accessed from the door on the street marked 105A. My guess is the lead car and the Range Rover were hit by four bodies on two more bikes. The driver to get you up there fast and the pillion to lob in the ordnance.' He made an openhanded gesture. 'That means eleven or twelve of them, a lot on bikes. All of them knew what they were doing.'

Swann nodded and looked at each of their faces. The

door opened and the commander walked in with a superintendent from Special Branch. Swann pasted four enlarged photographs on the wall and stood back, one hand in his trouser pocket. 'Our dead biker,' he said. 'Distinctive beard.' He tapped the man's face, then went on to explain about the blood group tattooed on his ankle and elbow. 'A soldier would do that,' he finished.

As if in affirmation, McCulloch rolled up his right sleeve, revealing a thickly muscled forearm coated in blond hair. He tapped the blue ink at his elbow. 'Six years in the Green Jackets,' he said.

For a while, everyone was silent. 'Soldiers,' Colson mused. 'That would make sense considering how they handled their weapons. Not many people know about suppression fire.' He was looking at Christine Harris now. 'The weapons were all Russian, Chrissie. And we haven't come across their type very often before.'

'Hardly at all.' She cleared her throat. 'Some of them we don't even have pictures of.'

Colson chewed his lip and glanced at the commander. 'Russian weapons, motorcycles and a dead, unidentified soldier.'

'We can ID him now,' Swann said. He looked at McCulloch. 'The army will have a record of his fingerprints. Right?'

'They certainly will.'

'Excellent.' Colson clapped his hands together. 'There's another thing that the teams have thrown up in their searches. Two motorbikes were parked close to the Fox pub early on the morning of the attack, along with a small van of some type. The make or index number isn't known. The Fox is in Hanwell village, close to the canal. The bikes were the scrambler type. Later that morning, an old woman was almost knocked into the canal by two bikes that were racing along the towpath. Apparently, it happens quite often.' He paused then and turned to the map on the wall, tracing the line of the canal. 'The towpath'll get you most of the way to the M4. On a motorbike, it'd take no time at all.' He tapped the map. 'What a great way to escape.'

Webb studied the map. 'They may've dumped the bikes.'

'I know.' Colson looked back at him. 'I've organized the underwater search unit to look for them in the canal.' He turned to Harris once more. 'What about the weapons, Chrissie. They're from Eastern Europe. Our Polish friends, perhaps?'

'It could be connected, but there's no evidence to suggest it other than the coincidences we've already discussed.' She glanced across the table to where Julian Moore was watching her. 'We've lost our informant.' She sighed heavily. 'Got scared and went home to Poland.' Again, she looked at Moore. 'Nothing we could do about it, I'm afraid.'

'She's better off away, anyway,' Moore put in. 'There's no doubt the information was duff. It was the first time, but it scared her badly. Vaczka's a bad boy to cross. She couldn't believe the charity mission. As far as she knew, he'd never done anything that somebody didn't pay him for.'

'Charity clothes to Polish missions,' Webb said. 'Not his style then, eh?'

'No.'

'We know from Box 850 that he has had, maybe still does have, serious links with Abu Nidal. Nidal lived in Poland, remember, between 1981 and 1984. He sells weapons from there.'

'ANO-supplied weapons?' Colson said.

'Possibly.'

Colson stood up again. 'We'll look at Brynn Morgan's sister,' he said. 'And do some work on this dead soldier.

186

As far as the Poles are concerned, there's not a lot we can do right now.'

Tal-Salem watched *Newsnight* in his hotel room at Hyde Park. He rolled a skinny joint, wetted the gummed edge of the paper and twisted up the ends. The presenter was debating with Benjamin Dubin, sitting in a studio somewhere in Scotland. Tal-Salem lifted the remote control unit and increased the volume a fraction. He lay back then, arm crooked behind his head, and watched out of half-closed eyes.

'In your opinion, Dr Dubin, what's he likely to do?' the programme presenter asked him. Dubin pressed one finger to his earpiece, as if he could not hear very well.

'That's difficult to say,' he replied. 'Last time we saw Storm Crow, it was the worst chemical attack in the history of peacetime, other than what we know went on in Iraq, of course.'

'You're referring to the Kurds.'

'Yes, the Kurds and the Marsh Arabs.' Dubin gestured with an open palm. 'The break-out was obviously planned in minute detail. My guess is Boese's now somewhere very safe, amongst friends, possibly in Lebanon, or maybe the Yemen. Libya could be an option.' Again, he put a finger to the earpiece. 'He might, of course, do nothing. He's spent years cultivating secrecy. Now all that has changed. He might disappear again completely. Who knows? But he might come back for revenge.'

'Revenge?'

'He's been identified, hasn't he. Caught. Incarcerated. The Jackal, if you remember, waged a terrible vengeance on France in the 1980s, just because they put his girlfriend in prison.'

Tal-Salem flicked off the set and blew a thin stream of

187

smoke at the ceiling. 'Revenge,' he muttered. 'Now that would be interesting.'

The Irishman sat in the White Lion student bar in Washington D.C. He drank a pint of Guinness and watched the same interview, which had been broadcast by CNN to the States. Around him, the students talked, none of them much interested, although the bartender studied the screen, as he dried glasses on a cloth that hung to his chest from his shoulder.

'Now that is one nasty sonofabitch,' he said.

Down the length of the bar, somebody lit a cigarette and the Irishman wrinkled his nose as the smoke drifted into his face. He looked round, but the female smoker was so deep in conversation with what looked like an errant boyfriend, he could not catch her eye.

'They say he's an American.' The bartender seemed intent on holding a conversation with someone. 'That fella on the TV just now. They say he's from over here.'

'Is that a fact?'

'Oh, yeah. Can't remember where exactly, but somewhere Stateside, for sure. They say he delivers crows' feathers to his intended targets.'

'Do they now?'

'Oh, yeah. Serious sonofabitch.'

The Irishman moved from the bar to a table and looked out into the February rain. Ismael Boese out; and Benjamin Dubin talking on British television. He rubbed a thumbnail along the underside of his lip and stared at the condensation gathering on the inside of the window. The hubbub behind him subsided, as he concentrated slowly and allowed his mind to think. The word from Britain was that the police had stopped a motorcyclist, a good motorcyclist at that. He had died in hospital, which was interesting, if a little unfortunate.

Strange thoughts crisscrossed the quiet places of his mind, thoughts he had not entertained in years. But they were there now – unfamiliar, but there. He moved in his seat, jeans sticking to the plastic chair for a moment, and sipped the dark beer from his glass. Outside, the rain rattled in a fresh wave as the wind blew across Pennsylvania Avenue from 19th Street. Cars backed up at the lights and he saw the blacked-out windows of a secret sevice vehicle head down past Lafayette Square and the White House. Dubin had mentioned revenge. Dubin was very knowledgeable. He scratched slowly at the sweat gathered on the palm of his hand.

George Webb had never been to Hawick before, a dour market town in the Borders of Scotland. Once upon a time, farmers from all over the north of England, as well as Scotland, had travelled to the livestock market at the eastern reaches of the town, which nestled between two hills, with the River Teviot running between them. Now that market was a Safeway superstore and the livestock went somewhere else. Years before that, border clansmen, like the Armstrongs, had mustered as many as three thousand horsemen to terrorize the English as far south as Carlisle, stealing cattle, killing and raping as they went. By the time James V was the seventeen-year-old King of Scotland, Henry VIII was demanding action against the brother of the incumbent master of Maingerton, the ancient Armstrong seat near Newcastleton. James, however, was powerless. Johnny Armstrong of Gilnockie commanded both sides of the border from his tower on the banks of the Esk. It was not until 1530, when James summoned him to a bogus truce, that the power of the clan was broken. Johnny and fifty of his men were hanged from the trees at Carlenrigg.

Webb and McCulloch booked into the Station Hotel in

the high street, posing as mobile telephone engineers, and did a brief reconnaissance of the town. Morgan's sister, Catherine, lived at the eastern end. Bourtree Terrace was a narrow street which led up from the high street, where it separated for Galashiels and Jedburgh respectively, beyond the statue of the weary bronze horseman. At the south-western end of town, they found the park and playing fields, and Hawick Rugby Club, and closer in, the high school. The river cut right through the middle of the town and under the bridge, where the rapids were fast and yellowed, frothing water gushed over rocks and grey slabs and the odd shopping trolley. Many of the shops were closed, bars were dotted here and there, and, at night, the Lothian and Borders police patrolled in strength.

Catherine Morgan lived in an old flat, number 6, which was on the right-hand side of Bourtree Terrace as it rose up the hill. To the left was a small warehouse for antique furniture and an open piece of ground for private parking. Beyond that, a house and then a car repair workshop which, according to the local in the baker's at the bottom of the hill, had once been Rettie's Taxis. The three converted flats were in the last grey block on the right, before the road bent at ninety degrees, rising to a small cottage and a large residence right at the top of the hill. Garages and workshops lay stacked together down the left-hand side, as far as the car workshop. It was not an easy place to recce covertly, so Webb and McCulloch drove up, parked by the side of the road and looked at the bogus plans they carried, laid out on the roof of their car. Then Webb took a brief walk down past the flats and checked the external door. It was open and he climbed six worn stone steps and found number 6 on the first landing. The steps wound on in a cold spiral to two more flats further up. He rang the bell of number 6, standing with his breath coming in clouds of steam in the refrigerated atmosphere of the landing. Nobody answered. He rang again and still nobody came. Then he bent and peered through the letterbox. He could see nothing – a heavy velvet curtain covered the back of the door. Carefully, he inspected the keyholes, two of them, one a Chubb lock, the other for a bar key of some kind.

Back in the car, he looked at McCulloch from the corner of his eye. 'There's nobody there,' he said. 'I can't tell if she's away for a while or just out, because I can't see any post on the floor.'

They turned the car and trundled slowly down the terrace, turning left into the town once more. They drove out on to the A7 and south again. Five miles further on, they phoned back to the Yard and spoke to Harris in the Special Branch cell. Webb told her what they had found.

'I've got a request going in for production orders under Schedule 7,' Harris told them. 'As soon as I get them, I'll let you know what her bank account looks like.'

Back in town, they went into the Spar where they knew Catherine worked. It was literally round the corner from her house, the first shop beyond the pink-painted bar by the baker's. Webb asked the salesgirl if Catherine was working today.

'No, she's away just now.' She was small and thin and young, freckles smattering her face.

'Any idea when she'll be back? I've got a parcel to deliver for her.'

'Och, she'll no' be back for a while yet, another week at least. Gone away for a holiday wi' her bairn.'

'Has she?'

'Aye. Listen, if ye want to, ye could drop yon parcel off wi' us. Or better still, put it in wi' the bins.'

'Bins?'

'Aye. Yon door, down one from hers. That's what folk do if she's out.'

'Thank you,' Webb said. 'Thank you very much.'

# 12

They sat in the bar and drank single malt whisky. Webb told McCulloch it was to guard against the cold later. 'Sure it is,' McCulloch muttered as he knocked back a third and chased it with a pint of 80 Shilling. 'Here's to the cold.' They had conducted a brief recce and found that the dustbins were located in a small concrete shed that bordered the broken cobbles of the pavement. Three of them, one for each flat, along with three disused coal cellars. They were clearly marked and Catherine Morgan's bin was full.

'Away for two weeks,' Webb said. 'Be interesting to see the state of her bank account. They can't pay much for part-time in that shop.'

McCulloch glanced at him in the mirror. 'You want to get a locksmith up here?' he said.

Webb swilled whisky round the inside of his mouth. 'Let's see what's in the bins first, Macca. Then we can decide.'

They went back after midnight, when the last bar had closed and the activity of the local police had dulled to the odd Land-Rover patrol. McCulloch drove up Bourtree Terrace, dropped Webb off and turned the car round. Webb slipped into the shed and flicked on his pencil-light torch. He checked each bin for the number, crudely painted in blue emulsion, then he took the two well-tied plastic liners from Catherine Morgan's dustbin. McCulloch flipped open the boot on the hire car and he dropped them inside. They drove through the town and crossed the bridge over the river, then headed down past the high school before turning into the park. Here, they had excellent all-round visibility and would be able to spot anyone approaching from some distance away. Webb took the first bin bag from the boot and slipped on a pair of rubber gloves. He sat in the back seat while McCulloch sat in the front, holding open a second plastic sack, the same type as the ones from the dustbin. Piece by piece, Webb shifted the rubbish from one bag to the next. He found the usual sorts of stuff: old tins, milk cartons and plastic bottles, scrapings of food, which stank out the inside of the car. In the front, McCulloch wrinkled his nose in the torch light.

'Hertz are going to wonder what the fuck we've been doing,' he said.

'Old police fetish. Rubbish-lined plastic.' Webb sifted through the remaining contents then screwed up the bag and placed it in the one that McCulloch was holding. McCulloch tied the top and Webb fetched the second one.

They went through the same process, Webb's expert eye looking for something that would tell him what she had been doing – letters or notes maybe, something scribbled on the back of an envelope, food packets out of the ordinary, something that perhaps she ought not to be able to afford. He sifted and sifted and the bag in McCulloch's hands became heavier. Then Webb pulled out a rolled-up holiday brochure of farmhouses in France. He looked through the torch light at McCulloch, then laid the brochure on the seat beside him. He dug deeper and came up with some sort of timetable. Turning it over in his hands, he shone the pencil-light torch again. 'Ferries, Macca,' he said. 'Car ferries from Portsmouth.'

Swann went to the offices of the National Criminal Intelligence Service at Spring Gardens, for a meeting with Sergeant Williams – prematurely grey, and from the Vale of Glamorgan. They knew each other from skiing trips they ran for disabled RUC officers, who had been maimed or paralysed by gunfire or bombs in Northern Ireland. Williams was ex-SO19, having done a five-year stint with the armed response vehicles before joining NCIS. Swann had not seen him for over a year.

They shook hands and Williams offered Swann a seat across the desk from him.

'How's things up at SO13?'

'Right now? Up to our necks in it.'

'Storm Crow's rapid exit.' Williams drew his brows together. 'Should've had a full team on him, Jack. No question about it.'

'I agree. But the SEG took tactical advice and decided against it. They determined no specific threat.' He chewed his lip. 'Having said that, I'm not sure the outcome would've been any different if they'd had SFO back-up. The team that hit them were in and out in about two minutes. So far, twenty-one people are dead and we've collected over five hundred shell casings.'

'Jesus Christ.' Williams sat back in his chair. 'You know what'll happen now, Jack.'

'What's that?'

'The old "arm the police" call will go up again.'

Swann moved his shoulders. 'They were all armed, Ray!'

They sat in silence for a few minutes, then Williams said: 'I suppose Boese's long gone.'

'We think so. So far he's been sighted in Germany, Chile and South Africa. All at the same time.'

'Usual story, then. Interpol are on it, though?'

'For what it's worth. Boese's got more disguises and more passports than you could shake a stick at.' Swann clasped his hands together on the desk. 'We've got a body, though, Ray. Dead. One of their team, he was hit by a car on his motorbike.'

'Any ID?'

Swann shook his head. 'Not obviously. But he's got his blood group tattooed on his ankle.'

'Soldier.'

'That's what we thought. We should be able to ID him from his fingerprints. The military will keep a record.'

Williams nodded.

'One thing about him,' Swann went on. 'He could really handle a motorbike. The four/two that followed him said he was stonking along like Max Biaggi.'

'What're you thinking?'

'There had to be other bikes involved. We think they may've escaped along the towpath running from Hanwell village.'

'Biker gang?'

'Could be, couldn't it.'

Williams stood up then. 'Wait here a minute, Jack, would you.'

Swann sat and looked across the open-plan office – detectives and civilians and spooks from Box, all working hand in hand, trying to place and establish patterns of activity on nominals all over the country. He recognized one of the men from Special Branch, who was permanently seconded on terrorism.

Williams came back with a file in one hand and a video cassette in the other. He sat down and passed over the file, blue and curling now at the edges. 'Funnily enough, we've been gathering a bit of intel' on a relatively new bike gang, or at least new to us.' He looked keenly at Swann. 'We heard that they were burying one of their dead up in Newcastle last year, so I got an SB contact to run a surveillance video as they crossed the Tyne Bridge.' He paused and tapped the cassette case. 'No helmets. They always like to take them off for the funeral run.'

'So you got their faces?'

'We did. The SB contact has a mate at the BBC. They ran the film as a news piece, so the quality is good. He passed the tape to SB who passed it to me.' He handed it to Swann. 'Yours to borrow, Jack. I need it back for the library.'

'Who's the gang?' Swann asked, as he picked up the black plastic box.

'That's the really interesting bit, given what you've just told me. They call themselves The Regiment.'

'Regiment?'

'Yeah. They rarely wear their colours, but when they do, the insignia is a death's head between two crossed M16 rifles. We haven't ID'd them all by any means, but the ones we have are ex-soldiers.'

Swann stared at him.

'The leader is a man called David Collier. He spent three years with 22 SAS.'

'Hence, The Regiment.'

'Exactly.'

Swann opened the file. 'This what you've got on them so far?'

Williams nodded. 'I'll get you a copy done.' He gestured to a girl sitting in the typing pool behind his desk. She took the file and brought back a copy for Swann. 'That, you can keep,' Williams said. 'The video I need to get back.'

Swann sat at his desk and read the file in its entirety. The Regiment, according to the intelligence gatherers at NCIS, had been formed three years previously by David 'Dog Soldier' Collier, thirty-three years old, and a former badged member of 22 SAS. He had served for long periods in Ulster and went behind enemy lines during the Gulf War. He had left the army in 1995 and travelled for over a year, spending a considerable amount of time in the United States, Chicago and Texas, particularly. According to his file, he had always ridden a motorcycle, but had never affiliated himself to any club or gang. NCIS believed that while he was in the States he made contact with two notorious biker gangs. One was The Outlaws, who had upwards of forty chapters worldwide, and whose dubious motto was 'God forgives, Outlaws don't'. They had done battle with Hell's Angels all over the world for control of drugs and criminal empires. The other gang he contacted was The Bandido Nation in Texas; again, a worldwide group who were known to run drugs and operate other criminal activities. Bandidos and Outlaws had signed a non-aggression pact in 1980 and referred to themselves as sister organizations. NCIS knew that they had affiliated groups in England.

When he got back to the UK, Collier attended meetings (as a probationer) held by the Midland Outlaws, even though he lived in London. But he soon left them. Many of his former friends were leaving the army, and by 1996, he was forming his own motorcycle gang who were affiliated to no one. They bought a four-bedroomed, end-of-terrace house in Hounslow, West London, and fortified it as their clubhouse. Swann studied the surveillance photographs which clearly indicated the CCTV cameras that Collier had set up against intruders. Only three members lived full-time in the clubhouse, one of whom was Collier; but forty others were dotted round the country, covering most of the major cities. They operated much the same rules as other clubs, but they were very much an MG – motorcycle gang rather than a club. Their bikes had to be 750cc or over, strictly British or American. The gang members who did not live in London had to phone the clubhouse at least twice a week and attend meetings or events twice a month.

The surveillance photos were few and far between – a couple of long-lensed shots of two members leaving the clubhouse, but apart from that there was very little. NCIS pointed out that The Regiment operated antisurveillance measures as a matter of course, came out of the clubhouse in twos, and checked the vicinity scrupulously for observation points. They rode their bikes in pairs, with an obvious 'third eye' scouting for surveillance. Unlike other gangs, they were not believed to be involved in drug-running, but were thought to be dealing in stolen motorbikes. Two import/export companies had been registered with Companies House, one of which had a subsidiary in Petersburg, Virginia. Swann looked at the single picture they had taken of Collier: a slim, wiry man, with dark, short hair and hard grey eyes. He was coming out of a house wearing Levis and a regular biker's jacket. No colours, no earrings and no obvious tattoos.

Christine Harris was in the Special Branch cell when he took the videotape to the senior officers' room, where they had a television and video. Swann liked her; she had been their liaison with the sixteenth floor for the past six months and he knew she would've liked a more active role. Swann had often told her to transfer downstairs. The problem was, her bosses knew how bright she was and they wanted her in a role where she could strategize long-term operations. Swann showed her what he had got and together they went to view the film. Colson came in while they were watching it. Swann was seated forward in his chair, with his elbows on his knees and knuckles fisted under his chin. 'What've you got, Jack?'

'Biker gang, Guv. The Regim—' Swann broke off. 'Chrissie, rewind that,' he said. She picked up the remote control handset and wound the tape back. 'Stop.' Swann pointed at the screen. 'Forward again.' She moved on and a biker came into view – no helmet, short-cut hair, with a neat black beard. 'Freeze it.' Swann got up from his seat, and, bending, he studied the image on the screen. 'That's our dead soldier,' he said.

Webb listened to all Harris had to tell him, then met McCulloch in the bar. 'SB,' he said as he put the phone back in his pocket. 'Our bird's got bugger-all money. She gets about two pounds fifty an hour from the Spar, plus her income support, child benefit and single parent benefit. The father is absent and the CSA have no record of him. She gets a rent allowance and her council tax is paid in full by social security.' He arched his eyebrows. 'She's skint, Macca. No money at all.'

Swann briefed everybody working on Operation Crow's Flight, as the Boese break-out had been dubbed, including Webb and McCulloch when they got back to the Yard. Colson had decided that they had enough on Catherine Morgan to ask her some searching questions when she got back from wherever she was, without making a covert entry into her house. Webb had been assured by her workplace that she would return by the end of the following week. If she didn't, they could break in then. Swann passed on all the information that he had gathered from NCIS. The technical support unit had broken the video down into stills, so they were able to check out, at least visually, each face that crossed the bridge. Five members of the troop crossing the Tyne had been identified as ex-soldiers by NCIS, each from a different regiment.

'Their clubhouse is in Hounslow,' Swann told his colleagues. 'Gives them good communications for the M4.' He paused, letting his sentence hang in the air. 'NCIS have gathered quite a bit of intelligence on them and some of it has been looked at by SB. They don't appear to have any major UK affiliations, but nobody rumbles with them. The Midland Outlaws have been known to associate with two

199

Regiment members in Birmingham. NCIS also believe that a delegation from both the Texas and French Bandidos have visited Collier here in London.'

'What's their form?' Webb asked. 'Drugs?'

Swann shook his head. 'No. Legitimately, they bring in US import motorbikes, as well as greys from Japan and Italy. NCIS reckon they are heavily involved with stealing bikes as well, and supplying over in Europe. Bikes are nicked and probably sold pseudo-legally through their legitimate firms.' He broke off then and his face sharpened. 'They are, however, ex-soldiers. Collier was 22 SAS. Nobody can prove anything and the intel' is scant, but it's rumoured among biking circles that if you want a contract carried out, you pick up the phone to The Regiment.'

Colson cleared his throat. 'It's possible that this gang performed the hit on the SEG,' he said. 'The attack was planned and executed with military precision. The escape on motorbikes tells a story. So far, we've recovered three powerful machines, all of them ringers, the index numbers don't match the engines. The underwater search unit has recovered two more from the canal down by the Southall recreation ground. They've also recovered two full-face crash helmets, which are down in Lambeth right now, being swabbed for hair samples.'

McCulloch looked doubtful. 'They won't get any, surely.'

'They will,' Webb cut in on him. 'Hair sticks to the inside of crash helmets, Macca. The water won't shift it.'

'DNA,' Tania Briggs put in.

'When we've got something to match it with, yes.'

Later, Swann and Webb had a drink in Los Remos, well away from the Yard, with Roberto lining up *tapas* and San Miguels for them. 'The biker gang'll be a bastard to look at, Webby,' Swann was saying. 'They've got CCTV set up and they operate a third eye every time they're out.'

Webb nodded, and stabbed at a piece of garlic potato with a cocktail stick. 'There's ways and means for everything, Jack.' He looked sideways at him then. 'You did bloody well.'

'No.' Swann shook his head. 'NCIS did well. Right result that was, getting a video of them all.'

Webb chewed potato. 'Bikers like to show respect when they bury their dead,' he said. 'No doubt they phoned the Newcastle Old Bill and told them they'd be doing it.'

They bought more beer and sat at a table. 'How you doing, anyway?' Webb asked him.

'I'm all right.'

'Missing the kids?'

'Course I am. Flat's so fucking empty without them.'

'There's no way Rachael will let you have them back again?'

Swann lit a cigarette, inhaling sharply, and shook his head. 'No chance. Her life's on the rails again, isn't it. Besides, I'm never home. I can't remember the last time I didn't pull any overtime.' He drained his glass and caught a glimpse of himself in the mirror. His face looked old and empty. He looked away. 'I still think about Pia. With Boese getting out, I think about her even more.'

'She was more of a victim than anything else,' Webb said gently. 'She *was* genuine, Jack. Anyone could see that.'

'You think so?'

'Yes, I do. So does Caroline.' Webb touched him lightly on the shoulder. 'Anyway, it's history now, mate. Time to move on.'

'Yeah, I know. I need to.' Swann sucked on his cigarette and crushed the butt in the glass ashtray on the bar.

Webb and McCulloch went through Catherine Morgan's bank account with a fine toothcomb. They contacted the special secure unit to speak to her brother Brynn, but he refused to talk to them. Swann went back to NCIS with the photographic stills and the file. He sat with Ray Williams and the NCIS Special Branch liaison, and began to track the handful of members they had started to profile. One week had passed since Ismael Boese had been broken out of prison, and later that morning, Swann heard that the twenty-second victim of the shooting had died; after clinging to her eighteen-year-old life for a week.

'Bike gang members never speak to the police,' Williams told him. 'It's part of their code, goes for all of them, right across the board – Angels, Outlaws, Bandidos, Cycle Tramps, Satan's Slaves, the lot. They never ever give statements. There's been a few successful infiltrations, one from SO10 in Manchester and one good one in the States: an FBI agent named Tait joined the Angels' chapter in Anchorage, Alaska, of all places.'

'What about this firm?' Swann asked him.

Williams made a face. 'Doubtful. We've got no source there at the moment, though SB have looked. They're too new and Collier's an old hand. He's done plenty of UC work himself. Box 850 used him for at least one deniable operation in South America, the year after he came out of the army.'

'Where'd you find that out?'

'DEA Intelligence in El Paso, Texas. It's highly possible they still use him from time to time.'

'I don't care if he's a full-time spook,' Swann said. 'If we can pin this on him, I'm going to cut his legs from under him.'

Williams regarded him thoughtfully for a moment or two. 'I hear the feather you lot received was addressed to you,' he said quietly.

'How the hell d'you know about that?' Swann looked

sharply at him. 'We haven't even released the fact that we got one.'

Williams tapped the side of his nose. 'This is NCIS, remember.'

Swann relaxed and again looked at the file. 'Who's the girl?' he asked. 'This Janice Martin?'

Williams placed both hands behind his head. 'Gorgeous, isn't she.'

She was, with blonde hair that shone like gold, even in the photo, and a classically carved face with full, almost pouting lips. 'That picture's from her modelling days, before she started to hang around with the gang. We think she was Gringo's old lady for a while.' He sat forward. 'His steady girlfriend. Property, if you like.'

'Who's Gringo?'

Williams tapped the stills from the video: a biker with longer hair than the rest, riding directly behind Collier on a chopped Harley Davidson. 'George Beresford, Gringo,' Williams said. 'He lived in a flat with Janice for a while, then moved back to the clubhouse. She still lives in the flat. We think she's just a mamma now, but she's the daughter of a pretty wealthy antiques dealer from Norfolk. They use her on their trips to the States now and then, to courier over paperwork and other stuff. She can come across as very upmarket English.' He scraped at his cheekbone with a fingernail. 'Trouble is she has a major cocaine habit, which they don't like at all.' He cocked his head to one side. 'If they have a weak link, it's her.'

Again Swann looked at her picture. 'She's certainly a babe,' he said. 'What's a mamma exactly?'

Williams made a face. 'I once heard a mamma described as someone who has to "pull the train"; in other words, sleeps with any gang member, at any time of his choosing. No doubt, she's fucked the lot of them.'

Swann stared at him for a long quiet moment. He was

thinking about the hairs that Lambeth had found in the crash helmets.

Tal-Salem smoked a Turkish cigarette and drank his third cup of coffee in the Internet Café in central London. He logged on and waited, and smoked and waited, and then tapped into the system. Carefully, he scrolled the bulletin boards, first the FBI web site, and then, checking the address in his notebook, he dialled into 'Alt. Constitution-alist', the main US militia web site. He waited, then worked his way through the pages until he found what he hoped he would. The FBI had alluded to it in general terms in their own recent bulletins. He sat back and looked at the picture, which was grainy, in black and white, but the man's features could just about be made out. 'This man is dangerous and a traitor to the United States constitution,' the inscription read. 'Free Americans beware, Special Agent John Dollar worked undercover for two years in Idaho. Because of him Jakob Salvesen is in custody await-ing federal trial, on trumped-up federal charges. Guard against such FBI/ATF activity occurring in your territory. Remember Randy Weaver.' Tal-Salem printed the page, complete with the picture, and folded the sheet in his wallet. Then he logged off and went back to his hotel room.

Ismael Boese lay in bed in an old farmhouse in the Dordogne, listening to the rain rattle the corrugated metal of the roof. The boy, Ieuan, who lived in Scotland, was asleep in the next room. Beside Boese, Catherine slept soundly, lying on her back, her face framed in the light from the window and her white breasts rising and falling with each breath. Red hair was spread on the pillow. He tried to remember the last time he had slept with a woman but could not. He had not intended to sleep with her, but there she was and the desire was in him, so he did. Carefully, he eased the blankets down her belly to her thighs, revealing the mound of thick red pubic hair which was not shaved at the bikini line, as with other women he had known. This intrigued him. Magda, a Romanian he had been with for a while in the early days with the Jackal, did not shave her armpits, and her pubic hair, though black, was thick and curling and across her inner thighs, like this one. Lightly, he brushed his index finger through the coarseness and tasted it. She stirred but did not wake, and he straightened the blankets again before slipping out of the bed.

In the kitchen, he sat at the big wooden table and took the Gyurza apart. Next to the pieces, he laid his leather wallet and from it took the selection of diplomatic passports that Tal-Salem had given him. There was a Chilean one, one from Mexico, one from Venezuela, and the prize – one from the United States. All bore different names, but the same photograph, his own. He could move about the world as often as he liked. Along with the Gyurza he had been given a PSS silenced pistol, which he considered using now. There would be no sound and the distance was not an issue. He took it from his jacket pocket and considered its merits. The Poles were good and they had Abu Nidal to thank for the guns. He would buy him alcohol the next time he saw him. Abu Nidal liked alcohol. The PSS was nicknamed the Vul, and he had used the type before, favouring the special SP-4 round for the six-shot box clip. It could penetrate two millimetres of steel at a distance of twenty-five metres and still inflict a fatal wound. He slipped the clip out now, checked each round, holding the shells in his palm, before re-inserting them and snapping the clip into place.

He stood at the door to the boy's room, with the gun held loosely in his right hand, arm dangling at his side.

The boy stirred, snuffled and rolled on to his side. Boese walked silently across the wooden floor in his bare feet and looked down at him – red hair like his mother and the same gathering of freckles across his nose. Boese glanced at the gun in his hand. Even his mother would not hear the shot. But then he paused and looked again and for a moment saw himself and heard his parents talking in the sitting room. He could not make out the words, but he listened, and that was the only memory he had of them. They were imprisoned for ever when he was thirteen. He should have more memories, but he didn't. Idealistic fools, the pair of them. Again he looked at the boy, and lightly brushed the muzzle of the gun through his hair, letting it rest against his exposed temple. For a long moment he stood like that, then he paused, cocked his head to one side and considered. She would go home. They would check Griffiths's assessment book. They may have done that much already. He considered for a moment longer and then smiled.

Turning silently on his heel, he left the boy's bedroom and went back to the kitchen. He dressed quietly and stepped out into the rain, with both the pistols stuck in his belt. It was a two-mile hike along the narrow country lane to the telephone kiosk and the rain fell in steel rods on his shoulders. He barely noticed it, watching the grey-black of the sky and the way it shadowed itself against the horizon.

At the phonebox, he fumbled in damp pockets for change, then dialled the code and number he had memorized on the ferry. 'Room 313, please.'

There was a pause, then a voice said. 'This is the night porter. It's three o'clock in the morning.'

Boese gripped the receiver more tightly. 'I shall ask you again. Room 313, please.' He heard a sigh, then a series of clicks, then the repetition of a soft ringing tone in his ear.

The phone was answered. 'Yes?'

'It's raining.'

'Is it?'

'Yes. Did you cast the net?'

'One dollar. John.'

'The watcher in the hills?'

'The same.'

'Then I'll ask in the hills.'

Boese replaced the receiver and stood for a few moments in the kiosk, watching the tufted grass at the kerbside being kicked into waves by the wind.

# 13

The oiled and muddy water of the Mississippi River slapped against the broken stones that sloped down the bank from the wooden walkway. On a bench, two aging bikers sat drinking Lite beer from plastic cups. One of them, bandanna wrapped about his head, strummed a six-string guitar, half of the third finger missing from his fret hand. His voice was gravelled and he sang the blues for anyone passing who would drop a dollar or two in the box at his feet. Boese gazed across the three currents of the river, which kicked the surface into waves, then clashed in a flurry of surf. One week previously, all he could see were the bars on the windows of his cell and the wire roof of the exercise yard. Now he watched the tanker labour round the bend, sending out a wake which rattled the wooden boards at his feet. He watched for a long time, observing the length and breadth of the vessel, low in the water, still weighed down with its cargo of crude oil. He had considered some of the more noxious chemicals that he knew were carried up and down the delta, but this would suit his purpose.

Behind him, the blues singer's voice lifted in a final crackle and the music subsided. Boese turned and the singer grinned at him, bright blue eyes and white teeth. 'Need a cigarette for my voice,' he said, and took a pack of Basic 100s from his shirt pocket, then snapped open his lighter. Boese dropped two dollars into the box and walked down the stone steps and across the railroad tracks and then up past the iron cannons of Washington Artillery Park.

Sunday, and below him, three black acrobats were entertaining the crowds massed along the steps. One of them was telling people not to stand on the sidewalk, but to sit down or the cops would stop the show. Boese ignored them, ignored the crowds, and gazed across Decatur Street, beyond the artists and fortune-tellers and people posing as statues in Jackson Square Park. A black-haired man lit a cigarette. He was standing in the doorway of the cathedral, a white stone building with twin slate spires lifting against the cloud-strewn New Orleans skyline.

Boese hesitated for a moment, looking east and west along Decatur, then he moved through the crowds seated and standing on the steps, and crossed in front of a mule-driven wagon, in which a group of Japanese tourists were being shown the sights. A skin-headed girl flapped a set of tarot cards at him as he crossed the park, but he ignored her, eyes intent on the black-haired man, still smoking his cigarette in the cathedral doorway. It had been hot and sunny earlier in the day, but now the clouds massed like smoke-seared stone and the wind lifted the branches of the trees. A storm was blowing in from the Gulf of Mexico.

The black-haired man caught his eye as he crossed the square. Boese had been careful, told him on the phone to expect a fellow Mexican, wearing a short black jacket and white shirt. He wore the jacket, but his shirt was blue. The man looked him over once, flipped away his cigarette and let smoke drift from his nostrils. Boese moved past him, close enough to smell his aftershave, and stepped into the cathedral. Candles were lit in glass bowls to his right, and a woman dipped her fingers in holy water. A sign told visitors they were not allowed in the main church area without a guide, and Boese paused. The man still stood behind him, watching the square. Boese nodded and smiled to the lady crossing herself with the holy water, then turned, and as he walked out, he spoke to the man without looking at him. 'The ticket,' he said, holding out his hand.

For a moment, the man hesitated but still Boese did not look at him. Then he fumbled in his pocket and dropped a parking-lot ticket in Boese's palm.

The car was a blue Buick and was parked on the raised platform in the Park and Lock on Camp Street. Boese handed the ticket to the attendant, who selected a set of keys from the hooks hanging in his kiosk and went to lower the ramp. He came back with the car; Boese paid him and got behind the wheel.

It was dark when he left New Orleans, taking Interstate 10 west towards Baton Rouge, but only as far as 310. Here, he left the freeway and headed south-west along the raised concrete carriageways which ran over the swamplands. He drove leisurely, one hand on the wheel, in no particular hurry, heading towards the river and St Charles Parish. He pulled off 310 before the bridge that spanned the river, and watched the red tail-lights of the sheriff's deputy as he rattled past. He slowed at the bottom of the slip road and glanced at the signs for the Destrehan Plantation to his left, before pulling right on to the river road. Now he was trundling past huge, well-lit, southern mansions that had long since been turned into hotels; darkened, perfectly manicured lawns stretching to the lip of the road. They were followed by smaller wooden dwellings and then gas stations, the odd diner and the first tentacular pipework of the refineries. He drove for five miles or so, passing the chemical companies and oil companies, with their fat metal pipelines stretching over the road to the levee, where they fed oil or waste or whatever into the tankers moored in the river.

Finally, the road petered out, then swung right from the levee and arced round to the Bonnet Carre Spillway, a mile and a half of wooden-slatted dam. Twin cranes were perched at this end, ready to lift each individual piece of planking out and let the river water run off to Lake

Pontchartrain, if spring floods threatened the height of the levee. He knew the Army Corps of Engineers looked after the spillway, but there were none there now, though their building stood squat and flat on the raised section of open ground that lifted to the right of the levee. Boese drove on to the dirt road that led all the way to the waterline and pulled over. The spillway was on his right now. He sat for a while with the engine off, his lights dulled to nothing, and looked beyond the levee to where three tankers were moored in the middle of the river. Six hundred yards from the shore, fully visible from here, with no raised riverbank to block the view. Far in the distance, he could make out the lights of Waterford 3 nuclear power facility.

Lights behind him suddenly lit up the river road and he swung the Buick round, turning left and driving beyond the spillway itself, where the road ran right across the belly of the valley. Sometimes water seeped, as it had done now, with the ice-melt from further up the delta raising the height of the river. It was silver and black in the moonlight, like dull patches of mercury. Boese stopped the car on the blindside of the spillway and went round to the trunk. Inside, he found the weapons and the night-vision glasses he had requested. Quickly he climbed back, up past the army engineer's building, and on to the wooden spillway, hidden in the lee of the first crane. The lights he had seen were from a taxi van and he could hear it now, lumbering along the river road. He watched its steady approach, then his attention was diverted to the lights that showed on the side of the tanker.

The cab pulled up on to the stretch of unmade road and stopped. Boese crouched with the night-vision glasses to his eyes and watched. For a while nothing happened and he wondered if his information was correct. Then he heard the faint chug-chug of an outboard engine and he shifted his line of vision to the water. A launch, lit at the front,

211

was cutting a path towards the shore. At the same time, the side door of the taxi van was slid back and Boese heard women's voices. He looked to the van once again and saw the black cab driver helping the whores down one by one. They teetered in their high-heeled shoes on the loose stones, and slipped purses over their shoulders, tugging at the hemlines of skirts that barely reached their stocking tops. The engine from the launch grew louder and the cab driver was looking nervously back along the river road for any sign of a sheriff's deputy.

Boese stayed where he was until the boat hit shore and he witnessed two crewmen help the whores on board. He saw money change hands between one of the crewmen and the cab driver, and then the boat headed back towards the tanker. Boese lowered his glasses. The first weighted drops of rain began to spatter against his skull.

Harrison and Penny drove away from their meeting with Rene Martinez, who was much chagrined by his current predicament. They had put it to him straight, for the second time now – the good-guy/bad-guy routine. Harrison with his lean arms folded across his faded denim shirt and his hair hanging loose, with his Tunnel Rat stare set deep in his eyes. Penny playing the clean-cut FBI agent, but with the same steel in his voice.

'You got two choices, Rene.' Penny made an open-handed gesture. 'Either you set up a meeting with Manx, or you go to the farm for the rest of your life. It's really very simple.'

Harrison thought about it now, riding in Penny's car, with one arm resting on the open window ledge, back through the projects north of Rampart Street. Black women and children were still selling ice cream and candy through their open windows, though darkness had fallen, and, with it, the threat of a storm.

212

'Do a lotta that down here, don't they,' Harrison said.

Penny looked where Harrison looked and grunted. 'Had a probationer I was training one time,' he said. 'He figured they were doing crack deals right there in the open.' He laughed to himself. 'You never make a rapid entry through a back door in the projects, Harrison. You'll find a fucking great freezer stacked up against it.'

Harrison scratched the hairs on his leg, where they itched above the ankle holster. His snub-nosed .38 fitted snugly inside his boot. 'Put me down on North Rampart and I'll walk,' he said. 'We'll pick up on Martinez again tomorrow.'

Penny let him out on the sidewalk, gunned the oversized engine and roared back towards Highway 10 and his home out in Kenner. His wife had been away for a few days and he had to get the house cleaned up. The trouble was he always needed an incentive to clean the house and he had a six-pack of cold Guinness on the back seat. Harrison knew he'd be loaded by the time his wife got home. Clean one room – have a beer, clean another – have a beer.

Harrison watched his car swing right and then he stuck his hands into the pockets of his jeans and started walking. The rain grew stiffer, falling straight down, though the wind howled through the narrow streets of the French Quarter. Two black guys eyed him from a doorway on the far side of the street. Harrison met their eyes and they looked away. He thought about going straight home, but he knew that once there, the loneliness that he never admitted to would creep up on him; so what was the point. Bourbon Street was beginning to think about Mardi Gras and the tourists would be out in force. But on the other hand, Maria might be playing in the Jazz Café tonight. Not that it did him any good – except maybe to look at her. He needed to avoid women in the quarter, especially after getting his butt chewed off over Lisa Guffy. Getting a woman in Idaho had not been part of the UCA deal, and he knew he could've been fired if the suits at the zoo had not had Tom Kovalski to deal with. Once again, he had realized how useful it was having such an influential ally at headquarters.

He walked the length of Conti and paused on the corner of Bourbon. He thought about it for a minute or two, then headed on down to Decatur and made a left on to Frenchman. The sign in the window of the Apple Barrel glinted appealingly. It was early yet and Joey wouldn't have any women lying on the bar doing belly-button shots. Joey must've seen him, because a cold bottle of Miller was waiting for him on the chipped wood of the counter.

'Hey, Harrison, what's happening, bro?'

'Hey, Joe.' Harrison slid on to a stool and picked up the bottle of beer, cool under the sweat of his palm. 'Storm's gonna blow like a trumpet player tonight.'

'Sure looks that way.'

The only other drinker was Tom, the English jazz promoter, who was waiting, as usual, for his hamburger from across the street. It was a local bar, used by local people and well away from the tourists. Harrison had not taken long to find it. Nobody knew what he did. Nobody ever knew what he did. He was looking forward to getting off the drugs squad and on to the SOG, so maybe he could one day tell them. He had avoided the bust that 10 Squad had made on Café Brazil down the street.

He sucked on the beer, and thought about a Jack Daniel's, but decided against it. Instead, he plucked a Merit from his top pocket and Joey lit it for him. 'How come you smoke two brands of cigarette, Harrison?'

Harrison looked sideways at him. 'Got hooked on the menthol in Vietnam. Cooled my hashish throat.'

'Right on.' Joey smiled. 'You couldn't quite quit on the Marlboro, though, huh?'

214

'Guess I'll always be a cowboy at heart.'

Harrison shook the rain from his shoulders and ordered a bowl of soup, silently chastising himself for the quality of his meal habits. Sometimes he went till dinnertime without eating. The door opened behind him, rain washing in for a moment, before it was closed again. He looked over his shoulder and saw a small-boned Mexican standing there. A Buick was parked outside that had not been there when he came in. The Mexican looked at him, then at Tom, and sat down on a stool. The waiter clattered down the wooden staircase and placed the bowl of soup in front of Harrison. ⸻ ⸻ved the Mexican with a beer which he sat and nursed quietly, looking at the array of different countries' banknotes pasted on the wall behind the bar. Harrison looked sideways at him, then concentra⸻d on his soup.

Boese considered Harrison, seated now only two stools along from him. He had only remained in France for three days, then he had flown to Idaho. There were many Mexicans in Idaho. He had not been there very long; just long enough to sit in the diner in a town called Westlake and ask about the FBI man who'd been undercover there for two years. The talk was cheap and easy. It didn't take long before one of the girls told him about another girl who'd been involved with the FBI man. Together they had gone north, then south to New Orleans, which was where he'd been posted. There, the girl had left him, perhaps there were too many lies between them.

Harrison pushed away his soup plate, finished his beer and took another from Joey. He glanced at the Mexican. 'Wild night out there, huh.'

'*Si*.' The Mexican looked at him. He had thick black hair and a drooping moustache. 'Sticky.' He held up his bottle. 'Need you cold beer.'

'You betcha.'

The Mexican nodded and smiled and Harrison looked

215

away. He yawned, glanced at his watch and thought about the Sweet Sensation Band and Maria's black eyes in the Jazz Café. He shook the beer bottle at Joe. 'Put this in a "to go" cup for me, will you, bro?'

'You got it.'

Joe dispensed the beer and Harrison slid off his stool. 'Later, Joey.' He stepped out into the rain.

Boese could see him seated on a stool in the Jazz Café, with a beer bottle in his hand, watching the black girl singer in the band. Lust in his eyes. Boese smiled thinly – another tourist among the thousands that thronged Bourbon Street at night. He lifted his camera, sighted, zoomed in on Harrison's face and pressed the shutter. Harrison saw the flash from the corner of his eyes, blinked and looked up. He saw no one on the street he recognized.

It took the army a week to come up with the identity of the dead biker from the fingerprints supplied to them by the Antiterrorist Branch. His name was John Stanley and he had served with the Scots Guards. His family were informed and they travelled from their home in Manchester to see the body. It would be a while before it was released for burial. Swann and Webb spoke to them at their hotel. They had no idea that their son had been involved with a motorcycle gang, let alone anything like what had happened at Hanwell Green.

'Rough on them,' Swann said, as they drove back through a wintry London to Scotland Yard. Hyde Park Corner was choked with traffic and they sat amid the fumes, engines idling all round them.

'Especially the mother.' Webb sighed and smoothed a hand through his hair. 'It's always worse for the mother.' He looked sideways at Swann. 'Mothers will love their sons, no matter what. They may be the worst kind of bastard walking, their mothers may not even like them, but they always, always love them.'

Swann lifted one eyebrow. 'Even yours?' he said.

The traffic began to move at a crawl and Swann drummed the steering wheel with the flat of his hand. Webb watched him out of the corner of his eye. 'Colson is talking about re-interviewing Pia, Jack.'

Swann suddenly went cold. For a moment he did not say anything. The traffic had eased and they were heading ~~down Grosvenor Place with Buckingham~~ Palace Gardens on their left.

'Makes sense,' Webb continued. 'Maybe there's things she hasn't told us yet.'

'Like what?' Swann stared through the windscreen.

'Like anything.' Webb breathed out audibly. 'We're back to square one, Jack. Nothing can be discounted.'

'I suppose.' Swann pulled on to Victoria Street and sped up. 'Who's going to see her?'

'Not been decided yet.'

'Tell the old man I want to do it.'

Back in the squad room, he sat at his desk and thought about a night in Scotland when he had poured out his heart to Pia, told her the innermost fears in his soul, how he had tried to climb Nanga Parbat in the Himalayas and ended up cutting the rope that held himself and his partner together. His partner fell to his death. That dark night was with him now as he sat in the squad room, with the afternoon fading outside. He could hear the others, the hubbub of the office, phones ringing, keys tapping on computers; but in his mind he was still out there in the storm, with the rope freezing and the snow falling, and above him the unsteady lurch of the ice screw, pulling itself free from the wall.

He opened his eyes, not realizing he had closed them, and he was aware of the stickiness on his brow. Getting up, he went out to the toilets and washed his face in cold water. Bill Colson came in behind him.

'You OK, Jack?'

'Yeah. Sure.' Swann stood up quickly and flapped his hands to dry them.

Colson washed his own hands and regarded him, almost like a father would his son. 'You sure?'

'I'm fine.'

'You look a bit pale, that's all.'

'Tired, Guv. We're all tired.'

'Tell me about it.' Colson poured a plastic cup of drinking water from the tap at the far sink and swallowed it down.

Swann waited for him to finish. 'Webb told me you're thinking of re-interviewing Brigitte Hammani.'

Colson looked squarely at him. 'That's right.'

'It makes sense,' Swann said. 'She's a lead. Maybe Boese told her something that might give us a clue about this biker gang.'

'Or the Poles, perhaps.'

'If they're connected.' Swann leaned against the sink. 'From what Box told us, the Poles are more than capable of carrying out a hit like that. Why use somebody else?'

'The informant.'

'Possibly. It could be unrelated, though.'

Colson tilted his head slightly higher. 'Is this leading somewhere, Jack?'

'Yes, sir. I want to interview Hammani.'

For a long moment Colson was quiet, then he said: 'I'm not sure that's such a good idea.'

'I want to do it, sir.' Swann held his gaze evenly, arms folded across his chest.

'I'll think about it.' Colson turned and the door swung closed behind him.

*

Pia looked tired, pale and drawn; a darkness crawling beneath her eyes that Swann had never seen before. Colson had not agreed to let him see her on his own. Webb was with him, the three of them in the police interview room at Holloway Prison for women, in North London. Pia – Brigitte Hammani – was still on remand. Swann was choked. His anger still burned from time to time, but he had loved this woman, had even asked her to marry him, and he was shocked by her appearance. All at once he was

moment and leaned over the desk.

'How you doing?' he asked.

Pia looked from him to Swann, looked in Swann's eyes until he looked away, then sat back in the seat. 'I'm doing all right.' Her voice was softer, broken almost.

Swann looked up at her. 'You look like shit,' he said.

She half smiled. 'What did you expect, Jack? I can't afford make-up.'

Webb cleared his throat. 'You know about Boese, obviously.'

'Of course. Everybody knows about Boese.' She looked at Swann again. 'How're you, Jack? How're the kids?'

'They're living with Rachael again.'

'Oh. I'm sorry.'

Swann shrugged. 'They're better off with her. You know I'm never home.'

'Pia,' Webb said. 'Brigitte. Shit.' He sat back and suddenly smiled. 'This is difficult for all of us, right.'

'Right.'

'We need to know about Boese.'

'I've told you everything there is, George. I confessed. Remember?'

Webb glanced at Swann. 'I know. But is there anything else you can think of. He clearly intended to get caught. He always knew he could get out. All he had to do was let

219

someone know the time he'd be in transit between the prison and the Bailey. He must've set it up way in advance. Is there anything else you can think of that he might have said?'

Pia passed a hand through her spiked black hair and shook her head again. 'George, you're talking about Storm Crow. He was the nastiest, most thorough person I ever had the misfortune to come across. He didn't say anything to me that was not relevant to me. Nothing. Not one time in nearly ten years.'

'Absolutely nothing?'

'I'd remember. I would've included it in my confession. We made contact. He told me what to do. He provided the money. And I did it.' She lifted the flat of her hands. 'That's it. There is no more.'

Swann and Webb both looked at her then, weak and small and suddenly terribly vulnerable. Swann wanted to say something, something that would encourage her, something that would ease the ache inside him. But there was nothing he could say.

'This is very hard,' she said quietly. 'I've told you all that I know.' She looked at Swann then. 'I've seen you, Jack. I'm glad.' She scraped back her chair and stood up. 'I'd like to go back to my cell now.'


Boese got out of the cab in the loading zone of the Mobil Oil building and walked up to the main entance. On his left, an escalator carried people up to a mezzanine floor. Other people in business suits milled here and there, making their way to their correct floor or back to the Amoco building. Boese took the escalator and then waited for the elevator which only stopped at the twenty-second floor, the FBI field office. The doors opened soundlessly before him. No one inside. He pressed the button and the elevator began to rise. He stood and looked at the metal of the doors, at the envelope between his palms, and then the doors slid back and he saw blue paint and twin leather couches and the FBI shield on the wall. A receptionist looked up and smiled at him from behind her glass partition. Boese returned her smile, then very deliberately stared into the face of the CCTV camera mounted above the door. He handed the receptionist the envelope. 'Some papers,' he said. 'For Special Agent Dollar.'

'Thank you.'

He walked back into the lift.

Harrison parked his car on the seventh level and made sure the chain lock was secure on the trunk. He sucked the last out of his cigarette and ground the spent tobacco under his heel before walking to the elevator. Penny was already at his desk, on the phone. A tin of snuff was upended on the desk, and he was rolling it back and forth like a wheel. From the tones of the conversation, Harrison could gather that he was talking to the dicks downtown about another group of crank dealers they were looking at. Harrison scratched his head and sat down, and his gaze then fixed on the slim, brown envelope on his desk. He looked at it – delivered by hand for his attention. Taking his pocket knife from his jeans, he sliced open one end and looked inside. Spider's legs crawled on his spine.

He took the stairs to the twenty-second floor and the ASAC's office. Charlie Mayer, the special agent in charge, was talking to Fitzpatrick, as he knocked on the door. Both his bosses together.

'What is it, John?' Fitzpatrick asked him.

'I think we got a problem, boss.'

'We do?'

'Yeah.' Harrison tipped the envelope up and the contents dropped on to the desk. 'This was delivered by hand for me this morning.'

Fitzpatrick and Mayer both stared at the items on the desk: a photograph of Harrison with a bullet hole in his head, and a single, black crow's feather.

For a moment none of them spoke, then Harrison looked again at the picture. He was sitting on a stool in the Jazz Café, watching the band playing. He tried to place when it was, then remembered the other night, the flashbulb going off on the street. When he had looked up, no one was there. He had dismissed it; flashbulbs went off on Bourbon Street all the time.

'Delivered by hand?' Mayer said.

'This morning.'

Mayer looked at Fitzpatrick. 'Get the videotape out of the security camera, Kirk. Let's see what we got.'

They took the tape into the conference room and set it up in the huge, flat-screened TV. Harrison sat in one of the high-backed blue chairs with the FBI logo embossed in gold on them, and looked again at the picture on the table before him. One of the evidence response team had been over it for prints and any fibres, and it and the feather were sealed now in separate plastic bags. They rewound the videotape, then played it through and slowed it when a man came into reception. Nobody spoke. The man turned his face deliberately to the camera – short dark hair, dark skin, wearing a two-piece business suit. Fitzpatrick moved in his seat. 'Charlie, I think we better get on to head-quarters,' he said. 'I wouldn't swear to it, but my guts tell me that is Ismael Boese.'

Harrison was still staring at the screen, Boese's black eyes on his. Unnerving; even with his experience. 'Johnny.' Mayer laid a hand on his arm and indicated the feather and photograph. 'You've just become a member of a very elite club. The only other guy in the States to get a set of those is Lucky Louis Byrne.'

Harrison didn't hear him. He thought back over the past

222

day or so. That picture had been taken the night before last. He had been with Penny in the projects and then he had walked in the rain. The Apple Barrel, then Bourbon Street long enough to piss himself off in the Jazz Café. The Apple Barrel – the little Mexican man at the bar. Fitzpatrick had frozen the image and Harrison stared again at those eyes. 'There was a Mexican in the Apple Barrel the other night,' he said quietly. 'Came in out of the rain. Might've been driving a blue Buick.'

'You think that was Boese?'

'Coulda been.' Harrison tapped the photograph with a fingernail. 'This was taken about an hour later.' Getting up, he walked to the window and looked out over the business district. He could see the crescent of the river in the distance; the day was clear, with the February sun beginning to burn in the sky. Looking down at the streets, he thought about Mardi Gras, almost upon them. Already the bleachers were being set up, green and gold and purple on the streets below him. They would run all the way along St Charles Avenue. Mardi Gras, and the Storm Crow in the city.

Louis Byrne was having lunch with his wife in the Old Ebbitt Grill, just around the corner from her office on New York Avenue. He looked across the table at her, statuesque and serious as she always was. He'd hate to face her across a courtroom. 'So, how'd it go this morning?'

'I'll get him off.'

'He's an embezzler, Angie.'

She looked coldly at him, ignoring the playful light in his eyes. 'No, he's not, Louis. He's a wronged corporate executive. I'm his attorney and I'll get him off.' She picked at the caesar salad, then laid the fork down and swallowed her carbonated mineral water. 'Shall I cook tonight?'

'Will you be home in time?' Byrne said.

'Seven-thirty, I guess.'

'I'll cook.'

'Whatever.' She folded her hands in her lap.

Byrne's pager sounded on his belt and he unclipped it. 'Gotta call the office,' he said. He went outside to make the call, the restaurant disallowing the use of cellphones on the premises. Angie watched him go, his cropped hairline and straight back, and she smiled. Outside, Byrne spoke to the SIOC.

'This is Byrne,' he said.

'New Orleans field office are trying to locate you, sir.'

'OK. Patch me through.' Byrne waited, looked at his watch, then through the restaurant window. Angie was in conversation with a couple of lawyers at the next table. New Orleans answered.

'SAC please.'

'One moment.'

A pause and a click, then, 'Mayer.'

'Charlie. Louis Byrne.'

'Hey, Louis. What's up?'

'You're looking for me.'

'Yeah. We might have a situation going on down here.'

Byrne stood very still, listening to what Mayer was telling him, no longer aware of the traffic noise. He stared at the agents guarding the White House.

'We thought you'd want to know pretty quickly, Louis,' Mayer finished.

'I'll be down on the first available flight.' Byrne switched off the phone and placed it back in his pocket. The wind flapped at his jacket and all at once he shivered. The sky was growing overcast, with clouds rolling in from the west. He went back inside the restaurant and sat down.

Angie stared at the sudden chill in his face. 'What is it?' she asked.

'We gotta cancel dinner.'

224

Back at headquarters, he took the elevator from his office on the fifth floor to the eleventh floor and the Domestic Terrorism Section. Like his own, this part of the building was a SCIF, secret compartmented information facility, and the windows that looked out over 10th Street were permanently blinded, the walls specially concreted to interfere with any covertly planted listening device. He walked through the array of sectioned desks and saw Tom Kovalski on the phone in his office. Kovalski had just been promoted, now deputy section chief. Byrne tapped lightly on his open door and Kovalski beckoned for him to come in. He sat and waited as Kovalski put down the phone, his eyes resting on the booklet-sized copy of the constitution that lay on the desk. Kovalski never let anyone forget that the FBI was set up to protect the constitution, particularly when he was dealing with the ever-growing problem of the militia.

'Goddammit,' he said. 'You know the bomb in St Louis?'

Byrne nodded.

'Local PD gave us a skunked licence plate and now the fucking ATF are sniffing around.' He shook his head. 'What is it with those guys? They're so fucking desperate to stay in existence, they break all the goddamn rules. They poke their noses into another agency's jurisdiction, and now they're trying to muscle in on my turf.'

'Bombs, Tom.'

'Right. But, Louis, terrorism is an FBI problem. The chosen weapon of the terrorist just happens to be the bomb. The ATF can butt the fuck out.' He ran his fingers through his hair. 'Sorry,' he said. 'Shooting off at the mouth. What d'you wanna see me about?'

Byrne looked deep in his eyes. 'The Storm Crow just showed up in New Orleans.'

# 14

Jack Swann rested his head against the seat back, as the aircraft wobbled violently again. Next to him, the elderly lady gripped the twin armrests with hands that boned white at the knuckle. Swann looked out of the window at the bruise-coloured thunder heads, and the turbulence hit them again, dropping the plane so much that his stomach was left in his chest. The pilot came on the intercom once more and assured them that they would be landing in a few minutes and the storm was nothing to worry about. Swann glanced at his seating companion and saw the disbelief etched in her eyes. He looked again through the window, and the land appeared below the mist, grey and black, trees here and there, and the crisscrossing intersections of roads. He could barely make out the traffic, as the plane banked high, the wing dipping almost vertically. The Yard had had a call from the FBI terrorism team telling them what had happened in New Orleans. Swann had been on late turn that day, and was at Regent's Park Zoo with the kids, when George Webb phoned him. He had dropped the children home, much to Charley's dismay, then he had scuttled into the Yard. There would be an SO13 liaison and he was determined to be part of it.

As it turned out, he was *it* in its entirety. He thought there would be two of them, as there normally was for overseas stuff, but they were up to their necks in London, with Operation Flight and the other things that were happening. He had called Cheyenne Logan, who told him that a team from Washington had already been dispatched to New Orleans. Swann had got the first flight he could. Now they were trying to land at Dulles Airport in this storm. Logan should be waiting for him and he had a little tingle in his stomach when he thought about her. They would collect his luggage, then ride to the National Airport and fly on to New Orleans. He sat there now, with the panic-stricken woman next to him, as the pilot brought them in low, the rain lashing against the window.

Logan was waiting for him as he came through customs. He spotted her immediately, jet black hair, ebony skin and a red two-piece suit. She smiled widely at him, lips parted, showing the brilliant flash of her teeth.

'Hi, Jack. How you doing?' She kissed him lightly on the cheek and he could smell her perfume, rich in his nostrils. She took his small briefcase from him with long-fingered hands, and guided him outside.

The rain beat against the earth with a vengeance. Fortunately, her car was parked in the lot directly across from the main terminal building, but his hair was still plastered to his scalp when they got there. He stowed his luggage next to hers in the trunk and then they left Dulles for the National Airport.

'We coulda flown from here, but the connection's better at National,' she told him. 'It's only about forty-five minutes' drive. This evening we'll be in New Orleans, honey.'

Swann shook the rain from his clothes and settled into the passenger-seat as they headed towards Washington D.C. on Highway 261. The rain battered the windshield and the wipers were clicking back and forth at maximum speed. Spray hissed from passing vehicles, making the wipers work that much harder. Swann shivered and Logan turned the heating up higher.

'Bad flight?' she asked. 'Was it like this all the way?'

'Just when we got here.'

'I know. It's been steel-rod raining for days. Cold too.

Still, the weather's so messed up these days, it could be eighty in the shade tomorrow.'

Swann smiled to himself. A long time since he had ridden in a car with a woman. He glanced at her as she drove, skirt riding up her thighs as she worked the brake and accelerator pedals: he could hear the faint rustle of her stockings. Her legs were long and black and shapely, her face strong. He had noticed her before, of course, when they worked together the previous year, but then he had been blissfully ensconced with Pia.

Maybe Logan perceived his thoughts because she suddenly looked sideways at him and smiled. 'So, how've you been, Jack?'

'I've been OK,' he said. 'We've been busy since Boese escaped.'

'I bet you have, baby.'

'I still can't quite believe it,' he said. 'Twenty-two people killed. It was an outrage, Chey. A total fucking outrage.' He shifted round then and laid his arm across the back of her seat. 'Tell me what happened down in New Orleans.'

She told him again as they drove, about how Harrison had received the feather and the photograph with the bullet hole in his head. Swann recalled the day when he had received the same package, and how he had carried a sidearm for weeks afterwards. 'That was the day before yesterday?' he asked.

'February 16th, yes.'

'And you've heard nothing since?'

'Zilch, hon. Silence. Everyone's on high alert down there. But we've heard or seen nothing of him since.'

They got to the National Airport and parked the car before checking in their bags. Swann had been given one week initially by SO13, and was booked to fly back directly from New Orleans. They ate a meal in the airport restaurant, sitting across from one another, making small talk. Logan told him that she was originally from Alabama; her father had been a working man, two jobs to put herself and her brothers through college. She was the youngest of four, and two of her three brothers were cops in Birmingham. Her third brother, the youngest apart from her, was living in New Orleans, and she hoped to see him while they were down there. Unlike the rest of them, he had avoided law enforcement and worked with the Kingsley House project as a social worker.

Harrison sat in the conference room with Mayer, Fitzpatrick, Byrne and Kovalski. Initially, the terrorism people had restricted their liaison to just those two, technically Byrne's remit rather than Kovalski's, because, as yet, Boese had committed no crime on US soil. Kovalski had come down too, though, as a link with Jakob Salvesen and his now-disbanded group of followers could not be discounted. Byrne was speaking and Harrison stared at him across the table. They had never met in person. Lucky Louis Byrne, the apple of the Director's eye. Tall and slim, still under forty, and the most famous special agent since Joe Pistone. Byrne had ridden the promotion train without pissing off the suits at the zoo. He was a fast tracker, a 'blue flame' promotion boy, but still had the respect of the hump agents out on the street. He had done his share in the field, before this Storm Crow thing had blown up. Yet there was something about him that got under Harrison's skin. Maybe it was the fact that he was a GS15 at thirty-nine and his wife one of the top defence attorneys in D.C., earning upwards of a million dollars. Harrison had heard through the grapevine that they lived in a million-dollar home in old town Alexandria, and were invited to some of the White House parties. Angie Byrne's law firm represented the President.

'Mexican?' Byrne was saying to him.

Harrison studied his face and nodded. 'I think so. Same size, same build. He just came outta the rain on Frenchman Street and bought a beer in the Apple Barrel.'

'Did he say anything to you?'

'Just about the rain and shit.'

Byrne glanced at Kovalski and then at Mayer and Fitzpatrick. 'It's certainly his style,' he said. His jacket was over the back of his seat and his sleeves were pushed up, revealing Caribbean-tanned forearms. 'Mexican is easy for him. Half-caste skin, short-cut hair. He's used it many times. Fort Bliss, we think. Certainly in London last year.'

Mayer sat forward. 'What I want to know is, what's he doing here in New Orleans. Mardi Gras is less than a week away. This city's gonna be bursting at the seams with tourists.'

Byrne breathed out heavily, his closely shaven jaw flecked with red dots of concentration. He lifted his shoulders. 'I wish I knew. We've got the Scotland Yard liaison flying in this evening,' he went on. 'Maybe he can tell us more.'

'Just the one of them?' Fitzpatrick said.

'Yes. Detective Sergeant Swann. He knows the case better than anyone else over there.'

Harrison sat very still, his hands held loosely together on the tabletop in front of him.The conversation dulled into the breaking of blood at his temple. Suddenly, he was back in Jake Salvesen's courtroom, when the militia passed their death sentence on him. He saw again the red madness in Salvesen's eyes, the cold stare of Jesse Tate, the former Green Beret; and then he was underground, crawling for all he was worth, with the gunfire booming behind him.

'He's flying in with Logan,' Kovalski said. 'Can somebody meet them from the airport?'

Harrison thinned his eyes. 'I'll do it,' he said.

Downstairs in the squad room, he sat with Penny and John Earl Cochrane, spat tobacco juice into an empty Coke can, and told them about Swann flying in from London. 'I don't want this guy knowing that I know about him,' he said. His voice was low and his eyes hard. 'Tell the other guys who know about it to keep their traps shut, will you, Matt. I don't want any fucker letting this guy know I got his marker.'

‾ [illegible] in the cool of the evening, outside the lower baggage claim section of New Orleans Airport, with the roadway raised above their heads and the line of airport shuttle buses getting shorter. 'Where're we staying, Chey?' Swann asked her.

'The French Quarter, a hotel Tom Kovalski always uses. The Bureau likes us in the Hilton or the Holiday Inn, but New Orleans is New Orleans and you can walk to the Mobil Oil building in less than twenty minutes from the quarter.'

A car drew up then, a big grey Ford which bumped against the kerb. Swann looked at the driver as he got out – not very tall, with a tanned and beaten face, grey hair tied in a ponytail dangling from under his faded baseball hat. He stared first at Logan, then at Swann and his eyes were cold as steel. 'You Logan?' he said, glancing back at her.

'Yes.'

'Harrison,' he said and picked up her bag. He looked at Swann then. 'You gotta be the limey.'

Swann smiled and offered his hand. 'You the Harrison that was undercover in Idaho?'

Harrison looked him deep in the eyes and nodded.

'Good to meet you.'

Harrison squeezed his hand tightly. 'Likewise, duchess. Likewise.'

231

Harrison opened the trunk of the car and moved his MP5 and pump-action shotgun to one side, together with his SWAT body armour and gear belt. 'Not much room in the back,' he said. 'I got more shit stowed on the back seat, so y'all have to shift up.'

Swann climbed in the back and Logan got in the front. Harrison got behind the wheel, rolled the window down and pinched a cigarette from his shirt pocket. He pressed the lighter button on the dashboard and accelerated away from the kerb. 'Where ya staying?' he asked. 'Hilton?'

'Hotel Provincial,' Logan told him.

Harrison squinted at her. 'Down there on Chartres? Right on.'

He drove them in on Highway 10, then pulled off by the Superdome and headed down Poydras, before cutting across Camp to Canal Street and finally along Chartres. Swann had never seen anything like it: the town was lit up in the darkness, with raised concrete carriageways and buildings scraping the skyline, great wide roads and honking cars. Then all of a sudden the buildings receded and the streets narrowed, and he could have been in some French port at the turn of the century. The hotel was in classic Napoleonic-style and there was even a picture of the old emperor in the lobby. They checked in and Harrison parked his car in the lot, telling the bellboy that he would leave it there till the morning.

'You live here?' Swann asked him.

'Burgundy and Toulouse.' Harrison placed a fingerful of chew under his lip. 'Don't go up there at night.'

'Why not?'

'Because this is New Orleans, duchess. Someone'll have your kidneys.'

The receptionist smiled at them across the counter. 'You're from England?' he said.

Swann nodded.

'He's right. Stay on Bourbon or below. Stay with the crowds. There's nothing but residential places up there, nothing for you to see. New Orleans is a great city,' he said. 'But it's like anywhere else, there's places you don't go at night.'

Swann eased the breath from his cheeks. 'You ever been to London?' he said.

They met up with Byrne and Kovalski, and ate dinner at Irene's on the corner of St Philip, reputedly the best restaurant in the French Quarter. Swann liked Kovalski immediately; an easy-faced man in his mid-forties who, despite his senior position, seemed to have lost none of his street sense. Kovalski told him that he had been a helicopter pilot with the 82nd Airborne Division and, after that, briefly a lawyer, before joining the FBI in 1981.

Harrison lit a Marlboro after the meal and told them a bit about New Orleans, mentioning, amongst other things, the fact that the law in Louisiana was different from the rest of the United States. All the other states based their statutes on English common law, whereas Louisiana had its legal roots in the Napoleonic Code.

'Has Boese shown up since the feather?' Swann asked him. He could sense something in the man, some hint of hostility, but he ignored it.

'Nope.'

'But you recognize him as this Mexican?'

'Maybe. I wouldn't put my life on the line for it, but I figure it makes sense.'

'Boese's hard to recognize.' Swann looked at Byrne as he said it. 'He walked right past me once, in the middle of London.'

'I'll bet he did,' Harrison said, with no hint of a smile in his face.

After dinner, Byrne and Kovalski had things to do, and Logan was going to telephone her brother. Harrison told

233

Swann to take a walk up Bourbon Street, and have a look at the titty bars. 'You not coming?' Swann asked him.

'I live here, bubba. I got other places to go.'

'Whatever.' Swann stuffed his hands in his pockets and headed for the door.

Harrison scratched one unshaven cheek. 'Good place to grab a beer is the Café Lafayette in Exile,' he said. 'You'll enjoy it in there.'

'Thanks.' Swann opened the door and walked up St Philip.

'Dumb limey fuck,' Harrison muttered, and headed for Frenchman Street.

Swann got to Royal, and then another block and he was on Bourbon Street – the name that was known all over the world. Jean Lafitte's bar was across the street, dimly lit, all but dark inside. He thought of the shadows and he thought of Boese and he headed left on Bourbon. The street was narrow, with two- or three-storeyed buildings on either side. One-way traffic, and further up, the road was cordoned off with bollards, for pedestrians only. Here the crowds swelled; one week to Mardi Gras and already the people were in party mood. Jazz music and Cajun music rebounded from open bar doorways, electric guitars and violins.

Swann saw the bar that Harrison had mentioned. Men crowded the doorways and looked at him strangely as he went inside. And then the darkness opened up and he saw the bald-headed bartender swinging his arms over his head to the music. Swann was crowded, jostled against the bar, and as he looked around his worst fears were confirmed, not a woman in the place and all eyes on him. The bartender was right in his face now, all smiles and gold teeth, and he had no option but to order a beer. Mercifully, it was poured in a 'to go' plastic cup. Swann paid his two dollars and felt someone run fingers over his buttocks.

234

'Just got into town?'

He looked round to find a sandy-haired man in a leather jacket standing behind him.

'That's right.' Swann thought of Harrison and wondered what kind of joke this actually was, good-humoured or cruel. Again he looked at his questioner. 'I'm a cop,' he said quietly.

'Right on.' The man faltered, then looked beyond him, saw somebody he knew and excused himself. S~~~~ ~~~~ on a stool to drink his beer.

The following morning he met Logan in the lobby and they drove over to 1250 Poydras Street in Harrison's car. He parked in the underground car park and led them upstairs in the freight elevator. 'Suspect transportation,' he explained.

'D'you have cells up here?' Swann asked as the elevator opened on the twenty-first floor.

'No. Only interview rooms.' Harrison led the way to the stairs and the next floor up.

Byrne and Kovalski were already in the conference room. Byrne was on the telephone and Kovalski was working at documents laid out on the table before him.

'I'll get the bosses,' Harrison said, and went in search of Mayer and Fitzpatrick.

When they were all gathered, Mayer briefed them on the situation. 'Ismael Boese has to be considered public enemy number one,' he said. 'So far, we've notified no one about what's happened here, except FBI personnel and you guys in London.' He glanced at Swann. 'That was a considered decision. I guess you could argue that we should've informed the precinct houses in the city at least, but until we know why he's announced himself to us like this, there's little point.' He paused and sighed. 'Mardi Gras's next week and we do not want panic running through the

235

city.' He looked squarely at Swann again. 'He's capable of almost anything, apparently.'

'He certainly is,' Swann said.

Byrne then gave them a full run-down on Storm Crow, his activities logged to date. He mentioned everything from the first recorded incident in Israel in 1989 to Benjamin Dubin's assertion that he was a protégé of Ilyich Ramirez Sanchez, a.k.a. Carlos the Jackal. He broke off for a moment and looked at Swann. 'A couple of your boys visited with him again, didn't they, Jack?'

'Carlos? They did, but Boese's name didn't come up.'

'OK.' Byrne rolled up his sleeves. 'That's his history. I'm with Dubin on the Jackal theory. Boese was definitely part of the "Friends of Carlos" in 1982. It's where he learned to master his trade. Our problem is – why has he shown up in New Orleans? But before we can answer that, we need to know the details of how he got here.' He asked Swann to fill the gathering in on what had happened in London.

Swann stood up and exchanged cool glances with Harrison. Nothing had been said this morning, except the usual pleasantries. Harrison sat a little further down the table from him and Swann could see his gun poking out of the slim-fitting holster in the top of his boot. He told them what had happened, fully briefing them on what Ismael Boese had done in the UK the previous year: how they had discovered him in what looked like an IRA bombing in Soho, and then the investigation which had led them to a house in the west of the city. After that there was the death of an American militia sympathizer, called Bruno Kuhlmann, in Northumberland, and finally the abortive chemical attack in the City of London itself. Here, Swann paused and exchanged a smile with Logan. Harrison caught the look and glanced at her himself.

'We arrested him on the M1 motorway,' Swann

explained finally. 'He was making a mobile telephone call and we took him out with a firearms team. We believe that his arrest was at his own instigation. He had every opportunity to get away; he had access to a number of different passports, many of them diplomatic. He's a master of disguise.' He looked directly at Harrison now. 'He makes a good Mexican, for instance. In London, he was a Greek Orthodox priest, a South American businessman, etc. etc. He didn't get away when he could have ... ... ... evacuation of London, for example. Instead, he hung around till everything died down and returned to a long-term storage car park, and a vehicle he would've known we'd track. There never was any chemical in the device in London, but enough panic was created to evacuate huge areas. When he was in custody, he set another ball rolling when he telephoned his lawyer. The next thing we knew, the Rome incident happened. That killed two hundred and eighty people, and the streets round St Peter's Square are unlikely to be the same again.' He sat down before he continued. 'Boese allowed himself to get arrested, because he knew beyond any doubt that he would get out. What happened in West London with the special escort group was planned a long time ago.'

'Any ideas who might be behind that?' Logan asked.

'A few.' Swann smiled at her. 'The point is, Boese knew he would do a little remand time, but that on one of the occasions he was transferred to court for a hearing he would be broken out. He doesn't care how many people he kills, we know that from Rome. The Hanwell Green shooting was a continuous burst of suppression fire from four different shooters, while others cut through the truck. We recovered in excess of five hundred cartridge casings; Russian most of them, some 9-millimetre, some 7.62, and we think the guns were Vikhrs. They used a 50-calibre machine gun to get rid of the escort helicopter.'

'So why show up here?' Fitzpatrick asked him.

'I don't know.' Swann looked across at Kovalski. 'Militia?'

'It's possible.'

'The chap you had in Idaho?'

Harrison moved his shoulders, shifting the chew in his mouth. He held an empty Coke can in one hand and spat a trail of tobacco juice into it. 'Salvesen's one powerful motherfucker,' he said quietly. 'He's still got friends on the fringes of Congress. If he wanted to do something from the inside, it wouldn't be difficult.'

'Boese *will* be planning something,' Byrne stated flatly. 'That we can count on. Mardi Gras.' He sucked breath, then turned to Kovalski. 'Tom, we could go public on him now. Smear his face across every newspaper, get him on *America's Most Wanted*. See if John Walsh will devote a programme to him.'

'You mean, put the pressure on right from the get-go.'

'It's worked with others before.'

Swann was shaking his head. 'I know I've got no jurisdiction here,' he said. 'But I don't think that's a good idea. Boese walked in here and gave a feather to him.' He poked a finger at Harrison. 'He did the same at Scotland Yard. Tell the other law-enforcement agencies by all means, but going public won't achieve anything. He'll have his plans and no amount of publicity will change them.'

For a little while they sat in silence. Harrison sucked tobacco juice and watched Swann from half-closed eyes. What he had just said made sense. It was also his own opinion. Swann looked across the table at him and Harrison looked back. Logan shifted in her seat. Her legs were sticking to the fabric of the chair. Louisiana was much hotter than D.C. and she had removed her stockings. Swann sat next to her, trying not to look at the shine of her skin. He noticed the colour was lighter at the knees and elbows, and at the joints in her fingers: it gave her skin the impression of glowing.

'Jack's right, Louis,' she said. 'I think the policy the SAC's adopted so far has gotta be the best one.' They all looked at her, the only black face in the room, and a female black face at that. Logan had told Swann already, she would have her work cut out down here, even with some of her fellow agents.

Byrne sat back and folded his arms. '... thinking of Mardi Gras,' he said quietly.

Mayer glanced from him to Swann and then back again. 'I think we should sit on it for a few days at least, see if we can come up with anything. He's been sighted in the quarter, so we should let the Vieux Carre Precinct in on it. Give them his picture and put it to them as an "unknown subject" at the moment. We could do that with the rest of the city and the parishes too.'

Kovalski rubbed a palm over his chin. 'I guess we might luck out,' he said.

Logan was given desk space in the squad room. The white-collar crime squad were in the process of relocating, so a number of desks were spare. Swann attached himself to her and Harrison went back to his drug-squad deals with Matt Penny. Byrne occupied part of the SAC's office upstairs, and Kovalski had to fly back to D.C. Logan would remain as the representative from domestic terrorism.

Harrison sat at his own desk, with his foot resting against the leg of Penny's chair, and watched Jack Swann. He watched the way Swann looked at Logan. She was pretty, really pretty, reminding him of Maria, the object of his own lustful desires in the quarter. He could already see the chemistry between Swann and Logan. In their own way, they were both outsiders down here. Swann must have felt the intensity of his stare because he suddenly looked up from his conversation and met Harrison's eyes across the

239

squad room. Cochrane walked up behind Harrison and laid a hand on his shoulder. Harrison looked up at him.

'That the English guy?'

'Yep.' Harrison spat tobacco juice into his empty Coke can and set it on the desk.

'You said anything to him?'

'Nope.'

'You gonna?'

'When I'm good and ready, John Earl. When I'm good and ready.'

Boese sat in the Buick, watching the cab driver start his van. It was a green Ford, quite recent, with the name of the cab company emblazoned on the side. Next to Boese sat the girl with cropped blue-black hair, the butt of a Vikhr submachine gun sticking out of the canvas bag at her feet. That bag also contained a second Vikhr and various pistols and spare clips. Behind them sat two black-eyed Puerto Ricans, each with a similar bag across his lap. Boese glanced at their silent faces in the rearview mirror and shifted his position in the seat. God help any traffic cop who pulled them over.

Ahead, the cab driver pulled away from the kerb and threaded a path through the projects, north of the French Quarter. A girl on this corner, another on that, very young, all of them black or Hispanic. They wore short skirts and only a bra or bikini-type top. Legs up to their armpits. He collected six of them, before heading west out of the city.

He left 310 at the river road and Destrehan Plantation sign. The Buick pulled ahead of him, and passed a St Charles Parish sheriff's cruiser coming the other way at the lights. Boese watched as it pulled on to 310 to cross the bridge for Hahnville, then he gunned the Buick forward and headed north-west, the levee on his left, taking the river road for the spillway.

Fifteen minutes later, the Buick was parked in the seeping puddles of water on the eastern side of the spillway, out of sight of the road and the river. Boese lifted the hood and tied a white handkerchief to the strut that held it up, and then the four of them, each carrying a black canvas bag, made their way on foot round the lip of the spillway. No sound came from their rubber-soled boots. They passed the US Army Corps of Engineers' building and stared across at the tanker settled high in the river. Cloud had blown in from the south and it massed above their heads. There was no moon, no stars, and the smell of rain and cypress trees hung in the air. On the waste ground, which ran beyond the levee to the water's edge, they halted. Boese listened, looking back over the lights of the petrochemical plants towards the road. Headlights washed in the distance. He glanced to his right, where the grey shadow seemed to squat, a silent hulk in the water. The bows were high; the superstructure, a tower block against the waterline. The cargo of crude oil had been unloaded and the fresh cargo of refined would not be loaded until tomorrow. No cargo, but a threat was a threat, and it was the location that suited him most. Far in the northern distance, the lights of Waterford 3 speckled the skyline.

They melted into the massed rubble and brush grass that topped the levee, as the van bumped off the tarmac on to the metalled part of the road. It ambled down to the waterline, with no headlights showing. The driver had clearly done this many times before. Boese moved first. Already he could hear the mosquito-like hum from the outboard motor, as the crew member from the tanker negotiated the six hundred yards of black river to get to them. He could hear the cackled laughter of the coke whores as they waited, with the first mists of rain beginning to sprinkle them from the clouds. Boese felt the sudden damp on his skin. He looked to each side of him, at the black-eyed Puerto Ricans and the girl with blue-black hair. They moved as one, silently, all holding weapons. The boat was nudging the gravel at the edge of the river. Boese waited till the crewman was ashore, then he stepped forward and turned on the flashlight he carried. The Kalashnikov was slung by its strap and aimed at the crewman's belly. 'Good evening, ladies and gentlemen,' he said. 'My name is Ismael Boese. You may know me better as Storm Crow.'

Frans Thyssen, captain of the oil tanker *Rotterdam*, stared down the barrel of Boese's gun. They stood on the bridge: Boese and one of the Puerto Ricans, the girl with the blue-black hair, seventeen crew members and six whores. The cab driver lay with his face in the rank, oiled water, hidden from view by the levee. The second Puerto Rican was placing magnetic signs over those of the cab company on the sides of the van. Boese smiled at the captain. They had not had to round up the rest of the crew, as he thought at first they might, because they were all gathered at the side of the ship, eager to assist the ladies of the night on board. Only the captain and first mate had remained on the bridge.

'A little crowded, isn't it.' Boese thinned his eyes and moved the barrel of his gun slowly over the frightened faces before him. 'Now,' he said. 'Like all good shows, I need a volunteer. Nationalities, please.' He aimed at the cook, clearly an Oriental. 'You first,' he said. One by one he went through them. Dutch and Indonesian. No Americans. His gun barrel came to rest on a stout little man in his fifties, with a well-spoken British accent.

'Englishman,' Boese said. 'What do you do here?'

The man was red-faced, his long thin nose broken up with blue veins.

'I'm the engineer,' he said.

'Good.' Boese crooked his index finger at him. 'Come

242

along with me.' The man's face paled then and he seemed unsteady on his feet. Boese nodded to the girl and the Puerto Rican, then he moved the chubby Englishman before him and together they stepped out into the night.

When the girl left him alone, the Puerto Rican made them all sit down. He was vigilant, but easy. He knew there were no weapons on board this vessel, none of the tankers carried any. Their cargoes made the accessibility of firearms a risk the own... ... not prepared to take. The only real danger of piracy was in the South China Sea and many of the larger vessels were now accompanied by a military escort through the more notorious waters. He watched the captain's eyes for signs of heroics, but saw none.

The girl moved about the ship on the decks below the bridge, and smashed windows, choosing ones with curtains, in particular.

Further down the ship, Boese was laying charges, the wind in his face, the deck slippery now with rain. At the bows, he clipped himself into a sit harness and climbed over the side. Holding his flashlight in his teeth, he checked his watch – a little after two in the morning, five hours before dawn. From the pocket of his jacket he produced twin conically shaped charges, half a pound of Semtex in each. He fashioned them some more, then pressed the pliable material between the links in each anchor chain, and primed them with twin Iraco detonators. He climbed up on to the deck again and laid out the single timing and power unit – a black and grey plastic box with twin screw terminals and a light-emitting diode between them. His trademark, his own perfected creation: two integrated circuits, two transistors and a ten-position decade switch linked to a Spanish clock. Carefully, he set the decade switch to zero, then looked at the electronic digits displayed on the clock.

243

# 15

Harrison and Penny looked across the patio to where Rene Martinez was sitting with the Cuban, Manx. Harrison sucked on a bottle of Miller and wiped the froth from his lips.

'What d'you reckon?' Penny said.

Harrison pursed his lips. 'I reckon it's bullshit.'

Penny looked at his watch. It was almost one-thirty. 'I'm crashing at your place.'

'Whatever.'

Across the patio, Manx was drinking vodka, deep in conversation with Martinez. Every now and again Martinez would glance briefly in their direction, before looking away again. Harrison suddenly yawned. 'I'm outta here,' he said. 'We'll see the little fucker tomorrow.'

They left the bar and walked back up St Peter and across Bourbon, north towards Harrison's apartment. The streets were empty, save the odd stumbling drunk.

'You're making it a mite obvious with Swann,' Penny told him.

'Yeah, well he's in America now. He's all growed up, Matt. He can handle it.'

'He know why you hate him so much?'

'Nope.'

'That Cheyenne seems pretty tight with him.'

'It's the English accent, man. Works every time with American gals.'

They walked up the steps to Harrison's apartment on Burgundy and Toulouse.

'Do I get the bed or the couch?' Penny asked him.

'What do you think?'

Swann ate dinner with Logan in the Café Nu Nus on Decatur Street, down the road from the French Market and across from Governor Nicholls Wharf. Louis Byrne was eating at Charlie Mayer's house.

'So what d'you think of the Big Easy?' Logan asked Swann.

Swann looked through the window to the café across the street, where a single trumpet player was climbing the scales. 'It's nothing like the film. I don't hear too many Cajun accents.'

She smiled. 'The New Orleans accent sounds almost New York, doesn't it. Sorta Italian-sounding. The Cajun people are out in the bayous.'

Swann gazed across the table at her, hair loose and long to her shoulders, a hint of auburn dyed into it. 'You ever been married, Cheyenne?'

She shook her head. 'With my hours, I'm lucky if I keep a steady boyfriend.'

'Domestic Terrorism's getting busier over here, then.'

'Militia types mostly; they're moving away from their religious fundamentalism, Jack. Not so much of the anti-black, anti-Jew rhetoric any more. They know that turns the regular people off them. Most important thing, from our point of view, is that up until now they haven't had any real groundswell of public support. A lot of people were pissed about Randy Weaver and Waco, but not enough to join in. Now these groups direct their focus on us, the federal government agencies, and the government itself. It's getting worse and they're popping up everywhere.'

'So, no steady boyfriend, then?' he said, changing the subject back again.

'Not right now, honey.' She looked at him with slanted

245

eyes, her head slightly to one side. Swann felt the shiver in his loins and he shifted himself in his seat. The waiter came over and they ordered two more bottles of beer.

A little later, her brother, James, arrived, and had a final drink of the night with them. He was a big, heavy-set man, with lights in his eyes and a twinkle to his smile. He told Swann about his work with Kingsley House and the disaffected people of all ages and colours: black, white and Hispanic. He clearly enjoyed his work. He looked a little like Cheyenne, and Swann thought about the family, their two-job father, working all hours to keep them in school; the pleasure he must have got seeing how they turned out. Two cops, a Fed, and this gentle giant, the social worker. That night, Swann sat on the edge of his bed and gazed through the tall uncovered window at the grey snake of the river, spanned by the wrought-iron bridge that crossed to the west shore. Somewhere, a tanker's horn sounded as fog settled against the onyx black of the water. Swann lay back, thought about Logan next door, and fell asleep with his clothes on.

Boese sat in the captain's chair on the bridge of the tanker, holding the ship-to-shore telephone in his hand. The captain sat on the floor before him, trussed like a turkey for Christmas, a gag stuffed in his mouth. Boese considered him a moment longer, then gazed the length of the ship, beyond the oil holds, to where the bows jutted against the gathering dawn. He half closed his eyes and looked again at the captain, shifting the weight of the pistol that protruded from his belt. The rest of the hostages were locked in the television room, two floors below them. He could smell diesel fumes and oil, and, though the bridge was clean enough, he imagined the day-to-day grime and the soiled crew cabins where the coke whores rolled on top of their johns. He went to the starboard window and looked out over the spillway. The van was parked there, freshly signed and waiting. The Buick would be parked a few miles back up the road. He returned to the ship-to-shore and dialled the Coastguard.

'United States Coastguard, New Orleans.' The voice was clipped in his ear.

Boese breathed into the receiver. 'This is the *Rotterdam*. We're moored up at the Bonnet Carre Spillway and we've been hijacked. Th~~~~~~ ~~~ ~~~~~ ~~~~~~~~ ~~ ~~~~~, six of them women.' He hung up, patted the captain on the head and stepped outside the bridge.

From his cellphone he called the TV stations, 4-WWL, 6-WDSU, 8-WVUE, then the radio stations, WWL, WCKW and WADU. He also called CNN in Atlanta, and told them all the same thing: a tanker had been hijacked on the Mississippi River, only a mile from Waterford 3 nuclear power facility.

At dawn, Kirk Fitzpatrick was at his desk, covering the early duty with a handful of agents downstairs. The phone rang on his desk.

'Fitzpatrick.'

'This is the Coastguard. We've just received a ship-to-shore communication from the tanker, *Rotterdam*. They're moored up at the spillway and they claim they've been hijacked.'

Fitzpatrick felt sweat form in the palm of his hand.

'We're stopping the river traffic,' the Coastguard told him, 'and I'm trying to get some of the big tugs on standby.'

'OK. We're on our way.' Fitzpatrick put the phone down, then picked it up again and spoke to Gerry Mackon, the SWAT team leader. 'Gerry,' he said. 'I think our bird just landed.'

*

Penny and Harrison were woken by their pagers at exactly the same time. Harrison sat up straight, sleep in his eyes, hair falling over his face. He grabbed the pager and checked the reader message. *SWAT Roll. Muster – 1250, parking lot.*

'You get that?'

'Yep.' Penny was already pulling on his pants and strapping his ankle holster round his leg. His car was parked downstairs, Harrison's at the office. Within three minutes, they had the light flashing on the dashboard and the siren howling as they tore the wrong way along Burgundy Street. Three minutes after that, they were parked underground at the office, and Harrison was untying the chain on the trunk of his car.

Mackon, the SWAT team leader, was already suited in black coveralls and rubber-soled boots, his body armour in place. FBI SWAT was pasted over his breast pocket, and the New Orleans badge, the laughing Mardi Gras masks, on his arm. Kirk Fitzpatrick was down in the lot, talking to him. The SWAT team was split into two sections – gold and blue. Harrison and Penny formed one of four sniper observer teams, two in each section.

Fitzpatrick disappeared back upstairs, and Mackon gave them their instructions.

'The tanker's up at the spillway,' he said. 'The *Rotterdam*. The Coastguard's making a fly-by now, but get up there as fast as you can. I want "eyes-on" threat assessment at the double.'

The snipers piled into the first panel van, eight black-suited men sitting in the back, screaming up Loyola and then on to the freeway. The carriageway was bathed in early morning sunshine, the concrete road, lifting over the swamp, in brilliant white. The glare bounced off the windshield, and Harrison fished in his pockets for sunglasses and hooked them over his ears. He stared out of

248

the window, feeling the adrenalin beginning to grip him. The swamplands flashed by underneath them, cypress trees dotted every few yards, like a mass of thin and speckled hair. He glanced at Penny, squatting on the bench beside him, MP5 across his knees. Penny shook his head slowly. 'Oh, boys,' he muttered. 'I can feel my spider's senses tingling.'

They left 310 at the Destrehan Plantation sign and headed up the river road. Already, press vans were moving. They passed the 4-WWL van, a mile up the river road.

Harrison shook his head. 'How the fuck do they get here so fast?'

Swann was summoned from his bed by the phone ringing. Logan, in the next room, told him what had happened.

'A tanker?' Swann frowned. 'What does he want with a tanker?'

'Maybe it's not the tanker. Maybe it's where it's moored.'

'Where's that?'

'Bonnet Carre Spillway, about a mile from Waterford 3 nuclear facility.'

'Oh, my God.'

'You're not kidding, Jack. The Wackenhutt boys'll be creaming their pants.'

'Who're the Wackenhutt boys?'

'Private security firm. They guard the nuclear facilities. They're ex-special forces, SWAT-trained, big time.'

They met downstairs and were in a cab to the Mobil Oil building within a few minutes. They jumped out at the front entrance and took the elevator to the twenty-second floor, then walked down one flight of stairs. The squad room was already heaving with agents. Logan told Swann that they would be coming in from all over the southern United States for an emergency like this.

'OK, people, listen up.' Mayer was at the mini-lectern with the 'Fidelity Bravery Integrity' shield underneath it. He tapped the microphone. 'We believe that Ismael Boese, a.k.a. Storm Crow, has taken possession of an oil tanker on the river. It's up at the spillway, which gives us a potential horror story with Waterford 3. Right now, we don't know what the tanker's carrying. We're trying to talk to the owners. SWAT sniper teams should be at the scene about now, so we'll get an initial threat assessment in the next few minutes.' He paused for a moment and bit his lip. 'We're forming a critical incident response group, with the unified command center upstairs in the command post. The tactical operations centers are on their way now, and the mobile command post will roll immediately after this briefing. The ASAC will be "on-scene commander", reporting back to me here. I want a hostage negotiation team on the scene and one more back here. We've got regional SWAT response flying in from Memphis, Jackson, Mobile, Little Rock and Houston. The DOD have given us access to Blackhawk choppers, so they should be on-site within the hour.

'We've notified FEMA, the public health departments, Department of Energy, Transport, and, of course, the Department of Emergency Preparedness in St Charles Parish. The sheriff there will have the perimeters in, but the press seem to be rolling already. We need to know what's in that tanker before we can fully assess the threat to the local population, and hence, who and where to evacuate. I've been in touch with D.C. and the Director's ordered out the Hostage Rescue Team. They should be here within four hours. The National Security Council are on standby, at least until we've determined the threat.

'The media rep's had every damn assignment editor in the country on the phone already, demanding to know what's happening. It seems that some of the TV networks were called up right after the Coastguard. Nice of them to call us ahead of time, huh. On the positive side, they don't seem to know anything about Ismael Boese or the feathers or anything. That's how I wanna keep it for now.'

He paused and turned to Byrne. 'That make sense, Louis, just stick to "unknown subject" for press releases?' Byrne sat with his arms folded, his face grim, and nodded. Mayer continued: 'Louis, I want you, Agent Logan and Jack ᴀ ᴀ ᴀᴀᴀᴀ ᴛᴏ ᴏ ᴡᴀᴀᴀ ᴛᴀᴇ ᴍᴏᴀᴀᴇ ᴄᴏᴍᴍᴀᴀᴀ ᴘᴏᴀᴛ. He looked directly at Swann. 'Is that OK with you? You have specialist knowledge, sir.'

'It's fine with me,' Swann told him.

He followed Logan back to the elevator, and a couple of minutes later, the three of them were clambering into the black Chevrolet Suburban, with the blacked-out windows and a mass of electronic equipment set up in the back. An intelligence analyst was already working as they rolled out of the parking lot and on to Loyola, lights and sirens going.

'This mobile unit connects via computer with the SIOC in Washington,' Logan explained to Swann. 'That's our strategic command post. The command post upstairs will do the same. We've got a programme called Rainbow that kicks in when this sort of thing happens. Everything from now on will be recorded on Rainbow and can be analysed by the guys back at the puzzle palace.'

Boese watched the first FBI van arrive and the SWAT sniper teams begin to deploy amid the rubble and brush grass on the levee. A second group took up a position halfway down the spillway itself. Already the sheriff's cordons were in place, but there were TV vans backed up on the vacant lot parallel to the spillway. Boese smiled to himself and checked the array of mobile telephones he had on the floor in front of him. He would use each one at random. He knew they might be using their Triggerfish

251

system, trying to get an exact fix on the electronic serial numbers that were flashed up into the airwaves. But he had done his homework, and there would be so many signals going up at once, with all the world's media gathered, it would be almost impossible. As an added precaution, however, the cellphones were digital and had been procured in Mexico.

Harrison was out of the van at a crouch, fully suited now, respirator in place, ballistic helmet on, and the weight of twenty-four layers of Kevlar plus a ceramic breastplate pulling his crouched run even closer to the ground. He moved in front; the Kevlar body bunker before him, MP5 carbine gripped in his free hand. His Sig-Sauer handgun was attached to his gear belt, along with extra clips, handcuffs and a series of flashbangs. Behind him, protected by him, Penny had his rifle in the drag-bag, like a heavy black tail between his legs, attached to a karabiner on his gear loop. He also carried his MP5. The second sniper observer team was being deployed on the spillway, and a third were heading for the west bank of the river.

Harrison moved forward along the gravel road, out of sight of the three tankers that were lying at anchor in a line up the river, a hundred yards between them. The levee sloped to their left, where water seeped from the river this side of the spillway. The press were gathering in force on the raised section of ground, just before the army engineers' building. Already TV cameras were up and helicopters could be heard, buzzing like so many flies. Harrison hoped to God that the Department of Transport had implemented their no-fly zone. He moved again, into the grass and boulder rubble that topped the height of the levee. Once he had established the cover, he moved off with the body bunker, allowing Penny to move in front. Penny pulled Excalibur from the drag-bag, set the tripod and lay flat in the grass. Harrison, still using the body bunker, took up the six o'clock position behind him.

Penny lay in the grass, adjusted his scope and tried to see the names on the tankers. So far, they had not been able to identify which one was the *Rotterdam*. 'Oh, Jesus,' he said.

'What is it?' Harrison squinted over his shoulder. Penny did not reply for a moment, then he spoke into his radio. Sniper TOC from Penny. The frequency was encrypted, the signal only picked up by the SWAT and sniper tactical operations centers that were rolling across the bridges of Highway 310. The sniper frequency could be further encrypted for when they were about to order the attack.

'Go ahead, Penny.' Mackon's voice in his ear.

'Eyes on target. Repeat. Eyes on target. There's three tankers lined up bow to stern, heading upriver towards Waterford 3. The middle one's the *Rotterdam*. I can't see the name, the hull is too dirty. But there's a body hanging by his neck from the side of the ship.'

Harrison eased breath through his teeth and, using his binoculars, took a brief look at the hull. He could make the man out plainly against the raised and blackened ironwork. 'Hull's high, Matt,' he said.

'Right.' Penny spoke again to the TOC commander. 'The hull is high in the water. Whatever they were carrying, it looks like they already dumped it.' He lay on his belly, with his respirator mask down, so he could see through the scope more easily.

Harrison sat behind him and watched the comings and goings on the river road. The TOCs had arrived now and were setting up forward of the inner perimeter which would be guarded by FBI agents as soon as the back-up arrived. The outer perimeter was the sheriff's responsibility. The TOCs would sit in the hollow between the levee and the

253

spillway, below the line of vision of anyone on board the tanker. The press were banked above them, and already agents he recognized were arriving in cars and panel vans and the black Chevy Suburbans. On the spillway, photographers were taking pictures with zoom lenses and flashguns.

Penny was scanning the superstructure of the tanker through his rifle scope. 'Penny to CP. I got windows out on the superstructure. Four/one, three/two, six/two, three/four and seven/five, all on the green. Repeat. All on the green. Drapes on the windows.' Suddenly, he tensed. 'Oh shit. I got movement.'

Gunshots rattled from the tanker. Penny pressed his face into the ground. 'Engaged. Gunfire from the ship. Cannot identify crisis site. Repeat. Cannot identify crisis site.' He looked up. 'I got movement on the bridge, light on, light off. That's window six/three, on the green. Double-tap firing. Cannot locate target to return fire.'

The mobile command post took up position in the hollowed section of land where there was some water underfoot between the levee and the spillway. Fitzpatrick, the on-scene commander, Byrne, Logan and Swann, together with the hostage negotiator and the intelligence analyst, were crammed in the back of the Suburban. The other two TOCs were parked alongside, doors opening on to doors to allow constant access between the three vehicles. Swann could not see the tanker, but he could see what looked like half the world's media gathered on the raised section of open ground only a hundred yards behind him. FBI agents now patrolled that perimeter and twin Blackhawk helicopters squatted on the river road where it was blocked. One was from the Department of Defense, the other was painted in the white of the US Coastguard.

Byrne was talking to the hostage negotiator. 'I can do this if you want me to,' he said.

254

The young agent looked back at him out of flat green eyes. 'I'll try first, sir. It's my job, after all.'

Swann glanced at Byrne and then at the calm face of the negotiator. Fitzpatrick sat alongside him and dialled the ship-to-shore line that the tanker's owners had provided them with. They knew now that the holds were empty, but there was a crew of seventeen on board. Boese, if indeed it was Boese, had indicated twenty-three, so where six more had come from they did not know. Apart from the gunshots, there had been nothing from the ship by way of communication. So far, the snipers had not returned fire, for fear of who they might hit.

The Suburban was cramped and Swann stepped outside with Logan. He was thoughtful, watching the hubbub of activity around him – agents running here and there, sheriff's deputies trying to stop the press from breaking the line of the cordon. Swann was thinking hard. Why would Ismael Boese hijack an empty tanker?

Harrison looked over Penny's shoulder at the body of the hanged man on the side of the hull. 'That poor bastard's family are gonna see him dangling there like that,' he muttered. 'This fucking deal'll be beamed all over the world. They're gonna see him on TV and recognize him.'

Back in the SWAT tactical ops center, a detailed plan of attack would be formulated. They could do nothing yet, however. Fifteen SWAT guys were nowhere near enough to attack a ship of that size. Harrison looked at his watch, the adrenalin still pumping. Not long now before the regional response teams arrived, but hours before the HRT. If this thing blows, it'll be us up there, anyhow, he thought.

In the command post back at the office, Mayer was sitting with people from the New Orleans Fire Department hazardous materials handling unit, two men from the Department of Energy, and others from the Departments of Defense and Transport. Mayer had an open line to the FBI Director in Washington, who had agents from both the international and domestic terrorism sections with him, along with the Attorney General. The President was also being kept informed by an open line, direct to his office. The fear was Ismael Boese, what he had done in London and in Rome, and the proximity of that tanker to Waterford 3. Mayer was speaking on a conference line to the Director and Attorney General, as well as other members of the National Security Council.

'The tanker is empty,' he said. 'So even if he blows it all to hell, we should be able to handle the situation.'

'What about London, Charlie,' the Director said. 'And Rome? There's no way of knowing what he's got on the boat.'

'That's true, sir. But *he* is on it, too. I don't think he'll set off any chemical device if he's still on board. So far, we've had a brief firearms exchange, that's all. Or rather, someone from the ship fired on one of our sniper observer teams. The team is intact and we've not returned fire. I doubt he's going to blow the tanker, sir.'

'How long's he been in the United States?' The Attorney General's voice now.

'We don't know, mam. We received his calling card here in New Orleans, two days ago. That's as much as we know. We got nothing from customs or immigration, so we don't know. Having said that, it can't be long. We're only talking ten days since he escaped from prison in England.' He paused then for a moment. 'I guess you're wondering if that's enough time for him to have planted some kind of dispersal device anywhere else in the country.'

'I am, yes.'

'Well, mam, it's possible. Right now, we're trying to

contact him ship-to-shore, but he doesn't answer his phone. I've got negotiation teams at the scene and here at the command post.'

Swann was back at the TOC and talking to Byrne. 'What's he doing, Louis?' Swann said. 'We both know this isn't his style.' Byrne's normally calm face was lined and red. His brows knitted together in a frown and he scraped his lip with a thumbnail.

'Shit, I don't know, Jack. If he'd talk to us, we could ask him.'

Just then more gunfire rang out, three short bursts, then three more. The sniper team on the spillway reported that they were under fire this time. The SWAT supervisor ordered them not to return fire. They still had no way of knowing where the hostages were. Swann could hear him talking into the radio.

'Have you got visible contact on the crisis site?'

'Lights on the bridge is all. We got drapes blowing, but can't see what's in back of them.'

'Do not fire. Repeat. Hold your fire unless you have eyes on target.'

Swann looked at Byrne. 'Like London all over again,' he said.

Angie Byrne stood in the shower, letting hot water cascade all over her body. Louis was still in New Orleans and she had a busy day ahead of her, starting the embezzlement case proper. She could hear the phone ringing by the bed, thought about ignoring it at this early hour, but her instincts would not allow it. She switched off the shower and reached for a towel. The phone still rang, a single shrill tone, and she picked it up with one hand, while holding the towel to her hair.

'Angie Byrne.'

257

For a moment nobody said anything, but she could hear the echo of a cellphone.

'This is Angie Byrne. Speak up or hang up. I don't give a damn which.'

'Turn on the television.' The voice was low and soft in her ear.

'What?'

'You heard me. Switch on the TV. Where are you? Bedroom? You must have a TV in your million-dollar home.'

A shiver ran the length of her spine. 'Who the fuck is this?'

'Angela, you're an attorney. Try and behave like one. You shouldn't use such expletives with a client you barely know.'

Something in his voice disturbed her, stirred up a sense of fear deep inside her. She knew little about fear, but this voice seemed to drag it up from the depths. She took the phone with her, crossed the Persian rug and switched on the TV set.

'OK,' she said hoarsely. 'What channel?'

'CNN.'

She flicked the button on the remote control handset and stepped back. The Mississippi River came into view, a tanker with a man hanging by his neck over the side. She gasped audibly.

'See him?' His voice again. 'Pity. He was quite pleasant really. But they had to know which boat, didn't they.'

'Who the hell are you? What're you calling me for?'

'Have you ever looked in the sky and mistaken a turkey vulture for a big black crow?' She could hear his breathing. 'Some people have. You see they look alike from the ground.' He paused again. 'I'm calling you because I need an attorney and under the circumstances you're the best option.'

The phone went dead then, and she stood for a moment, before she realized she was shaking. Goosebumps had broken out on her flesh and she had the urge to urinate. She dialled her husband's cellphone.

Byrne took the call, standing at the back of the Suburban, while the intelligence analysts punched information through to the SIOC. Swann watched his face whiten, his eyes widen and a droplet of sweat form on his brow as he listened.

'OK, honey,' Byrne said. 'Don't worry. I'll get someone over to the house right away. Just stay where you are.'

He hung up and stared at Swann, face very red. 'Sonofabitch,' he said. 'That bastard just called my wife.' He phoned through to the SIOC and requested a technical team to get a wire tap on his phone line right away. If Boese was going to call his wife, they needed to hear what was said. He spoke to Fitzpatrick then, who requested that the line be patched through to the command post.

Suddenly, the phone rang on the computer console and the intelligence analyst flicked a switch. 'That's the SIOC,' she said. 'He's on line to D.C.'

Fitzpatrick shifted where he sat, Byrne crouched beside him, Swann and Logan stood in the breeze by the door. 'You got that, boss?' Fitzpatrick spoke to Mayer back in New Orleans.

'I got it.'

Fitzpatrick nodded to the analyst. 'Put him on conference.' He looked from Byrne to Swann to Logan, and then at the negotiator. Fitzpatrick spoke first. 'This is Special Agent Kirk Fitzpatrick,' he said calmly. 'Who am I speaking to, please?'

No reply.

'This is Fitzpatrick. Who am I speaking to, please?'

They heard a hiss, like sudden air from a tyre, then a

259

soft, ice-clad voice. 'You're speaking to your "unknown subject".'

'Boese,' Byrne said, and Fitzpatrick glared at him.

'Oh dear. A conference line.' Boese hung up.

'Nice one, Louis.' Fitzpatrick threw his hands up. 'Fuck. You of all people ought to know better than that.'

Byrne's neck burned red. 'He just phoned my fucking wife.'

'Yeah? Well get a handle on it or get outta here.'

The phone rang again. Again Fitzpatrick spoke. 'Is this Ismael Boese?' he asked.

'Let me speak to Byrne.'

Byrne glowered at Fitzpatrick, clasped his hands together and leaned forward. 'What do you want?' he said.

'I just spoke to your wife, Byrne. But no doubt, you know that already. I expect by now you've arranged for one of your Title 3s to be set up on your own home phone. That's ironic, isn't it. You're used to listening to other people's conversations.'

A helicopter made a high pass above the tanker, a Blackhawk from Montgomery National Guard base, south of Meridian, Mississippi. It was bringing in the Jackson field office SWAT team. They all heard the sudden rattle of gunfire, and then Boese hissed at them over the air-waves. 'Get that helicopter away from this tanker, or I'll start killing hostages.'

'You got it,' Fitzpatrick said. 'Sorry. Listen, Ismael, speak to us on the ship-to-shore. It'll be easier.'

'I don't think so. I prefer it this way. I'll just call when I want you.'

'What is it exactly that you want?' Byrne asked him.

'What do I want? I want a lawyer, you fool.' He hung up.

Byrne ran the tips of his fingers across his scalp. Swann stood at the door and frowned.

*

260

Harrison and Penny had been in position for an hour now. One more hour and they would be rotated, assuming back-up snipers from the other regions were on hand to replace them. Penny still lay prostrate, talking without looking round to Harrison behind him.

'I got movement on these windows, JB, but I can't fucking see anything.'

'Windows are small, Matty. Small and dark. You ain't gonna see anything.'

'Bridge is the crisis site. I figure he's up there, though he don't show himself.'

Harrison wanted a cigarette. He could not have one, but he peeled off his respirator and placed a plug of chewing tobacco in his cheek instead, like a baseball player. He sucked and spat and shifted the body bunker slightly. 'We'll go in by air,' he said. 'Nobody's gonna swim in that.' He pointed with his MP5 to the grimy, swirling water. 'Gotta be by chopper. Up and drop and go.'

'Hope we make the team,' Penny said. 'We've been here an hour already.'

'I'm too old to make the team.'

'Bullshit. You passed the fitness test, though God only knows how, with the amount you smoke. Your lungs gotta be made of iron. Besides, you're the last guy in the office to actually shoot anybody.' He spoke into his radio again. 'Penny to CP. I got lights again. Window, five/four, on green.' He cradled himself into his gun Excalibur.

Louis Byrne spoke to his wife. She was still wrapped in the towel in her bedroom in old town Alexandria. The shutters were open now and early morning sunlight breathed through the frost on the window. She sat on the edge of their bed, with the drapes pulled back, her knees close together.

'Listen, honey, if he calls again, just stay calm. OK?'

'Louis, don't patronize me. I'm one of the best goddamn attorneys in this city. I can handle the odd conversation.'

'OK. OK. I'm just looking out for you. Everything that he says to you, we'll be able to hear. If he wants to talk, let him do so. While he's talking, we can maybe figure out what he's trying to do here. But listen, honey, hostage negotiation is tough, and it might be that he wants to negotiate with you. I've got back-up guys from Pennsylvania Avenue on their way over now, so make sure you let them in.'

'OK.' She hung up and rubbed a hand through damp hair. She would have to wash it all over again after this. The phone rang. Her stomach tightened into a knot and then she picked it up. 'Hello?'

'I want you to be my attorney.'

'Get somebody else.'

'No. I want you.' He laughed then. 'Are they listening now? No, it's still too soon, isn't it. Next conversation, I guess. That's if you allow them. Client confidence is everything, Angela. You know that.'

Angie switched hands with the phone. 'Fuck client confidence. You're not my client. What d'you want? Why have you taken hostages?' She was calmer now, her sense of professionalism beginning to return. He did not reply and she thought hard for a moment. 'Let me speak to one of the hostages, the captain. I want to know they're all right.'

'And then you'll represent me?'

'Represent you how, exactly? You're on the run, wanted for trial in the UK. How can I represent you? I can't work in the UK.'

'Nobody asked you to, Angela. You see I have other endeavours.'

She bit her lip. 'We can talk about it maybe. But you got to let me speak to the captain.'

The doorbell rang and she jumped. Getting off the bed, she put on her dressing gown and carried the phone downstairs. A breathless-sounding man with a European accent came on the line. 'Hello,' he said. 'This is Captain Thyssen. He's got hostages, seventeen crew, six women.'

'Women?'

'He'll kill us. Do what he says.'

'Captain . . .'

Boese's voice came back on the line. 'Think about this, he whispered. 'When the prey is down, does the jackal or the crow eat first?' He hung up.

Angie opened the door to three special agents from her husband's technical department. 'Wait here,' she said. 'I need to get dressed.'

In the mobile command post on the banks of the Mississippi, the on-scene team regarded one another. The SWAT supervisor stood between the two Suburbans and considered his position. He now had three full teams, with agents arriving from Mobile and Jackson. The Memphis and Little Rock guys were on their way, as were the team from Texas. The HRT were one hour out from Andrews air force base in Virginia. Angie Byrne had phoned through Boese's message. Anything he said now, they would hear directly, with the technical team set up in Byrne's house.

Byrne looked at Swann. Of all of those gathered, between them they knew most about Boese. 'What d'you think, Jack?'

'I don't know. The jackal and the crow. Prey down. Turkey vultures.' Swann hunched his shoulders into his neck. 'I don't know, Louis.'

Byrne scratched his lip. The Director was patched through to them then from the SIOC. 'Seems he's picked his own hostage negotiator,' he said. 'Is your wife gonna be able to handle this, Louis?'

263

'Sure she is, sir. She's tougher than I am.'

'OK. The D.C. crisis negotiation team have arrived. They're on-site at your house, as we speak.'

'Good,' Byrne said.

Swann stepped away from the Suburban and rubbed his eyes. He lit a cigarette, pondering hard. A flashgun went off from the line of reporters above his head and he blinked. Gunfire rattled from the ship.

The phone rang in the TOC, and everybody tensed again. Boese's voice came at them over the airwaves. 'I heard another helicopter. You send any more and I'll shoot them down. Do you understand?'

Swann listened intently.

'What do you want, Ismael?' Fitzpatrick asked him. 'Why have you hijacked the tanker?'

Boese was quiet for a moment. 'It's close to Waterford 3, isn't it.'

Swann felt the sweat break out on the nape of his neck.

Fitzpatrick was concentrating. 'Is that your intention – Waterford 3?'

Boese did not reply.

'Ismael, is Waterford 3 your intended target?'

But he had gone. The phone clicked dead and then silence.

Swann moved to the SWAT tactical operations center. Something was wrong, but he didn't know what. He stared at the river, the tanker, the hanged man, and screwed up his eyes. He remembered a house in London, a year and a half ago, when an SO19 firearms team was held down by gunfire for a full six hours before storming the building. He looked at the SWAT supervisor, dressed like a ninja in black, earpiece in, listening to the reports coming in from his sniper observer teams. The siege had been going on for an hour and a half now.

'I'm Jack Swann,' Swann said to him. 'British Antiterrorist Branch. What've you got, exactly?'

'Got?' The supervisor squinted at him, toothpick set in the corner of his mouth. 'Movement at windows. Light. You heard the gunfire. That's semi-automatic.'

'What kind of movement?'

'Windows are out on various levels of the superstructure. We got drapes blowing or being moved on the green, the same thing on the red.

'What about the white?'

'Nothing so far. I've got nobody deployed directly on the white. That'd mean getting on board that tanker yonder, and I can't do that right now.'

'Thanks,' Swann said and moved away again. He stood, letting cigarette smoke drift from his nose. He looked at the sky and then at the line of TV reporters and pressmen. He could see the FBI media representative trying to answer their barrage of questions. The sky was blue and clear and the sun was fully up, the day was indeed bright enough for sunglasses. Suddenly, he thought of the flashgun going off. Who would need a flashgun on a day like this? And then he went cold. He stared at the line of pressmen, but could not identify anyone using a gun. Lots of cameras had them mounted, but he could not see them going off. He moved up the hill, closer to the perimeter line, and stared. Hundreds of people, fifty, sixty vans maybe, with scaffold platforms on top of them. TV cameras. There were helicopters outside the no-fly zone with long-mounted lenses, no doubt picking up every inch of the tanker. The body on the side would be identifiable to someone. He went back down to the TOCs. Boese had not called again, neither directly to them, nor to Byrne's wife in Washington. He could almost taste the tension.

He stood at the back of the van, close to Logan, who was biting the knuckles of her right hand. Swann looked at

Louis Byrne, then at Fitzpatrick. He was talking to Mayer back in New Orleans.

'Boese's not on the ship,' Swann said quietly.

They all stared at him. Fitzpatrick stopped talking.

'What was that?' Swann heard Mayer's voice over the conference line. He climbed into the back of the truck.

'This is Swann,' he said. 'I don't think Boese is on the tanker. I don't think anyone is except maybe a group of dead hostages.'

Silence.

'What d'you mean, Swann? We heard the captain just now.'

'Did we?' Swann hunched forward, his face intent upon Byrne's. 'We heard his voice, yes.'

'What're you saying, Jack?' Fitzpatrick asked him. 'That what we heard was a recording?'

'It could've been. Listen,' Swann went on, 'there's somebody out here using a flashgun, yet the sun's high and the day is bright and clear. In 1997, we had Boese pinned down in a house in West London. He fired on SO19 as they tried to breach the door. Six hours went by, we had listening probes in the walls and had sound and movement, doors closing, muttering, coughing, lights going on, the toilet being flushed. But when we went in, there was nothing there but movement sensors, tape recorders on timers and remote-controlled switches.' He broke off. 'Boese's made no demands. He's toying with us, with Louis Byrne's wife. Why? Why hijack an empty tanker and surround yourself with Feds and cops and the world's media, if there's no way off the boat. There is no way off that boat and Boese doesn't deal in zero options.' He paused and bit his lip. 'Like I said just now, somebody amongst the press corps is using a flashgun in bright sunlight. The IRA have set off remote devices up to six hundred yards away, using a radio signal built into a flashgun and slave flash unit. That same signal can turn the cam in the trigger guard of any weapon you choose.'

Harrison and Penny were relieved by a sniper observer team from Mobile, their badged insignia clearly showing on their sleeves. They made their way back down to the sniper TOC where they were fully debriefed. The supervisor handed them coffee, and Harrison lit a cigarette and sat Swann talking at one of the other Suburbans. The sun was hot now, and Harrison could feel sweat crawling the length of his body under the fire-resistant suit. The body armour was heavy and he unstrapped it and laid it at his feet. This side of the levee, two Blackhawks squatted with their rotors whirring on idle.

The supervisor told them that the two helicopters from Little Rock and Memphis were also set and waiting with full teams on the western bank. When the word came to go in, they would attack from the air. Four choppers would drop the SWAT teams on to the deck using fast ropes. They would clear in field office teams, New Orleans and Jackson taking the superstructure, top down, half the clock face each. The other SWAT teams would work the rest of the ship.

Penny chewed on a sandwich, hungry and not hungry. Perspiration blackened his face. The adrenalin would not let up. Every minute that passed brought them closer to the point of contact.

The supervisor pointed to the first Blackhawk, the white one provided by the US Coastguard. 'When you're through with the coffee,' he said, 'take your place in the stack.'

In the mobile command post, the FBI team were considering what Swann was telling them. Fitzpatrick scratched his head. 'I don't know,' he said. 'I guess you could be right. But right now, we've got to believe he is on board. There's a crew up there and, by the sounds of it, a few

267

coke whores somebody shipped in.' He broke off. The word came through that Boese was on the phone to Angie Byrne again. The call was patched through and they listened to the cruel cold voice.

'Have you thought about it, Angela,' he said, 'does the jackal or the crow eat first?'

'I don't understand what you're saying.'

'You will, eventually. After all, you are my attorney.'

'I'm not your attorney. I will never be your attorney.'

'You know something, Angela. This is getting tiresome.' They could hear him suck breath, then he spoke directly to them. 'Gentlemen, I'm bored. I think it's time we moved on.'

Then they heard another man's voice; begging, pleading. Swann's eyes widened. A well-spoken British voice. 'Please,' he said. 'Just let me go. Please. I have a family . . . They need me . . . Please.' The voice rose in pitch, almost screaming now. Then a single gunshot and silence.

'Jesus Christ.' Mayer's voice on the conference line. 'Send the teams in. Now. Compromise authority granted. Send them in now.'

# 16

Harrison felt the tension like a knot at the base of his spine. The rotors were screaming now, the chopper about to lift off the ground. He stared at Penny through the eyeholes of his respirator, as the team leader's voice called the attack in his earpiece.

'Phase line yellow.' The final covered position. Harrison tightened his grip on the MP5. He had fully automatic firepower if he needed it. The voice sounded again in his ear.

'Phase line green.' Attack. The helicopter lifted above the levee and swung across the water, coming at the tanker from the stern.

Thirty seconds later, two helicopters were hovering above the deck in unison, the New Orleans team closest to the superstructure. Harrison fast-roped to the deck, brought up his carbine and crouched, as they formed a hasty perimeter to guard both the chopper and the men still coming down. Further back along the tanker's deck, the other field office teams were dropping, contact with one another and the SWAT TOC maintained through their radios.

Harrison and Penny had their guns trained on the crisis site, the bridge high in the superstructure. New Orleans SWAT would take the port side twelve to six o'clock, and Harrison and Penny moved off as the breachers came up with the battering ram. They stacked up at the external port side door, the breachers in front, Harrison second in the line, with Penny behind him. Harrison's breath came as fog in his respirator, the air high and hoarse in his throat.

269

His eyes were intent on that white metal door, as the breacher reached for the handle. It wasn't locked and he wrenched it open. As he did so, Harrison slapped him on the shoulder and grabbed the two flashbangs from the back of his belt. 'TWO UP,' he yelled and lobbed the stun grenades over the first man's shoulder. They burst in nine separate explosions, the boom echoing in the metalled confines of the hallway.

Harrison was inside, crouching with his MP5, as the others came in behind him. They saw nothing, the hallway empty and silent. Smoke filled the confined space, but as it cleared they saw the flight of metal-runged steps that rose all the way to the top.

Two-man clears, top to bottom and room by room; they would use flashbangs in every one of them. They moved off, up the stairs, keeping the line of the stack, each man covering his partner. Harrison and Penny started at the very top. They breached the door, tossed in the grenades, then entered the smoke-filled confusion. Nothing, the room was empty. They gradually made their way down. Still nothing – doors kicked open, smoke in their faces, weapons trained on emptiness. Then they came to the bridge. Harrison was lead man, Penny taking the grenades from him. Harrison bent and twisted the handle, then kicked the door open, foot sliding on the grimy metal step as he did so. Penny threw in the grenade and they entered, MP5s sighted, red lasers seeking for targets in the smoked grey of the bridge. Harrison saw two men trussed up on the floor, both of them in uniform.

On the bank, the Puerto Rican reporter got behind the wheel of the KYZ Radio van and the woman with the blue-black hair sat next to him, long-lensed camera with a flashgun on her lap. The Puerto Rican fired the engine over and backed his way through the mass of panel vans at the

270

very lip of the spillway. The sheriff's deputies watched
them for a moment, then stood back to let them through
the perimeter, and they drove slowly back along the river
road towards Highway 310. A Mexican sat in the back,
four cellphones at his feet and three separate tape recorders.

Swann stood and watched as the helicopters dumped the
SWAT teams down the ten-inch-thick, fibred fast rope.
Like a long . . . poles from the chopper to the deck. One
by one, black-suited men slid down, then took up the cover
position on deck. Beside him Logan stood tense, replaying
in her head the last phone call from Boese, the pleading of
his victim. Swann could still see the now-bloated body of
the man hanging over the side. He felt sick. Byrne was
watching with them, Fitzpatrick still inside the TOC, on
the conference line to the SAC in New Orleans. It was
three hours exactly since they had had the call from the
Coastguard, too late for the elite Hostage Rescue Team.
Swann glanced at Byrne, who looked on with a strange
expression on his face. Then they heard the explosion.
Swann stared at the ship as it lurched, but could not see
anything immediately.
    Logan lifted a set of binoculars to her eyes. 'Oh, my
God,' she said. 'He's blown the anchor chain.'
    Swann took the glasses from her and scanned the length
of the ship. She was right, it was loose, the chains were
blown at their deck housings, and the ship, high in already
high water, was adrift on the river. Logan passed the word
to the TOC and they scrambled the Coastguard. There were
other ships and chemical installations downriver, not to
mention the bridge by the Destrehan Plantation. Already,
Swann could see the swiftness of the current begin to
swing the ship fractionally. He left the TOC and moved up
to the press corps, moving among them, walking between
them, eyes peeled. He had seen this sight before – only not

271

here in this macabre Louisiana sunshine, but on the streets of London. He looked at every face he passed, scanned every van, car, truck. He saw nobody he recognized, but the spectre of Storm Crow hung on his shoulders like a rancid shroud. He had the strange sensation that Boese could see him. A great clanging sound went up, then a shriek from the assembly and Swann looked back. The loose tanker had clipped the one behind it, as it was pulled downriver by the strength of the current.

On board, Harrison was standing on the bridge with his gun at the heads of the trussed men, while Penny ensured the rest of the area was clear. Penny had found a sub-machine gun, set on semi-automatic and fixed in the broken window of the bridge.There was an electronic cam motor in the trigger guard, and, dangling outside, a slave flash unit. Penny spoke into the radio. 'A team. Bridge now clear. Two found. Possible hostages.'

Harrison still held the two tied men under the barrel of his gun; the echo of the flashbangs in his head, the shouting of SWAT men in his ears, yet there was the total concentration on his own line of vision. He didn't hear the explosion, but he felt the sudden movement under his feet. He stared into the blue-green eyes of the grey-haired man on the floor and saw the sudden fear. He pulled the gag down and the man gasped for breath. 'We're moving,' the man said. 'Let me up.'

Harrison just looked at him. Then the word came in his ear from the SWAT supervisor.

'All teams blue and gold. You are adrift. The anchor chain is blown.'

'I'm Captain Thyssen,' the man said. 'Untie me, for God's sake.'

Harrison stepped back, still levelling his carbine at the captain's heart, and thought for a moment. The ship rolled

272

ever so slightly, and he spread his feet for better balance. Then he gestured for Penny to untie him. The captain snatched up the radio and relayed the mayday message to the Coastguard.

'Can you start the engines?' Harrison asked him, his respirator hanging loose at his neck now.

The captain spoke without looking round, his hands fixed on the wheel. 'Not like this.' He looked down at the ~~~~ ~~~~ ~~~ up on the floor. He's the first officer. For God's sake, untie him.'

They freed the first officer, and again the captain was on the radio, talking about dimensions and boat width and the strength of the current. Above his head was a chart on which all the installations on this stretch of the delta were listed. Then he and the mate were talking about tugs. Harrison felt suddenly helpless. One by one the calls came in on the radio from the other teams, as each area of the ship was given the all-clear. Two of the New Orleans boys had located twenty people locked in the television room, six of whom looked like coke whores from the projects. All remained under guard, but from what they could make out, the terrorists were gone.

Harrison spoke to the captain again, then took the ship-to-shore radio from him and spoke with the Coastguard. 'This is Special Agent Dollar, FBI SWAT,' he said. 'I'm on the bridge of the *Rotterdam*.'

'OK. I need to speak to Thyssen again. That guy just talking to me. He's the skipper of that boat.'

'Maybe. But I need to know what's going on. We've got sixty FBI guys, plus twenty-two civilians on this vessel and it's wheeling out of control.'

'OK. We've got the big tugs coming up from New Orleans, but they'll take a while to get there. In the meantime, we got smaller tugs from Shell and Amoco out by you now. They're gonna attempt to shepherd you into

273

the bank, before you start moving too quickly.' He paused for a moment. 'Listen, we're on line to your command post in New Orleans about this, but that guy talking *is* Frans Thyssen. I know. I get shitfaced with him whenever he's in the quarter.' Again he paused. 'Now if you wanna get off that mother alive, you got to let me talk to him.'

Harrison handed the phone back to the captain and looked up as the SWAT team leader came up the steps. 'Ship's cleared,' he said.

'Yeah, and now we got this crazy situation.' Harrison took his tin of snuff from one of the many pockets on his black tunic, and placed a fingerful under his lip. He stepped out into the wind and watched the river far below them. They were moving, not quickly to the naked eye, but other ships and the petrochemical installations were growing ever larger behind them. Fortunately, the river was four hundred yards wide here, and all shipping traffic had ceased as soon as Boese struck. But they were stuck on this massive iron monster, which seemed to bob like a top with no cargo to steady it. Harrison sucked tobacco juice and spat on to the diesel-smelling deck. Penny moved beside him, MP5 slung over his shoulder. Harrison stared at the eastern shore and the world's gathered media. 'You know what, I feel really fucking dumb,' he said. 'That sonofabitch set us up pretty good, didn't he.'

The team leader came outside. 'We're in for the Mississippi riverboat ride, boys,' he said. 'They're taking the other teams off by chopper, but we gotta stay with the crew.'

'Ain't that just the ticket.' Harrison spat into the wind.

The captain fought to steer the ship, engines still off. Harrison and Penny were down on deck, watching the Blackhawks whirl in from the shore and drop the winches and ladders for the other SWAT teams to get off. Harrison shifted the weight of his carbine to his left shoulder and

274

then he and Penny reached over the side and began to reel
in the dead man on the bulwark. He weighed a ton, it felt
like, and they hauled him up, hand over hand with the
rope. Finally they made it, and struggled between them to
lift him over the side. He lay on his back, face blue, lips
swollen, eyes glassy and staring. His teeth were long and
yellow and feral. He had been shot twice in the head.

The tanker ploughed its crazed path downriver and
Harrison watched with his heart high in his chest, as the
first of the tugs came alongside. From where he looked,
the tug looked tiny indeed. But it bulldozed up against the
hull and was joined quickly by another. Harrison glanced
at his watch: it would be another half-hour before the big
tugs got upriver from New Orleans. They would hit the
Destrehan bridge before then. He had a sudden vision of
sinking to a watery death in the grey swirl of the river.

Penny was still looking down at the dead man. 'Only
one killed,' he muttered. 'Rest are just dandy.' He squinted
at his partner. 'Why'd he do that, ponyboy? And what the
fuck was this all about?'

'Beats me.' Harrison looked down at the tugs.

The tanker was carried along by the current. The captain
was trying to keep the bow straight, but already it had
turned and they were flatter against the wind than he would
have liked. They rounded the bend where the river road
fed out beyond the levee on the eastern shore, and the first
of the feed pipes from the chemical installations threatened
their path. Two tugs were on the port side now, pressing
their combined weight against the hull, trying to steer the
ship away from the shore and into the middle of the river.
With no traffic, that was their best hope, merely to guide
them on to a safer path until the big tugs arrived and could
manoeuvre them into the bank, between the installations.
Harrison watched, his heart in his mouth, as they negotiated

275

the first of the chemical plants, with the tugs just a hair's breadth away from the feeder pipes.

Penny stared further down the river and grimaced. 'Look,' he said, pointing.

Harrison twisted his head and saw the 310 bridge, looming grey in the distance.

The minutes ticked by and the 310 bridge grew larger. Both of them went back inside, where the captain and first officer were sweating. They talked among themselves, ignoring the two black-suited FBI men, concentrating their efforts on steering the stricken vessel and keeping in tight radio contact with the skippers from the small tugs below, that were trying desperately to keep them away from the shore. Harrison lit a cigarette and blew a steady stream of smoke at the window.

'I can't stand this,' Penny said all at once. 'I gotta watch what happens.'

They went back outside again, and watched from the height of the superstructure, as the grey span of the bridge grew closer and closer. The first three tugs had been joined by two more, and Harrison used his binoculars to scan the horizon for the big ones. All at once, the boat juddered and a tearing sound split their ears. Harrison almost lost his footing. 'What the . . .' he started.

Penny was looking over the side. 'Barge,' he said. 'We just hit a barge.' They could see the crumpled mass of metal suddenly spin loose from where the hull had trapped it, and zip out to the bank, like a stick tossed by a child.

'You see that?' Penny said. 'Jesus, Harrison. What if we hit the bridge?'

Harrison laid a hand on his shoulder. 'We won't hit the bridge,' he said.

They rolled on, slowly being sucked by the current, and the height of that grey mass of concrete drew closer and closer. Harrison could see the press gathered in droves on it, before the sheriff's deputies moved them on. 'Surely they gotta close it,' he said to himself. Sure enough, all vehicle movement was halted, and now his heart surged as he took in the dimensions of the footings and the position of the tanker in the water. The tug captains had steered them away from the eastern shore and into a more central position, but he still could not gauge whether or not they would make it. He thinned his eyes, and the bridge got bigger and bigger. He could feel the saliva draining from his mouth. Penny was standing very still alongside him. The bridge got closer still. Two helicopters buzzed overhead: the Coastguard monitoring their position. Tugs on either side of them pressed their combined weight against the high sides of the hull, gradually squeezing them further into mid-river. And then the bridge was upon them, and Harrison could see the height of the carriageway, and he imagined that amount of concrete falling on to the ship. But the tugs still pushed and the captain tried to steer, and Harrison spat tobacco juice into the wind, as they passed through the central section with ten feet to spare. He looked the length of the bows and knew then they would make it.

Penny's hand suddenly rested on his shoulder. 'Look,' he said, and, as Harrison turned, he saw the bows of the first big tug steam into view downriver.

Winter rain fell almost as sleet, accentuating the grey of the grey-roofed town that straddled the banks of the Teviot. Webb and McCulloch watched from their car as Catherine Morgan delivered her only son to school.

'Two weeks out in term-time,' Webb said. 'Lucky little sod, isn't he.'

McCulloch pushed a meaty, red-knuckled hand through his hair and looked at the car through cat-green eyes. 'Where did she get the money, Webby? That's about three grand worth of car she's sitting in.'

Webb looked sideways at him. 'We'll ask her, shall we.'

They followed her back through town and she turned into Bourtree Terrace and parked outside the door to her flat. She was locking the car when Webb walked up to her.

'Catherine Morgan?' he said. She started, and turned and stared at him. 'My name's Webb,' he went on. 'Detective Sergeant Webb, from Scotland Yard. This is Detective Constable McCulloch. Enjoy your holiday, did you?'

They sat inside the flat. There was a very small, narrow hall with a bedroom on the left, then a sitting room, one further bedroom at the end of the hall, and a shower room and tiny kitchenette on the right. In London, they had checked with the ferry companies and found her booked in her own name, coming into Portsmouth the previous Saturday. She had driven all the way back to Scotland in her Volkswagen Passat. Webb stared at her now – eyes blue, but still kindly – as she sat with her hands in her lap, a cigarette burning between her fingers. Pictures of her son lined the mantelpiece and there was one of her and the boy and her brother Brynn. Webb watched her face, the pale skin, the freckles faint against her nose, and her thick red hair.

'Close family, are you?'

'Sorry?' She squinted her head sideways at him.

Webb flicked a pudgy finger at the photograph. 'Close family. You and Brynn and Ieuan.'

'Brynn's my brother, not my husband.'

'We know. We spoke to him.' Webb smiled at her. 'After Ismael Boese was broken out.' He leaned forward in the seat. 'You know how many people got killed that day, Catherine? Twenty-two.' He paused then and looked at McCulloch. 'Boese doesn't care who he kills, so how come she's still alive?'

McCulloch shrugged. 'Beats me. How come Boese didn't kill you, Catherine?' he said.

She blanched then and stared at him. 'I don't know what you're talking about. I don't know anyone called Boese.'

'Yes, you do.' Webb inched himself further forward on his seat. 'Sure you do. You just went to France with him, yourself and Ieuan. We don't know where you stayed yet, but we'll find out.'

She looked down at the floor.

Webb sat back again. 'Who bought the car, Catherine?'

She looked up sharply then, chin high, head back, nostrils flaring slightly. 'I bought the car. It's my car.'

'Where did you get the money? We reckon it must be all of three thousand pounds worth.'

'I won the money. Cash. I bought it at an auction. Got it cheap.'

'Which auction?'

'The one over in Gala.'

'And you've got the papers, the receipt for it and everything?'

'Aye.'

'Good. We're going to need them.' Webb stood up, looked at his watch and heard the grinding engine of the low-loader as it faltered down on the high street. He looked at McCulloch. 'D'you want to go and check them, Macca? We'll never get the truck up here. I'll suit up and drive the Passat down. They can throw the tarps over it on the high street.'

Catherine stared at him. 'What're you talking about? You can't drive my car.'

'I can,' Webb said. 'Catherine Morgan, I'm arresting you under the Prevention of Terrorism Act.' She stared goggle-eyed at him, as he went on to read the rest of her rights. When he was finished, he shook his head. 'Conspiracy to murder police officers, Catherine. That'll get you twenty years, at least.' He smiled and patted her on the shoulder. 'Never mind, we can talk about it later.'

They drove her to London in silence, talking between themselves, but never addressing a single word to her. She was in the back, with her hands cuffed. Webb and McCulloch chatted about football and the upcoming five nations rugby tournament all the way down to London. At Paddington Green police station, Webb got her out and two WPCs were there to greet her. They frog-marched her to a cell, then strip searched her, put her in a paper suit and somebody else's shoes, before locking her up for the night. She sat, saying nothing, not allowed to smoke, and biting down on her fingernails.

Webb and McCulloch got into the Yard at six p.m. and met Colson in the squad room. 'Is she tucked up for the night?' he asked them.

'Snug and cosy, Guv,' Webb said. 'Snug and cosy. Have we heard anything from Swann?'

Colson looked grave. 'Yes, we have. That tanker was Queen's House Mews revisited. Boese wasn't on board. He blew the anchor chains and set it adrift on the river. Four FBI SWAT teams were trying to do a clear at the time.'

Webb arched his eyebrows. 'You know, I'd forgotten how clever he was.'

Colson sat down on an empty desk and fisted his hand to his chin. 'The thing I don't understand is – what exactly is he doing?' he said.

They went to get a drink in Finnegan's Wake. Webb bought Guinness and sucked off the froth. 'Catherine Morgan's a tough old bird,' he said. 'She's not going to buckle. Depending what Lambeth find in the car, we can go in hard and then soften if we have to. She says she won the money for the car playing bingo, but SB already checked that out and it's bullshit. Schedule 7 gave us access to everything financial and we know she's worth tuppence ha'penny at best.' He shrugged his shoulders.

'She can't account for the cash, or the holiday she's just had, so we've got a good starting point, even if we blow out on forensics.' He broke off for a moment then. 'I wonder why she's still alive. She's in a weak position and I wonder why Boese allowed that. He must've known we'd catch up with her.'

'George,' Colson said, sliding his finger up and down the condensated side of his glass, 'nothing that bastard does makes any sense to me.'

McCulloch sipped from his pint, his hand like a paw round the glass. 'Did the search turn anything up?' he asked.

Colson stood straighter, where he leaned against the bar. 'Nothing particularly incriminating. There were a few back copies of the *International Herald Tribune*, which strikes me as odd, though.'

The following morning, Webb and McCulloch interviewed Catherine Morgan. She looked pale and tired, seated across the table at Paddington Green. Next to her, the duty solicitor sat with a pad and pen before him, his suit a little crumpled, as if he had been working all night. They had got the initial swab results from her car from the scientists at Lambeth. Ismael Boese's fingerprints had been lifted from a road map of France they found in the glove compartment. 'The map could have been placed in the car, Sergeant,' the solicitor was saying. 'You know that. It doesn't prove he was there.'

'No.' Webb held his eye evenly. 'It doesn't.' He reverted his gaze to Catherine. 'But it's coincidental in the extreme, isn't it, Catherine?' She did not reply, gave a brief twist of her lips and sucked on the cigarette she was holding. Webb glanced at McCulloch, then he said: 'Where did you get the money for the car, Catherine, and what made you take a trip to France at that particular time?'

281

McCulloch butted in: 'How did you pay for the trip? It must've been expensive.'

'I already told you. I won the money at bingo.' Her solicitor touched her on the arm, but it was too late.

'No, you didn't,' Webb said, teeth set together. 'We checked with every bingo hall in your area, nobody has won that kind of money in years.'

'I didn't win it all at once.'

'No?'

'Over how long then?'

'A couple of years.'

'Really.' Webb sat back and folded his arms. 'Then how was it that your brother had to pay your train fare to visit him with his prison money?'

She glared across the table at him. 'He wanted to see me.'

'Did he?' McCulloch jutted his chin at her. 'What did he want to see you about?'

She faltered.

'Come on, Catherine. If he wanted to see you that badly, you must remember what it was about. It was only last year.'

'Things,' she said. 'Just family stuff and that.'

'Family stuff?' McCulloch twisted his head sideways.

'Where did you keep this money, Catherine?' Webb asked her then. 'Not in the bank. We've checked your accounts. Not to put too fine a point on it, you're skint. Hardly a penny to your name, and then suddenly a car, a holiday in France, the works.'

'I never kept it in the bank.'

'Why not? You wouldn't pay tax on it if you won it. What's safer than the bank? It's not as if you didn't have a bank account.'

She did not answer him, looked at her solicitor and looked away again.

'Gentlemen,' the solicitor said. 'Perhaps I could have a word in private with my client.'

Webb slowly nodded, then he leaned across the table and looked Catherine in the eye. 'Sure you can,' he said quietly. 'But maybe you'd like to remind her that, as it stands, I'm looking to charge her with aiding and abetting Ismael Boese's escape from the SEG in Hanwell Green. Twenty-two people were massacred that day, sixteen of them police officers.'

He stood outside with McCulloch, while McCulloch smoked a cigarette. 'The brief's not stupid,' McCulloch said. 'She's going to squawk.'

'What d'you reckon? She'll go for the coercion routine, a poor single mother from Scotland, hounded into action by her big bad brother.'

'Something like that.'

Webb's face creased in a wide smile. 'Swallow it, shall we?'

'I think so. We've got bigger fish to fry.'

Swann sat quietly on his own in the FBI squad room in New Orleans. The helicopters had winched off the remaining SWAT team, the crew and six prostitutes from the deck of the tanker, after it was finally shepherded into the riverbank by the big tugs. The evidence response team were now crawling all over it and the reactive squad had begun the initial interviews with the hostages. The one dead man was William Richards, the chief engineer from Gloucester, England. Swann now knew that the voice pleading over the telephone was a recording of him before he was shot. Boese was sicker than ever.

He felt isolated – the procedures, people, alien to him. He could sense the weird atmosphere, almost of mistrust, from the FBI agents, apart, that was, from Logan. But she was isolated too – a woman, a black woman from headquarters. He stared out of the window and across the city. He could see the New Orleans Superdome, a vast enclosed stadium where the Saints played. He suddenly missed his children.

The FBI Hostage Rescue Team had finally landed from Virginia and were currently debriefing the SWAT team members and their supervisors. There was an air of relief, if puzzlement, about the office. The special agent in charge was knee-deep in meetings with other government bodies, and via telephone conference with the FBI Director and Attorney General in Washington. Tom Kovalski had flown down with the HRT, and was using the ASAC's office upstairs, along with Louis Byrne. They had already put in an affidavit for a UFAP warrant from the district attorney's office.

Logan touched Swann on the shoulder. 'You OK, Jack?'

He looked up at her and smiled. 'Fine, Chey. Just fine.'

'God, I love your accent. You English guys. It's so sexy.'

'Get me the phone book. I'll read it to you.'

She laughed, then looked up as Harrison came over, still wearing his black SWAT fatigues, sweat dripping from his hairline. 'They wanna talk upstairs,' he said. 'See how this is gonna be played now.'

'You coming, too, Harrison?' Logan asked him.

He cocked his head to one side and laid his body armour on the desk. 'Anyone with specialist knowledge is requested. I worked the Idaho end of this click, remember.' He looked briefly at Swann and shifted the roll of chew in his mouth. 'The sharp end, eh, bubba.'

Swann looked after him as he sauntered away to change his clothes. 'What's his problem?' he said. 'Is he pissed off because we lost Boese or something?'

'I don't know, Jack. I'll try and find out.'

284

'I'd appreciate that, Chey. The man is beginning to irritate me.'

Again she laid her hand on his shoulder. 'Take no notice, honey. Harrison's old school. Regular dinosaur.' She bit down on her lip. 'The trouble is, people respect the hell out of him, even the ultra-tight suits back at the zoo. We needed a home run against the militia and he hit out of the ballpark.'

They went upstairs and sat in the padded blue chairs in the conference room. The room was pleasantly cool, air conditioning on. Outside, the pavement steamed. Mayer came in with Fitzpatrick. The SWAT team leader was there from the tactical arm of the critical incident response group they had set up, together with the senior agents from the evidence response team, although nothing forensically was back from the ship as yet. The criminal investigation people, who were still interviewing hostages downstairs, sent Cochrane up, as the violent crime co-ordinator.

They sat round the table and drank coffee. Mayer passed a hand through his fine, grey hair. 'Well,' he said. 'What was all that about?'

Nobody responded at first. Swann rested his elbows on the tabletop. 'He's done it before,' he stated. 'Announced himself publicly, before disappearing.' He glanced at Byrne. 'He did it to us in London, remember.'

Byrne nodded.

Logan sat forward. 'Jack figured he wasn't aboard that tanker back at the spillway, Charlie,' she said.

Harrison looked closely at Swann then, something like surprise in his eyes. Swann seized his opportunity. 'You found three separate weapons mounted strategically, right?' He spoke directly to Harrison. 'They had slave flash units attached to them, the type that pick up a radio signal.'

Harrison stared back at him.

'Boese was on shore all the time,' Swann continued. 'He

285

probably set himself up with a TV van or something, sat in the back with a couple of mobile phones, so you couldn't get his electronic serial number. His accomplices, one of whom could be Tal-Salem, stood outside with cameras and all the press paraphernalia. They took pictures using a flashgun. The day was bright and clear, no need to use a flash. But it sent a radio signal to the slave unit and turned the cam in the trigger guard on the guns. Double tap. Then again, double tap. Your snipers are suddenly under fire.' He rapped the table lightly with his fingernail. 'PIRA have used the same method to remotely detonate IEDs in Ulster.'

Kovalski cleared his throat. 'You told this to the on-scene commander?'

Swann looked down the table at him. 'I did, yes.' He glanced at Fitzpatrick then. 'But he was right. As far as we knew, the tanker was under siege and there were hostages. What could he do but go with it?'

Fitzpatrick steepled his fingers. 'The question is, why did he go to all that trouble? He didn't make any demands.'

Swann wrinkled his lip. 'He's got something else planned, Kirk. This is just his way of saying hello.'

'Reserved kinda guy, ain't he,' Harrison muttered.

Mayer scratched his head. '*What else* could he have planned? Jesus, he had Waterford 3 right there.'

Swann spoke to Byrne. 'Why your wife, Louis?'

Byrne looked back at him, sitting slightly slumped in the chair. 'I don't know. I need to listen to the tapes.' He broke off and glanced at Kovalski. 'I guess this is a domestic deal now, Tom. I'd like to stay closely involved though, however you decide to play it.'

'Of course.' Kovalski held his fountain pen between the ends of his fingers. 'New Orleans is the OO, so we'll run the investigation from here, but with heavy D.C. input. It's a specialist field and this guy is like nobody we've ever seen.' He looked at Swann then. 'Office of origin, Jack. That's how we play things over here.'

Harrison interrupted him. 'A team on the ground?'

'Probably.' Kovalski looked again at Swann. 'If Jack is right, then we're looking for a TV van. Let's go public on that. Get Fugitive Publicity to spread the word on the six o'clock news.'

'Are we gonna name Boese?' Logan asked.

Kovalski pursed his lips, and looked for opinion around the table. 'I don't think we should,' he said. 'He didn't announce himself to the press or the Coastguard, so I think we'll stick with "unknown subject" for now.'

'What about the crew?' Cochrane put in. 'The coke whores and the crewman running them out there told us he called himself Storm Crow.'

'Ask them to keep quiet for now,' Kovalski said. 'If one of them lets it out, then we'll have to go public.' He frowned. 'But it looks like we're in some kinda game and we need to know what the rules are before we show our hand.'

Boese lay back against the pillow in his room at the Holiday Inn, in Meridian, Mississippi. His eyes were closed but he was not sleeping, merely resting his limbs and allowing his mind to clear. The van was parked outside. Across the road was a Howard Johnson bar and a diner where he could eat later. The Puerto Ricans, old Machetero contacts from days gone by, had gone back to New York, and the girl back to her compound in Arkansas. He had asked the Macheteros openly, but they knew nothing of *El Kebir*.

He pondered the FBI in New Orleans. An interesting footnote had developed. While seated in the back of that van, watching through the tinted windows as the panic slowly developed, a face from the past had climbed out of one of the Suburbans. Sergeant Swann from Scotland Yard.

Lazily, he got off the bed and leant on one elbow. He switched on the TV and watched CNN. The main story was his of course and they showed shots of the tanker, complete with the dead Englishman, hanging by his neck from the side. They now knew, of course, that he'd been shot, but that did not matter. Nobody was mentioning him by name, there was nothing of feathers or his calls to Byrne's wife. The three of them that had been seen by the crew, the two 'Mexicans' and a black-haired girl, had been sketched by an FBI artist. The drawings were pretty accurate, but his disguise had changed. He was a negro once more.

He slept till six o'clock and then watched the news again. Things were getting interesting. The FBI were looking for a TV company van, either abandoned, or parked in an odd place – motel parking lots, outside diners, on the roadside, perhaps. He looked through the window at the taxi van, the magnetic KYZ Radio signs were missing. He glanced at the clock again; six o'clock in Mississippi meant five in Washington D.C. He picked up his cellphone and dialled.

Angie Byrne was working in her office on the eleventh floor of 1440 New York Avenue. Bill Trellis poked his head round her door. 'How long you gonna be here till, Angie?'

She looked at her watch. 'Seven, seven-thirty, I guess. Why?'

'Just the Williams & Howells deal. I wanna brief you on it before you go.'

'Today?' Angie clicked her tongue. The matter should've been discussed two days ago, but Trellis had a

288

habit of putting things off. 'I can give you a half-hour at best.'

'That'll work. Conference room at six-thirty?'

She went back to her keyboard, then looked up again as Joe Dunn came in, a tall white-haired man in his sixties, who'd spent twenty-two years as a Washington PD lieutenant before getting the job as head of security here. 'Hey, Joe. What's up?'

Just about to go, Mrs Byrne. Anything I can do for you first?'

'Nope. We're set for the senator's deposition?'

'Yes, we are. Saturday, eight o'clock.'

'I don't want anyone here except you and me,' she said. 'He's particular about the situation, and he's a United States senator with an eye on the Democratic nomination.'

'Yes, mam.' Dunn half saluted and left her alone. The phone rang and she clicked her tongue in exasperation. 'Hello. Angie Byrne,' she said.

'Hi, honey. It's me. How are you?'

'Busy, Louis. Any developments?'

'We found a dead black man in the river. Apart from that, nothing. I was just checking you were OK.'

'I'm fine. Don't worry about me, Louis. I'm a big girl.'

'You talk to anyone there about it?'

'No.'

'OK. Great. We want to keep it under wraps for now.'

'No problem. When you coming home?'

'I don't know. Couple of days, I guess.'

'Talk to you later, then.' She hung up and went back to work.

The phone rang again and she was almost tempted to switch to voice mail, but didn't.

'Angie Byrne.' More than a hint of irritation in her voice.

'My attorney.'

289

A coldness dripped through her. 'What do you want?'

'Fair representation.'

'Get yourself a lawyer, then.'

'I've got one.'

'No, you don't.'

'Did you see the news just now? They're looking for a TV van. The unknown subject got away, they believe, in a television van.'

Angie sat back, the tape running on her phone. She taped all her calls as a matter of course. 'Why d'you think they called me "unknown"?' he said.

'You tell me, asshole.'

She heard him click his tongue. 'That's no way to speak to a client.'

'You're not a client. You'll never be a client. I'm busy, so what do you want?'

'We can talk about that later. For now, just remember the parable of the jackal and the crow.'

He hung up then, and Angie sat back, shook her head and switched off her computer screen. Concentration gone, that ball of knots in her stomach for the second time today. She rewound the tape and picked up the phone to New Orleans. 'Louis,' she said. 'He's got my office number. I received a call right after you put the phone down.'

'He's calling you at the office now?' Her husband paused on the other end of the line. 'Maybe we could . . .'

'Don't even think about it, baby. This is the President's attorney's office. The partners will never allow it.'

'OK. Just a thought. What did he say?'

'I taped it. I'll play it to you.'

The New Orleans team were still gathered in the conference room, and Byrne put the taped conversation with Boese through the conference line, so they could all hear it. When it was over, he said goodbye to his wife and told

290

her to get an FBI escort home. She told him audibly to fuck off, she could look after herself.

Harrison cocked an eyebrow at Byrne. 'Sounds like my kinda gal,' he said.

Swann was pensive. 'Jackal and crow again. What's he talking about?'

Nobody could give him an answer.

Darkness had fallen in Meridian, Mississippi. Boese crossed the street and ate buffalo wings and french fries in the diner next to Howard Johnson's. When he was finished, he left a five-dollar tip and went back to the hotel. He already had his eye on a grey Ford sedan parked two up from his van. He had number plates in the back, which would take him no time to fix. Back in the hotel room he closed his eyes again. An hour later, he switched the number plates on the Ford. Quietly, he moved his equipment, then took the magnetic KYZ Radio signs and refixed them on the side of the van. He got behind the wheel of the Ford, hot-wired the ignition and pulled out on to the highway, heading west. He wondered how long it would take them to find the van.

Kovalski had decided on his course of action, and he called a late meeting to announce that he was going to run a team on the ground, initially out of New Orleans. Two or three people with specialist knowledge, headed by Cheyenne Logan. Everyone stared at her as he said it.

'Logan was in London with the FEST last year,' Kovalski explained, 'and she also worked the Salvesen case from the US. She's had four years in Domestic Terrorism and will be the ground liaison with the SIOC.' He looked then at Swann. 'If you want to tag along, your knowledge will be useful, Jack. You've got no jurisdiction, of course, but you can participate in the investigation other than fugitive contact.'

'I'll clear it with SO13,' Swann said. 'But he's on the run and we want him, so I'm sure they'll let me stay.'

Mayer interrupted them. 'What about from this office, you want some agents on temporary duty?'

Kovalski nodded. 'I'd like a couple of co-ordinators based right here,' he said, 'and whatever intelligence analysts you can spare.' He looked then at Harrison. 'Apart from them, I want Johnny Buck on the ground.'

Harrison sat back, gazed hard at Swann and spat into his empty Coke can.

## 17

The following morning, they gathered in the conference room. Kovalski suggested that Logan brief the people back cast as to what had transpired. Byrne had flown back to Washington first thing that morning. It was suggested that they might want to get the behavioural science people involved, as well as the fugitive and violent crimes units.

Harrison pursed his lips. 'Don't we got enough people involved already?' He sat up straighter. 'What can they tell us anyway, goddammit? We know who the fucker is.'

Kovalski glanced at him and winced. 'We'll think about it,' he said. 'If we need them later, we'll bring them in. Right now, we need to find the TV van or whatever vehicle he used.'

'What about the identities of the other two with Boese?' Swann asked.

Logan answered him. 'I've run the pictures through the NCIC and we've got a couple of possibles, but nothing definite.'

'We have to talk to Jakob Salvesen again,' Kovalski stated. 'I'm asking two agents outta Salt Lake to go see him. We might luck out and get something, but I doubt it.'

Swann scratched his temple. 'None of this makes sense,' he said. 'Why do what he did? Why announce himself quite so spectacularly, without actually going for the full vanity trip and plastering his name all over the television stations? He rang the local ones down here. He even rang CNN in Atlanta. So why not tell them who he is? He told the crewman and the hookers. He sent you a feather. Why not go all the way?'

'I thought you said this guy was the ultimate enigma,' Harrison said.

Swann did not answer him directly. 'Even bearing that in mind, it doesn't answer my question. He was made public, after years of secrecy, last year.' He looked round the room. 'He's got nothing more he can hide. What's the reason behind it?'

Logan cut in on him then. 'Jack, yesterday, you told us how he likes to put people on warning without giving them a reason.'

Swann folded his arms across his chest and nodded. 'I know I did, Chey. But somehow this feels different.'

'"Feels different."' Harrison cocked an eyebrow at him. 'Just exactly what does that mean, bubba?'

The phone rang on the side cabinet and John Cochrane, who would be the office of origin ground liaison, leaned over and picked it up. His features stiffened and he nodded. 'OK. Right.' He put the phone down and looked across the table at Logan. 'Guess the debate's over,' he said. 'That was the Jackson field office. They think they've found the van.'

Taking Harrison's car, they drove out of the city on Interstate 10, crossing the bridge which clipped the south-eastern corner of Lake Pontchartrain. Swann looked out across the expanse of the water, the surface shimmering, crystal blue in the Louisiana sunshine. He could see the causeway more clearly now, the cars moving up and down. He had seen it from the air when they flew in to the airport at Kenner, lit up in the darkness. Twenty-four miles long, and when you got to the middle, you could not see land in any direction.

Logan sat up front with Harrison; Swann in the big back seat of the silver Crown Victoria. Harrison had attached a blue light to the inside of the windshield and traffic moved

294

out of the way as he raced up the highway at 110 miles an hour. The car moved effortlessly.

'It's got the basic police package,' Harrison told him, when Swann asked. 'Up-rated suspension, reinforced floor and an oversize engine.' He indicated the overdrive switch on the gear shift. 'Alls I gotta do is press that and she really kicks ass.'

Logan had her lap-top open and was scrolling through pages of the notes and reports she had on file. Swann leaned over the front seats. 'All the stuff from London, Jack.' She turned her face to his and smiled.

Harrison looked sideways at her, then in the mirror at Swann. 'How come you let this mother get away in the first place, duchess?' he said. Logan flashed dark eyes at him, but he ignored her.

Swann stared at him in the mirror. Harrison was fifteen years older at least, with a battered, lined face, like old leather, and his hair long and grey down his back. The baseball hat was grimy at the peak, and in his denims and boots, he looked like a roughneck from the oilfields.

'We didn't let him get away,' Swann said quietly. 'Strangely enough, we don't do that. He employed a bunch of ex-soldiers to shoot up the escort taking him to trial. Close-range suppression fire in a crowded London street. Have you ever been to London, Harrison?'

'Never had any call to.'

'I don't suppose you have. Well, twenty-two people got killed that day. Sixteen of them policemen. Machine-gun fire and phosphorus grenades. Ugly sight. Not one I want to look at again.' He pressed his lips into a line. 'I think I want Boese a bit more than you do.'

They drove for half an hour in silence. Harrison plucked a cigarette from an unseen packet in his shirt pocket. He popped a match on his thumbnail and Logan wrinkled her nose, but said nothing. Her hair fell across her face and

295

Swann was filled with the desire to hook it behind her ear. She did it herself, exposing a high, chocolate-coloured cheekbone. She looked back at him again. 'I've got everything logged here, Jack.' She indicated the computer. 'Copies of all your files. We can check through it later if you want to rerun anything. We're in twenty-four-hour contact with the SIOC. I can download whatever I want, either to them or from them. All I need is a phone line.'

They got to Meridian at the top of Highway 59 just before noon. The SWAT team from the Jackson field office had been deployed and had opened the van with KYZ Radio flashed along the panels on its flanks. Logan sought out the SAC, and he explained that the van had been sighted in the parking lot by one of the guests. After the Jackson agents got there, they discovered that another car, a grey Ford Taurus, had been stolen sometime during the night. The driver of the van had been in room 202, and, as they spoke, it was being scoured by evidence response agents.

Logan walked over to the van. Two ERT guys in paper suits and sterile gloves were conducting a fingertip search. 'You guys come up with anything?' she asked them. 'I'm running the ground force team for D.C.'

'Oh, right.' One of them sat back on his haunches and indicated the floor of the van. 'A couple of fibres is all. No fingerprints yet.'

Swann stood at Logan's elbow and scanned the empty back of the van.

The hotel manager was hovering behind them with the SAC from Jackson. Logan turned to him. Harrison was standing looking at the van, with one hand on his hip.

'Who drove it?' Logan asked the manager. He was a big, fleshy man with a red face and broken veins in his nose. His hair was thin and black, and little globs of perspiration bedecked the pink of his scalp. He looked at her, then at Swann, and spoke as if he should be talking to Swann.

'Black guy. I mean a negro.'

Logan nodded. 'What did he look like?'

The man frowned. 'Well, I don't know . . .'

'We all look alike, don't we,' Logan said, shaking her head. 'But was he black black, like I'm black, or lighter?'

He scratched his arm with his middle fingernail 'I guess he was lighter'n you.'

'What about his hair?'

'Afro, you'd call it, I guess. Short though, not big on top.' He patted his own head lightly and smiled at Swann.

Harrison came up behind them and spat a stream of tobacco juice. 'The van,' he said to the manager. 'Did it come in like that?'

The manager looked puzzled. 'Like what?'

'Like it is now.' Harrison waved a hand at it. 'KYZ Radio.'

'I guess. I didn't see it.'

'But you checked the guy in, right?'

'Yeah, but I didn't notice the van.'

'You mean you didn't *see* or you didn't *notice*?' Harrison walked over to the van, and, putting on a pair of gloves, he took hold of the radio station sign and peeled it off.

'Magnetic,' he said to Logan. 'It's a taxi cab underneath.'

'*The* taxi cab,' she said.

'Right.'

The manager looked bug-eyed at them, almost a little sheepish. 'No wonder I didn't notice,' he said.

They looked through the room: unmade bed, nothing in the drawers, the closets or the bathroom. It was a standard, run-of-the-mill Holiday Inn bedroom. Swann stood with his hands in his pockets, feeling the presence of Boese.

Harrison stood by the door, smoking. 'He drove in without the magnetic signs on,' he said. 'Then he ups and puts them back on.' Swann looked round at him. Harrison was looking at Logan, who leaned against the window. 'Why do that?' Harrison finished.

'Because he wanted us to find it,' Swann said.

Webb and McCulloch had left Catherine Morgan to sweat a bit longer. Her solicitor had told them she was ready to resume the interview, but they let her go another night. They were both at the Yard, listening to the early morning briefing given by Colson.

'We need to get sound into The Regiment's clubhouse in Hounslow,' he was saying. 'We're going to create a diversion, get everybody in that street out and get a technical unit from Box inside.' He looked at Webb. 'George, I'll want you to do the sneaky beaky, so the sound men can do their job properly.'

'No problem,' Webb said. 'Just tell me when.'

'We're set up for tomorrow with the gas board. There'll be a leak in Wellington Avenue, which is a parallel street to theirs. The whole area will be evacuated for a period of two hours.'

'Plenty of time,' Webb said.

He and McCulloch drove over to Paddington Green in McCulloch's car. 'Have you spoken to Jack?' McCulloch asked him.

'Not since the tanker thing, no.'

'Wonder how he's getting on over there?'

'I'll speak to him later today.'

McCulloch rasped a palm over his jawline. 'Good that he could get out of London in some ways. He was struggling, wasn't he.'

Webb looked sideways at him. 'Who wouldn't be in his position, Macca?'

Catherine Morgan was brought down to the interview room after a second night in the cells. Her face was pinched and white and darkened hollows accentuated the depth of her eyes. 'I want to speak to my son,' she said.

Webb stroked his moustache. 'Well, maybe we can think about that. Talk to us first, Catherine. Tell us why Ismael Boese's fingerprints are on a map in your car.'

She glanced at her lawyer, tugged at her lip with her teeth and lit a cigarette. 'I went to France with him and my son,' she said.

Webb breathed out heavily. 'Go on.'

She made a face. 'I didn't want to. I had to.'

'How did you get the car?'

'The money was sent to me. I was told to go and buy something practical and half decent, you know.'

Webb nodded. 'How did it begin, the contact, I mean?'

'My brother. He'd not wanted to see me for over a year, then he writes me a letter and sends the money for me to come down on the train.' She looked at Webb then, a little bit of pleading in her eyes. 'We've never been the closest of families. He was always the bad one. Violent. He's hit me more than once.'

'What did he tell you to do?'

'Messages. I was to put messages in the newspaper on a certain day of the month.'

'Which newspaper?' Webb was leaning further over the table.

'The *International Herald Tribune*. I'd never heard of it before.'

'We found some copies in your flat,' McCulloch said.

'Aye, that's right. I kept them. My brother passed me the messages written on a piece of cigarette paper. I put the advert in and paid for it. Then I had to copy out the reply and take it into the prison.' She sat back. 'It was

299

pretty easy really. Nobody thinks to check a packet of Rizlas.'

Webb pushed his chair back and folded his arms across his chest. 'What about after?'

'I had no part in the killings. My brother told me that he was going to get a lot of money if I helped. He was due out in a year or so, and he said we'd be set up for life on the money. He also told me if I didn't help he'd send somebody after me.'

Webb cocked one eyebrow. 'Your brother did that, threatened you?'

'Aye. He's done it before now, I'll tell you.'

'So what did you do?' McCulloch asked.

'I just drove to Portsmouth and waited for him to come. Then we all went on holiday to France. One of them farmhouses, but he only stayed a couple of days.' She shook her head then and started crying. Webb rolled his eyes to the ceiling.

'You'll have to protect us now,' she sobbed. 'He threatened to kill my son if I ever said anything.'

Back at the Yard, they got the copies of the newspapers which had been brought from the flat, and Webb and McCulloch sat in the squad room, scouring the advertising pages.

'Listen to this,' McCulloch suddenly said, 'November, last year: "To sell bookcases to engines to xylophones. And shortly to be in York and Birmingham and Brighton. In Kendal next year. For beds or Queen Anne oval mirrors, xylophones or violins, call British and Anglian."' He frowned heavily, the lines creasing his face. 'What the hell is that about?'

'Code, Macca,' Webb said, patting him on the arm. 'We're going to need Box to look at it.'

\*

Christine Harris scrolled through the notes on her computer screen in the Special Branch cell. Before he had flown to the United States, Jack Swann had passed over the information he had obtained from NCIS on the biker gang, The Regiment. Harris had a sheaf of photographs at her side, the stills taken from the funeral parade across the Tyne Bridge, some of which had been already scanned on to the computer. She studied Collier's face now. Dog Soldiers, a warrior faction and ... young men of the Cheyenne Indian nation. Collier had served time in the most elite regiment in the British army.

Flicking through Swann's notes, she picked up on Janice Martin again. She had been considering her, and considering the whole subornation process in the wake of Amaya Kukiel. Since she left the country, Vaczka had been silent. The surveillance was cancelled and, so far, that was that. But every instinct she had ever relied upon told her that Jorge Vaczka and his little Polish army were linked to the events in Hanwell Green. But by travelling up to Ellesmere Port, Vaczka, Stahl and the others had managed to procure themselves the best alibi possible: how could they have been involved, when they were under surveillance in the north of England.

Again, she looked at Janice Martin's picture, reading the notes that MI5 had dug up on her background. She was the only daughter of a wealthy antiques dealer, who, Box believed, still allowed her some money a month, notwithstanding the company she was keeping and the cocaine habit he was inadvertently feeding. Everything else they had on The Regiment indicated that, unlike other bike gangs, they were not dealing in drugs. Stolen motorcycles shipped out of the US possibly, but nothing to do with drugs. Janice Martin was a mamma, which meant she slept with any gang member at any time. As Swann had done previously, Harris considered the hairs recovered from the discarded crash helmets in the canal. Those hairs could give them DNA, but only if they had something to match it with. She wrinkled her face at the thought. But what other way was there? Janice Martin was the weak link in The Regiment's armour. Again, she looked at the pictures. Gringo, ex-marine commando and second in commmand to Collier. Then there was Fagin, the skinny one, who had been in the Guards, like the deceased John Stanley. She looked back at Janice again, a very pretty blonde-haired girl in her mid-twenties.

'The master of illusion.' Swann sipped his bottle of MGD and looked across the table at Harrison, who was rolling a cigarette around in his mouth. The three of them were sitting at a table in the diner across the highway from the Holiday Inn. 'When I first interviewed Boese in London, he was reading a book about Geronimo, the Apache. According to my boss at the Yard, Geronimo was the master of illusion. It's why he evaded capture for so long.'

'Like the van and the tanker.' Logan sat next to him, spreading barbecue sauce on her hamburger. 'Illusion.'

Harrison sighed audibly. 'That's a great hypothesis, limey. But it don't answer the question why.'

Swann stared at him for a moment. 'Look, Harrison,' he said. 'You don't like me. I don't know why. Maybe you're just prejudiced against the English. Fourth of July or something. Maybe your grandad can't find a record of him fighting with us in World War Two, I don't know. But stop calling me limey.'

Harrison looked across the table at him, a faint sneer on his lip. 'You know something, asshole,' he said, 'you really shouldn't talk about stuff you don't understand. You never fought in any goddamn war. You wanna pull all that "Yankee over here" shit on me and I'll show you a fucking Yankee.' He lit the cigarette and drew smoke in harshly.

302

'Harrison.' Logan's voice was clipped and cold. 'You get off whatever trip you're on, baby, or I'll call you in with Kovalski. You might be his Shenandoah buddy, but *I'm* running this show.'

'You know what.' Harrison stood up. 'I need a real drink.' He stalked over to the bar, where he perched himself on a stool and tipped back his hat. Swann stared after him.

'What's his problem, Chey?'

She hissed out a breath and tugged at the hem of her skirt. 'I never got round to telling you, did I.' She flapped out a hand. 'I had a word with Cochrane back in New Orleans.'

Swann bunched his eyes at the corners. 'What did he say?'

'Honey.' She touched his cheek with long fingers. 'Harrison thinks you're the reason he got burned in Idaho.'

Swann stared at her for a long moment and she nodded. 'Salvesen arrested him under their mock common law. They tried him and would've hanged him if he hadn't known about the tunnels. They chased him clear across the county, Jack. He ended up taking three of them out in a mine shaft. He nearly got killed, and I'm afraid he really does hate you.' She shook her head then. 'I think Kovalski might be running some kinda dumb joke, having put you two together. But the Bureau owes Johnny Buck big time. He can do no wrong after what he did to the militia. You got to watch yourself, Jack. Harrison's a KMA. That's a "kiss my ass" agent. He's fifty years old and doesn't give a damn any more.'

Swann felt as if someone had taken a punch at him, a sucker punch right under the ribs, knocking the wind from his body. He sat and looked at her, lips scrunched up, eyes half-closed, then he exhaled a long breath. 'I don't understand,' he said. 'How can he think that *I* was responsible?'

'Your ex-girlfriend, Jack.' Logan covered his hand with hers. 'Pia Grava. Brigitte Hammani. Harrison got burned right around the time you and Byrne went to Paris. You told Pia you were going, remember? She would've known why.'

Swann thought about it then. He had gone to Paris while the army EOD men were trying to render safe the bomb in the City. There, he had identified Pia. It made sense. All it would've taken was one phone call from her. She was owned by Storm Crow; and Storm Crow, at the time, was employed by Salvesen.

'Oh, Christ,' he said. He laid his hands open, palm up on the table and looked across the bar at Harrison's stiff back. 'No wonder he's pissed off.'

'I'm sorry, Jack.' Again she touched his hand and this time he squeezed her fingers.

'I'm OK.' He looked again at Harrison. 'What can I do about it?'

'Nothing, hon. Not a damn thing. He might get over it. He might not. But don't call him out on it, Jack. He fought the VC, one to one, lying on his belly underground. They don't come meaner than that.'

They stayed in the Holiday Inn. Swann lay in his room and stared at the ceiling. The loneliness was as intense as he had ever known it. His mind worked over itself; clouded images, the past, the present, Harrison's tough face, those blue steel eyes, and the knowledge that *his* involvement with Pia had nearly got the man killed. God, no wonder he hated him. Guilt lifted from somewhere in the pit of his stomach and the weight was so fierce he had to stand up. He switched on the light and lit a cigarette. Then, pulling on his trousers, he opened the door on to the balcony.

Harrison stood there, leaning on the rail and smoking. Swann opened his mouth to say something, but stopped himself. Harrison was staring out over the highway, the lighted roads running crossways towards downtown Meridian. He flipped away the butt of his cigarette, blew a stream of smoke and looked round.

'Logan got a call from the ERT guys in Jackson,' he said slowly. 'Last thing tonight. The prints they lifted from room 202 were definitely Storm Crow.'

'Right.' Swann avoided his eye.

Harrison moved off the rail and opened his door. 'I'm getting some shut eye. Better get some yourself.' He looked coldly, once, right into Swann's eyes, and closed the door to his room.

Webb spoke to the briefing at Scotland Yard. That morning, the operatives from MI5 had come back to him with the coded messages broken. They had turned to one of their academic contacts at Oxford University. He had worked on the tail end of the Enigma programmes during World War II and had broken this code easily.

'Apparently the code was used by Caesar,' Webb explained. 'Anyway, the eggheads have broken it. There's three messages. Two going out and one coming in. I don't know who they were going to, but we all know Tal-Salem was never captured.' He paused. 'The first one is weird, from Boese to whoever was outside. It says: "We have been betrayed."' He broke off and looked at Colson. 'Why would Storm Crow say *we*? And also, how was he betrayed? I mean it's not as if he didn't get out of prison, is it.'

He went on to tell them the second and third messages: Greer dead TJ CC and the trial date. 'I'll phone Swann with these,' he said. 'They might be relevant over there.'

Harris stood up then and told them what she and her Special Branch colleagues planned to do about The Regiment. 'Janice Martin is the key,' she said. 'Or, at least, the weakest link we can find. They all sleep with her because she's so good-looking. If she wasn't, I doubt they'd tolerate her coke habit, considering their apparent aversion to class A narcotics. We're putting a team on her. We'll need to be bloody careful, because they operate a third eye most of the time. But I doubt she's accompanied when she scores gear, so that'll be prime time. I'm going to try and bust her on a possession charge and get her to lay down.' She chewed on her lip for a moment. 'She's already got two previous convictions for possession and this time she's looking at a stretch.' She sighed then. 'Boys, you're going to love this bit. I'll admit it was Swann's idea, not mine. But Janice Martin is a mamma, which, like I said, means she sleeps with any gang member at any time of his choosing. I'd say she was regular fodder, and she has the privacy of her own flat. We've got some hair from the crash helmets, which will give us DNA if we can get something to match it with.'

'Oh, God.' Webb rolled his eyes to the ceiling. 'Jack Swann's mind.'

'I know, but it might work. We can get semen samples from her and ID the owner. If we get a DNA match with the hairs, we might start to create some waves.' She looked at Colson. 'That'd make the sound in the clubhouse interesting listening.

'The point is,' she went on, 'if we can ID the helmet-wearer, then we can start a little psychological warfare. We can listen in to conversations inside and put a tap on the phone. Gang members who live out of the area have to phone in at least twice a week.' She broke off again for a moment. 'My instincts tell me there is a connection between the Poles and The Regiment. I've no idea what it is, but that trial day's events were just too coincidental. The Poles were planning something. Box 850 said possibly Ulster Loyalist links, but maybe it was something else. One thing is interesting, however, and it might give us a break if we can ever get to it: biker gangs operate written contracts. They do it over drug territories, lines of supply, etc. The word from NCIS is that The Regiment might just do requests. If they do, they'll be contracted on paper. The details are only known by one or two, and it stops flapping mouths. I'm getting a Schedule 7 search warrant to look at their financial activities, some of which are in America. I've already contacted the US Secret Service.'

Swann took the call from Webb at 5 a.m. in his room. Every time he moved, he paged London with a contact number. He was fast asleep, and dreaming that he was back on Nanga Parbat, but it wasn't Steve Brady he was killing, but Harrison. He woke to the sound of the phone ringing, with sweat on the sheets and a clamminess to his skin.

'Hello.'

'Jack.'

'Hey.' Swann rubbed his eyes. 'It's five o'clock, Webby.'

'It's elevenses here. How you doing?'

'I've been better. I'm working with this ground task force the FBI have got going. Three of us: me, Logan and Harrison.'

'Logan? You lucky bastard.'

'Yeah, I think I fancy her, Webby. I mean, I do fancy her. I mean, I like her a lot.'

'Never shit where you eat, Jack.'

'No, right. I've got enough problems, eh.'

'What d'you mean?'

'Harrison. He's the UCA from Idaho? The one who was nearly executed by the militia.'

'What about him?'

'He thinks I'm responsible for it.'

'What?'

307

Swann fumbled for a cigarette, the ache back in his gut. 'He thinks I got him burned, George. I went to Paris with Byrne. That meal receipt, remember. I told Pia I was going, and the next thing you know, Harrison is compromised.'

Webb was silent for a moment. 'Shit, Jack.'

'Yeah, I know. Harrison is one pissed-off man, an ex-Tunnel Rat for Christ's sake and enough service with the FBI to not give a shit any more.' Swann exhaled cigarette smoke and pulled the blankets up to his chin again. 'We never asked Pia about compromise, Webby. We didn't have to.'

'I suppose it's obvious.'

'Yeah. I suppose it is.'

'Can you deal with it?'

'I'll have to, won't I. I'm not running home with my tail between my legs.'

Webb was silent for a moment, then he said: 'Listen, the reason I'm ringing is because we've worked out how Boese got messages out of Reading. He used Brynn Morgan's sister. You know we picked her up. Well, she coughed yesterday morning.' Webb told him about the coded messages. 'We cracked the code through Box. The first one is strange, Jack. I can't understand it.'

'What is it?'

'"We have been betrayed."'

'We?'

'That's what I thought.'

'Why would Storm Crow say *we*?'

'Exactly.'

'And who in their right mind would betray him?' Swann lay back against the wall, a pillow behind his head, and put out the cigarette. 'He knew he was getting out,' he said. 'He must've done. He'd never have been caught otherwise.'

'Right.'

308

'So why betrayal?' He could hear Webb's breathing down the line.

'I agree, it makes no sense.'

'What did the others say?'

Webb told him the second message and finally the date of the trial.

Swann wrote them down and he was about to put the phone down when another thought stalked across his mind. 'How did Boese *know* he'd been betrayed, George?'

'Sorry, I'm not with you.'

'How did he know? Something must've happened to tell him.' Swann paused for a moment. 'No calls, no letters, and only one visitor.'

'Benjamin Dubin,' Webb said.


Swann went over to breakfast in the diner with Logan. They had had a brief telephone conference with Kovalski and Byrne, who were both back in Washington. The stolen Ford that Boese had used had not, as yet, been sighted. Undoubtedly, he would have changed the licence plates. Harrison came in a few minutes after them and sat down to eggs, bacon and hash browns. He looked as though he'd had a skinful of whisky, and drank his coffee hot and black with no sugar. Swann thought about the events of the early morning and his long-distance phone call with Webb. All of it disturbed him and he did not know what, if anything, to say to Harrison.

'So, what's the plan, Stan?' Harrison squinted at Logan. 'We gonna sit here, go to Jackson, back to New Orleans, or what?'

'I wanna go over to Jackson field office and talk through everything the ERT have got.'

'Your call, baby.' Harrison looked at Jack. 'Sleep well, did ya, bubba?'

'No. Actually.' Again Swann wanted to say something,

but Harrison turned his attention back to his plate. 'SO13 phoned me at five o'clock this morning,' Swann said in the end.

'Up with the roosters, were you?'

'Something like that.' Swann told them about Boese's escape and the messages in the *International Herald Tribune*. He took the slip of paper he had written them on and read them out. 'Second one was: "Greer dead. TJ CC."'

Harrison stopped eating, fork halfway from the plate to his mouth. 'Run that by me again.' His eyes narrowed and he set the fork down. Swann passed him the slip of paper. Harrison sat for a moment, then squeezed a white filtered cigarette from his shirt pocket. 'Cheyenne, pass me that cellphone, would you.'

She handed it to him and he flipped it open, then dialled, waited, cursed and dialled again. 'Hey, bro. What's up?'

'Martinez came through.' Penny's voice in his ear. 'We got a meeting set up. But I need you, man. I told them you're outta town looking at supply lines. I need you in New Orleans.'

'No problem. I can fly in for a night. I'm trying to get hold of John Earl right now, but he don't answer his phone.'

'I'll page him for you. What number you on?'

Harrison told him and switched off the phone.

Logan looked at him. 'What gives, Harrison?'

Harrison picked his teeth with a cocktail stick. 'That note. TJ CC. I think I've seen it before.'

The phone rang almost immediately and Harrison spoke at some length with Cochrane. 'Check it for me, will ya, buddy?' he said, then waited, drumming his fingers on the tabletop. Cochrane came back on the line. 'Right. OK.' Harrison hung up and looked at Logan. 'Baby, you ever been to Georgia?'

'I'm from Alabama. What do you think?'

He explained the situation in the car. They were two states west of Georgia and the part they wanted was all but in South Carolina. It would take them most of the day to drive, but it would still be quicker than finding an airport, waiting for a plane and flying. Swann listened intently as Harrison told them about John Earl Cochrane being the VICAP co-ordinator, and how they had had a call from the Georgia Bureau of Investigation, with similarities between a murder in the small town of Royston and a series throughout the south. 'Gal from the CASKU came down, but there were too many differences,' he said. 'Method of strangulation was wrong, for one. This dude used a ligature of some kind. The guy we were after has been dubbed "The Garbageman".' He squinted at Swann as he drove. 'He left the bodies in dumpsters – used his forearm.' He sucked on his cigarette and trailed smoke from the side of his mouth. 'Not only that, but the age of the victim was wrong. They got all kinds of psychological theories up there in Virginia and most of the time they're right.' He paused and scratched his head. 'There was something else too, but I can't remember. Oh, yeah. The GBI dicks found the butt end of a joint in the yard at the back of the store.'

Swann tensed all at once. 'A joint?' he said.

'That's right, bubba. You know, a cigarette with drugs in.'

Swann ignored him. Logan leaned her arm over the back of the seat. 'What is it, Jack?'

'Yeah, what is it, Jack?' Harrison mimicked.

Logan glanced sideways at him. 'Harrison, why don't you shut up and listen to what he's got to say for once in your fool life.'

Harrison grimaced and pressed his foot to the accelerator pedal. Again, Logan looked round.

Swann sat hunched against the window, fighting the desire to punch Harrison in the back of the head. 'There's a killer I mentioned when we were in New Orleans,' he said. 'His name is Tal-Salem, and he's the only one of Boese's gang we couldn't scoop up.'

'What's your point?' Harrison cut in.

'My point, Harrison, is we now think that this murder in Hicksville, Georgia, as you put it, may be linked to Boese.'

'So?'

'So Tal-Salem always smokes a joint before he kills someone.'

Louis Byrne was due to meet them at the offices of the GBI in Athens. They got there first, Harrison shaking hands again with Agent Gabriel Chaney, the big, bull-necked detective who had worked the case. He introduced Jack Swann as a limey from Scotland Yard and again Swann bristled. He remembered Logan's words. Harrison would needle him and needle him until something snapped and then he would punch his lights out. He wondered how he'd do against a fifty-year-old.

Chaney looked Logan up and down and talked above her head. 'Yeah, we still got the joint,' he said. 'Why?'

Swann sat on the edge of the desk. 'Because the BKA in Germany and the DST in France have got Tal-Salem's DNA. We've already matched it with a stub end of a spliff we found in London.' He looked back into Chaney's big, flat face then. 'If there's dried saliva on that butt, there'll be DNA. We can maybe put an identity to it through London.' He picked up the phone. 'I'll get them to send the configuration over.' He looked at Logan. 'Where shall I have it sent?'

'Domestic Terrorism in Washington.'

Logan turned to Chaney, who was chewing on a cigar stub and talking to Harrison.

'Did you make any progress with the case?' she asked him. He replied without looking directly at her.

'Not really. Our main suspect was a black guy who claimed to be from Alabama. Rode into town with a broken truck and got set up over at one of the autoshops there. He was in the jewellery store the day before Mary Poynton was murdered.' He looked at Swann. 'Greer was her maiden name. I guess y'all will want to talk to her old man. That'd be Jim Poynton. He was interviewed by the Carnesville sheriff's dicks and myself. But he couldn't say much, except give us her background history. Y'all go on and talk to him, but she didn't do a whole lot. He'll tell you.'

Swann put the phone down and leaned against the wall, folding his arms, as Chaney continued. 'The black guy reconnoitred the joint, I reckon. He drove outta town in the tow truck. Only other vehicle sighted was a blue Toyota with tinted-out windows. Nobody tagged the plate and the body wasn't discovered till five hours after the crime was committed.' He made a face and clamped his teeth over the cigar. Still he looked at Harrison and Swann as he talked, his eyes never alighting on Logan's face, though he dropped his gaze to the curves in her skirt more than once. 'Sure shook them people up, up there. They got no history of crime to speak of. Place is where Ty Cobb grew up.' He squinted at Swann. 'Baseball player from way back. Only other claim to fame is Tony Jones Street. Tony was from there too, or had a house there or something. He plays football for the Broncos.'

Byrne arrived and was shown into Chaney's office. He wrinkled his nose at the combined cigar and cigarette smoke and introduced himself to Chaney. Chaney got the file from his cabinet and spread the papers out on the desk. 'We need to speak to the husband,' Byrne said. 'You know where we can locate him today?'

'I ain't sure. Give Van Clayburgh a call. He's the Carnesville sheriff. Poynton did work for the Chevy dealer up there, but that may've changed. If y'all don't mind, I'll let you get on up there by yourselves.' He glanced briefly at Swann. 'You want that butt end of the reefer, buddy?'

Swann nodded.

'OK.' Chaney took a nylon evidence bag, with the stub of cigarette inside, from the drawer, and parcelled the papers into a blue file. He handed them both to Harrison.

'Guess it was federal, after all,' he said. 'Get the sonofabitch and I'll book him for you.'

# 18

The FBI ground team drove up Highway 29 from Athens to Carnesville and the sheriff's department on James Little Street. Clayburgh remembered Harrison, probably from his long hair. He was talking to one of his detectives when the team came in.

'Hey, Sheriff,' Harrison said. 'What's happening?'

'How y'all doing?' The sheriff shook hands and glanced briefly at Logan.

'Sheriff, I'm Special Agent Logan,' she said, offering her hand.

'Uh huh.' He shook her hand and looked at Byrne.

'We need to speak to James Poynton,' Logan went on.

'You do, huh.' Still Clayburgh looked at Byrne.

Byrne introduced himself and then Swann.

'Scotland Yard, uh?' Clayburgh scratched his nose. 'No shit.'

Logan interrupted them, her voice calm, no hint of irritation. She let it all just blow over her head. 'Sheriff, apart from seeing Mr Poynton, we need to go back to Royston and look at the crime scene.'

'Thought y'all decided this wasn't a federal case.' Clayburgh addressed Harrison.

'Things have changed,' he said.

'All righty,' Clayburgh said. 'Be my guest. Ain't nothing changed over there. The store closed down after Mary passed on. Nobody wanted to run it any more and the owners don't need the money. Seemed like the right thing under the circumstances.' He squinted at Logan now, not so much in her eyes as looking her up and down. 'The GBI

315

never did catch that black feller. Had to be him that done it, I figure. He was the only out-of-towner we saw that day. And it weren't a local deal.'

'Of course not.' Logan looked him right in the eye.

They checked into the Royston motel and Byrne set up conference lines. Swann told him about his conversation with Webb. 'Something happened, Louis, after Dubin visited him. Why would he send a note out right then? And why *we*? What does he mean by *we*?'

Byrne rubbed a palm over his marine-style haircut. 'Figure of speech, Jack.'

'What, like the royal *we*?' Swann looked at him with one eyebrow lifted.

'No.' Byrne shook his head. 'If your DNA test proves positive, then we know Boese is working with Tal-Salem again. The *we* is referring to them.'

Swann cocked his head to one side. 'Could be that, I suppose.'

'Can you think of anything else, Jack?'

The four of them took Harrison's car from Carnesville into Royston. 'Small-town, Georgia,' Byrne said, as they drove past the Chevy dealership. Poynton still worked there, but they had decided to visit the original crime scene again before they spoke with him. Logan wanted to see if, given what they now knew about a connection in London, a motive might be more apparent.

They parked on Church Street and Swann looked out of the side window at the jewellery store. Logan was sitting next to him, and she leaned across him to see, her hand brushing his thigh. The building was single-storey in pale brick, with a sheet of corrugated iron as a canopy, and pink woodwork round the windows. The door was pink and Swann could make out heart-shaped cushions, probably for display cases, beyond the glass. The twisted trunk of a naked tree grew out of the concrete on the sidewalk.

Harrison switched off the engine and adjusted his ankle holster. 'You guys go take a look-see,' he said, 'I'll see if I can round up old Mack, the police chief.' He took a cigarette from his shirt and popped a match, cupping both hands to his face.

Swann turned up his collar against the chill wind that drifted the length of the street. He glanced at the darkened windows of the Western store, and the business premises giving way to domestic ones, as Church Street cut a straight line into the distance. The three of them crossed the road and Swann peered through the shop window, cupping his hand to the glass. The display cases were intact, but bereft of anything to sell. Logan moved alongside him. 'See anything?'

He shook his head and they joined Byrne in the alleyway behind the shop.

'The GBI file states she was found in the dumpster back here.' Logan pointed to the green dustbin on wheels, which was set in the small space behind the back door. She looked the length of the alley to where the water tower dominated the rapidly greying skyline. 'Took off this way, maybe.'

Swann glanced at Byrne, who was standing by the dumpster, deep in thought.

'Louis?'

Byrne looked round at him. 'The killer put the body in here,' he said slowly.

'That's right.' Logan checked the file. 'Just like the garbageman in Louisiana.'

'Right.' Byrne still looked at the dumpster. 'And New Orleans had someone from the CASKU out here?'

'Special Agent Mallory. I graduated with her, Louis. She's got a master's in criminal psychology.'

Harrison came back with Mack, the aging, yellow-toothed chief of police. 'GBI boys never came up with nothing,' he was saying. 'I ain't gotten in here in a while now, but the owners left me a set of keys. Reckoned I'd need them till this thing got figured out.' He stopped on the sidewalk and glanced at the other three as they looked at the area out the back.

'They all with you?' he said to Harrison.

'You bet. Got us a limey back there, too, Mack. International now. Gonna put this town on the map.'

'No kidding.' Mack unlocked the front door and showed them inside.

Swann took in the surroundings; Harrison remained by the door, chewing tobacco. He had been right through this building when he came in Cochrane's stead the last time. He watched Swann, as he walked about the salesroom with one hand in his trouser pocket. Swann caught Logan's eye and made a face. The room smelled musty, damp and old. The door to the rear section, the kitchenette, stood open and it looked as though nothing had been disturbed since the murder happened. Dust lay thick and grey on the work surfaces. The police chief stood and watched them, particularly Logan, as they paced the room, none of them saying anything. Byrne looked closely at everything, face cold as if he was calculating every step the killer must've taken. Swann looked to where Harrison remained by the door.

'Seen it before, bubba. Don't need to see it again.'

'Why?' Byrne said suddenly, looking directly at Swann.

'Good question.' Swann touched the layers of dust on the glass cabinets and rubbed the ends of his fingers together. 'If this was Tal-Salem, he went to a hell of a lot of trouble over this woman.' The police chief was watching him. 'Our intelligence told us that Tal-Salem was back in Spain. We were making attempts to try and get him back to the UK.'

Byrne looked beyond him to the street outside, where a pick-up truck rumbled slowly past. 'Helluva lot of trouble.'

He turned and spoke to Logan. 'Let's go talk to the husband.'

They found Jim Poynton at the Chevy dealership and his boss gave him some time off to talk to them. Logan wanted to do it at his home. She told him she wanted to see some of Mary's things, get a feel for her surroundings.

'GBI did that already, mam.'

'I know that, Mr Poynton. But this is a federal case now and if we're gonna apprehend your wife's killer, I need to be thorough.' She smiled at him and laid a long-nailed hand on his arm. 'This musta been real hard on y'all and I thank you for giving us this time. I can promise you, Mr Poynton, we've got the best FBI agents there are working on this one.'

'You do?'

'You can count on it, sir.'

He drove Logan in his car to the house, and the rest followed in Harrison's. 'First time her black face made an impression that wasn't the wrong one,' he muttered. He glanced at Swann. 'You get that shit in London, duchess, the black/white thing?'

'It's around. Not like it is down here.'

They arrived at Poynton's house and followed him and Logan in through the screen door. The drapes were still pulled and the sitting room lay in darkness. Swann could see two mock leather couches and a reclining chair, all arranged round a TV set and video. A black cable box squatted on top of the TV, and the time stared out at them in liquid crystal letters.

'Sorry about the mess.' Poynton scooped last night's dinner dishes off the coffee table, and placed them in the sink, set round the corner in the open-plan kitchen. He opened the drapes and sat down in the reclining chair with a beer he had got from the fridge. 'Only got the one,' he said apologetically, and sucked off the froth. 'Goddamn. Four FBI agents in my house. What would my daddy say?'

'Your daddy?' Logan asked him.

He stood his beer on the arm of the chair and pushed a hand through his hair. 'My daddy was sheriff's deputy in Hart County.'

'So, y'alls a Georgia boy,' Harrison said.

'Yessir, I am. Born and raised.'

'And what about Mary?' Logan asked him. She had the file from the GBI on her lap.

'Alls in there, I guess.' Poynton nodded to it. 'I done told everything I ever knew about her to Agent Chaney in Athens.'

The Poyntons had been married in 1985, and had lived since then right there in Royston. Mary had been born in Clarksville, Virginia, fifty-three years previously, and her parents had run the Lakeview Motel. She had graduated from high school, then worked for a while in the Winn Dixie food hall right across from the police department. Logan read the file, then looked up at Poynton, who was nursing his can of Coors.

'Mary's maiden name was Greer,' she said. 'Where'd you meet her, Jim?'

'California.' Poynton put the can of beer down again and took a tin of Smokey Mountain snuff from his pocket. He sucked noisily, looked for somewhere to spit and swallowed instead. 'I was over in Orange County there for a while. Mary went to Berkeley.'

Logan glanced at her notes. 'She arrived in California in 1970.'

'I don't know. I guess.' Poynton poked himself in the chest. 'Me, I was just a surf bum. I don't remember a whole lot about the late sixties and early seventies. It was all just the Beach Boys and party on. I never hooked up with Mary till just before she moved to Nevada.'

Harrison stared at him: plump, middle-aged. He imagined him lying on his couch every night, watching HBO or Showtime, eating potato chips and drinking beer. It was hard to equate the person seated before them with the waves off Laguna Beach.

Logan sat forward in her seat. 'Have you got any pictures of Mary?' she asked.

'There's none there?'

'There is, honey, but only this one.' She smiled again, as she held up a portrait of his wife, taken, according to the inscription on the back, in 1997. 'You got any albums, Jim?' she asked. 'Any of her stuff. Did she collect stuff? Women like to collect stuff.'

'Are you kidding me? We got boxes up in the attic.'

'You do?'

'Sure we do. You wanna see some of it?'

'You bet.'

Harrison stood up. 'I'll give you a hand,' he said.

Swann smiled at Logan and she flicked her eyebrows. He had to hand it to her. After all the implicit shit he had watched her eat, she had this man wrapped so tightly round her little finger, he couldn't move. Swann bet with himself that Logan would find out more about who Mary Greer was in five minutes than Chaney would in a month.

Poynton and Harrison rummaged about above their heads for a few minutes, then came down carrying a cardboard box between them. They set it on the coffee table and Byrne stood up. 'Cheyenne,' he said. 'I'm gonna get back to D.C. I've got my car at the motel and you guys can handle things here. If you want help from Atlanta, let me know.'

'OK, Louis. I'll call into the SIOC later. You sure you don't want to stay?'

'I'm more use in D.C., trying to co-ordinate the other

offices with Tom Kovalski.' He shook hands with them all and left.

'That's Byrne,' Logan muttered. 'Flutters in and flutters right out again.'

'Guess he wanted to see for himself, though, huh,' Harrison said.

'I guess.' Logan was sifting through the box of memorabilia that Mary Greer had kept. She glanced at Swann. 'He knew her as Greer,' she said.

Swann thought for a moment. 'The note, you mean. Yes, he must've done.'

'What note?' Poynton was looking puzzled.

'Mr Poynton,' Logan said to him. 'The reason we got involved again is because there's more to your wife's death than the random killing you were perhaps led to believe. We don't know for sure, but we think we might be able to identify the killer.' She hesitated for a moment, then laid a warm hand on his knee. 'Right now, sir, this must be for your ears only. We'll make our findings public when we have to, but I don't want to do that yet.' She nodded to Swann. 'This man is from the British Antiterrorist Branch, and we think that Mary's death might be connected in some way with events you may have read about in Europe.'

'I don't read much about Europe. What events y'all talking about?'

'Terrorist stuff,' Swann said. 'Suffice to say, there's a bigger picture here, Mr Poynton. None of us know how that picture gets completed, but we're looking at some of the pieces.'

'We believe the killer knew your wife, or of her, before she married you,' Logan finished.

'Hell, that was fourteen years ago.' Poynton's face reddened about the ears. 'Y'all telling me this guy's been waiting to kill her for fourteen damn years?'

'We don't know. All we do know is that he used her

maiden name in a note that we discovered, and she wouldn't have used her maiden name since 1985.'

She turned back to the others. Each of them had a pile of Mary's papers and books from the box. 'So we're looking pre-1985,' she said.

Harrison had a yearbook in his hands and was flicking through the pages. High school 1963; Mary would have been seventeen. He browsed every page, looking for some clue, something that caught his eye.

Logan looked over at Poynton again, who had got another beer from the refrigerator. 'When did Mary leave California, Jim?'

'I can't remember. I was still there. I guess 1979, maybe 1980. She went to Reno and worked on the tables there for about six years. Matter of fact, she only quit when I brought her back here.'

'Reno?' Harrison said.

'Yeah. She worked the blackjack tables. Dealer. She was pretty good.'

'Did she know anybody with the initials TJ?' Logan asked him. 'Or CC, maybe?'

'Beats me.' He flapped his arms at his sides.

Swann sifted through his pile of papers: old letters, some perfumed from lovers, cuttings from magazines and photo albums. Some of the photos had come loose and he gathered these separately and worked his way through them. One caught his eye and he stared at it for a long time – three women, one black, and a dark-skinned boy of about nine or ten. The picture was taken in a park and the three women were leaning on wide-fanned grass rakes, the boy huddled between them. He turned it over and read the inscription on the back. *Me, Gabby & Oko. Park attendants one and all – 1970.* He showed the picture to Poynton. 'D'you remember this?' he asked.

Logan looked up then. Poynton took the picture and

regarded it thoughtfully. 'Before I was on the scene,' he said. 'In 1970, I was still surfing at San Clemente. I guess this is Berkeley, though. She attended classes there, worked as a park warden-cum-gardener for a while. These gals musta been her buddies, I guess. I don't know who they are, though.'

Logan took the picture from him and studied it carefully. 'Mind if I keep this for a while, Jim?'

'Be my guest. Matter of fact, you can take all this stuff if you want.' He looked at his watch. 'I got to get back to work about now.'

They took the box of papers back to the motel room and Logan spread them out on the bed. The photo she laid on one side. 'I want to get this put through the system,' she said. 'Gabby and Oko, that might tell us something.'

Swann was looking closely at it again, at the boy standing shyly between the women. He wore shorts and a T-shirt and his skin had an ebony tint, but his face was downcast and all that showed was the black hair on his head. He looked up at Harrison, who was looking back at him. 'What?'

'Nothing, duchess. Quit being so paranoid.' Harrison spoke to Logan then. 'Cheyenne, I need to get back to New Orleans for a night. My partner's set up an undercover drugs buy and I need to be in the quarter.' He looked at his watch. 'If I haul ass now and highball a bit on the freeway, I can make Atlanta and still get a plane to New Orleans. You want me to run any of this stuff through the computer?'

'Great idea, Harrison,' she said. 'In fact, the best you've come up with so far. Take the picture and some of these letters and see what you can find out.'

Harrison stared at her for a short moment, then scooped up the papers and stalked off.

Swann relaxed; with Harrison gone, the atmosphere

eased perceptibly. He heard him tear away in his car, and then he lay back with his head against the pillow of the other bed.

'God, that's better. He's winding me up like a top.'

'Don't go for it, Jack. Whatever happened was not your fault, no matter how that asshole chooses to see it.'

'You don't like him, do you?'

'He chews tobacco and spits the juice in a Coke can. He's arrogant, rude, a Midwestern hill-billy in an FBI raid jacket.' She broke off. 'I don't know, maybe it's me. Everybody else seems to worship the ground he walks on. To be fair, he's been our most productive UCA since Pistone infiltrated the Mob. Tom Kovalski rates him and I rate Kovalski, so is his judgement fucked or mine?'

Swann smiled at her then and laid his hand across her arm. 'D'you think we can find anything to drink in this town?'

'I doubt it, but why don't we try.'

They found no liquor, but the BP garage sold beer and Swann bought a case of Miller Lite. They packed ice around it in the sink, then ate dinner in the diner, with every eye in the place on their table. There were black people and there were white people, but none of them were sitting together. Swann felt just as much intimidated by the blacks as the whites; each group looked at them with equal disdain. Logan touched the ends of his fingers with hers. 'Don't let it bother you, honey. This is Georgia, remember. Folks here don't get around too much.'

Swann finished his hamburger and looked across at the table of a tanned-faced man in his forties, who was constantly giving him the eye. Swann stared at him and the man eventually looked away. 'You know what,' he said, leaning forward. 'I've been undercover on the Falls Road in West Belfast, and I wasn't anywhere near as intimidated as I feel right now.'

325

'Let's go,' Logan said. 'I'm done if you are.'

They went back to her room and broke open the beer. Swann stood in the open door and smoked a cigarette. 'You miss Pia, honey?' Logan asked him suddenly.

He looked back at her, lying on the bed with her jacket off, the height of her breasts pushing against the material of her blouse, skirt riding slightly on naked thighs. Her feet were bare and her toenails painted cherry-red. 'I don't miss her, Chey. No.' He looked away again. 'I miss something, but I couldn't tell you what it is.'

'Closeness.'

'What?'

She propped herself up on one elbow. 'You know, closeness, intimacy. How long were you with her – eighteen months, wasn't it?'

'About that, yeah.'

'It's a long time, Jack.'

'Yeah, you're right, it is. Especially when she seemed so much in love with me.' He looked away. 'Ah, I don't want to talk about it. I got stiffed, Chey. It's time I got over it.'

He didn't hear her get off the bed, didn't feel her come over till she slipped her hands around his waist from behind. His heart began to pulse and he could feel a tickling sensation in his loins. He turned to face her, there in the doorway of the motel room, with the Georgia sky huge and purple above his head. He kissed her, lips yielding under his own. He pressed himself against her. She gave and then moved against him, lifting one leg to rustle against his. He kissed her again, more deeply, reaching both hands behind her, cupping the arc of her hips. Deeper and tighter. She kicked the door closed and Swann felt the breath stick in his throat. He lost himself in her, tugging at her lips with his teeth, brushing her cheek, forehead, the long line of her neck, like velvet under his tongue.

Carefully, he undressed her, easing each button from its housing till her white lace bra was brilliant against the swell of her breasts. Her skin was rich and dark, like smooth chocolate, with a depth of scent that he could only associate with black women. There was something almost regal about the arch of her back. Her hands caressed him, nails in the soft flesh at the back of his neck. She got up and wriggled out of her skirt. And then she was naked and dark, with a mound of thick, black hair rising at the top of her thighs. She laid him on his back and undressed him completely. Then, rolling him over, she took some aromatic oil from her bag. 'Lie still and relax,' she said softly. 'I'm going to spoil you.'

She oiled his back and rubbed his skin into ruffles with the points of her fingers. Swann groaned and sighed and felt the cares of the past year begin to subside. The gentle, loving touch of a woman – a woman he trusted not to hurt him. He felt himself sinking into the bed, allowing her to roam his body with hers; his back, his legs, buttocks, kneading him gently and firmly in turn. Then she turned him over and eased her hands over his stomach to the tops of his thighs and worked him till he was hard. She kissed his face, his chest, his belly and the tip of his penis, and then she lowered herself on top of him.

Afterwards, they stood in the shower with hot water rinsing the soap from their bodies. Swann washed every inch of her, her flesh easy under his touch. They dried, shared a beer and lay together till morning.

David Collier looked at the CCTV screen at the clubhouse in Victoria Avenue, Hounslow, West London. Gas vans were rolling down the street. He rubbed at his jaw and frowned. One parked right outside and a man in British

327

Gas overalls came up to the house. It was an end-of-terrace house, with CCTV on both the side and the front, and a final camera set up over the tiny patch of garden at the back. There were four bedrooms, and they'd built a small extension at the back to enhance the size of the clubroom. When out of town members came down, they slept in sleeping-bags on the floor.

The control panel was in the master bedroom, overlooking the street at the front. The brickwork and windows had been reinforced and there was space for two bikes at the front. They were in no danger of being stolen.

Only Fagin was with him in the clubhouse. Gringo, the other resident, was down at the shop working on a '56 panhead Harley they had acquired in Texas. The gas man came right up to the door and rang the bell. Fagin would answer. Collier kept the camera on the man's face, zooming the lens in for a close-up to see if he had seen him before. There was nothing there he recognized and he relaxed. He had smelt gas that morning when he went out for cigarettes. He heard Fagin's feet pounding the stairs and then his head poked round the door.

'The man says there's a gas leak, Dave. We've got to clear out the house.'

'Fuck him.'

Fagin pulled a face. 'The leak's across the road, man, in Wellington Avenue. They're clearing everyone out of three parallel streets, as well as Penderel and Rossindel.'

Collier looked again at the screen. The gas man was looking at his watch and hopping from one foot to another. He lifted his finger to the bell once more. 'Ah, fuck it,' he said, and lifted his jacket from the bed.

They were shepherded down the street along with all the other residents. Collier wanted to take the bikes, but the gas man said he couldn't. The action from the spark plugs was enough to send everything up. Collier walked along the street with Fagin, eyeing everyone that he passed. He could definitely smell gas in the air. More vans were arriving and men in breathing apparatus and equipment.

George Webb and a locksmith from MI5 walked right past Collier and Fagin, carrying their tool kits with them, suited and booted as gas men working on the leak. They looked back and Webb was given the all-clear by the observers in the evacuation area. Then the two of them went to work. The locksmith stripped off his mask and Webb let his sit under his chin, while they assessed the front door.

'Bloody hell,' the locksmith said. He was a small man with a black moustache and hairs sticking out of the neck of his shirt. He rubbed his finger back and forth under his nose, while he studied the variety of locks that Collier had set in the door. 'What about the back?' he said at length. 'No one guards the back door like they do the front.'

There was no gate to the garden, the rear wall jutting on to the neighbours' garden in the parallel street. The wall was brick and six feet high and there was razor wire curled on top. Webb went back to the van for a ladder and Kevlar blankets.

In the garden, the locksmith breathed a sigh of relief. 'That's better,' he said. 'There's only three on this one and they're all bar keys.' He took a soft metal probe from a package in the breast pocket of his overalls, and set about the first of the locks. It took him twenty minutes a key, but he made three and they all fitted, the tumbler markings being worked out partly from the pattern they made on the probe and partly from the expertise of the man. Webb had known him as long as he had been in the Branch, and they must have made in excess of twenty covert entries together. 'What about alarms?' the locksmith said.

Webb shook his head. 'They didn't have time to set them.'

'Right. There you go then.' The locksmith fitted all three keys and Webb had access to the house. They were joined by two other specialists from the technical support unit, and a search team who accessed the building over the wall. One of them spoke to Webb.

'You need to check if that CCTV is taped,' he said.

'Right.' Webb went upstairs and found the control unit in the master bedroom. There was a taping facility, but no cassette in the cartridge.

Tania Briggs joined him. 'We'll need to reshape the razor wire when we're done, Webby,' she said. 'They're the sort that'll notice.'

He patted her lightly on the shoulder and produced a Polaroid picture of the top of the wall. 'Ahead of you, Tania. Ahead of you.'

The technical men put in the sound-listening probes, wired into the light switches. They considered the television in the lounge, but that had a downside if the TV was on. All the listeners would hear was the burble of whatever was showing. They worked quickly and expertly. Even David Collier, with his SAS background, would never know they had been there. The whole process took them an hour and a half, and for once there was no chance of being compromised, with the roads cordoned off and the gas board genuinely checking for leaks.

Webb and Briggs and the rest of the search team went through the property with a fine toothcomb, checking every drawer, every nook and cranny, and Webb even disturbed the kick boards on the kitchen units, looking for hides. They found nothing, which puzzled him. Normally, there would be something.

Webb moved out into the yard. It was crazy paved and he stared at each section for a long time. Nothing. He looked at the small shed and inspected the dry space beneath it with a pencil-light torch. Still nothing. Again he looked at the paving, one step raised to the kitchen door. He knelt beside the step and checked the brickwork for loose mortar, but found nothing. He scratched his head and whistled to himself, and then he saw it – one line of cracked mortar in one small section of paving close to the wall. Bending over it, he looked very carefully round the edges of the cement to see exactly how it was joined. He tested it with the weight of his palm, but it didn't feel loose. Yet his instincts told him it was. He could see that the mortar was cracked all the way round, now that he was bent right over it. He beckoned Briggs as she appeared in the kitchen doorway. 'Give me a hand here,' he said.

They stood either side of the slab, and Webb slipped a tiny metal probe into the crack. It gave. Very carefully, they lifted it between them, without disturbing the dried mortar any further. A shallow hole in the ground, no more than eight inches square. Webb squatted on his haunches and smiled. 'Oh, Tania,' he said. 'I think we're finally getting somewhere.'

A single sheet of paper was folded in a transparent polythene bag. Webb lifted it out and carefully unfolded it. Taking his Polaroid camera, he laid the paper flat and studied it. 'Looks like an inventory for motorbike parts,' he said. He snapped it up close, ensuring that all was legible. It was on a sheet of company-headed paper that had originated in the United States. Webb looked at Briggs. 'Tell me something, Tania. Why would anyone go to so much trouble to hide a bike-part inventory?'

They replaced the stone exactly as they had found it. Then their gear was cleared out, the sound system tested and the door relocked. The locksmith carefully dusted away all trace of metal filings with an airbrush and then they climbed over the wall. The last thing that Webb and Briggs did was to reshape the razor wire, wearing padded leather gloves.

331

Later that afternoon, Webb went with Christine Harris to see the US Secret Service at the embassy in Grosvenor Square. They met Special Agent Combes in the leg-att's office. Harris had already given him the information on the US companies operated legally by Collier, and now she passed him the inventory.

Combes was in his forties, thin-faced, with the kind of slow eyes that had seen most of everything before. He was a veteran money-laundering investigator for the Treasury Department and liaised between London and Washington. 'No problem, Christine,' he said. 'I'll get it across to the States, see what we can make of it. We'll run the handwriting through our systems and see where we come out with that as well.'

'Great,' she said. 'We've already got a warrant for UK production orders on their bank accounts over here.'

'The only thing is, this might take a while,' Combes warned her. 'Lot of man hours here. I guess you're in a hurry.'

'We're on top of what we have, and there's other pieces we need to put in place, Peter. What we need is the right information.'

'Oh, you'll get that. You can count on it.'

Webb walked down the steps with her. 'Seems like a good guy,' he said.

'He is. We've used him before. He wrote the manual for them, George. I mean quite literally. What he doesn't know about cleaning up dirty money isn't worth knowing. All he's ever told *me* are the three basic principles: "placement" – that's getting the dirty money into the system initially; "layering" – moving it around; and finally, "integration" – that's where it becomes part of the normal economy.'

*

332

Boese had stolen the white Nissan truck in Arizona. Now he drove it under the shadow of Slide Mountain, whose one bald side had slipped down to the valley ten years previously. Bears roamed its height, along with mountain lion and white-tailed deer. Boese drove casually, one hand on the wheel, till the turn for Eastlake Boulevard. He pulled into the outside lane and halted at the sharp uphill left, while the traffic coming from Carson City rumbled past him. He waited, drumming his fingers on the wheel, then pulled across the oncoming carriageway and up the short hill. Eastlake Boulevard stretched ahead of him. On his right, Washoe Lake was glassy, low and flat, with the water higher than he remembered it. He had been here once in his life before, but that was a long time ago.

The road drifted for a mile or so through Washoe City, then cut under the lie of the hills and edged the lake all the way back to the highway on the western shore. From there, he could get into Carson. He slowed the truck and pulled off to the right, where he parked and wandered in the dust to the shore. He was in no hurry; they were light years behind him and there were things he needed to think about. He squatted and skimmed pebbles on the lightly breaking wavetops. His hair was long and thick, a Mexican moustache drooped to his lower jaw, and a straw cowboy hat was perched high on his head. He wore Wranglers and sloping-heeled Mexican boots. He had fresh ID in his pocket and a story for any state trooper who happened to pull him over.

There was much on his mind, many thoughts, emotions, questions. He could feel nothing yet and he wondered why. He was public after all, but interestingly enough, they had not named him. The FBI knew who he was, because he had allowed them to witness his arrival, undisguised, on the twenty-second floor of that oil building in New Orleans. Yet he remained an 'unknown subject'. They would not make public the incident with the photograph or the feather, because that would only generate a million copycats. But why not name him? After Rome and London, the world knew Ismael Boese.

It was not overly important, though it remained puzzling. No matter, the unknown subject would do for now. He would finish what he had started – until someone or something altered the path he was walking.

He heard a sound behind him and looked back to see a cowboy sitting on a horse, shaded by the sun. '*Buenas tardes*,' he said.

The cowboy looked at him for a moment. Boese could not see his face. The horse was all of seventeen hands, and the cowboy sat in the saddle with a straight back and was but a shadow against the sun.

'*Buenas tardes* to you.' The cowboy rested both hands on the saddle horn. 'That your truck up there?'

'*Si.*' Boese straightened, and, shielding his eyes with one hand, tried to get a look at the speaker.

'Y'all wanna move it for me. I need to get my horse trailer down here in a while. Wanna run some beasts in the lake there.'

'*Si.* No problem.'

'Obliged.' The cowboy touched his hat and wheeled the horse away.

Boese drove further along Eastlake Boulevard, almost to where it curved at the head of the lake. A pair of red-tailed hawks fanned the air as they settled in the upper branches of a white-barked cottonwood tree, close to the water's edge. Boese turned right on Pintail Way, past an unfenced property: a single-storey house and corrals where a number of horses grazed on hay that had been dumped for them in truck tyres laid sideways in the dust. A cowboy, with red hair and sunglasses, his jacket loose at his shoulders, was hauling more hay into the corral. Boese drove the length of

Pintail Way, almost to the lakeside itself, and slowed when he came to the ten-unit trailer park. Mail boxes lined the fence at the entrance in a single rack. He turned the truck so the driver's side was close to them, and carefully inspected the names. He paused at number 9, and a cruel twist worked the line of his lips. A copy of *USA Today* protruded from the open flap, Teniel Jefferson's name on it.

# 19

Swann woke up with Logan in his arms, and lay for a few moments staring at the ceiling. Logan was still sleeping, the warmth of her body wrapped in his. He touched her face, easing away the fallen strands of hair, and kissed the lids of her eyes. She was beautiful; tough, yet as feminine as he had known a woman to be. He felt easier, lighter, than he had done for a long time. Then he thought of Harrison and his mood soured a fraction. It was barely six-thirty and only just struggling to get light outside. He would have to do something about Harrison, but quite what, he did not know. His grudge was very deep indeed and he was in no hurry to bring it to a head. Again he looked at Logan. This had been bound to happen. He had known it since she first agreed to meet him in Washington, and fly with him down to New Orleans.

She stirred and he wondered what her reaction would be when she came to. As soon as Harrison had gone, they both, perhaps, knew that it would end up like this. She stirred again and flicked one eye open, saw him, smiled and lifted a silky thigh over his, pressing her breasts against him. The telephone rang and she sat upright, covers falling back. She sat half naked and swept a hand through her hair. 'Better let me get it, honey.' She leaned over, away from him, the sheet slipping so he could see the curve of her buttocks.

'Logan,' she said, and moved closer to the table. The sheet slipped away completely now, and Swann let his fingers wander the flesh of her bottom.

'What did you say?' She sat upright and looked back

over her shoulder at him, her eyes bright all at once. 'OK. We'll be there. What time's Harrison getting back from New Orleans? Right. See you later.' She put the phone down and rested the spread of her fingers against Swann's chest. 'That was the Atlanta field office,' she said. 'The picture you found, Mary Greer and two gals – Gabby and Oko?'

'Yes?'

'Gabby is the a.k.a. for Camilla Christina Hall. She was a member of the SLA in the 1970s.' She paused for a brief moment. 'Oko was also a member of the SLA. Right now, she's serving fifty-five years for conspiracy to murder. Her real name's Leona Boese.'

They sat in one of the interview rooms at the FBI field office in Atlanta, a thick, heavily stapled file on the desk between them. The report had been prepared by the Los Angeles Police Department and was entitled 'The Symbionese Liberation Army in Los Angeles 1974'. Swann was reading about Gabby: Camilla Christina Hall, born 24 March, 1945. She had been active with the SLA in Los Angeles and was killed during the LAPD SWAT raids at 1466 East 54th Street on 17 May, 1974, an attack which all but ended the activities of the SLA. Logan tapped her finger at the top of the following page. Leona Boese a.k.a. Oko. She and her husband Pieter had been active throughout the history of the SLA, which had its roots in the Venceremos movement which was prevalent on the Berkeley campus between 1972 and 1973. Swann then cross-referenced against the file that the GBI had furnished them with, which confirmed that Mary Greer had been around the Berkeley campus at that time. The file mentioned nothing about any revolutionary activity, however.

Pieter Boese (Ismael's father) had been involved closely with Joe 'Bo' Remiro, who was subsequently arrested for the murder of Marcus Foster, the superintendent of Oakland school, and the attempted murder of his assistant, Robert Blackburn, in November of 1973. Pieter Boese was also suspected of involvement in those shootings, but was not apprehended until May of 1974. He and his wife took part in the robbery of a sporting goods store in Inglewood, Los Angeles, before planting an improvised explosive device at the county courthouse, where two other SLA members were being held. Both the Boeses were taken into custody before the SWAT team's attack on 1466 East 54th Street. Logan put down the file and looked up at Swann.

'Nothing about Mary Greer,' she said.

'On the fringes, maybe.' Swann sat back in the chair. 'There's always lots on the fringes, Chey. You know that. Especially on a university campus.' He picked up the file again and flicked through the pages. It documented every known SLA member, including the infamous Patty Hearst, and listed the number of LAPD and FBI personnel who took part in the main raid on 1466 East 54th Street. 'We need to talk to Leona Boese,' he said. 'She and Mary Greer were obviously friends. Why would Boese have one of his mother's college friends killed?'

'I'll find out where she's serving her time.' Logan again looked at the file. 'She got fifty-five years, Jack. That was twenty-five years ago. She'll be due for parole soon. Maybe she'll want to talk to us.'

Logan updated Kovalski's team as well as the fugitive unit in Washington. They were busy trying to co-ordinate all supposed sightings of Boese with police departments around the country. The Ford that he had stolen in Meridian had been found abandoned west of Amarillo, Texas, but the search by state police and the Texas Rangers could find no trace of the driver. Logan also linked the phone line up to New Orleans, where Harrison was preparing to rejoin them. She arranged for an intelligence analyst to set about trying to locate Leona Boese's whereabouts with the Federal Bureau of Prisons. Swann phoned London and told Webb what they had discovered.

'That's a result, Jack,' Webb said.

'We think so. I'm waiting to find out which pen' she's banged up in, then we plan to go and visit her.'

'How's it going with the UCA?'

Swann gazed out of the window. He could see Highway 85 splitting the city in two, with the buildings looming like great concrete sentinels on either side of the road. 'He's been in New Orleans the last couple of days, some deal he's got with his partner, so that's been fine. But he's intent on winding me up, Webby. There's not much I can do about it.'

Webb was silent for a moment. 'Keep your hands in your pockets, Jack. Sounds like he wants a confrontation. Don't give him the pleasure.'

'I'm not planning to. What's happening back there?'

'We've got sound in the clubhouse.'

'You have?'

'Yeah. We did a mean old sneaky beaky, got the gas board out and everything. Worked like a dream. We're going to apply a little pressure through a snout that SB are trying to suborn, so we'll see. I don't think it's going to be easy, though, Jack. You know what these gangs are like, and this one's tighter than any I've seen before.'

'The discipline of ex-soldiers,' Swann said. 'Makes a hell of a difference, eh.'

'We've got other irons in the fire.' Webb told him about the visit to the US Secret Service agent and then Swann put the phone down.

Webb returned to his desk. He had taken Swann's place in the squad room, but was still officially attached to the exhibits office and his desk remained there. He spoke to

339

the duty sergeant looking after the Bomb Data Centre and asked him again for everything they had on Storm Crow. Boese's words were on his mind: *We have been betrayed.*

He looked again at the information they had collated. Some of it had been updated from Louis Byrne's files at the FBI, and there was the odd anecdotal incident that had been given to them by Ben Dubin. He had been in Israel when the first recorded attack by Storm Crow occurred. A triacetone triperoxide grenade thrown at the US Ambassador's motorcade. Webb looked through the other listed events and tugged at his lip.

'Jesus, I can hear the wheels turning.' He looked over his shoulder and saw Colson standing half in, half out of the door. 'What've you got, Webby?'

'Storm Crow stuff, sir. Bits and pieces I pulled from bomb data. Movements, activities, normal kind of thing.' He cocked his head to one side. 'Why would the baddest man in the world allow himself to get caught, even if he knew he could escape?'

'Vanity.' Colson looked at him over the rim of his glasses. 'Ten years of anonymity, then on to the world scene with the worst chemical incident in Western peacetime history. It put him in the papers, George, and, as you said, with an escape plan whenever he chose to use it.'

'But the message to Tal-Salem, Guv. "We have been betrayed."'

'Who could betray him?'

'Member of an escape team maybe, somebody in the background or something.' Webb lifted his shoulders. 'I don't know.'

'Then what's he doing in America?'

'That's another good question.' Webb looked again at the papers in front of him. He was searching for clues to something, but he didn't know what it was.

\*

340

Boese watched Teniel Jefferson working in the autoshop, on the Fallon Road in Carson City. He had taken the Nissan in for an oil change, and right now Jefferson was checking the suspension, shining a flashlight up from the pit he was standing in. Boese was a long-haired Mexican, his skin slightly darkened, with a latex nose, bigger and more hooked than his own. He leaned against the office wall and watched Jefferson sweating his way through the work. He was a big man, bigger than Boese had thought, broad-shouldered with a squat, square trunk and thighs like small trees. His blond hair was shaved up his neck like a grunt; he was forty-two years old and clearly hated beaners. He had been polite enough when Boese drove in, but the eye contact was minimal and the sentences short and stunted.

Boese considered his IQ to be reasonably high, but he was uneducated and his bulk was probably some form of over-compensation for other inadequacies. Jefferson came through to the office, wiping his hands on a rag. 'You're all set,' he said. 'You wanna watch the rear offside suspension, the shock's on the way out.' He shifted a lump of chewing tobacco from one side of his mouth to the other. Boese paid him and climbed behind the wheel of his truck. As he backed out of the garage, Jefferson was on the phone, sipping from a pint of peppermint schnapps.

Back at his motel, two blocks off Main Street, in a quieter section of Carson City, Boese took his make-up case from his bag and prepared another latex mould. He sat before the mirror, enjoying himself. He had learned the art of stage make-up in college, as a side study to his more conventional curriculum. It had served him well over the years. Now he applied the liquid rubber and worked the dye into a paste. When he was finished, two hours later, he was as black as the ace of spades: face, neck, hands. His nose was thick and rubbery, lips heavy and the colour of a

341

summer storm. He put fresh ID in his wallet and stowed the PSS pistol in his waistband holster, before stepping back into the night. Across the street a Ford 250 pick-up truck was parked, and, as Boese walked to his Nissan, somebody inside struck a match. Boese did not see him, or if he did, he did not show as much. The man lifted the match to his face as if to light a cigarette. He wore a wide-brimmed cowboy hat.

Boese started the Nissan and headed out of town towards Gardnerville, driving as far as the turning for the Indian Correctional Center. Behind that was the Nevada Highway Patrol training facility; and further still, nestling amid the foothills, Stallions whorehouse.

He parked his truck next to a big grey Dodge with a blue flash running the length of the sides. Carefully, he locked his doors and watched the road for a moment. A set of headlights were coming up the hill, some distance back on the highway. Boese heard the soft peal of laughter coming from behind the drapes, which only half covered the lighted windows in the single-storey building. He walked through the wire gate and up to the front door, where a burly man with no hair stood in a penguin suit. He stared at Boese for a long moment, eyes dull and sus-picious. Boese had gold about his neck, and gold on his negroid wrists. He looked the man in the eye and, taking his wallet from his pocket, ran his thumbnail over the stack of bills before peeling off a twenty. He stuffed it in the breast pocket of the penguin suit, patted the man on the shoulder and went inside.

The front door opened into a small lobby where an older woman was seated behind a desk. She smiled at him. 'Good evening, sir. How are you today?'

'Just fine, thank you.'

'Can I take your coat?'

Boese looked down at the heavy winter sports jacket he

was wearing and shook his head. 'You know what, I think I'll keep it on. I don't guess I'll be staying a whole lotta time.'

'Just here for a drink, sir?'

'I think so.'

'Bar's right through in back.' She smiled at him again. 'You know what, though, I bet you change your mind.'

He went through the bead curtain into a bar area with couches and armchairs set around drinks tables that were knee-high to the floor. The bar was dimly lit: soft, pale lampshades hung at eye level from the ceiling over the bar. A blonde girl, wearing a leather waistcoat which forced her breasts together, was serving cocktails.

'Sir,' she said, as he sat down on a stool. 'What can I get you tonight?'

Boese looked at the array of bottles behind the counter and caught sight of himself, unrecognizable in the mirror. 'I'll have a Tom Collins and take one for yourself.' He peeled off another twenty and looked to his right. Two whores dressed in lace and silk were seated together on the couch against the far wall. One of them was black and she smiled at him. He returned the smile, but concentrated on his drink. Teniel Jefferson, wearing an open-necked shirt that revealed matted hair on his chest, sat with his arm about a young Mexican woman on the couch in the far corner. He was laughing at some private but raucous joke. Clearly, he had been here before.

Boese stared at his strange reflection in the mirror and sipped the gin. He could see Jefferson's reflection in the glass further down the counter. Jefferson *had* been here before, many times in fact. He could afford it, not because he worked as a mechanic for the autoshop, but because he was an ex-Carson City prison warder who sold cocaine on the inside. He was careful, not drawing attention to himself, and he lived modestly in the trailer park by Washoe Lake.

343

He had two vices that Boese knew of, both of which were expensive – the blackjack tables in Reno and here at the cat house. Boese looked up as the black whore left the couch and slid on to the vacant stool next to him.

'Hi, honey.' She laid a hand on his shoulder. 'What can we do for you tonight?'

Boese looked sideways at her. 'You know what, baby doll,' he said. 'I'm feeling kinda tired right now. Maybe I'll just sit a while and have a few drinks.'

She stroked his nappy hair with slim, long-nailed fingers. 'OK, hon. You just holler when you want something.'

The door opened then and a cowboy walked in. He wore black jeans and pointed boots and a high-necked purple shirt, buttoned down at the cuffs. His hat was faded and dusty and he took a seat two stools from Boese, and ordered a Coors Lite and a shot of Jagermeister. Boese glanced sideways at him and the cowboy touched his hat. 'Howdy,' he said.

Boese nodded, sipped his drink and watched Jefferson rise from his seat. He stretched, then curled his index finger at the Mexican whore who sat next to him. They disappeared into a back room and Boese half closed his eyes. Next to him, the cowboy toyed with a book of matches in his left hand, easing it in little somersaults between his fingers, like a cardsharp does with a deck. He sipped at the beer, then swallowed the shot in one, and wiped his beard with the back of his hand.

The same girl who had approached Boese approached him, and, like Boese, he declined. For a moment their eyes met and Boese caught the cold, hard stare, and for the first time in as many years as he could remember, he felt a little uneasy. The cowboy drained his beer glass and looked at the whores lining the couches behind them. All of them were young and firm, all of them were pretty. He looked again at Boese, the same cold stare. Then he slipped the matchbook into his shirt pocket, paid his tab and left. Boese finished his drink and sat for a while longer. Again the girl approached him and again he sent her away. He ordered a glass of 7Up, drained it and walked back outside.

He parked the Nissan in the shadows by Washoe Lake and closed his eyes, listening to the water lapping at the broken cottonwood limbs that lined the shore. Two hours later, he heard the rumble of Jefferson's grey Dodge with the blue flashes on the sides, and he eased himself more upright. Jefferson, he decided, was one of those professional drunk drivers who make an art of riding home after drinking too much: never running a stop sign and keeping exactly to the speed limit. He'd check his tail-lights on a daily basis, to make sure there was no reason for a cop to pull him over.

Boese slipped lower in his seat, then lay crosswise as the headlights shone full against the windshield. Jefferson swung into the park with a bump against the kerbstone, then trundled the length of the road to his trailer. Boese opened his truck door, adjusted the handgun that was settled against his spine, and then walked the length of the park with silent, expert footsteps. Now his eyes were still, cold and glinting in the fragment of sickle moon that crested Slide Mountain. He could hear Jefferson moving about and grunting to himself, like a pig, inside the trailer. Boese had his hand on the screen door; the inner door stood open. He could see Jefferson just inside, TV remote control in one hand, an empty glass in the other, with a bottle of Black Velvet whisky crooked under his elbow. Boese pulled back the screen door. Jefferson turned, gawped, and Boese pressed the muzzle of the gun against the sweaty skin of his forehead.

Fifteen minutes later, he reloaded the clip with fresh ammunition. Two hulls had been left with Jefferson, and he pocketed the other four, before loading six fresh ones.

Then he made his way back up the road to the cottonwood trees and his truck. The name *El Kebir* rang inside his skull, and his features were set in a scowl. He was closer and yet he was no closer and the irritation showed in the tick at the corner of one eye. He got to his truck, opened the unlocked door and climbed in. He sat on something that had not been there when he got out. He cursed silently and felt under his backside. His fingers brushed something soft and then a small square of card. He remained absolutely still, his free hand creeping to the butt of the pistol. His eyes scanned every inch of what could be seen through the darkness. He saw nothing, no movement. He heard no sound. The night was still, the valley sleeping soundly. Switching on the interior light, he looked at what he had sat on, a single black crow's feather and a book of matches.

Benjamin Dubin was in Washington D.C. He was due to give a lecture, as he regularly did, to FBI recruits at Quantico. Tomorrow's lecture was on the political beliefs and objectives of Hizbollah and the current stuttering status of the Oslo Peace Accords. Tonight he was dining with Louis and Angie Byrne in the Oyster Bar in old town Alexandria. Byrne had offered to put him up in his own house, which was only a couple of blocks from here, but Dubin always preferred the anonymity of hotel furniture. The two of them went back a long way; 1985, in fact, when Byrne was about to leave the marine corps, after his experiences in Beirut. Angela, he knew less well, but he was aware of her reputation. They were talking about Boese.

'So far the media has backed off,' Byrne was saying. 'Our Fugitive Publicity office have released minimal information. We're not confirming it is Storm Crow, and we've said nothing about feathers.'

'But you received one in New Orleans.'

'That's right. John Dollar got it. His name's been public since Jakob Salvesen got indicted.'

'That, I can never understand about our legal system,' Dubin said. 'Puts the man in danger.'

'His name had already been bandied about on the militia Internet web sites,' Byrne said. 'They issued a death threat, tacitly of course, but somebody somewhere's putting up a million dollars reward.' He smiled wryly then. 'JB doesn't seem to be worried by it. Even the Mob think twice about contracts on FBI agents. After all, we're the biggest, meanest gang in the country. Nobody fucks with us.' He smiled at his wife who was playing with, rather than enjoying her oysters. 'Remember the DEA agent who got killed by the Mob in New York? He was a close friend of one of the old-timers in our field office up there. Well, our guy and some of the other agents grabbed one mobster a night, and beat the living shit outta them. They told them to tell the wiseguys that this would continue until the killer was given up. A week or so later, his head was delivered in a box to the field office.' Byrne sipped white wine and laid a palm on his wife's smooth and naked arm. 'You doing OK, honey?'

'I'm fine.' She smiled at Dubin and laid down her fork. 'Don't pay any attention to me, Ben. I've got work on my mind as always.'

'And how is the President?' he asked her.

'Not my client personally, I'm afraid, so I couldn't tell you.'

'I'd like to come up to your offices one of these days, Angie. Must get a great view of the White House.'

'White House, Washington Monument, Jefferson Memorial, all the way down to Woodrow Wilson Bridge on a clear day.'

Dubin was quiet for a moment, finishing the last of his oysters and refilling his wine glass. He had been in the

States for a couple of days already, spending some time at the State Department on Virginia Avenue. There were one or two diplomatic security guys he needed to speak with. He had always found they had their finger on the world pulse much more effectively than the CIA, which was somewhat ironic. They were on the spot in the embassies and most of the intelligence they fed back was sound. He looked across the table at Byrne's blue eyes. 'How's the hunt going, anyway?' he asked.

'So so.' Byrne sat back, fingers entwined in his lap. 'There's been no sightings since New Orleans. No doubt he's got his make-up bag with him. He can *be* just about anyone, given enough time: Mexican, black, Chinese. Makes him damned hard to track.'

Dubin tapped his lip with one finger. 'I'm not sure if I'm supposed to talk about this,' he said, 'but Scotland Yard interviewed me.'

'I know.' Byrne lifted his eyebrows. 'We got Swann over here on liaison, right now.'

Dubin nodded. 'He interviewed me after Boese escaped,' he said. 'Apparently, I was the only one to visit or even speak to him from the outside all the time he was on remand.'

'He was smuggling messages through the sister of one of the inmates,' Byrne told him. 'Scotland Yard know that now.'

'Do they? Perhaps they think the messages and me have something in common.'

Angie looked sharply at him then. 'Did you know he's been calling me?' she asked. 'He says he wants me to be his attorney.'

Dubin nodded slowly. 'So I understand.'

'So what does that mean?'

'I hunted him,' Byrne said. 'Above anyone else on the planet, *I've* hunted him. He's a professional, Angie, been playing the game all his life. His intel' is excellent.' He shook his head. 'That's why he was able to give the Brits the run-around for so long. I mean, look what he did with Swann. How long had that been planned? Brigitte Hammani in Swann's bed for six months, before anything started to roll.'

'That doesn't answer my question.'

Again Byrne touched her arm. 'He's just playing games, honey. Getting at you to get at me.'

'But his attorney? Why does he want an attorney?'

Byrne sighed then. 'Who knows what's going through his mind. It's a pity your people won't let us wire up your work phone.'

'It's a law firm, Louis. What'd you expect?'

He made a face. 'I said, it's a pity, that's all.'

Dubin looked at him for a moment, sitting back as the waiter brought the next course. 'What d'you think about the message to the outside,' he said. ' "We have been betrayed." What d'you think that means?'

'You know about that?'

Dubin smiled. 'I have my sources. Who would betray the Storm Crow, Louis? Or, alternatively, who *could* betray him?'

Byrne was silent. Then, 'Swann says he always intended to get caught. Maybe he didn't. Maybe that was the betrayal.' He sat forward, gesticulating. 'Or maybe the phrase was coded in itself, intended just to get Tal-Salem on the move.'

'Tal-Salem is still involved?'

Byrne nodded. 'Right now, we're checking DNA on him over another matter. If the profile checks out, then that message was undoubtedly meant for him.'

'The *we* could refer to him and Boese together, then,' Dubin said.

'What about the jackal and the crow,' Angie said softly.

'When the prey is down, does the jackal or the crow eat first? That's what he said on the phone.'

'Carlos?' Byrne suggested, eyes intent on Dubin.

'I'd say so, yes.'

'Why is he talking about Carlos?' Angie asked.

'They have an association. Carlos was his mentor.'

'So what does it mean, eating first, when the prey is down?'

'It could mean all manner of things.' Dubin picked up his fork.

Angie widened her eyes then and looked at the gathered food on her plate. 'You know what, guys, I'm not really hungry.' She scraped back her chair. 'This is real rude of me, Ben, but then I'm a court lawyer, so what the hell. I'm going to go home. It's been a long day and I've got a longer one tomorrow. You guys go ahead and eat.'

Byrne looked up at her. 'You want me to get you a cab, honey?'

She shook her head. 'It's two blocks, Louis. I'll walk.'

It was raining outside and a chill wind was blowing in tight gusts off the Potomac River, only one block to her left, as she walked along Union Street. The cobbles on Prince were slippery underfoot and the wind lifted to batter her from behind as she climbed the slope to their home. She had left lights burning in the lounge and in their first-floor bedroom, where the three arched windows were like triple eyes looking out from the middle of a black face in the darkness. She loved the house: three floors, with a paved yard out the back, and an underground garage, housing three cars and Louis's Harley Davidson. She climbed the stone steps to the front door and went inside. After the phone calls, Louis had wanted protection agents assigned to her, but she had refused. Something in Boese's voice told her that she was not a target – at least, not yet

350

anyway – and she prided herself on being an excellent judge of conversation and motive.

She closed the door, leaned on it, and thought about a herbal bath. The telephone rang on the small table beside her. 'Angie Byrne,' she said, trying to keep the yawn from her voice.

'You sound weary. Another long day defending the wrong people?'

She stiffened. 'You know,' she said, steeling herself. 'I've just been talking about you.'

'My ears must've been burning. Tell me, how long d'you think I can stay on the line without the FBI catching up with me?'

'I don't know. You tell me. I guess if you were really worried about it, you wouldn't keep calling.' She paused for a moment. 'You tell me something,' she said. 'What d'you mean when you talk about the jackal and the crow? Is the jackal Carlos?'

'Ah, Angela. We do so well together, you and I. That's why I picked *you* to represent me. You see, the jackal has fur, it runs on the ground, but the crow – the crow has feathers, black feathers, and the crow can soar like an eagle.'

'So what does it mean?'

'I've already told you, who eats first?'

'But I don't understand.'

'They both eat carrion, Angela. Surely you know that. But did you ever see the crow on a kill before the jackal?'

The phone clicked dead and she held the receiver for a moment or two. Uneasy now, she walked to the window and looked out. Where was he? Here in Washington? Close by perhaps, in some silent hotel room. Could he see her? What exactly did he mean? Why should he choose her to represent him? And represent him in what? Switching the phone on again, she paged her husband in the restaurant.

*

Christine Harris observed the undercover buy in London. Janice Martin had been watched round the clock ever since they had identified her as their way in. Cocaine had a way of destroying people and she could not get enough of the stuff. Six days previously, she had made a purchase from her usual dealer in Camden Town, travelling by tube train up from Hounslow in the west of the city. Two Area drug squad had an informant who could put them on to the supplier, and they were ready to scoop up both him and Martin, the next time she tried to score. Twice now it had failed because she had turned up at the usual flat in Camden Town only to find him not at home. She had bitten down her nails and gone a little paler. Then GCHQ heard her make an illicit telephone call from The Regiment's clubhouse.

Now Harris sat with Julian Moore, as the SO19 firearms team plotted up the flat. It was a daytime buy, which gave them more problems because the team would have to attack quickly and very hard. The flats were difficult in themselves, in that there were no friendly faces, and three flights to get up before the reinforced door could be breached. It was tactically very difficult to deploy a full team wearing hidden body armour and carrying MP5 carbines in and around the site. It had been achieved by a five-man band of council workmen, working for three full days on the road outside the building. Three days was long enough not to arouse suspicion.

Harris had no input on the SO19 attack. It was their call and anything could go wrong. As much as they had been able to recce the building, gain the plans and assess the threat and possible escape routes, it was still touch and go. They had to get Janice Martin with the gear in her possession and eradicate the source at the same time. Undoubtedly, word would get back to The Regiment. But if Martin played it straight enough, and they were careful, it might still work. She was pretty and she was a mamma, and all they needed her to do was to sit in her flat and wait.

Harris and Moore were sitting in a Fiat van, parked one hundred yards down the road from the subject premises. They had the local drug-squad arrest team already primed with what was needed on standby, and the SO19 firearms officers were digging up the road, wearing bulky black donkey jackets. Janice Martin appeared at the tube station and made her way north-east up Camden Road. Harris pressed the transmitter on her radio. 'Eyeball on target,' she said. 'Walking up Camden Road. ETA at subject premises in approximately five minutes.' She stayed where she was, glanced at Julian and sighed. 'The lengths we actually go to,' she said.

The SO19 team, who were working outside the small block of flats, observed her approach on foot. Five of them, with three more backing them up in their van. The team leader gave the instructions over the encrypted Cougar radio from the rear of the van. Information was relayed to him from the full team of observers that picked her up at various points along the way. She moved past the workmen, a deliberateness to her gait, looking good in skin-tight jeans and short leather jacket. Just beyond the workmen, she paused and looked back up the street, then, feeling in her handbag for her purse, she strode up the first flight of concrete stairs.

'Stand by.' The team leader's voice in the ears of the SFO team. Harris could hear everything on her own Cougar set, back in the Fiat van. She listened as the armed officers moved off, deploying swiftly and quietly up the stairs to the flat. She could see nothing from here, and she cracked the little bones in her fingers, with Moore looking on in disgust. They both felt the adrenalin. You never got used to any kind of a raid, and this one was more important than most. Twenty-two people's families were quietly urging them on.

On the balcony outside the flat the SFO team gathered, with the battering ram held by the method of entry man – short and squat and built like a bear. He checked in with a click of his radio transmitter and the team leader called the attack. The door crashed after two blows, and armed officers swarmed into the premises. The dealer stared and paled, then dived for the toilet, only to be round-housed by a baton-wielding officer, and knocked to the ground. Martin was the only customer. Eleven-thirty in the morning and it looked as though the dealer had traded some of his wares in kind. She squatted, half naked, breasts hanging loose. In her purse, they found a small polythene bag filled with white powder.

It had taken the ground team three days since the Leona Boese discovery to actually get to meet her. She was caged in a federal penitentiary, close to the port of Eureka, California, on the Pacific coast. Harrison had flown directly there to meet them, and Logan and Swann flew in from Atlanta. They were driven out to the prison by one of the resident FBI agents. It was set on the side of a hill, close to where the redwood forests began, and surrounded by three wire fences, eighteen feet high, with barbed and razor wire along the tops. Bulls with rifles and shotguns watched their approach from goon towers, and from ten miles back on the highway, they saw 'No Hitchhiking' signs.

The resident agency office had been notified, as they had been nationwide, concerning the ground team and the assistance that they might require. Tom Kovalski had phoned Logan to inform them about the latest contact with Louis Byrne's wife and Swann was mulling over the words. 'The jackal eats first,' he said. 'That's what he's saying, but what's the significance of that? Carlos came before Storm Crow. Well, we already knew that.'

'It beats me. The guy talks in riddles.' Logan sat in the back with him, Harrison in the front, window down and smoking. He had been pretty quiet since he got back from New Orleans.

Right now, Harrison stared out of the window as they cruised up to the outer perimeter gates, watching the rifled guards in the towers. Two nights ago, he and Penny had made progress in the quarter, but Penny had criticized him in the morning for his attitude. His mind had been elsewhere: this guy Swann, Lisa Guffy up in Idaho, only two states from here. All of a sudden, it was like his age had caught up with him, as he looked across the table in Jean Lafitte's at the worthless piece of shit that was Rene Martinez, and the even more worthless Cuban dealer, Manx. The part seemed to be harder and harder to play these days, when there was so much else in the world. And maybe now he had Swann and unfinished business in his sights, he might take that pension early.

He could smell Logan's perfume while he held the door open for her as she got out of the car. The shine on her skin reminded him of the fruitless, disallowed nights, pursuing Maria in the Jazz Café on Bourbon Street. Last night he had been there again, before finally getting hammered with Joey in the Apple Barrel. The early morning flight to San Francisco and then up here had been accompanied by a pounding head and no food in his stomach. He caught Logan's eye as she moved past him, then he looked across the roof to see Swann looking carefully at him. Harrison held his eye, glanced behind at Logan again, and immediately he knew. Limey sonofabitch, he thought.

Logan's cellphone rang and she lifted it to her ear. 'Logan.'

'Cheyenne, this is Tom Kovalski.'

'Hey, Tom. What's up?'

'DNA. The profile the British sent us? It matched the sample lifted from the reefer. Tal-Salem smoked that butt. That's another round to Swann.'

Leona Boese was fat and black with big hair and different-coloured nail polish on each hand. Harrison sat next to Logan, across from her in the interview room. Swann, who was not allowed to participate, sat behind with his ankle crossed over his knee.

'I only agreed to talk to you because I'm up for parole,' she said. 'It's my second time. Man said no the last time. This better make a fucking difference or I ain't talking at all.' She folded thickly fleshed arms across her one-piece overalls. There was something gross about her that turned Harrison's stomach. He could smell the sweat on her, gathered in the folds of her flesh, where no amount of soap and water could shift it.

'We'll talk to the parole board,' Logan said, leaning across the table. 'But what we say will depend on what you tell us. That's the deal. You understand, Leona?'

Leona nodded, then lifted her snout-like nose to the ceiling. Swann watched her from where he sat, thinking to himself that this was Ismael Boese's mother. The man who had sat across from him at Paddington Green, the man who had engineered the mass evacuation of London, the man who killed 280 people in Rome. That man had come from the womb of this gross, sassy black woman, who had spent the last twenty-five years in prison. As if maybe she guessed his thoughts, she looked directly at him for the first time. 'Who's he?' she said. 'What's he doing here?'

'His name is Swann,' Logan told her. 'He's from Scotland Yard.'

'Scotland Yard?' Her face broke up in a grin, thick lips parted, pink tongue pushing at the white of her teeth. 'No kidding. I used to love them Scotland Yard shows on the TV. You an English bobby, honey?'

'After a fashion, maybe.' Swann stared at her. It was hard to believe that this person had ever been on the campus of Berkeley. But that had been twenty-five *prison* years ago.

'Leona,' Logan said. 'Why would your son have Mary Greer killed?'

The fat, black woman sat still, her body weight balanced on both sides of the chair. 'Mary Greer's dead?'

Logan nodded. 'She was killed in the jewellery store where she worked. Somebody sent by your son strangled her, then left her body in a dumpster. He wanted it to look like the work of a serial killer we were hunting, but the method of strangulation was different.'

'Ismael had Mary Greer killed?' Something moved in Leona's piggy eyes, set deep amid the rolls of pinking flesh in the dark moon of her face. She picked her nose, inadvertently, and searched her pockets for cigarettes. 'Anybody got anything to smoke?'

Logan looked sideways at Harrison. 'Jesus Christ,' he muttered, and tossed her the pack of Marlboro from his pocket. 'Lady, just answer the question, will you. Why would he do that?'

Leona looked strangely hurt. 'Mind your manners, Mr Ponytail. I don't got to say nothing to you.'

Harrison's lips thinned into a line of white tissue. Logan touched him on the arm and leaned forward. 'Leona, remember we have a deal going here. *We* can get what we want elsewhere. Can you?'

'OK. OK.' Leona puffed little clouds of smoke at the ceiling. 'You got to remember I ain't seen Izzy since he was a bitty little kid. God, I don't even remember how old he was before the Maguires took him on.' She glanced at

Swann. 'You get that Irish business took care of yet, mister?'

'We hope so.'

'There you go.' She laughed aloud and sucked on the cigarette. 'I was twenty-nine years old when I saw my son the last time. I'm fifty-three now, nearly fifty-four.'

Logan interrupted her. 'How did you know Mary Greer?'

'Worked in the park. She came to the university.' She glanced at Harrison then. 'Yes, Mr Ponytail, I went to Berkeley University for a while.'

Harrison didn't say anything.

'Mary, Leona. Tell us about Mary,' Logan prompted her.

'Mary's a good gal. She was from back east. Virginia, I think. We worked together in the parks, me and her and Gabby.'

'Camilla Hall?'

'That's right. Mary was part of the prison reform group.' She snorted ironically. 'She never joined us, though.'

'Us being the SLA?'

'Yeah. Me and Gabby were in, yeah. Gabby got shot by the cops in LA. My husband, Pieter. He dead now, died in the pen', just like I will, unless y'all can get me that parole. I tell you, I'd be a model citizen now. I got education. I could get me a job and I wouldn't have nothing to do with no terrorism. Hellfire, I'm an old lady. What kinda harm could I do? I could be somebody's grandma.' She stopped and stared closely at Logan. 'My boy got any kids?'

'You don't know?'

'I don't know a damn thing. He never once come to see his momma. Never made me no calls. And I never get no letter.'

'Did he know Mary well?'

'Not well. He was nine when Mary and me started hanging out. I think he might've stayed with her for a week or two after we got popped. Pieter, that was my old man, he'd already set it up with the Irish, if anything ever happen to us. Well it did, and I guess they took Ismael in.'

'They did,' Harrison said. 'And it worked. The little mother became the meanest sonofabitch on the planet.'

Leona looked pained again. 'He just a kid, Mr Ponytail. No call to badmouth him like that.'

'He killed your best friend, for God's sake.'

She wagged her head at him. 'Well if he did, he musta had a reason.'

'Leona,' Logan pressed a hand over her wrist, 'can you think of any reason why he might have wanted to do that?'

'Nope. I can't say I can, honey.'

'What about the initials TJ and CC?' Harrison said. 'They mean anything to you?'

'Nope.'

Logan's pager was going off, vibrating against her flesh through her clothes. 'Leona, that'll do for now,' she said. 'But we might want to see you again.'

'Whatever you say, girlfriend. I ain't going no place. Don't you go forgetting what we agreed now, y'hear. The parole board, remember.'

Outside, Logan phoned the SIOC and when she hung up her face was grave, eyes set back in her head. Harrison cocked an eyebrow at her. 'What gives, baby?'

She looked beyond him, back through the prison fence to where one of the bulls was still watching them from his tower. 'Kovalski and Byrne are on their way to Carson City, Nevada,' she said quietly. 'A guy called Teniel Jefferson has just been found in his trailer. Gunshot. Coroner says he's three days cold already.'

# 20

The ground team flew into Reno and were met by a young FBI agent, who briefed them on what had been discovered by the Nevada Highway Patrol. Somebody had checked on an autoshop worker called Teniel Jefferson, after he hadn't shown up for work for three days. His screen door was open and the front door unlocked. She had found him shot between the eyes from close range, sitting in an armchair as if he was watching television. The Highway Patrol officers had found a black feather in his shirt pocket and one of them had been sensible enough to run it through the NCIC right away. The FBI had picked it up and alerted their field office immediately. The agent looked sideways at Harrison as he drove.

'You guys got a clean shot at this one. Crime scene's as it was found. Only the ME's done his bit. We got our ERT boys along there right now.'

'Good,' Logan said from the back. 'Maybe we can learn something this time.'

'Teniel Jefferson,' Swann said, half as if to himself. 'Who was Teniel Jefferson?'

The FBI agent looked over his shoulder. 'Redneck. I don't think he was from around here originally, but he used to work out at Carson City Jail. We're doing a background check on him right now. I'll be able to let you know more pretty soon. We got agents and support staff checking on him. One thing that's interesting, though, we found a key of low-grade nose candy, right there in the trailer. Killer just left it right there.'

He drove them out of Reno in the direction of Carson

City and Harrison rode up front, thinking again about the future and Lisa Guffy. She was only a day's drive north of here and he could not get her out of his mind. He did not know why he should suddenly start feeling mortal all at once, suddenly start to wonder about any of it. Maybe it was just the Englishman bugging him, particularly after what he smelled on him with Logan. She had handled herself pretty well so far, a broad on the ground, running a team with an old hick like him along for the ride. She had weathered the storm from the sheriff's office and the GBI in Georgia, as well as the odd look here and there in New Orleans. He glanced at Swann in the mirror. He was clean cut and good-looking, young, and, of course, English. Why did American women always go for the limeys?

'You're Harrison, aren't you,' the young agent said, as he pulled off the highway and drove round the edge of Washoe Lake.

Harrison squinted at the lake. 'My name's Dollar, bub.'

'Yeah, but everyone knows you as Harrison. You were UCA up in Idaho.'

'Was I?'

'Come on, man. I was in Pocatello at the time with Kirk Fitzpatrick. I was fresh outta Quantico and working on computer stuff up there. Reno's my first posting. Course, I report into Vegas like everyone else.'

'Course,' Harrison said.

The young agent paused. Swann listened to the conversation and could see the sweat gathering in a little red patch at the nape of his neck. 'You really take out those three guys in the mine?'

Harrison took his chew from his pocket and placed some under his lip. He sucked and spat juice out of the window. 'Two in the mine,' he said. 'One just outside. Used my knife on him.' He looked sideways at him. 'Killing ain't all it's cracked up to be, bubba.'

361

The young agent was quiet after that and he parked his car in the trailer park, beside other FBI vehicles and two cruisers from the state. Swann got out the back and stretched his legs. The state troopers eyed him cautiously, one of them chewing on a wooden toothpick. Harrison tied his ponytail and turned his collar up. The wind blew in from the west, only half checked by the mountains, and whipped the slate-coloured surface of the lake into flat-faced waves that shucked against the sunken boughs of the cottonwoods. Harrison lit a cigarette and let the smoke drift in the wind. He exchanged glances with Swann as they walked to the steps of the trailer.

'Be kinda sniffy in there, duchess,' he said. 'Man's been dead seventy-two hours already.'

Swann walked shoulder to shoulder with him. 'You know what, hick. I think I can manage.'

Harrison looked coldly at him then. 'You wanna watch yourself, bubba. That stiff upper lip's getting loose.'

They moved into the trailer and the air was thick with death. Swann had smelled it many times before. He watched Harrison watching him carefully for his reaction. Death smells quickly, especially if the body has been lying in a confined and airless space like this one. Jefferson sat in the chair, arms flopped on the sides, feet straight out before him, quite as if he had been watching TV. Only the grey-blue of his skin and the small hole between his eyes gave his death away. The trailer was dishevelled; clearly, only a single, middle-aged man had lived here. Grease-coated pots were stacked up in the sink along with plates and bowls and spoons, with mould growing in blue fur on some of them. A cage sat to one side of the sink with a tarantula spider inside it. At first, Swann thought it was two spiders, but a discarded skin lay cracked and dried in the sawdust. He looked closely at the live one – assuming it was alive. It stood absolutely still, red patches on all of its knees. Harrison came up alongside him. 'Watch he don't bite you.'

Swann looked over to where Logan was carefully considering the body. Harrison moved next to her and studied Jefferson's open, blue eyes, the colour fading in them now. He bent to his knees and considered the fingernails, before the agent from the evidence response team put the plastic bags back over them. Harrison's gaze settled on the feather in the left-hand shirt pocket.

'Been out on the town,' Logan said quietly.

Harrison looked down at the white silk shirt and black jacket over a pair of black slacks and shiny black shoes. 'I'll get the local boys to start asking around. We can bring in help from the Highway Patrol and the county sheriff if we need it.'

Logan moved through Jefferson's home: two bedrooms, both in darkness, with the blinds pulled right down. They were musty and smelled now of the death that reeked in the trailer. She glanced at Swann, who stood by the washer and dryer which were set against the wall before the second bedroom. Two ERT agents were busy inside, photographing and beginning to dust for samples. 'What the hell's Boese doing, Jack?' Logan said. 'I can't figure this at all.'

Swann did not answer her. From where he stood, he looked the length of the corridor and could see Jefferson's prostrate body with the feather sticking out of his shirt. Outside, blue lights flashed and Logan came up beside him. 'That'll be the medics,' she said. 'Jack, get someone to take the feather out of his pocket. I don't want anyone outside this room knowing about that.'

Swann went over to the body and relayed Logan's order to the ERT agent working the floor area close to the body. He had two shell casings in an evidence bag and Swann squinted at them. The ERT man put the feather in a separate bag and stowed them both in the plastic evidence case, having marked their zone location on his pad of paper. Swann stepped out of the trailer, where he found Harrison with another bag in his hand, a postcard inside it. He looked round at Swann. 'Hey, duchess,' he said. 'Reckon I know where this mother hung out of an evening.'

They went together, Harrison borrowing the car of the young, wide-eyed agent. 'Have you been here before?' Swann asked him, as they drove round the lake.

Harrison steered with one hand, the window partially rolled down, and a cigarette burning between the fingers of his other one. 'I been through Carson a few times.' He looked out of the side of his eyes. 'I got the whorehouse directions from a state trooper, if that's what you're thinking.'

Swann snorted then and shook his head. 'Jesus, Harrison. When're you going to grow up?'

Harrison stamped on the brakes and the car shuddered to a halt. One hand still gripped the wheel and the other lay fisted in his lap. His eyes were cold and for a moment he did not say anything. 'You wanna call me on that, bubba?'

'Don't be a jerk. We're working together. You don't like me. I can live with that. I certainly don't intend getting into a fist fight over it.'

'You know *why* I don't like you?'

Swann curled his lip. 'You're jealous of me and Cheyenne?'

'You smart-assed sonofa . . .' Harrison lifted his fist and Swann looked him in the eye. Harrison stopped, shook his head and spat tobacco juice out the window. He started the engine, revved hard and squealed the tyres in the dust.

They drove then in silence all the way to the cat house, high in the hills above the Stewart facility complex, Swann feeling that somehow he had gained a victory. Harrison parked the car, slammed the door and stalked inside. Swann followed him. Two long-legged girls, clad only in underwear, were seated on barstools, while a white, Italian-looking guy polished glasses. The room was hot, oppressive, lifeless. In a strange kind of way, Swann was reminded of Jefferson's trailer.

'Gentlemen,' the bartender said. 'What can we do for you today?'

Harrison leaned on the counter and waved his shield under the bartender's nose. 'You can get me the boss, brother. We ain't here for the company.'

Swann sat and listened while Harrison questioned the manager, a woman in her fifties, bosomy, who did her best to look as though she were still in her forties. She was reluctant to talk about clients.

'Ah, Jesus,' Harrison said, after five minutes of stalling. 'We're the fucking FBI, lady. I'm pissed off already today, without you yanking my chain. Either tell me what I wanna know or I'll have the guys downtown roll this place for drugs every night for a year.'

She looked at him. The bartender looked at him. The two hookers in underwear looked at him. Jack Swann looked at him: beaten, weathered face, long grey hair, and the hint of spittle on his lip. He meant it. Every one of them knew that he meant it.

'OK,' she said. 'He was here two nights ago.'

'On his own?'

'He arrived on his own. He drives a grey Dodge with blue stripes on the side.'

Harrison nodded and lit a cigarette.

'Can I offer you a drink?' she asked.

'No. Just talk. Then we can all get outta here.'

She seemed to physically bite down on her tongue. 'You know,' she said. 'We have excellent law-enforcement relations round here.'

'Not with me, you don't.' Harrison stared at the bartender. 'I'm sure I could find shitloads of something if I bothered to look.' He looked back at the manager. 'You were saying, lady.'

'He drank. He fooled around. He left.'

'Who'd he fool around with?'

'I'm not sure. I'll check.'

'Do that.' Harrison sucked on his cigaretfe. 'What about other customers? Anyone else in here when he was?'

She glanced at one of the whores at the bar, a small girl with pale skin and freckles on her naked shoulders. 'Jenna, you were working that night, weren't you?'

Harrison got up and walked to where she sat at the bar. 'Well?' he said. Jenna looked frightened, shrinking back, as if from his breath. 'Who else was in here?'

'Just a cowboy. And a nigger I hadn't seen before.'

'Nigger?' He cocked his head at her. 'You mean negro, don't you?'

'Yeah, right.'

Swann was on his feet now, wanting to interrupt but unable to. Harrison took her by the arm, not squeezing, just holding her firmly. 'Tell me about him.'

'What's to tell? Nappy hair, black skin, big nose. He didn't wanna party, just drink a cocktail, have a gawk and fuck off again.' She shook her arm free. 'We get a lot like that, mister. They're either afraid of their wives or just can't get it up.'

Harrison asked about vehicles and someone remembered a white Nissan truck. As they were about to leave, the blonde girl pointed at Swann. 'Hey,' she said to Harrison. 'Your partner's cute, mister. How come he don't talk?'

Harrison looked coldly at Swann. 'He ain't from round here, girlfriend. He don't get to talk.'

*

Webb sat in on the interview with Janice Martin. She was seated across from Christine Harris, smoking cigarettes, very pretty, except for bitten-down fingernails.

'Third time, Janice. I think it's bye-bye this time.' Harris studied the nervous lines in her face. 'We might charge you with intent to supply. There was a lot of crack in that flat.'

'*His* not mine.'

'There were two of you there.'

Janice rolled her eyes to the ceiling, but Webb saw the fear in the pupils. He could always detect the fear, sometimes he could smell it, even in the toughest. 'You'll do five years at least,' he said.

She looked at him for the first time and gnawed at the edge of her little finger.

'Tell us about The Regiment, Janice,' Webb went on. 'Tell us about David "Dog Soldier" Collier.'

Her face paled, eyes watery all at once, as if suddenly afflicted by the pain of some bad memory. Webb leaned his elbows on the table and thrust his chin at her. 'What d'you know about the morning of February 5th?'

'February 5th?' She screwed up her eyes. 'Nothing. What's so special about February 5th?'

'It's the day that the terrorist known as Storm Crow escaped from the convoy taking him to trial. It's the day that twenty-two innocent people, including sixteen police officers, were shot or burned to death. It was all over the news, Janice. You must have seen it.'

'I did see it,' she said, her accent beginning to show through. 'I just wasn't aware it happened on February 5th.'

'We think your friend Collier was behind it.' Webb was staring at her now. 'He's an ex-soldier, they're all ex-soldiers. They know about weapons, they know how to plan attacks.' He was watching her face as he spoke, the slight inward turning of her mouth, the way she avoided his eyes. 'What d'you know about it, Janice?'

'I don't know anything.'

'Nothing? Come on. You were Gringo's old lady for a year.'

'Well, I'm not any more. I don't get to know any business. No girl does. They don't talk business while women are there.'

'What exactly is their business, Janice?' Harris asked her.

'I don't know.' She shrugged her shoulders. 'Motorbikes or something.'

'Or something.' Webb shook his head at her. 'If you know something about what happened that day and you're not telling us, you're going to be in even more trouble.'

'Well, that's fine, because I don't know anything.'

Harris clasped both hands together on the table. 'OK,' she said. 'We can either charge you now or talk about something else.'

Janice listened while Harris explained the situation to her: two choices, either be charged with possession of crack cocaine and perhaps intent to supply, both of which would mean a prison sentence with the two convictions she had on record already, or she could go to work for them. 'You play it cool,' she told her. 'Collier will know that you were arrested, his sources will tell him as much. Don't try to hide it. Tell them your father put up bail for you, and in the meantime we'll speak to the CPS on your behalf.'

Janice flicked at a long strand of hair which hung down over her eyes, and lit another cigarette. 'What d'you want me to do exactly?' she asked.

'You've got your own flat, haven't you.'

'Yes. My father owns it.'

'Do you let the boys come round?'

'Yes.'

'Good. That's all I want you to do. They get to sleep with you, don't they? Any of them, whenever they want.' Harris took a plastic bag from her case and laid it on the table. Inside were a dozen or more specimen bottles. Janice Martin stared at them for a long moment and then she burst out laughing. 'Fucking them is going to keep me out of prison?'

Harris held up a bottle. 'If you bring us these, marked with their names on, yes.'

Back at the Yard, she had a phone call waiting, and she picked up the phone at Webb's desk. It was Combes, the US Secret Service agent from the embassy. He told her that he had sent the inventory over to Washington and they were checking it now. From what they could gather, the company who supplied the parts from Texas was legitimate.

'We found that inventory in a plastic bag under a paving slab in the garden,' Harris said. 'There must be more to it than just motorbike parts.'

'Hold on a second. I said we *think* the company is legitimate. It is on the face of it, but it's owned by the Bandido Nation. We're looking further, Christine. That company has a lot of dealings in Mexico, and they bank with Banco De California. We've been interested in them for a long time. They have branches throughout South America, Mexico particularly; and they also have some in the southern states of the US. That's all I can tell you right now, but I'll call as and when we make progress.'

'Thank you, Peter. Thank you very much.' Harris hung up and relayed the information to Webb, who sat toying with a pencil on his desk.

'What d'you reckon about the girl?' he said.

'I think she'll go for it.' Harris sat down opposite him.

'If you think about it, what have we asked her to do?' She spread her palms. 'Exactly what she has always done, let the biker boys sleep with her, only we get semen speci- mens. She doesn't know why. In her mind, she won't be informing on them. I think Collier will keep tabs on her for a while. She may even be banned from the clubhouse, given his attitude to drugs and the police. But that won't matter. I think it'll work, George.' She smiled. 'And if it does, we might just get a DNA match on the hairs we found in the crash helmets. Then we can really sow the seeds of panic.'

Tal-Salem was in Shrivenham, in Oxfordshire. He had never visited this part of the country before, confining his activities to London and Birmingham. He sat in the small hotel where he had rented a room, using a false Kuwaiti passport, and began to thumb through a copy of the *Yellow Pages*. He stopped when he got to car hire companies and ran his finger down the page. There were not that many of them: the major ones, of course, and a few smaller ones. He picked up the telephone to Avis. 'Good morning,' he said, when the receptionist answered. 'This is Detective Sergeant Webb of Scotland Yard. Could you tell me, please, how far back your records go? I'm interested in vehicles rented from you in August of 1997.'

Byrne and Kovalski had arrived from Washington by the time Harrison and Swann got back from the whorehouse. The crime scene had been cleared now and they moved back to the resident agency office in Reno. Logan briefed them on what they had got so far and then she ran through the rest of the case, trying to assemble some order. They conference-linked the briefing to the fugitive unit in D.C. and the field office in New Orleans, so everyone could be updated. Logan laid her notes in front of her and started running through them.

'February 5th,' she said, 'Ismael Boese was broken out of a prison truck on his way to trial in London. February 16th, he shows up in the field office in New Orleans, walks into reception and delivers a feather and a photograph of Special Agent Dollar with a bullet hole in his head. This is classic Storm Crow behaviour, having first done it to Louis Byrne at Fort Bliss in March 1995.' She looked across the table at Swann, seated between Kovalski and Byrne. 'He did the same in London to three Antiterrorist Branch officers. It's his calling card, his way of telling the authorities that something is about to happen.

'Within three days of that delivery, he attacks an oil tanker on the Mississippi River, tricks us into believing he's on board with hostages, and then he blows the anchor chain with four FBI SWAT teams still aboard. All the time this was going on, he was actually in the back of a radio station van by the spillway, negotiating through Louis Byrne's wife in Washington. We find the van in Meridian, Mississippi, the following day, and the ground team is set up.' She paused for a moment. 'Back in the fall of last year, a woman called Mary Poynton was murdered in Royston, Georgia. The VICAP team in Quantico call John Earl Cochrane, the VICAP co-ordinator in New Orleans, because New Orleans had been looking at a series of similar crimes. John Dollar goes up to see what the situation is and meets with Special Agent Mallory from the CASKU. Between them they agree that this is not part of the killings perpetrated by the so-called "garbageman", but a copycat. The case is left with the GBI, whose number one suspect is a negro driving a tow truck. He is never apprehended. We can now link that killing to Storm Crow, the killer being Tal-Salem. DNA from a reefer butt confirmed his presence in that jewellery store.'

She paused for a moment and looked round the table. 'The victim was known to Boese from his childhood. She was a friend of his mother during her active days with the Symbionese Liberation Army in Los Angeles in the 1970s. Boese stayed with her for two weeks before being adopted by the Maguires, IRA sympathizers.' She paused then and asked, 'Why kill *her*?'

No one answered her. Harrison sucked on his tobacco. 'Maybe he wanted something,' he suggested.

'Like the name of Teniel Jefferson.' Byrne rested his elbows on the desk.

'But why, Louis?'

'Cheyenne, if we knew that, we wouldn't be sitting here.'

Harrison spat tobacco juice into an empty Coke can. 'Why do all that shit in New Orleans?' he said. 'That was a helluva lot of trouble for very little. And why drive your stolen cab into the Holiday Inn at Meridian, then leave it for us with the radio station signs put back on the sides?'

'Why indeed?' Kovalski looked across the table at him. 'He picked you out, JB, which to my mind indicates something to do with the past, and that has to mean Salvesen. But we've re-interviewed him and, as far as I can tell, this is nothing to do with him. We can't be sure, of course, but my instincts tell me this is Boese's own agenda.'

'"Other endeavours."' Logan chewed on the words. 'He said to Angie Byrne that he had other endeavours.'

Nobody spoke for a few moments, everyone mulling over their own thoughts, then Swann said: 'He went to an awful lot of trouble to say hello to the FBI. He wanted you to be aware that he was in this country, just like he did to us in London.'

'In London he was planning something really big,' Logan said. 'What's he planning here?'

372

'The jackal and the crow.' Harrison was staring at the ceiling. '"When the prey is down, does the jackal or the crow eat first?"'

'The jackal does,' Byrne said. 'In the pecking order, the crow gets the scraps the jackal leaves behind. The jackal is Carlos. That much we know. Ben Dubin was in D.C. recently and we talked about it again. He can confirm beyond any doubt that Boese was the protégé of Carlos. Boese might've denied it when interviewed, but then he was on remand in the UK. The jackal is Carlos and the crow is Boese. He's linking the two in riddles. What he's trying to tell us, I don't know. Maybe they're planning something together?'

Swann shook his head. 'Carlos is tucked up tighter than a drum in Paris. They bring him to interviews chained to a pole. He isn't going anywhere.'

'But he is trying to tell us something about Carlos.' Logan gesticulated with a red-nailed finger.

Swann looked at Byrne again. 'Why should he ask your wife to be his attorney? What does he need defending against other than what we know about already?'

'Maybe the motherfucker wants to turn himself in,' Harrison said drily. 'Whatever he's up to, he's giving us the run-around.' His eyes narrowed, then glinted in the light that shone through the window. 'There's something else we need to think about. If he got Jefferson's name from Greer, what did he get from Jefferson?'

The Reno agents were working hard on Teniel Jefferson, along with the city and state police. He had lived in the area since 1984, moving there from Virginia. He had worked as a prison guard at Carson City Jail, on the outskirts of town. Harrison, Swann and Logan went to see the governor. Swann stared at the wire fence and wondered at how strange life can be. He had never been anywhere near an American penitentiary in his life before, and here he was, visiting his second one in as many days. Harrison pointed out a separate brick building with double bars on the windows, set slightly back from the rest of the compound. 'Death row, bubba,' he said.

The governor was in his sixties, a big man with a tanned and lined face. White hair was brushed back from his scalp, exposing a forehead dappled with liver spots. He had liver spots on his hands and looked as though he had spent too many years in the sun. He sat behind his desk, with an elk head mounted behind him. Harrison counted six points per side. 'How much meat you get?' he asked.

'Six hundred pounds. Weighed near on nine when I shot him.'

'You get him round here?'

The governor shook his head. 'North, almost in Idaho.' He looked at Logan then and fisted his hands under his chin. 'I knew Jefferson,' he said. 'He was a warder here for ten years. I fired him in 1994.'

'Fired him?' Logan looked across the desk at him.

'Yes, young lady. Fired him.' He stretched his hands out on the desk. 'I run a clean ship here. Any infraction of the rules is taken very seriously. Jefferson bent those rules just about as far as a man could. He ran all kinds of rackets in this prison and it took me four years to figure him out. I shoulda had him indicted.' He paused then, pushing himself back in the seat. 'On the face of it he was a good man, but that was just bullshit. He ran drugs, cigarettes, whisky, the odd whore now and again. You name it, young lady. That man did it.'

'Cocaine?' Harrison said.

'I could never prove it, but I imagine so. All I ever could prove was some illegal cigarettes and a buncha chewing tobacco. It was enough to get him fired, which was all I needed to clean house. That's exactly what I did.' He sat back. 'I can tell you, I'm not a bit surprised to hear he wound up with a bullet in the head.'

Logan crossed her legs and Swann saw the governor's gaze waver a little. 'We need to look at your records,' she said. 'Inmate records. We need to run the names through our computers and see what we can come up with.'

He stared at her. 'You're talking about all the names of all the inmates during the period he worked in this facility?'

She nodded.

'That'll take you a while, lady. You're lucky this is a state facility, otherwise you'd be asking the Bureau of Prisons and they'd hold you up for sure.' He laughed then. 'Ringing my own bell again, aren't I. Like I said to you, I run things clean and tight. You'll have the information by this afternoon. We got it all on computer disk.'

'That'd be great.' Logan looked at the pictures behind his head, some of his predecessors, some other men in uniform. 'I'd like a list of the warders here during that same period,' she said. 'We'll need to talk to any still serving that knew him. Can you set us up with an interview room?'

The governor reached for the phone.

They talked to various different warders, none of whom seemed to have a good word to say about Jefferson. After the fourth one had gone back to work, Harrison ran his hand over his scalp in frustration. 'Goddammit. They musta been briefed or something. Governor's so concerned about his fricking reputation. There must be one guy in this joint who liked him.' He stood up. 'You two can stay here if you want. I'm going back up to the cat house. Betcha the guy had his favourite hooker. She'll tell us more than these guys ever can.'

They met up with him later that evening, Swann wondering if he had got *everything* he wanted from the whorehouse. They were in the field office in Reno, using the conference room to go through some of the information they had gathered. The computer records had been downloaded to the team back in Washington, who were also trawling every inmate's card, looking for quite what, they did not know. Harrison sat down across the table from Swann.

'Get what you went for?' Swann asked him.

Harrison cocked his head at him. 'Yes, duchess. I got what I went for. You got a problem with that?'

'Harrison, if you don't crawl back under your stone, I am gonna bust your ass.' Logan's voice was sharp and cold. Kovalski and Byrne were working in the next office and Swann saw them look up. Logan lowered her voice but the tone was as cold as before. 'If you got a problem with Jack, then get it aired, motherfucker, or keep your damn mouth shut.'

Harrison stared at her, then hissed air through his teeth. 'I talked to a Mexican gal, Suela,' he said. 'Jefferson's favourite whore. She told me he went up there at least twice a week, sometimes three times, so he was making more money than what he'd been getting in the autoshop.' He took some chew from his chin and flicked off the unwanted strands. 'My guess is, he was still running stuff into that prison – through one of the other bulls, maybe. There's no way Carson City Jail is cleaner than any other. Stuff gets in, people get paid. That's the game. The whore confirmed that he sold coke, but she didn't say where he got it, and, of course, she never used any.' He rocked back on the legs of his chair and rested his head against the glass partition. 'His other vice was the blackjack tables.' He let his words hang for a second before going on. 'According to the whore, he played in the Big Whisky casino in Reno. Sometimes on her days off, he would take her.' He sat forward again, with a bump of the chair legs.

'Check the file, Cheyenne. Ten years ago, Mary Greer was a dealer in that casino.'

Byrne and Kovalski took a night flight back to Washington. Logan and Swann ate dinner together at the hotel. Harrison said he had things to do. Swann laid a hand on Logan's arm. 'Can I come to your room tonight?' he asked her.

She laughed then, touching his nose with the tip of her tongue. 'Honey, you don't have to ask.'

'What about the others?'

'What others?'

'You know. The team working on this thing.'

'Well, baby doll, the D.C. contingent have gone back to D.C. The Reno people have homes to go to and who gives a shit what Harrison thinks? Besides, I can sleep with who I like, just as long as it doesn't interfere with my work. Jack, we got agents married to each other who work in the same office, some on the same squads. We call them GS26s.'

'Why?'

'Hump agents are mostly GS13 in service grade.'

'And two together is 26.'

'That's right.'

She pushed her plate away and took his hand. 'How long they gonna let you stay over here, d'you think?'

'I don't know. I'll have to call in again and check.'

'You been in touch though, huh.'

'Oh yes.' He looked beyond her and saw Harrison walking purposefully towards the table. 'I'm going to sort this thing with him,' he said. 'One way or the other.'

'Watch yourself, baby.'

Swann leaned over and kissed her. 'I'm tougher than I look, sweetheart.' He got up from the table. 'You fancy a game of pool somewhere, Harrison?'

Harrison looked in his eyes. 'Why not,' he said.

They left Logan and walked three blocks down the street to a small, dimly lit bar in a side street. Harrison pushed open the door and Swann followed him inside. A group of bikers sat at one table, some women with them. Working men lined the barstools, in checked shirts and baseball hats and grubby-looking jeans. Swann felt various sets of eyes on his back. He still wore his suit and tie and felt distinctly out of place. Two pool tables were set back-to-back on a raised section away from the bar. Harrison tossed him two quarters and jerked his thumb at the table. 'Rack 'em,' he said.

Swann walked past the table where the bikers were sitting and placed the money in the slots. Then he racked for a game of eightball. Harrison dumped his jacket over Swann's, where he had laid it on a chair, and selected a cue from the wall. He rolled it on the table under the flat of his hand, then did the same with another. Satisfied, he chalked the end and nodded to the twin bottles of Coors he had brought over from the bar; then he settled himself to break. 'We play for a beer a stick,' he said.

Harrison broke and dropped both a striped and a spotted ball. 'Still open,' he said. 'One ball, right here.' He slapped the pocket next to him and played a double off the top rail. Swann watched the ball drop into the hole. Harrison lit a cigarette and did not remove it from his mouth as he bent for the next shot, which rattled into the middle pocket. Swann sat down with his beer. One of the bikers, big-bellied and bearded, was watching him. Harrison hit three more down before Swann got to play a shot.

They played four games and Harrison won them all. 'You're not very good at this, are you, limey?' he said, as Swann went to the bar for more beer. Swann just smiled at him. He bought another round and carried the bottles back to the table. One of the bikers was on his feet, talking to Harrrison.

'He challenged, bubba,' Harrison told him. 'You got to sit this one out.'

The biker was big and tattooed and mean-looking. Swann watched the way he watched Harrison closely with each shot, looking for some sign of cheating. Harrison beat him easily.

'Another,' the biker said.

Harrison shook his head. 'Play somebody else, bro. I'm all done here.'

'I wanna play you or him.' The man staggered a little as he jerked his thumb over his shoulder.

'Listen, partner. He don't wanna play, and I don't wanna play. You understand?'

'Son-of-a-fucking-bitch.'

Harrison was suddenly in his face, FBI shield in his hand. 'Go away, asshole.'

The biker blinked and looked at him, then at the badge. 'Fuck it,' he said, turned on his heel and left the bar. Harrison sat down with Swann and tossed the shield on to the table.

'Has its advantages,' he said. 'FBI, can't lie to get in, gotta lie to stay in.'

'What?'

'Forget it. Just an old cliché.'

Swann stared at him. He looked beaten and tired, and unimpressed with his life. 'You better get whatever it is that's bugging you off your chest, Harrison,' he said. 'Because it's eating you up.'

Harrison poked a finger at him. 'You, brother. You are on my chest.'

'So, what're you going to do about it?'

Harrison lit a cigarette and blew smoke at him. 'Last year, I nearly got my ass burned for good because of you.'

'So I've heard.' Swann could feel a pulse jerking at his temple. He leaned forward. 'I'm sorry about that. It wasn't my intention. I went to Paris with Louis Byrne to check on a receipt you got from Salvesen's office. I told my girl-friend I was going. I had no idea who she really was at that time.'

'You were an asshole.'

Swann opened his mouth and let the blocked air go. He thought back over the last few years, the dreams, the cold sweats, the fear. All of it topped by Pia and Ismael Boese. He could see Boese's eyes in his mind. He could see Pia's eyes, dark and big and looking longingly at him. Even now he wanted to believe her, believe what Webb had told him, that a part of her was genuine. But he could not, not quite. If she had not forced him to talk that night when he had been dreaming of Nanga Parbat, then perhaps.

'You know something, Harrison,' he said suddenly, 'you can go to hell for all I care. If I was responsible for getting you compromised, I'm truly sorry. But I never was and never will be an *asshole*.'

Harrison was staring at him still, the drink evident in the edge of his eyes. 'I was almost hanged, Swann.'

'I can't do anything about it.' Swann flapped his hands at his sides.

Harrison plucked a cigarette from his shirt pocket and scraped a match head on the heel of his boot. He flapped it out and ran the burnt end across the back of his hand. 'Why'd they pick *you* over somebody else?' he asked.

'It's none of your business.'

'Come on, bubba. What was the deal there, why'd Boese pick you out from the crowd?' Harrison rocked on his stool. 'Come on, man. Don't you think I got a right to know? I mean, they got to you, didn't they. They musta picked you out for a reason.'

'I'm not going into that, Harrison. Just leave it alone.'

'Come on.' Harrison slapped him lightly in the chest

380

with the backs of his fingers. His eyes were tight and cold. 'Talk to me, duchess. I got a right to know.'

'Fuck you.' Swann got up and went for his jacket. Harrison half rose and caught hold of his wrist.

'Let go.' Swann was tense now – back on the Falls Road, being compromised himself, with only Webb to back him up. Harrison did not let go. And then Swann hit him, a right cross, flush on the jaw. Harrison reeled back over the pool table. The bar was absolutely silent. Swann picked up his jacket and walked across the floor, out of the door and on to the street.

Harrison got up from the pool table and rubbed his jaw where the blow still sang in his teeth. He shook his head to clear the fog behind his eyes. The other drinkers were looking at him. Ignoring them, he stuffed his shield away and picked up his jacket. When he got to the street, Swann was nowhere to be seen.

Swann took the elevator to their floor and paused outside his own door. Maybe he just ought to be alone, lie in his own bed and think his own thoughts. But Harrison had rattled him, shaken up all the emotions he was so desperately trying to smother. He knocked on Logan's door. She answered it with a towel wrapped round her, very white against the black of her skin. She saw his face, the trouble burning quietly in his eyes, and touched his cheek with her palm. 'Hey, baby doll. What's up?'

Swann kissed her, then took her to bed. They made love for a long time, and gradually the tension eased like sweat from his pores. He explored every inch of her body, holding her, breathing her into him, touching her skin with his fingers, his body, his tongue. He drew tight black nipples into his mouth and sucked them till they were hard. She worked her thighs against him, long fingernails raking his scalp. He spread her legs wide and entered her, resting on his fists, while she held his waist. He closed his eyes

381

and dreams flooded his skull. Back on that mountain. Snow and ice and the wall stretching above him. The Diamir face. The Merkl Gully and Steve Brady's twisted features. And then the horrible, high-pitched wail, as the snow ledge collapsed and Brady fell to his death.

Swann cried out as he came, and his eyes were wide and staring. He rolled on to his side with the sweat pouring off him. Logan was up, sitting next to him, her hand on his face, smoothing the crescent of lines in his brow. She touched his hair, brushed his face with her lips, then kissed him gently on the mouth.

'I can never get it out of my system, Chey,' he said. 'No matter what I do, I see that hill. I see that fucking ice cliff and I see myself sawing and sawing that rope.' He sat up, scrabbling for cigarettes. 'Steve begged me not to kill him, pleaded with me.' He lit the cigarette with trembling hands. ' "Don't kill me, Jack." That's what he said. "Please don't kill me." '

Logan got up, poured them both a shot of whisky and handed him a glass. Swann drank, gagged, then pulled her towards him again. 'If I hadn't told Pia,' he said. 'If I could've just kept that bit to myself, they wouldn't own me like they do.' He shook his head. 'When Boese was inside, it was bearable. I had won – at least, I thought I had. I was on tenterhooks all the time he was on remand. I promised him thirty years, and I was desperate to get him away and out of my head. I was dealing with the Pia thing, slowly, in my own way, without getting too fucked up.' He stopped and sucked on the cigarette. 'Then Boese gets out and it all goes to ratshit.' He sat up again, resting his palm on her thigh. 'Then this thing with Harrison to cap it all.'

'What happened tonight?'

Swann laughed. 'He called me out and I hit him.'

'You did what?' She sat up. 'What happened?'

'Nothing. That's it. He called me out, and I whacked him. He went flying. Best punch I ever threw.' He rubbed at the raised skin on his knuckles.

They lay together quietly after that and then made love again. Swann got up for a shower and let the hot prickles of water burn the weariness from his skin. He went back to the bedroom, towelling his hair. Logan was sitting up in bed with the sheet below her breasts. 'God, you are beautiful,' he said. 'Will you marry me, Chey?'

She burst out laughing and he sat down on the bed, laughing himself. 'Better?' she said, laying the warmth of her palm on his leg.

'Much.'

'George Webb called while you were in the shower. He wants you to call him back.'

Webb had gone to see Pia Grava again. Christine Harris had the situation set up with Janice Martin, and GCHQ were monitoring everything that was said in the clubhouse, which was not very much. No business anyway, other than stuff about motorbikes. Collier was careful, very careful. He made sure nothing was said on the telephone when out of town members made their twice weekly phone calls.

Webb had reread the entire notes made on Operation Stormcloud, right up to where they apprehended Boese. He checked the back files again, then the events leading up to the situation in Rome. It began with the car bomb in Soho, an IRA timing and power unit, but no coded warning, which was something they had not done in years. A successful controlled explosion and then the investigation that followed. Boese led them to a house in West London, where they laid siege only to find him gone; guns set up, the floorboards taken up. The Syrian passport, triacetone triperoxide crystals in felt-tip pens. Boese wanted them to find him, but remained one step ahead of the game right

383

up until the very end, when he allowed himself to get caught. Pia always able to slip him bits and pieces of information because of her relationship with Swann.

He sat at his desk and checked everything they had on her. They had her cellphone records, and there were two numbers that they had not initially been able to account for. One, they had discovered, was Boese's cloned mobile, and the other given to her so she could make a return call to him on an aeroplane. Webb looked at that number now and it troubled him a fraction. They had never traced it to its source. There had been no need, with Boese in custody and a full confession from Pia.

He laid the bills out on the table, as he sat across from Pia one more time. She looked better than when he had last seen her with Swann. Her skin had more of a glow to it and she did not look quite so weary. She asked him about Swann and he told her, gently, that she had to forget about Swann.

'I have, George.' She drew in her lips. 'In my way. I saw him. I needed to see him. There was nothing we could say. I feel better for it. But it's hard, though, especially in here. I got attached to him. I got attached to his children. How are they?'

'Good. He doesn't see so much of them now, of course.'

'That must be very hard. He got very used to having them.' She clasped her fingers together. 'Did you know my trial is set for April 15th?'

'Good.' He looked at her, his blue eyes soft. 'Everything you've helped us with will go into the file, Pia.' He shook his head. 'I'm sorry. I mean, Brigitte.'

She laid a hand on his and squeezed. 'Don't worry about it. I've been Pia for so long, I think of myself as her.'

Webb looked at the notes in front of him, the words in his head again: *We have been betrayed.* 'I need to ask you some more stuff,' he said. 'With Boese getting out we're back to where we started.' He tapped the phone bill with one finger and spun the page so it faced her. 'Can you remember this call?'

'To an airphone. I think I told you.'

Webb nodded. 'It might be important now. It wasn't before, because we had Boese. But the more this goes on, the more my guts tell me something is wrong. This was Boese you called, yes?'

She lifted her hands. 'I assume so, George. Why shouldn't it be?'

'No reason. It was definitely the man, the voice, that gave you your orders.'

She nodded.

'Did you speak to more than one person?'

She took both his hands in hers. 'George, I can't tell you that. I don't know. I spoke to one man or many men, every time a different voice, a different accent. I really couldn't tell you.'

'OK. Had you received any land-line calls around the time you took and made this one?'

'I don't remember. I don't think so.'

He looked at the phone bill again. 'All these other numbers are accounted for?'

'Yes. We've been through them.'

'Right. I need to find out what flight this was and where, then get the passenger manifest.' He spoke half as if to himself. 'I should've done it at the time. Maximalist, Webb, remember.' He smiled at her then. 'Getting senile, Pia. I've started talking to myself.'

She smiled at him and he stood up. 'Take care,' he said. 'And remember, when that trial comes up, the full facts will be told. Believe me. You'll do time, Pia, but no one's going to hang you out to dry as some kind of scapegoat, with Boese over the wall.' He walked to the door and knocked. 'Oh, by the way, one thing I meant to ask you.

385

When Jack was in Paris with Louis Byrne, you phoned and told Boese, didn't you.'

She bit her lip. 'I should've done. I was supposed to report all Jack's movements. But I was sick of things then, and, besides, I was at your house with Caroline and the children.'

Webb felt a little shiver trickle the length of his spine. He sat down again. 'Tell me that again.'

'I didn't tell anyone about Jack being in Paris,' she said.

'No one at all?'

'No one.'

Webb's eyes were narrow slits in his head, and he stared through her to the wall. A key rattled in the metal door behind him.

Swann phoned Webb from the hotel bedroom and listened intently to everything he had to say. His breath got stuck as he learned that he was not responsible for Harrison being compromised. 'You're joking,' he said at last.

'No, I'm not.' Webb's voice was chipped and edgy. 'Why would she lie, Jack? What could she possibly gain now?'

'You're right. She wouldn't lie. There is nothing to gain.'

'Think about it. Whoever called Salvesen was covering his tracks. Harrison got burned at that particular time in order to deliberately implicate you.' Webb paused for a moment. 'There's someone else on the inside, Jack. There always has been. And the only people who knew you were in Paris were people on the team. That's the security group, Box, and the FBI liaison.'

Swann was quiet for a moment, then said: 'Another thing occurs to me, given all of this.'

'What's that?'

'If you were Storm Crow, would you allow yourself to

be caught so you could make one dramatic phone call? Or would you send someone else in your stead?'

He put the phone down and turned to Logan. For a long moment he looked at her, a mixture of fear and relief in his eyes. He could bury this thing with Harrison. But there *was* somebody on the inside. Storm Crow had penetrated further than just Jack Swann. It was, as Webb said, either the UK security services or the Foreign Emergency Search Team. Logan had been part of that team.

'Good news?' she said, with a smile.

'I think so, Chey. I think so.' He swallowed and looked her right in the eye. Could it be possible for two women to betray him? 'I didn't blow Harrison's cover,' he said.

# 21

Angie Byrne ate a breakfast sandwich in the sunshine on the roof of her company's building on New York Avenue. She sipped coffee and picked at the bagel, letting her gaze wander to the Washington Monument. Her cellphone rang on the glass-topped table and she picked it up.

'Hello,' she said.

'How's my attorney today, ready to represent me?'

'How did you get this number?'

'I can get whatever I like. I had a very good teacher. Tell me something. D'you think the jackal and the crow ate at the same time?'

'What did you want with Teniel Jefferson?' she asked him.

'They found him, then. I haven't watched the news.'

'What did you want?'

'It's not good to talk on the phone, Angela. But one day I need to tell you something about that – interesting thing with feathers. Very strange, but not entirely unlooked for.' His voice was suddenly cracked and cold. 'Tell your husband to think about what I said, tell him to consider the jackal and the crow.'

Louis Byrne was sitting at his desk when Angie called him with Storm Crow's latest message. 'Goddammit, Angie. That sonofabitch.'

'Keep your shirt on, honey. It was just another phone call.'

'Yeah, but Jesus, you're my wife.'

'I can handle it, Louis. He's just another wacko on the phone.'

'He's a very dangerous wacko.'

'So, you want I should live my life in fear?'

'Why don't you let me put a watch on the house?'

'No, Louis. No way. Fuck him and his delusions. If anybody breaks into my house, I'll shoot them myself.'

'OK, look, I'll pass this on to Kovalski's team. Where are you, by the way?'

'Sitting in the roof garden, keeping an eye on the President.'

Byrne laughed and hung up. He scratched his lip with his thumbnail, rocking from side to side in the chair and staring at the black feather that hung on the wall.

Swann slept soundly for the first time in a long while after Webb's phone call. He lay close to Cheyenne, his body outlining hers. He awoke still pressed against her, her back to him, her hair in his face and the warmth of her flesh on his. He did not want to move, did not want to get up. But the red digits on the clock read 6:45 and he eased himself away from her. She joined him in the shower, soaping his body till he stiffened and they made love standing up, with the water cascading over their heads.

Swann dressed first and went down to breakfast. He found Harrison seated in a booth on his own, stirring sugar into black coffee. His hat was beside him on the seat and his hair was long and silver and untied. It hung on to his shoulders. Swann looked at him, still lean and fit, and he wondered what would have happened if Harrison had hit him back.

'Ah, Mike Tyson,' Harrison muttered.

Swann sat down opposite him. 'Why didn't you hit me back?'

Harrison touched his jaw, where the skin was tinged red.

'Why?' He opened his eyes wide for a moment. 'I don't know why. I guess I was being polite. Neighbourly, we call it.' He looked at his coffee cup. 'I don't know, Swann. I guess it ain't gonna solve anything.'

Swann stared at him then. 'That's the first time you've called me anything other than bubba, limey or duchess since I arrived in this country.'

'I call everybody names, duchess. It's just my way.'

'Listen,' Swann said. 'I had a phone call last night after I got back to the hotel.'

'Did you now?'

'From the UK.' Swann shook his head at him. 'I wasn't responsible for you getting burned, Harrison. Brigitte Hammani did not tell anyone about me going to Paris. Nobody outside the job knew except her and she did not pass the information on.' He paused for a moment and looked closely at him. 'My partner spoke to her again. She had no reason to lie. She can gain nothing now.'

For a long quiet moment, Harrison stared at him, his eyes thin and fixed in concentration.

'You bullshitting me?'

'Fuck, am I.'

Harrison closed his hand over Swann's fist and squeezed. 'You wouldn't bullshit me, just to deal with this thing between us.'

'No.' Swann looked him right in the eye. 'I wouldn't. The point is, Harrison, if it wasn't me, then who the hell was it?'

'John Henry Mackey.' Harrison looked through him now, eyes edged in shadow.

'Who?'

'Militia man in Idaho. He took the call. It came from a payphone in London.'

Logan was on her way over to the table and Harrison sat up straighter. 'She know we had a fight?'

390

Swann nodded.

'Shit. Now I got that to deal with.'

'She'll be cool.'

Logan had stopped to talk to the waitress. 'She was part of that FEST,' Harrison said.

'That thought crossed my mind last night.'

'Sweet on her, ain't you.'

'Yes.'

'You got no worries, bro. This was nothing to do with Logan. She's one of the best they've got back at the puzzle palace.'

'So who, then?'

Logan was almost at their table, and Harrison lifted a finger to his lips. 'Talk about something else. This is between you and me, right now. I'd appreciate it if you kept it that way.'

Logan said nothing about the previous evening. She could see as soon as she sat down that the tension had eased between them. When they got to the field office, there was a message for her to call Washington, and Kovalski told her about the latest phone call to Byrne's wife.

Harrison was quiet, sitting in the room they had been allocated and checking the various reports that had come in from the intelligence analysts, regarding the inmates of Carson City Jail. He laid down the papers and looked at Swann. 'Nothing jumps out at you, does it?'

Swann, too, had been reading, and he shook his head. 'All we know is that Jefferson knew Greer through the blackjack tables at the casino.'

Logan came through then and sat down. 'That was D.C.,' she said. 'Boese's been on the phone again.'

'What did he say this time?'

'He asked Byrne's wife if the jackal and the crow ate together?'

Swann screwed up his eyes. 'Ate together?'

'Carlos again,' Harrison said.

Swann got up and walked to the window. ' "When the prey is down, does the jackal or the crow eat first?" ' he said, half to himself. 'The jackal eats first. Then the crow.' He turned and looked at them. 'They don't eat together. They never ate together.' He felt a little chill ripple through him. 'Ben Dubin believes that Boese was with Carlos in 1982. He probably was. Dubin was the one who first put forward the theory that the John Doe at the Paris–Toulouse train bombing was the man who eventually became Storm Crow. Ismael Boese.' He leaned against the glass behind him. 'The jackal and the crow do not eat together. They never did.' He stared from Logan to Harrison, then back again, aware of a coldness which began at his scalp and worked the length of his body. 'Did it ever occur to you that Boese might not be Storm Crow?'

Logan had already started looking into Teniel Jefferson's life. Before he went to Nevada, he had been a prison warder at Ellis Island Correctional Center on the Virginia/ North Carolina state line. It was logical to assume that if he had been running contraband in Carson he would have done the same at Ellis Island, only he had never been caught there. She got the team in Washington to start looking at prison records for Ellis Island, which meant getting into the computers at the Federal Bureau of Prisons, as Ellis Island, unlike Carson City, was a federal penitentiary. She spoke to Harrison and Swann.

'We've drawn a blank here, apart from identifying how Jefferson knew Mary Greer,' she said. 'I'm going to speak to D.C. again and then I think we should ship over to Virginia.'

Harrison cocked an eyebrow. 'Regular globetrotters, ain't we. I haven't covered this much soil in years.'

Logan went to call Washington again, and Harrison looked evenly at Swann, then took his battered leather briefcase from where it lay by the desk. He rummaged around for a moment, then pulled out a file bound with elastic. Swann squinted at it and Harrison took out a large paper evidence envelope.

'What's that?'

'Operation Bubble Burst.' Harrison laid it on the desk. 'My copy of the entire file on Salvesen. Undercover in Passover, Idaho.' He sat down again and sighed. 'I've had this mother with me every day since I left the place. I kept my goddamn trap shut and let Kovalski make his enquiries.' He hesitated, thinking hard for a moment. 'Interesting point he came up with.'

'What was that?'

'It was Louis Byrne who told him you went to Paris, right about the time my product got over to you.'

Swann thought about that, as Harrison leafed through the photographs he had taken, looking for one in particular. He found it, chewed on his lip and reached for his snuff tin. Swann looked over his shoulder at the picture of the receipt for a meal for two in Paris. Poking out below it was the scrap of paper with bits of handwriting on it.

'What do you think that is?' Harrison said.

Swann felt a rush of adrenalin. 'Winthrop directions to a dead drop.' He paused for a moment. 'At the Virginia City overlook.'

Harrison nodded slowly. 'That's what I figured.'

'We assumed the money was paid to Boese,' Swann went on. 'We did a partial financial investigation on him, but got nowhere. Somewhere, he's got a lot of money stashed.'

'You didn't find it?'

Swann shook his head. 'We already had him in custody,

remember, enough forensic evidence to get him his thirty years. It wasn't that important.'

Harrison took a notebook from his bag and flicked through it. 'I gotta make a phone call,' he said. 'Shoulda done it months back, but I let the Bureau handle things and look what happened.'

'Who're you calling?'

'Old buddy of mine from 'Nam. Marine colonel.' Harrison picked up the phone and dialled. 'Bill,' he said, after a moment's wait. 'This is Johnny Buck. Where can I find The Cub?'

The sky over London was white with cloud, weighted over the city. It had snowed in light flurries the previous evening and it looked as though it would snow again today. Collier and Gringo sat on their chopped motorcycles and watched Janice Martin window-shopping.

'There she is,' Gringo said. A twist of the throttle and they roared away from the lights. Janice heard the rattle of engines and instinctively looked over her shoulder. Collier pulled up alongside her, a helmet flapping from his left elbow. He shoved it at her. 'Get on,' he said. She looked at him, fear suddenly sharp in her eyes. She put the helmet on, glanced at Gringo, then climbed behind Collier.

They parked the bikes in the little yard at the front of the clubhouse and got off. All the way across London, they'd both been scanning for surveillance and were satisfied that no one was following them. Collier tripped the alarm and unlocked the front door, then pushed Janice ahead of him. Gringo got beer from the fridge and they sat in the living room, the three of them. Nobody spoke; Collier staring at Janice.

'You got nicked,' he said after a while, voice low, grey eyes like chips of broken ice. She bit down on her lip. Gringo watched her, resting his can of beer on his belly.

'What did you say to the police?' Collier spoke again.

Janice looked at him sharply then, the fear gone from her eyes. 'What d'you take me for?'

He smiled thinly. 'I take you for a rich bitch with a very bad habit.'

'I don't talk to coppers, David.'

'You're on the street. How is that?' He jutted his chin at her.

'Bail. It was only possession. I had enough on me for one line of coke, that's all.'

'You've been nicked twice before. How come they let you out?'

'My rich daddy, remember.'

Collier still stared at her, eyes not wavering. She had to look away, the gaze was so intense.

'When's the hearing?' he said.

'I've had it.'

'When does the case come up?'

'I don't know yet.'

'Did you tell them anything about this place?'

'Of course not. I've got my own address. I never even mentioned you.'

He was quiet for a moment, then he glanced across at Gringo. 'What do you reckon?'

'I'd say she's cool, man.'

Collier shook his head. 'Your trouble is, you think with your dick.' He squinted once more at Janice. 'You're banned from this place for a month. If you weren't such a good lay, I'd expel you altogether.' He was quiet for a moment. 'Go upstairs and wait for me.' When she was gone, he looked again at Gringo. 'What do you really think?'

'I think she's cool. OK, so she snorts a little coke. But she's not a talker, man. I know it.'

Collier was still again. 'Did she ever ask you anything about anything, when she was your old lady, I mean?'

'The usual stuff. Nothing I wouldn't want her to ask.'

'Contracts?'

'She doesn't know they exist.'

Webb's eyes lit up when GCHQ told them that Collier had mentioned the contracts. He and Harris were on their way to Grosvenor Square for another meeting with the US Secret Service, when McCulloch phoned and told them.

Combes, the secret service agent, offered them chairs across the desk in his office, and studied the papers in front of him.

'Banco De California,' he said slowly. 'As you probably know, Mexico does not adhere to any of the banking or financial regulations that the likes of our countries do. That makes it fertile ground for dirty money. Russia, Turkey and Estonia are the same. Russia, particularly, because it's a cash economy.' He paused. 'We've been looking at the Banco De California for years, I think I told you.' He held up a copy of the inventory that Webb had taken at The Regiment's clubhouse in Hounslow. 'This company – TCX,' he said. 'It's a junkyard in San Antonio, Texas. They bank with the Mexicans. This list of motorcycle parts, receipt, whatever, is some sort of code. It's possible goods changed hands, but the amount of money is paltry, and why would anyone hide it under a paving stone?' He scratched the side of his face. 'We can link TCX to the Bandido Nation in Texas. They run legitimate businesses, but fundamentally they're into organized crime. They use the Mexican bank all over the southern states, and we're pretty confident that a whole string of senior management are involved. The DEA have been working with us for years, looking for a weak link we can exploit.' He tapped the inventory again. 'TCX are involved in selling motorcycles and motorcycle parts, for certain. But we think they're into the Colombian drug cartels in a big way. And we also believe they're a clearing house, a financial go-between, if you like, for motorcycle gangs doing business worldwide.'

Webb smoothed the tips of his fingers over the line of his moustache. 'NCIS told us that when David Collier left the army he spent some time in the States. He had links with the Bandidos and the Outlaws.' He stabbed a finger at the inventory. 'Could that be some kind of coded contract, maybe?'

'Easily.' Combes looked at it again. 'It's been done before. Biker gangs like their transactions on paper. It stops tongues wagging, but they have to be careful. This could be a contract. It could be for drugs. It could be for weapons.'

'The Regiment, as far as we know, don't deal in drugs.'

'Then it's something else.' Combes sat back in his chair. 'We're going for production orders on TCX's bank accounts. Normally, we'd never get them from Mexico, but San Antonio's in Texas, so we will. We've been looking for a way in for ages. This might just be it. We can check everything – electronic transfers, in and out. We can then get orders on accounts where they've made or received payments, assuming the countries are cooperative.'

'If somebody paid The Regiment to hit the special escort group, it will have cost a small fortune,' Webb said.

Combes shook his head. 'They'll be smart, George. Instalments, small payments, but they'll be a regular size, and we've seen the like before. If there's something there, *we can* find it, believe me.' He smiled then. 'You've done us a favour here. Like I said, we've been after these Mexicans for years. Any chance we get to have another pitch at them, we'll take it.'

Christine fished in her bag and brought out the information her colleagues in financial investigation had got on Jorge Vaczka's organization. 'These might be useful,' she said. 'We think there might be a link between Vaczka's gang and the SEG break-out. You may have come across him before. Nasty piece of work. He's got an operation based here at the moment. We think he might be linked to Abu Nidal.'

They left Combes then and went back to the car. Two red diplomatic protection group vehicles buzzed down Upper Grosvenor Street with their lights flashing. Webb got behind the wheel. 'Any word from our little girl?' he asked.

'Nothing so far, but it's only been a few days.'

'She's got guts, I'll give her that. Messing with Collier is dangerous.'

'She'll be all right. No doubt, she'll get the third degree about the drugs bust, but you saw the way she looks, George. We might just get lucky.'

Webb's pager sounded on his belt, and he picked up the mobile phone and dialled McCulloch at the Yard.

'What is it, Macca?' he asked.

'Where are you?'

'US Embassy. Why?'

'Get back here, will you. We've just received a call from Avis in Shrivenham. They were calling *you* back. Apparently, a Detective Sergeant George Webb of Scotland Yard has been requesting vehicle rental records from August 1997.'

Angie Byrne took a hot soak in the tub. Darkness had fallen long ago and Louis was still stuck at the office. He had called her an hour ago, saying he might be in for an all-nighter. Everyone was working round the clock, trying to find something from Teniel Jefferson's past that could give them a clue as to what Boese was doing. Angie's day had been long and hard, most of it in court with Judge Arnold T. Benson, who was a moody sonofabitch at the best of times. He must've lost his golf game over the weekend because he'd been moodier than ever today. Angie had poured herself a glass of white wine and was sipping it now, wrapped in herbal oil and bubbles, the water lapping about her chin.

She dried herself, her hair still piled on her head, and closed the white slatted shutters over the windows. She sat on the bed in her dressing gown, flicked on the TV set and idly surfed the channels. Then she switched off the over-head lights.

Outside, a figure stood in the shadows, saw the lights go off, then caught the flicker of blue reflected off the win-dows. He moved down the street towards the Potomac River.

Angie flicked through the channels and found nothing she wanted to watch. She untied her hair, shook it over her shoulders and slipped the bathrobe off her shoulders. Standing before the full-length mirror, she inspected her breasts, tweaking a nipple in each hand, straightening her back, then patting the flat of her stomach. 'No kids, girlfriend,' she said. 'It shows.'

An hour later, the windows were in darkness. The figure stood in the silence and watched. Nothing, nobody on the street; late February and cold. His breath came in clouds, his eyes were narrowed. He wore black gloves and a black sweater. He climbed the steps, and watched again from the top. Then he slipped the ski mask over his head and ran his fingers round the rim of the door.

Silence inside. The kitchen, metalled and spotless in the half-light from the street. Across the wide hall, the staircase rose in a sweep of white pine. The lounge door was closed. In his soft-soled shoes, his steps made no sound as he climbed the stairs, with his head held high like a wolf;

watching, listening. No sound, no movement, no sudden light. He moved to the master bedroom door, where he paused for a moment on the balls of his feet, eyes darting this way and that. He could hear the steady rise and fall of her breathing. Sleep: deep and peaceful sleep. What was she dreaming tonight?

He moved a step closer, watching the floor, polished wooden boards and a rug. The bed before him, raised on a platform, was an iron four-poster with muslin drapes pulled back and tied. A chink of light broke the weight of the shutters. He moved closer and closer. Then, reaching the bed, he slid back the drawer in the nightstand. A loaded .38 special lay in its box, the lid open. He lifted it out, effortlessly, soundlessly. Then he took a small black feather from his other pocket. He smiled under the mask, bent over the flawless white face, and drew the fanned end of the feather over her nose. She wrinkled her nostrils, sudden lines in her forehead. And then she was awake, eyes wide and staring, a scream rising in her throat. He flattened red lips with gloved fingers, and pressed the gun against her temple.

He could feel her trembling under his hand, the rise and fall of her chest – swift now, erratic, as if the breath was stuck in her throat.

'Hush,' he whispered. No accent, voice cracked and gravelly, way back in his throat. Slowly, he lifted his hand from her mouth, but still rested the barrel of the gun against her flesh.

'My attorney,' he said. 'Pretty as well as tough. You're much better looking close up.'

'What d'you want?'

'Ah, conversation,' he said. 'The subtle art of conversation. That's our trouble, Angela. We don't talk. You don't listen to what I say. You don't seem to understand.' He said the words very slowly, very carefully, his voice back in his throat, ugly. 'You must know that where the crow flies, only bad tidings follow.' He looked at her through the slits in the mask and he could feel her fear as something tangible. He could smell it. It excited him. His eyes widened. 'But the crow can bend the laws of the physical universe, Angela,' he whispered. 'You didn't know that, did you? He's a shape-shifter, becoming something else at will. Long, long ago, the Indians knew that the crow had perfected this art of doubling. He can be in two places at once. He is that fly on the wall. He can observe what's happening far away.'

'What're you saying? I don't . . .'

'Hush.' He let the word slip in a tight hiss to linger between them, his face close to hers now. She could feel something hard and sharp pressing into her shoulder. She thought it must be the gun barrel, but he still held it against her head. Then he drew the bedclothes back with it, and traced the skin between her breasts, pausing to look at the nipples.

'You're excited, Angela,' he whispered. He moved the gun lower and she gasped and felt sure she was going to urinate. She lay there, rigid, naked, staring at him as he lifted the pistol back to her face. 'Shape-shifter,' he said, and walked out of the room.

She could not move. She wanted to scream, but when she opened her mouth no sound would come out. She didn't hear him leave the house, didn't know if he was still there or not. She lay rigid, not even lifting the bedclothes. Her mind was racing. Shock. She could feel it numbing her senses. Her body would not move, nothing seemed to work. How long she lay like that she did not know, but then something snapped in her head and she reached for the gun in the nightstand. It wasn't there. She spasmed, controlled herself and picked up the phone. She dialled her husband's cellphone. No answer. Switched off. She looked at the clock. One a.m. She rang his office and a voice she didn't recognize answered.

'This is Angela Byrne. Is my husband there?'

'No, mam. I haven't seen him for a while. I don't know if he took off already, we been working pretty solidly here.'

'Who is this?'

'Agent Randy Shaeffer, mam.'

'Storm Crow has just been here.'

'What?'

'Boese. In my bedroom. Just now. Get my husband. Get somebody over here now. Now, dammit. Now.'

She put the phone down and forced away tears. She would not cry, would not succumb to the terror, the humiliation that built inside her. The phone rang by the bedside.

'Hello?'

'Angie. What's going on?'

'Louis, where are you?'

'On my way home. They just paged me. What's up?'

'Boese's been here.'

For a moment, Byrne was stunned into silence. 'What?'

'Here. In our house. In our bedroom. Just now. He's only just gone. I don't even know if he has gone. I never heard him leave.'

'I'll be right there. Just stay calm. Lock the bedroom door.'

He hung up and she stared at the black hole where the door stood open. She looked for a long time, trying to penetrate the darkness. Then she leapt up and slammed it shut. Twisting the key, she leaned against it, sobbing.

Byrne raced the length of King Street, with his blue light on and siren wailing. He took the corner of Lee with wheels screeching and pulled on to the cobbles outside his house. He was out of the car in a flash, jacket flapping

402

behind him as he wrenched his gun from the shoulder holster. He raced up the steps, fumbling for the key, and burst through the front door. Training. Clear each room. No matter that it was *his* wife up those stairs. The hall was clear. He checked the kitchen, the lounge. Then he took the stairs, inching his way up, gun in both hands, back against the wall.

'Louis, is that you?' He could hear her call him, hear her fumble with the lock.

'Don't open the door. Stay in the bedroom.' He moved on, eyes everywhere, hair lifting on the back of his neck. At the landing, he stopped, again in the crouched position. He eased himself up the wall and switched on the landing light. Nothing. No movement. He checked the dining room, the other bedrooms and bathrooms, before finally knocking on their bedroom door and telling her to open it.

She fell into his arms and he hugged her. She squeezed him, blinked back tears and then pushed herself away from him. 'Where were you? Your phone was switched off.'

'It's OK. I'm here now. The phone was off while I was in the office. I forgot to switch it back on. Randy Shaeffer paged me.' He held her at arm's length and stared. 'How did he get in here?'

'I don't know. I didn't hear anything. I just woke up with something tickling my nose and then his hand was over my mouth. And his voice. Jesus, his fucking voice, like broken glass in his throat.' She sat down on the bed, hugging herself like a child.

Byrne picked up the phone and called headquarters. 'Randy, this is Byrne. I want an ERT down here right away. Get hold of Kovalski and tell him what's happened. I want an APB put out on Boese. Every cop in the city, not just Washington – the parks, the counties, the Metro police, everyone. I want someone in Fugitive Publicity on this *now*. I want his name, his goddamn face, splattered over every TV screen, every fucking newspaper in the country. Get Kovalski to call me here.' He put the phone down and turned back to his wife. 'You OK, honey?' He sat on the edge of the bed, arm about her shoulders, and pulled her gently towards him.

'I'm fine,' she said. 'Really. I'm over it now. It's just the shock.' She looked at the bedside table, drawer open, gun missing from the box. 'He took my gun, Louis. He walked in here and took my gun. How did he know it was there?'

Byrne stared at the empty drawer, then at his own gun, still lying where he had dropped it on the bed. He could hear the howling of sirens in the distance. The phone rang and he answered it: Tom Kovalski. Byrne told him what had happened. 'We need to go public on this now, Tom. We've got him right here in Virginia.'

'OK. But there's not much we can do till the morning. You got an ERT on its way over there?'

'Yeah.'

'Let them do their thing. Then I suggest you dose Angie up with sleeping tablets. In the meantime, I'll make sure his picture's sent down the line to every station house in the city.'

Byrne put the phone down and saw Angie getting dressed. 'What you doing, hon?'

'What does it look like? I'm not gonna stand here in my dressing gown while your agents dust my bedroom for fingerprints.'

Byrne smiled at her. 'OK. I'm sorry, baby. You know it's gotta be done. Sooner the better, eh.'

'I know it.' Angie pulled on a pair of jeans and pressed her T-shirt into the top of them. She stopped and looked at him. 'I've had a shock, Louis. Somehow that bastard got in here. But I tell you now, I do not want this house turned into a fortress, you hear me?'

'He took your gun, darling.'

'I'll buy another. I'll keep it under the pillow. If he ever comes back, I'll blow his fucking head off.'

Kovalski called Logan's room in Reno. Swann was sleeping next to her, and when the phone rang, he picked it up by mistake.

'Logan?'

'Hang on.' Swann passed the phone to Logan who was yawning and rubbing her eyes.

'Sorry,' he said. 'Shouldn't have picked it up.'

'Whatever.' She took the phone. 'Logan.'

'What's going on, Chey?'

'None of your business.'

Kovalski laughed. 'Right.'

'Why're you calling me at midnight, Tom?'

'I want the three of you on a plane first thing in the morning. If you can't get a civilian one, then get on to the DOD and organize something else. I want you in Washington tomorrow.'

'What's happening?'

'Boese just showed up.'

The snow was falling hard now, fluttering against the fifteenth-floor window of the squad room at Scotland Yard. Webb sat at a desk on the telephone to National Car Rental, writing notes as he spoke. Colson and McCulloch stood next to him. 'Right. OK,' Webb said. 'Thank you very much.' He put the phone down, frowned at the sheet of paper he'd scribbled on and shook his head. 'What the hell is going on?' he said.

'What?' Colson sat down opposite him.

'That's National, Avis and Hertz,' Webb told him. 'They've all called me back about my enquiries regarding cars hired in August of 1997.'

405

'From Shrivenham?'

'And the surrounding area.' Webb blew the air from his cheeks. 'D'you know what,' he said. 'I never knew I could be in two places at once.' He took a picture of Tal-Salem from the blue file on his desk. 'And I never knew I looked like him.'

For a few moments, nobody spoke, then McCulloch scratched the skin under his jaw.

'Tal-Salem, back in the UK.'

'Maybe he never left.'

Colson picked up the file. 'What happened in Shrivenham in August '97?' he asked.

Webb looked in his eyes. 'The international conference on terrorism.'

Harrison phoned his contact again, while they waited for their flight at Reno Airport. He leaned in the booth and watched Swann and Logan steal a kiss across their coffee table.

'Hey, Bill,' he said, when the colonel answered. 'You manage to locate him for me?'

'I did.'

'Good man. Where's he at?'

'Paris.'

'What happened to Idaho?'

'It's not elk season till the fall.'

Harrison laughed. 'How can I get hold of him?'

'You can't. He'll contact you.'

'Same old Cub. Listen, I'm going to D.C. this morning, Bill. Tell him to page me with a number I can call.'

On the flight to Dulles, while Logan was in the toilet, Swann asked Harrison about The Cub. Harrison told him he was a wetboy, a killer for the CIA; to all intents and purposes, a special operations mercenary. 'He's about the best they ever had,' he said. 'Half Indian, half Chinese-

406

American. He's made it his business to know everybody there is to know on the inside. They've used him all over the world. Nearly lost him once or twice, but it's hard to lose The Cub. He is very careful, trusts nobody, especially his masters. It's done on his terms or it's not done at all.

'I don't know what his real name is, but he was born on the Nez Perce Reservation in Idaho. His momma died when he was six months old, and his old man took him to live with the Hudderites in Montana for a while. They moved back to Idaho, when, I guess, The Cub was about seven. Back to the reservation up near Kamiah. They say he slept in animal skins for the first twelve years of his life, and he had a habit of getting into things he shouldn't. One day he brought home a baby mountain lion from the woods. You can imagine, all hell broke loose when momma lion came a-looking. Anyways, that's how he got his name.'

'How do *you* know him?' Swann asked.

Harrison licked his lips. 'You know what – sometimes I wish I didn't. You probably figured there ain't a whole lot in the world that bothers me. But that guy.' He shook his head slowly. 'Just glad he's on our side.' He blew out his cheeks. 'Anyways, there was a Nez Perce Indian in our unit in Vietnam. That was before I went underground. We were patrolling one night and he took two in the chest. Deep jungle, Jack, the dust-off was two miles back.' He glanced sideways at Swann. 'I carried him out of there, kept him alive. Never thought no more about it. But it turned out he was The Cub's uncle. One day I get a call from my old colonel. This Indian was an important *hombre* back on the reservation, some kinda medicine man. I guess The Cub reckoned he owed me. Lifetime thing, I figure. Whenever I've needed him, he's been there.'

'Why d'you need him now?'

'Because there isn't anything about anybody he can't find out. If we're lucky, you'll get to meet him.'

They all gathered on the eleventh-floor conference room used by the Domestic Terrorism Operations Section. Kovalski, Byrne, Harrison, Logan and Swann, together with back-up agents and the support staff from Fugitive Publicity. Byrne was absolutely bristling, his face red and eyes edgy. Swann had never seen him so agitated.

'She won't have any damn protection,' he was saying. 'At her fucking desk by seven this morning. She says she's safer there than anywhere else.'

'She probably is, Lou,' Logan said. 'She's a tough lady, your wife.'

Byrne relaxed a fraction and unbuttoned the cuffs of his shirt. 'It's time to go public,' he said.

Kovalski nodded. 'How much do we want to release?'

'Just his name and his picture,' Logan said. 'We can name him as the suspect in the Mississippi tanker hijacking, but we keep the feathers and the fact that he's been calling Mrs Byrne out of it.'

'And calling on her.' Byrne spat the words from between his teeth. 'He took the fucking gun from our bedside drawer. How did he know it was there, for Christ's sake?'

Harrison was watching him from across the table. 'Where else you gonna keep your piece, Louis?'

'I guess.' Byrne looked at Kovalski then. 'I agree with Cheyenne. Release the minimum to the press. What about *America's Most Wanted*?'

'I think we should do that. Maybe we could get the network to shuffle their schedule around. Get a programme put together just on Boese. Do the stuff in London, Rome, the full history. Put some pressure on him.'

Ed Leary, the representative from Fugitive Publicity, said he would begin working on it right away. He already had a copy of the file on Boese and he left the meeting to contact the television networks. Byrne said he would try again with Angela's law firm about a wire tap on her office phone. After last night, they might just agree. Swann was thoughtful, saying little during their deliberations. Webb had left three messages for him in Washington and he had phoned him as soon as he got there.

'Tal-Salem is in England telegraphing messages to SO13,' he said quietly. Everybody stared at him. 'He's visiting the major car hire companies in a place called Shrivenham, in Oxfordshire. He's got some false ID and is asking for the records to be sent to Detective Sergeant Webb of Scotland Yard. George Webb is my partner.'

'You know it's Tal-Salem?' Logan asked him.

Swann nodded. 'Undisguised, the description fits every time. There's no question.'

'This is the guy that killed Mary Poynton?' Harrison put in.

'Yes.' Swann was looking at Byrne. 'We've got two terrorists on both sides of the Atlantic trying to tell us something, Louis. Shape-shifting – Boese's never mentioned that before. Why now?' He thought for a moment. 'The crow being able to double, to be the fly on the wall, the unseen observer. I've looked that up,' he said. 'It's Indian animal totem mythology. Many tribes believed that the crow was the archetypal shape-shifter. He could become something else, and be in two places at once. Boese reads books on Geronimo, but why should he mention this now, and what does it mean?' No one interrupted him. Byrne was watching his face. 'The jackal and the crow,' Swann went on. 'Boese *was* with the Jackal, we know that. Dubin believes that Boese became Storm Crow. But the Jackal and the Crow never ate together. That's what he's telling us.'

'Which means what, exactly?' Kovalski asked him.

Swann glanced at him. 'If you were Storm Crow, would

409

you allow yourself to be caught, after you had spent a lifetime hiding your identity?'

'What's your point, Jack?'

'I think Boese's trying to tell us that he's not who we think he is.' Silence. All eyes were on him now. 'He talked to Louis's wife about "other endeavours". He wants an attorney to represent him. He said something interesting happened to him with feathers.' He broke off again. 'I think he's trying to tell us we've got it wrong. We're looking at the wrong man. Boese is not Storm Crow.'

It took a moment for them all to digest what he had said. Byrne scratched his cropped hair at the scalp. 'Jack,' he said. 'Why in heaven's name would he want to do that? Right now, he's still the most wanted man on the planet.'

'I know, Louis. But he's been misrepresented. Yes, he was with Carlos in 1982, he may well have been a protégé. But he is not Storm Crow. That's what all this jackal and crow stuff is about. You're the man who has hunted Storm Crow like no other. Your wife just happens to be a defence attorney. What better way of making his point than by spinning riddles to *your* wife?' He sat forward now. 'Think about that first coded message in the *International Herald Tribune*. "We have been betrayed." Boese went to prison on the orders of somebody else.' He looked round the table. 'I was there. I arrested him. The real Storm Crow would not risk that. But somebody had to do it, so the point could be made in Rome. Whoever is behind Boese was showing us the kind of power he wields. His own vanity; yet he still didn't make the mistake that Carlos did, by allowing his identity to become public. He's thrown us a curveball, as you people would say. He's made us all believe something that's total bullshit.' He looked at Logan now. 'I think Boese was expecting his "Get out of jail free" card, but he didn't get it. Hence the message to Tal-Salem. They must've had a contingency plan of their own.'

410

He stopped talking and thought about it for a moment or two. Suddenly, he felt certain that Jorge Vaczka and his Polish gang were the original choice to break Bocse out. 'The real Storm Crow would have to prove to Boese that he could and would get him out, after he became the sacrificial lamb,' he continued. 'That would mean two things – money and know-how. We never found the money. The know-how, I believe, was a gang of Polish hardmen who were operating in the UK.'

He thought hard again. 'Boese must've been told he would be broken out, but that promise was broken. Hence the betrayal message. Tal-Salem must've gone to have a look at the Poles to see what had gone wrong. We had an informant . . .'

Then, all at once, he knew where the original tip-off that went into MI6 had come from. A shudder rang through him as he considered the implications. 'The Poles were looked at by MI5,' he said. 'And if Tal-Salem hadn't shown up, we'd have caught them trying to get Boese out.' He stood up then. 'I need to use a phone,' he said.

Kovalski motioned to the one on the table. Swann dialled the Yard and got Campbell McCulloch. 'Macca, it's me. I want to speak to Chrissie in the SB cell.' McCulloch put him through.

'Harris.'

'Chrissie. It's Jack Swann.'

'How are you, Jack?'

'Making progress. Listen, I think I've figured something out. Jorge Vaczka was the original choice to get Boese out of the nick. He knew he had been looked at, hence, the shit we went through with his charity run to Liverpool. Do me a favour, will you, talk to Box, get them to check with 850. The original source, Chrissie. Try and find out who it is. I know they won't tell you, but check the reliability. Have they had information from that source before, you know

411

the sort of thing. Get Julian on it, he's old school tie. If I'm right, Boese is not Storm Crow. But whoever tipped off Box 850 just might be.'

He put the phone down and looked at the FBI agents, talking now around the table. Byrne was staring at him. 'You seem pretty sure, Jack,' he said.

'I am. Boese is telling us that we're looking for the wrong man. That's why he made such a public appearance in New Orleans. He could gain nothing from hijacking that tanker other than our attention. He did it spectacularly. And he effectively did it in the name of Storm Crow. If I *am* right, think how the real Storm Crow would've reacted to that.'

Logan folded her arms and looked from Swann to Byrne. 'If Jack is right, it raises another question,' she said. 'Who *is* Storm Crow?'

Harrison pushed one booted foot against the leg of the table. 'And why hasn't he done anything about Boese?'

After the meeting broke up, Logan, Harrison and Swann set about the files that had come in from the Federal Bureau of Prisons, still searching for the elusive connection between Jefferson and Ismael Boese. 'What about going down to Ellis Island?' Harrison suggested to Logan.

'If we have to. But Boese might still be in D.C. Let's see what we can come up with here first.' She thought for a moment. 'What we need is the patsy. We must be able to trace him. Jefferson was only there between '82 and '83.'

'Who's gonna talk, Cheyenne? They're all cons. Who's gonna talk to the Feds?'

'Cowboy up, Harrison,' she said. 'Leona Boese was looking for parole. She talked, didn't she.' She slapped him on the shoulder. 'There's gotta be some old con down there who knew what was going on, maybe even one of the bulls.'

Harrison's pager went off and he made a call from

Kovalski's office with the door closed. When he came out, he looked thoughtful. Swann bought coffee from the machine and Harrison joined him in the corridor. 'How you doing?' he asked.

'Fine.'

'You did good in there this morning. I think you got the respect of the people. That takes some doing. Especially for a limey.'

Swann laughed and sipped frothy coffee. 'Thanks,' he said.

Harrison looked at him then, and stuck out his right hand. 'I guess I owe you an apology.'

Swann cocked his head to one side. 'Yeah, you're right. You do.'

'I'm sorry for being an asshole.'

'Don't mention it.' They shook hands and Harrison slapped him on the shoulder. 'What's this Shrivenham conference thing? You mentioned it and then you didn't mention it.'

'It's an annual conference on terrorism. Tal-Salem asked for car hire records from August 1997. Three months later, we had our first chemical crisis in Northumberland.' He chewed his lip for a moment. 'Louis Byrne was at that conference, Harrison.'

Harrison stared at him for a long moment. 'Byrne?' He cocked his head to one side. 'You're not telling me you think Byrne's got something to do with this, are you, Jack? Lucky Louis – he's about the most celebrated FBI agent in history.'

Swann pulled a face. 'I know he is, Harrison. I'm just saying – he was at Shrivenham, that's all. So were a lot of other people.'

Harrison leaned against the wall and folded his arms. 'He *was* part of the Foreign Emergency Search Team, though, wasn't he.' He looked left and right down the corridor. 'We need to talk, bro. But not here. If you can keep your hands off Logan for one evening, I'd like to buy you a beer.'

'I'll try. But she's better looking than you are.'

Harrison laughed. 'Listen,' he said. 'That was The Cub just now on the phone. He's got a two-hour stopover in Dulles tomorrow. I'm driving out to meet him. You can tag along if you want.'                           •

Boese checked into the Best Western Inn and Tower on South Glebe Road, in Arlington, Virginia. He was bearded, long-haired and Venezuelan, booking in under the name Sanchez, which he thought was a good joke considering all this talk of the 'jackal'.

Chucho Mannero cleaned rooms and drove the shuttle bus. He had picked Señor Sanchez up when he arrived at the National Airport, and they had driven from there to Pentagon City Metro station, before arriving at the hotel. Chucho was in his forties, small and grey-haired and Puerto Rican. He told Señor Sanchez that the bus left the hotel on the hour, stopped at National Airport on the quarter hour, and Pentagon City on the half. It was back in the hotel parking lot by fifteen before.

Now, Boese lay back on his bed and relaxed, two new encrypted cellphones beside him. They would be getting the heavy equipment out for him now. The more he called Angela Byrne, the closer they would get – Triggerfish II, or whatever they called it. He switched on the television news and saw his face fill the screen. He was slightly taken aback, and turned the volume higher.

'Ismael Boese, alias the international terrorist known as Storm Crow,' the news anchor was saying. 'The FBI have just released this picture of him. Formerly a member of the "Friends of Carlos" group, Storm Crow took over the mantle of the world's most wanted man after Carlos faded

414

into obscurity. The name first surfaced in 1989, when the US Ambassador's motorcade came under fire in Tel Aviv, Israel. Since then, Storm Crow has appeared in many parts of the globe, although only once before in the United States. He was responsible for the mortar attack on Fort Bliss, Texas, in March 1995. That, according to DEA sources, was drug-related. Until recently, nobody even knew for sure who or what Storm Crow was. An individual, a group. But last year he was positively identified as Ismael Boese, the only son of Pieter and Leona Boese, two active members of the Symbionese Liberation Army in the 1970s. According to FBI sources, Boese is the archetypal terrorist – an idealogue, born to it, brought up in it, then perfecting his trade at the knee of Ilyich Ramirez Sanchez, alias Carlos the Jackal.' He paused and smiled. 'Tonight, I'm delighted to say, we're joined here in Washington by Dr Benjamin Dubin, a leading academic on terrorism, and the most recent biographer of Carlos.'

Boese stared at the screen now, eyes dull in his head. Such a sudden turnabout. And Dubin again, the little man with the strange eyes, who spoke fluent Hebrew and Arabic, and had surfaced at just about every terrorist event in the world, offering his considered opinion.

'Dr Dubin,' the anchorman was saying, 'can you throw any light on what Boese, Storm Crow, is doing in the United States?'

'I wish I could.' Dubin shook his head. 'It could be anything. When he attacked Europe in such a devastating way a year ago, the authorities there did not know what was happening until the last possible moment. That's his style. As you rightly pointed out, he first surfaced in his own right ten years ago, but he *was* a member of the so-called "Friends of Carlos" group in the early eighties. A very young man then, but already he had been weaned by two SLA parents, and then supporters of the Provisional

415

IRA. I had a brief interview with him, following much longer sessions with Carlos himself, in Paris.'

'Fool.' Boese spoke aloud at the screen. 'You learned nothing from the Jackal. He played games with you. He toyed with you, let you think you were important.' He spat in disgust on the floor and cast his mind back to the last time he had seen Carlos himself: sitting on the balcony of his well-guarded flat, under the protection of Assad in Syria. January 1991, just after the Americans launched their attack on Saddam Hussein. The Jackal was fatter, his features even more rounded. He drank brandy and smoked cigarettes and let the sun warm his face. Boese sat next to him, watching the guard with the AK47 in the street below. He sipped Café Arabi and told Carlos about the feather he had just received.

Carlos smiled then, his boyish face open. 'Storm Crow,' he said, as if tasting the word. 'Take up the feather, my friend. I hear he pays very well.'

Boese gazed at the sun-bleached buildings that stacked against the blue, almost purple sky above them. 'I would,' he said. 'But I don't know who he is.'

Carlos thinned his eyes and looked, for a moment, through him. 'I heard a whisper about him only the other day,' he said, voice soft in his throat. 'From friends on the Gaza Strip. The name they gave was both interesting and a little troubling.' He broke off for a second and drew heavily on his cigarette, inspected the end and tapped off the ash. 'I had heard the name before, you see; fifteen years ago now, after I walked away from Entebbe.' His gaze shallowed at the memory. Boese was intent on his eyes. 'Apparently, there was a plot to kill me. There were always plots to kill me. The French would've cut off my head if they'd caught me in the Rue Toullier. This one was different, though; somebody from the PFLP had turned, somebody who knew me. To this day I do not know who it was.' He tasted the brandy in his glass. 'It was a CIA plot, to be carried out by this PFLP turncoat, but engineered by an agent of the Americans called Josef El Kebir.'

# 22

Boese watched the news for a little longer and learned that a special programme of *America's Most Wanted* was to be dedicated to him. He laughed out loud, then his eyes clouded. He thought he heard movement outside the door, and, leaving the television with the volume high, he moved towards it on the balls of his feet. He recalled the chill he had felt when he climbed into the truck in Nevada. He thought of the cowboy in the whorehouse, the cowboy sitting on his horse by the lake. He peeked through the edge of the curtain, but only the late evening sunshine winked back. He let the curtain fall across the window once again and stood for a long moment, watching the images on the TV screen. Then, picking up his coat, he left the room, and found Mannero standing at the desk in reception.

'Chucho,' he said. 'What time does the bus leave again?'

'At the top of the hour, *señor*.'

Boese rested a hand on his shoulder. 'I think I need a ride.'

Mannero dropped him outside Pentagon City Metro station, where Boese bought a five-dollar pass. He caught the blue line and got off at the Federal Triangle, then switched on his cellphone. Now, the electronic serial number was active and could be identified within a given area, depending on the beacons. They would triangulate, and they could be starting now. He dialled Angela Byrne in her office.

'Hello?' Her voice in his ear.

'Different tactics,' he said. 'Suddenly, I'm famous. What happened to the "unknown subject"?'

'You motherfucking sonofabitch.'

'Such a foul mouth.' He tutted. 'Is that any way for an attorney to talk to her client?'

'I'm not your fucking attorney and after what you did to me last night . . .'

'Last night?' The hairs lifted on the back of his neck. 'What about last night?'

'You ever come near me again and I'll kill you.'

'Of course you will.' Boese was thinking hard.

'You sorry, sick bastard. What was all of that crap about shape-shifting and being in two places at once? What happened to the jackal and the crow, you fucked up sonofabitch?'

Boese looked at his watch; the phone had been on for thirty seconds now. 'I'll speak to you later, when you're in a better mood,' he said.

'I'll never be in a better mood.'

He switched the phone off, looked at his watch and stood for a moment on the sidewalk. The J. Edgar Hoover building was only two blocks from here. Shape-shifting, being in two places at once. The game had finally changed, and with it all of the rules.

Janice Martin sat in her flat in Pimlico. Cushions on the floor, biker posters on the walls and a pile of unwashed crockery on the stove. He father had bought the flat for her when she first moved to London; which seemed like a lifetime ago now, in the days of art college and grand ideas and some kind of progress. But then she had met Gringo, big, muscle-bound, dumb-as-a-fuck Gringo. Somehow he had risen to the ranks of second in command of this biker gang. The gang was cool and different and the thrill of it touched some dormant part of her being, which had been

stifled by her father and the county set and the smashing of
port glasses on public commons in Norfolk. She waggled
the end of her thumb in her mouth and watched TV
mindlessly. She did not seem to be able to concentrate on
anything these days. Maybe it was the coke, maybe it was
the hash or the booze, or the combination of all three. The
doorbell rang and she looked out of the window. Fagin's
thin, fox-like features leered up at her. She really didn't
fancy Fagin at all – of all of them, he was the least
attractive. But he always gave her money for a score and
she needed a score right now. Then she remembered the
specimen bottles in the bathroom cabinet. God knows what
they thought they were doing with them, but she had had
to give them a sample of her saliva, so they could separate
her DNA.

She didn't bother to undress; Fagin was on his way to a
meeting in the clubhouse and just wanted a quickie. 'I
heard you got busted,' he said. 'Not a good move with
Collier, sweetheart.'

'Oh well.' She shrugged her shoulders, unzipped him
and worked it hard, then dropped her knickers and knelt on
all fours so he could take her doggy style, the way he liked
to. She had a box of tissues in the bathroom, and when he
was done, she waited for gravity to take its course, then
placed the soiled tissue in the specimen jar and wrote Fagin
on it in felt pen.

He was zipping himself away when she came back to
the lounge, and she noticed the twenty-five pounds on the
table. 'Can you spare another tenner, Fagin?' she asked,
stroking his hair. 'I could really do with it.'

He looked down at her, then lightly kissed her nose. 'Go
on then, but not a word to any of the others. By the way,
you might get a few visitors this weekend. A lot of the lads
are in town for the meeting.'

'Whatever.' She flapped an arm at her side. 'I'll be

here.' He left then and she closed the door and spread the notes on the table.

George Webb tried to get hold of Benjamin Dubin, but his secretary told him that Dubin was in Washington again for a brief lecture tour. Webb hung up and looked across the desk where McCulloch was watching him.

'What d'you want him for, Webby?'

'Tal-Salem's trying to tell us something about cars being hired in Shrivenham, isn't he.'

'Yeah.'

'I want to know if Dubin was at that 1997 conference.'

'Phone the organizers and ask them.'

Webb smiled at him, shaking his head. 'Don't want to do that, Macca. It won't do any harm for the man to know we're wondering.'

Whatever game Tal-Salem was playing with them, the August 1997 rental records had already come in from National and Avis. Each individual car and hirer from all their branches in and around that area. Webb and McCulloch read through them, checking each one in turn for anything that might stick out. They waded through the papers, but really had no idea what they were looking for.

'What's he trying to tell us, apart from the fact a car was hired?' Webb said, after an hour or so of sifting.

'I don't know. Why should he want to tell us anything?' McCulloch yawned and scratched his head. 'By the way, that flight manifest you asked for.'

'What about it?'

'What was the date?'

'Of the flight?' Webb checked his notes. 'August 21st. Why?'

McCulloch made a face. 'No reason. It's three days after the Shrivenham conference finished, that's all.' He thought for a moment. 'When's it coming through, by the way?'

'It's an internal US flight, Macca. Washington D.C. to Detroit. It'll come whenever they send it.'

Christine Harris came into the squad room and sat down opposite Webb. 'I've spoken to our girl again,' she said. 'First one's home. Fagin. Number three in the gang.'

'Is he one that NCIS identified?' Webb asked her.

'No. But I'm showing the stills we've got to Janice again, the next time we set up a meet. She can pick him out for us.'

'How long will it take to compare the DNA?'

'I don't know yet. I'll have to talk to Lambeth. In the meantime, there's a big club meeting this weekend, which should be worth our while eavesdropping.'

The Irishman sat in a grey Chrysler on South Glebe Road, and watched the comings and goings in the Arlington Valley Project, across the four lanes of carriageway. Red brick dwellings, built in square, flat-roofed blocks, rising back up the hill towards the raised section of Highway 395. Hispanic children ran around on the grassy areas. Women stood in the doorways, four apartments per block, with God knows how many families living in each of them. Section 8 government housing. The Irishman was only interested in one – 445, apartment B – the home of Chucho Mannero. Chucho was not at home right now, he was working up the road at the hotel. A thought struck the Irishman: perhaps he would wander up there this evening for a drink. Again he looked at the grimy little block where Chucho lived with his alcoholic girlfriend, and wondered what it would be like after dark.

Boese phoned Angela Byrne again on her mobile. 'Calmed down?' he asked her.

'You're a sick sonofabitch. Cut and dried asshole.'

'Remember,' he said savagely. 'All may not be what it

seems.' He could hear the sharpness of her breathing in his ear then. 'Tell me, Angela, who can get to Pentagon City, the airport and home again in forty-five minutes?'

'Don't start your fucking games . . .' she began, but the line was already dead in her ear.


Louis Byrne told the ground team what his wife had just told him. 'Pentagon City, the airport and home in forty-five minutes,' he said.

'Anyone, depending where you live?' Logan wrinkled her eyes at the corner.

'That's brilliant, Chey.'

Harrison looked at his watch. The Cub was due to arrive from Paris in thirty minutes. He nudged Swann and coughed. 'Tom,' he said, to Kovalski. 'I've got to meet somebody out at Dulles in under an hour.'

'Who?'

'Just somebody flying in. Somebody who could throw some light on what's happening here.' He looked at Cheyenne. 'I want to take Jack with me, Chey. He might be able to help.'

Byrne was watching him. 'We're busy, Harrison. People have been checking prison records round the clock.'

'I know it. But there's other ways of skinning a cat.' He nodded to Swann and they left.

Kovalski laid a hand on Byrne's shoulder. 'Don't worry about it,' he said. 'That's just Johnny Buck.'

Byrne folded his arms. 'Not exactly a team player, is he.'

Harrison got a car from downstairs and started the engine. 'So talk to me, bubba,' he said.

Swann lit two cigarettes and passed one across to him. 'I'm thinking about Dubin. And I'm thinking about the FEST.'

'Who'd you have most to do with?'

423

'You mean workwise? Logan and Byrne.'

They headed out of the city on Highway 29. Harrison sat leaning against the window, one knee drawn up, chewing tobacco, the lines bunched in the leathery skin of his face.

'You fought in Vietnam,' Swann said.

Harrison pushed up the sleeve of his shirt and showed Swann the tattoo – a rat standing on two legs, holding a whisky bottle and gun. 'Underground,' he said. 'Musta had a death wish or something.'

'Cu-Chi?'

Harrison nodded.

'I read about it.'

'Yeah? They never interviewed me.'

Harrison worked the chew in his mouth and flipped the butt of his cigarette out of the window. They left 29 at Falls Church and jumped 66 up to the airport road.

'What was it like?' Swann asked him. They were cruising, Harrison's foot only lightly on the gas.

'Dark. Hot. Dangerous.' Harrison looked at him out of the corner of his eye. 'Not a nice place to go hunting.'

'So why'd you do it?'

'Buddy of mine got all blowed to hell when a gook popped outta one of those holes. Hell, I volunteered right there. Did all right, till the one time I fucked up.' He shook his head. 'You only get the one crack at it, Jack.'

'That's what I heard.'

'Loosed off six shots all at the same time.' Harrison pulled a face. 'My second tour. Got drummed out and within a few months I was back over here.' He looked at Swann again and cocked his head to one side. 'I killed three men in Idaho, Jack. I crawled tunnels for the first time in thirty years, faced down the ghosts, and I won.'

Swann looked enviously at him and Harrison nodded. 'I know, brother. Cheyenne told me about what really happened to you back in the UK. You got fucked over big time, didn't you. That sonofabitch really suckered you in.' He paused then. 'You ever think about that, Jack? I don't just mean your emotions. I mean the planning, the forethought that went into that one thing alone. He must've studied every face that ever went into your outfit, looking for someone he could exploit. I wonder how long that took him?' He checked his watch and accelerated past a U Haul truck in the centre lane. 'You know what else that makes me wonder?'

'Yes,' Swann said quietly. 'How he had that kind of access.'

They parked at Dulles and took the shuttle bus to the airside terminal. Harrison showed his shield to the security people and they were allowed across without having to go through the metal detector. 'Why over here?' Swann asked him, as they climbed into the strange bus that lifted itself on hydraulics to reach the door of the terminal.

'Very simple. They've got a half-hour connection time and there's a smoking room this side of the building. These days, smoking rooms are private,' he said.

They got to the far terminal, which was one long corridor of gates, and Harrison turned right and they walked past the duty-free shops to the end. Two men sat behind the glass door of the smoking room, one of them lighting a cigarette. The other one stared through the glass at them. He looked like a younger version of Harrison, only his hair was very black and his skin the copper of Native Americans. He wore a faded blue baseball hat and his eyes were the coldest, blackest lumps of ice Swann had ever seen. The man smoking the cigarette was taller, thinner, perhaps a little older. His eyes were blue, no expression in them whatever. He wore jeans and the dusty desert boots favoured by ex-soldiers. His hair was long and looped in a ponytail, which hung over one shoulder.

425

Harrison opened the door and the black-eyed man continued to stare at Swann. 'It's cool, Cub,' Harrison said. 'He's with me.'

Swann stood a little awkwardly, hands in his pockets. Harrison closed the door behind him and sat down sideways in one of the forward facing chairs, plucking a cigarette from his shirt pocket. Still The Cub stared at Swann, and Swann looked back at him.

'He's a cop, Cub. British.'

The other man looked up then. So far, he had ignored them.

'Jack Swann. Antiterrorist Branch.' Swann offered his hand.

Outside, a business-suited man looked as though he wanted to come in. The Cub stared at him, eyes widening slowly. The man looked at him briefly, checked his pockets, then turned on his heel and walked back up the corridor. Harrison took a fresh pinch of chew from his tin and popped it under his lip. He offered the tin to The Cub, who shook his head.

'I wanna know if you could check out some names for me,' Harrison said. 'There's five of them. Cheyenne Logan, Larry Thomas and Louis Byrne. They're all with the FBI. Bob Hicks is diplomatic security, and a guy called Ketner from your outfit.'

The Cub nodded slowly. 'The FEST that went to London,' he said.

Harrison laughed then and glanced at Swann. 'What did I tell you?' He stood up. 'Can you figure it for me, buddy?'

'We're going duck hunting,' The Cub said. 'But I'll put feelers out first. Where can I get hold of you?'

'Just page me, bro. I can get to a secure phone.'

They shook hands and turned for the door. 'It was nice to meet you, Swann.' The other man spoke for the first

426

time; cultured voice, the accent very English. Swann turned and nodded to him.

'Likewise,' he said.

They rode back in Harrison's car, and he was quiet and thoughtful.

'Weird guys,' Swann said, breaking the silence.

'Uh?'

'I said, a couple of weird guys.'

'I don't know the other guy, but I heard a rumour. Something to do with the British army, behind Soviet lines, before the Berlin Wall came down. May've been in the Legion after that. I guess he's for hire now. Gotta be, if he's hanging out with The Cub.'

'Psychotic eyes.'

'The Cub? I'll tell you something about him,' Harrison said. 'He got married when he was first in the marine corps, back in the eighties. Did reconnaissance work, special forces. He had a buddy stay in his basement for a while, and one day his wife took off for a weekend vacation with her girlfriend. The guy was gone too. So The Cub, being a suspicious sonofabitch, checked with the girlfriend, and, of course, his wife wasn't there.' He sighed. 'Anyways, one thing led to another and he got dumped. Three months after that, he ran them down in his pick-up truck. He just saw them in the street, the red mist came down, and he rolled the rig right over them.'

Swann was staring at him.

'He did twenty-six months in Leavenworth for attempted manslaughter. Had to fight for his life every day for the first eight months. Course, he was dishonourably discharged from the marine corps. But he's very bright, and as far as deniable ops go, he was one of the very best. Didn't take long for Langley to pick up on him.'

They got back to Pennsylvania Avenue and found Logan in a state of excitement. She was in the conference room with some agents from the fugitive unit, trying to work out a plan of campaign. Swann and Harrison joined the meeting and Logan told them what she had discovered. 'We've found the inmate who Jefferson supplied in the Ellis Island Correctional Center,' she said. 'We got lucky with some parole violators who were looking for a favour. The guy was an inmate from 1979 to 1986. His name is Chucho Mannero.' She laid her palms on the tabletop. 'The problem now is nobody knows where he's at.'

Chucho Mannero was in the hotel on South Glebe Road, only a few miles from FBI headquarters in the Federal Triangle. Ten p.m. and he was preparing to go home, having done the last trip back from the Metro. Tips had been good today and he was enjoying one bottle of beer before he walked home. Teresa had gone earlier. She said she would cook dinner, but she was probably already drunk by now.

Boese watched Mannero from where he sat, sipping 7Up, at the far end of the bar. Another Mexican had been in earlier. One of the other guests, he assumed; although he had not seen him before. He had watched *Jeopardy* on the television and answered a lot of the questions.

Boese looked at Chucho now, and considered the other drinkers. There was Bill, the ex-naval man, who talked a lot and saluted everybody. He lived in one of the apartment blocks and came in every evening. Apart from him, a fat guest from Michigan, who ordered pitchers of beer, and a couple of suntanned oldies from California. No one who set his spine tingling. Leaving the last of his drink, he went back to his room. He had already checked out, telling the staff at reception that he would be driving off early in the morning. He lay quietly on his bed till one o'clock, then he changed his clothes to black sweater, jeans and a zipped jacket. He stretched black leather gloves over his fingers

428

and took his weapons from the canvas bag. Under the jacket he wore a double shoulder holster, and he slipped the silenced pistol into one and a Beretta into the other. In the back of his jeans, he had a third gun tucked in the waistband. Now he was ready and he sat quietly for a moment to compose himself. He thought of the Mexican in the bar, and tried to think if he had seen the man before. He observed everyone; he always had. But he did not know that man. He stowed the rest of his things in the concealed section he had fashioned in the trunk of his car, then he got behind the wheel, pulled out past reception and glided down South Glebe Road. Across the street, a Chrysler fired its engines.

Rain hissed against the tarmac as Boese let the car trundle down the hill, under Highway 395. He drove past the projects, along South Glebe, being careful to watch the movement of traffic behind him. He left the road a little further on, made a series of lefts, and then two rights before two more lefts, and he was back on South Glebe, coming the other way at the lights. There was nobody following him; he was expert enough to know. He drove more speedily now and pulled off in a side street, close to the edge of the Arlington Valley Project. Here he stood in the rain, which was sheeting down now, hazy in the orange light from the streetlamps. Traffic still rumbled on 395 and Boese watched for movement in the projects. These were deadly places at night. He could see a group of teenagers smoking hashish by one of the buildings. They had built a small fire and were huddled round it, trying to shelter from the rain.

A state trooper rolled by in his cruiser and glanced at the group on his left. He was alone, though, and he did not stop. Boese crossed the road and walked into the projects. It was 2 a.m. now, and the grass was soft and mushy under his feet as he crossed between the first two apartment blocks. He wanted 445, apartment B. He knew exactly where it was, butting up against the road, about four blocks in from South Glebe. He moved cautiously, doubly aware tonight. His eyes darted, like black coals in his head, adrenalin high in his veins. Two youths moved from the shadows to his left and he paused. They looked at him, big Mexican eyes dulled by crank. He ignored them and walked on, off the grass now and on to wet pavement. He turned right and walked up the low hill, with 395 on his left. Boese watched the numbers; 445 was the next block on his right. Now he tensed and stopped moving altogether. He was standing in the shadow of the first block, and his hand was on the butt of the automatic on the left side of his chest. One jerk of the holster would free it. No movement. No sound. He moved on; 445 directly right now, the main door standing half ajar. Where there had been glass it was missing.

Boese paused again, scrutinizing the doorway, looking for anything that shouldn't be there. His heart bumped in his chest, and he looked back the way he had come. Then he stepped up to the door. The inner hall was concrete and cold, smelling of urine and dried sex. There were two apartments on the ground floor. He moved just inside the main door, looking at the concrete steps with the metal rail rising to the first floor. The wind blew rain against the outside door, making it creak. He drew the Beretta from its holster, and his gaze rested on the door of apartment B, where the letter hung at an askew angle. He crossed the hallway on the balls of his feet and waited, watching the main door, listening for movement upstairs. Then, taking a set of keys from his pocket, he began to work at the lock.

It took him a little while, longer than he would have liked, but the lock finally clicked and he pressed gloved fingers against the wood and stepped inside. Debris greeted him: clothing, two old bicycles, a broken dresser in the narrow hall. Four doors led off it, and a light glowed under the one at the far end. Boese moved past the bicycles and the dresser, the rancid stink of the place in his nose. He stepped over the piles of dirty clothing and stopped outside the door where the light showed. He put the Beretta back in its holster and took out the silenced pistol. He put one ear to the door and could hear the low hum of the TV. Silently, he turned the handle.

Bedroom: bed facing him with two people in it; a woman lying on her back with her arms flopped by her sides and her mouth open. Thick gurgling snores emanated from the cavity. Chucho was propped up on pillows watching TV – only he wasn't. His eyes were closed and he did not open them until Boese placed the barrel of the gun between his lips.

Outside, a figure moved in the shadows, silent, watchful, like a hunting cat. He had seen Boese enter and he made his way to the back of the building.

Inside, Boese had what he wanted. Chucho Mannero was still propped up in bed, only his eyes were open and blood flowed over the whiteness of the pillow, where Boese had blown the back of his head out. He had taken the gun from his mouth just long enough to learn what he wanted. There had been an unexpected bonus. In a desperate bid for his life, Chucho had told him more than he needed to know. He stood over him now, watching his fat, drunken girl-friend, still snoring beside him. He considered shooting her too, but there was no need. If she had woken up he would've done, but the drink he could smell on her breath had dulled her senses to nothing.

Weighing the gun in his hand, he looked one more time at Chucho's shattered face, then walked back down the hall. Outside, the rain still beat at the streets and Boese paused briefly before stepping on to the sidewalk. He moved back the way he had come, watchful, listening. At the corner of the first block, he saw a grey Chrysler sedan which had not been there before. Steam rose from the hood, as the rain hissed against hot metal. Boese's hackles rose and he felt in his shoulder holster for the Beretta. He stared at the car as he moved slowly past it. Silence, save the rain and the hum of the slowing traffic on the highway to his right. He knew the car had not been there when he walked in, and there was something about it that bothered him. Then he realized what it was – it was too new to be parked there for the night.

'The master of illusion.' The voice was thin and cruel and came out of nowhere. Boese whirled and crouched, breath coming short in his chest. Laughter, low, and edged by the wind.

Boese fired the Beretta into the darkness; two shots, two more. He heard the laughter again, and then he was running for cover. No lights came on. Nobody came to their windows. Nobody wanted to know about gunfire in the night. He paused in the lee of the next block and looked back. He could not tell where the voice had come from. Then he realized why. He stared at the fire escapes bolted to the walls of each block and saw that they climbed to the flat of the roof. He heard an engine start, then saw headlights, and somebody drove the Chrysler between the buildings. Boese raised his gun again, but did not fire. Two turns and the car was out of sight.

Teresa woke with the very first cracks of dawn filtering through the inadequate blinds and the grime that stained the window. Her head fizzed with last night's booze. She yawned and opened her eyes. Something stuck to her back; her nightdress was clinging to her skin, and, for a moment, she thought in horror that she must have peed herself. Then she saw Chucho's rolling eyes and the choking mass of drying blood that had soaked through half the bed. Her throat was so tight she could not get the scream out.

Byrne woke to the sound of Angie taking a shower, yawned and stretched and looked at his watch. He was later than he wanted to be, but this investigation was wearing everybody down. Throwing off the bedclothes, he joined his wife in the shower.

They ate breakfast together, wearing matching white dressing gowns, at the breakfast bar in the kitchen. Byrne watched the early morning news on TV. Three murders overnight, one in Arlington, two in Georgetown. 'Only three,' Angie said. 'That's not bad.'

Byrne brushed her neck with his lips. 'How you doing now, after your ordeal?'

His wife looked at him, dressing gown open to the waist, tanned muscular chest with the dark curling hair. His wedding ring hung from the silver chain she had bought him the last time they were in New York together.

'I'm a tough guy, honey, you know that.'

'Yeah, I do. But this is a little different.'

'He's just some jerk with a hard-on.' She patted him on the cheek. 'Thanks for the concern, darling, but really I'm all right.'

Byrne looked back at the TV screen. He started as a picture of Chucho Mannero flashed up. The news anchor reported his shooting the previous night.

'Oh, fuck,' Byrne said. 'That's the guy we're looking for.'

The ground team were already at the scene when Byrne pulled up and parked. Kovalski was back at headquarters, and Logan was running things on the ground. The evidence response team had been scrambled and they were on their way now to join the agents from Arlington County. Logan caught sight of Byrne and came over.

'Shot through the back of the mouth, Louis, while he lay in his bed. Goddamn girlfriend didn't even wake up.'

'That's three,' Byrne said. 'What the hell is he doing, Chey?'

He followed her inside, and the bedroom looked as though a barrel of red paint had exploded, only the smell told you it hadn't. Harrison stood at the window, smoking a cigarette. 'Made a helluva fucking mess,' he said.

Swann was outside, looking at the area in general. He could feel Boese here, almost sense his presence. Logan touched his arm. 'You OK, honey?'

'Fine. Just trying to figure him out, Chey. None of this makes sense.'

'What gets to Pentagon City, the airport and home again in forty-five minutes?' she asked him.

'I don't know. Tell me.'

'The Best Western courtesy bus. Chucho Mannero drove it.'

'He worked up there?' Swann pointed to the hotel on the hill.

She nodded. 'Will you and Harrison go check it out?'

Harrison drove and they parked in front of reception. The manager had been summoned and was on his way in now. The staff looked very distressed, and already a number of them had been questioned by the Arlington County detectives. Harrison nodded to a couple of the dicks, but they merely eyed him suspiciously. 'Can't say I blame 'em,' he muttered. 'FBI takes everything and gives nothing back.' He spoke to the receptionist. 'Can we look at your guest list, please?'

He and Swann sat down and began to peruse the list while they waited to speak to the manager about Mannero.

One name jumped off the page at Swann. 'Here we go,' he said. 'Mr I. R. Sanchez. Venezuelan.'

'So?'

'Ilyich Ramirez Sanchez. That's Carlos, Harrison.'

They summoned a second ERT from Pennsylvania Avenue, who went through Mr Sanchez's room with a fine toothcomb. They came up with a set of fingerprints on top of the television, which were lifted electronically and sent down the computer line. Within a few minutes, they were identified as belonging to Ismael Boese.

Back at the crime scene, the FBI team were deep in conversation with the Arlington detectives. Logan was talking to Kurt Leuze, the evidence technician, while Randy Shaeffer was organizing a fingertip search of the area. Harrison and Swann pulled up and Logan beckoned them over. 'The residents are being quite helpful, considering this is a project, they're all Spanish and we're the FBI,' she said. 'Apparently, shots were fired around two-thirty this morning.'

'Have we got a time of death yet?' Harrison asked.

'Somewhere between two and two-thirty.'

'There you go, then.'

Logan shook her head. 'Look at this.' She held up a transparent evidence envelope with a buckled shell in the bottom. 'This was dug out of the wall where it came out the back of Chucho's head.' She looked at Swann then. 'It's from a Russian Vul, Jack. The PSS silenced pistol. The same as was used on Teniel Jefferson.'

'So?'

'So, don't you get it? Other shots were fired, right after this one. Only these could be heard. A different weapon must've been used.'

In London, Christine Harris had the first genetic fingerprints from the DNA samples provided by Janice Martin.

435

She spoke with Webb and Superintendent Colson. 'Negative. No match, I'm afraid.'

'Have we got any more coming?' Colson asked her.

'Three. She gets around quite a bit. They're all out of town members.' She pointed to three pictures she had laid out on the desk, stills from the funeral parade. 'Marco, I suppose because he looks Italian.' She tapped the other two in turn. 'Fatboy and Gib. All three of them slept with her over the past couple of days. Fatboy's real name is Frank Burroughs, ex-Royal Green Jacket, now living in Portsmouth. Marco is ex-Green Jackets too, living in Maidenhead. And Gib was a para who now lives with his mum in Northampton.'

Colson glanced at Webb. 'Has anything come from the meeting over the weekend?'

'Couple of titbits.' Webb looked at a transcript of the tape that GCHQ had given them. 'Two references to contracts,' he said. 'And the word "hide" was mentioned.'

'Excellent.' Colson rubbed his hands together. 'I want a team standing by.'

'There's a lot of them, Guv. Have we got the manpower?'

'Box have,' Harris said.

'See what you can do?' Colson leaned on fisted knuckles. 'If we can just get a positive sample, we can really wind them up.'


Swann phoned them from Washington and spoke at length with Colson. He explained what had happened in Arlington and that Chucho Mannero was now being investigated in terms of possible links with Boese. Colson told him what they had accomplished, and updated him on the financial investigation. Swann said that Tom Kovalski was in touch with the secret service case officers who were looking into

436

the situation, and there was a hive of activity down the street in Washington.

'Did they ever find out what happened to the ten million dollars that Jakob Salvesen shelled out?' Colson asked him.

'Not as far as I know.'

'Jack, do us another favour, will you. According to St Andrews University, Ben Dubin is in Washington on some lecture tour. Webb wants to know if he was at the 1997 Shrivenham conference. He's on the list of proposed delegates, but no one can confirm whether or not he actually attended.'

Swann hung up. Logan had called a full briefing and set up flip charts at the front of the eleventh-floor conference room. Byrne was there, with Harrison, Kovalski and the other agents working the case.

'Listen up,' Logan was saying. 'We got three stiffs. Mary Greer, Teniel Jefferson and now Chucho Mannero. Two Caucasians and one Puerto Rican. So far, the only one we can link directly to Boese is Mary Greer. Her friendship with Leona Boese, who's flipped out now in prison. If ever there was someone gone stir-crazy, it's her.'

She paused for a moment to collect her thoughts. 'Mary Greer must've known Teniel Jefferson,' she said, 'if only from dealing his cards at the blackjack tables. Jefferson knew Mannero from Ellis Island Correctional Center, where he supplied him with illicit gear before moving to Nevada.' She looked at Swann then, as if for support. 'Something else happened last night. Something which makes me re-evaluate all Jack has said about Boese's identity.' She stopped and glanced at Byrne. 'Something he said to your wife, Louis. Something like "interesting thing with feathers".' She rubbed her knuckles against her mouth for a moment. 'I think Boese killed Mannero last night. Then I think he came out of that apartment building and right into something else. We recovered four shells, all the same type, all fired from the same weapon.'

'A single shooter,' Harrison mused. 'Not a shoot-out.' He frowned heavily, the lines creasing up in his forehead.

No one spoke for a few minutes, then Byrne said: 'Greer, Jefferson, Mannero. We still don't know why he killed them.'

Swann sat forward. 'If Boese isn't the Storm Crow, maybe he's trying to find out who is.'

Silence.

'By killing Greer, Jefferson and Mannero,' Byrne lifted his eyebrows. 'How does that work?'

'Three links in a chain,' Harrison said quietly.

Swann nodded slowly. 'I think he's tracing the line of his own recruitment.'

Again silence. Logan let breath escape audibly through her nostrils. 'Greer knew Jefferson back in 1985,' she said. 'Jefferson could only've known Mannero between 1979 and 1984. Jesus, if this is correct, whoever's behind this thing has been working on it for years. Just to get Boese on his team.'

A chill, almost tangible, replaced the heated atmosphere in the room. 'Only one weapon got fired last night,' Logan went on. 'Outside the building, I mean. Either someone tried to kill Boese, or he tried to kill them.'

'No blood. No corpse.' Harrison rolled his snuff tin back and forth on the table. 'But another player's joined the game.'

Swann was still for a moment, watching each of their faces. He looked from one to the other of them and spoke very quietly: 'There's something else we have to address,' he said. 'Whoever is behind all this has got access to intelligence that I can hardly believe. Not only have they engineered incredibly complex situations, like myself and Pia Grava, for instance, they have access to gangs like

Jorge Vaczka's. If what we think is correct, they can also access the British Secret Intelligence Service, and be a reliable enough source to set a whole surveillance operation going on the UK mainland. They'll have shown Boese the strength of Vaczka's operation, before completely double-crossing him. They then double-cross the Poles by tipping off MI6. Think about the influence, the power, the money, and, above all, the inside information you need to have to be able to do all that. You've got to know how every secret service, every terrorist group in the world, virtually, operates. How many people can do that?'

'Any one of us,' Byrne said bluntly. 'Tom Kovalski. Me. You, Jack. Your commander, any commander of any security group in the world. Lots of politicians. Lots of businessmen. Diplomatic security. CIA. You name it.'

'You're right, Louis.' Swann looked evenly back at him. 'There's one thing you're forgetting, though.'

'What's that?'

'Harrison.' Swann jerked a thumb at his friend. 'He was compromised in Idaho, right around the time you and me went to Paris. Most people thought, logically so, that because I told Pia Grava I was going, that's how it happened. The trouble with that theory is, she was with my kids at a friend's house all the time I was there. She's on remand in England right now, and she's given us everything she possibly can on Boese. She categorically denies telling him I was ever in Paris. What reason could she have to lie?' He stopped speaking for a moment and glanced at Harrison. 'I wasn't responsible for the compromise,' he stated. 'But somebody certainly was.'

# 23

Swann, Harrison and Logan had a drink in the hotel bar. Logan sat on a stool next to Swann, with her hand resting in his lap. Swann was eyeing Harrison. 'Time it was said, JB. I hope you don't mind.'

Harrison sighed heavily, lit a cigarette and flipped the match into the glass bowl of the ashtray. 'It's the only reason I'm still an agent. When this is cleared up, so am I.'

Logan cocked her head to one side.

'It's true, Chey. Like you said, I'm a fifty-year-old dinosaur, and I got a lotta lake fishing to catch up on.'

'Jack.' Logan tugged at his arm. 'What you said in there implicates a lot of people. The whole of the FEST for starters. *I'm* part of that FEST.'

Swann squeezed her arm. 'That's all right, love. He tells me you're on the level.' He winked at Harrison. 'It implicates everyone at the Branch too, and SO12. Hundreds of people, Chey.'

'It's the handwriting,' Harrison stated. 'There's nothing like seeing something as personal as your own handwriting to spook you, no matter how tough you think you are. The scrap of paper that was under the receipt. We concentrated on the receipt, Jack. But it was the bit of paper underneath it that mattered. I should've photographed it on its own. Directions to a dead drop, like you say.' He looked keenly at Logan now. 'Think about it, Chey. If we'd busted in on Salvesen after the covert entry, we would've had that paper. Whoever saw the product knew that. That's why I got burned. There was jackshit in Salvesen's drawers when the HRT got there.'

Swann undressed while Logan spoke to her mother on the telephone. She put the receiver down with a smile. 'She's gonna be a grandma,' she said, with a flash of her teeth. 'My brother Dale's wife is gonna have a baby. God, I can all but hear her jumping up and down right now.' She wriggled her hips out of her skirt and kicked it away. Then she sat on the bed and traced lines on Swann's chest. After a while, she said: 'What're we gonna do when this is over?'

'You mean about us?'

She nodded.

Swann drew in a deep breath. 'I don't know, darling. I suppose I'll have to go back to London.'

She pulled at her lip with her teeth. 'A transatlantic telephone relationship. Sounds just wonderful.'

Swann sat up and held her by her small, delicate shoulders. 'Chey, I think I might be in love with you.'

She drew up her brows. 'Might?'

He smiled. 'You know what I mean.'

'I do, yes.' She unclipped her bra and her breasts swung free. He threw back the bedclothes and eased her out of her knickers.

Later, lying in their own sweat and breathing hard, she curled herself against him, wrapping her arms about his neck, and kissed him several times on the cheek. 'You still dream, Jack?' she asked. 'You remember how you told me you dream?'

'Oh, yeah. I dream. I dream a lot more than I did.'

'Have you spoken to anyone?'

'You mean professionally?'

She sat up, resting her chin on his chest. 'Yes.'

'No, Chey. I haven't. I should've, I suppose.'

441

She lifted her eyebrows. 'It might help, honey. Sure as hell can't hurt.'

Swann placed one arm behind his head. 'I don't know. Somehow I think it's going to take more than just talking to put the death of Steve Brady behind me. You see, after what happened with Pia, it's ten times worse. I mean the whole thing, the whole episode in my life was punctured again. It was like somebody rubbing salt into an open wound.'

She kissed him again and lay back, looking at the ceiling. 'Where *do* we go from here?' she asked.

'I've got kids in the UK, Chey.'

'I know.'

'And you've got your job over here.'

'My life.' She sat up again. 'It's all I do.'

'You've got your family. Look at you just now, talking to your mum.'

She got up and poured them each a drink. 'It's funny, isn't it,' she said. 'You get so wrapped up in things, your job, I mean, you forget other things. I mean, look at me.'

'I am.' Swann watched her walking about the room, naked, with the drink clutched in her hand, other arm crooked beneath her breasts. 'You're beautiful.'

'You know what I'm saying, dumbfuck.' She flicked fingertips dipped in whisky at him. 'I've done nothing these last few years except work for the FBI. I've got no hobbies. I don't socialize except with other Feds, and I haven't had what you'd call a satisfying relationship for years.'

Swann was still watching her, pacing back and forth like a restless black leopard.

'What d'you want from your life?'

'A satisfying career.'

'There you go, then.'

'Not just that. There's things I don't have. I want to be

442

with someone, Jack. I don't want to spend the rest of my life on my own.' She sighed again and sat on the edge of the bed. 'You know what, it's only through meeting you, doing this, being lovers like this, that you realize what you've missed. You shut off the intimate side of your life, the tenderness goes. All you do is look for one bad guy after the next, and, unless there's someone special in your life, you get too tough.' She looked him in the eyes then, and set her whisky glass down on the nightstand. 'I guess what I'm saying is, I'm scared what's gonna happen after you go back to England.'

Swann sat up, took her in his arms again and buried his lips into hers. 'Cheyenne,' he said when they broke, 'like I said, I think I love you. Let's just get Bocse and see.'

Harrison was alone at the bar, smoking cigarettes and thinking. He watched the couples round the room, saw the little touches of intimacy, and missed Guffy. He caught a glimpse of his reflection in the mirror and thought how old he was getting. He looked like some hippy bum from the west coast, who could never quite get over his surfing days. Ragtail hair, tanned and lined face, denim clothes. His Chippewa boots were busted at the heel and the handstitching was coming apart at the seam. He took another cigarette from his shirt pocket and wondered how long it would be before they killed him. His cough was a hack and he chewed too much tobacco. He had never cared before, but suddenly he did and he didn't know why. For thirty years he had struggled with a bit of himself that was missing; his courage, whatever, left underground in the tunnels of Cu-Chi. That bit he'd finally gotten back last year, after Salvesen tried to take him out. Since then, two things had struck him: one was the need to find out who had compromised his cover; the other his own mortality.

He bought another bottle of Miller and thought about

Swann and Logan upstairs. She was one tough lady; holding her own, openly having a relationship with a member of her ground team without so much as a who gives a damn? Swann had stood up well under the pressure that he himself had exerted. Weird that too, when finally confronted with him, what the hell could he do – punch the limey's lights out? He sipped beer and considered his future, he considered all that he and Swann had said, and he thought again about the handwriting on the slip of paper. There was not much of it, just scraps of words, but a handwriting expert, and there were one or two at Quantico, could give you a definite opinion if they had something to match it with. He thought about Boese too, going to all this trouble. He could've done it quietly, but he chose not to. The stuff he was doing with Byrne's wife, and his cohort in London, sending in vehicle rental records. Why do that – unless he figured that the cops in London, or the FBI over here, could somehow help him find his prey? Swann was right, he was tracing his line of recruitment. His pager suddenly vibrated and he looked at it, squinting, and thinking on how he should finally succumb to the optician's chair. He went to the payphone and called the SIOC, nodding to a black man, who sat on a stool at the far end of the bar.

Boese nodded back to him, black hands clasped on the counter, an orange juice before him. He could have left this morning, last night even, but things had changed and he wanted to stick around and watch. He had enjoyed his evening, being this close to Jack Swann again and without Swann even knowing it. He looked over his shoulder to where Harrison had hunched himself into the phone booth and was fishing in his jeans pocket for quarters. Harrison's room was only three doors down the corridor from his own. Swann and Logan were in rooms above him, though he knew they were only using one of them. That thought reminded him of Catherine Morgan and her red pubic hair. Tal-Salem had spoken with him earlier in the day. She was free on bail, no doubt having done some deal or other with the police. It was what he had expected, what he wanted; that was why she still lived. Tal-Salem had told him something else that was very interesting. Both Louis Byrne and Dr Benjamin Dubin had attended the Shrivenham conference in 1997. There had been one free afternoon, the Thursday. Boese had always wondered how the pirillium derivative had found its way to the farm in Northumberland.

Harrison spoke to the people in the SIOC and they gave him a payphone number to call. He fumbled for more quarters and dialled. The Cub's voice answered.

'Hey, partner. What's up?' Harrison said.

'You had another killing.'

'Arlington, yeah.'

'Too bad.'

'He's playing the tune, man. We're just dancing to it.'

'So I see.'

'You got information for me?'

'I do.'

Harrison nestled closer to the phone, looking back across the bar. The black man had gone and he was the only one left, save the bartender himself.

'Shoot,' he said.

'OK, listen up. Hicks is not in the game. A definite no-no. Logan the same, non-player. Thomas, the guy from Weapons of Mass Destruction, gets about, but his first time abroad operationally, was the UK deal with Byrne. Ketner's a footpad, a regular Company guy and I can't find anything about him that worries me. But then, that's what they thought about Aldrich Ames.'

'Which leaves Byrne,' Harrison said softly.

'Right. Lucky Louis Byrne. That mother is one golden

445

boy, Johnny Buck. The whisper is, he could even be the first FBI Director appointed internally since J. Edgar Hoover.'

'That'll be the day.'

'Maybe. But he is very good. Ex-US Marine Corps. He got blown up in Beirut in 1983, up with the roof and down again, with nothing but a few cuts and bruises. Luck of the devil, wouldn't you say?'

'Go on.'

'He was supposed to be shipped home in 1984, but stayed on for a while. I don't know why yet, but it didn't last more than a year. When he got home he joined the Feds and you know the rest, the guy blue-flamed a trail to the top. One interesting thing though, Johnny, he was in Beirut the same time as somebody else you might be interested in, one of the best agents we had at that time. This guy was ISA, that's intelligence support activity, part of the CIA, set up when Operation Eagleclaw fucked up in Iran. Ground intel', special forces mostly, but some support people too. This guy was fluent in Arabic and Hebrew and could've passed for either to look at. He was based in Lebanon for a few years. He's moved on now, but he's still an asset. He spent a little while in Israel after Reagan bombed Tripoli, and we worried about him for a bit. You know what Mossad are like. He's had more aliases than you could shake your stick at, but you'll know him as Benjamin Dubin.'

Harrison stared across the empty bar room, thinking hard, and seeing nothing.

'Listen,' The Cub went on. 'He's still highly thought of, so keep this to yourself. I might need a job again some day. If I hear any more, I'll get in touch with you.'

'Where you gonna be?'

'I told you already, duck hunting with my buddy.'

'What kind of ducks, Cub?'

'My kind, Johnny. The sitting kind.'

In the morning, Swann phoned Louis Byrne from the hotel and asked him if he knew where Ben Dubin was lecturing.

'He's through, Jack. Last one was yesterday. I think he's flying out today.'

'You don't know where he's staying?'

'No, but he's gonna call me before he goes. You want me to have him call you?'

'I'm on my way in now with Harrison and Logan. Maybe you could let me know when he phones.'

They walked the short distance from the hotel down Pennsylvania Avenue, with the wind blowing hard in their faces. Two or three black homeless guys were ambling along the sidewalk, sharing jokes and a bottle wrapped in brown paper. Something was going on at the White House and black-windowed secret service cars were shuffling between there and Capitol Hill. Harrison was thoughtful, walking with his thumbs hooked in his belt. The sky was a dull iron colour and rolls of smoky cloud inched their way across the rooftops. They entered the Hoover building by the side door and took the elevator to the eleventh floor. Kovalski was deep in conversation with Randy Shaeffer. The conference room table had a fresh pile of computer print-out hard copy stacked on top of it. Logan stripped off her coat and flicked the topmost page.

'I guess this is the rest of the information from the Federal Bureau of Prisons,' she said. She looked at Harrison and Swann, both of whom were looking in dismay at the mountain of paper.

'Don't we have support staff for this kinda shit?' Harrison muttered.

Logan clicked her tongue. 'We do. They're looking at the rest of it.'

The phone rang on the desk beside her and she picked it up, spoke for a few moments, then passed it to Swann. 'Louis Byrne,' she said.

'Hello?'

'Jack, I got Dubin on the line. You still wanna talk to him?'

'Yes.'

'Hold on.' Swann heard a series of clicks and then Dubin's New York accent was thick in his ear.

'Dr Dubin, this is Jack Swann.'

Harrison cast a glance in his direction.

'Hi, Jack. I heard you were over here. What's going on?'

'Oh, the usual. Listen, I need to ask you a question. Something they wanted to know at the Yard. They tried to get hold of you, but you'd already left the country.'

'Whatever I can help with.'

'August 1997,' Swann said. 'Did you attend the international terrorism conference at Shrivenham?'

Dubin was quiet for a few seconds, then he said: 'I've been to so many, Jack. I can't remember.' He paused again, thinking. 'Yes, I think I did, but only for a couple of days. That's right. I flew out here on the Friday, missed the last few sessions.'

'Thank you.'

'That it?'

'That's it for now. Thanks for your time.'

Harrison looked across the table as he hung up. 'That Ben Dubin?' he asked.

'Yes. You know him?'

'Never had the pleasure.'

George Webb was considering the latest 'correspondence' from Tal-Salem. Ever since the information that he had been in Oxfordshire had hit the fifteenth floor, every police officer in the country had been looking for him. But they did not know what he currently looked like. He had learnt the art of disguise from Boese and could be masquerading as any number of dark-skinned nationalities. Webb sat with Harris and McCulloch in the Special Branch cell and considered what they'd been sent. 'Detective Sergeant George Webb of Scotland Yard' had been asking questions again, this time in Northumberland. Rental car transactions, particularly one-way drop-offs. Avis had contacted him by telephone five minutes earlier, and told him that there had been no one-way drop-offs in August of 1997 for that area of the country. Webb picked up the phone to Special Branch at the Northumbria Police headquarters in Ponteland. He spoke briefly to DC Newham, whom they had met at the back end of 1997, after the chemical incident at Healey Hall Farm. He told him that Tal-Salem had been in the area and fresh pictures would be scanned to them via computers. He put the phone down again and sniffed. He had developed a cold over the past few days and his head had pounded all afternoon.

'What's he telling us?'

'And why is he telling us?' Harris echoed.

McCulloch said nothing. He pushed back his long, red-blond hair, then he rubbed his jaw. 'He's suggesting that somebody drove a hire car from Shrivenham to Northumberland,' he said quietly.

The phone rang again and Harris answered. Swann. 'Hello, Jack, how are you?'

'Fine. Is Webby with you?'

'Yeah, I'll pass you over.' She handed the phone to Webb, who listened while Swann told him what he had got from Dubin. Webb put the phone down and looked at the others. 'Thursday afternoon was free,' he said, 'so Dubin would've left the conference centre at lunchtime.' He scratched his head. 'I think it's time we had another chat with him.'

He and McCulloch walked back to the squad room, where they found Tania Briggs, from the exhibits office, talking with Colson. Colson beckoned them over.

'What've we got?' Webb said.

'DNA match.' Briggs's eyes were shining. 'The hair in the helmet they dumped belongs to the biker they call Gib.'

They were all gathered in the conference room and a buzz of excitement charged the atmosphere. This was the first major breakthrough they had had.

Gib was ex-Parachute Regiment, and he lived in North-ampton, which suited their purposes perfectly. His real name was Anthony Gibson and his acquaintance with David Collier went back some ten years. They had been in the same regiment together, before Collier joined the SAS.

'We've matched DNA from Gibson's semen with the hairs found in one of the crash helmets dumped in the canal,' Colson told the gathering. He paused and looked at Harris. 'Chrissie?'

She cleared her throat and said: 'We believe that The Regiment were subcontracted, for want of a better expression, to take out the SEG. Originally, I think Jorge Vaczka was employed to do it, but that was before we were tipped off about his activities. We know what Swann has come up with in the States, and the general belief now is we never did have Storm Crow in custody. His identity remains unknown. Our prime objective, however, is to get those responsible for the deaths of our colleagues. So far, we're scratching the surface of The Regiment's financial activities, and this new development represents the best opportunity we have.' She paused again and Colson nod-ded for her to go on. 'We're going to release a photograph of Gib to the press, put it on the *Six O'Clock News*, etc.

The stills from the video, blown up to show his face as clearly as we can get it. The gang are bound to recognize it, and with the sound we've got in the clubhouse, we might get some form of result.' She broke off again and turned to Colson. 'What about the weapons hides?'

Colson looked at the rest of the officers gathered. 'Opinions?'

'Go for broke,' Webb said. 'Put out a statement, saying we believe that the gang responsible have connections in America and have Polish-supplied weapons cached over here. Somebody's nerve will go.'

Colson turned to Harris once more. 'What about surveillance?'

'We'll need Box.'

'Why don't we just raid the clubhouse?' McCulloch suggested. 'We've got the DNA.'

Webb shook his head at him. 'Covertly. You know it's not enough, Macca.'

'But there's bound to be weapons there.'

'We never found any before. Even if there are some, I doubt they'll be the ones they used on the SEG. Collier's a smart boy, he won't have them stashed anywhere that could implicate him.'

Colson shook his head. 'Webb's right. Go for broke with publicity and put them in a spin.'

'We could do something else,' Harris suggested. 'Put out more than just Gibson's picture. Why not do Gringo and Fagin as well?'

Colson looked back at her out of thin and thoughtful eyes. 'Why not indeed?' he said.

Webb went back to the squad room with McCulloch and found an envelope on his desk, marked United Airlines. Inside was the passenger manifest for flight UA323, dated 21 August 1997, from Washington D.C. to Detroit. Forty-seven people had been on it. Pia Grava had been called from this aircraft and given a number, which she called back again. He ran his finger over the list of names, none of which he recognized.

> Smith M.
> Latimer K.D.
> Richardson M.
> Levenson P.D.
> Callis J.M.
> Brown P.
> Redgard L.
> Mason T.H.
> Kebir J.L.
> Williams F.G.
> Collins E.

He checked the rest, then passed the sheet of paper to McCulloch. 'Anything familiar?'

McCulloch looked through the list and shook his head.

'I'll fax it over to the FBI,' Webb said, 'see what they can come up with.'

The phone rang in The Regiment's clubhouse and Fagin picked it up.

'Where's Dog Soldier?' Gib's voice.

'Hey, man, what's up?'

'Haven't you seen the news?'

'No.' Fagin's voice dropped an octave. 'Why?'

'Because your face has just been plastered all over it. So has Gringo's and so has mine.'

'You're fucking kidding me.'

'Do I sound like I'm kidding, you jerk? Where the fuck is Collier?'

'Wait. I'll get him.'

Gib waited for a few minutes, then Collier's chill tones came over the line. 'What the hell is going on?' he demanded. Gib told him and Collier was quiet for a few moments. 'Get in here now,' he said. 'We need to talk about this.'

Webb and Harris sat outside Gib's mother's house and listened to every word. The front door opened and Gib appeared, fighting with the arms of his leather jacket. He got it zipped up and pulled his crash helmet over his ears. He straddled his bike and kicked it into action. As he roared past them, Webb pretended to snog with Christine Harris.

He pressed his radio transmitter. 'Webb to Control. Mummy's boy is on the move. Repeat. Mummy's boy is on the move.'

They followed, keeping well back, other vehicles tracking the Harley Davidson into London, without Gib ever knowing they were there. If he had been trained in antisurveillance, it did not show now. He concentrated on getting from Northampton to Hounslow as quickly as he could, without getting stopped for speeding.

Webb parked four streets from the clubhouse, in a suburban, terraced road, with only dull streetlamps lighting it. The sound from the clubhouse was relayed to them in the car and he and Harris settled down to listen. 'Have we got spotters on Janice Martin's flat?' he asked.

Harris nodded. 'Two bodies, one in a fixed OP and one car. SO11. They're both shots and they're armed just in case. We've also got two ARVs on standby.'

They heard Gib's voice in the clubhouse. The doorbell had sounded and Fagin answered it. Webb listened intently, recognizing both Collier and Gringo. Two others were also there, Marco and Fatboy, both spoken to by name. Collier had just watched the television news, with the newscaster referring to the pictures of Gib, Fagin and Gringo that the police had released. He had switched the set off after that and the room had been silent. Now Collier was speaking. Harris pressed her earpiece in tighter and listened.

'Two reasons,' Collier said, 'Janice Martin's talking. Or the Poles still have a leak.'

Gringo answered him. 'I don't think Janice would say anything.'

'They know about us from John Stanley,' Fagin said. 'If he hadn't fucked up, they'd never have got anything.'

'Initially, maybe.' Collier's voice, tight in his chest. 'They've got more than that, now, though. They have to, or they wouldn't have made this move. *You* think with your prick, Gringo,' he said. 'Janice is on the street and look what happens – we get our names in the paper.'

In the car, they heard him get up. Then Webb bunched his lips, as he heard the distinctive sound of Collier taking the phone apart.

'He's going to look everywhere,' he said. 'Tell me he won't find it, Chrissie.'

Harris looked through the gloom at him. 'He won't think of the lights, Webby.'

They heard him curse and then put the phone back together again. 'Get me a Philips screwdriver,' he said. 'I want to check the TV.'

'No one's been in here,' Gringo said. 'We're secure, man.'

'It pays to check. We had that gas leak, remember?'

'Yeah, and you phoned the gas board and it was confirmed. Fucking police can't leak gas into a street and evacuate people.'

'Can't they?'

In the car, Harris twisted her features into a grimace.

'We need to check our situation,' Collier was saying, 'discreetly though. No panic. That's what this is about. They're trying to put the shits up us.'

'They're doing a good job, then.' Gib's voice again.

'Chill out, Gib. You start chasing round like some headless fucking chicken and they *will* get you.'

'What about the guns?'

'Not our problem, are they.' Collier stood up. 'I'll talk to the Poles.'

Webb looked at Harris through the darkened interior of the car. 'Poles must control the hides.'

She made a face. 'Supplied, used and returned.'

'Have we got anyone watching them?'

She shook her head, then picked up the phone and spoke with Colson, telling him that they needed a team on Robert Stahl, the Polish commander of operations. She switched the phone off again. 'We'll follow Collier when he moves,' she said.


Gringo rode his motorcycle to Janice Martin's flat and parked under her window. He did not ring the bell, but let himself in with the key he'd kept. He climbed the stairs slowly, quietly, thinking. Outside, the armed surveillance officers from SO11 were on high alert. They had sound in Martin's flat, so if things went wrong they could hit it. The team leader spoke to the SO19 armed response vehicles over the encrypted Cougar radio and briefed the officers as to the situation. Back in the operations room at Scotland Yard, Colson chewed his knuckles and waited.

Janice had a visitor, one of the other London gang members, using her services for the night. Gringo let himself into the flat and watched them, hard at it on the living-room floor, before Janice looked over the shoulder of the other biker and saw him. Gringo kicked the biker in the backside. The man sprawled across Janice. He twisted his head back and Gringo leered at him. 'Get out,' he said. 'Now.'

'You fuck . . .'

Gringo hauled him off her. 'You heard me. Go.'

Janice snapped her knees together, pulling down her T-shirt to cover herself. Gringo leaned in the doorway with his arms folded while the other man buckled his jeans, then left.

Janice was in the kitchen now, T-shirt not quite covering her buttocks as she bent to get beer from the fridge. Gringo lit a cigarette and sat on the couch.

'You that desperate, darling?' she said, as she handed him a can of beer. 'Pulling rank like that.'

Gringo sucked from the can and said nothing. She sat down next to him, the T-shirt riding up her thighs. She leaned against his arm. 'I'll have to take a shower first.' Standing up, she peeled the T-shirt over her head and walked naked, hips wiggling, to the bathroom. Gringo let her go and when he heard the water start to tumble, he got up and searched the flat. Living room, kitchenette and bedroom. In the bedside drawer he found two specimen bottles, looked at them briefly, then closed the drawer. He lit another cigarette and waited till she came through.

Her hair was wet and her skin red and hot, nipples bunched into wrinkles of jutting flesh. She towelled herself in front of him, rubbing between her legs with a smile on her face. 'You're quiet tonight.'

'We need to talk.'

'Do we?' She stopped the motion of the towel and held it limply in her hands; shoulders low, breasts heavy.

'You've got a big mouth, haven't you, Janice.'

She stared at him, and lifted the towel to cover herself. 'I don't understand.'

Gringo got up slowly and faced her. 'You got nicked. Now you're out. You've got two previous convictions.' His features twisted into an ugly grimace. 'That doesn't make sense. And now my face and Fagin's and Gib's are suddenly all over the news.' He took one pace towards her.

456

She watched him carefully: he always carried a switchblade knife in the inside pocket of his leather jacket.

'Gringo,' she said. 'I don't know what you're talking about. I'm on bail. My father's rich, remember. He's got connections. You know that.' She gestured at the walls around them. 'He bought this, didn't he.'

'I think you're lying to me.'

Outside, the surveillance officers were tense, listening to every word. The first ARV turned the corner at the end of the street and stopped. Two armed officers climbed out, both in plain clothes. They started walking along the street.

In the flat, Janice had sat down and was puffing nervously on a cigarette. 'Gringo,' she said, brain clicking fully into gear now. 'First of all, I said nothing to the police. I've been bailed by my father and when I go to court, I'll more than likely do time. But in the meantime, I'm not a danger to the community. They *let* people like me out on bail.' She looked at him, wide-eyed and evenly. 'Secondly, what could I tell them anyway? I don't know anything. Mammas get told nothing. Jesus, all you guys do is buy and sell motorbikes. I'm the rebel here.' She poked herself in the chest. 'I'm the one on the white powder panty remover. I piss off Dave Collier more than my own father. Jesus, Gringo. Get a life. What could I bloody tell them?'

Gringo pivoted for a moment on the balls of his feet, one hand still bunched in a fist. Then suddenly his shoulders dropped and the breath went out of him. He picked up the telephone and spoke to Collier at the clubhouse.

'She's cool, man.'

'Bullshit.'

'No, really. She is cool. I know when she's lying, man. And she ain't lying.' He put the phone down and cupped his hand round the back of Janice's neck. 'If I find out I'm wrong, I'll cut you up myself.'

Jeconec checked the newsagent's window on the corner of King Street, as he always did. He saw the card placed by The Regiment and the hairs rose on his cheeks. He walked back to the POSK, where Vaczka was teaching the Stanislavsky class. Harris and Webb followed him. Stahl was sitting in the cafeteria, drinking coffee. Jeconec looked at the clock on the wall; still fifteen minutes before Vaczka was finished. He told Stahl what had happened.

Stahl nodded his blond head, eyes set like stone. 'I saw the news on TV.'

'What about the hides?'

'I'm checking them.'

'You think there's any way we can be linked to the bikers?'

'No.'

'What about the dance we led the cops? What about Amaya Kukiel?'

Stahl shook his head. 'Jorge set her up. They stopped watching us ages ago.'

Vaczka came into the cafeteria with a dark-haired girl on his arm. He sat down and Jeconec looked at the girl. Vaczka frowned, then patted her on the bottom and sent her to get some coffee. He leaned over the table. 'What is it?'

'Message from The Regiment. Collier wants to talk.'

Vaczka sat back again and smiled at Carmen behind the counter. He drummed his fingertips on the table. 'Panicking, is he?'

Stahl looked sideways at him. 'Never struck me as the type to panic, Jorge.'

'Send word,' Vaczka said. 'I'll meet him.'

That afternoon Stahl drove his van to Wimbledon and

parked on the common. Webb and Harris walked hand in hand, with their dog gambolling before them. A kite-flier was desperately trying to get the wind to lift his craft, but to no avail. Joggers ran here and there, and a woman rode a horse at a trot. Stahl walked, straight backed, his Rott-weiler running for sticks ahead of him. He was photo-graphed every step of the way. At a copse in the middle of the common, he paused, bent for a short stick and threw it into the trees. His dog raced after it. Stahl had a brief glance left and right and followed him. Webb watched him from behind his long-lensed camera. When Stahl was gone, followed again by other spotters, Webb called the Yard and requested that an RAF aircraft fly over the copse and scan for ground disturbance. Colson told him it would take some time to organize.

Stahl was followed to two more sites: a grove of trees near Beaconsfield with an electricity substation in the middle of it, and then to a lock-up warehouse in Highbury. Every location was logged. Back at the Yard, the following morning, Colson had the results of the aircraft scan. Defi-nite ground disturbance in the copse on Wimbledon Common, the same at the Beaconsfield substation. The ground disturbance could be as innocent as a badger's sett, but somehow they did not think so. It was decided that they would make a covert entry to the lock-up in Highbury.

Webb and Phil Cregan sat in the back of the van outside the massive warehouse, which completely covered the individual lock-up units. The locksmith from MI5 set his equipment on the main entrance electronic lock and over-ruled it. Then he created a second digital combination and they went in. The driver backed the van up to the unit where Stahl had gone. Here there was a roll-up steel door, with a single entry swing door set into it.

Webb got out and held the pencil-light torch for the locksmith, while he checked the heavy padlock that secured the unit. Webb could hear him breathing as he studied it, setting a soft metal probe to work out what he needed. Half an hour later, they were inside. The lock-up was half empty. All they could see were a couple of motorcycles with no number plates on the back, three or four metal filing cabinets lining the walls, and an old carpet which lay across a bunch of weathered cardboard boxes. Webb inspected the motorcycles, a Honda and a Yamaha. Cregan looked through the cabinets – papers mostly. He called Webb over, who bent to look over his shoulder. Blue paper files secured with elastic bands. Lifting one carefully, he slipped off the bands and checked the contents. Business papers, bank statements, various companies. Christine Harris would love this lot, he thought.

Cregan had partially lifted the carpet and was studying the array of boxes. Most of them were worn and squashed against one another, nothing in them except yellowed curling papers. He looked more closely. 'If there's anything here, it'll be at the bottom,' he said. 'We'll have trouble putting stuff back as it was.'

Webb curled his lip. 'Fuck it, Phil. It's a mess anyway, isn't it. We can do a pretty good job. They might suspect, but they won't know. And there's no point in being here if we're not going to check everything.'

Between them, they lifted back the carpet and set about moving each box individually. Most of them contained paper, but then, as they got towards the bottom of the pile, the boxes became squarer, more uniform. Webb felt the adrenalin beginning to pump, and then he lifted the lid on one and saw a gun in a polythene, ziplock bag. They stared at it for a few moments, then Cregan unzipped the bag. 'That's a Vikhr Whirlwind,' he said.

Collier rode out of London to meet Vaczka. Gringo and Fagin backed him up, with Fagin acting as third eye. A helicopter tracked them high overhead, a full team of surveillance vehicles interchanging behind them. They chose a circuitous route, riding hard and fast through the side streets close to the clubhouse, but were tagged by surveillance riders. They headed west on the M4, before cutting south towards Bracknell. They crossed the M3 at Hook. Collier rode on towards the village of Odiham, before pulling into the Swan pub car park on the left-hand side of the road. The lead surveillance car went straight on, as did the second. The third pulled in and parked. A man and his girlfriend went inside for a drink.

Vaczka sat on his own with Collier. Gringo and Fagin stayed at the bar, watching the door and trying to vet anyone that came in. The surveillance couple walked in, sharing a joke between them, and Gringo stared hard into the eyes of the man, a big, rugby-playing number 8.

'What's your problem?' The rugby player said, and looked directly back at him.

Gringo ignored him and looked over his shoulder at the door as another two men came in.

The girl tugged the rugby player's arm and they moved to the bar, bought beer and sat down at a table.

Vaczka sat with Collier on the other side of the table, two booths down from them. Gringo watched every person in the bar. There was no way to covertly take a picture. Collier had been careful. He had deliberately avoided a seat where anyone could photograph him from outside. He sat with a pint of Guinness settling in front of him and stared at the Pole out of steel-grey eyes. Vaczka stared back. Blunski and Stahl drank together at the bar.

By now, the surveillance team had covert photographers set up and were snapping everyone coming out of the pub. They would not get the bikers and Poles together, but they could get them leaving the same establishment, and the date was automatically stamped on the pictures.

Vaczka sipped his drink and looked at Collier. 'So, why the urgency?'

'You don't watch television?'

Vaczka smiled. 'Of course I watch television. But it's not my problem. You should never have lost your soldier.'

Collier's eyes were cruel and a vein lifted at his temple. 'It's more than that,' he said. 'That gives them a little, but no word is spoken outside my clubhouse. No women know anything and everything, as you know, goes down in code on paper.'

'Maybe Special Branch bugged your clubhouse. I heard there was a gas leak.'

Collier shook his head. 'I'd know if they'd bugged my clubhouse.'

'Yes. I think you probably would.' Vaczka lit a cigarette and blew smoke out the side of his mouth. 'So what do you want?'

'I think you still have a leak.'

Vaczka flared his nostrils. 'Me?'

'That was the reason you came to us in the first place, remember. You had an informant, a mole in your organization.'

'Yes, and she's gone now.'

'Is she?' Collier shook his head sadly at him. 'Are you fool enough to think there's no legacy?'

'Listen.' Vaczka leaned towards him. 'My organization's been operating without serious interruption since 1980. My paymaster is Abu Nidal. We think we know what we're doing.'

Again, Collier shook his head. 'I know Abu Nidal. Sabri al-Banna. He's been infiltrated by Mossad for years. His war council's made up of Algerian-Israeli agents. I'm telling you again, I think you've got holes in your boat. If the water leaks on me, you'll wish we'd never met.'

Vaczka snorted at him. 'Fuck you, man. Who d'you think you're talking to?'

Collier had been sitting with one hand resting on his thigh, and as he spoke, a stiletto knife worked down the sleeve of his jacket. All at once he reached under the table and pressed the sharp end against Vaczka's testicles. Vaczka's eyes were suddenly orbs in his face.

'All I'm telling you is to check your firm,' Collier said softly. 'Now, which bit of that don't you understand?'

Vaczka looked sideways to where Stahl and Blunski were watching them. They could see what was happening. They did not move, their gaze shifting between Collier and his sergeants. Collier was still staring into Vaczka's eyes.

He stood up. They looked at one another one last time, then Collier turned on his heel and his sergeants followed him out to the bikes. They were snapped three times by photographers in the trees across the road.

In the pub, Stahl and Blunski slid into the seat opposite Vaczka, whose face was a rash of scarlet and his lips white against it.

'Was he doing what it looked like he was doing?' Blunski asked.

Vaczka looked witheringly at him. 'A knife against my bollocks, yes.' He lit a cigarette and sat back, then fisted his hands on the table in front of him. He smoked in silence for a few moments, then very savagely he crushed the cigarette in the ashtray. 'Move the guns,' he said.

It was growing dark on Pennsylvania Avenue as Swann stood in the Domestic Terrorism Section in the FBI building, studying the fax that Webb had sent over.

Byrne moved at his shoulder. 'What you got, Jack?'

Swann showed him. 'Passenger manifest,' he said. 'Flight from here to Detroit in August 1997. Pia Grava made a phone call to one of the passengers. It might've

463

been Boese. It might've been somebody else. Can you do anything with it?'

Byrne plucked it from his grasp. 'Sure we can. We can see who these people are. I'll get somebody on it.' He took the paper with him and went back to his own office on the fifth floor.

Swann looked after him, then turned as he felt someone staring at him. Harrison was leaning against one of the desk partitions, spitting tobacco juice into a Coke can. The female ATF agent, who occupied the booth, was grimacing. Harrison ignored her and pushed himself off the partition. He walked past Swann and touched him on the shoulder. In the corridor outside, he paused. 'Let's go get us some coffee, Jack.'

They sat opposite one another in the canteen, two large paper cups of coffee steaming between them. Harrison looked at Swann across the table. 'The Cub called me up last night.'

'And?'

Harrison sat back, drumming his fingers on the table. 'This is strictly between you and me, Jack. It goes any further and other people could get compromised.'

'So why're you telling me, then?'

'*Touché*, duchess.' Harrison's face creased into a grin. 'You can't even tell Logan.'

'No problem. What is it?'

Harrison's features sharpened again. 'Ben Dubin's a CIA agent.'

Swann stared at him.

Harrison told him what The Cub had said.

'How does he know?'

'Told you before, bubba. He's got the inside track. Kinda missions he goes on, he needs to know what's cutting and what ain't. Life depends on it, Jack.'

Swann thought hard. 'ISA?'

464

'He used to be very active. Probably still is. Jack, think of the access he gets with a background like that. Think of his job right now.'

'And who he knows.'

'No kidding.' Harrison sat back again and sipped his coffee.

'So where does that leave us?'

'I don't know.' Harrison flapped a hand. 'All I want is the sucker's ass who fucked me.'

'But Dubin could be Storm Crow, Harrison.'

'He could be, yeah.'

'And if he is, then maybe the CIA know about it.'

'That's possible too.'

Swann sat back. 'The MI6 tip-off. Jesus Christ, Harrison.'

'You got that right.' Harrison sipped at his coffee and arched his eyebrows. 'Between us, bro. Got it?'

Swann poked himself in the chest with his thumb. 'You think I'm going to broadcast this?'

Logan walked into the refectory then, spotted them and hurried over. 'That's where you're at. Jesus, since you two kissed and made up, you're about inseparable.'

'D'you want some coffee?' Swann asked her.

'No, I don't want coffee. I want you guys upstairs right now.'

'Both of us?' Harrison looked incredulous. 'At the same time?'

'Kiss my ass, baby.' She cracked a long polished finger-nail against the surface of the table. 'I think we've found where Chucho Mannero fits in.'

Upstairs, one of the intelligence analysts handed Swann and Harrison a copy of a thin, paper file. It was headed up United States Department of Justice, Federal Bureau of Investigation, New York City and dated 23 November 1981. Swann furrowed his brow. *Fuerzas Armadas de*

*Liberacion Nacional Puertorriquena.* (Armed Forces For Puerto Rican National Liberation or FALN.)

'That'll give you some background,' Logan explained. 'The important factor is this: Chucho Mannero was Puerto Rican, FALN. He didn't leave the island until 1978 – where he had been a Machetero; a machete-wielding, independence-seeking, bad guy.' She looked to the door of the conference room, where Kovalski now stood with his arms folded. 'The FALN were active on the mainland United States from 26th October, 1974. It's all in the document there. They bombed various sites in various cities – New York, Chicago, Philadelphia. In 1978, we popped Willie "Fingers" Morales for the first time. He was making a pipe bomb and it went off prematurely, blowing off most of his hands. You'd think that'd be enough to get a guy to hospital, but Willie is still tearing FALN documents up with his teeth, when the NYPD show up.' She leaned against the back of a chair. 'Anyways, for a while after that, there was a threat to break the leaders out of jail, which we took very seriously. In 1982, we had Henrique Valentin, one of the main bomb-makers, on Rikers Island, New York. He'd worked with "Fingers" Morales before, and the FALN were trying to bust him out, so we had him moved around the country.' She paused for a moment. 'He's out now, only served ten years. But one of the facilities we shipped him to was Ellis Island Correctional Center.'

Harrison stared across the desk at her. 'Where Chucho Mannero was serving time,' he said.

466

# 24

The UK security services kept up their surveillance on
Jorge Vaczka's gang, as well as The Regiment. Resources
were stretched thin and officers were working round the
clock. Webb and McCulloch co-ordinated the movement
of teams and a fixed observation point was set up in the
Highbury warehouse. On the Monday afternoon, following
Vaczka's meeting with Collier, Stahl and Jeconec arrived
at the lock-up unit with a van. The information was relayed
back to the Yard and an SO19 firearms team immediately
deployed to Highbury.

Stahl and Jeconec backed the van right into the garage
and began shifting the old carpet and papers and everything
else to one side. Then they started to hoist the guns into the
back of the van. They followed that with the papers from
the cabinets, before throwing the carpet over what was left
and slamming the van doors. Webb and McCulloch were
outside the warehouse, two streets away, running parallel.
Every move the Poles made was relayed to them by the
observation team. The Poles drove the van out of the
garage, rolled the door shut and left the warehouse. They
were vigilant, but obviously preferred to do this in the
daytime, when suspicion would not be aroused. The surveillance teams followed them south through London,
down to the Angel from Highbury, then to Old Street and
the City, before crossing the river on Tower Bridge. They
took the South Circular Road, heading west.

Webb drove, McCulloch next to him. 'Wimbledon?'
Webb said. 'In the middle of the day?'

Stahl and Jeconec drove on, bypassing Wimbledon, and

467

headed south on the A3 carriageway. At Guildford they took the right fork, the road for Farnham and across the Hog's Back hill. The firearms team were now part of the surveillance, their orders to detain the Poles when they got to wherever they were going. Webb relayed that order to the firearms team leader in the lead Range Rover. Messages crackled back and forth over the radio, the lead car falling back to allow another to take over. The rest of the convoy were still some way back, but bunching now and gathering pace, in order to close the gap. The Poles might pull off the road at any of the towns or villages they passed through.

At Farnham they did turn off. Webb received the message and the firearms team moved up. Webb and McCulloch were right on the tail of the second SO19 Range Rover, and they speeded up, blue lights on now, but no sirens, still two miles back from the motorcycle courier who had eye contact. The Poles pulled into a side street, which narrowed where the flow of traffic was calmed, before widening out again and leading them into an industrial estate. 'This is it,' Webb said to McCulloch, as they heard the directions given.

Stahl slowed for a mini-roundabout, Jeconec checking his side mirror as he had done all the way from London. 'I don't know why we're doing this,' he said. 'Vaczka's worrying about nothing.'

Stahl looked sideways at him. 'I don't think so. That Collier is unpredictable. If he gets pulled, we've got no way of knowing what he'll do. Better to be safe than sorry.' They crossed the next intersection and slowed for an articulated lorry that was pulling out of the gates to a builder's yard on the left-hand side. Behind them, the Range Rover was lead car now. Jeconec glanced at it; three men inside. He frowned, then looked forward again as Stahl pulled round the lorry and turned right to the self-storage units. The firearms team took the left turn. Webb's car drove past the lock-up, which was similar to the one they had in London, only not enclosed inside a warehouse. Stahl, the blond-haired hard man, was fiddling with the key to the padlock. Jeconec had moved to the driver's seat and was spinning the van round so they could back it up to the door.

The firearms team deployed, two of them initially; clad in jeans, long jackets and soft-soled boots. Leaving the cars, they walked down towards the unit where Jeconec had the van parked with the back doors open. Webb and McCulloch were parked round the corner, ready to come up as soon as the all-clear was given by the SO19 team leader. The first two officers were armed only with handguns. The rest would mobilize when they drew level with the garage. The Poles were busy, lifting boxes between them and stowing them into the lock-up, oblivious to two long-jacketed men making their way down the street towards the hamburger stand on the corner. Webb listened to the radio and waited.

Stahl could feel the first threads of sweat on his brow, though the day was cold. The boxes were heavy and there were a number of them. He looked over Jeconec's shoulder and saw two men, laughing about something as they drew level with the front of the van. He backed into the garage, Jeconec on the other side of the box. They set it down with a mutual grunt and straightened up again.

'ARMED POLICE. STAND STILL.'

Stahl stared in disbelief at the two men training automatic pistols on them. Moments earlier they had been bareheaded, but now they wore black baseball caps with the chequered banding of the police. Stahl froze, half lifting his hands, and watched as four more officers, each carrying an MP5 carbine, leapt out of the black Range Rover that pulled up next to the van. The officer who had shouted took a pace forward. He held his pistol one-handed now, and his eyes were fixed on Stahl's.

'Now,' he said. 'Do exactly as I say.'

They did; they had no choice, each staring into the six gun barrels. Behind them was all the firepower they could ever need, but they could not get to it. They were forced to drop on to their knees, arms outstretched, then fall forward on to their hands, before lying prostrate on the cold concrete. People were watching them now, from the hamburger stand, from the upstairs windows of the offices around them. They were secured with plastic handcuffs and handed over to the arrest team.

Webb and McCulloch searched the boxes and discovered an array of Eastern European weapons, including Gyurza pistols, and the Vikhr submachine guns. Webb looked Stahl in the eye as he was being bundled towards an arrest car. 'Private collection, is it?' he asked.

Stahl said nothing, his mouth was twisted and set, eyes betraying no emotion. He was placed in one car, and Jeconec, his eyes troubled, was placed in another.

Special Agent Combes, the secret service liaison at the US Embassy, slit the seal on the large envelope that had come across in the diplomatic pouch that morning. He spread the papers on his desk and read the report from his counterpart in Washington. The motorcycle inventory that Special Branch had furnished him with was a fake – fake in that the sale had never happened, the parts did not exist and the values on the notice of receipt were deliberately missing zeros. The same thing had been seen in the United States, all of them transactions between various motorcycle groups. TCX was indeed a third-party financial clearing-house, and the banking link was with Mexico. He looked further, sipping at a cup of hot coffee, which steamed on the desk before him. His counterpart had drawn up a spread sheet for him, showing the links that the production orders, so far received, had thrown up. Separate amounts of money going through the account and into the Banco De California in San Antonio. TCX had paid over $1,200,000 to a total of six different companies, which had been traced back to three main holding companies, two in the US and one in the UK, that were owned by The Regiment. He sat back and scratched his nose, then he began to follow the trail going the other way, sensing great excitement in the words written from Washington. The trail was far from clear, but the UK link had allowed the US Secret Service to look at the Mexican bank from a different angle, and a number of new leads had arisen. One of them became apparent when tracing the electronic transfers into TCX and its subsidiaries from different parts of the world. Companies from Poland, from the British Virgin Islands, from Jamaica, and one from London. Combes picked up the phone to Christine Harris at Special Branch.

Jorge Vaczka was teaching class at the POSK. He sat on a stool, tight-fitting jazz shoes on his feet, with his arms folded and a trail of sweat on his brow. The class were studying Ibsen and he wanted them to consider a single night's performance for the university. His reputation in and outside the POSK was growing, and more and more prominent members of the community were approaching him. Respectability: it provided excellent opportunities. There was a new girl in the class, English, with light skin and dark brown hair, and she could act. She had poise and held herself well and Vaczka caught her eye now, as she went over her lines in the far corner of the room. His gaze was disturbed, however, by movement in the glass panel of the door, and then the door was opened and two men in suits walked in. They stared at him. He stared at them and felt cold all of a sudden. Webb and McCulloch crossed the floor and Webb stopped in front of him.

'Can I help you, gentlemen?' Vaczka said.

Webb flapped open his warrant card. 'Police, Mr Vaczka.' He took a set of handcuffs from McCulloch. 'I'm afraid you're under arrest.'

Webb and Harris sat behind the two-way mirror in interview room 5 at Paddington Green. They had them all now: Vaczka, Blunski, Jeconec, Stahl and Herbisch, locked in cells awaiting interrogation. They had undergone the humiliation of body-searching, of their clothes being taken, and paper suits and other people's shoes being given in their place. Webb watched Vaczka now, as he waited for his solicitor. He glanced at Harris beside him. 'His brief is McAlinden,' he said. 'Doesn't come cheap.'

'Maybe Abu Nidal's paying.'

The Section 18 searches had already been carried out: Vaczka's flat, the others', the lock-ups in both Farnham and London. Teams had been sent into the copses on Wimbledon Common and near Beaconsfield, to dig up the other hides. More weapons had been found, cached and wrapped in plastic. 'D'you think we've got enough?' Harris asked him.

Webb pulled a face. 'That'll depend on whether we can match the cartridges from Hanwell Green to the guns.'

At that moment, three firearms teams from SO19 were deployed outside the clubhouse on Victoria Avenue in Hounslow. Collier sat in the living room, listening to their loudhailers. Fagin stood next to him, and alongside him, Gringo. All of them were armed with pump-action shotguns that Collier had brought in the day before. He wore a holster on his hip, with an old FBI Sig-Sauer 9mm inside it. He looked at the floor, then up at the others' faces.

Fagin's was sallow, haunted, half circles of grey in the hollows below his eyes.

'I don't want to fight,' he said.

'Fagin.' Collier spat out his name. 'You don't have a fucking choice.'

Fagin drew breath stiffly through his nose and glanced at Gringo. He was quiet, fingering the wooden stock on the shotgun. Collier could sense the fear in him and closed his eyes to a slit.

'They've arrested the Poles,' Gringo said. 'They must be talking.'

'The Poles won't talk.'

'You said yourself, man. We can't trust them.'

They had called other gang members earlier, including Gib. Gib's mother told them that the police had come in the early hours of the morning and driven him into London.

'What've they got on Gib?' Fagin was asking.

'Nothing.' Irritation chipped at Collier's voice. Again, he looked through the curtains and spotted the black-suited ninjas that once upon a time he had trained with. He considered their tactics; sooner or later they would storm the place. Birdshot through the upstairs windows, CS gas and then assault ladders and flashbangs. He had done it many times himself. His respirator lay on the floor at his feet. He wished he'd had the chance to bring in more firepower.

'Dave.' Fagin had a hand on his arm. 'There's hundreds of them out there. We won't stand a chance.' He shook his head. 'We don't know what's going down. Maybe we can make a deal.'

'Deal?' Collier stared at him. 'Are you fucking mental? We killed their mates, sixteen of them. Every copper we see is going to give us a kicking you wouldn't believe. When they lock us up, they'll throw away the key.' He shook his head very savagely. 'No way,' he said. 'I'm fighting.'

Again, the call to surrender crackled from the street. Throw their weapons out of the windows and come out with their hands over their heads. Fagin scratched nervously at the palm of one hand. 'I ain't dying,' he said. 'I wasn't even there that day.'

Collier's eyes glowed, seeing the treachery already etched into Fagin's face. 'You take one step towards that door,' he said, 'and I'll shoot you in the back.'

Fagin paled, then glanced at Gringo, who was shaking his head. Collier went to the window again. He glanced out, then looked back at the others. 'Upstairs,' he said. 'We need the height advantage.' They looked at one another, then back at him. Neither of them budged. 'Come on, you fuckers. Move.'

Gringo got up, swung the shotgun on to his shoulder and stuffed more cartridges into his pockets. He sucked on his cigarette, wetting the end, and then flicked away the ash. They all heard movement outside, booted feet on the pavement. Collier took the stairs two at a time, Gringo behind him. Fagin paused at the bottom. Collier had no time to worry about him. He was in the front bedroom, crouched by the window, watching the gathered forces outside. They had come at dawn, but his alarm systems had tipped him off in advance. He was at the window with a shotgun and firing on them before the method of entry man could get anywhere near the front door. He was surprised they had gone for the frontal attack, given the extent of his security. They must've imagined they still had the element of surprise. The shotgun rounds he had peppered them with sent them scurrying for Kevlar blankets and cover, and then the siege had begun. They had tried to speak to him on the phone, but he ripped it out of the wall.

He had made up his mind as soon as those rounds were exchanged, and he was not about to change it now.

Gringo squatted next to him, the windows closed in front of them. 'What about the back?' he said.

'What does it matter?' Collier reached for his respirator and half pulled it over his head. 'We're not walking out of here.' He indicated the street below. 'They'll punch out these windows and then it's tear gas. You better put your mask on.'

Gringo hesitated. Then they heard the front door open and the clatter of Fagin's gun hitting the pavment. 'Little fucker.' Collier lifted his head. Outside, the police officers took cover by their vehicles, where Kevlar blankets were thrown over the doors. Fagin was walking out of the gate, past the parked bikes, with his hands clasped together on the back of his head. Collier curled his lip and smashed the window with the butt of the shotgun. He spun the weapon in his hand and aimed at Fagin's back.

The sniper's round hit Collier clean in the forehead. His body went limp, the gun falling away from him, and he crumpled like a rag doll on the floor. Gringo stared at him, the rubber of his mask, bloodied and smoking where the round had smashed into his face. Blood spilled from the back of his head and began to seep into the carpet. Keeping his own head down, Gringo threw the shotguns out of the window, then crawled on his hands and knees all the way to the stairs.

Angie Byrne lifted the ringing telephone with a sense of trepidation. She could not help it, tough as she thought she was. She stared across her desk, where another of the partners was watching her. 'Yes?' she said quietly.

'So they found Chucho Mannero.'

The voice was strange again. She thought she had got

used to the intonations, notwithstanding the variety of accents, but now it seemed different.

'That's another person you've killed. What does it do for you, give you a bigger erection?'

'You know for an attorney, you have a foul mouth.'

'Tell me something I don't know.'

'Sometimes things are not what they seem, Angela.'

'You don't think I know that?'

He laughed then. 'Are you frightened of me?'

'What do you think, butthead?'

'You should be.'

'That'll be the day.'

'Shall I put an end to it now, finish it once and for all?'

'Finish what, exactly?'

'What I started. I'm getting close now, close enough to walk away.'

'You'll never do that. They'll hunt you to the ends of the earth.'

'I don't think so. I don't think so at all. Remember what I told you, the crow is a shape-shifter.' He hung up.

Angie replaced the receiver and looked at her colleague. 'We should let them tap this phone, Bill. He's calling me here because he knows we won't allow it.'

'Don't take the calls, then. Make him call you at home.' He rested the elbows of his thousand-dollar suit on the table. 'It's not up to me. Everyone is agreed, our clients are never going to stand for an FBI wire tap on the phone. They'd leave us for the competition in droves.'

She sighed and picked up the phone again, already rewinding the tape to play to her husband.

Boese, now a fat, balding Mexican, glanced at the woman who occupied the seat next to him. Three nights since he killed Chucho Mannero, three nights since whoever it was lay on the roof of the building and could have shot him dead. Benjamin Dubin in Washington. The jackal and the crow. He closed his eyes and thought again about all that Chucho had told him. It made so much sense now, and this flight to New York was not altogether necessary. But he was going anyway, because he needed to know just how far ahead he was, if indeed he was ahead at all. The death of Mary Greer and the mischief on the Mississippi River had telegraphed his intentions. That night in Arlington could have ended it all. Why wait so long? And why, when the opportunity best presented itself, did it not happen?

He looked out of the window again, suddenly feeling like a rat between the paws of a cat. But the rat is cunning and smart, and his teeth are very sharp. Who was following him? Who whispered to him from the roofs of buildings? Shape-shifter, doubler, the ability to be in two places at once. The cowboy in Nevada, the Irishman in London last year. Dulles Airport drifted below like a strange grey carpet, as the nose of the plane stretched skywards. He would need to take even greater care from now on. The pace of the game had sharpened considerably.

Benjamin Dubin was back at his desk in St Andrews, watching the lunchtime news on television while he ate his sandwich. He considered all that had gone on in Washington, considered his latest conversation with Swann and the overt suspicion in his voice. He thought about Louis Byrne and he thought about the jackal and the crow. Boese's dark eyes suddenly filled his mind, not from the television pictures, but from when they had been separated by a table in the prison interview room. He finished his sandwich and folded the waxed paper carefully, before dropping it in the bin.

The TV newscaster was describing the events of the morning, when scores of detectives from all over the country had raided the homes of members of the biker gang known as The Regiment. Their clubhouse in Hounslow had come under siege when other police officers had been fired on. Later, it was also confirmed that their leader, David 'Dog Soldier' Collier, had been shot dead by a police sniper. He was the only casualty, and two other members of the gang had been arrested at the premises. Dubin watched as officers from the Antiterrorist Branch, some of whom he knew, milled about behind their white vans at the clubhouse. Exhibits officers in blue one-piece suits were going in and out of the front door, carrying evidence bags with them. The phone rang at his elbow.

'Dubin.'

'Christine Harris, Dr Dubin. Special Branch.'

Dubin felt the hairs lift on the backs of his hands. 'What can I do for you?'

'We'd like to talk to you again.'

Dubin stared at the box files on the walls. 'Are you coming up here?' he asked. 'Because I'm due in London the day after tomorrow.'

For a moment, Harris paused. 'That'll be fine,' she said.


Fagin was talking. Vaczka had said absolutely nothing to anyone, other than to deny any involvement with Stahl or Blunski or Herbisch or Jeconec. Halfway through his first interview, Lambeth contacted Paddington Green to confirm a ballistics match between the shell casings recovered from Hanwell Green and four Vikhr submachine guns. Webb looked coldly into Vaczka's arrogant eyes. 'Weapons found in a van driven by your people,' he said.

Vaczka shook his head. 'Not my people. Acquaintances, yes. But we all have those, Sergeant.'

Webb smiled at him, then took one of the surveillance photographs taken after his meeting with David Collier, and set it before him. 'Acquaintances?' he said, tapping it.

'I think that looks more like a commander and his lieutenants, don't you.'

'That, Sergeant, can have no basis in anything other than your own opinion,' McAlinden, his solicitor, stated.

'Fair enough.' Webb sat back and folded his arms. 'Tell us about Amaya Kukiel.'

'Girlfriend,' Vaczka said. 'I have a number of them.'

'Tell me about February 5th.'

'I don't remember February 5th.'

'Yes, you do. You were in a van with Blunski and Stahl. You drove up north and gave away a whole bunch of old clothes on behalf of the Polish mission. Why did you do that?'

'Because I'm charitably minded.'

Webb burst out laughing.

Vaczka wagged his head now, a slow smile on his face. 'Sergeant, you obviously know very little about me. Speak to the Polish community. They'll tell you about Jorge Vaczka. You'd be surprised just how much I do for charitable causes.'

'I'll tell you about Jorge Vaczka, shall I.' Webb sifted papers before him and laid them out sheet by sheet. 'Jorge Vaczka, Polish activist. Jorge Vaczka, terrorist. Jorge Vaczka, gunrunner, the puppet of Abu Nidal.' He tapped the photographs of the weapons they had recovered at the lock-up. 'These guns have been used in a number of terrorist activities over the last five years,' he said. 'We have ballistics links in Serbia, France, Germany, here in the UK, and a Loyalist murder in Northern Ireland.' He shook his head sadly. 'And here they are in your possession, in a garage rented by one Peter Francis, a.k.a., Pieter Jeconec, who just happens to work for you.'

Again, Vaczka shook his head. 'Sergeant, you can prove nothing that links me personally with any of these weapons.'

'No?' Webb stood up. 'I tell you what, Jorge. You go back to that nice little room we rented you and we'll talk about it later.'

Christine Harris was upstairs with Combes from the US Secret Service. She was all smiles, and showed Webb why. 'Electronic money transfers,' she said. 'It was a circuitous route – here, the USA, Jamaica, Poland.' She shook her head. 'National pride or whatever, some kind of vanity.'

Combes explained it to him. 'We can trace the payment of one million two hundred thousand dollars from companies run and owned by Vaczka, all small amounts, but ultimately ending up in the bank accounts of companies operated by The Regiment. Electronic transfers have to be requested on handwritten forms. We can access those forms with the right search warrants, depending on how cooperative the countries are *vis-à-vis* international banking regulations.' He produced a photostat of one of the forms that they had ultimately traced, via a discretionary trust in the Cayman Islands, to Jorge Vaczka.

'That's Vaczka's handwriting, George,' Harris interrupted. 'We got a sample from his flat that's been given a "high probability" definition by the Questioned Document Section at Lambeth. They want us to do some more sampling, before they'll give it a "was written".' She sat back and rested her hands in her lap. 'Fagin is spouting off like a whale coming up for air. He wants immunity and lots of protection, but he's prepared to identify the rest of the shooters.'

Combes was looking pleased with himself. 'Now we've been able to identify these bank accounts, we can make the connection with our Mexican friends,' he said. 'We'll check the money trail into Vaczka's companies back in the States for you.'

Harris looked at Webb. 'Fagin has confirmed that The

Regiment was approached because Vaczka's own team was compromised,' she said.

Webb drew his brows together and turned to Combes again. 'If Vaczka was compromised, effectively double-crossed, then Boese himself will have funded the payments to The Regiment.'

Combes nodded. 'We've got access to all the accounts we can, so far. But we're looking at applying some State Department pressure on the governments of some of the more dubious countries. Most of them owe us favours. We'll turn something up.'

Back at the Yard, Webb had a message to get in touch with Swann in Washington. He phoned him immediately and Swann told him what they had discovered regarding the latest of Boese's victims, and what they thought he was planning next.

'Henrique Valentin,' Swann said. 'Ex-FALN, Puerto Rican independence terrorist. The trouble is, he's been out of jail since 1990 and nobody knows where he is. He served out his parole time, never got in trouble again, so I suppose he gave up the cause.' He paused for a moment, then added: 'Listen, I'm not sure how much you can use this, but I've found out something very interesting about Dubin.'

'He's coming in here tomorrow,' Webb said. 'We're going to talk to him informally about the Shrivenham conference thing.'

Swann dropped his voice to a whisper. 'Well, you need to be aware – Dubin's a CIA agent.'

Swann hung up and went back to the conference room where the team were gathered.

'Valentin is next on Ismael Boese's list.' Logan was standing, one hand fisted against her hip, addressing the rest of those gathered round the table. 'He has to be. We're fortunate this time, we've figured out who we're looking for before Boese's had a chance to deliver his head on a plate.'

'We did that with Chucho Mannero,' Byrne said. 'Look what happened to him.'

Harrison cocked an eyebrow. 'Chin up, Louis. We might luck out this time.'

Byrne ignored him and concentrated on Logan. 'What we have to do is find him before Boese does. It's possible that Mannero gave him a name, but not a location.'

Harrison interrupted. 'Boese knows where he's at. That's been the way of it, so far.'

Byrne squinted at him now. 'Now who's being negative?'

Harrison looked at him for a long stiff moment and the atmosphere, already tense, crackled all but visibly. Kovalski spread his arms in a calming gesture. 'OK. OK. Let's all just chill out a little,' he said. 'We need to think clearly here.'

Byrne was still looking at Harrison. 'We could think more clearly if we all had the same agenda.'

Harrison stared into Byrne's eyes. 'You got something you wanna say, old buddy?'

'John, take a walk, huh. Go give yourself five.' Kovalski glared at him across the table. Harrison stood up and stalked out of the room, back straight, hair falling over his shoulders. Kovalski turned to Byrne. 'Louis, play it cool, huh?'

'I tell you what, Tom.' Byrne was on his feet now. 'That guy has had one thing on his mind ever since this deal started.' He stabbed a finger at Swann. 'First it was him, now it's somebody else. All he gives a flying fuck about is what happened in Idaho.'

'Understandable, though, isn't it?' Swann spoke quietly.

Byrne flashed a look at him. 'Hey, Jack,' he said. 'Ever

hear the word professionalism? My wife is being hounded, goddammit. D'you hear me busting my balls about it?'

Logan stared at Byrne. 'The way I heard it, Louis, it was you who put Harrison on to Jack in the first place.'

Byrne coloured. He looked at Swann. 'Nothing personal, Jack,' he said quickly. 'It made sense at the time. Now, maybe, it doesn't. I'd've discussed it with you if there wasn't the Atlantic between us. Boese and Salvesen were both in jail, and what we didn't need over here was someone like Harrison chasing shadows.'

Swann stood up then. 'If you don't mind, I'll get some air,' he said.

He walked the length of the corridor, then took the lift to the ground floor and found Harrison sitting on the wooden benches in the quadrangle, gazing absently at the 'Fidelity Bravery Integrity' statue and smoking a cigarette. Swann looked over his shoulder.

'What's happening?' Harrison asked him.

'Oh, the usual tension.'

Harrison exhaled again with a sigh. 'Should learn to keep my fool mouth shut,' he said. He flipped away the cigarette and stood up. 'Byrne's right. It's the only thing on my mind.' He looked Swann in the eye. 'I don't give a horse's ass about Ismael Boese, Jack. Alls I want is the sonofabitch who stiffed me.' He looked across at the FBI statue again, the three figures before the American flag, two crouched, a third standing, arms wide to protect them. 'Not much integrity in that.' He looked glassy-eyed for a moment, then led the way to the entrance. 'Let's get back up there,' he said. 'I might even apologize.'

Logan had effected her plan by the time they reached the eleventh floor. The meeting had broken up and Byrne and his colleagues from International Terrorism had gone back down to the fifth floor. Kovalski called Harrison over, and they spent half an hour in his office with the door closed. Voices were raised, then lowered, then raised again. Logan squeezed Swann's hand as she passed him. 'Just another day at the zoo,' she said. 'I think old Tom's considering how he can send Harrison back to New Orleans.'

Swann asked her what was happening.

'We're putting Valentin's face on the front page of every newspaper in the country. See if anyone calls in with information on his whereabouts.'

'He's finished parole. Perhaps he'll call himself.'

Logan curled her lip. 'Somehow I doubt that, Jack.'

The door to Kovalski's office opened then and Harrison walked out. He winked at Swann and sat on the edge of the desk. 'Detention,' he said, and took a tin of Smokey Mountain from his pocket. He placed some in his cheek, compressed it, then slid off the desk again.

'Going down to Byrne's office to straighten things out.' With that, he left them and walked to the elevator, smiling at the support staff girls, who were strolling back from lunch. He went down to the fifth floor and rapped on the locked door of the International Terrorism Section.

Byrne's office was open, but he wasn't there. Harrison looked at the feather and photograph on the wall, together with the seven commendation certificates, and a photograph of him and the Director, with President Clinton between them. That had been taken on the White House lawn, after Boese was imprisoned in England. Harrison sat down to wait for him. Papers settled like so much debris on the desktop and one piece caught his eye. He glanced at the agents milling about the outer office, then, picking up the sheet of paper, he crossed between their desks and photocopied it. When he was finished, he looked over the partition and smiled at Byrne's secretary. 'Tell Louis, I'll catch up with him later,' he said.

\*

Boese was on the street in Spanish Harlem. His clothes were rags, soiled greatcoat dragging the floor as he shuffled, half limping, behind his wheeled shopping trolley, where his plastic bags were piled. His hair was long and one eye was half closed and his beard stuck to his chin in little, flat strands. Across the street, a man in his late forties sat on the steps of the tenement, watching the world go by.

Henrique Corazon Valentin, one-time bomb-maker for the FALN. He had spent ten years in various state penitentiaries, for what he considered minor offences, and for which he was still bitter. The others had tried to contact him after his release: Morales, Torres, Luis Rosa. But he had resisted. The organization had petered into nothing with the arrest of its five leaders. He had gone straight since getting out of the pen, had drifted for a while, before ending up back here where he came from, the Puerto Rican population of Spanish Harlem.

Leaning wearily on his trolley, Boese watched him. It had not been difficult to locate him. Mannero had kept in touch throughout his parole and knew Valentin was in New York. From there, it was simply a matter of recalling Valentin's speciality: electronics. Now he ran a small shop in the basement of one of the more run-down tenements, doing favours, more than anything else, for his friends; fixing their TVs and VCRs, etc. He made enough to get by, his tastes had always been modest. Last night, Boese had followed him to a little bar two blocks from the attic apartment he rented. It seemed he was a regular, drifting in at around five o'clock most days, and heading home for some dinner at seven-thirty. As far as Boese could gather, Valentin lived on his own.

That evening, Valentin was back in the same bar, seated on a high-backed stool, while two young guys shot nine ball pool behind him. The room was dim, with a dark wood counter and an array of brightly labelled bottles standing high against the mirrored glass behind it. Valentin drank rum with a beer chaser, and watched the sport on ESPN. Boese slipped in quietly. He had a moustache, long hair dripping over his shoulders, and wore a fur-lined denim jacket. He took a stool two seats down and ordered a glass of beer. The bartender looked at him out of pink and bloodshot eyes, then placed the drink before him. Boese gave him a two-dollar tip and he rapped his knuckles against the counter.

Valentin nodded to lots of people, but kept himself to himself; a small man, with thin hands and pockmark scars on his face. The bartender flicked the TV over to the *Six O'Clock News* and suddenly there was the younger Henrique Valentin, with a 'Have you seen this man?' question coming from the lips of the news anchor. Nobody paid much attention; the bar was quite crowded. One group of young bucks around the second pool table were being particularly noisy. Boese saw Valentin's face blanch, though, and a minute or so later, he slid off his stool and stepped back on to the street. Later that evening, Boese watched his lights burning on the top floor of his tenement. Again he was the bum on the street, lying in the doorway opposite.

Angie Byrne was making love to her husband. The windows were open slightly, allowing in just enough breeze to cool the heat in their bodies. Byrne lay under her, holding her by the soft flesh just above her hips, as she arched her back, palms behind her on his thighs. The phone rang and she looked down at him, thrust some more, then sighed and rolled off. She leaned over to pick it up, but Byrne moved against her, reaching over her shoulder.

'Byrne,' he said, the receiver to his ear.

'Louis Byrne. Storm Crow hunter. Have you found him yet?'

'Boese.' Byrne leaned against his wife as he moved one elbow under him, his grip tight round the handset. 'Where are you?'

'Me. I'm in New York. The Big Apple, Louis. If you talk to your technical boys, they'll confirm it. I called to talk to your wife.'

'You're not talking to my wife. You're talking to me.'

'Shape-shifter, Louis. Has she figured it out? Have you?'

'What're you trying to prove here, exactly?'

'Prove. You mean you *haven't* figured it out yet? You of all people.' Boese sighed in his ear. 'Anyway, tell Angie I called. Oh, and by the way, I saw the *Six O'Clock News* tonight. Valentin's in Spanish Harlem.'

He hung up and Byrne leaned over his wife again to put down the phone. Angie was lying on her side. Fear snapped in her eyes. She could feel a sharpness against her shoulder. The wedding ring that Louis wore round his neck cut into her flesh.

# 25

No sooner had Boese hung up, than Byrne's cellphone rang. It was the technical team in the SIOC. 'We got a trace, sir,' they told him.

'Don't tell me. New York City.'

'Payphone. Spanish Harlem.'

'Somebody on their way?'

'Field office and NYPD.'

'OK. You better get hold of Kovalski.'

Byrne called Logan in her hotel room. She pushed moist hair out of her eyes and picked up the receiver. 'Hello?'

'Get your clothes on, Cheyenne. Then get to Andrews airforce base as fast as you can. Boese's in New York City.'

They woke Harrison, or rather they didn't: he was lying in his room watching TV. Within five minutes, they were in a car to the airbase, siren blaring, lights flashing and the police package kicking in. Swann rode up front, Logan in the back, already tapping away at the keys of her lap-top computer.

'Why ring and tell us?' Swann was saying. 'What's he playing at now?'

Harrison looked sideways at him. 'Valentin's dead already.'

They met Byrne and Kovalski at Andrews airforce base, where a fifteen-seater, propeller-driven fixed wing was already on the runway. The three of them got on board and Harrison and Byrne exchanged a glance, as the engines started and the big three-pronged props began to whip the air.

'Have we heard anything from the NYPD?' Logan asked Byrne.

He shook his head. 'They're trying to locate Valentin.'

Swann sat in one of the single seats on the other side of the aisle, Harrison in the row behind him. He looked out across the lighted runway. One a.m. and cold. His jacket was buttoned to the neck and his thoughts were suddenly of England and the children he hadn't seen for what felt like ages. He looked across the aisle, where Logan was busy with her lap-top again, scrolling through the prison program she had downloaded. She glanced up, caught his eye and smiled.

Boese lay huddled in the doorway once more, blankets wrapped round him, hood pulled over his head, and a paper-wrapped vodka bottle beside him on the top step of the tenement. From here, he could see the lights of Valentin's attic apartment in the block directly across the street. Cold tonight, and not much activity. A couple of young hoodlums roamed the street, but they didn't bother the bagman. He was lying on his side, knees curled to his chest, when the first police road unit cruised up the street. He could hear the crackle of radiospeak as the driver slowed, his window half rolled down. They stopped right by the phone booth he had used. One of the cops got out, shone his torch into the booth and went back to the car, letting the beam of his torch fall across the steps where Boese was 'sleeping'. The torch shone in his eyes and he yelled at them in Spanish.

'Hey,' one of them yelled back. 'Keep it down, or we'll book you.'

Boese muttered something unintelligible and rolled over. The cops called in on the radio and sat there for a moment. Boese knew the FBI would have passed Valentin's name to them, and right now they would be running all kinds of checks to try and find his address. Knowing the kind of privacy that Henrique Valentin liked, they would have plenty of trouble. Boese lay there only until the cruiser pulled away from the sidewalk, then he got up, packed his belongings and made his way down the street.

The ground team flew into JFK Airport and an agent from the airport resident agency was there to meet them. Vehicles had been laid on and the SAC was waiting for them in the Manhattan field office. The agent told Logan that both the police and the FBI had been patrolling the streets of Spanish Harlem in numbers, ever since they received the call. As yet, they had neither sighted anyone who could be Boese, nor located the address of Henrique Valentin. They drove with lights and sirens into Manhattan. Stanley Gerard, the SAC, greeted them. They got coffee and settled in the conference room, where he told them that he had scrambled agents from Staten Island, Bridgeport, Queens, New Rochelle, and Brooklyn; effectively the entire area.

'The guy with the feathers, huh,' he said to Byrne. 'Storm Crow.'

Byrne merely nodded. Nobody outside the working team knew what they really feared. Harrison shifted in his seat and spoke to the SAC: 'Don't you got a snitch up there in Spanish Harlem?' he said. 'Your hump agents must've got drugs connections and stuff. That's the only way you're gonna locate someone like Valentin, even if he's dead already.'

Gerard looked him up and down. 'We're working on it now. The word's gone out to the precincts and we're just waiting on a call.'

Harrison stood up. 'Well, if it's all right with you guys, I'll hit the streets myself. I got my own contacts in this city.'

Byrne looked at Kovalski, who looked at Logan. 'I got

no problem with that,' she said. 'I guess it beats sitting around.'

'You wanna come, Chey?' Harrison asked her.

She shook her head, pointing to the lap-top. 'I got things to do here.'

Harrison turned to Swann, who scraped back his chair. He glanced over at Logan. 'Like you say, Cheyenne. It beats hanging around here.'

Harrison made a phone call from one of the agents' desks in the squad room. He asked for Detective Lopez of the 85th Precinct and was given a pager number. He hung up, and looked at his watch: 5.30 a.m. He cursed softly and dialled, gave his number and hung up again. 'I knew Lopez years back,' he said, 'when I was undercover in the Florida Keys. We worked for two weeks together on a Cuban connection up here. He's drugs squad, great street cop. DEA have had their eyes on him for years, but he don't wanna leave the job.' The phone rang and Harrison smiled as he listened to the voice on the other end.

'This had better be fucking good.'

'Get up, ya lazy sonofabitch.'

'Who the fuck is this?'

'Feds, Rio. Don't you recognize the number?'

'The middle of the fucking night is what I don't recognize.'

'This is Harrison, Rio. I need a tour of Spanish Harlem.'

Lopez picked them up at six-fifteen. There was snow in the air and the roads were crisp with frost. Swann looked up at the sky, little bits of it, broken and chipped between the square grey towers of downtown Manhattan. Already the city was busy. It had been busy all night, but he could see the gradual swell in the traffic, a flood of yellow cabs crowding the streets.

Lopez was about thirty, with bushy black hair and an engaging smile, where he showed you one gold tooth. He wore chains round his neck and a bracelet on each wrist, and the cut of his clothes was sharp. Harrison got in the front, and introduced Swann.

'England, eh? You're a long way from home, *amigo*.'

Swann explained the situation and Lopez drew his lips into a little hole in his face.

'Boese. I heard of him. Passes himself off as Spanish a lot of the time.' He looked at Harrison. 'What's he doing in New York?'

'We think he's trying to kill, or more than likely already has killed, Henrique Valentin.'

Lopez scrunched up his face. 'Should I know the name?'

'Henrique Corazon Valentin. Former FALN.'

'Those guys went down the river years ago, Harrison.'

'Valentin's out. He was only busted for burglary.'

Lopez drove them uptown to a diner, where they stopped for bagels and coffee.

'What did Valentin do in the FALN?' he asked Harrison, as he slid into a booth from where he could watch the car.

'Bomb-maker.'

Lopez smiled at Swann. 'Guess you guys come across a few of them, uh?'

'One or two. We always liked the ones that blew themselves up the best. Saved us a lot of trouble.'

Lopez sipped coffee and winked at the Spanish girl serving. He chatted to her for a few moments and then smiled again. 'So, we're probably looking for a guy who can fix electronic stuff. An ex-FALN member and convicted felon ain't gonna get a regular job, even round here. He'll be working for himself someplace, that's if he's here at all.' He frowned then. 'How come you guys think he's here, if you don't where he's at?'

Harrison looked at him over the rim of his cup. 'We get calls from Boese, Rio. But that don't go no further than this table, you dig?'

492

'Got it.'

'He's been calling Louis Byrne's wife on the telephone and leaving all kindsa cryptic messages. He told Byrne *himself* that Valentin was here.'

Lopez sat back then, a puzzled expression ringing his eyes. 'Why would he wanna do that?'

Harrison looked beyond him again. 'Boese isn't the Storm Crow, Rio. We think he's looking for whoever is, and he wants us to help him.'

'I don't get it.'

Swann spoke then: 'Boese worked for Storm Crow,' he explained. 'He broke out of jail in England after Storm Crow double-crossed him. At least, that's what we think. He's been running round killing people, and at first we couldn't understand why. But we've been piecing it together and we think he's tracing the line of his own recruitment. If he's doing that, he cannot be Storm Crow.'

Lopez was silent for a few minutes. 'Wait a minute, this guy Boese has been dubbed public enemy number one. And I mean, like worldwide, not just in the United States.'

Swann nodded. 'Right. And if *he's* not Storm Crow, then there's somebody else out there who's twice as bad as he is.'

Lopez sat for a moment longer, then he switched on his cellphone and stepped on to the street. 'Good guy,' Harrison said. 'If *he* can't find Valentin, then the guy ain't here.'

Lopez was still out on the sidewalk, talking into his phone. Swann could not help but note how many people he nodded to, and how many nodded or spoke to him as they passed. Lopez switched off his phone and came back inside. 'Finish up and let's roll,' he said.

Back in the car, they cruised the streets. Lopez explained that he had put the word out on Valentin and now it was a case of wait and see. All the hospitals had been checked for John Does, but none of them had any who might fit his

493

description. 'I tell you what, Harrison,' Lopez said, nodding to various suited figures in Fords driving up and down the blocks. 'Your guys hang around like this for too much longer and nobody'll be on the street.'

Boese could see them too – the FBI agents – from his vantage point, pushing the shopping trolley along the sidewalks, a stagger in his step, and his face puffy and hooded. He walked past the very coffee shop where Harrison, Swann and Lopez were talking in the booth by the window. He pushed his trolley up the street, then he turned and pushed it down again, passing their window twice. Nobody seemed to notice him. He watched vehicles. He listened for unexpected sounds. His sixth sense was alive and tingling, anticipating. This was why he was here. In Arlington, he had been deliberately spared. Why? Why not take him out then? Storm Crow dead and the case finally closed.

Valentin had also seen the gradual build-up of police officers. He had identified at least two FBI agents by the cars they drove, and he was considering his position. Not only had that old picture, taken when he was in prison, been broadcast on every TV station in the city, it was on the front page of the *New York Times*. But it *was* an old picture and nobody here knew him as Henrique Valentin. He had changed his name when he came back, so he could sink into anonymity. Now he was plain Rico; Rico who mended your electrical stuff when it broke. He sipped coffee and watched the street from his attic window, not wanting to venture out, but knowing there was work to be done, and if that work did not get done, then the rent would not get paid. He finished his coffee and hit the streets, wearing a black reefer jacket with the collar up, and a wool cap pulled tightly over his scalp. On the corner, he saw the homeless guy pushing his shopping trolley. He lurched into a doorway and squatted with his head on his chest. Valentin ignored him and crossed the street, skipping between the cars. Two blocks further on, he was safe in his basement workshop.

He had not even bothered to consider what the FBI wanted with him. His past experience with the Feds was very bad. He knew he was clean, having served his time and not violated his parole. There was nothing anybody could pin on him. He even paid his taxes on time. His shop was messy and small, with very little sunlight creeping in. But he liked it, and the clutter gave him a sense of purpose as he worked on broken wiring or old valves and transistors. From his bench, he could see the street at about knee level. He settled down to work, with the heater on and a cigarette burning in the ashtray beside him. He heard the rattle of wheels and, looking up, caught a glimpse of a shopping trolley and then the grimy, half-laced boots of the old rummy that pushed it. He stared into space for a long moment, realizing that he had only been aware of that guy over the last few days. He had seen him every day during that time, but before that, he did not remember him at all. Insect legs tickled his spine and he went up on to the street. He looked left and right, but the rummy was nowhere to be seen.

Byrne met Harrison and Swann in Spanish Harlem. Harrison introduced Lopez. They were still waiting for some information. 'What you doing, Lou?' Harrison asked him.

'Thought I'd hit the bricks. Not been done in a while.' Byrne smiled at Swann. 'Logan's got that office turning somersaults for her. She doesn't need me there.'

'You wanna hang out with us?' Harrison said.

Byrne shook his head. 'No. Figured I'd take a look round for myself. I want to check in with the dicks at the

495

precinct house, see if there's anything they've come up with.' He looked at Lopez. 'Nobody's been found dead that fits the description we put out, right?'

Lopez shook his head. 'Nothing that I've heard.'

Byrne cocked one eyebrow. 'He must be dead. What's the point of dragging us all the way up here, if he isn't.' He left them then and walked off up the street, camelhair overcoat reaching almost to his ankles.

Lopez looked after him. 'Dresses well, don't he. Even for a suit.'

'Wife's a big time attorney, Rio,' Harrison told him. 'Earns a million dollars a year.'

Boese had changed clothes, and was sitting in Valentin's favourite bar, watching the customers come in. His face was the same, still old and careworn, but he was now dressed in normal working man's clothes, a Yankees hat perched on his greying head. FBI agents were crawling all over the place, he could pick them out a mile away. Valentin was at his work bench, doing whatever it was that he did, and they still had no clue where he was. He was not coming forward, not answering their pleas in the newspapers. Obviously, he had no idea that the one organization he hated most in the world was trying to save his life. Boese sat and nursed the beer as the afternoon wore on. The sun had finally broken up the clouds and sat in pale yellow against the sudden blue of the sky. But it was not bright enough or high enough to penetrate the fine spaces between the buildings, and the streets stayed chill and cold.

And then Boese felt something, sitting where he was, staring at himself in the mirror behind the bar. Something moved on his skin, lifting the hairs on his cheeks. He sat very still, conscious of the leg holster and the waistband holster and the three knives in his pockets. He moved forward a fraction on his stool, and looked the length of the bar. It was long and dark and crowded now with drinkers. Every high-backed stool was taken and the bartender was serving fast and furiously. One man sat about eight stools down from him. Boese could not see his face without leaning much further forward, but he could see his hand as he lifted the glass of beer to his lips. FTQ tattooed in blue on his fingers. The tingling heightened in his veins and Boese swivelled on his stool again, perspiration gathering at his hairline. The same feeling he'd had in Arlington, with the rain beating down on him and the apartment blocks cast in shadow. Again he moved his head, almost imperceptibly, and again he saw the fingers, the inky-blue tattoo. He tried to use the mirror to match a head to the hand, but the rows of bottles were mounted on wooden shelves that occupied most of the glass.

He sat a while longer, finished his beer, then slipped off the stool and saw the men's room sign in the far corner, beyond the pool tables. The door to the street opened suddenly and Valentin came in. Their eyes met and Valentin looked vaguely puzzled. Boese recovered himself and turned for the men's room. He walked behind the backs of the drinkers, hunched shoulder to shoulder like so many pigs at the trough. He couldn't tell; straight backs, working clothes, coats, long hair, short hair. But he sensed the presence, like something deep in his veins. He had sensed that presence so many times over so many years; this street, that street; in parks, bars, and particularly in churches, like Westminster Cathedral in London. He went into the men's room and closed the door. Sitting on the toilet seat, he checked his guns. He heard the door to the bar swing open, two paces on the flagstones and then silence. No unzipping, no sound of anyone pissing. The sweat dribbled from the line of his hair and the gun felt weighty against his palm. In silence, he bent until he could

497

see, at least partially, under the door. A man stood facing the panel of the box he was in, and the saliva dried in his mouth. Boese eased himself up again and gripped the pistol in his right hand, listening intently. Nothing, no more sound, not even the rasp of a breath. And then the door opened a second time. Somebody walked in and coughed, and then he heard the trickling sound of urine hitting the pan.

He flushed the toilet, opened the door and stepped out, hand in his coat pocket, covering the butt of his gun. An old man stood at the urinal. No sign of anyone else. Boese moved back into the darkness of the bar, walking carefully, watchful. His stool was still unoccupied and he slid back on to it, aware of Valentin seated on his own in the corner. Boese looked the length of the bar once more, searching for those three blue letters on somebody's hand. But he could not see them anywhere.

Lopez took the call. They had been cruising the city most of the day and Swann had seen just about everything he could from the side window of a car. Lopez spoke rapidly in Spanish, then hung up and beamed at Harrison.

'Homer,' he said. 'Valentin runs a basement shop on Galena. He goes by the name of Rico, and drinks in Garcia's bar.' He spun the wheel under his hand and drove north again. Swann looked at his watch, five o'clock now, and the once-pale sky was beginning to darken. It took them over half an hour to negotiate the traffic and Lopez pulled up a block from Valentin's store. 'He won't be working now,' he said. 'He'll be over in the bar.'

They walked, the three of them, shoulder to shoulder, and Harrison looked at Swann.

'How come he ain't dead?' he said.

The bar was crowded with afternoon drinkers and filled with smoke. Swann manoeuvred his way to the counter while Lopez and Harrison circulated. Harrison spotted Valentin, still on his own, head down, waggling a glass of rum in his hand. Harrison nodded to Lopez, who in turn nodded to Swann. Swann bought the drinks and then all three of them sat down at Valentin's table.

'Hello, Henrique,' Harrison said. 'Why didn't you answer the call?'

For a long moment, Valentin just looked at them. Then he tried to get up, but Harrison had a hand on his arm. 'Hey, bro. Relax,' he said. 'You're not in any trouble. In fact, we're watching your butt.' He smiled again. 'Strange world, ain't it, the Feds looking out for an FALN bomb-maker.'

Valentin's eyes were hot now, a small fire smouldering amid the coals. 'I'm not in the FALN any more,' he said. 'I serve my time. I serve it in four different prisons.'

'Well, we had to move you, bubba. Your buddies were plotting to get you out.'

Valentin flapped out a hand. 'I do my time. I work my parole. Now I'm free. I pay my taxes and I pay my rent. I hurt nobody and nobody hurt me.'

'Well, that's the point, Henrique.' Harrison leaned much closer to him. 'Somebody's looking to hurt you. And he's about as mean a sonofabitch as it gets.'

At the US Embassy in London, Christine Harris had occupied a desk in Combes's office, where they were both digesting the information that was coming through in dribs and drabs from the US Secret Service. It was making interesting reading. The bank accounts held by both The Regiment and Jorge Vaczka's organization had been investigated, and production orders obtained on every single electronic money transfer since the accounts were opened. Money was being paid from Poland, under the guise of invoices and goods delivered, but Harris checked with

NCIS and then with MI5, who confirmed the probable activity of Abu Nidal. The link was much stronger than she had first imagined. Some of the accounts paying money to Vaczka's banks were not accessible, because they were in Russia and Turkey. But others were, particularly an account in Israel and another one in Japan. Combes sifted electronic transfer requests that had been shipped to him via the diplomatic pouch, and scrutinized them under a magnifying glass. They were all handwritten and he went through them one by one. After an hour he sat back, frowned, then looked at Harris. 'Funny thing,' he said.

'What's that?'

He handed her two separate slips from two separate banks. 'Two different companies, one in Japan and one in Israel,' he said. 'The banks are in Australia and Jordan respectively. One of the companies lets vacation property on Australia's Gold Coast, the other offers sailing holidays off Haifa.' He made a face. 'The directors are different, names, etc., but—'

'The handwriting on both the slips is the same,' Harris finished for him.

Neither of them spoke for a full minute or more, then Harris said: 'Vaczka's account in the United States received ten thousand dollars. Five thousand dollars from each of these accounts.' She cocked her head to one side. 'Why would someone do that?'

'Why indeed?' Combes reached for the phone and called his office in Washington.

Ben Dubin called into Scotland Yard as agreed. At the front desk, he waited by the eternal flame and put in a call both to the fifteenth floor and to the assistant commissioner for specialist operations. They had been friends for a number of years and he wanted to let him know he was there.

Webb was in conference with Colson and Harris, who had just brought her findings back from the embassy. 'The US Secret Service has requested the bank details of the two accounts in question,' she said. 'We'll get sight of them, as and when they do.'

'Interesting, though, isn't it,' Webb said. 'Somebody paid Vaczka a total of ten thousand dollars in May of last year. Right around the time we arrested Ismael Boese.'

The call came through from upstairs, telling them Dubin had arrived.

'I want to be in on this,' Harris stated.

'No problem,' Colson told her. 'But we're keeping it informal. We've got nothing but coincidence so far.'

'Right.' Webb pursed his lips. 'That and a terrorist data base going back fifty years. Not to mention the CIA.'

Colson shook his head at him. 'That part we don't tell him. The last thing I want right now is a diplomatic incident.'

Dubin was shown up to the conference room on the Special Branch floor. Webb, Colson and Harris traipsed up the stairs and found him standing at the window, with his back to the door, looking out at the Palace of Westminster. He turned as they came in – his smile easy, his manner relaxed – and shook hands firmly with all of them. They sat down and Webb arranged for coffee to be brought in.

Dubin steepled his fingers before him. 'So,' he said. 'Here we are again. How can I help you this time?'

'What do you think Ismael Boese's doing in America?' Colson asked him. 'So far he's killed three people, if you include what Tal-Salem did in Georgia.'

'Four, if you include the English engineer in New Orleans,' Dubin corrected him.

'You're right. Four.'

Dubin sat back, stretching his legs out under the table. 'I

don't know. It depends on whether or not you believe he's the Storm Crow.'

'We don't any more,' Webb said quietly.

'Neither do the FBI.'

'And you?'

'I don't know. I'm a theorist, an academic. I've not been privy to the details of the case, as you have.'

'You're good friends with Louis Byrne,' Webb said.

'I am, yes. But Byrne's the consummate professional. He doesn't tell me much.'

'You still believe that Boese is Storm Crow?'

Dubin smiled then. 'You know, it's hard,' he said, 'when you've publicly espoused a theory, to see it come under such scrutiny. I always believed that the John Doe with Carlos at the Paris–Toulouse train bombing was whoever became Storm Crow. Byrne identified Boese as that man.' He paused and licked a drop of saliva that stuck to his lower lip. 'To me, it proved my theory, especially after I was given the opportunity of interviewing Carlos last year.' He held up his hands. 'I don't know now, is the answer.'

Webb looked carefully at him. 'You attended the Shrivenham conference on international terrorism in August 1997,' he said.

Dubin nodded. 'Your Sergeant Swann asked me that in Washington.'

'But you only stayed till Thursday lunchtime.'

'That's correct. I had to fly to the States. I was due to give a lecture at Langley.'

'Langley, Virginia,' Colson said. 'CIA headquarters?'

Dubin nodded. 'I've lectured to them many times over the years.' He rested his elbows on the table. 'What's the significance of Shrivenham?'

'How long were you in the States that time, doctor?' Harris asked him suddenly.

He snapped a short glance at her. 'Ten days, I think. Or thereabouts.'

She nodded, exchanged a glance with Webb, and sat back.

'What's the significance of Shrivenham?' Dubin asked them again.

Webb looked briefly at Colson before he answered the question. 'Doctor, Tal-Salem remained in the UK after Boese was broken out. We didn't know he was still here – until a man answering his description turned up in Oxford-shire. He claimed to be me, and he was scouring the major car hire companies, asking about rentals around the time of that Shrivenham conference.'

Dubin screwed up his eyes. 'Why?'

'We don't know. We only knew he was doing it when Avis, Hertz and National phoned here to let me know that the information I had requested was ready.' He paused for a moment, then said: 'The next thing we know – I'm getting the same calls from those companies' offices in Newcastle. Apparently, I'd asked about one-way rentals from Oxfordshire.' He shook his head. 'We couldn't work it out. But the man asking the questions answered Tal-Salem's description. What d'you think he could be trying to tell us?'

Dubin stared at him. 'He thinks somebody might have rented a car in Oxfordshire and driven it to Newcastle. I would say that's obvious, isn't it.'

'That's what we thought. What we don't understand is why?'

'And you think I can help you?'

Webb cocked his head to one side. 'Can you?'

'Not that I know of, Sergeant. No.'

They were silent. The bark and growl of traffic lifted from Victoria Street, but in the room nobody spoke. Colson cleared his throat. 'We think Tal-Salem believes that someone who attended the Shrivenham conference rented a car and drove it to Northumberland,' he said. 'A couple of months after that date we had the death of Bruno Kuhlmann and the discovery of pirillium E7/D10 at Healey Hall Farm.' He scratched his eyelid with his index finger. 'We know that Kuhlmann was there and we know that Boese was there. We also know that the pirillium was there in a sealed copper tube.' He looked from Webb to Harris, then back again at Dubin. 'What we don't know for sure is how the derivative got there. The FBI believe it was manufactured by Abel Manley, the Minuteman chemist from the sixties.'

A shallow smile spread across Dubin's lips then. 'You're suggesting that I rented a car and took the derivative to Northumberland.' He poked his chest with his thumb. 'I could've done, couldn't I. Because I left the conference Thursday lunchtime and I didn't fly to the States till Friday evening. Plenty of time to get to Northumberland and back again to Heathrow.'

All three of them were looking him in the face.

He sat back then, hands resting easily in his lap and laughed out loud. 'Wonderful,' he said. 'I've got a data base. I worked with RAND. The Israelis. I had access to the CIA, the DIA, Diplomatic Security, the FBI, British Intelligence. You people here.'

Webb wasn't laughing. 'And you're the only person who spoke to Boese while he was in prison,' he added.

'I thought you discovered he'd got messages out via codes in the *International Herald Tribune*.'

'He did,' Harris said. 'But something happened to spark that off. It seemed to coincide with your visit last year.'

Dubin crossed one ankle on his knee and looked at them out of slightly hooded eyes.

'Well,' he said. 'What can I say? Apart from *what a coincidence*.' He paused for a moment. 'Why don't you just say it, though it's the most absurd notion I've ever come across in my life? You think I'm Storm Crow, don't you.'

Swann watched through the two-way mirror while Henrique Valentin was interviewed by Logan and Byrne. He sat across the table from them, with his shoulders hunched to his jowls and his chin down, arms folded tightly across his chest. He had been here over an hour now and had hardly said a word.

'Henrique, believe it or not, we're trying to help you,' Logan told him for the umpteenth time. He looked up at her, shrugged his shoulders and looked down again. 'You were in Ellis Island Correctional Center with Chucho Mannero,' she went on. 'Not for very long, but something happened while you were there, something that links you to Ismael Boese.'

'Please,' Valentin said. 'You say you are helping me. OK. But you know, I don't need your help. I did what I did. I was caught. I go to prison and I keep my mouth closed. Even when you move me this way, you move me that way. I say nothing. I do nothing. I make no trouble. Then I am released and I don't jump my parole. I stay where I am for three years. Then I come home. I work. I pay taxes. I live a quiet life.'

'We know all that, goddammit.' Byrne thumped the table. 'Listen, you stubborn sonofa . . . we're trying to help you here.' He jerked a finger at the window. 'There's a psychopath out there called Ismael Boese. Storm Crow, Henrique. The fucking Storm Crow. You know what, your name's on his hospital list. He already killed your buddy, Chucho. He killed a guy called Jefferson and an old woman called Mary Greer. You telling me none of that bothers you?'

Valentin closed his mouth, lips set in a line, and sat back

505

in the chair. Byrne stood up, ran a weary hand over his scalp and opened the door. 'Chey,' he said, gesturing for her to follow him. 'We're gonna let you think about it, Henrique. It's for your own good.'

'You can't keep me here,' Valentin said. 'I do nothing. I would like you call my attorney now, please.'

'Later.' Byrne shut the door on him and they all went back to the conference room.

Swann left the anteroom after taking one last look at Valentin's stiff features, and joined the others. One of the New York-based intelligence analysts brought in a fresh batch of information from the Bureau of Prisons. Rikers Island, where Valentin had been held before they moved him to Virginia. Everyone was weary, nobody seemed interested in any more paperwork.

'Stubborn fuck,' Byrne muttered.

'Why didn't Boese kill him?' Harrison asked. 'He definitely called you from Spanish Harlem, Louis. So how come he didn't kill him?'

Byrne stared at him and shifted his shoulders. 'I don't know, Harrison. I wish I did.'

'Why come all the way up here and not do what you came for?' Harrison upended a pack of cigarettes on the table. 'Makes no sense at all.'

Swann was not listening. He had picked up the list of inmates that had been sent from Rikers Island, and was leafing through them. The information was laid out year by year – transfers, new intakes, releases, parole violations. He didn't look hard, merely skimming the entries. He set the papers down, as Logan asked if they could keep Valentin overnight.

Byrne shook his head. 'You know we can't, Cheyenne. It's a violation of his human rights. We can't put him in protective custody without his permission. If he wants to hit the streets and die, that's his decision.'

Swann had picked up the papers again and was scanning more entries.

'We'll have to let him go then,' Logan said wearily.

'So put him on the street and get the special ops group to tail him,' Harrison suggested.

Swann skimmed a prison record entry, kept reading, then stopped. Adrenalin rushed in his veins. 'Chey,' he said, quietly.

'Yes?'

'When was Valentin moved out of Rikers?'

'March 1982.'

Again Swann stared at the page. 'There's a new inmate record here,' he said, 'January 15th 1982.'

'And?' Harrison said.

'Jorge Marius Vaczka.'

# 26

Swann sat in with them this time, a chair set back against the wall, while Byrne and Logan pressed themselves against the edge of the table. Valentin was weary, rubbing his eyes with the heel of his palm. Harrison brought them some coffee. Valentin stared at it.

'I don't want coffee,' he said. 'I want to go home. I do nothing. I see nothing. I don't care who you say is looking for me. I am Puerto Rican. I have many friends. I don't need FBI protection.'

'Shut up, Henrique.' Byrne's eyes were grey ice. 'You've fucked with us long enough. I could bust you right now for obstructing justice. You know damn well what we're talking about. You know what went down with Chucho Mannero, because somebody paid you to take your place in the line. Come on, Henrique. Tell us about your experiences on Rikers Island.'

'I don't know what you talking about.' Valentin rubbed his face again, shadows creeping now beneath his eyes.

'Sure you do. Tell us about Jorge Vaczka, the Pole.'

Valentin stopped then and stared at Byrne. He half closed his eyes and then his body sagged and he let go a heavy breath.

'Better,' Byrne said. 'A couple of words, Henrique, and you're outta here.' He sat forward, making a beckoning gesture. 'Come on, *amigo. Diga me.*'

Valentin told them that before he was arrested, the leadership of the FALN had been in contact with various organizations throughout the world. They had been supported by some Middle Eastern states that were hoping to

508

create a terrorist capability on US mainland soil. They were short of explosives and short of weapons, particularly at the beginning of the eighties, having suffered serious setbacks in 1976 when the Chicago PD discovered their bomb-making factory. Then, in 1978, they lost Willie Morales when his hands got blown off. Contact was made with Abu Nidal in Poland.

'And Vaczka came over here,' Logan said.

Valentin nodded. 'He was the contact between us and the ANO. He was very young, too young, I think. But he speak with us about weapons, about bombs and blasting caps. We say, blasting caps we don't need. But guns, we need a new supply of guns.'

'Jorge Vaczka was arrested for being in possession of an unlicensed firearm,' Byrne said. 'He only served a short amount of time, but you met him on Rikers Island.' He leaned forward then. 'Didn't you, Henrique?'

'I speak to him, yes.'

'And what happened then?'

Valentin pursed his lips, bit down and sighed again. 'He contact me again when I get out of prison. He send me a little money and ask me to speak to Chucho Mannero, who I know from the Macheteros and from Ellis Island.'

'And you did?'

'*Si*. Yes, I did.'

'What did you say?'

'I tell him he must speak with Teniel Jefferson, who was once his guard.'

Byrne sat back. 'And that's all you know?'

'Yes.'

Logan watched his face for a moment, then she scraped back her chair. 'OK, Henrique. You can go,' she said.

Valentin stood up. 'You think this Boese really does look for me?'

Byrne stared for a moment, then slowly shook his head. 'Not any more he doesn't.'

Logan led Valentin out of the room, and Swann stood up with Byrne. 'So that's why Valentin is living?' he said. 'Boese got more than he needed from Mannero.'

'Looks that way. But it doesn't explain why he's here in New York.'

Swann lifted his eyebrows. 'No,' he said. 'But at least it explains where he's going.'


What Boese could not know, or at least Swann hoped he couldn't, was that Jorge Vaczka was right now in custody in London. He thought about it as he and Harrison had a quiet drink in the hotel bar, while Logan showered upstairs.

'Why call us up here when he already had the information?' Swann sipped cold beer from the bottle. 'Why bother to come himself?'

Harrison leaned his elbows on the bar and drew a cigarette from his shirt pocket. 'Maybe he just wanted to see what would happen,' he said slowly.

'What d'you mean?'

Harrison made a face. 'Maybe he wanted to see who would show up?'

Swann was quiet for a moment. 'Somebody tried to kill him in Arlington.'

Harrison nodded.

'The real Storm Crow, maybe?'

'Not personally. He hasn't shown his face so far, Jack, why should he start now?' Harrison sucked on his bottle of beer. 'He's got access to just about anybody he wants, let them do the dirty work.'

'Right. But he would've known long ago what Boese was doing. Why wait till Arlington? Why not do something in Nevada?' Swann looked over Harrison's shoulder as

Logan came into the bar. 'He must've known what Boese was doing right from the start.'

Harrison crushed his half-smoked cigarette in the ashtray. 'Maybe he's waiting for *us* to get him, Jack.'

Swann made a face. 'Meaning that the real Storm Crow can go back to his retirement plan? It's too late for that now.'

Harrison shook his head. 'He'll have a contingency. Something you said one time, he doesn't believe in the zero option.'

That night, Swann lay in bed with Logan, one hand resting on the warm skin of her stomach, and thinking that soon this would be over. The net was getting tighter and he knew that once he was back in the UK, he would not be coming back here for a long time. That thought disturbed him, and he gazed through the darkness at Logan's face, and already he missed her. Lying back, he stared at the patterns cast in shadow on the ceiling. He thought of his children and Pia Grava, and the death of Stephen Brady. He thought of Boese, always one step ahead of them, playing his games, allowing them snippets of information here and there. The cryptic messages to Byrne's wife, the jackal and the crow. Shape-shifting, being in two places at once. Who had he been expecting to come with them to New York?

Ismael Boese, dressed in the flowing robes of an Arab, passed through JFK International Airport and saw the FBI agents watching for him. He took a direct flight to Charles de Gaulle in Paris and was met by Tal-Salem, who was driving a stolen, replated Peugeot. His bags stowed in the boot, Boese settled into the seat next to him.

'*El Kebir?*' Tal-Salem said.

'Close.'

'How close?'

Boese looked sideways at him. 'One more question to ask.'

Tal-Salem started the engine and they pulled out into the traffic. He knew Paris well, having worked there many times, and he drove them to the Latin Quarter and the little apartment he had rented. 'Vaczka's in prison in England,' he said.

Boese stared through the windscreen. 'That's inconvenient.'

Tal-Salem nodded, then fished in his jacket pocket for a photograph. He passed it to Boese. An aging Catholic priest, grey-haired, with his neck hanging in folds over the white dog collar. 'That is Anton Graucas,' he said. 'Jorge Vaczka's priest. He will visit Vaczka the day after tomorrow at Paddington police station.'

Boese put the photograph in his pocket and smiled.

At the apartment, he rested and Tal-Salem prepared some food. Then Boese opened his case and took out the mirror and his latex moulds. He set the picture of Anton Graucas on the small table before him. He inspected the smooth dark lines of his own face, working his fingers over his jaw and massaging the tight skin under his chin. Again, he looked at the priest: blue eyes, they would not present any problems. He took the latex mix and then a mould, and set about his work.

The following morning, he drove from Paris to Calais and booked the Peugeot on the car ferry to Dover, England. He was Jean-Paul Giroux, area sales manager with Peugeot Europe, and going to England on business. His disguise was minimal, a slight hook to his nose and thick eyebrows. Heavy-lensed glasses finished it off. The security was lax at Calais and he drove on board, parked his car, and was soon on deck with the wind in his face, as the vessel slipped into the English Channel. He leaned on the rail, gulls crying above him, grey against the more brittle grey of the sky. The last time he had been on such a boat had been five weeks previously, after making his escape from prison. He thought about that now: only forty-two paces in any one direction. He thought about the building, the dead space between the airlocked doors; the exercise yard with the wire-mesh top, like being locked in a chicken run.

In the restaurant, he chatted to the English waitress about the weather and the crossing and the usual kinds of things that English people talked about. His French accent was good and he told her about his aged mother in Lyons, and his sister and brother in Paris. She said she had never been to Paris, but one of these days she would go. Twenty minutes before they docked, he stood once more on the deck and watched the white cliffs approaching. Then, with a tingling in his veins, he went back to his car. Security was much tighter at Dover and he knew the English knew he was coming. The FBI must've got what they wanted from Valentin. He easily picked out the plain-clothes Special Branch officers at the dock; they were more visible and perhaps more vigilant than usual. His papers were checked, but the car not searched, and soon he was driving up the A2 towards London.

Tal-Salem took a flight from Paris to Amsterdam and then a connecting one to England. He flew into Stansted, north-east of London, carrying only hand luggage. It was searched and his papers checked. Negro, bearded, Dutchman; he was only here for a few days to visit some friends. Armed uniforms were everywhere. He smiled and was polite and calm with the immigration officials, and soon he was on a train to London. At Liverpool Street Station, he took the Underground Central line one stop to Bank, and then walked to Monument tube station and took the District and Circle line heading west. He got out at St James's Park and checked into St Ermin's Hotel, a fifth-floor room, overlooking the entrance to Scotland Yard. Diplomatic Protection Group officers, armed with handguns, stood on each corner, and the road was marked off with cordons to stop anyone from parking. Tal-Salem sat down on the bed and switched on the television news.

Across the road on the fifteenth floor, George Webb was reading the statement made to them by Fagin, third in command of The Regiment. Every member had been scooped up now, and the clubhouse taken to pieces. They had found more paperwork under the floorboards, coded details of other outstanding contracts, and their stock of motorcycles had been seized. Webb had given the financial information to Christine Harris and she had passed copies to the US Secret Service.

Swann was flying in this evening and everyone at the Branch was on edge, because sooner or later Ismael Boese would turn up. They knew he would try to see Vaczka, unless he knew something that they didn't. Vaczka was still at Paddington Green and would remain there until Swann had interviewed him, before being remanded in custody somewhere else. The day before Boese phoned Louis Byrne from Spanish Harlem, Vaczka's priest had contacted the custody suite at Paddington and requested to see him. He had been vetted and cleared and was due to visit tomorrow. Webb looked at the clock on the wall and checked it with his own watch. Swann's flight was due to land at 6 p.m. and he was looking forward to seeing him.

Boese drove to Ravenscourt Park and the Church of St Peter and St Paul. He parked three streets away and walked back to the building. It was cool and dark inside, and he took a seat quietly in the second to last line of pews. The altar cloth was green, twin golden candles set at each end, with a gold crucifix as the centrepiece. He sat with his head bowed and his hands in his lap, the silenced pistol fixed in his waistband. Tal-Salem had done his work well, and right now Anton Graucas was terrified that his sister in Warsaw was about to be murdered. Tal-Salem had also made contact with the lower echelons of Vaczka's now-defunct gang, and would be meeting with them about now.

The door to the vestibule opened and an old man in robes came out. His hands had liver spots and one foot shuffled slightly behind him as he made his way up the aisle. He saw Boese and the fear broke out in his eyes. He faltered, one hand on the rail, said something in Polish, then cleared his throat with a liquid rasp.

'You people,' he said, voice hoarse and sharp. 'I don't know who you are, but you should not threaten an old man's family.'

Boese stood up, eyes black as night, and laid a hand on his shoulder. 'Father,' he said. 'All men are sinners. There are a lot of things we should not do, and yet,' he squeezed his fingers into the bony flesh, 'we do them.'

He stayed the night at the priest's house, first sitting across the sparse living room from him while they ate a frugal meal, and then locking him in his bedroom, after divesting him of black trousers, shirt and dog collar. Having seen him in the flesh now, he could put the final touches to the latex face and begin the process of whitening the skin of his hands. It would take a long time to get this right. The police had been sent a photograph, albeit a bad one, and he had to be very thorough. So he locked Graucas in for the night, took his car keys and set about his work. In the morning, he would drive to the same police station from where he had caused so much havoc in Rome.

Swann, Logan and Byrne flew directly to Heathrow from New York. Harrison remained behind; nothing for him to do in London. He stood with Swann in the bar at JFK and had a quiet word. 'I may not see you in the flesh again, buddy, at least not for a while.'

Swann shook his hand and all at once he realized that he was going to miss this grizzled, tobacco-chewing long hair. 'I'll let you know what we get from Vaczka,' he said. 'And anything else we come up with.'

'Likewise, duchess.' Harrison cast a brief glance to where Logan and Byrne were both talking on mobile telephones. 'I'm gonna talk to The Cub again,' he said. 'See if he can dig up anything else on Dubin.'

'OK.' Swann shook his hand again. 'I'm going to miss you.'

'Ah, you'll see me again. You never know, one of these days I might just show up in England.' Harrison glanced at Logan. 'Besides,' he said, 'I kinda get the feeling I might be seeing you again over here.'

Swann looked where he looked and smiled. 'I hope something works out.'

Harrison laid a hand on his shoulder. 'Things work out, bubba. But only if you let them.'

'Are you really going to quit the Bureau once we've sorted this thing?' Swann asked him.

'I don't know.' Harrison pressed a ball of tobacco into the well of his cheek. 'There's a lot of things I never done in my life, Jack. I reckon it might be time to start doing them.'

'What, like get married, you mean?'

'Oh yeah, right.' Harrison shook his head. 'No, I don't mean that so much. Though you never know. Had me a gal up in Idaho. I don't know. I still got family in upper Michigan, though not many. We'll see what happens.'

The flight was called and Byrne and Logan came over. Swann shook hands with Harrison one last time and then made his way to the departure gate. Harrison stood and

516

watched them go, then he turned and headed for his own gate and the flight to Washington.

Webb met them, parking his car right outside Terminal 3, with the Met warrant book stuck under the windscreen. Byrne had ordered a car from the embassy, which picked him up, diplomatic flags flying on the bonnet. Logan wanted to travel with Swann, however, and Webb stowed their cases in the boot, then drove them into London. 'Have you seen my kids?' Swann asked him.

'A couple of times. Though your ex doesn't like me checking up on her.'

'You're not checking up on her, you're checking on them.'

'Not as far as she's concerned.'

Swann looked over his shoulder at Logan. 'You want to meet them, Chey?'

'Of course I do.'

Webb looked at him out of the corner of his eye. 'You two an item now, then?' Swann smiled and said nothing. Webb glanced back at Logan. 'I warned you about him last year, remember?'

He dropped Logan at the Marriott Hotel, round the corner from the US Embassy, then drove Swann to his flat. Swann had been hoping that she would stay with him, but she had a lot of calls to make to the SIOC in Washington. Webb parked the car and came upstairs with him. 'I checked it once or twice for you,' he said. 'Nothing to report except the usual stack of bills on the mat.'

The flat felt musty and cold. The heating had been off and the windows shut, and the February weather had been damp and chill. Swann turned the heating on and took two bottles of beer from the fridge. He passed one to Webb, then sat down heavily on the settee.

'So, what's the story?' he said.

517

'You know most of it. We scooped up Vaczka and The Regiment, got a full confession from Fagin, and the financial investigation looks promising. In fact,' he added, 'the more they look, the further the trail seems to spread. I told you about the two payments to Vaczka.'

'Ten thousand dollars. Yes.'

'Well, that trail is proving interesting. The handwriting on both electronic transfer forms is the same. The US Secret Service are doing the legwork because it all involves this Mexican bank they've being trying to crack for years. They've now got access to other bank accounts that have dealt with the ones in Japan and Israel. Three more so far, and guess what, the handwriting on the forms is the same as the other two. Different directors in each case, different companies, different countries. But the handwriting is always the same.'

'What about Dubin?' Swann asked.

'We had a little chat. Right now, he thinks we believe he's Storm Crow.'

'And is he?'

Webb lifted his hands. 'You tell me, Jack.'

'Did you talk about the CIA?'

'No. The old man didn't want to ruffle any diplomatic feathers just now.'

'We can't prove anything yet,' Swann said. 'All we know about Dubin is that he has access and that he was in Shrivenham.' He paused. 'But the biggest thing against him is what happened after he saw Boese.' He paused again and made a face. 'Byrne was in Shrivenham too. Tal-Salem was definitely telling us that somebody went from Shrivenham to Northumberland.'

'But how does he know that? And why tell us?'

'I don't know the why. Perhaps they've got something else planned for us. We've been led by the nose from the start, and we still don't really know why.' Swann swallowed beer. 'As to the how, maybe he doesn't know for sure. Maybe he's just guessing. But Boese's canny, George. He'll have worked this whole thing out. Somebody as good as Storm Crow must have had access to intelligence at the highest level.'

'Like the CIA, you mean.'

Jorge Vaczka's priest was shown into the interview room where he would be allowed to speak to his parishioner. He stooped, leaning heavily on his cane, his neck hanging in folds of grey flesh from his tattered dog collar. His black jacket, shiny at the elbows, smelled of a bachelor's sweat and pipe tobacco. His blue eyes were yellow at the edges and age lines crisscrossed his face. He had to be helped into the chair by the young constable. 'Thank you. Thank you.' Boese patted his chest and wheezed into a handkerchief.

'You won't have very long, I'm afraid, Father. He's being interviewed at length today. You're lucky to get this chance at all.'

'I know. I'm very grateful. But you see, his mother is ill in Warsaw. She may not last and I need to break the news to him.' He looked up then, eyes watery. He dabbed at them with the handkerchief. 'I suppose two minutes of privacy is out of the question.'

The constable made a face, and Boese coughed again, then laid a hand across his chest.

'I'll see what I can do,' the constable said. 'But it'll be up to the custody sergeant.'

He left him alone then and Boese stared at the walls, the walls he had seen before, when he had sat across the table from Swann, and made his telephone call. That had been then, however, and many things had happened since that day. He had been paid, had been assured, had seen the depth of the Polish operation, and then he had been betrayed. Again, he saw Mannero's face when he gave up the names of Valentin and Vaczka. Abu Nidal selling guns to the FALN and using the young Pole to do it. Ironic, but it made perfect sense now that all the pieces, but one, were set in place. From the Pole to him; via Valentin, Mannero, Jefferson and poor Mary Greer, the girlfriend of his mother.

The door opened and the young constable stood there, smiling. 'They're bringing him down now, Father. And you're in luck, you can have that two minutes, but literally only two. You'll need to tell him straight away.'

'Thank you. Thank you very much.' Boese cracked a smile. 'It's nice to know there is still a sensitivity about these things, even in circumstances such as these.' A few minutes later the door opened a second time and Vaczka was brought in, hands cuffed together in front of him. He stared at Father Graucas. He knew him, but had never set foot in his church. He looked old and tired, at death's door almost. His cane leaned against the leg of the table.

The custody sergeant pressed Vaczka into a seat. 'Two minutes only,' he said.

'Thank you.'

The door closed, the room slipped into silence and Boese stared at Vaczka.

'Father,' Vaczka said. 'What is it?'

Boese leaned towards him, then crooked his index finger, drawing Vaczka closer. 'Look closely,' he said, his voice a sliver of ice.

Vaczka's features sharpened, and then he frowned. 'I don't understand.'

'Josef El Kebir.'

Vaczka's eyes grew wide, and the light of unease settled deep in the pupils. '*Corneja Tormenta*?' he whispered.

Boese nodded once.

Then cold fear filled those eyes and Vaczka shrank back

from the table. 'We were betrayed,' he said. 'But I did what you asked. *I* provided the soldiers.'

'I know.' Boese looked at him again, arms folded now. 'The guards here think your mother is dying, so be sad when the time comes.' He paused for a moment. 'You know what I've been doing?'

'On the TV, yes.'

'You understand why?'

'No.'

Boese paused again. 'Tell me, who is the Irishman?'

'I don't know.'

' "Fuck the Queen" tattooed on his fingers. He spoke to you?'

'Yes. To set up your escape.'

'No. No. He spoke to you once before, long ago, perhaps?'

'No.'

'Never?'

'No.'

'He told you to speak to Henrique Valentin.'

Vaczka shook his head. 'I was in prison with Valentin by coincidence.'

'Yes, but you spoke to him again, later.'

'Yes, of course.'

'Who commanded it so?'

Vaczka stared at him, his eyes bunched, as if unsure of himself. 'You did.'

'Me?'

'In the cathedral, the Greek Orthodox priest.'

Boese sat very still, aware that time was short. He thought hard for a moment. 'Listen very carefully,' he said. 'Soon you will be interviewed by a detective whose name is Swann. The FBI may be with him.' He bent forward then, as the keys rattled in the lock. 'I want you to tell them this.'

*

Swann was at the Yard early, and briefed the team on everything that had happened in the United States. Logan arrived with Byrne shortly afterwards, and they prepared to go and interview Vaczka. Webb told them about the visit from the priest that morning.

'Priest?' Swann looked carefully at him. 'Has he been vetted?'

'Of course he has, Jack. Something about Vaczka's mother. She's dying, or very ill anyway, in Poland.'

'You're sure that's all it was.'

'They are. That's all that matters.'

They were unaware of it, but Tal-Salem watched Byrne and Logan get out of their taxi at Scotland Yard, and he also watched them all leave the underground car park in Webb's car. He picked up the phone, dialled a cloned cellphone and reported everything to Boese. They had decided to let the priest live. He would not talk all the time he thought his sister was in jeopardy, and even if he did, it would not harm them now. Tal-Salem then made two more phone calls to the remnants of Vaczka's gang, who were only too pleased to assist them.

Swann stared out of the window of Webb's car at the familiar, yet unfamiliar streets of London. 'Nothing changes, does it,' he said.

'No.'

He looked at Byrne over his shoulder. 'Boese's here, I can feel it.'

Byrne nodded, briefcase on his lap. 'It's more than likely, yes.'

'No. I can feel him, Louis. It's like cancer returning. They say you *know* when you've got it again.'

They pulled up the ramp at Paddington Green and got out of the car. Swann questioned the custody sergeant about the priest, and was satisfied. Vaczka was already in the interview room, with his solicitor, waiting for them. He sat with his arms folded and his face sullen and closed. Swann sat down, Byrne alongside him. Logan was seated against the wall. Swann opened the file and placed a fresh tape in the machine. He went through the formalities and then looked hard at Vaczka.

'Tell us about Henrique Valentin, Jorge.'

'I don't know him.'

'Yes, you do. You were in Rikers Island Prison with him in New York.'

Vaczka said nothing.

'Don't tell me you can't remember.' Swann pointed to Byrne. 'He's with the FBI. He remembers.'

'Selling weapons to the FALN,' Byrne said quietly. 'Or trying to anyways.'

'You were working for Abu Nidal,' Swann went on. 'You still work for him. He funds you all the time you're in this country. Tell me something, Jorge. Did Storm Crow borrow you from the ANO, or were they in on it too?'

Vaczka's face was sour. He glanced at his solicitor. 'So I did some time in the States. So what.'

'So everything.' Swann leaned closer to him. 'You met Valentin in prison, and my guess is, a little later on, somebody asked you to contact him again.'

'Did they?'

'I think so.' Swann pressed the ends of his fingers together. 'I'll tell you what else I think, Jorge. You broke the wrong man out of jail.' He paused for a moment, then said: 'Have you ever wondered who told us you were here?'

Vaczka stared at him.

'Ah, a nerve at last.' Swann bent his head towards him. 'Boese isn't Storm Crow, Jorge. Didn't you know that?'

'I don't know what you're talking about.'

'Sure you do. You see, you're one of the main links in the chain. Somebody spoke to you, you spoke to Valentin, Valentin spoke to somebody else, and a little way down the line, we have Ismael Boese, the protégé of Carlos.' He paused, arms folded. 'But not Storm Crow. We were handed Boese on a plate, so the real Storm Crow could retire without any fuss. The only thing that spoiled it was you subcontracting. Put the cat right among the pigeons, that did.' Swann sat back in the chair. 'He double-crossed you, Jorge. He tipped off the security services about you – guns to the Loyalists in Ulster, Abu Nidal, the whole nine yards.' He stopped talking and looked Vaczka in the eye. 'You went and spoiled his plan and now Boese is out there looking for him. You know something else, this is probably the safest place for you right now, because he knows exactly what you did.'

Vaczka was staring at him, a strange light in his eyes.

'Who spoke to you, Jorge? Who spoke to you all those years ago?'

For a moment Vaczka just sat there, saying nothing, looking through Swann at the wall. Suddenly he sat forward. 'I'll tell you what, Swann,' he said. 'Geronimo was the master of illusion. Ask the Jackal if he ever ate with the Crow. And who is *El Kebir*?'

Swann stared at him for a long moment. Vaczka was smiling now, laughter, merriment almost, in his eyes. Swann could feel the tingling across his back, the sweat in his palms. He did not say anything, just kept looking at Vaczka's smiling eyes, then he nodded, switched off the tape and stood up. They took Vaczka back to his cell and Swann brooded quietly. Logan rested the flat of her palm on his shoulder. He got up then and they followed him to the custody sergeant's desk, who looked up from the report he was writing. 'I want the address for that priest,' Swann said.

They found him locked in his bedroom, a frail old man

with weak, water-filled eyes that he dabbed at constantly. He was dressed in a faded, striped dressing gown, and he told them what had happened. 'They threatened my only sister in Poland,' he said, a choked breath in his voice. 'What could I do?'

'It's OK,' Swann told him.

'I had to lie. I had no other choice. They made me get in contact with the police, took pictures of me and then *he* came.'

'He?'

'A small, dark man with black eyes.'

'Ismael Boese,' Swann said.

'He didn't tell me his name.' And then the priest's face buckled into itself. 'The Storm Crow. The man that was responsible for killing those poor people in Rome?'

'I'm afraid so.'

He stared round the room. 'He was here, in this house, wearing my clothes. He ate my food.' He shook his head, as if not believing his own words.

Swann got up. 'Look,' he said. 'I'm going to arrange for someone to come down here and get a statement from you. OK?'

The priest nodded. Again Swann patted him on the arm. 'And don't worry. It really wasn't your fault.'

Tal-Salem saw them drive into the underground car park and he picked up the phone.

'They're back,' he said. 'They went to Paddington, then on to the priest's house.'

On the other end of the phone, Boese stared at the wall. 'Keep a watch at the airport,' he said.

On the fifteenth floor, Swann and Webb sat with Colson, Swann briefing him on what had happened with Vaczka, the priest and everything. Colson shook his head wearily.

'To be fair to them, we know how good Boese can be,' Swann said. 'Apparently, he was a dead ringer for the priest – face, hair, the lot.'

'Must've gone to make-up college or something,' Webb muttered.

'The question is, what're we going to do about it,' Swann went on. 'Ask the Jackal if he ever ate with the Crow. And who is *El Kebir*.'

Webb furrowed his brow. 'I've heard that somewhere.' He left them then and went back to his desk, where he started going through papers. He had seen it or something like it, but he could not remember where.

Swann was still talking with Colson. 'Sir, Boese has been leading us by the nose throughout all this. He's telling us that in one way, at least, Dubin was right – the only person who knows the true identity of Storm Crow is Carlos the Jackal.'

Colson tilted his head to one side. 'Jack, are you asking me what I think you are?'

'Yes, sir. I want to get permission to go and interview him.'

Colson went to put the diplomatic wheels in motion. Antiterrorist officers had interviewed Carlos before, over the shooting of Edward Sieff in 1974, so it ought not to be a problem. Meanwhile, Swann had other things to consider. He went back through the Storm Crow files and found the copies of Harrison's product from the time he was in Idaho. Byrne was working with Logan on reports for the FBI, and Webb was still looking through his own files. The phones were quiet today and an air of concentration filled the squad room.

Swann found what he was looking for: the photograph of the receipt and the Winthrop directions beneath it. He went looking for Christine Harris in the Special Branch cell. She showed him everything that they had got so far from the US Secret Service regarding the movement of money.

'I'm interested in the money that was paid to Vaczka,' he said, 'the two lots of five thousand dollars from Japan and Israel.'

Harris located the electronic transfer forms, and Swann studied the handwriting carefully, then he looked at the scraps of letters from Harrison's product. 'What're you thinking, Jack? That whoever wrote those, wrote on these bank forms?'

Swann did not say anything for a moment. He had a magnifying glass and was looking at the slant of the letters. 'These are capitals,' he said. 'So are the bank forms.' He laid the magnifying glass down then. 'You said the US Secret Service had uncovered more of these, more companies with the same handwriting on the transfer request forms?'

'That's right.'

'A Mexican bank involved?'

'Yeah, branches in the southern United States.'

'Can I copy these?'

'Sure.'

Swann photocopied the forms and went back to his desk. Byrne was talking to Webb. They were studying a single sheet of paper.

'What's that?' Swann asked them.

Webb showed him. It was the passenger manifest from the Washington to Detroit flight in August 1997.

Swann ran his index finger down the list of names and felt gooseflesh rise on his cheeks. J. L. Kebir. He stared at Webb and Byrne in turn.

Webb spoke quietly. 'I knew I'd seen it before. It's not *El Kebir*, but too similar for comfort.'

Byrne's face was grave. 'Dubin was in Washington. That flight was two days after the Shrivenham conference.'

Swann turned to him then. 'What happened to the copy I gave you, Louis?'

'I passed it on to Kovalski. His team were checking on it.'

'D'you want to make a call, see what's going on?'

'You bet.' Byrne picked up a phone.

Swann showed Logan the transfer forms. 'I'm going to fax this lot over to Harrison,' he said. 'I'm going to get him to give it to CJIS and see what they say. I'm going to do the same with the Questioned Document Section at Lambeth.'

'You think there might be a link?'

'I wouldn't, if there hadn't been those two payments to Vaczka. It still might be nothing, but nobody has ever got a handle on the money trail after that ten million dollars was dumped at the Virgina City Overlook.'

'It's a good idea,' she said. 'By the way, if you get to go to Paris, I want to come with you.'

'Deal,' he said, and kissed the end of her nose.

He went down to the exhibits office to phone Harrison. Quite why, he did not know, he just felt he wanted the privacy. He told him what he planned to do and then faxed the copies of the bank forms over to him. Then he packaged the rest and sent it down to Lambeth, priority one.

That evening, he introduced Logan to his children. Rachael, his former wife, brought them over, and they came bounding up the stairs and into the living room. Logan dropped to one knee. 'Hey, how you doing?' she said.

Charlotte, the youngest, shrank back from her for a moment. 'You talk funny,' she said. Joanne was watching her carefully, as if not sure what to say.

'Cheyenne works for the FBI,' Swann explained. 'She's from America, Charley.'

'Cheyenne's an Indian name, isn't it,' Joanne said.

Logan nodded. 'That's right. It is.'

'But you're not an Indian.'

She sat down on the settee, with the girls on either side of her. 'No,' she said. 'I'm African-American.'

That started them into a great conversation about America and the people and what happened to the Indians, slaves and everything. Swann made some food and poured wine into two, full-bellied glasses. The phone rang as he was about to dish the food.

'Swann,' he said, as he picked it up.

'Colson, Jack. You've got the all clear. The DST will meet you when you get to Paris.'

# 27

The following morning, Harrison phoned Swann before they left for Paris. He told him to stand by the fax, as he had a sample of handwriting coming over. Harrison had already sent it to his own people in Virginia, but he wanted a second opinion on whether it matched the bank transfer forms and maybe the Winthrop directions. When the page came through, Swann packaged it and sent it off to Lambeth. Then he, Webb and Logan were driven to Heathrow Airport.

They were met at Orly Airport by Yves Mercier from the DCPJ, together with an officer from the DST. Swann and Mercier knew each other from various operations in the past, most notably when Mercier's police artist drew the likeness which exposed Pia Grava as Brigitte Hammani, the Palestinian terrorist. They had a brief discussion with the DST officer, then Mercier drove them to the prison on the outskirts of Paris, where Carlos the Jackal would spend the rest of his life. Twenty-two years after murdering three DST agents in the Rue Toullier, he had finally been caught and convicted.

The prison was old: eighteenth century, according to Mercier. Swann gazed up at the battlement-like ramparts as the steel doors were opened and they were driven inside. Their ID was checked and rechecked, before they were led to a police interview suite in the west wing.

Swann stood with his hands on his hips, considering the table with two chairs on one side and a third bolted to the floor on the other side. Bars crisscrossed the reinforced glass of the window, both vertically and horizontally.

Swann could see pigeons huddled together on the guttering of the opposing wing. They waited for fifteen minutes, then heard the sound of heavily booted feet in the corridor outside. Somebody cursed softly, then the door was unlocked and Carlos the Jackal was carried in on a pole.

Swann stared at him, suspended like a piece of dead meat, with manacles keeping him in place. Two thickset guards held him, and they set him in the bolted-down chair. One of them watched, hand on his gun, while the other knelt and fastened the chains to the bolt loops set in the chair. All the time Carlos looked on impassively; hair brushed straight back from his head, pudgy, with still-boyish features, and a crinkled moustache lining his upper lip. He wore a blue prison overall, one piece with a zip fastener. He ignored Swann and Webb, but looked lasciviously at Logan, his tongue touching the edge of his teeth. The guards went outside and relocked the door. Carlos sat before them like a condemned man in the electric chair, his hands clasping the arms where the chains held them in place.

'What do we call you?' Swann said. 'Carlos? Ilych? Mr Sanchez?'

The Jackal was still looking at Logan, who stood by the window. 'My friends call me Carlos,' he said to her, voice soft with a Spanish accent. His eyes were dark and a little yellowed at the edges. 'What's your name, my dear?'

'Logan.'

'And where are you from, Logan?'

'The United States. I work for the FBI.'

'FBI? Their special agents are much prettier than I remember.'

'Carlos.' Swann's voice was sharper. 'My name's Swann, from Scotland Yard. We'd like to speak to you about *El Kebir*.'

Carlos looked at him now, directly in the eye, and Swann knew he had struck a chord.

'You know who he is, don't you?'

Carlos cocked his head slightly to one side. '*El Kebir*.' He seemed to mull over the words for a moment.

'You know who he is,' Swann repeated.

'Josef El Kebir.' Carlos tried to shift position in the seat, but the chains restricted him. Again he looked at Logan. 'So undignified,' he said.

Swann glanced at Webb. That was the first time they had heard 'Josef'. Now the name on the passenger list made total sense. J. L. Kebir.

Carlos looked at Swann again. 'You clearly want something from me. What can you possibly offer me in return?'

'Nothing.'

'That's what I thought.' Carlos smiled at Logan.

'*El Kebir* is Storm Crow, isn't he,' Swann said.

'Is he?'

'You know he is.'

'Do I?'

'I think so.' Swann leaned back in his chair. 'What've you got to lose, Carlos? Why don't you talk to me. They say *El Kebir*'s more dangerous than you were. That must piss you off.'

Carlos ignored him, letting his eyes and his slow smile roam the contours of Logan's body.

Swann breathed stiffly, audibly. He looked sideways at Webb, and then at Logan. Carlos sat on the other side of the table, impassive. Again he looked at Logan. 'You really are very pretty,' he said.

Logan moved to the table. Webb got up and she sat down in his seat, resting one elbow on the wood and cupping her cheek with her palm.

'Am I?' she said. 'You think so?'

'Oh, yes.'

'You like black women, Carlos?'

'My dear, I like all women.' He tried to lean forward, but couldn't. 'They like me. I'm very experienced, you see.'

'I bet you are, honey.' She smiled at him, lowering her gaze so her eyelashes brushed her cheek. 'It's just a shame you're chained up.'

He laughed now, showing the white of his teeth. 'And that we're not alone.'

She looked from Swann to Webb, then back in his eyes. 'Pretend they're not here.'

He made a face. 'I don't think I can. You see, a man likes his privacy.'

'I understand.' She reached over and touched the back of his hand. His eyes softened. She touched him again, then sat back and folded her arms. 'I wish there was something I could do for you.'

'Talk,' he said. 'Talk is enough for now. Just to hear a woman's voice, and such a pretty woman too.'

'You know, you say the sweetest things.'

'Do I?'

'You know you do. All the ladies loved you. Carlos the Jackal, the most dangerous man in the world. What happened, baby doll, you disappeared off the face of the planet?'

'I have many homes, my dear. I like to relax, to party, see friends, girlfriends. I grew tired of the spotlight, the world's press speculating on my whereabouts. What I was planning next, my links with the KGB.'

'That was all bullshit, wasn't it,' she said.

'The KGB? Of course. I hated Russia, and Russian women. There, I don't like Russian women.'

Logan laughed. 'Tell me about Ismael Boese,' she said. 'You can do that much, can't you?'

533

Carlos did not reply. He was looking at her now as if Swann and Webb were not there.

'It's my job, honey,' Logan went on. 'Did you hear what he did in New Orleans?'

'A tanker. Impressive.'

'You trained him, didn't you, Carlos. All those years ago, when he was still just a kid. He was something of a protégé, wasn't he?'

Carlos looked a little wistful.

'You must've trained him well, because he's giving us the run-around.'

'He is?'

'Oh yes. He's led us all over the place.'

Swann was watching her, trying to decide if she was making progress or not.

'Tell me something, Carlos,' Logan said.

'What's that?'

'Did the Jackal ever eat with the Crow?'

He looked slantedly at her then and laughed, low in his throat. 'You're very clever, Logan.'

'You think so?'

'Yes. I do. They should promote you, the FBI.'

'Why don't you write and tell them?' Logan flashed her eyes at him. 'Well, did he? Did the Jackal ever eat with the Crow?'

Carlos looked at her for a long moment, then breath escaped his nose in a sigh. 'No, my dear, he did not.'

'Is *El Kebir* the Storm Crow?'

He smiled again. 'You *are* very clever, so I'll tell you something for free,' he said. 'Because you're pretty and you smell so good, and I haven't smelt a woman for what seems like eternity.' He paused, cocked his head to one side and looked longingly at her breasts. 'In 1976, Josef El Kebir tried to kill me. Right after I walked away from

Entebbe. Your own President Ford put a stop to it.' Again, he tried to lean forward. 'You see, *El Kebir* was CIA.'

Harrison was in Tom Kovalski's office. He was working his way through some files when Randy Shaeffer came in and told him that Swann was on the line from Paris.

Harrison reached across Kovalski's desk and picked up the phone. 'Hey, Jack. What's going on?'

'I'm still in Paris. We just interviewed Carlos.'

'How'd you get on? Did the old fart tell you anything?'

'He told Logan. She was brilliant, let him think he could get in her knickers. Listen, the stuff The Cub told you about Ben Dubin?'

'What about it?'

'Ask him if Dubin ever used Josef El Kebir as a *nom de guerre*?'

'Kebir?' Harrison thinned his eyes. 'That was one of the names on the flight manifest you got.'

'Right.'

'That guy don't exist, Jack. We've checked everybody and he doesn't exist.'

'Harrison, Carlos told us that *El Kebir* was a CIA agent. Ben Dubin's a CIA agent, and he was in the States on the 21st August. He could've been on that flight.'

For a moment Harrison was still. 'I'll try and get hold of The Cub. When you back in London?'

'First thing in the morning.'

'I'll call you.' Harrison put the phone down.

Tal-Salem had observed Swann, Webb and Logan leave Scotland Yard. Two Algerians, known of old to Boese, had followed them to Heathrow Airport and watched them check in for the flight to Paris. They phoned the information back to Tal-Salem. Now, he watched them return, and then he phoned Boese, who was waiting patiently in his small hotel in Perth, Scotland.

'They went to Paris,' Tal-Salem said.

Boese was thoughtful on the other end of the phone. 'We have no way of knowing what they're doing now, no way of knowing what they've discovered. Not until they move. Watch and wait. The timing will be everything.'

Swann and Logan were in the Special Branch cell, talking to Christine Harris. The door was open and Byrne and Webb stood in the corridor, listening. 'Josef El Kebir,' Swann said. 'Storm Crow is a man called Josef El Kebir.' He paused and looked across at Byrne. 'According to Carlos, *El Kebir* was CIA.'

Byrne was still, face grave, greying hair cut so close the artificial lights reflected off the pink of his scalp. 'And you're thinking Dubin.'

Swann nodded. 'Dubin was ISA, Louis. That's pretty serious stuff.'

'You're not kidding. Special forces, Jack. I guess Dubin would've been ground intel', though, embassy-linked. Official.'

'He's got a data base in Scotland the length of that corridor.' Swann flapped a hand. 'Every single incident that's ever happened anywhere, as far back as the Stern Gang in the forties. Every bad guy, every government agency. He's in and out of the State Department, Langley, and your headquarters all the time.'

Logan chewed her lip. 'You know something, Louis,' she said to Byrne. 'I've got this most weird feeling. Carlos was allowed to roam the world by a whole bunch of governments, including ours, until his usefulness ran out. It's possible that the CIA know about Dubin and are, at best, turning a blind eye, or, at worst, actually sanctioning it.' She stared at Swann. 'It wouldn't be the first time.

Special relationship or not. Friendly countries stiff each other all the time. Israel tried to fuck with us in the past. Tom Kovalski was a spy hunter before he fought terrorism. He busted two State Department guys who spied on us for Mossad.'

A cold silence fell then. Outside, the wind was blowing and it seemed to send a chill through the little room. Harris had her computer running. 'January 1976,' she said, indicating the screen. 'CIA plot to assassinate Carlos the Jackal. An ex-PFLP terrorist was hired for ten thousand dollars to carry out the hit. The deal was brokered in a hotel room in Athens. It was only aborted after President Ford decided to cancel all future CIA liquidation operations.' She thought for a moment then. 'Leave me alone a minute,' she said. 'I want to talk to Box.'

They left her and trooped back to the squad room. 'What do we do now?' Webb asked.

Swann stared out of the window. 'I don't know.' He glanced at Colson. 'What d'you want to do about Dubin, sir?'

'Nothing yet.' Colson lifted his hands at his sides. 'What can we do, Jack? You've told me that Storm Crow is a CIA agent called *El Kebir*. You haven't shown me how that man is Dr Benjamin Dubin.'

Swann took Logan down to the canteen and they ate some food. Swann picked at his, not really interested, but poured his third cup of coffee. Logan looked over the rim of her cup at him.

'Jack, your insides are gonna rot.'

'Probably.'

His pager sounded at his side and he turned the display to look at it. 'Chrissie wants us upstairs,' he said.

The squad room was a buzz of excitement when they got back up there. Christine Harris held a sheet of printed computer paper in her hand, and Byrne stood reading it over her shoulder. Harris looked up as Swann and Logan came in.

'What is it?' Swann asked her.

Harris handed him the paper. 'I talked to Box 500,' she told him. 'Then I did some checking of my own. Special Branch airport-entry records, February 1976.' She cocked one eyebrow. 'MI6 received a tip-off in February 1976 that a CIA operative was passing through Heathrow on his way to Athens. Seems *we* might've been in on the deal to kill Carlos, as well. Why not, he'd already shot Edward Sieff and bombed an Israeli bank in the City.'

'What're you saying, Chrissie?'

'I'm saying that Josef El Kebir came through Heathrow on his way to call off the PFLP hitman in Greece. Box 500 told us, and the Special Branch team pulled him at the airport. They had a little chat, as we like to do. Then they sent him on his way.'

'And?'

'And later we identified him through MI6. His name was Benjamin Dubin.'

Boese rang St Andrews University. Nothing had happened since Tal-Salem had contacted him after the police returned from Paris. Boese had decided to gamble. If he was wrong, it would not matter. He would just move on to other options. 'I'd like to speak with Dr Dubin, please,' he said. 'Department of political relations.'

'One moment.' The operator connected him and he waited, moisture on his lip, recalling the darkness of the Spanish projects in Arlington and the chill voice from the rooftop. Dubin had been in Washington at that time. Dubin had interviewed the Jackal and Dubin had been in the special secure unit at Reading Prison last October.

'Dr Dubin's office.' A woman's voice.

'I'd like to speak with Ben, please.'

'I'm afraid you can't, sir. He's away.'

Boese closed one hand into a fist. 'I'm sorry,' he said. 'This is Dr Burden at Columbia University in New York. I was really hoping to catch him.'

'That will be impossible for the next couple of days, at least. He's taken some of his students on a walking trip to Ben Nevis.'

'Thank you. I'll call him when he gets back.' Boese hung up, picked up his bag and walked downstairs.

Swann phoned Harrison in Washington. 'Forget my last request,' he said.

'Why, what's happened?'

Swann told him. 'It's Dubin, JB. We got it from Carlos, and it was confirmed by Special Branch over here.' He let air hiss from between his teeth. 'No wonder he wanted to perpetuate the myth about Boese. It all makes sense now. The prison visit. That's when Boese knew he'd been betrayed. He was waiting for something, some sign. Dubin never gave him one. He just wanted to gloat. Think about it, JB. He'd already written a book on Carlos. Add to that, one on Storm Crow, and suddenly he's got a reason to start having a lot of money, all those royalties flowing in.'

'Makes sense, Jack.' Harrison paused for a moment. 'You heard anything on that handwriting I beamed over?'

'Not yet.'

Swann put the phone down and then dialled the number of St Andrews University. He spoke at length with Dubin's secretary. She told him that Dubin was up north and then she said: 'You're the second person to ask about him in as many minutes.'

Swann felt sweat break out on his brow. 'I am?' he said quickly. 'Who was the other one?'

'Somebody from Columbia University in New York. Dr Burden, he said his name was.'

Swann thought for a moment. 'Did he sound American?'

She hesitated. 'Well, I suppose so, yes.'

'Where exactly *is* Dr Dubin?'

'He's staying in Fort William, the Eil Hotel. It's beautiful, right on the banks of the loch.'

Swann put the phone down and wiped the moisture from his palm on his thigh. He turned back to the others. 'Dubin's on a walking holiday and I'm the second person to ask about him in as many minutes.' He sat for a moment longer, looked at his watch, then picked up the phone again. He spoke to international directory enquiries and asked for the number of Columbia.

'Dr Burden, please,' he said, when the line was answered.

'What department, sir?'

'I don't know.'

'One moment.'

He waited while the telephonist checked her listings.

'I'm sorry, sir,' she said. 'We don't have a Dr Burden registered at this campus.'

'You sure?'

'Absolutely positive.'

'Of course you are.' Swann stared at the faces of his colleagues 'Thank you,' he said, and put the phone down.

He took the briefing in the conference room, planning exactly what they were going to do. Boese had led them to this: primed Jorge Vaczka, and probably watched them fly to Paris. After that, it didn't take a genius to figure things out. Black team from SO19 had been tasked and they had got to the Yard as quickly as possible, vans and Range Rovers all ready to go. The commander was on the telephone to the local police, letting them know that he was sending an armed team into their area to make an arrest. His Scottish counterpart was not very happy about a bunch of armed Londoners on his turf, but Garrod reminded him of his nationwide terrorism jurisdiction. A nice way of saying there was nothing he could do about it. When the short briefing was over, Swann looked at his watch: two-thirty already. The team would be helicoptered from the roof of the Yard to Lippetts Hill, north-east of London. From there, they would fly in a fixed wing to Inverness and drive south.

Logan phoned Kovalski and told him what had happened. She told him about the CIA connection and almost felt the shudder run down his spine.

'Oh God, Chey,' he said. 'Let's just hope he's a lone wolf gone bad.'

'You'll soon know if he isn't,' she said. 'Because we're about to pop him.'

'He's a rogue player, Chey. He's got to be. There's no way the CIA would sanction an attack on London.'

'You sure, Tom? I don't know that I am.'

'Don't even think about it. What about Boese?'

'He led us to the Jackal. He must've been hoping we'd lead *him* to Storm Crow. There's been no sign of him so far, but we think he tried to contact Dubin.'

'So he's gonna try and kill him.'

'Well, I guess he's not going up for a lecture.' Logan paused for a moment. 'Dubin was in D.C. when Chucho Mannero bought it.'

'You're right. He was.' Kovalski ran a hand through his hair. 'You going along for the ride?'

'Course I am. My boyfriend's running the show.'

Kovalski laughed. 'Don't you get any ideas about staying in England, Logan. I need your ass back here.'

'Aye, aye, Captain.' She put the phone down on him.

# 28

Angie Byrne had a sickness deep in the pit of her stomach. Ghosts were haunting her; they were there when she fell asleep at night and there again in the morning. The night when her home had been invaded grew in intensity in her mind. The passing time had not served to diminish the experience – she relived it again and again. And now she was stalked by a new fear and she did not know what to do with it. She was having lunch in the partners' dining room in the offices on New York Avenue, playing with the food she had been served, only half listening to the conversations going on around her. She watched Steve Nelson, one of the younger partners, directly across the table from her, as he cut his meat with his fork. His left hand was resting on the whiteness of the tablecloth, a thick, gold wedding band on his finger. Angie pushed her plate away and excused herself. Back in her office, she closed the door and leaned on it. Case files stood like mini-towers on her desk. She walked to the window, rested her forehead against the cool of the glass and looked out across the Federal Triangle. She could see the height of the clock tower on the old post office building, and the time seemed to be ticking away from her. She looked back at the desk, at the telephone, which almost seemed to beckon her. She bit her lip, pressed her hand against the glass and pushed herself away. Again she looked at the phone, then she cursed and picked it up. She dialled and waited.

'FBI. Domestic Terrorism,' a woman's voice in her ear.

*

The team that flew to Scotland consisted of the eight members of specialist firearms officer black team, plus Webb, Swann and Logan. Byrne was staying in London to liaise with Washington and clear up some outstanding issues with the leg-att. The helicopter took them from the roof of Scotland Yard, north-east across London. Logan sat next to Swann, looking down on the spires of the city. They swung low in an arc over the M25 motorway and settled on the landing pad at the SO19 training facility at Lippetts Hill. Quickly now, they transferred to the fixed-wing aircraft, which was already idling on the runway. The firearms officers, dressed in plain clothes, threw their black canvas kit bags ahead of them; weapons, ammunition, distraction devices and equipment for gaining entry. Neither Swann nor Webb was armed. Conversation was minimal, the adrenalin pumping as soon as the briefing was over. Swann thought long and hard about it all. Two situations to deal with: Boese, the man who attacked England and Rome with chemical weapons, and Dubin, the mastermind behind it.

He let a little air escape his lips and glanced at Logan, sitting next to him. When this was over, she would be going back to the United States and the loneliness would overtake him once more. He looked forwards again, not wanting to confront that level of desperation, with both Boese and Storm Crow still at large. Maybe they would kill each other and save them all some trouble. He thought back to when Boese had been apprehended the previous May, the doubt that had fixed in his gut even then, a doubt that had proved to be right. He thought back to the past few weeks in the United States, with Boese leading them all over the country. Dubin could have struck at him earlier than Arlington, but to strike would be to explode his own myth. Better just to watch, and see if the FBI could get him.

He glanced at the SFO team, who were relaxing now. There was enough time, when they hit Fort William and loaded up in the vehicles, for the adrenalin to flow again. They had telephoned Dubin's hotel in advance, to try to get an idea of his whereabouts. The receptionist told them that he and his party of students had walked on to Ben Nevis that morning, and were intending to spend the night in the mountain hut just north of the observatory ruin. Swann had considered his options, given that information, and discussed them with Mick Rob, the SO19 team leader. The party was six in total – Dubin and, potentially, five hostages. Swann did not doubt that he would be armed. He would know that Boese was still out there, and would be taking no chances. Perhaps that was why he had chosen *now* to make such a trip, to draw Boese to him. As far as Swann was aware, winter walking was not one of his preferred hobbies. The students were the problem, though. Neither Dubin or Boese would baulk at taking them hostage.

Swann left his seat and joined Mick Rob, whose winter jacket was unzipped and the butt of his Glock protruded from the quick-release holster under his arm. Swann had a map of the area with him and spread it on his lap. He indicated the mountain hut where Dubin and his party would be staying.

'It'll be dark if we go in today,' he said. 'We've got a long hike from the distillery car park.'

Rob scratched his lip. 'What's the trail like?'

'It's OK. But no mountaineer or mountain rescue man would recommend walking round the Ben in the dark.'

'What about Boese?'

Swann didn't reply for a moment. 'I don't know,' he said. 'I don't know for sure that he'll have Dubin's exact location, but we ought to assume he will.'

'Given what you told us at the briefing, he'll want to get the jump on us.'

Swann nodded. 'He may have back-up as well. Tal-Salem's never been caught.'

Rob studied the map. 'The other option is to sit tight in the cars and attack at dawn.'

'Be bloody cold,' Swann said.

'So what. We've done worse.'

'It's your call, Mick.'

'Let's see what the weather's like when we get there. Any idea of the forecast?'

'Snow and more snow.'

'Why did I think you'd say that?'

Swann moved back to his seat next to Logan. Webb was seated across the aisle and was chatting to her. 'Really?' he said.

'Possibly, yeah.'

'What's that?' Swann asked her.

She laid her hand over his. 'Nothing, hon. I'll tell you about it later.'

Swann leaned across her then and told Webb what he and Rob had discussed. 'Suck it and see, then,' Webb said. 'It'll be dark even before we load up in the cars. Boese isn't going to attack in the dark.'

'Isn't he? We don't know that.'

'Jack,' Webb said. 'You and me are climbers. We wouldn't walk in the dark.'

They were quiet again then, the country slipping by underneath them, hidden by dark swathes of cloud. The weather had been foul in the north and Swann doubted very much whether they could make the mountain hut that night. They had brought plenty of gear with them. Before the briefing, he had raced home and collected ropes, boots, crampons and his ice axes, just in case. If nothing else – they needed to look like a party of hikers.

*

Boese drove north from Perth, two hours up the A9, then the A82 to Fort William. Time was on his side. The Antiterrorist Branch would send their own team up from London, he knew that much. Storm Crow was *their* prize and their arrogance would not allow the locals to interfere. He had phoned the hotel and had learned that *El Kebir* and his party of five were spending the night in a mountain hut near the old observatory ruin. That gave him options, although flurries of snow were already falling against the windscreen of the hire car. In the back, he had warm clothing and stout boots, a set of crampons and an ice axe. He had studied the map in some detail, and intended to walk in, kill *El Kebir* and walk back to his car, like any other hiker. Contingencies were difficult; his only other option was to hike for miles to the north. He could do that if he had to: he was fit and strong and had spent many months sleeping on the cold floor of the prison for just such eventualities.

Tal-Salem was on his way north right now, but he was flying and that would take time. He had waited in London long enough to see a helicopter first land, then take off from the roof of Scotland Yard. He had contacted Boese on the cloned mobile phone. The helicopter was all Boese needed to know. His plan had worked. They had got something from the Jackal. Probably they'd appealed to his vanity, that had always been his undoing. No doubt he bragged to them.

Boese thought about Swann then, the stupid English policeman, who trailed in his wake like some broken shadow. He had watched him for many months before they put the plan for Jakob Salvesen into action. They had sucked him in well, but to his credit, he was fighting back now. A strange irony occurred to Boese then, and it was the one factor that disturbed him. Storm Crow had picked Swann out because of his weakness, his vulnerability emotionally, after the death of his climbing partner on the cliffs of Nanga Parbat. Here they were almost three years later, and heading for the mountains. He knew then that he had to get to Dubin first, tonight if at all possible. If this snow kept up, they would not send their team in till morning. Swann, with his mountain experience, would not allow it.

But he would get there first; no matter the weather – if not tonight, then at first light in the morning. He glanced in the rearview mirror at the case on the back seat of the car, the broken-down sniper's rifle inside it.

He got to Fort William and stopped to buy coffee, which he poured into two Thermos flasks, and stowed them in the backpack he would carry. It was three-thirty now. It had stopped snowing, but the sky was still dulled white with the threat. Back in the car, he checked his food rations and sleeping-bag. Again he looked at the map, and noticed that there were a number of mountain huts dotted around the area. He might have company, but if he needed it, there was shelter. He sat in the car with the engine idling, his 9mm in the waistband holster, and the rifle that Tal-Salem had procured for him stowed safely in its case. That case would fit in his backpack, and he could dispose of it when the time came. He checked his appearance in the mirror and smiled. Swann would never recognize him. He engaged first gear again, and trundled up the main road until it crossed the river. Here he turned off, the River Nevis on his left, and took the minor road that would eventually bring him to the car park. No more than two miles north of that point, *El Kebir* was waiting, oblivious of his presence.

Halfway along the minor road, just beyond the Glen Nevis Hotel, the snow began to fall again. Cloud settled like a stained bandage over the land and the sky grew dark, as if something old and long dead had been disturbed. The wind lifted, tossing at the branches of trees, and the snowfall became a blizzard. Boese scrunched his eyes and drove on.

The arrest team landed at Inverness where the hire cars were waiting for them. Swann drove with Webb, Logan, and Rob, the SFO team leader. The snow was falling heavily and halfway down the A9, Rob looked over the seat at Swann. 'Blizzard.'

Swann looked at the sky. 'Looks like it's set for the night. Shit.' He bit his lip and thought hard. Fort William was still half an hour away and the car park they wanted another half-hour beyond it, following the course of the river. 'What d'you reckon, Webby?'

'Is there anywhere we can spend the night other than in the car park?' Webb asked him.

Swann looked at the map. 'No. Nothing's marked till you get to the climbing club hut.'

Webb hit the accelerator and the Range Rover lurched forward. 'Let's see what it's like when we get to the distillery,' he said. 'You never know, the snow might stop.'

The convoy of vehicles sped along the road to Fort William, then Webb turned sharp left, with the River Lochy coursing the valley on their right.

'How far from here?' he asked. The snow was banked on the side of the road, but patches of black still showed on the lower flanks of the mountains out to the east.

'No distance.' Swann looked at the darkening sky, the swirl of the blizzard cutting visibility in half. 'Not much daylight left,' he said. 'It's a two- to three-hour hike even in good conditions. And that only takes us as far as the hut.'

Rob leaned against the glass, trying to see through the whirling clouds of snow. 'We'll bivouac at the distillery,' he said. 'Go in at first light.'

\*

Harrison parked his car in the half-empty parking lot of the Criminal Justice Information Services Division, in Clarksburg, West Virginia. He had decided to drive here in person rather than get them to send his answers over. He flipped away his cigarette, took some fresh chew from his tin and tucked it under his lip. He sucked and spat and tugged his hair where it was stuck in his collar. He showed his pass at reception and made his way to the Questioned Documents Section. He was deep in thought, for some reason remembering the tunnels under Jakob Salvesen's property, and the boom of a 454 Casull tearing at his eardrums.

He walked the length of the corridor to the technicians' lab, and pressed the buzzer. An operative let him in, glancing at Harrison's shield, which was flipped open in the pocket of his shirt. Harrison wanted to spit tobacco juice, but there was nothing to spit in. He swallowed, grimaced, and was shown to the technician's desk.

'What you got for me, bro?' he asked.

The technician took the file from the stack on his desk and opened it. 'The bits of words photographed under the receipt you gave me,' he said. 'They're difficult. There's not enough of them really.'

'So you can't say?' Harrison felt his heart sink in his chest.

'No, I think I *can* say. But a defence lawyer would tear me to pieces in court.'

'OK,' Harrison said slowly. 'We'll worry about that when the time comes. Right now, I want to know what you think.'

'I think the hand is the same.' The man sat back. He was in his forties, balding, with a gold and black ring on the little finger of his right hand. 'I've been checking documents for years, Harrison. I'd say the same hand wrote them. An accurate assessment for prosecution purposes would be "probable".'

'For all three samples?'

'No. The other sample you gave me is, in my opinion, unquestionably the same as that on the bank transfer forms.'

Harrison sat still for a moment, letting the information sink through him. He was cold and yet at the same time his blood burned like a slow fire. Deep inside, emotions were beginning to stir, the type of emotions he doubted he'd be able to keep a lid on.

'Can I take this with me?' He indicated the file.

'Sure. I got copies.'

'Thanks.' They shook hands and Harrison walked back to his car. In the parking lot, he spat juice and wiped his mouth, a small pulse beginning to work at his temple. He took the cellphone from where it lay on the seat and called headquarters. He got Randy Shaeffer. 'Randy,' he said. 'Give me the number of that secret service agent the Brits have been talking to.'

Angie Byrne looked out of her bedroom window as Tom Kovalski pulled up in his car. He parallel parked, then got out on to the cobbles. The wind was whipping the street hard from the Potomac River, where little surf breakers chipped away at the road. She met him at the door, smiled and showed him inside.

'What's going on, Angie?' he said. 'You sounded real down on the phone.'

She led the way into the living room and stood in front of the white marble fireplace. Kovalski sat on the red leather couch, the other side of the coffee table.

'You wanna drink or anything, Tom?'

'No, thank you. I'm fine.' He sat forward, elbows on his knees, fingers entwined, and looked at her. Her face was pale, shadows etching the skin below her eyes. There was a light in her eyes, though, that flickered now and then, like an animal being hunted.

'All this has got to you, huh,' he said gently.

She sat down heavily in the armchair, then shifted herself to the edge, as if she could not get comfortable. 'You could say that, yeah.'

'I'm not surprised, Angie.' He tried to offer encouragement with a smile. 'Anyway, you called me. What's up?'

She looked at him now and her lower lip quivered; none of the toughness he normally associated with her was evident. She looked more like a frightened child and he had to fight the desire to hug her. 'You said on the phone, you think two people are calling you,' he said.

'I do, yes.'

Kovalski nodded slowly.

'You don't think so?'

'I don't know, Angie. It's hard to tell from the tapes.' He made an open-handed gesture. 'But you were the recipient. Your emotions were played with. Only you can know for sure.'

'I do know, Tom. I'm absolutely positive.'

'OK. Then I accept what you say.'

'There's something else.' She broke off, voice getting caught in her throat. 'The person that broke in, got in, whatever. The one that paid me the visit . . .' Again, her voice dribbled away from her.

'Boese.'

She shook her head. 'No, Tom. Not Boese.'

'You're sure?'

'Yes.'

'Why?'

'Because there was no sign of forced entry. Because he took the gun I kept by my bed.'

Kovalski was staring at her now. 'What're you saying, Angie?'

'He leant against me, when he ran the gun over my body.' She shivered violently as she said it, the moment of disgust coming over her again. 'Something round and hard pressed against my shoulder. That's happened to me since, Tom.'

He shifted to the edge of his seat. 'Since? What d'you mean?'

'My husband wears his wedding ring round his neck.'

Dubin watched with a certain amount of pleasure as one of the students got the fire crackling in the stove. The walk had been arduous, cutting a path between the mountains, with the splendour of the amphitheatre all around, and Ben Nevis itself to the south. They would return by the same route in the morning, making their way back to the distillery, north of Fort William. He sat on his sleeping-bag by the fire and watched as the students prepared the food.

'You sit there, Ben,' one of the girls told him. 'You're getting a little old for this, aren't you.'

Dubin smiled at her, a light in his eyes. 'You should speak to my wife,' he said. 'She'll tell you if I'm getting old.'

Outside, the snow fell against the walls of the hut and lay thick on the ground like a fresh white carpet. Dubin stood and looked out into the gathering darkness; another half an hour and it would be fully dark. There would be no moon tonight. He looked back at his students, some of whom would go into industry when their course was completed; some the military and a few of them the security services. The odd one might plump for a Ph.D. and enter academia, but he would not recommend that.

Tina handed him a bowl of soup. 'There you go, Ben. Just what the doctor ordered.'

*

Boese parked in the empty car park at the bottom of the Glen Nevis road. From here he could make the quickest entry to the Coire Leis, where Dubin would be walking tomorrow. But the route was also the steepest and most treacherous. He considered the snow and waited, engine off, his breath coming as steam. *El Kebir* was in the shelter north of the observatory ruin, but there was another hut to the north of that, on the ridge of Carn Mor Dearg. In good visibility it would take him two hours. He was fit and fast and strong. But there was no visibility and he considered his options. The team from London would not make their approach this way, he was sure of that. Few people did; only seasoned climbers who wanted to abseil from the Carn Mor Dearg Arete into the Coire Leis. He had no need to abseil: what he wanted was height, and he could traverse the ridge as far as he desired to find a suitable place to settle. Once it was over, he could go north on foot or back along the ridge to his car. They would be on the valley floor and could never overtake him. They would not even see him. Taking his sleeping-bag from the back seat, he worked his legs inside, and poured hot coffee from the Thermos flask.

Fifteen miles north-east as the crow flies, Swann lay huddled with Logan in the back of the Range Rover. Rob and Webb had settled themselves in the front, passing back coffee and sandwiches. The windows misted with condensation and they could no longer see any movement from the other cars. Logan talked softly to Swann through the darkness. No moon and no stars. They could not see if the snow was still falling. Webb was reminiscing with Rob, about the many times they had lain up in vehicles in the dead of night, waiting for the 4 a.m. takeout.

'Jack, there's something I want to talk to you about.'

Logan's voice was low, her head on his shoulder, the warmth of her breath against his neck.

He sipped coffee and passed the cup to her. 'What?'

'I need to ask you something.'

'So ask.'

'It's difficult.' Her voice was almost a whisper now. Swann nestled down more closely, so her lips brushed his ear. 'I need to know how you feel about me.'

He was silent for a moment, his children's faces in his mind all at once. He felt the snow outside, thought of Pia and betrayal and slipping deeper into the abyss. He sighed heavily and twisted his face to hers. 'Chey,' he said. 'I think I love you. But I'm fucked up in the head. I've been burned as badly as I think it can get, and to tell you the truth I'm scared.'

'Why?'

'Because *this* has happened to us and after tomorrow you're going back to Washington.'

'And that scares you?'

'Of course it does. I might never see you again.'

She kissed him then and sought out his hand with hers. 'Let me tell you something, Jack. I was attracted to you the first time I came over here. I wasn't about to tell you then – you were with Pia. But she's gone, so now I can tell you.'

He squeezed her fingers, smelling the scent of her close to him. They slouched like high-school lovers on the back seat of a bus. 'Jack,' she went on, 'there's an opening in the London embassy for a deputy legal attaché. One of the guys there, right now, is going back to Washington.'

Swann was stunned. 'You mean you want to apply?'

'I could.'

'Would you get it?'

'I've already spoken to Bill Matheson, the current leg-att, and he's keen. He knows my work. I don't think Tom

554

Kovalski would stand in my Way either. There'd be other applicants, sure. But, honey, I think the work I've done over here ahead of time has got to give me the edge.'

'Jesus, Chey. You mean this?'

'Jack, all I've got in the States, apart from my blood family, is the FBI. If I get this posting, I can still have the FBI, but I can do my job over here, with you.'

'How long's the posting?'

'Who cares.' Again, she kissed his cheek. 'A day at a time, baby. That's all we can do.'

'Take it. Apply. I'll help you write the letter.' Swann clutched her to him and whispered in her ear. 'I love you, Cheyenne Logan. I don't want you to leave.' He was suddenly aware that the conversation up front had stilled to nothing. 'You earwigging, Webby?' he said.

'What do you think, Flash? I was trained in surveillance, remember.'


Kovalski sat in his office with Harrison, the door firmly closed, neither of them saying anything. The information Harrison had got from CJIS lay on Kovalski's desk, next to the ever-present copy of the constitution. Kovalski fisted his knuckles against his chin and looked over the ridges at Harrison. He sat holding an empty Coke can, a lump of tobacco in his cheek. 'Our secret service,' Kovalski said.

'Yeah. They were looking at the US accounts for the British and came up with two five-thousand-dollar payments. They looked further and further and pretty soon they find bank accounts all over the world for companies that don't exist. The directors are all different, but every time an electronic transfer's requested, the handwriting on the form is the same.' He pointed to the Winthrop directions from Salvesen's study. 'The fella over at CJIS hasn't got enough there to get a conviction, but his guts tell him it's the same.' He broke off for a moment rolling the chew in his mouth.

Kovalski snaked his tongue across his lips and frowned. 'OK,' he said. 'Make the call. See what you can find out.'

Harrison nodded and got up. In the outer office, he sat down at Schaeffer's empty desk and called the ordnance museum in Baltimore. Colonel Atwood answered.

'Bill? Johnny Buck again. The Cub told me he was duck hunting. I need to know where he's at.'

The first strands of light played across the snow-covered car park and Boese moved in his sleeping-bag. He was stiff and sore, but his eyes were sharp. He kicked his booted feet out of the sleeping-bag and checked his handgun. Then he climbed out of the car and stamped his feet, flapping his arms against his sides in the cold. He was alone; nothing save himself, the sudden height of the mountains and the crows that circled the trees. From the back seat, he took the rifle case and checked it, wiping the thin layer of condensation from the barrel, before sliding the case into his backpack. He fitted his crampons, then swung the pack between his shoulder blades. His breath steamed, warm against the cold of the day. He pulled on military issue gloves and studied the guidebook he had bought. The sun lifted above the mountain and he raised a hand to shade his eyes, studying the line of the horizon. He would take the diagonal route up the side of the hill to where the saddle lay between Meall Cumhann and Ben Nevis itself.

He started walking, using the lengthy axe to gauge the depth of the snow, his boots sinking at first in the spindrift, until he hit higher ground where the ice lay in slabs. His calves ached with the sudden exertion, having been immobile for twelve hours. If the police were also moving, he knew he was ahead of them, because their three-hour walk would only take them as far as the climbing club hut. *El*

*Kebir* was well back from there, on the Observatory Ridge. When he started back, he would either traverse the ridge for a while and drop into the coire from there, or, more likely, use the hard-packed snow to angle a path down the easier slopes. Boese climbed on; the fullness of his plan now stretched across his mind. Whichever option *El Kebir* took, he would be waiting. No need for open confrontation – too risky with Swann and his team of firearms officers making their own approach. Just get the job done with the minimum of fuss, then head back to the car. Tal-Salem would have passports and plane tickets, and within a few more hours, they would both be history.

At the saddle, he headed north-west, following the line of the ridge. An hour from here it merged into angled slopes, and he would turn north-east on to the Carn Mor Dearg Arete, where the climbers abseiled in.

SFO team leader Mick Rob woke everyone an hour before dawn. The night air was freezing, but still, and the cloud cover had been replaced by an inky-black sky patterned with slivers of ice. Half a moon winked weakly over the hillside and the snow bounced back in reflection. 'What d'you think, Jack?' he said.

Swann was out of the car and standing with gloved hands in his jacket pockets.

'Visibility is good. The first section is easy enough, so long as you can see. It's going to take us a good three hours, though, Mick.'

'That's why I wanted to move now. If Boese is here and he's got the drop on us, we might make up the time.' They checked their equipment: PX back-to-back radio sets; no contact with the outside, except a hand-held Cougar that linked them with the local police. So far, they had made no contact other than to confirm their presence. When

Dubin, and hopefully Boese, were arrested, they would be flown straight back to London.

They set out, eleven of them, Swann leading the way; boots on his feet, three-quarter shank in leather, with gaiters over the top. If he needed to, the crampons he had stowed with rope and axes in his pack could be strapped on to them. The snow was packed hard along the line of the railway. They crossed the main line and then negotiated half a mile of heathland that was always boggy after the spring thaw, but now served as no great obstacle, other than having deeper snow. The walked in single file, the SO19 officers carrying MP5 carbines, which were shoulder-slung under their coats. Swann wished he was armed. Logan walked behind him, her hood down and her face very black against the snow.

Beyond the heathland they struck another disused railway line, and headed north a few hundred yards to a small bridge over the burn, which burbled quietly through the trough, its passage set in the snow. At the bridge, Swann stopped and looked back. The team were fit and strong and moved quickly despite the conditions. He checked his map and watched the line of the path creep between the trees, gradually climbing the hill. Where the hill browed, the Allt a'Mhuillinn was dammed, and from there they would work their way up the glen on the track. He stared at the summit of Ben Nevis lifting to scratch the sky in the south. Ahead, the amphitheatre rose in a circle of ice-crusted crags. He could smell the snow in the air, the crispness of mountain air, and for a moment he was back on the Himalayan glacier with the Mummery Rib above him. He felt colder than he should have done and Webb came up beside him. 'Penny for them, Jack,' he said.

Swann glanced at him. 'What? Oh, nothing, Webby. Ignore me.' He set out again, matching Mick Rob stride for stride, their breath coursing in clouds.

Webb and Logan followed, along with the rest of the SFO team.

Boese had twisted north-east now, following the line of the ridge, like a lone Indian in bygone American days. The hut where *El Kebir* was staying was behind him now, and he would walk for another two hours before settling down to wait. He considered the movement of the police and asked himself how early they had set off. If it was earlier than him, which it might have been, they would hit the climbing hut before he was in position. But he would see them, a group no doubt, making their way up the Coire Leis, long before they saw him. They would be looking to take *El Kebir* out with the least possible fuss, because he had five potential hostages with him. Boese sharpened his pace, eyes on the ridge, mapping out the steps he would take. One slip and he would fall: it was not sheer, but he would roll all the way to the bottom, fifteen hundred feet below. He gauged the distance in his mind, working out the skinny line of the track deep in the valley. He needed to get lower, within six hundred yards for his best shot. He looked back at the easier slopes that led from *El Kebir*'s hut to the Coire Leis below. He might make a shot from here, but the path was blocked by buttress and gully alike. He looked ahead again and decided he needed to be north of Carn Mor Dearg, somewhere on the lower slopes, a thousand feet or so above the valley.

An hour after dawn, Dubin led his group of students from the observatory ruin hut. He checked his compass and map, plotting the safest route along the ridge, then down the lesser slopes, when they would use their axes as both stick and brake. Once in the coire, the track was easy and they would be back at the hotel for a late lunch. The sky was blue crystal, no hint of yesterday's cloud, but he had been here enough times to know that the weather could change in the time it took to walk off the mountain. He checked their equipment and then they set off in single file, roped together for safety.

Swann led the team along the track, three miles now from the dam and the sun getting hot overhead. They had crossed the burn where it joined the main flow of the stream and he bent to drink some water. They all stopped to rest, the climbing hut almost in sight at the end of the track. Rob called the firearms officers together. 'We'll deploy at the hut,' he said, holding the map so all of them could see. 'It's where the track ends or begins, depending if you're going in or coming out. Dubin will bring his party down the easy slopes to join it. We need to be at that hut and in position before he gets into view.' He looked the length and breadth of the valley. 'We haven't seen Boese,' he said to Swann. 'No car, no hikers, nothing.'

Swann half closed one eye and considered the map. 'He could have come from the south,' he said slowly, then bunched his eyes. 'I doubt it, though. That ridge is treacherous in these conditions.' He lifted his shoulders. 'Maybe he's not coming at all.'

Webb looked doubtful.

'Keep alert,' Rob said to his men. 'Watch each other's backs. We have to assume he'll come.'

Boese settled in a lay-up point, one thousand feet above the valley floor. He was protected from the sun by a rocky overhang above his head, and could rest his elbow in a patch of loose snow. He sat on his haunches and watched as the group of tiny specks made their way along the broken line of the track. Within twenty minutes, they would be there and deploy. That was the obvious place. It's what he would do. Taking the gun case from his pack, he laid it in the snow, and, working slowly, began to piece the weapon together. A 7.62mm Magnum hunting rifle. He had practised with it many times. He pressed his tongue against his teeth; eyes glassy, like doll's eyes, soulless holes in his face. His hat was pulled low over his ears and his breath steamed as he screwed the barrel into the stock. He looked below again and then to his left, and he paused. A party of six people moved down the snowy foothills to the valley floor and the track. They were converging on one another, neither knowing the other was there.

The gun complete, he screwed on the 10 power scope and sighted, adjusted and sighted once again. He watched each party through the scope. *El Kebir*'s was still too far distant to get off a decent shot. The police, however, were closer. At the hut now. He lay prostrate in the snow and thought about his escape route. There would be no hurry. If he was lucky, he would get the shot off, lie low, and they would not even know where it came from. He could pick his way carefully along the ridge and be back at his car in four hours. They would be below, and if a helicopter flew in, he was just another walker traversing the Ben. By now, cars would be arriving in both car parks, and the more people around the better. He watched the firearms team deploy, taking up positions around the climbing hut – in the trees, and behind the rocks and scrub heather on either side of the track.

Swann and Webb took up their position with Logan, to the north-west side of the hut. Rob had deployed his team in twos along the line of the track, taking advantage of the best cover they could find. Swann watched them now, backs to him, out of sight of the main track. They would secure Dubin and then he would read him his rights. The students still worried him, however. Surprise would be all. If Dubin got in a position to take a hostage, things could go very wrong indeed. His heart thumped, the old adrenalin twisting round in his veins. Webb's eyes were wide and bright. Logan watched the track.

They waited, ten minutes, fifteen, and then they heard voices in the distance. Swann crouched on his haunches, aware of the desire to urinate. It was always the same in takeouts – the moment they were over, you either had to piss or shit. He glanced at Logan and smiled. The voices were growing louder. He could see the party now, and his eyes searched for Dubin.

Boese had the party in his sights now, and a new thought made him smile. He lay as still as the grave, his finger already crooked round the trigger, applying the faintest pressure. The barrel of the gun lay on a ledge of snow he had fashioned to act as a tripod, and his breathing had stilled to something so shallow it barely existed. *El Kebir* in his sights, he could feel the tingling in his veins, the spider's walk on his spine. The police were deployed, well hidden. *El Kebir* walked the track, ahead of his students. Boese could make him out now, so small of stature, but with eyes that betrayed his past. *El Kebir* who had arranged to assassinate the Jackal, only to write a book about him twenty years later. He walked into not one but two traps: one would surprise him, the other he wouldn't even know about till he looked on the face of the devil.

Swann saw Dubin crest the path in front of his students. His manner was relaxed, but his gait brisk, just another hiker enjoying a cold winter's morning. He was almost level with the attack team. Swann could feel his pulse thicken against the side of his head. Webb shifted in the snow alongside him. And then the first SFO was up, MP5 at shoulder height, aimed at Dubin's head.

'ARMED POLICE. STAND STILL.' His shout

resounded in an echo that battered off the bluffs and buttresses to come back at him like a ghost from his past. Dubin froze where he stood. The other officers were up, guns pointed, eight of them, at Dubin's head and body.

'No one else move.' The leading officer spoke to the students, who stared at him, dumbfounded. Again he spoke to Dubin, voice quieter now. 'Put your arms wide at your sides. Do it now. Look me in the eye. Do not look away from me.'

Dubin did as he was asked, his jaw set, confusion in his eyes. He opened his mouth to say something.

'Do not speak to me. Do exactly as I tell you.'

Dubin did, first dropping to his knees, then falling prostrate and setting his hands in the small of his back, fingers interlocked. The firearms officers dropped on him, clasping his hands so he could not move. Then a few seconds more and plastic handcuffs secured him. They searched him, found no weapon, then wrestled him to his feet. The team leader made the shocked students sit down in the snow, while he called the arrest team up.

Boese saw them pop up from nowhere. He heard the shout and felt it reverberate around him. He saw them drop *El Kebir* to his knees, and the temptation to kill him like that was so strong, his finger tightened on the trigger. But no, not yet. Not just yet.

Swann, Webb and Logan came out from the side of the hut and marched across the packed snow to where Dubin was now on his feet and watching their approach. He faced Swann, saying nothing, but wearily shaking his head. Swann cautioned him. Webb stood to his right, Logan slightly away to the left. The firearms officers still held their weapons ready, and the team leader was questioning the students.

'You're making a mistake, Sergeant,' Dubin said wearily.

A shot rang out from the hillside. Swann saw the shock in Dubin's eyes, as blood spurted from the left side of his chest. Then someone else cried out. For a moment, Swann was too stunned to take it in, but then Dubin crumpled at the knees. Swann swung round and saw Logan lying on her side in the snow, eyes glazed with shock, blood seeping from a wound below her collarbone. The round had gone right through Dubin's chest.

'Jesus Christ.' Swann dropped to his knees beside her. The SFO medical technician rushed over to her and drew back the tattered edges of her jacket.

Swann looked at Webb, who was kneeling by Dubin with two fingers against the side of his neck. 'Dead,' he muttered, and turned his attention to the radio.

Swann got to his feet again. Logan was breathing heavily and the medic was working away at the hole in her flesh, trying to stem the flow of blood leaking out of her. The other firearms officers were scanning the skyline for movement.

Boese lay where he was. He knew *El Kebir* was dead, and he had got two in one, which was a bonus. It looked like the black FBI agent, but he could not be sure. The gun was already in the bottom of the crevasse to his right, and he lay for a few moments more, before working his way backwards behind the lee of the rock.

Swann saw the movement, just a flicker at the corner of his eye. 'There.' He pointed towards Carn Mor Dearg on the north-east side of the amphitheatre. Webb was alongside him, binoculars to his eyes. Rob considered his options. Swann dropped to his knees beside Logan. Already the sweat was lifting on her brow and she was shivering. The medic had a foil survival blanket open, and he and Swann wrapped her in it, while a second officer staunched the flow of blood.

'How bad is it?' Swann asked.

The medic made a face. 'Hard to tell. Went straight underneath the collar bone.' He gently prised her over and Swann could see the width of the exit wound, like a fuzzy star shape, with the flesh flaring at the edges of the hole.

'You're OK, darling.' He kissed her brow, easing the flecks of hair back from her eyes.

She shivered. 'I'm cold.'

*Cold, Jack. Cold.* Words from the past. Words from nightmares. Steve Brady's plaintive voice, just before he cut the rope that held them together. Swann was there now, eyes tightly closed, images blurring his mind. And yet rational thought broke in. He spun where he stood and scanned the ridge. He could see no movement, but knew that Boese would be traversing that ridge, back the way he had come, heading south. He must have taken his chances on the Carn Mor Dearg Arete. He looked at Webb, then at Rob and finally at Logan. Rob had fanned his men out across the valley, in the direction of the north-eastern buttresses.

'You won't catch him,' Swann said. 'Webb, get on that radio and tell the locals to swamp the southern car park.' Dropping to one knee, Swann scrabbled in his backpack for his mittens. He threw them on the ground, then untied his crampons. His twin short axes already lay in the snow. 'Where's the guidebook?' he said. 'Where's the fucking guidebook?' He found it, flipped through the pages and looked again at the ridge. 'It'll take him two hours or more to get round this valley,' he said. 'Two more, at least, to make it to his car.'

'You don't know he's going south,' Webb said.

'Where else is there to go?' Swann stared at him,

burning now, a rage growing inside him. He found what he was looking for in the guidebook and stood up, trembling slightly. The wind howled across the Diamir face in his mind and Brady wobbled on the rope below him.

Webb moved alongside. 'What're you thinking about, Jack?'

Swann looked back at Logan, where the medical technicians were already doing all that could be done for her. 'There's nothing I can do here,' he said. 'The only way to cut Boese off is to climb.' He scanned the page of the guidebook, then gauged the distance to the bottom of the route on foot. Webb took the book from him and Swann tramped to where Mick Rob was standing. 'I want your guns,' he said.

Rob stared at him. 'What're you going to do?'

'Climb Zero Gully and cut him off on the ridge.'

'Jack.' Webb's voice from behind him. 'Zero Gully is a thousand feet. There's no fucking belays. It'll take you three hours.'

Swann shook his head at him. 'I don't need belays. And it'll take an hour and a half, because I'll be climbing solo.'

Webb stared at him. 'Jack, it's grade five.'

Swann ignored him and turned to Rob again. 'Guns.'

Rob hesitated.

'I'm a shot, Mick. Pink ticket. It's called instant arming, remember.' He held out his hands. 'There's no other choice. Keep your boys after him if you want to, but you're not going to catch him. Now give me your fucking guns.'

Rob unhooked his MP5 and passed his pistol as well. Swann swung the carbine over his shoulder and stuffed the pistol inside his jacket. He bent and kissed Logan and then he turned, looked at Webb and hesitated. 'I have to do this.'

Webb nodded. 'I know you do. Good luck.'

Swann left them then, heading for the Observatory Ridge, to climb Zero Gully alone.

Boese was moving freely now; good cover and no way they could catch him. The rifle lay somewhere in the belly of the mountain and he still had his pistol. They would get choppers up, but already clouds were drifting ominously across the sky and he had all the documents he needed if he got stopped. The valley was out of sight now; the wind had lifted and he picked a careful path along the line of the ridge. There was a feeling of quiet satisfaction inside him, revenge was indeed sweet – all the sweeter by the unexpected bonus of two in one. Poor Jack Swann, another girlfriend down.

Swann hiked to the base of Zero Gully, not thinking about the climb. Sweat on his arms, on his calves, and gathering in his groin. He relived that moment again, having a hand on Dubin's arm and then *bang* and Dubin down and with him, Cheyenne Logan. The gully was dead ahead now, and he had no rope and no partner, just himself and his need and his fear. He did not know how badly Logan was hurt, but the rescue helicopter needed to get here quickly. Still he could hear no engine.

He knew the climb from other people, but had never made the ascent himself. First climbed in 1957 by Hamish MacInnes. One thousand feet, the most serious of the big three in this area. Nowhere to belay properly and very exposed. He stared up the slopes to the face, the snow still deep here, and the wind seemed to howl in his head. The trees were barely moving though. Cloud was rolling in, and he wondered how much of it was in his head. Thoughts buzzed like flies and he could do nothing to quiet them. The others were out of sight now, and again he thought of Logan, then of the futility of Rob sending his men after

Boese. He was too far away to catch, and he might yet turn north and fool them. But somehow Swann didn't think so. He would have figured that any attack team would use the climbing hut to deploy, and he had deliberately circumnavigated the ridge to be on the north-east side. Maxium effect, as always with Boese.

The ground steepened beneath his feet and he had to invert his axes and start driving the picks into the hard-packed ice. His breath bounced off the wall, and he was aware of the tiny icicles that were forming on his lips. He licked them away and concentrated on looking up, feeling the sudden gradient as his crampon points dug home and his calves began to feel the strain. He climbed up the gully, hand over hand, aiming for the stance below the chimney. Here he was exposed, there he would be less so, but it was still three hundred feet above his head. He got higher and higher and Boese's features lay etched in his mind.

One hundred feet below the chimney, the wind got up, and his left foothold was looser than he would have liked. He paused, breathing hard, and leant his weight on the points of his right boot, while seeking securer ground. He kicked in with his left foot and tested the hold, lying against the ice for a moment. The wall was not sheer, but he was high up, and if he slipped, his axes could do nothing to save him. He saw again the blood that leaked from Logan's wound and it mixed with the bloodied features of Brady, his foot all bent up, and the weight on the rope unbearable.

Swann felt that weight now and Boese's face began to break up in his mind. In its place, flashes of red and white tissue, the puffed and half-closed eyes. He shook his head, steeling himself, and climbed on. Almost to the chimney now, and he swung with his left-hand axe. It bit and splintered and fell away, the loop only saving it from slipping off his wrist altogether. He felt the rush of adrena-

568

lin from his skull to his toes, and hung there on one axe and one point, while an arm and a leg flailed free. He bit down on his lip, forced the seizure of trembling from his limbs, then swung the axe again. It bit and held. He cursed under his breath and kicked in with his cramponed foot.

Boese was watching the skyline as he heard the drone, then *whump whump* of rotor blades. The orange helicopter swung in low over the amphitheatre. He ignored it, keeping out of sight, and then moved on when it dropped below the horizon. He would hear it again taking off, and the next one after that would be the police looking for him. He kept his eyes fixed on the ridge and pressed on, nimble-footed, glad of the rigorous years of self-discipline. Not much further now and he would be at the abseil arete. There, he would need to be careful, go a little more slowly, the mountain walls were steep.

Swann was in the chimney, climbing for all he was worth, the sweat rolling in little rivers off his forehead and soaking his clothes. The sun was gone and the clouds were massed and the wind had risen still further. He knew then it would snow, and images of blizzard and the shoulder of Nanga Parbat filled his mind. Brady had wanted to go on. He had wanted to go back, but had bowed to Brady's experience, though the clouds settled about them.

'You crazy fucking fool,' he said aloud, forcing the words from between his teeth. 'It was your own fault.' He climbed on, sweating up that chimney, suddenly aware that he was climbing as freely and well as he had ever done. He did not know how much time had passed, an hour or so, maybe, of hard slog up that shaft, with the wind on his back and the valley eight hundred feet below. No rope, nothing between himself and all the forces of gravity. One wrong move and he would die in Scotland today. But he had two kids and he still had Logan, and Boese was out there waiting. Brady faded, like mist in the early morning, and Swann reached the top of the chimney. He paused, resting on his axes, and the valley swam before his eyes. The sweat had dried to a frozen point on his nose and he shook his head to clear the block in his ears. Now, traverse right to the amphitheatre and narrowest gully. After that, he was almost home.

He moved right, slipped again and shouted at the top of his lungs. Far, far to his left, Boese heard the cry and paused, his head cocked like a hunting dog. He felt in the waistband of his trousers for his gun. Swann climbed on, moving across the wall now, taking sideways steps like a spider. He could see the gully and the funnel that lifted from it, and he no longer looked at the ground. Brady was gone now, faded to dust, nothing in his mind but thoughts of his daughters and Logan, and a calmness he had never known before. He felt renewed, as if climbers of old were watching him with pride in their eyes. One thousand feet of grade five ice-climb, with no rope and no partner to protect you. He knew then he would make it, knew then that Brady was buried for ever; and, above all else, he knew he would be ahead of Ismael Boese.

Another twenty minutes and he was on the easy slopes that led to the top of the ridge. Now he moved more cautiously. For the first time, he was aware of the carbine slung across his back. He listened, head away from the wall, for sounds that should not be there. But all he could hear was the rush of the wind and the ice-crack as it shifted.

Boese was beyond the arete now and moving more swiftly again. He had his rhythm and, as yet, had heard no police helicopter. The first flurries of snow were falling. If it got any worse, they would not come. He had heard one shout bouncing off the mountain walls, but then nothing. He was cautious, however, even though his instincts told him there was no way anyone from the valley floor could get to him before he reached his car. He moved on, picking out his footholds and working the line of the ridge.

Swann saw a hiker work his way along Observatory Ridge, as he crested it fifty yards away. He must have climbed for an hour and a half at least, and now his limbs were weak and he still had work to do. He looked for an ambush point, keeping his head low. He worked his way to the south, away from Ben Nevis itself, cutting a path through the boulders and snow. The hiker was heading away from him now. He could still see him, and if they both kept going, they would ultimately converge. He ducked his head once more, the carbine in his hands, and eased himself below the line of the ridge. The hiker had his head down, concentrating, unaware of the danger. Swann's mind stilled and all memory was banished. This was just himself and his prey. His anger was gone and he was a police officer again. He kept moving across the ridge and knew he would come up ten yards behind the hiker. It had to be Boese, the timing was just about perfect, given the movement he had seen. He slowed still further, aware of the scraping sound his crampons made on the flakes of ice. The hiker moved ahead, small, nimble, like a goat. Swann saw blond hair, long and tied in a ponytail under the woollen hat. All at once he wondered. He saw no gun, no sniper's rifle and suddenly his resolve faltered. He climbed back on to the ridge, fifteen yards behind the hiker.

'Armed police. Stand still,' he said. Not loud, just sharp and firm. The hiker stopped where he was.

Swann's ice axes hung from his wrist loops, like two appendages to his gun. The man stood still, back to him, and slowly he raised his hands. Then he turned, a silly

571

smile on his very Caucasian face. Swann baulked for a second, but he did not lower the gun.

'*Bitte*?' the young man said, blue eyes, blond hair, his hands still over his head. 'Please. I do not understand.'

Swann stared at him, unable to believe the coincidence, and yet it was possible. Many walkers travelled this path: climbers, going to and from the abseil point on the arete. He stared at the man, looking at his eyes, taking another three paces forward.

'Please,' the man said again and gestured very slowly with his hand. 'The snow is coming. We have to get off the mountain.'

'Who are you?' Swann demanded.

'*Ich bin* . . . Sorry. My English is not so good. Please, sir. The gun. I am very frightened.'

'Who are you?' Swann demanded again.

'My name is Rudy Maaber. I'm German. Holiday. Walking.' He indicated his backpack and Swann lowered the barrel of the gun. Fear stalked the young man's eyes and Swann silently cursed himself.

'I'm a police officer,' he said more gently. 'There's been a shooting here today. I need to see some identification.'

'Of course.' The young man was trying to smile. 'Please.' His hand started to snake towards his back. Swann lifted the gun barrel once more.

'Please. Please. You are frightening me, sir. I have a package. How you say, a belt. My passport is in a belt.'

'Money belt,' Swann said.

'That's right. Money belt.' He smiled again. 'I'm a student from Hamburg University. I have my papers. Please, do not point the gun.'

Swann relaxed, exhausted by the exertions of the climb and the disappointment in his own judgement. He stood taller and let the barrel of the MP5 swing towards the ground. The German's hand inched behind him, slowly,

slowly, the smile still on his face, hope suddenly in his eyes. Swann watched him wearily and then a strange thought rode across his mind, why doesn't he use both hands? He'll need both hands to work the belt to the front, so he can open the zip.

And then the hand moved fast. Swann brought up the barrel of the MP5 and shot him, double tap, right in the chest. The man jerked and his arms flailed, the hand behind him coming away empty. Swann saw the look of surprise in his face and then the blood running over his lips, and he knew he had hit his lungs. The man fell to his knees, clutching his chest, and looked Swann in the eyes. He muttered something in German and then, 'You have killed me. Why have you killed me?' He rocked on his knees, blood dripping from his nose and mouth. His eyes had begun to glaze, yet still he knelt, seeming to scrabble or scratch at his back. Swann took a pace towards him, the carbine a dead weight in his hands. Then the man stopped moving. He did not fall, but Swann saw the life vanish before his eyes. Again, he was alone on a mountain, with the stench of death in his soul. He stood a long time, the wind tugging at his hair. Finally, he laid the carbine on the ground, pulled his ice axes from their wrist loops, and knelt before the German. His eyes were still open, but they were dull, like cold glass. No breath played against Swann's palm when he lifted it to the bloodied mouth.

Gently, he took the dead man in his arms and laid him face down on top of the ridge. He felt the threat of tears as he fumbled with the backpack, reaching to the base of his back for the money belt and passport. He lifted away the jacket and saw the butt of a 9mm pistol pushing against the waistband of his trousers. With a cry in his throat, he rolled the body over. He stared at those dead eyes, the blond hair, the white skin. And then he prised his thumb into the flesh of that face. His thumb stuck, then gave and came away with strips of pink latex sticking to it, like flaps of dead skin. Swann tore at the face, pulling away the mask, until Boese's dark skin was exposed. His eyes were still blue and they were still open, but they were no longer laughing at him.

# 29

Webb and the firearms team flew straight back to London, but Swann remained behind. Logan's bleeding had been stopped by the rescue team as she was airlifted to hospital. The wound was clean, with minimal muscle damage, but she was going to be in hospital for a few days at least, before they would allow her to move. Swann was floating – the rush of adrenalin, the death of both Storm Crow and Boese. He would've liked to see them in court, but they had escaped him twice and perhaps justice had been done today. He sat by Logan's bed and held her hand while she slept. Then he dozed too, and when he lifted his head, she was looking at him with a softness in the black of her eyes.

'Hi, baby,' she said. 'You OK?'

Swann nodded. 'What about you?'

'Just fine.' She smiled. 'You made the climb?'

'I did, didn't I.' He paused, looking beyond her for a moment. 'Boese's dead. I shot him on that ridge.' He looked back at her then. 'Brady's dead too, Chey. He died in that ice chimney, right there. His fault, his idea. All I ever tried to do was save him.' He sat back in the chair and all of a sudden he laughed. Then he leaned over the bed and kissed her. 'I love you,' he said.

She touched his face and winced, shooting pain rippling up her arm.

'You OK?' He cupped her cheek with his palm.

'I'm fine. A little uncomfortable is all.' She laughed then, lightly. 'You know what's funny, Jack?'

'What?'

'I've been a Fed for seven years now and I've been in

lots of bad situations. I've had my gun out more than once, but it takes a second-hand bullet to plug me.'

Atwood called Harrison and told him The Cub would meet him in a bar off 21st Street. Harrison went up to the eleventh floor and collected Kovalski. The Cub was on his own, drinking from a bottle of beer in a corner, where he could keep an eye on the entire room. He wore jeans and boots, a Pendleton hat set low over his eyes. Harrison bought beers, and he and Kovalski sat on stools for a while, checking who was watching whom, then they slid into the seat opposite him. The Cub stared into Kovalski's eyes. Harrison took a Marlboro from his shirt pocket and introduced Kovalski. The Cub continued to stare into his eyes. Kovalski looked right back and then The Cub extended his hand.

Harrison tapped the ash from the end of the cigarette. 'So, what did you get for me, bro?'

The Cub bunched his eyes and sat back, tapping a tin of chewing tobacco against his thigh. 'Dubin wasn't on that flight on August 21st,' he said. 'D.C. to Detroit. The Jonathan Institute was told he was flying from the UK to the States, but that was just cover. I know, because he was in Pakistan with me.'

Harrison stared at him.

'That's number one,' The Cub went on. 'Number two. He only used the name of Josef El Kebir twice.'

'You're sure?'

'As far as I can figure. The first time was in 1976. You know about that. He ran the operation to kill the Jackal until Ford told us to quit it.'

'And the second time?' Harrison asked him.

The Cub smiled, but not with his eyes. 'The second time is real interesting, Harrison.' He placed a fingerful of chew under his lip. 'Beirut, 1985. Dubin had been put in after

576

the marine barracks got blowed to fuck. I told you already, the guy speaks Arabic like a native and he can pass for Middle Eastern with no problem at all. Anyways, he dug around a little bit, gathering intel' here and there, and he found out who was behind the suicide attack. A guy called Sheik Mohammed Fadlallah. Given that he killed two hundred and thirty-eight of ours, we decided to hit him.' He paused long enough to sip from his beer bottle and check the tables closest for potential eavesdroppers. 'Interesting thing happened,' he went on. 'About that time, the DIA were considering recruiting a young marine, who'd been at the barracks when it was bombed. I guess the suits figured Dubin could use some help, and military intelligence wanted to see how this young guy performed in the field. On March 1st, 1985, thirty-six US citizens, who were working with the UN, got evacuated real quick. One week later, a motherfucker of a car bomb goes off right in the middle of the Shiite suburb where Dubin had located Fadlallah. Eighty people got killed and two hundred more were injured. Unfortunately, not Fadlallah. I guess an hour or so later, a banner was hung up on one of the bombed-out buildings. It said: "Made in the USA."'

The Cub stopped talking as a cocktail waitress offered them more drinks, then he sat forward again. 'I don't know why they fucked up, boys, but it sure as hell wasn't Dubin's fault. That guy's intelligence was as good as anybody's ever seen. He *was* and *is* a prize CIA asset. The marine on the other hand, well, he never did cut it with the DIA. Dubin sent a report back on him, saying he wasn't suitable for covert operations.'

'So he came back to the States and joined the FBI.' Kovalski's face was grey. 'Louis Byrne,' he said.

'You got it, daddy.' The Cub looked him in the eye. 'Dubin ain't your bad guy,' he said. 'But I figure you know

577

that already. Byrne knew the name *El Kebir* as far back as 1985.'

They met Angie Byrne in the Seaport Bar in old town Alexandria, after they left The Cub. Kovalski told her what they had discovered. 'The British are convinced that Ben Dubin was Storm Crow,' he said. 'Case closed as far as they're concerned.'

'You've said nothing to them?' Angie asked him.

'Not so far.'

Angie was very quiet, but the tiredness had gone from her eyes. She looked at the sample handwriting that Kovalski had shown her from copies of the bank forms. 'This *is* his handwriting,' she said. 'He likes to print capital letters. He always has.'

'There's millions of dollars in those accounts, Angie,' Kovalski said.

She made a face, lip quivering just fractionally. She sucked at a breath. Neither Harrison or Kovalski spoke; the silence awkward and stretched.

'Louis was always bitter about not going further in the service,' Angie said at last. 'He had a yearning to work overseas, and he thought he could do everything so much better than anyone else.'

'Well, he sure did a number on Dubin,' Harrison said. 'For such a top CIA guy, he was suckered in big time.'

'Without him ever knowing it,' Kovalski added. 'Louis's worked him over ever since 1985, Angie. He knew that if we ever got through the myth that Boese was Storm Crow, there was always *El Kebir* in the background.'

'It's terrifying.' Angie shuddered. 'My own husband. He's been bad since before I ever met him. I never had any idea till that night in my bedroom. He should've taken his wedding ring off.'

Harrison lit a cigarette. 'He shouldn't have come at all,'

he said. 'But he knew what Boese was doing. I guess
wanted to push us towards the second person – Dubin.'
blew cigarette smoke at the ceiling. 'Some of it was vanity
though. That's what Boese figured on. Vanity fucks you
over in the end. It got to Louis, just like it did to Carlos.'
He sipped at his bottle of beer. 'He should've let things
run their course. But I guess Boese musta pissed him off.'
He broke off then. 'If Boese hadn't got his own contingency plan, he would have rotted in jail as Storm Crow.
Louis would've kept his millions, killed his own creation,
and been fêted as the best FBI agent since Joe Pistone.' He
paused for a moment and blew the air from his cheeks.
'Was he jealous of you, Angie, earning all that money?
That why he did this?'

'He's been jealous of somebody all of his life,' she said.
'His father, his elder brother, me. Clearly, Benjamin
Dubin.' She sipped from her glass of wine. 'He'll have
guessed that Dubin sent back a bad report. And he'll have
nursed that grudge from that day to this.'

'Can I ask you another question?' Kovalski said.

'Sure.'

'Tal-Salem, Boese's cohort, was digging into the events
surrounding the first chemical strike in England.' He
looked at the notes laid out on the table. 'The records say
that Louis used the diplomatic pouch when you and he
went over.'

'That's right, he did.'

'What did he put in it, d'you know?'

'Only his attaché case.' She paused then for a second.
'No. A pair of binoculars.'

'Binoculars?' Harrison screwed up his face. 'In the
diplomatic pouch?'

'Yes. He had them in London, but we didn't pack them
at home.' Angie looked at Kovalski again. 'Why?'

'Did you see them?'

'What d'you mean?'

Did he use them, take them out of the case?'

'I can't remember. Come to think of it, I don't think he did.'

Kovalski looked at Harrison.

'You're thinking pirillium crystal,' Harrison said. 'And how it got to England.'

Swann flew back to London with Logan, her arm in a sling, but ready to travel home. The case was officially closed and the souls of sixteen police officers and six civilians could finally rest in peace. Swann felt happier than he had done in years. He, Logan and his children spent a gloriously relaxed weekend together, before she flew back to Washington.

The morning Logan and Byrne were due to leave, Swann received the information he had requested from the Questioned Document Section at Lambeth. He read their report carefully and then phoned Harrison.

'It's the same, JB,' he said. 'They *think* the Winthrop directions match, and are *certain* of the transfer forms. Whose writing is it? Dubin's?'

'Watch CNN, duchess. Make sure you're sitting down.'

'What's going on?'

'I'll explain later, buddy. Better that way, believe me.'

Swann looked across the squad room at Logan. 'Does all this mean you're going to leave the Bureau?' he asked.

Harrison's voice was low. 'Well, let's just say I don't got no reason to stick around any more.'

Swann was all at once disturbed. 'What aren't you telling me, Harrison?'

'Not a good time, Jack. Later.'

'OK. But are you going to leave?' Swann asked.

Harrison sighed heavily. 'You know what – I never

worked abroad, Jack. And there's a deputy leg-att's job coming up in London.'

Swann didn't say anything for a moment and then he smiled to himself. '*You* know what, JB,' he said. 'If I were you, I wouldn't bother going for it.'

'No, why's that?'

'Because you'd have to cut your hair.'

'Is that right? Nothing to do with the fact that I ain't beautiful, black and female then, huh.'

They both laughed then.

'She's coming back here first, though, right?' Harrison said. 'Kovalski'll chew her butt off if she don't.'

'She's coming back. Tell him not to worry.'

'What time they get in?'

'Three-thirty, your time.'

'Tell them we'll be at Dulles to meet them.'

Swann shifted the phone to his other ear. 'Listen, Harrison, much as I hate to, I have to tell you. Even with your fits of pique, it was a pleasure working with you.'

'Likewise, duchess. Later.' Harrison put down the phone.

Swann drove them to Terminal 3, and Byrne discreetly made himself scarce while Swann said his goodbyes to Logan. They held each other for a long time and Swann was careful not to disturb her shoulder. He felt sad and yet more hopeful than he had ever felt, and he kissed her tenderly on the mouth. Everything was ahead of him now. Some doors had been closed for ever and others had been opened. Logan touched him on the lips with a finger. 'I love you, Jack Swann,' she said. 'Don't you ever forget it.'

Swann held her in his arms one last time. 'Just get the job, and get yourself over here.'

'I will. Just you wait for me.' She kissed him again. Byrne was looking at his watch. 'Gotta go. Love you, baby. Always.'

Swann stood with his hands in his pockets, staring after her until she disappeared into the departure lounge. Then he walked back to his car.

On the flight, they relaxed in business class. Byrne ordered single malt whiskies and they touched glasses. 'Here's to a job well done,' he said. 'And remember, Cheyenne, the Director's a friend of mine. That leg-att's job is yours.'

'I know it is, Louis.' She settled back then, exhausted again, and quickly fell asleep.

Byrne covered her with a blanket and watched the world below through the window. He ordered another shot of whisky and smiled to himself. 'Here's to *El Kebir*,' he whispered, and drained the glass in one.

At Dulles Airport, they transferred into the high-wheeled shuttle bus and crossed the tarmac to the arrivals lounge. Byrne was smiling as he loaded both their cases on to a trolley and pushed them through the customs hall. He saw Kovalski and Harrison and waved across the concourse. Kovalski, stony-faced, lifted a hand. Harrison just stared at him and spat into a Coke can.